GWENNA
THE WELSH CONFECTIONER

Books by Vicky Adin

The Cornish Knot
Portrait of a Man

Brigid The Girl from County Clare
Gwenna The Welsh Confectioner
The Costumier's Gift

The Disenchanted Soldier

The Art of Secrets

"An absorbing read. This fast-paced novel once again demonstrates the author's trademark flair for telling great historical stories."

– Erin McKechnie, author

"Adin is a master of her craft. Gwenna, the confectioner; charming, irrepressible and utterly unforgettable. A must read for those who love historical fiction."

– Jenny Harrison, author

GWENNA
THE WELSH CONFECTIONER

Inspired by a true story

VICKY ADIN

Cover Image:
Sir George Grey Special Collections,
Auckland Libraries, 7-A4799

Queen Street, Auckland, c. 1895(?)

DEDICATION

To Janice,
who, like Gwenna, battled the odds
and never gave up

1

LOCKED IN THE PAST

Auckland, New Zealand
March 1899

For the moment, she felt free – deliciously free – only too aware the illusion would pass soon enough.

Gwenna Price hurried along busy Karangahape Road towards Turner's, the greengrocer. Her boots crunched along the hardened grit as she swung her basket and called a cheery good morning to shopkeepers preparing for the day ahead. She loved watching them sweeping footpaths, cleaning windows or winding out the shop awnings, unless they were lucky enough to have a fixed verandah. Other merchants set their wares out in doorways and along their shopfronts, seemingly indifferent to the rattle of trams and clink of harness, or the clomp of horses' hooves and bicycles whirring past.

Gwenna delighted in these sounds as the day came to life, exhilarated by all the hustle and bustle. She waved to the girl changing the window display in the milliner's shop, and stopped to pat a horse munching on oats in its nosebag, wishing her life could be as contented. In the distance, the sails on Partington's Mill slowly turned in the breeze.

One day, she promised herself, she would be a part of all this busyness. One day.

She continued down the street, mentally ticking off her shopping list, thankful for the wide-brimmed bonnet shading her face. Her cool dimity blouse and pale grey skirt swishing around her ankles were a blessing in the warm air on a cloudless autumn day.

She pushed the niggling worry of her ailing half-brother Charlie to the back of her mind as the far more pressing worry of the charming and persistent Johnno Jones entered her thoughts. She was tempted to give in to the young man's pleas, if only to escape life at home, except for one troublesome detail – his father, Black Jack Jones.

She and Johnno had known each other once in childhood days, when his father had been the local carter and used to do odd jobs for her pa, but they'd disappeared years ago. She'd all but forgotten about them until Johnno returned over the summer.

Deep in thought, Gwenna hadn't seen Johnno appear, as if from nowhere, as he was wont to do. He'd grabbed her hand and spun her round like they were dancing, before his smiling face came into focus. His cap was set at its usual rakish angle. "How's my favourite girl doing?"

She slapped his arm playfully, laughing, elated at the sight of him. Readjusting her hat, she tried to ignore the melting feeling that swept over her whenever he was near. As a youngster, with his impish smile and cheerful ways, Johnno had been a popular lad for running messages. He still found occasional work, but nobody hired Black Jack any longer.

"What are you doing here at this time of day, Johnno? You near scared me to death," she teased.

"Hoping to see you, of course. How can you 'xpect a man to go for so long without seeing yer pretty face?" Johnno twisted one of her freshly curled ringlets around his finger as he leaned closer.

At his touch, a flutter ignited in places too intimate to think about. "Away with you now. Enough of your flattery, and it's not much more'n a week since you saw me last. I've work to do, ev'n if you don't."

"Aw, Gwenna. Don't be like that. Walk with me aways. You make my heart glad, that you do, and I need some cheering."

"So you always say."

His glorious brown eyes, glowing with desire, threatened to devour her, and she couldn't resist their unmistakable message.

"All right, then, but only a wee ways. I need to get the groceries home before that stepbrother of mine thinks I've been gone too long. I don't want to feel the sting of his hand this day if I can avoid it."

"Run away with me, sweet Gwenna, and I promise you'll never feel the sting of a man's hand ever again."

He led her off the main road and down a couple of twisting alleyways until there was not a soul in sight. Gently pushing her back against the warmth of the brick wall, he kissed and caressed her with a lightness of touch that sent shivers through her body. The more she quivered, the more amorous he became. She lost her heart, as well as her hat, as the fiery passions of youth flared.

"Ah, Gwenna, me love. I wish you'd come away with me. What have you got to lose? Jack and me, we're leaving this night to try our luck down south." Johnno always called his father by his nickname. There were far too many John Joneses, even in Auckland, not to differentiate them in some way. "The wagon's all loaded and only needs you to decorate it."

Gwenna had heard this argument before, more than once, and it was enticing, but not if she had to be anywhere near his father: something evil burned in that man's dark eyes.

If only Pa were still with us, she wished fervently. *He would advise me.* She shook her head to chase away her futile thoughts. Her stepbrother, Elias Hughes, was head of the household now, and life had changed.

"We've been through this afore, Johnno. Sometimes the devil ya know is better than the one you don't. And I can't leave Mam just yet. She's enough on her plate caring for young Charlie. He's mighty sickly, and Elias wouldn't care whether he lives or dies."

Never to be undone and always philosophical, Johnno shrugged his shoulders. "Well then, give us some more of those tasty kisses to take with me on me travels. I'll have to store 'em up till I return."

"Wherever have you been?" whispered Bethan as Gwenna eased the latch to the door, hoping she could pretend she'd been at home for a time before Elias found her. "He's been looking for you."

A trickle of fear turned Gwenna's stomach sour, but the sight of her stepmam's tired, wan face unsettled her more. Sitting in the big armchair next to the fireplace, Bethan nursed the sleeping Charlie on her knee. He was almost seven, but small and scrawny enough to be mistaken for a four-year-old.

A lump rose in Gwenna's throat as Bethan began to sing softly in Welsh 'Ar Hyd y Nos' – the old hymn 'All Through the Night'.

"Charlie's so peaceful there, Mam. Don't disturb him. You stay put and I'll start the soup."

"Be quick then, chook. He'll be wanting you to make the sugar ready – not doing *my* chores. Charlie had a rough go earlier, coughing his little lungs out till he were sick. Poor fellow."

Gwenna placed the basket of groceries on the kitchen table before going through to the scullery. She filled the pot with water from the butler's sink and set it on the coal range to heat. Chatting away to Bethan about the gossip she'd picked up at the grocer's, Gwenna sorted the vegetables.

She didn't see the blow coming. As she stood up from getting a few parsnips from the bottom of the pantry, Elias slammed the door against her face, sending her staggering into the table. Before she could gather her wits, he was leaning over her, forcing her back into a painful arch. She could smell him. The foul odour of stale beer and sweat made her gag, and his cold, hard stare frightened her. Most times when he lost his temper and spittle flew from his mouth in his rage, he was content to push and shove, and sometimes slap her, but nothing like this.

Even as the blood seeped from a cut to her cheek and pain exploded in her nose, she refused to show her fear.

"I'll break you in two one day, I will, if you don't learn to do as you're told. One hour, I said, then back here and ready the sugar. But what do I find?" Elias's temper was rising and Gwenna's body relaxed a fraction. He ran out of steam quicker when he was angry and often mistimed his blows. "I find you missing for more'n half the morning, the ol' woman in there caring for the crybaby an' you doin' *her* chores instead of yer own, that's what. An' I won't have it. Do you hear me? I'm head of this family now, and you'll do what I tells ya."

The open-handed slaps jerked her head first to one side then the other. As she prepared herself for the next blow, he turned away. Crossing to his mother, he grabbed her by the bun at the back of her neck and forced her to her feet. She barely had time to put the now wide awake and whimpering Charlie down before Elias shoved her in the direction of the scullery. "Get in there and do ya chores."

Tripping from the force, Bethan would have fallen had Gwenna not caught her.

Elias's hand was raised to strike again when the sound of the adjoining door stopped him in his tracks.

Hugh Powell filled the doorway. His muscles bulged under the rolled-up sleeves of his collarless white shirt, as he wiped his hands on a towel. His jaw clenched within a grim face.

"What do you want?" snapped Elias, spinning around and combing his fingers through his hair.

The women stood silent, watching from the safety of the scullery door, waiting for Elias's next move. Hugh was broader than his employer and a good half-head taller. Elias had never challenged him, but there was always a first time.

"I've finished that batch of boiled sweets," said Hugh.

Wise to his boss's temper, Hugh said little. He had become a thorn in the other man's side and someone Elias viewed as a necessary evil – someone with both the strength and skill needed to keep the business viable, but who saw what he shouldn't.

Elias glared between the two women and Hugh, before pushing past him, and stormed into the back room where the large sugar-boiling kitchen was housed. Hugh followed, closing the door behind him.

"Let me see, Gwenna, *bach*," Bethan coaxed, as she soaked a towel under the tap.

Gwenna, pale with shock and pain, leant against the door frame, holding her hands to her face, unable to control the trembling in her legs. At times like this, she sorely missed her pa George, who had died two years earlier of the bronchial disease Charlie now suffered from. Elias would not have dared touch her or Mam had Pa been alive.

"Come, sit down," Bethan said, pressing the cold compress against Gwenna's nose, and led her to the table. Gwenna's sky-blue eyes filled with tears as she gaped in bewilderment at her beloved stepmother – the only mother she'd known.

"Why, Mam, why? He's never been that vicious before."

Bethan subdued her own tears as she fussed around inspecting the damage to Gwenna's face, cleaning up the blood amongst the tears and runny nose. "I can't answer you, my dear. I don't understand him any more. He wasn't like this as a child. You remember, don't you? He was never moody and bad-tempered. Not until his father died. But now – since your pa's gone – he seems to have lost his way."

Gwenna's memories of Elias's father, Owen Hughes, were few, except as a funny, kind man. She'd been six years old when her widowed pa had taken his two daughters to live with the Hughes family in Treorchy, in the Rhondda Valley of South Wales. Their life had been blissful for two whole years – until the accident.

Owen and Pa had built up a healthy trade together, boiling and stretching the sugar to make medicinal lozenges and every variety of sweets she could imagine. Every month Elias would hitch up the wagon and happily traverse the hills and valleys with his father, selling their goods for days on end.

One day, Owen didn't come home.

In time, Gwenna had been told the full story of how, on a wet day, the wagon had got stuck in a muddy rut on a hill. How Owen had put his shoulder to the back, yelling at the boy to drive the horse forward, but the squealing, terrified animal kept slipping in the mire. As the cart lurched backwards, Owen was crushed under the wheels. Even now, Gwenna could picture the scene and hear the screams of both man and horse. She felt the agony of a young Elias who could not save his father. The scene had haunted her for years.

"Do you remember how inconsolable he was?" asked Bethan. "Elias blamed himself for his father's death, and his grief was unbearable. Overnight he changed from my happy-go-lucky boy into a morose young man."

Gwenna understood how barren Elias had felt, now she had lost her own father – and guilty. She understood guilt too.

"I remember, but that's no excuse. Elias shouldn't treat you like that, Mam. It's not right."

Nor me, she thought, as she ran her finger down Charlie's cheek and smiled at the silent boy sitting on the chair next to her. His eyes, too big for his thin face, were troubled.

Bethan put ointment on the cut on Gwenna's face, and placed a fresh, cold cloth over the girl's throbbing nose. "He says I betrayed his father's memory. Betrayed him, too. It was bad enough when I sought your father's advice to keep the business running, but when I married George, and Charlie was born ..." Bethan drew another shuddering breath. "... Elias never forgave me."

Once Bethan had finished tending to Gwenna, she tidied up and returned to the scullery. Picking up her favourite knife, Bethan began to chop the vegetables, the knife blade flashing as she vented her anger. Still holding the compress to her face, Gwenna watched.

Elias's bitterness had festered, eating deep into the soul of the tormented sixteen-year-old. Nothing but memories remained of his father after George changed the name of the business to G Price & Family, and they emigrated to New Zealand. While Gwenna understood his sorrow, she could never forgive the young man whose wrath had become a beast that grew with each passing year. If only she and Mam could get away, but they had few choices; the law was on his side.

She sighed; she would never fulfil her pa's dreams under Elias's roof.

"Maybe you should get married again," ventured Gwenna. "It'd be a way out of this mess." Gwenna bit the side of her fingernail while she thought through what she wanted to say. "What about Hugh? I'm sure he's got a real soft spot for you. I've seen the way he keeps an eye on you."

Bethan stopped chopping to glare at Gwenna. "Rubbish. And you can put those ideas right out of your head, young lady," she said, pointing the knife tip at Gwenna. "But it's you he has a fancy for, not me."

Gwenna wasn't sure how old Hugh was – somewhere between her eighteen years and Bethan's mid-forties, she suspected. He was considerate, dependable and likeable, and she trusted him, but she'd never thought about him like that, not when she had Johnno. "Never!" Gwenna shook her head, denying Hugh's interest. "You're dreaming, Mam."

"I know what I see, girl," said Bethan. "And if you took more notice you'd see it too. I'm too old for all that nonsense now, but you should think about getting yerself away, our Gwenna. Before it's too late."

Unbeknown to Bethan, Gwenna *had* been thinking about it. She'd thought a lot about Johnno and his constant urging to go away with him.

"You don't need to put up with Elias," continued Bethan, dropping the chopped vegetables into the pot. "He's no kin to you. Why, even Samuel, his own brother, won't have nowt to do with him any more."

This wasn't the first time she and Bethan had had this conversation, but Gwenna was torn. She wanted to get away but, almost with his dying breath, Pa made her promise to care for Bethan and Charlie after he'd gone.

Pa had understood Elias's loyalty to his father's memory and watched his resentment grow over the years but he could never have imagined Elias becoming quite so angry and obsessed. It wasn't until her older sister Matilda married Tom Griffiths the previous year that Gwenna's sense of responsibility for Bethan and Charlie weighed so heavily on her shoulders.

Oh, how I miss Tillie.

To take her mind off the things she couldn't change, Gwenna rolled up her sleeves and gathered the tools she would need to make a new batch of acid drops with her homemade lemon essence. Since her father had gone, she preferred to work in the scullery rather than the back kitchen where the men worked. Her family still made their sweets and lozenges by hand, despite the proliferation of modern machinery used by many other confectionery manufacturers. The Price family reputation rested on it, and on her.

George Price had taught his daughters well, but Gwenna had excelled. No one matched Gwenna's skill at boiling the sugar or pulling and stretching the mixture until it was smooth and pliable. She could flavour and colour to perfection and turn the finished length into sweets – or lollies, as they called them here – of any shape and size she chose. And while she didn't have the strength to lift the seventy-pound sacks from the Colonial Sugar Company across the harbour in Birkenhead, nor handle the large boxes of finished goods, Hugh did.

With difficulty, Gwenna reached up to unhook the six-pounder open pan from the collection of copper pots hanging from the rack swinging above the scullery workbench. Her back hurt and her muscles resisted the stretch. She fetched a long-handled roasting fork to help her dislodge the pan then set it on the range to heat.

With a practised eye, she measured out a good six pounds of sugar, added a pint of water and three pounds of glucose, and stirred it until it had all melted. Leaving the mixture to reach temperature and bubble for about half an hour, she poured boiling water from the kettle, permanently on the range, into the cast-iron hollow workbench Pa had made that better suited her height.

While she waited for the sugar to liquefy, she squeezed the lemons, grated the skin and put the mixture on to heat with a little confectioners' sugar. Stirring it all the time while it simmered, she felt the familiar ache in her jaw at the tart aroma. As soon as it was ready, she pushed the mixture through a sieve until she had the right consistency. Lumps of rind didn't go down well.

The heat rose in the enclosed space, and she wiped her forehead with her sleeve, bumping her sore nose in the process. "Ouch!" Her eyes watered with the pain, and she held her nose between her fingers until the throbbing subsided. She dabbed at her eyes with her hanky and checked the sugar mixture again.

Once the pan and workbench reached the right temperature and she settled into her routine, she could produce batch after batch without thinking. Only if she allowed herself to get distracted was she likely to make a mistake, resulting in a cut or burn to her hands. On occasions, she overheated a batch and it would crystallise, but it had been a long time since that had happened. Pa had taught her well. Pa had taught them both – her and Tillie – but for reasons never explained, Elias would not allow the sisters to work together. But then nothing about him surprised her any more.

Gwenna checked the temperature of the sugar mixture with the large thermometer, stirred in the lemon essence and decided it was ready. Picking up a padded woollen cloth in each hand, she felt every muscle protest as she lifted the pan from the range and tipped the contents onto the hot, greased worktable.

Using the wide scraper, she briskly folded the sticky substance in on itself several times, flipped it over, and folded it again until it was cool enough to handle. With a quick flick of the wrist, she threw the knot over the hook fixed on the wall above her head and started stretching and twisting the sugar mixture over and over again – pulling it out and turning it back on itself in a continuous motion – until it was the right consistency and turned a creamy colour.

"You do that so well, Gwenna," praised Bethan. "You have the right action. I used to watch Owen and your father in amazement, but you are as good as they were – and as quick. I can't say the same for Elias, but he already knows that. It's one of the reasons he's so hard on you."

Feeling comforted by the soothing action, Gwenna smiled her thanks at Bethan. She lifted the molten mass off the hook and dropped it on the table. Picking up her father's favourite wood-handled knife, she cut the sugar mixture into manageable chunks and, regularly dipping one hand into a bag of fine rice flour, she kept up a constant motion, kneading and stretching each piece back and forth between her hand and the heated worktop to make long rolls. Once satisfied with the length and thickness, she swiftly chopped them into smaller pieces using the oversized scissors that were almost as long as her forearm. She shaped each of them into little balls and laid them out on a tray to cool and harden.

A small hand pulling at her skirt interrupted her rhythm.

"Can you make me a lollipop? Please, Gwenna?"

" 'Course I can, Charlie," she smiled. She glanced over her shoulder towards the door, nervous about Elias coming in, but shrugged the thought away. It didn't matter. He would either get angry or he wouldn't, never mind what she did.

Taking a couple of portions, she added a drop of cochineal to one and kneaded the colour in. Twisting the two pieces together into a long roll, she curled it into a circle, put a wooden skewer through, and handed the red and white lollipop to Charlie. His grin was worth a thousand tears. He was beautiful when he smiled.

A memory of Pa flashed into her mind. He used to make special lollipops for her and Tillie when they were little. She missed him so much – and her sister. *Oh, Tillie, what shall I do? I'm torn. Can I afford to have dreams?*

A wave of loneliness washed over her. One by one the household had emptied. A few years ago, the oldest of her stepsisters, Louisa, had married Albert Evans the butcher. Then Janetta wed. She chose Percy Lewis, who worked for the ironmongers. They'd gone before Pa died and understood little of what their brother was like except from what they'd been told. Soon after, Samuel disappeared. Time and circumstances had put distance between them.

And now Tillie was married too.

The only chance the four girls had to catch up and talk without the pressure of life was when Elias was away, or sometimes after chapel on Sunday mornings. Gwenna and Bethan would walk past the two-storey corner house in Beresford Street where Tom and Tillie lived, on their way to the gothic-style wooden church in Wellington Street – not that St James's was chapel, as they knew it; the place was much fancier. And every time Gwenna walked past, she peeked into Tillie's front room and dreamt of turning it into a shop where the two of them could work together.

Gwenna tried not to dream too much and shut her heart and mind to the possibilities such thoughts opened up. Elias would never allow it.

⚬⚬⚬⚬⚬⚬⚬

2

FRUSTRATIONS AND REGRETS

April 1899

The following month, much to Gwenna's surprise, Elias decided to accompany Hugh on his rounds to the Franklin area. They had stock to deliver to regular buyers, as well as seek out new customers. Most times Elias serviced the local shops, leaving Hugh to do the travelling further afield. Nevertheless, every month Elias ended up in a state of indecision. Was Hugh doing the job well enough? Should he go instead and leave Hugh behind to replenish the stock? But he didn't trust Hugh enough to leave him on his own. Round and round, Bethan and Gwenna had heard these arguments, but they did not dare express an opinion.

"Whatever you decide is best, Elias," said his mother.

"Yeah, I'll go this time. We'll get it done in half the time and I might get a few new clients. We could do with some. The local market's gettin' too crowded."

Elias had a number of fixed ideas on why he was having problems. First, there was that vulgar American company, the Chicago Sugar Boilers, with shops at either end of Karangahape Road.

15

" ' ... due to unprecedented success', it said in their advertisement," Elias spluttered. "I'd like a bit of that 'unprecedented success' to come my way." He got to his feet and paced the floor, rubbing his hands through his hair. "Even Smeeton's boasts a confectionery section in his grocery store these days, never mind that the Chicago crowd is right next door to them. They've started demonstrating how to make sweets in the shop window too, giving away all the trade secrets. It's not right, I tell ya. Not right at all."

And second, according to Elias, their slump was all to do with the long-lasting after-effects of the 1886 stock market crash.

Gwenna had little knowledge of the crash or the Shop Hours Bill passed in 1894, except it had forced a half-day closing for all shops except pharmacists, confectioners and eating houses.

"Surely that must be better for us?" said Bethan. "If confectioners are one of the few shops open, won't they sell more goods and need more supplies? We sell medicinal lozenges and sweets for those who just want lollies for their own sake. Won't we benefit both ways?"

Elias grunted. Although many shops had begun selling confectionery to get around the law, his order base had not increased to match. Competition was fierce among the nearly six hundred sugar boilers and retail outlets in the city.

"Stick to what you're told, old woman, and leave me to manage the trade," said Elias, dismissing his mother with a wave of his hand.

Gwenna wished he *would* manage the business – and properly. Of late, she'd often thought to remind him of all the plans her father once had. If only Elias would listen.

Pa had built up a healthy manufacturing and distribution trade in the six years between their arrival in Auckland in 1891 and his death two years ago. In that time, her father's ideas had grown larger, and he'd developed plans to expand and open a retail shop.

In readiness, he had leased their large, two-storey house with its courtyard and stable for the horse and wagon, and he'd enclosed the lean-to at the back. There, he built a working kitchen where they could process larger batches of sugar, and where a young Tillie and an even younger Gwenna had refined their skills.

But Pa's plans never came to fruition. Too many drenchings while making the deliveries and too many long, hard hours with a recalcitrant Elias and an inexperienced Samuel had drained his strength. A cold, wet winter took its toll and Pa's dreams died with him.

Since then, Elias had chased Samuel away, irritated enough customers that they were losing sales, and split the family. Gwenna hoped he wouldn't lose the roof over their heads as well.

"Now, listen to me Gwenna. I want no nonsense while I'm away. No gadding off to the stores, ya hear? She can do all that." He pointed at Bethan. "You're to double the stock levels by the time I get back so I can do the local shops."

He pulled a list from his pocket: peppermint drops, Irish moss, barley sugar, aniseed balls, butterscotch, gumballs, humbugs and bullseyes, as well as toffees, jellies and caramels, and so it went on. Gwenna nodded and took the piece of paper – she was going to be busy if she was to fill those quantities – but resisted the urge to say anything.

A small tingle of anticipation flared. With Elias away, Gwenna could see more of Johnno, and she and Tillie could get together. Maybe she could also arrange for Louisa and Janetta to visit their mother.

Bethan prepared a basket of food while Gwenna helped with the loading and soon after, the wagon was ready to leave. They watched Hugh ease the horse and wagon around the turn at the end of the street until he was out of sight.

Gwenna whipped off her apron and wrapped a shawl around her shoulders.

"Are you going to see Tillie so soon? Don't go yet, Gwenna *bach*. He might turn around to check on you."

"Not with Hugh driving, he won't. Stop worrying, Mam. I'll be all right, you'll see. And I might have good news when I get back." Gwenna stooped to kiss the work-weary cheek. Within minutes she was knocking at Tillie's door.

Tillie's husband Tom worked in the men's department at the impressive new store of Smith & Caughey near the corner of Queen and Wellesley streets. The pair were a perfect match. Tom was a bright, cheery person who could sell coal to a coal miner if he wanted to, while Tillie was good-natured and a skilled needlewoman. She did piecework for Smith & Caughey, making handkerchiefs, cravats and shirts, and any other items they needed. The tailors, of course, made the suits. Tillie was happy with her lot, even if sometimes she wished she could make pretty things for the ladies, but those tasks went to the professional dressmakers.

"Gwenna, how wonderful!" exclaimed Tillie as she opened the door and hugged her sister. "But what are you doing here?"

"Elias is out of town for a few days. We need a family chat, Till. Bethan is in a poor way. Elias makes her life miserable and I fear for Charlie. Elias could turn on him any day."

Hand in hand, Tillie led the way through to the kitchen at the back. The sweet, warm smell of baking stirred Gwenna's taste buds – one of Tillie's other skills was making fudge.

"And what about *your* life? He's harder on you."

"But I'm strong enough to take it. She isn't," insisted Gwenna.

"Hmm. Maybe. But I'm not so convinced after his last attack. Your face is getting better and the bruise is fading at last, but you were lucky he didn't break your nose."

"I'm all right," said Gwenna, chewing the side of her fingernail, dismissing her sister's concern. "It's Mam and Charlie we have to worry about."

"But what can we do?"

"I'm wondering if Louisa or Janie could consider taking Mam and Charlie to live with them ..."

The kettle whistled, Tillie made tea and laid slices of fudge on a plate, and for a few minutes the two sisters chatted about the latest news and gossip as if there were no problems in the whole world.

Before long, they began to talk about the family.

Charlie was now attending the Beresford Street School. He had proved to be a quick learner when he was well enough to go, but he couldn't even raise his head when the coughing fits took him, and winter was yet to come. On those days, Bethan fretted over him, which only served to annoy Elias and make his temper worse. Neither was Tillie surprised to learn trade was not going as well as Elias wanted, since he was always so disagreeable.

"Janie couldn't take Mam. She's pregnant again," said Tillie. "I don't know how they're going to manage when the baby comes. Let's hope Mr Lewis gets a promotion or an increase in his pay and they can find a house of their own instead of living in lodgings."

"Of course. Silly me, always wishing too hard for a way out."

Gwenna bit into her second piece of fudge and closed her eyes as she let it melt on her tongue. "This is gorgeous. How do you get it so smooth?"

"Practice. As you well know. We both have the knack." Tillie sipped her tea. "Louisa might consider taking her, but not yet. They can't while they're living with his parents; however, she says they plan moving to a house of their own sometime in the New Year."

She agreed to talk with Louisa and get both her and Janie to visit their mother before Elias and Hugh got back.

"It would be wonderful if we could all be together again just for a little while," said Gwenna, fiddling with the empty plate, turning it round and round. "Pa had such dreams. We have to do something to save his dreams, Tillie. We have to."

<hr/>

3

DOORS OPEN; DOORS CLOSE

October 1899

One of the bright spots lightening Gwenna's darker days was Charlie – he had survived the winter. Despite a serious bout of bronchitis, he was well again now, and colour crept back into his cheeks as spring arrived.

Another bright spot was Johnno. His endless good humour and persistent wooing gladdened her heart and put a different sort of spring in her step. A secret smile tweaked Gwenna's lips at the memory of their frequent trysts over the winter months. Johnno had turned up at the oddest of times, with a message to meet him when Elias wouldn't notice her absence. He took her to the theatre where they sat in the cheapest seats at the back; they went dancing, and kissed in the darkest shadows; they made love and promised the impossible.

But what occupied Gwenna's mind the most as she packed a basket with soup, pies and cakes, were thoughts of the day several months earlier when Elias and Hugh were away and all the girls had got together.

Bethan had been cheered – happy even – having her daughters and grandchildren around her. She rarely saw them, despite living within walking distance. That day, though, small niggles and past resentments were put aside, and the women enjoyed each other's company, chatting about what was going on in their lives. Except it hadn't gone quite as Gwenna had wished.

"Do any of you know where my Samuel is these days?" Bethan asked. She always asked. She missed her middle son and always believed he'd return one day. The sisters glanced at one another, each waiting for someone else to speak.

"Last I heard, he was in Christchurch," Louisa shrugged. "Not that I care much. I've got far too many things to do than worry about him. What with my two, and all the social and charitable commitments I have, it's more than a body can cope with." Louisa took a bite of Tillie's fudge, peered at it sideways and put it down again.

Ungrateful cow, thought Gwenna.

"Didn't I hear you say something about wanting a larger house of your own?" Tillie asked, hoping the answer would help Bethan.

"Oh, you know how it is. Time will tell. We are rather overcrowded, but Albert's father has just taken on a new apprentice, so at the moment Bertie is far too busy in the butchery to consider it. I even have to help with the chores, of all things. Just look at my hands! Maybe we'll think about it in the New Year. Father-in-law has said Bertie is due for a promotion."

Gwenna thought she sounded far too smug, but any thoughts that Louisa might help Bethan had been thwarted.

Janetta wasn't much better. Not wanting to be outdone by her older sister, she retaliated. "Percy is

22

expecting a promotion, *and* an increase in salary in the New Year." The sisters shot a snippy glance at each other, but Janie had always been the more good-natured of the two. "It's nice, getting together like this, isn't it? But it'll be my last outing for a while. Percy says I'm getting so big with this child, it wouldn't be decent to be seen in public. I wish we had a place of our own, or at least a little outdoor space. A toddler in the house is so demanding." Her voice faded away with a sigh.

"Poor, hard-done-by Janie," muttered Gwenna under her breath, getting more cross with her stepsisters as time passed. "You don't come around that often," she said out loud.

"Well, no. I suppose not. It's Elias's fault. He is so rude, I simply can't be bothered."

Gwenna saw the way Bethan's face fell at Janetta's words, and when Louisa said something similar, her shoulders collapsed and she dropped her head.

The four sisters parted company, agreeing they'd had a lot of fun, and yes, they should do it again. Some day. Soon. Gwenna didn't have any expectations it would be soon enough. Sometimes she despaired of ever being allowed to live her own life. More and more, Bethan's daughters left it to her to enrich Bethan's life with news and companionship …

"Righto, Mam," said Gwenna when she'd finished packing the basket. "I'm away round to Tillie's. Are you sure you'll be all right?"

Elias's behaviour had worsened since his trip away. He'd always liked a drink at the local after work, and more so at the weekends, but of late his drinking had increased to the point where he came home drunk most nights. Gwenna worked harder than ever to appease his

23

demands, but nothing she did was good enough, and she and Bethan had taken to shutting themselves in their rooms at night to avoid him.

"Yes, yes, girl. I'm fine. I'll put Charlie to bed soon and then get away meself. Elias doesn't come looking for me. It's only if I'm in his way does he remember he's angry about something."

Gwenna was tired of being the brunt of her stepbrother's temper, and Hugh being away more often than not, trying to salvage the declining sales, was not helping matters. When questioned by Gwenna, Hugh reluctantly admitted the trip with Elias earlier in the year had been a disaster. While Hugh had not dared to say what had happened or what he thought, Gwenna pieced together enough to confirm her opinion that Elias was destroying the business.

Not that it made any difference. She liked Hugh. A lot. He was sturdy and reliable, but he was no talker – and no salesman either. Elias needed someone like Tom Griffiths to be the frontman.

As soon as the thought popped into her head, she dismissed it. Right now, Tillie needed Tom in a steady, well-paid job. She was expecting, which – after the best part of two years' trying – was a joy, but she was so ill every morning, she could do little else for the rest of the day. Cooking meals turned her stomach and she no longer made her fudge. To help out, Bethan baked an extra pie or made broth, and Gwenna took it around to them when Elias was out. Tonight was no exception.

With a shawl around her shoulders, Gwenna picked up her basket. "Take care then. He might be different tonight. He's been like a bear with a sore 'ead all day. He can't abide the thought that the new government might pass the forty-hour week into law." She stooped to kiss her stepmam on the forehead. "I'll be as quick as I can."

The heels of Gwenna's boots echoed between the buildings as she hurried along the street and turned the corner. Loads of people were still out and about celebrating 'Labour Day'. Not that everyone had heard of Samuel Parnell, the man who, in 1840, had successfully petitioned the government for an eight-hour working day, nor that it had taken fifty years – until 1890 – to commemorate his achievement. Thousands had taken to the streets that day to watch the parade. Government workers had been given the day off, and many businesses had closed for the first time. While the celebrations were now an annual affair, Labour Day would not be an official public holiday until next year.

Even so, the laws still allowed employers to make women and young people work up to nine and a half hours a day, as well as several late nights. Gwenna had read in the newspapers how many hoped the upcoming election on the sixth of December would change the situation. New laws would be passed so nobody worked more than forty hours, and shop closing hours would be regulated. She, too, hoped it was true.

She zigzagged her way between the people, laughing and saying hello to those she knew. She loved the bustle of Karangahape Road, harness jangling as the horse tram clattered past, cyclists ringing their bells to let people know they were coming, market sellers calling out their wares and the windmill looming above. They were all part of the fabric of life.

As she headed down the street towards Tillie's, she heard Johnno's voice.

"Wait up, Gwenna. Where ya going in such a hurry?"

She stopped to wait for him, smiling. "To Tillie's. She's not well, so I'm taking them supper, but I have to get back home before Elias."

Johnno took the basket from her and reached for her hand as they walked on. "Well, don't fret there. I've just seen him in the King's Arms along in France Street. He's already three sheets to the wind and has plans to be totally legless, by the sound of things. He'll not bother you tonight. Let's talk awhile."

Gwenna wasn't sure whether to be cheered by this news or more nervous. Sooner or later Elias would find his way home, and what happened then would depend on how bad he felt.

"That's a relief, but I still can't stay. He'll have a right sore 'ead tomorrow, and I don't want to give him any reason to be mad at me."

"I can make sure he don't make it home tonight, if'n you like."

Gwenna stopped in her tracks, letting go his hand. "What are you suggesting?"

Johnno tapped a finger to his cap. "Just that I know people who could take care of 'im."

"No," said Gwenna, shocked at the thought. "You can't. Elias has enough enemies of his own. I don't want to see him hurt."

"Gwenna Price, you're too soft-'earted. He won't hesitate to hurt you when it suits him. And he needs a taste of his own medicine."

Shaking her head, she tried to take the basket off him. "Leave it, Johnno. I'll just drop this off and head straight back."

But Johnno wouldn't let go. "I'll come with you then. And walk you home." The twinkle in his eye gave her some idea of how long the walk home might take, and what they might do on the way. She quivered at the thought.

While Johnno hovered in the shadows out of sight, she knocked on the door.

"Hello, love," said Tom, the lamp in the hall casting light on Gwenna as he held the door open. "Tillie's asleep. She's had a bad day. Do you want to come in for a few moments?"

"Thanks, Tom, but no. I won't tonight. Here's your supper."

"You're too kind, Gwenna. Tillie and I are so grateful to you and Bethan, but there's too much for one person. I still have some left over from last time."

"Isn't Tillie eating anything?"

"A little soup sometimes. I hope this passes soon, poor girl. She worries me."

"Don't worry too much. Mam says it's normal for women to get this sickness. It'll pass in a few weeks."

Tom disappeared for a few moments to unload the basket while Gwenna waited. Across the street, staring at her silhouette, stood Hugh.

A few minutes later Gwenna had linked arms with Johnno. They walked to the bottom of Beresford Street and turned towards Western Park.

Johnno peered over his shoulder. "You know the fella who works for you watches you, don't you? Unless you're with me."

"Hugh? Never," said Gwenna in disbelief, glancing over her shoulder. "Why would he?"

"Dunno. Making sure you're safe, maybe. He's gone now." Johnno shrugged.

Any thoughts of Hugh disappeared from her mind

as she and Johnno wandered into the shadows, heads together, whispering, giggling and stealing quick kisses.

Finding a cosy spot between the buttress roots of a large tree, Johnno spread his coat out for them to lie on. Wrapped in his arms, Gwenna believed her dreams of another life *could* come true after all.

⸙⸙⸙⸙⸙⸙⸙⸙

4

Life-Changing News

2 December 1899

Gwenna returned from her second visit to the privy and flopped into Bethan's armchair. The unmistakable aroma of baking bread was making her feel queasy again, and she put her arm across her forehead to block the light. "I don't know what's wrong with me, Mam. Must be something I ate, but I feel awful sick."

Bethan wiped floury hands on her apron before pulling up a dining chair. "I've a mighty suspicion what ails you, Gwenna, but I was hoping I was wrong. I was hoping you wouldn't get yourself in this position."

"What position?" Gwenna, feeling hot, flapped her skirt and undid a button on her blouse.

"You're expecting, girl. Did you not suspect anything?"

"Expecting!" Gwenna's head throbbed and she felt faint. "I can't be." Disbelief, denial and dread fell over one another as she digested the news.

"I see more than you realise, young woman," said Bethan. "And aye, you can be, if you've been doing what I think you've been doing, with that young fella who's

been hanging around. An' getting Hugh to pass you messages. Poor man. It must break his heart."

"But … it's not …" Guilt and uncertainty warred with each other in her brain. "How can you be sure?"

"For goodness' sake, Gwenna. Don't be so naive. I've had five of me own, remember, and I know the signs. I've been watching you these last weeks. You've filled out a little, and your skin has changed. And I bet your breasts are giving you trouble, too. Nothing much, and no one else would pay any heed. Ask Tillie if you don't believe me."

"But …" Gwenna hesitated, feeling the hot blush rise from her chest and burn her cheeks. Unable to face Bethan, she covered her eyes with her hands. "But … he said … 'twould be all right if he didn't go all the way," she finished in a rush. Removing her hands from her face, she pleaded with her stepmother. "And we didn't. Honest, Mam. We didn't. So how …?"

"It doesn't work that way, pet."

Embarrassed and chastened, Gwenna fell to her knees in front of Bethan, wrapped her arms around her stepmam's neck and burst into tears. "Oh, what have I done?" she wailed through the sobs. "What's to become of me?"

Bethan patted the girl on her back and let her cry.

In time Gwenna asked, "What should I do?"

"The only thing you can do, Gwenna, *bach*."

Elias didn't know about the baby – yet – but Gwenna needed a solution before he found out. And she didn't have long – Bethan reckoned she was six or seven weeks gone. She would start to show soon.

A few mornings later Elias grabbed her as she returned from yet another visit to the privy, pinching the soft part of her underarm as he pulled her inside. His grip tightened and Gwenna winced. "I won't have you shirking off like this. Don't think I haven't noticed how many times you disappear." He shoved her down the hall in front of him and she lurched into a side table. "Now get to work."

She didn't know whether it was the pain in her stomach from hitting the table, the fact she felt so terrible, or sheer worry that caused her to snap, but the tension inside her erupted. "You've no right to tell me what to do, Elias Hughes. You do next to nothing these days except shout and bluster and drink yourself to a standstill. I work hard enough and always have done. Now leave me alone."

She stormed back to the kitchen and started banging the pots and pans around and slamming cupboard doors as she prepared another batch of sugar. A shudder overtook her as she thought of what she'd done. Elias hadn't followed her, but that didn't mean anything. He could still make her pay later for her outburst. Although maybe facing up to him might make him change his behaviour. The idea left her as quickly as it had come. The reason the beatings had decreased in the last few months was because Elias was hung-over more often than not, and had no enthusiasm for anything. If it wasn't for the work she and Hugh did, the business would have folded. Or rather the work Hugh *had* done, but he was gone now.

Hugh had left for training camp six weeks earlier, at the end of October. Gwenna had been more than surprised when he volunteered to join the forces going

to South Africa to fight a war. The first contingent, with two companies, had left in mid-October, and it seemed no sooner had they gone than Hugh volunteered for the second contingent, due to depart in January. How he got accepted, as he wasn't a military man, she'd never know, but he was good with horses, so she guessed that was the reason.

Elias had been furious, but Hugh just stood there listening to the rant, his face impassive. Gwenna hadn't completely fathomed Hugh's reasons for leaving either, but his words echoed in her mind long after he'd gone: 'I can let go now, knowing you'll be safe with someone else to look out for you.'

What did he mean? Let go? But something Johnno had said months ago about Hugh came to mind. She just couldn't remember what it was. Something about watching her.

Gwenna was still banging pots around when Bethan walked in.

"My, it's warm out there. What's all the noise about, girl?" Bethan removed her bonnet, hung it on the coat rack and patted her hair into place.

"Nothing!"

Regretting taking her temper out on Bethan, Gwenna turned to apologise and saw her mam was wearing her going-out dress: a slightly old-fashioned but pretty mid-blue skirt, with navy frills and ruffles at the back over a small bustle, and a matching tapered-front jacket.

"Where have you been?" Surprise registered in Gwenna's voice.

"Don't tell Elias. I slipped along to the post office to make sure I was on the register for next week's election."

"Wouldn't you still be on their list from '93?"

Gwenna was confused. Women had been granted the right to vote in time for the 1893 election, with very little fuss. It had been a momentous decision and New Zealand had been the world leader. She'd read about the suffragette troubles overseas and assumed every woman here would have rushed to sign up.

Bethan shook her head. "I wasn't on the list. I didn't vote …"

"You didn't?" interrupted Gwenna shocked by the missed opportunity. "Why ever not? I would have."

"I don't know. Life was busy – remember, we'd not been here long, not even two years at the time – and we didn't know much about the way the country worked. Your father always talked to me about what he knew of politics and his thoughts on the matter. It just didn't seem necessary at the time, since I agreed with him. It does now."

"What about last time then, in '96?" Gwenna wished she was twenty-one and could vote. "You must have voted last time." She couldn't wait to have her say in how the laws affected women.

Bethan shook her head in sadness. "No. Not last time either. Your father was so sick three years ago I couldn't bear to leave him, even for a little while. You remember, don't you?"

Gwenna stopped mid-action. Placing both hands on the wooden bench scrubbed almost white, her head fell forward as her eyes filled with the tears she'd been fighting since her run-in with Elias. She remembered only too well how sick her father had been. They'd expected – hoped – the summer would help him get better, and although his coughing had eased with the warmer weather, nothing had saved him.

"What is it, child?" Bethan put her arm around Gwenna's shoulder. "What's happened?"

Gwenna shook her head.

"You've been ill again. I can tell by the colour of your skin. Has Elias found out?"

Turning her face towards Bethan, she let the tears fall. "No. Not yet. At least, I'm not sure, but I shouted back at him when he turned on me again this morning. I'm sorry, Mam. I hope he doesn't take it out on you."

Bethan placed both hands on the girl's shoulders so she could look directly at her, and smiled. "Listen to me now, our Gwenna. I'm glad you stood up to him. It's about time. But don't you go concerning yourself about me. I'm the least of your problems."

Gwenna nodded in agreement – Elias was proving the biggest stumbling block in her scheme.

"That boy's so lost in his own worries I doubt he notices my presence, or lack of it. As long as Charlie keeps out of his way, he leaves me alone. It's you he resents. And you need to start thinking seriously about your own life."

Gwenna found it such a relief to talk about Johnno and express her worries about marrying him, even if she had little choice. "I do so love him, Mam, and dream of our life together, but ..." Gwenna stopped, unsure how to explain everything.

"Have you spoken to Johnno at all?"

Gwenna shook her head. "Not yet. I'm scared he won't want me now, not like this." Gwenna spread her hands over her stomach. "But it's his father who worries me most. He won't want me or this child. He hated me even when I was little and he came to pick up the goods. He'd snarl at me in that growling voice of his and push

me out of the way. I saw him kick a dog once. You know what he can be like. Rude and surly and mean, and ..."

"I'm sure you'll win him over. He can't be all bad," coaxed her stepmother.

Gwenna wasn't convinced. Not from the things Johnno said about him. "And of course I worry about you – and Charlie," she insisted. "How are you going to cope alone? There's not enough orders coming in as it is. What are you going to do for money?"

Trade had been falling off even before Hugh had left, and Elias had not been able to find a man to replace him. It seemed no one was desperate enough. The sweet-making tasks had fallen on Gwenna's shoulders, while Elias did the deliveries and managed the accounts in secret. Elias tried to hide how bad things were getting, but Gwenna could tell by the quantities she was making that they were in trouble.

Unfazed, Bethan had another surprise for her stepdaughter. "I'll find a job."

"What? You can't do that." Gwenna's head buzzed with other ideas of how they could earn an income. Bethan was neither old enough to receive the pension, nor had she been in the country long enough to qualify for the new scheme passed into law a year earlier. Even so, her going out to work was not something Gwenna had considered. "And what about Charlie?"

Gwenna's forehead creased into a frown. Bethan had been a bright, capable woman, raising her own four children, being mother to Gwenna and Tillie as well as wife, housekeeper and confectionery maid for two husbands. And then she brought up another baby. But what did any of that qualify her for in the workplace?

Especially now.

35

These days Bethan seemed to doubt her every thought and move and had become more submissive as time passed. The thought she could find work didn't fit.

"That depends on you," Bethan replied with a touch of her old self.

"Me?"

"Yes, child, you. Don't be slow-witted now. You can't stay here. You know you can't. Elias will throw you out on your ear when he finds out, which means you can't keep making sweets for him either. Which is why you need to talk to Johnno."

The reality of her situation sank home with the truth of Bethan's words. Gwenna had been avoiding the obvious and she needed to take action before someone did it for her.

"We can help each other," continued Bethan, letting Gwenna pass to check the sugar boiling in the pan. "I can pay you a little to take Charlie after school, which would give you money of your own. Take my advice – start making your own sweets. Go into opposition with Elias. Take your father's reputation with you and build on it. It's not too late."

A ray of hope flared. Maybe everything was not lost after all. But what would Johnno say? And more importantly, what would Black Jack say?

<hr>

5

DREAMS AND SCHEMES OF LOVERS

4 December 1899

Johnno hugged her, grinning from ear to ear. "Now you can't refuse me. You *have* to come away with me, Gwenna, my girl." In his excitement, he started to bounce them both around.

"Johnno, stop," she begged, trying to push his arms away even while laughing at his antics. Gwenna was relieved and delighted by his reaction, but she had to make him appreciate the difficulties that lay ahead of them. "Be sensible. This isn't a game. We have to work out what to do. Time is short."

Johnno released her, tugged his jacket into place, shrugged his shoulders back and put one hand on his jacket lapel. "Is this better?" His smile belied the attempted seriousness of his pose.

Gwenna laughed again. "Much."

She took the arm he extended and they continued their walk through the park. The gentle breeze rustled the leaves over their heads, shielding the early summer sun, while birds twittered and flitted around them. Gwenna loved the park – their park, she now called it, recalling

37

that special night not so many weeks ago. She could see the waters of the harbour from the top near the Ponsonby Road end. The sense of awe and wonderment her ten-year-old self had felt as their ship had sailed into Auckland had never left her, despite the reality of life since.

The pair followed the steep, meandering path through the trees leading to the flat area people used for games and picnics at the lower end.

"And I *am* being serious, Gwenna. We can get married now. As soon as you say the word."

"But where we will live? You can't expect me to live with your father. He frightens me. And Onehunga is too far away. We need to find somewhere nearer Bethan so I can help with Charlie …" She couldn't stop, not now she'd started. All her worries came pouring out in a flood of words and ideas. "And I need to set myself up somewhere to make my own sweets. Mam says I should fight Elias at his own game. And you have to find a job. You won't be able to go off for days or weeks on end with your father any more. We'll have the baby to think of. Oh, how will I manage to make all those sweets with a baby as well?"

Johnno dismissed her worries. "Living with Jack will be all right to start with. At least you'll be out of Elias's reach. And Jack would never hurt you," he reassured her. "He's a rogue in many ways, and he's not fond of women – interfering busybodies, he calls them – but he'll more than likely avoid you."

Gwenna still didn't like the idea. "I remember what he was like. I wouldn't put anything past him. Nor do I want the police knocking on the door."

Walking perfectly in step, with her arm linked in his, Johnno folded his hand over hers. "He's a tough trader, and a man would be wise not to cross him in business, but trust me, he'll leave you alone. I promise. Not so sure about the bobbies, though," he smiled. "But I'll be there if they come calling."

"It's not how tough he is as a trader that worries me, it's the not-so-legal side-trade you told me about. I don't want you involved in anything like that. And, Johnno, I must have somewhere to make my sweets. It's important."

The conversation waxed and waned as they continued their walk, turning towards Hepburn Street and zigzagging their way towards the shoreline at Freemans Bay.

"I love it down here, close to the water's edge," she said.

On a bright summer morning eight years ago, they had sailed into the harbour shimmering under the sun as if someone had scattered jewels upon its surface. The Waitematā – place of sparkling waters – captured her heart. The greens of the land were colours she had never seen before, and the new city bustled with optimism. And nothing had changed as far as Gwenna was concerned.

Ships and coastal steamers lined the wharves or were tied up along the waterfront, loading and unloading goods; the steam from their engines rose into the sky, and the smell of coal and oil mixed with the salt-laden air.

"When I was younger, I used to wander out to Point Erin with my friends, to visit the Māori pā site or stand and watch the sawmillers handle those floating logs."

Johnno started to say something, but she stopped him.

"Listen. Can you hear the birds cawing and the waves lapping against the rocks?"

She'd learnt to love the sea in all is guises and seen it as angry as the howling winds or the moody skies above, but she never felt threatened by it, even through its wildest days – unlike the storms at home. Today, it was as peaceful as a lake under the bluest of blue skies.

"Not really," said Johnno. "There's too much other noise."

She shrugged, dismissing his indifference. "There's been a lot of talk about reclaiming the land at this end of the bay next. I wish they wouldn't. I love it as it is."

Over the last half-century, most of Commercial Bay, Official Bay and Mechanics Bay had been reclaimed, using fill from cutting back Point Britomart to create the rail link south. Wynyard Pier and the Queen Street wharf had been built back in the 1850s, leading to the formation of Customs Street and Quay Street by the 1870s. Now the authorities were turning their sights on the western end. They wanted to create flat land between the shore and hilly streets above for more industry.

"If you think it's noisy now, wait until they've done all that. They'll ruin it."

"It's called progress," said Johnno, not at all in keeping with her thoughts.

By the time they'd climbed their way back up Union Street to Karangahape Road, they'd agreed to a pre-Christmas wedding. "We've less than three weeks," Gwenna said. "We'd better hurry if we're going to get everything organised in time."

For a few brief moments, images of the sort of wedding she once imagined flashed through her mind, but she couldn't regret that now. She doubted Johnno would remember the age-old tradition of the man hand carving a lovespoon for his bride, let alone make one.

He'd been too young when his family had emigrated. But a wedding, even in a registry office, was better than none. She'd never live down the stigma of being an unwed mother, which would mean she'd never bring her pa's dreams – her dreams – to life.

With too many reservations still in her heart, she agreed they would move in with his father – if he would let her – until Johnno had saved enough money to lease a suitable property just for the two of them. Somewhere, she insisted, where she could make the boiled lollies and other sweet treats that would be the start of her business. Lost in her thoughts, she hadn't noticed Johnno avoided answering, never mind how many times she talked about what she wanted.

But, since neither of them was twenty-one, they needed permission from their head-of-household before anything could happen. Only then could they apply for a Notice of Intention to Marry and ask the registrar, or better still, a minister, to marry them.

Gwenna was less concerned about getting approval. "Mam told me she would give her permission, and since Elias isn't blood kin, I'll not need his consent. I'm almost tempted not to tell him at all and just disappear from his life, but it wouldn't be fair on Mam. She needs money coming into the house, and Elias won't be happy he has to find someone to replace me, what with Hugh gone as well."

"He won't try and force you to continue working for him, will he?" Johnno sounded anxious. "I don't want you near him once we're wed."

Anything was possible with Elias. Maybe he would stand back and let her go. Or he could threaten Bethan or Charlie and bully her into staying. Or he could decide she was a wanton, bringing shame on the family, and refuse to let her see them again. She fretted about what he would hold over her.

"Let's just wait and see. I'd better hurry, it'll be dark soon." And with a quick peck on Johnno's cheek she turned and ran the last part of the way home.

6

NOTHING CHANGES UNTIL
SOMETHING CHANGES

Gwenna stopped dead in her tracks the minute she opened the door. Her skin tingled a warning while her eyes scanned the room. Bethan sat in her usual chair by the fireplace, but her agitated fingers flew above her crochet work faster than normal. Charlie, sitting cross-legged on the floor beside her, leant as close to her legs as he could, resembling a statue more than a little boy. And there was no smell of cooking.

Her ears strained to hear the slightest sound out of place until a tiny flicker in Bethan's eyes alerted Gwenna to something behind her. She turned, but she couldn't move fast enough. Elias's fist skimmed past her jaw and slammed into the front of her shoulder. The force of the blow sent her stumbling.

She instinctively rolled into a foetal position as soon as she hit the floor, a matter of moments before Elias's boot struck. A searing pain shot up her spine. She flung her head back and arched her back away from the blow. Blood seeped from her tongue.

Within the veil of agony, she was vaguely aware of a loud, high-pitched scream. Was it her voice or someone else's? Charlie fell across her and a moan escaped her lips.

"Stop!" cried Bethan. "Elias, I said stop!" The tone she used brooked no argument. "This is too much, too far." She swept her arm towards the still prone figure of Gwenna, with a sobbing Charlie splayed over her.

"You … you're out of control." All her pent-up strain and anger burst forth. "Enough is enough. This bullying has got to stop. I will not tolerate it any longer."

Elias stared at his mother as if she was from another time and place. She hadn't spoken to him like that since his father died. Nor had she ever lifted a hand towards him. He took a threatening step towards her. "I'll do whatever I want, if I want …"

A resounding slap rang around the room as Bethan's hand connected with Elias's face. "No. You won't. Not any longer. I should have stepped in a long time ago, but I kept making excuses for you. Thinking you'd had enough hardships in your life, and I'd do nothing to add to them. But all I've done is condone your ghastly behaviour. It stops *now*."

Elias held a hand to his cheek. He opened his mouth to speak and then shut it again. Without another word he left the room, slamming the dividing door behind him.

Another groan from Gwenna brought Bethan to her knees beside the girl.

Charlie scrambled off his sister and started to wipe her brow. "You orright, now, Gwenna? Elias shouldn't have kicked you. He's bad."

"Yes, Charlie, Elias was bad, but we'll make her better, that we will," said his mother, holding Gwenna's hand as she tried to move. "Careful, don't get up too quickly," instructed Bethan. "Where does it hurt the worst?"

Still lying on the floor, Gwenna fingered her shoulder

where the first blow had knocked her over, but after moving her arm around in the socket found it wasn't too bad. Her elbow, which had taken the force of the fall, hurt as much. Both would mend soon enough.

"My back. Can you help me sit up?"

Bethan slid her arm under the girl's shoulder blades and lifted her into a sitting position against the chair leg. Charlie pushed a cushion behind her. They waited while Gwenna, biting her bottom lip to contain a moan, eased herself onto the side hurting the least.

By good luck, Elias's kick had landed on the softest part of her buttock. Bethan told her to expect a huge, painful bruise, and she'd find her joints stiff and bothersome as the days passed, but the damage could have been much worse. She could have lost the baby.

Bethan wiped away the tear trickling down the girl's face. "When you are ready, I want you to get off the floor and lie face down," she said. "I'll get some poultices for those bruises. Can you stand?"

Gwenna nodded. Gingerly, she folded her legs under and rolled onto her knees. Standing would have been impossible if not for Bethan's strong arms helping her to her feet. Still supporting her, Bethan watched her stepdaughter turn shades of white and green as she mastered the pain surging through her.

Beads of sweat popped out on Gwenna's forehead and upper lip as she stood. She released her breath and gave the faintest of smiles. "There, see. I'll be fine."

"Oh, aye? You will be, but not yet awhile." Bethan eased the outdoor coat Gwenna still wore off her sore shoulder. "Now come on, rest yourself on the sofa, and I'll make you a nice cup of sweet tea. And a slug of brandy won't go astray, neither. It'll help with the shock.

You can worry about getting up the stairs tomorrow."

Charlie was sent up to gather a pillow and a blanket. "And bring her house slippers with you," Bethan shouted after him before returning to remove Gwenna's button-up boots.

"I heard everything," whispered Gwenna. "Thank you."

Bethan shook her head. "No, don't thank me. It's me who should be saying sorry to you. I spoilt him. I let him pretend he was a man after his father died, although he was too young for the task. At some stage, I stopped teaching him right from wrong."

Bethan got to her feet and moved to the coal range to make the tea and start preparing a soothing poultice from brown paper soaked in sage and vinegar.

Gwenna raised her head enough for Charlie to push the pillow behind her. "Even so, you were mighty brave to stand up to him, Mam. He could have taken to you, the mood he was in."

"No, he wouldn't. He never hits me. Oh, yes, he'll grab me, and push and shove and be mighty rude, but he only strikes out at you."

Charlie tried to spread the blanket over Gwenna, but it was too big for him to manage and he put more over her face than anywhere else.

"Easy, Charlie," said Bethan, coming to his rescue. "Our Gwenna is real sore. Let me help you."

Once the blanket was in place and Charlie had tucked it around Gwenna's feet, Bethan took her hand. Her eyes carried years of sorrow. "I should have stopped him long before this. Forgive me."

Holding Bethan's gaze, Gwenna recalled all the years of mothering she had received from this kind, self-effacing woman. "There's nothing to forgive, Mam. You're trapped as much as I am." She stroked her stomach and thought about the child growing inside, and struggled to find a way to spring the trap.

Clothed in chemise and knickers, Gwenna lay curled on her side in an awkward position. She had no memory of undressing and could only guess what Bethan had put in her tea to help her sleep. Still feeling groggy, she opened her eyes a tiny bit, shut them, opened them again. Her stepmother sat asleep in the chair, and Gwenna could hear Charlie snuffling softly on the floor. A warm glow filled her heart at seeing them, like guardian angels protecting her.

A soft, grey light filtered through the window, and the embers in the coal range glowed through the blackness of its cast-iron door. Somewhere in the distance a horse snorted.

Aching and stiff, Gwenna tried moving one arm at a time. The left arm with the damaged elbow throbbed cruelly, but her right shoulder, where Elias's fist had struck, was worse. She was almost too scared to change position, fearing she'd aggravate the pain. Pins and needles gnawed at her skin, and one foot had gone numb. She couldn't stay still any longer.

She stretched one leg a bit at a time without making a sound. The burning sensation tearing through her lower leg and foot as soon as the blood coursed back was almost too much to bear, but she swallowed a cry. She tried to move the other leg.

Bethan was on her feet and kneeling beside her before Gwenna's deep-seated moan had come to an end. She whipped back the blanket and rubbed her stepdaughter's legs until the pain had eased. "Roll onto your stomach if you can, child. I'll put another poultice on the bruises and rub liniment into your back. It'll help with the soreness."

Gwenna had so many questions about what had happened after she fell asleep, but she scarcely had the strength to move, let alone talk. She needn't have worried.

"'Lias went out and hasn't come home," announced Charlie. "He won't hurt you any more, Gwenna. Mam says."

Bethan began to rub her home-made salve into Gwenna's skin. The sharp scent of camphor and peppermint tickled her nose, but it wasn't long before the heat from the ginger began to work its miracle and her muscles began to relax under her stepmother's gentle massage.

"Charlie's right. Elias hasn't come home all night. I hate to think what state he'll be in when he does return." Bethan stopped rubbing and pulled Gwenna's clothing into place. "Stay there and I'll put fresh poultices on your shoulder and under your backside."

Once they were in place and Gwenna lay propped up with cushions and pillows, Bethan handed her a cup of tea.

"What on earth did you put in the tea last night?" Gwenna smiled a thank you. "It must have been a powerful brew. Knocked me out completely."

"Never you mind. It did what it was supposed to do. You needed sleep so you can have your wits about you today. You'll need them."

The way Bethan spoke, the tone she used or maybe how she moved, set alarm bells ringing. Gwenna guessed the older woman had something more far-reaching to say.

"I'm worried for you." Bethan pulled her chair closer and sat with her cup and saucer on her knee. "I'm not sure I can keep Elias away from you," she said, staring at the tea swirling in the cup as she stirred it. "I took him by surprise last night, but when he's had time to think about it and fire himself up with alcohol and those … those *women* who can't answer him back …"

Gwenna snorted at Bethan's reference to the 'women of the night', as the local prostitutes were called. Although never spoken of in polite society, no one could deny either their presence or the fact they knew Elias rather too well.

But Bethan was serious. "He'll be madder'n a swarm of wasps when he does bother to come home, and I want you gone before then."

"It'll be all right, Mam. Don't worry. I'll just keep out of his way and make sure I don't do anything to annoy him."

Bethan shook her head. "It won't be enough any more, love. He knows about the baby. Don't ask me how, but he knows. He was waiting for you last night. He'd threatened to thrash Charlie if I didn't do what I was told." Bethan hung her head. "I'm sorry. I thought maybe if we did what he wanted, he wouldn't lose his temper. I was wrong. I'm ashamed of what I did."

Gwenna reached out and took her hand. Their eyes met. "It's not your fault …" she began, but Bethan shushed her. She hadn't finished.

"You're not safe here any longer. I want you to leave. Today. And I want you to take Charlie with you."

"Mam! You can't be serious." Gwenna's eyes followed Bethan's glance at the packed suitcases and holdall sitting by the door.

Bethan was deadly serious.

7

WHEN OPTIONS RUN OUT

Furious, and fired up enough to take silly risks when he found out what Elias had done, Johnno threatened to knock him through into next week and hope he'd never get up.

Tom Griffiths – dear Tom – managed to calm him down enough to listen to reason and hear Gwenna's side of the story.

"You'll put Bethan in danger if you go round there," she said, grateful for the sanctuary Tom had offered her. "I'm all right. Really, I am. And I'll be safe here at Tillie's for the time being. Elias won't come here, not into another man's home. He's too much of a coward."

When Johnno started to protest again, Gwenna handed him an envelope she'd taken from her pocket. "Stop your babbling now, and take this to the registrar – it's Bethan's permission for me to wed – and get us a licence as soon as possible."

Johnno didn't take the proffered letter; instead he let his eyes wander around the room to where Tom sat by the window, smoking his pipe and reading the paper. The headlines were full of news about the re-election of the Liberal Party and Richard Seddon as prime minister, and the war in South Africa. Tillie sat perched on the edge of her chair opposite, sewing.

Gwenna stared at Johnno, realisation clicking into place. "You've not spoken to your father. Have you?" she demanded, rising. "Have you?" He shook his head. "Look at me, Johnno Jones. Look me in the eye and tell me what game you're playing."

Johnno leapt to his feet and tried to reach out to Gwenna, but she backed away, her eyes flashing and her face white with disbelief.

"I tried to," he explained. "Honest, I did, but something's up with him. I don't know what 'tis, but he's not his usual self. And he was far too drunk to listen. I'll talk to him. I will."

But Gwenna wasn't ready to give in quite so easily. "You promised. The other night, you promised. If you can let me down once, how can I be sure you won't let me down again?"

He reached out for her a second time but let his hand drop. "You're the best thing ever happened to me, Gwenna, that you are. Give me the letter and I'll get us a licence, quick as a flash. You'll see. And I'll look after you for the rest of our lives." He crossed to where Tom sat. "Thank you kindly, sir, for taking care of Gwenna."

He extended his hand, but before Tom could stand or say anything, Gwenna added, "And Charlie. Don't forget Charlie."

Turning towards her, Johnno was confused. "What's Charlie got to do with anything?"

"He's at school right now, but Charlie comes with me – with us." Her pulse raced as doubts entered her head. They'd not talked about Charlie. Maybe Johnno wouldn't want him. Maybe Black Jack would refuse.

51

Twisting her fingers together, she spluttered, "It's not safe for him. He Pa's son, just like I'm Pa's daughter, and Elias hates us both. He'll hurt him. I just know he will. Please, Johnno. Please. For my sake. Let me keep Charlie with me." Moments before, her eyes had flashed with anger; now they beseeched him.

For too many long seconds not a sound could be heard except for the ticking of the clock.

The whole room stopped breathing, waiting.

Shuffling his feet awkwardly, Johnno cleared his throat. "I'm not so sure I could talk Jack into letting Charlie come."

Gwenna covered her mouth with her hand and her legs started to shake. What she was about to say could destroy her prospects. "If Charlie can't come, then I can't …"

Tillie was on her feet before Gwenna had finished her sentence. She placed her hand on her sister's arm to stop her from saying the wrong thing. "Don't listen to her right now, Mr Jones. She is too overwrought to know what she's saying. Let's just wait until after you've talked to your father before we say anything further."

Tom agreed. "Mrs Griffiths is right, lad. Talk to your father, get his permission for the two of you to wed and then we can talk about what happens next."

In time, they reached an agreement. Not the one Gwenna wanted, nor Bethan, but it met their needs for the time being, even if Gwenna and Charlie had little chance to say anything about their futures.

At first, Black Jack refused to give his permission

for his son to marry, but when Johnno threatened – no, promised – he and Gwenna would find somewhere else to live, and his father would be on his own in a household of one, Jack relented. His father needed Johnno to run the cartage business more than Johnno needed his father. How else would Jack have the freedom to expand the money-lending business but, Jack was emphatic – no children. Johnno omitted to tell him he'd have a grandchild before long, whether he liked it or not. That surprise could come later.

Tom came to the rescue before Gwenna could call everything off.

"Charlie can live with us, for the time being, at least," he announced. "He'll be a good introduction to having youngsters around the house."

Tillie had recovered from her morning sickness and was thriving in her pregnancy and, wanting to give the boy much-needed love and security, his big sister had readily agreed. "Charlie's closer to Mam here too," she added.

Bethan had disagreed. "Isn't it too close? I don't trust Elias, despite what he said. He could still decide to use Charlie as his punchbag. I can't risk it. He'd be out of reach with Gwenna. Elias wouldn't bother travelling to Onehunga to find them."

Tom's assurances swayed her decision. "He'll be safe with me. And you can come around anytime. Spend as much time with your children, and your grandchildren-to-come, as you like."

Dear Tom, always giving them strength and comfort.

Gwenna sat alone in Tillie's living room, weighing up all that had happened in the last few whirlwind days. Their first shock had come when Bethan had rushed around late in the afternoon the day after Gwenna had found shelter with her sister.

"You'll never believe it," Bethan blurted, ignoring the usual pleasantries as Tillie let her in. "Elias came home looking like he'd slept in the hedge and unable to string two words together." She'd waved away Gwenna's concerns and told her to listen. "I was in the kitchen, making bara brith, and all of a sudden he was there, staring at me, saying he was hungry. After I'd fed him and given him several cups of tea, he seemed a little brighter."

Tom arrived home then, interrupting Bethan's tale. Tillie made them all a pot of tea, and after Tom lit his pipe, they sat together listening while Bethan continued her story.

"He must have noticed how quiet the house was because he asked where you and Charlie were. I told him you were gone."

Gwenna held her breath, anticipating the worst.

"I expected him to demand to know where, or for him to lose his temper or something, 'cept he didn't. He just sat there staring at me." Bethan's voice faded; she seemed sad and far away.

"Mam! What did he do?" demanded Gwenna.

Bethan jumped. She viewed the trio before her as if she didn't quite know where she was. "He looked terrible, and my heart went out to him. I remembered the little boy he used to be and wanted to hug him and kiss it all better like I used to."

"After all he's done to you!" Gwenna's bitterness made her sharp.

Bethan sighed. "He's still my son. My firstborn.

You'll understand when you have children of your own, my dear. You both will. You never stop being a mother, and never stop loving your children even when they disappoint you."

Removing the pipe from his mouth, Tom brought the conversation back on course. "What did he say, Mrs Price?"

Bethan smiled for the first time. "He said, 'good'."

"Good?" echoed Tillie. "Just good?"

"To start with. Then he said, 'It's probably for the best. It'll be just you and me now, Mam, just like it should have been.' And then he got cleaned up and started to sort and tidy the storeroom."

In the days since, Bethan reported Elias was the happiest she'd seen him since his father had died all those years ago. "Long may it last," she said. "And he's willing for me to find something suitable to bring in a few coins. Only if I want to, mind. I'll ask around and see what there is. Neither of us are anywhere near as good as you with the sugar, Gwenna dear, and until Elias finds someone to replace you, we'll need something extra in the coffers."

Gwenna had accepted the arrangements must stand until after the baby was born and until she and Johnno had the time and money to make other plans. Her main concern now was getting through the rigmarole and paperwork of getting married before she started to show. No doubt the busybodies and gossips would put two and two together when the baby came, but they'd be married by then.

"I've got it." Johnno waved the marriage licence above his head as Tom let him in. "It took a lot of persuasion,

I can tell you. But the girl at the counter liked the idea it was a surprise Christmas present."

"Hardly a surprise," laughed Gwenna, relieved by his news.

"Maybe, but she didn't need to know that, did she?" Johnno grinned and knelt on one knee beside Gwenna. He took her hand, kissed it, his gaze not leaving hers. "So, my lovely girl. Will you please do me the honour of marrying me at 8 am on Christmas Eve?"

"Christmas Eve?" Surprise put a squeak in her voice, which didn't quite match her glee.

Put out by her response, he got to his feet. "And what's wrong with that?"

"Nothing." Gwenna jumped up and stood in front of him. "Nothing at all. In fact," she dipped her head in a flirtatious manner and placed her hands on his chest, "it's rather lovely." And smiled up at him.

Pacified, Johnno grinned back. "I'm glad. The minister's agreed to marry us first thing, before the normal church service."

If Tom and Tillie hadn't been watching, she would have kissed him but all of that would have to wait.

"There's no time to lose, then," Tillie said. "We've lots to organise. Who should we invite? I suppose we'll have to ask Louisa and Janetta, but let's not let on the reason just yet. They'll find out soon enough. We'll need food for the wedding breakfast …"

Both Johnno and Gwenna tried to protest it wasn't necessary, but Tillie put a stop to their arguments.

"Of course we'll celebrate. You're to come back here. And I'll have no more arguments about it. *And* I'll have no arguments about the dress I'm going to make you either."

"Tillie. No. You can't. That's too much. I don't deserve it."

Tillie took her sister's hands in hers and, bobbing her head to and fro, forced Gwenna to meet her eyes. "Listen to me, my girl. I never want to hear you say you aren't deserving ever again. It's absolute nonsense. You are the most loving, the most loyal and the most worthy person I know – apart from Tom." She paused long enough to smile at her husband, the glance they shared private and reassuring. "You will have a new dress. You will hold your head up high, and you will look forward to your new life with John Jones and the little one with pride."

With joyous tears coursing down her cheeks, Gwenna nodded, overwhelmed with gratitude. She croaked out a whispered 'thank you' and flung her arms around her sister's neck.

8

THE HAPPIEST DAY OF A GIRL'S LIFE

Christmas Eve 1899

On the morning of her wedding, Gwenna laughed as she twirled in her china-silk dress. Tillie had used the heaviest weight she could get and stitched the full skirt and contoured jacket to fit to perfection. Gwenna appeared taller and slim. Slim enough no one would guess her condition.

"It's beautiful, Tillie. Thank you so much. And I love the colour. It reminds me of summer roses." Her smile said it all. She turned first to one side, then the other, to see in the mirror the way the pleats fell over the small bustle.

"I must say the deep mauvish pink suits you well," agreed her sister. "I'm glad I chose it now. It puts colour in your cheeks."

A plain ivory cotton blouse with a lace jabot peeking out under the collar and lace cuffs completed the ensemble.

"Look," Tillie said. "It's practical as well as pretty. I've gathered and stitched it here and here at the waistband so you can let it out when you need to. And you can let out the blouse and corset. I purposely put the lacing at the front and gave you extra-long ties."

Tillie picked up the matching hat, decorated with a jaunty feather and a handmade rose and tilted it on an angle over Gwenna's curls. Pulling a detachable veil over her sister's face, Tillie glowed with happiness at the picture before her. "There. Perfect," she said, kissing Gwenna's cheek. "Shall we go?"

Tom escorted Gwenna down the aisle to where Johnno stood, with Charlie as her page. The ladies of the church had decorated it beautifully in readiness for the Christmas celebrations, but the only other people in attendance to witness their marriage were Bethan and Tillie. Black Jack hadn't been invited; they had not placed any announcement in the newspapers, which might have drawn onlookers, and no one was surprised when Louisa and Janetta declined the invitation. Although privately hurt and saddened, none of them said anything. Louisa thought only of herself, and Janetta always did as Louisa said.

The ceremony over, the bride and groom emerged. Charlie scattered rose petals on the ground while the others threw rice over the couple. Small it may have been, but no two people could have behaved more lovingly, and no one else could have wished them a happier future more than the four people there to watch: Gwenna's stepmam, her sister and two brothers by law and birth.

They sat down to a scrumptious breakfast of sausages and bacon on fried bread, with baked beans, eggs and fried potato, far more extravagant than their usual fare, and washed it down with copious quantities of tea.

"A meal fit for a queen," announced Tom, rubbing his stomach.

Charlie ate like a king, as if he'd never eaten before.

"Oh, how beautiful," Gwenna squealed when Bethan carried through the delicately iced and decorated fruit cake. Tom poured them each a glass of sweet wine and proposed a toast. "May you both have lasting happiness."

As soon as the clinking of glasses had been completed and the first sip taken, Tillie insisted they cut the cake. In high spirits, the couple fed each other a bite – a symbol that each would provide and care for the other for the rest of their lives. Amid applause from Tom and Tillie, and trying to suppress laughter as crumbs fell from mouths too full of cake, Gwenna felt fit to burst with a joyfulness she hadn't felt since before her pa died. The glow from Johnno's eyes warmed her to the core, and the day became a dreamy swirl of jubilation.

By mid-afternoon, Johnno was keen they get on their way. Bethan had delivered the last of Gwenna's belongings, and she and Tillie had packed the bags with bed linen, towels, tablecloths and other knick-knacks that would help turn a masculine household into a family home. Johnno and Gwenna said their goodbyes, picked up their bags and headed to the horse tram, which would take them to the impressive railway station, opened four years earlier, at the foot of Queen Street.

Their new life together was about to start. With only a 45-minute trip to Onehunga ahead, Gwenna couldn't decide if she was shaking with excitement or trepidation. She had no idea what to expect.

The house where Johnno and his father lived was far worse than she could ever have imagined. The ramshackle farmhouse, in desperate need of a coat of paint, sat up a long driveway and in the middle of nowhere as far as Gwenna was concerned. Wobbly fences and fields were all she could see. Even the animals were sparse. Some distance away, a neighbouring house was visible.

The isolation scared her, even if the house was within walking distance of the train station, along a rough dirt road. Its biggest advantage, from Johnno and his father's point of view, was the easy access to the road south for the goods wagon.

Hand in hand, she and Johnno walked up the driveway, around to the back of the house and up a set of steps. Battling the instinct to run, she entered the neglected and miserable house. She didn't want to be there – and definitely not on her own.

Wrinkling her nose at the musty smells redolent of mould, dirt and stale smoke, an eerie sense of sorrow passed through her. She tugged on Johnno's sleeve and whispered. "This place frightens me. It's got such a feeling of sadness about it."

He smiled down at her and patted her hand. "It's not that bad. You'll get used to it."

Gwenna doubted that was possible and clung tighter to Johnno. He had a habit of dismissing her concerns. An apparition arose at the opposite end of the gloomy kitchen. Trembling in fear, she emitted a loud squeal and buried her face in Johnno's arm.

"Shut that girl up before I do," growled a voice from the shadows. "Can't stand women's noises."

"Behave yourself, Jack," answered Johnno. "You scared her, that's all. Hiding there in the dark. This is my wife Gwenna. Your new daughter-in-law. Gwenna, my father Jack."

Gwenna could hear the pride in Johnno's voice as he made the awkward introductions, and smiled encouragingly as she raised her head.

"Make sure she's useful and keeps out of my way," the gravelly voice grunted.

As Gwenna's eyes adjusted to the gloom, she saw Jack, wearing an ancient military-style overcoat, and wide-brimmed hat, standing by a horsehair sofa spewing its contents through tears in the covering. She remembered him in an instant and shuddered. While of the same tallish and thin build as Johnno, hardly anything else about him was like Johnno. Gwenna could see little of his shaded face, even when he stormed past her and out the door.

In those small, black eyes, she saw menace.

Now they were alone, Johnno showed her the rest of the four-roomed cottage, except for the room where Jack slept and the room she assumed was the front parlour. "Jack keeps it closed," was all Johnno said.

There wasn't much to see. The room at the front, where they would sleep, was the best room in the house with windows on two walls, which would let in the afternoon sun. Johnno had made some effort to tidy up, but eyeing the grey walls and partly made bed, Gwenna was thankful Mam and Tillie had given her fresh linen and towels.

Too distressed to put her thoughts into words after seeing where Johnno expected her to live, they returned along the darkened corridor to the kitchen.

The room offered no comfort whatsoever. A higgledy-piggledy assortment of plates, bowls and mugs overflowed every surface, and the place was filthy. A rough wood table and three chairs filled the centre of the room; the single sofa was undoubtedly Jack's domain. Johnno moved the unwashed plates and stacked them on top of others on the bench under the window so they could sit at the table.

Supper that night was a sorrowful affair. All Johnno could find was some day-old bread, a chunk of hard cheese and the pitiful remains of a ham hock. Without any butter or pickle to help with the taste, Gwenna could do little more than pick at her food. Most of the time she stared at the cold coal range, hoping it worked and wishing for a cup of hot tea.

"It's Christmas tomorrow," announced Johnno into the silence that had grown between them. "I'll kill us a chicken, and I think I can find some potatoes to go with it."

Christmas.

Gwenna blocked her mind to what Christmas would be like without her family in this dismal house. She fought back tears.

"Aw, don't cry, Gwenna, my girl. Look on the bright side. You have me to make you happy."

He took her hand and led her to their bedroom. As Johnno shut the door to their small world behind them, Gwenna remembered today was her wedding day and supposed to be the happiest day of a girl's life. Yet the mood of the house, a mood she couldn't quite put a name to, had changed all that, and what she felt most was an unnatural foreboding.

"Everything will be all right, I promise," whispered Johnno.

He took her in his arms and her fears disappeared as they became one.

9

FUTURE HOPES

New Year's Eve 1899

Gwenna cheered and clapped at the loud crack of exploding fireworks. The colours and beauty of the sparkling shapes lighting up the sky filled her with wonder. Johnno had been his usual sweet self, suggesting they go to the Queen Street Wharf to watch the display at midnight. Seeing an old year out and a new year in was now a ritual, but for Gwenna being present at the change of a century was truly special.

She couldn't quite understand the articles in the newspapers where people argued how the new century would not begin until the end of 1900 because the Gregorian calendar did not start with the year nought. It didn't make sense to her. Tomorrow would be the first day of 1900; it was no longer the 1800s. It must be the start of something new.

For Gwenna, it would be the start of her new life. The year 1900 could only be a good one with Johnno at her side.

Dozens of boats crowded the harbour. At the striking of the hour, bells rang, horns sounded and whistles blew.

The cacophony continued for what seemed an endless time. People laughed and danced, lovers held hands and kissed, while children ran around without fear of reprimand for this one night.

"Didn't I tell you it would be fun?" Johnno spoke into her ear so she could hear him above the noise. His face was lit by another explosion, and the playfulness in his gaze gave her gooseflesh, and she tingled from head to toe. Delighted, she nodded her head, clapping her hands as yet another shower of glitter illuminated the blackness. Her face shone like a child's in awe.

Although she much preferred living in town to living in the country, Gwenna had never seen so many people in one place before. She would have believed it if someone had told her every citizen who lived anywhere within travelling distance of Auckland was crowded into the streets that night. The government reduced the rail and ferry fares so people could afford to travel, and thousands took the opportunity.

Earlier in the evening, the two of them somehow managed to find space on the top deck of the paddle steamer *Eagle* for an excursion around the harbour. From the water, the lights of the city twinkled as far as the eye could see. Every street and every window appeared to have been lit up specially for tonight. The new electric lights shone brighter than their traditional gaslight counterparts, and the outline of Partington's Mill stood tall and proud above everything else on the Karangahape Road ridgeline. Gwenna saw for herself how large Auckland had become.

Time passed in a flash until the sound of train whistles reminded them they must return home. Feeling more tired than normal, Gwenna climbed aboard. Sleep beckoned if she was to enjoy the planned picnic with Tillie, Tom and Charlie tomorrow. Resting her head on Johnno's shoulder, Gwenna crossed her fingers that Bethan would join them.

"Saying thank you seems hardly enough, Johnno. I've had such a good time tonight. I'm so glad we came." She pushed her arm through his as they sat in the overfull carriage surrounded by other tired but exhilarated passengers. She would never forget this night.

"Anything for you, my sweet girl." Aware of the many eyes around them, he patted her hand and winked. She flushed at the thought of how they would celebrate when they got home. No more hurried fumbling; no more dread of being found out; no more misgivings – they were husband and wife. Together. Forever.

As long as Jack wasn't there to spoil things.

"What did you tell Jack about tomorrow?" Gwenna avoided him as much as possible. He'd eaten with them once in the last week, but his mere presence put a damper on what she and Johnno could do together.

"Just that we'd be away for the day," Johnno replied. "Why?"

Jack came and went as he pleased, but Johnno had no such freedom. Every day Jack had chores for him to do. So far, they'd all been local, and Johnno hadn't been away from the house for long.

"Oh, no reason." Gwenna couldn't explain how much she dreaded the time when his father would take Johnno away on one of their long-distance trips and she would be left alone in that sad, lonely house.

Jack had not returned for two days after their first meeting. She'd made an ad hoc attempt to make the place seem less shabby for Christmas, but Gwenna decided she couldn't live in the place as it was. She had to clean it up, even if she ran the risk of incurring Jack's wrath. He couldn't be any worse than Elias, and Johnno was there to protect her.

She'd boiled the filthy rag rugs scattered on the floors in the copper in the outside laundry, washed and rearranged the assortment of crockery and cooking pots, thrown out all the stale and rotten food, and sent Johnno to buy fresh flour and other essentials to cook with.

Gwenna then cleaned the front bedroom she shared with Johnno, thankful she had fresh linen, since what she'd found was not fit to use. Although now clean, in her eyes their room remained cheerless.

When Jack came back demanding Johnno help him with some deliveries, he turned on her. "I'll have no women's fancy fripperies in my house. Keep your things out of my sight, and, by God, if you so much as touched a single item of mine, you'll pay for it."

Gwenna took him seriously. He made it only too plain she lived there under sufferance, and she'd be out on her ear faster than lightning if she got in his way. Within the first week, she sensed she was going to be worse off living with this bully than with the one she'd grown up with.

The train rattled its way along the tracks, and Gwenna put Jack out of her mind. She was excited at the thought of seeing her family again in the morning. They'd considered going to the monster picnic and camp day at Swanson, since the train fare was so cheap. She'd never been in native forest before, but in the end they decided to go to the Auckland Domain instead. Charlie was in the Sunday school parade, led by the Salvation Army band, who would march from the corner of Queen

Street and Karangahape Road, past the mill, down Symonds Street around Grafton Gully and back up the other side to Park Road and into the Domain. The forecast was for a fine day and, with all the shops closed, there was no reason why they shouldn't all attend.

The next morning, she and Johnno got off the train at Newmarket and walked the distance up Carlton Gore Road to watch the parade enter the Domain. They hurried as best they could, but even with Johnno carrying the hamper, Gwenna couldn't keep up. She couldn't understand why her legs dragged and she couldn't summon her usual strength.

From the top of the rise, they could hear band music floating in the air. Once they got closer they could see groups of children waving flags, both the traditional Union Jack and the informal New Zealand ensign, marching behind banners showing the name of their school. As each school group arrived at the spot where the band was still playing, the children dispersed and started shouting for their parents. Even from a distance, Gwenna could see Charlie looking lost when he couldn't see her.

As soon as she caught up with him, she wrapped him into a tight cuddle. "I'm here, Charlie, *bach*. Give us a *cwtch* then," she said, rocking him from side to side. Without realising it, she often slipped in Welsh words she'd grown up with, but which Charlie never used. She'd forgotten most of them herself.

Even when they'd lived in Wales, there were few enough Welsh speakers other than in the more traditional northern parts. With so many outsiders from England and elsewhere coming in to find work in the mines, the Welsh people had needed to learn English to coexist. Before the family had emigrated to New Zealand, they'd decided not to speak the language any longer – including Bethan, who'd grown up speaking Welsh. They needed English if they were to prosper, but sometimes the odd word crept in when she was being sentimental, like today, and no other word seemed appropriate. She remembered a little Māori girl from school had said the same thing was happening to her language. She spoke Māori at home with her parents and grandparents but was not allowed to speak it at school or at the milliner's shop. It seemed such a sad state of affairs; Gwenna liked mixing up words from both languages when she could.

Feeling the need to sit down soon, Gwenna kissed the top of Charlie's head and scanned the crowd for Bethan.

"Mam's not here," Charlie said, his voice muffled against Gwenna's belly. "She made sure I was in line and walked someways with me before she went back home to get the picnic."

Behind them, Johnno and Tillie spread blankets on the grass in the shade of a tree, and Tom helped Tillie sit down. With three months still to go, she felt ungainly and awkward. Johnno sat reclining on one elbow, leg extended and hat tilted back, watching Gwenna's every move.

"There she is," Gwenna pointed, as Bethan hurried towards them carrying a laden basket. Her heart lifted. She let go of Charlie and rushed forward to wrap her stepmother in a warm embrace. She missed her mam's steadfastness, even after a week.

The women unloaded their baskets onto the blankets, chattering away and vying to provide food enough to feed the entire gathering, rather than for the six of them. They laughed when each of them unwrapped a batch of Welsh cakes, a bara brith tea loaf and their traditional, skinless Glamorgan sausages made from vegetables.

"My favourites," shouted Charlie. He grabbed one of each from his mother and his sisters, and ran off to play with his friends.

"Don't go too far," Bethan called after him. He disappeared into a crowd of children all yelling at one another, kicking and tossing balls.

Once the adults were settled, the ladies handed the tins of food around. The conversation turned to what they had done since they'd last seen each other at the wedding a week earlier: Christmas Day services; the St Benedict's fair Bethan had attended; foods they'd prepared; cards and presents received and given. Gwenna managed to say little about her day, avoiding specifics other than 'we had chicken', but nodding in agreement when Bethan said she'd missed Gwenna.

The men were more interested in the Auckland–Otago cricket match, which Auckland had won a few days earlier, and the article in the morning paper stating: *'the year which came to a close yesterday will rank among the most memorable of the century'*.

In a semi-recumbent pose, Tom folded the paper to a manageable size so he could read it more easily. "Listen to this. Here's an interesting article about the state of affairs in South Africa which, I must say, I find unsettling. And it goes on about the Federation of Australia. I'm glad New Zealand didn't join. 'Twas a silly idea, in my opinion. And the war in Samoa caused by

German annexation. But what's *really* interesting," Tom explained, "is that it ends up stating the last century has been one of prosperity for 'the whole world' – England, the United States, the continent of Europe, and, of course, New Zealand. How about that?"

Tom sat up with his legs crossed to read the final paragraph aloud. "*The New Year, apart from the shadows of war, presents a bright and hopeful aspect, and we are justified in anticipating that it will prove as prosperous as the one that has now come to a close.*" He slapped the paper with the back of his hand. "Now, isn't that something to look forward to?"

The three women agreed with him; prosperity was good for everyone.

Johnno was the one to niggle. "I hope they're right. I 'eard more soldiers were going off to fight that crazy war, wherever South Africa is, and prices for basic goods would go up. I can't afford no more, what with a baby comin' 'n all." He reached for Gwenna's hand to reassure her.

Between breaths, sucking on his pipe to draw the flame of the match, Tom said, "Don't worry, lad. All will be well. You'll see. If prices go up, incomes will match it. They have to."

Charlie came and went, looking for something to eat while the adults tucked into the remainder of the food. More drink was consumed as the temperature rose and they moved the picnic blankets into the deeper shade of the tree.

"Tom," said Johnno, when everyone was sated. "Are you up to finding a friendly game of cricket or something? I'll go to sleep here otherwise."

Tom nodded. "I am that." Tapping out his pipe, he slipped it in his pocket, and the two men wandered

71

across the grass, under the cloudless sky, leaving the women to their own conversation.

"Going by the shouting and cheering I can hear, there's a game of something going on," said Tillie.

"More than one, by the sounds of things," said Bethan. "And the children are having fun. Whoever organised all those games and races deserves a day off to rest tomorrow. Look at them go."

The women watched the sack race, then the egg-and-spoon race followed by the three-legged race, laughing as much as the children when they fell over.

"Rather them than me," Gwenna said. "It's far too hot for such activities."

"I'm so glad Charlie's having fun," said Bethan. "There wasn't much laughter to be had over the last year." She reached into the pocket of her skirt. "I've brought something for you, Gwenna, dear." Pulling out a small bundle of envelopes – letters from 'the old country', as she called it – she handed them to Gwenna. "I saved them all."

Every Christmas and sometimes once in between, Bethan's sister would write with news of parents and other family or the 'goings-on' in the town. She was a poor letter writer. Her sentences were disjointed, and her spelling often made it difficult to work out what she had written. To make matters worse, she wrote both ways on the page – across, and up and down – to save paper, but it didn't matter. Bethan loved to hear the news and each letter was cherished and reread.

"There's a new one on top, but I found a couple of others I thought you might like to read again."

Gwenna took the letters and hugged them to her, knowing how precious they were to Bethan. "Thank you," she whispered, folding the older woman's hand within hers. "I shall enjoy reading them." Although, if she was being honest, she had little recollection of, and even less interest in what was going on 'back home'. She would always feel a bond with her homeland, and its spirit lived in her heart, but she couldn't relate to those days long gone. Her home was here now. Nevertheless, these letters were important to Bethan.

Gwenna felt tears prickle behind her eyelids and wondered, once again, what was wrong with her today. The raucous sounds of laughter, music playing, children screeching and overlapping conversations were swirling inside her head, making her feel weak and giddy, and her eyes ached from all the colours and constant movement. She hoped it was the effect of too much sun, but she could easily just lie down and cry. Except she had nothing to cry about, not when she had her family around her, and when her new life with Johnno was about to begin.

"I've got other news, too," continued Bethan. "In the last three months, ever since the day you left home, Gwenna, Elias is like a different person. He's stopped drinking so much. He comes home early, quite sober, and eats supper with me. He spends the evenings working in the storeroom, organising the stock and keeping good records of what's available and what's needed."

Bethan sipped the tea Tillie had poured, grateful to ease her throat. She hadn't talked so much in a long time. "I'm not as good as you, Gwenna dear, or you, Tillie, but I've got my own specialties and Elias has worked up a few batches to add to the stock levels. I don't quite know what he's doing about it all. I don't see much stock moving out, but he gave me a few coins for food, so everything must be all right. Mustn't it?"

Gwenna didn't answer, too distracted by everything around her to think about the change in Elias, but Tillie agreed. "I'm sure all is well, Mam."

Bethan nodded, appearing relieved. "I'm puzzled about one thing, though. For weeks, Elias has disappeared for long periods of time without saying a thing about where he's going or what he's doing. Whatever it is, he's like a new man when he returns. He's almost cheerful. I can hardly believe it."

"Well, I'm glad to hear it, Mam," said Gwenna, her head thumping, and feeling out of sorts at the news. "For your sake. You deserve a little peace. It's just a pity you had to pay the price of Charlie and me leaving home to get it." Had it been her fault Elias behaved as he had?

"Let's hope it lasts then, Mam," said Tillie, sensing her sister's unease. "My turn. I've got something for you, Gwenna."

She pushed a small, round tin with a typical English countryside scene on the lid towards her. Gwenna prised it open and let out an excited cheer. Her mouth salivated as the smell of butter and sugar wafted upwards. Hidden between pieces of waxed paper, the tin held three layers of Tillie's best fudge: vanilla, clotted cream and chocolate.

Gwenna couldn't decide which to try first. She drooled at the thought of them all, but it had been such a long time since Tillie had made any, she wanted to savour each one. Her hand hovered. Her fingers stretched into the tin and she selected a piece of the clotted cream. She considered it Tillie's best recipe. Taking a bite, she closed her eyes, tilted her head back and let her taste buds delight in the rich smoothness as it melted and slid down her throat.

"Tillie. That must be the best batch you've ever made. I don't know how you get it so creamy. Mine is never as good."

"Mine is made with love," Tillie responded. "For you."

Tears threatened again. Annoyed at her soppiness, Gwenna clambered to her feet and gave Tillie a hug. "I love you too, my dearest sister. Thank you. And I'm glad I'm such an inspiration. Especially if it means I'll never be without fudge ever again."

An idea took shape at the back of her mind as to how she could use Tillie's fudge to attract customers, if ever she could get her own sweet-making business started.

All too soon, the New Year's Day picnic came to an end. The band had long since departed, the games had finished and the children had become noisy and quarrelsome.

"I should be going," said Bethan. "I'm struggling to keep my eyes open. Too much sun, I fear, but it's been a great day."

"I've ordered a carriage," said Tom. "It's too far for Tillie to walk. You can have my place."

"Thank you, Tom. How thoughtful," said Bethan. "Are you sure?"

"Of course. Charlie and I will catch the tram. Or walk if it's too full. You ladies go ahead. We'll be there before long."

"We're heading the other way, back to the station," said Gwenna before Johnno could speak. They didn't have the money for a carriage, although she wished they did. Her legs wobbled, she was that tired. "It'll be good for me to get a bit of exercise. I'm getting lazy these days."

The women said their farewells with hugs and kisses, agreeing they'd all had an excellent time. Gwenna watched them go. She linked her arm in Johnno's, and they started their trek back to the train.

She shivered as a weird sense of foreboding surged through her.

10

LEARNING TO SURVIVE ALONE

January 1900

The honeymoon period came to an end more abruptly than even Gwenna anticipated.

They were barely inside the door after returning from the New Year's Day celebrations, when Jack insisted he and Johnno head south. "I've business to do," was all he'd say in explanation.

Johnno tried to argue it was too soon to leave Gwenna on her own. "She doesn't know the area, or met any of the neighbours. Let's leave it for a while, eh Jack? Let her get a bit more settled."

"We leave tomorrow." Jack thumped the table, ignoring Johnno. He glared at Gwenna, daring her to contradict him.

Feeling too weak to fight him, she dropped her gaze. It went against all her instincts to let him win, but now wasn't the time to pick a fight.

"Make yourself useful," he snarled at her. "Pack his stuff and get some food ready."

They ate their meal in silence. Resentment oozed from Johnno, while Gwenna began to regret jumping from the frying pan into the fire, even if she'd had no choice. Jack smirked and held out his mug or his plate when he wanted her to serve him. Once Johnno protested; only once.

"If you want her to remain under my roof, she does as she's told."

Later, in the privacy of their room, Gwenna begged, "Please, Johnno, we have to get a place of our own. Soon. I can't live here – not with him, and certainly not without you being here with me."

Johnno tried to comfort her. "Not just yet awhile, Gwenna love. You'll be fine. I'll talk to him while we're away. Make him understand I'm a married man now. He'll come round, I just know it."

He tried to kiss her, caressed her face with a gentle finger that wandered down her neck to her breasts, but she was too tense – and too upset to be persuaded. She turned away from him and, making as little noise as possible, cried herself to sleep.

When she woke in the morning, his side of the bed was empty.

With a start, she leapt out of bed and, grabbing her dressing gown, hurried towards the hallway. Before she'd taken three paces her head started spinning and nausea rose from her stomach. She slumped to the floor by the doorjamb, trying to take deep breaths and gather her senses.

"Johnno," she called, then again louder, but received no response. She willed herself to be still and quiet her breathing, straining to hear any movement. Anything, but no sounds reached her ears. Her heart was beating so hard she could feel it pounding and echoing in her ears. She pulled herself to her feet and, holding onto the wall, made her way down the dark, wood-panelled hallway leading to the kitchen at the back.

The early morning sun seeped in through the grimy window; an errant thought she'd have to clean it drifted through her mind as her eyes searched for evidence she wasn't alone. Any sign. Anything to quell the mounting terror, but she found nothing. No signs. No note. No fire in the range. She'd never been this alone before.

Shaking, and with the queasiness mounting, she opened the back door, ran down the steps and across the grass to the outhouse before she realised she was barefoot. The stench emptied her stomach in seconds.

Wiping her mouth on her sleeve, she tiptoed back across the grass, her feet now sensitive to every stone and foreign object in her path, and into the dimness of the house. Her teeth started to chatter, despite the warmth of the morning, as she stood by the door surveying the room. Clamping her jaw tight, she folded her arms across her body trying to calm her nerves while her mind listed what she should do next.

The square wooden table was as she'd left it last night, so the men hadn't had any breakfast. The hamper she'd packed for them had gone, so they'd not go hungry. Although why she should worry about whether they'd eaten or not when there were more immediate things to worry about, she couldn't explain.

Light the fire. At least then she could have a cup of tea. That might help calm her. As soon as she moved the dizziness came on her again; she reached for a chair and sat down, scared she would faint. And then what? How long would she lie there before someone found her? The quivering and shaking started again.

Sunlight shining into the room highlighted its dinginess. The sagging scrim-lined walls, yellowed with age and darkened with soot from the fire, closed in on her. Despite her meagre efforts, ingrained dirt still lay on every surface. Doorknobs wouldn't turn, window catches wouldn't shut, and the cracked and broken floorboards let the vermin in. She loathed the place, but she felt so weak and shaky at the moment she doubted she had the strength to do anything about it.

How she would tackle the outhouse on her own she had no idea, and the thought of carrying the water from the rainwater tank up the steps at the back seemed impossible. Johnno had done that for her. Tears fell as she contemplated her lot. They would have to get out of here before winter – before the baby was born. She couldn't, just couldn't live here any longer. Giving way to her unbearable gloom, she laid her head on her arms and sobbed.

She must have dozed off because when she next stirred pins and needles prickled her arm and her back ached. She stretched, easing her strained muscles, and this time she did light the fire. Johnno had left a pile of kindling, a basket of logs and a scuttle of coal for her.

Sipping on a cup of tea, she weighed up her options, her mind spinning with questions to which she had few answers.

Should she stay here, not knowing how long Johnno would be away? Could she introduce herself to the neighbour so she'd have someone to talk to? But her strength had deserted her in the last few days. She'd never felt so weak. She didn't know if she could walk the good half-mile to the nearest house.

And where were the shops? Johnno had collected what she'd needed when he'd taken the wagon out last time. Could she walk to the village to get fresh food?

Should she go to Bethan? She was sure her stepmother would be more than pleased to take her in, but Gwenna couldn't risk upsetting the precarious balance that existed between Bethan and Elias right now.

Should she go to Tillie? Her sister had enough to do, with her expanding girth and seeing to Charlie as well as caring for Tom who had his job. She was sure Tillie would welcome her in, but she couldn't put her in such a difficult position.

So, she was back to staying here – alone.

Every fibre in her body screamed, 'No!'

But stay she did.

Her father's words kept echoing in her head. "Gwenna, *bach*. We can do anything we put our mind to."

It was the argument he'd used when they'd moved to the Valleys to live with the Hughes family in the first place. He used the same argument after Owen was killed and he married Bethan and rose to be head of the household. He'd said the same thing over and over to push his argument about coming to New Zealand. Pa had had such hope.

At first, thoughts of her father deflated Gwenna's spirits further. If he hadn't died, life would be so different, but then her mood lightened. Pa said she could do anything. She just had to get on with it.

From somewhere in the centre of her being, she would find the strength. She had to. She placed her hands over her stomach. "I don't know who you will be yet, but you are Pa's grandchild and that means something. You are the future. For your sake, I will fulfill Pa's dreams. I will."

The house Johnno walked into the following Thursday afternoon was nothing like the one he had left. The open windows sparkled in the light. The newly blacked coal range shone, and the sink bench had been scrubbed almost white. A tablecloth covered the table, and the bright-coloured crocheted blankets thrown on the sofa hid the splits, despite Jack's warning about fripperies. It felt cosy and lived in.

"Gwenna?" He dropped his bag on the floor. "Where are you, Gwenna?" When there was no reply, he went exploring. He found her asleep on their bed, but it wasn't the same room he had left a little over a week ago either. He touched her shoulder and she stirred.

Turning over, she opened one eye against the glare of the afternoon sun and was awake in an instant. "You're home. Oh, Johnno. Thank goodness." She threw her arms around him so hard he lost his balance. "I thought you'd gone forever. Oh, how I've missed you."

"Steady on, Gwenna love." Sprawled half across the bed, he laughed as he disentangled himself. "Let me breathe."

Once he'd extricated himself, he sat beside her and held her in his arms. "I missed you, too." He planted several kisses on her forehead and face. "I've been worried about you, which is why I'm here. But I can't stay long."

Her face fell and she pulled out of his embrace to peer at him. "Why not? Where are you going? How long will you be gone? Don't leave me again," she gabbled.

"Slow down. I'll explain everything, but first, how about you tell me what's been going on here."

"Do you like it?" A smile of deep pleasure lit her eyes.

The furniture had been moved around, a new white candlewick bedspread covered the wrought-iron bed, lace curtains Tillie had made for her hung in the windows and a vase of flowers decorated the dresser making it smell clean and fresh. The whole room shone.

"It's very nice. Did you do all this by yourself?"

"Yes. Well, no. Not exactly. Oh, Johnno. I was in such despair I didn't know where to start."

She explained how tired she'd been and how sick. "I lay around for two days after you'd gone. Every time I moved I felt sick or faint, and I couldn't eat anything. I was that scared, but I felt Pa's spirit inside me, urging me on." She stopped, unable to explain what she meant. "Maybe the baby moved or something because I felt less sick and giddy, but I was still so weak."

She'd finally eaten an egg with a cup of tea and, with several rests along the way, had walked the distance to the neighbour's house.

"She was such a nice person. Mavis Milligan is her name. She said she'd get a message to Mam for me. I gave her the telephone number, but I suspect she sent a telegram."

She'd needed to explain to Mavis, who had never seen 'one of those newfangled things', how telephones worked. Elias, resistant at first, had agreed to install one since telephones had become popular for business purposes. For most people, telegrams were still the best way of getting in touch.

"The next morning Mam arrived on the doorstep. I've never been so glad to see anyone in my life. In the meantime, Mavis had given me some Dinneford's tonic. She said she could tell I was carrying and I was too pale. It worked wonders."

Choosing her words with care, she explained how horrified Bethan had been at the state of the house and had nearly forced her to return to North Street. But in the end, Bethan had agreed to help clean the place up a bit.

"She couldn't stay long – only for the day – because Elias was due home and she didn't want to upset him by not being there. She fed me some soup, and by the next day I felt stronger. She said I had to keep taking the tonic, and she'd get me some iron pills."

Gwenna willed Johnno to say something reassuring, but he didn't. While he could not have known how sick she had been, neither did he understand how miserable she was, and he'd ignored all her pleas to find a place of their own.

"So how did you do all this?" He waved his arm around the room.

"Mam helped me. She came back the next day, as she said she would, with those iron pills. They're wonderful, and I got stronger each day. We moved the bigger furniture around in here, and Mam carried water from the tank into the house. We filled all the buckets and bowls I could find and I heated it a pot at a time on the range. Can you fill more for me, now you are here?"

Johnno nodded. "I'll ask about installing a pipe to the door, too, if you like. But tell me what else happened."

She had so much to tell Johnno, words tumbled over each other.

"Mam made me promise to have a rest each afternoon, which is why you found me asleep now. I spent two days giving this room a thorough doing, but only in short bursts. Honest. And I rested. The bedspread was Mam's. She brought it for me, and Mavis picked the flowers. She's called in a couple of times, just to see how I'm doing. I need to pay her back for the Dinneford's, and I want to get some more. Have you got any money? Can you take me to town?"

Gwenna was so pleased to see Johnno she couldn't stop talking. She also explained how Bethan had brought her a box of lime, and together they had tossed it and heaps of ashes from the firebox, into the dunny.

"It stank, Johnno. Did you never notice? I couldn't bear to be inside the thing. Mavis also said to cover it each time with sawdust or straw, but I didn't have any. Bethan threw the vegetable scraps down into it. It's better, but you'll have to dig a new one. I've been using a potty."

"I'll add it to the list," he said, grimacing, repelled at the thought of tackling the job. "Anything else?"

"Did you see the kitchen? After I'd got this room looking nice I decided to tackle the kitchen. I just finished it this morning."

Gwenna ran out of steam and remembered Johnno had some explaining of his own to do.

"Can I at least have a cup of tea and something to eat, first? Please?" Johnno took her hand and led her towards the kitchen.

Gwenna put the kettle on the range to boil and whipped up a batch of Welsh cakes to go with their tea while Johnno stoked up the fire. Feeling safe and contented now he was back, she started humming as she creamed the butter and sugar, stirred in the eggs, flour and raisins, and dropped a spoonful at a time on the hot griddle. The smell of melting butter made Johnno's

85

stomach rumble. In a hurry to get home, he hadn't eaten that day.

"I don't know what happened to put Jack in such a bad humour, but whatever it was, he was keen to get away south. We'd been on the road for two days, calling into small settlements west of Pukekohe, and then he tells me to leave him. I'm to take the wagon and deliver whatever goods he still had on the back to Waiuku. Then I was to come and find him in Tuakau."

Johnno munched through several hot Welsh cakes and swallowed two cups of tea before he felt full enough. "We fought most of the way about leaving without telling you how long we'd be. He said he didn't know how long we'd be away, so I told him he could stay in Tuakau by himself. I wanted to come back here to see you." Johnno reached across the table and squeezed her hand. "I'm sorry, Gwenna. I should have prepared you better. I'm proud of you. You've done wonders."

Gwenna wasn't at all sure he understood what she was saying. He sounded indifferent to her fears, and she wanted to make Johnno feel bad for leaving her.

"I was that frightened, Johnno, when I realised I was on my own. I've never been overnight on my own before, anywhere, not ever. I didn't know what would happen to me if no one knew I was sick. I could have died." Feeling she was being a little overdramatic, she added, "I *am* better than I was, but you can help me fix up the scrim, and scrub these walls and the hallway to make up for it."

She saw his face change. Neither of them could be certain how Jack would react to the changes, but they suspected he wouldn't be happy about any of it. "I'll not touch Black Jack's room. I promise. And has anyone ever used the front room? There's furniture in there all covered in dust sheets, but beyond peeking in I've not been in there either."

She yelped in surprise when Johnno grabbed her arm. "Don't ever go in there, Gwenna. Jack'd come close to killing you if he found out." Johnno paused, releasing his hold, and stared along the corridor towards the front room and back at Gwenna. He took a deep breath. "It was my mother's favourite room. I was just a nipper when she told him she wanted to leave. Jack got himself into a right rage. He told her to get out and threatened he'd kill her, and me, if she ever came back. He wouldn't let her take anything with her either. He tied me to the verandah post and burnt all her belongings on the lawn as she watched and begged him to let me go. The front room furniture is all that's left. Jack refuses to use it." The painful memories clouded Johnno's eyes. "Don't say anything, Gwenna. Or ask about it again. Just leave the past where it belongs."

"I'm sorry, Johnno. I didn't know." His story at least told Gwenna a little about why Johnno was tied to his father. And why he lived for today, avoided making plans and dismissed her worries. It also told her a lot more about Johnno's father and why people called him Black Jack.

At a loss as to what to say or do next, Gwenna suggested they clean up after their tea, but Johnno had other ideas. Over the course of the evening and well into the night, they made love; she talked about the future, their child, her pa's dreams, the need for a home of their own and what Johnno would do for a job. He'd been more tight-lipped than usual about what Jack was doing and what it would mean for them.

"But he's a carter, isn't he?" Gwenna didn't understand what carting they did, since the boats and trains took most of the long-distance goods. "Can't you take over the carting side of the business and leave him to do whatever else he does?"

She'd heard rumours, too many rumours in fact, about the way Jack did business, and she didn't want Johnno caught up in any of it. Money lending was a nasty business at the best of times. Black Jack's rough methods made it worse.

"That's the plan," said Johnno, snuggling into her neck. "Enough talk for now. I've better things on my mind," and he let his hands do the rest of the talking.

11

THE JOY OF REUNION

March 1900

"Johnno's sent word. He'll be back tomorrow," Gwenna shrieked, grinning.

Most of the time, Johnno and his father were away for around seven to ten days, but this last time, Johnno said they'd be away for over three weeks.

Refusing to stay on her own for that length of time, Gwenna had gone to stay with Tillie, both for her own sanity, but also to help Tillie as she awaited the birth of their baby.

"I'll be sorry to see you go," said Tillie. "It's been wonderful having you with me for these past weeks. You've been such a help." Tillie gazed in awe at the little bundle lying in her arms. Only a matter of days old, her daughter slept peacefully, wrapped in the fine lace shawl Bethan had crocheted.

The radiance on Tillie's face melted Gwenna's heart. "I've loved being here. And I'm glad I've been of use, given I move like a blob of blubber. You've no idea how far I've let my stays out already."

Tillie and Bethan assured her she wasn't large at

all. In fact, they were worried she had lost weight and appeared to be all baby.

"You do look better, Gwenna, *bach*," said Bethan. "I was so worried about you back in January and the tonic and the iron pills have done their job. You're skin is blooming, but you're a little thin. Make sure you eat properly."

Gwenna didn't tell Bethan she found the heat of summer a strain and could scarcely eat a thing, but nothing could take away her delight at spending time with her family. Charlie had been thrilled to see her and keen to do her bidding, whatever she asked of him. Bethan had clung to her for an overly long time, studying her face intently.

Talking with Mam about what she'd done recently, how she felt about Johnno being away so much, and what to expect when her time came took her back to the old days when her pa was alive and gladness filled the house, but it was the joy of seeing Tom and Tillie together making Gwenna feel weepy.

To anyone watching, it was obvious they enjoyed each other's company and shared secret smiles and glances. Tom was solicitous, making sure Tillie had everything she needed and rested well, while Tillie cooked his favourite meals and ensured all was as Tom liked it. A relationship like theirs was what Gwenna wanted for her and Johnno. She yearned for a connectedness but something was missing. Johnno was too distracted. Until they had a place of their own, away from his father, and until she could persuade him to find a job in the city so he wouldn't have to travel, it wouldn't happen.

Gwenna gently ran her finger over the baby's brow. "Your Olwen is such a delight. You should be proud of her – and what a lovely idea to give her such a meaningful name. A new 'footprint' in a new land."

Gwenna had been relieved to find Tillie had had an easy time with the birth. The midwife even commented how unusual it was for a first time, but then the baby was a girl and quite small. Gwenna prayed it would be as easy when she came to her time – and that someone would be with her.

Over the last three months, Johnno and Black Jack had come and gone as often as the winds and the weather had changed. Sometimes Johnno returned alone, and they spent a few idyllic days together before he had to leave again. Life was quite different when Black Jack was there.

Gwenna had expected him to have something to say about the changes she'd made to the house, but he remained his surly and silent self in her presence. As time passed, it reached the point where she couldn't bear to be in the same room as him. Everything about him, from his glaring eyes and scowling face to the colour of his skin, even the smell of him, made her flesh crawl.

Seeing the growing antipathy between Gwenna and Jack, Johnno was cautious about repeating anything his father said. Somehow, Johnno had persuaded his father to let him extend the water pipe to fit inside the back door. It wasn't perfect but better than nothing. And she had a new outhouse too.

Saying her farewells to Tillie, Gwenna made her way home feeling lighter than usual, and her heart full of expectation and hope.

She couldn't believe her ears when Johnno told her he was on his away again the next morning. "I have to get back," he said. "I have to pick up a return shipment of goods from the wharf first thing. I'll be lucky if I can do the trip in two days. I hear the weather's supposed to turn bad."

"No, Johnno. No. You can't leave me again. Please stay home. I need you, Johnno, *bach*." She reached out for him. Hands on his arms, she peered into his face. He'd bent his head down to hers, but while she saw desire, she also saw defeat. "Don't go, Johnno. Don't go."

He shook her hands from his arms and backed away. "I must. Jack needs me to ..."

"Jack needs you?" she shouted. "What about me? I need you. Don't I count for anything?" Fear of being alone when the baby came, although that day was still several months away, drove her to scream at him, her voice shrill. "I need you. Here. With me."

She was unable to explain what was going on in her mind and, at a loss for the right words, couldn't begin to describe the loneliness, or how she felt like a different person in this house, and how she fretted and fussed while he was gone. How the story of his mother had upset her far more than he would ever realise. She just kept repeating, "I need you. I need you." But he was deaf to her pleas.

"We need the money, Gwenna." He took her by the shoulders and squeezed hard to bring her tirade to an end. "I can't stay against his wishes. He pays me to do what he tells me. I have to go."

Gwenna never considered herself one of the ancients who saw or heard strange things, but, studying Johnno's face, an unexpected and inexplicable feeling of dread drained the energy from her body. She slumped against him.

"Ah, Gwenna, my love. I'm doing my best." He wrapped his arms around her and held her close. "But we do need the money." He tried to catch her eyes, but they were downcast. Her head moved against his chest. "As soon as we've saved enough, I promise, we'll find a place of our own. And I'll find a new job – just to please you – but not yet awhile. Be patient. It'll work out all right in the end."

The next morning she rose early to say farewell and make sure he had enough food for the journey. She couldn't take her eyes off him. Following his every move, forcing her brain to remember every detail: every crease around his eyes, his mouth, his hands, his hair. She was filled with such love she thought her heart would burst.

Standing on the front verandah still in her nightdress with a shawl wrapped around her shoulders, she waved him goodbye. She remained standing there long after the wagon, with *J Jones Esq. Carter* painted along the sideboards, faded into the distance. He'd vowed to be home soon.

"In six or seven days, I promise. Saturday week at the latest."

She wished she could feel as certain.

12

HOME IS WHERE THE HEART IS

Early April 1900

Mavis dropped in now and then to bring her a bunch of flowers, a few veges from the garden or an egg or two. The days were bearable, but the silence at night set Gwenna on edge. Three days later, unable to stand her own company any longer, Gwenna took the train to Auckland. The walk to the station carrying her small holdall seemed a lot further than it once had, but at least she didn't feel so self-conscious travelling alone in public. Not now. Not wearing the maternity wrap dress she had borrowed from Tillie, which buttoned all the way down the front, softening her bumpy profile.

Getting off the train in Queen Street and catching the horse tram up to Karangahape Road felt like a homecoming. She smiled and found others smiling back at her. This was where she belonged. The isolation of the farmhouse was getting on her nerves, regardless of how much effort she'd put into making it look and feel as if it were 'her' place. It could never be hers. And she missed making sweets. She hadn't realised how much until now.

With only herself to feed, she had done little cooking and even less baking until word reached her that Johnno was coming home. After the first time, when they'd left in such a hurry and without saying how many days they'd be away, she made Johnno tell her before he left how long he'd be gone and to send word when he was on his way home. She'd needed something to look forward to, a time to prepare for, and tasks to take her mind off her loneliness. She'd whitewashed the interior walls, and the entire outhouse to brighten the place up, but it wasn't enough.

Tillie was pleased to see her. "You have no idea how often Olwen wakes and how little sleep I'm getting. But I mustn't complain. She's such a delight."

Gwenna sympathised. "Now I'm here, you can take a nap when you need to, and I can do some of your chores, but first things first. I'm going to make us a batch of butterscotch."

Setting aside her bonnet and gloves, and removing the wrap dress, now she was in the company of family, Gwenna headed to the kitchen with Tillie following behind.

"There's something about making sweet things by hand that is so satisfying, isn't there," commented Tillie, going to the pantry. She opened a cake tin and showed Gwenna the latest batch of fudge she'd made. "I was in a hurry because Olwen was crying. It's not my best, but it turned out all right."

As usual, Gwenna could not resist Tillie's fudge and popped a piece in her mouth. "Mmmm. It's still good. You're so clever," she mumbled through the gooey lump she chewed.

"Didn't Mam teach us not to speak with our mouths full?" teased Tillie.

Gwenna almost choked as the laughter caught at the back of her throat. She put her hand up to her mouth. *Oh, how good it was to be back home.*

"Have another piece."

Later in the day Bethan came around, delighted to know Gwenna was back in town again so soon.

"I'll stay for a couple of days. Mavis has promised to let me know if anything arrives from Johnno telling me when he'll be home. He's supposed to be back on Saturday, but he might come earlier." She sounded more hopeful than certain, but if he didn't arrive ahead of time, three more days wasn't too long to wait.

Over tea and scones the women chatted as if life was perfect – and for those few moments it was. All their cares and concerns faded into the background. It was not until Bethan mentioned stocks must be low, that either girl took notice.

"Elias hasn't asked me to make anything in a long time. He's away from home such a lot, and sometimes I don't know what I should be doing. He never tells me where he's been, but wherever it is, it's a dusty place. His clothes are covered in it."

Questions over whether Bethan had money for food, or if the bills were paid, came one after another, but she assured the girls all seemed well.

"The horse gets groomed, and there's plenty of hay, but the cart doesn't get used as much as it used to. Elias seems to do whatever trade he's doing either on foot or on horseback and I'm hearing the telephone more often. I don't like that thing, but Elias seems happy enough using it."

Gwenna pictured the black, box-shaped delivery cart with the protective roof jutting over the driver's head, which Pa had used. He'd had it varnished with several coats of high gloss and emblazoned G *Price & Family, Confectioners, Auckland* in white and gold on both sides.

He'd been proud of his purchase, pleased he had enough trade to warrant the expense, and considered it an investment. "Best advertising in the world, Gwenna, my love," he'd said. "Links me, our name and the business together in one."

Gwenna remembered something else he'd said. "All we need is a shop to make the business complete."

Now, according to Bethan, the cart sat neglected in the yard. It broke Gwenna's heart to think of it.

Two blissful days passed.

Each morning, Gwenna took a breakfast tray up to Tillie, insisting she stay in bed and rest after she had fed and changed Olwen. Gwenna would then walk with Charlie to school just as she had done when she lived at home. The mornings disappeared with chores, coping with the extra washing a newborn baby created and preparing whatever Tillie decided they were having for lunch and supper. The heaviness and lethargy Gwenna had felt in previous months seemed to leave her as her sense of purpose and worth returned. Sharing her days with her sister became the happiest she'd known in a long time – a time before Elias, before Black Jack, a time when she only knew lightness of heart.

On Good Friday as arranged, Louisa, Janetta and their children visited after church. Ostensibly to sing the praises of baby Olwen and offer congratulations to the mother, and to wish Gwenna happiness for her birthday in five days' time, but the day turned out less than cordial.

"Welcome, dear sisters, welcome," said Tillie. "Do come in. It's been so long since we saw each other. Mam's already here, and Gwenna's been baking since early morning." Hugs and fake kisses were swapped, bonnets removed and skirts swished as they moved to the sitting room.

The cups of tea and cakes began well, with gossip about husbands, their work, the latest fashions, or the newest appliances. The mood started to drift when Louisa's daughters, Ella and Lucy, aged three and two, became whiny and clung to their mother's skirts. Bethan considered them spoilt. George had been delighted with his first step-grandchild but didn't live long enough to enjoy her or meet his next one.

As best they could, they carried the conversation on around the grizzling children. Tillie excused herself once to clean up a spill from Olwen and refresh her nappy. No one asked Bethan about the business, or Elias, and Bethan refrained from sharing a precious letter she had received from Samuel.

Janetta laid the baby on a blanket on the floor beside her when she'd first arrived and wouldn't let anyone touch him. Refusing to play with girls, her two-year-old sat in the corner amusing himself with a few marbles and the wooden blocks Janetta pulled out of her excessively large bag. At least he was quiet. After a while, the girls began to poke each other and fidget, demanding their mother's attention.

"Isn't motherhood hard work?" Louisa commented to Tillie while trying to extricate her children. "Go outside and play, for goodness' sake." But after a pointed glance out the window onto the road frontage and seeing people and carriages passing, she sighed. "No. I'd forgotten, you can't do that here. Sit over there." Pulling a couple of cloth dolls out of her bag, she pointed to the hooked rug on the floor.

"Actually, I don't find it hard at all," replied Tillie as she watched the girls shoving each other and whispering as they headed towards Billy. "Well, not yet anyway. A little more tiring, maybe, but I'm enjoying watching Olwen develop. She changes so quickly." Tillie wondered what the girls would do to upset the delicate balance.

"Teach them to be seen and not heard," advised Janetta. "Children have to learn independence and to amuse themselves, like my Billy," she said with a smug smile. "Not like some I know."

Louisa took immediate offence. "What do you mean by that, Miss La-di-da?"

"Whatever you take it to mean, sister dear." Janetta sipped her tea and selected another dainty from the cake stand.

After their little outburst, tension simmered between the sisters; Louisa and Janetta were at odds over something. Tillie didn't quite know what to say to ease the way, and Gwenna bit her lip to stop herself uttering something she would regret. Honestly, sometimes they behaved worse than the children.

Seconds later, a scream from Lucy brought everything to a standstill. She and Ella had been teasing Billy, rolling his marbles away and hiding his blocks, so in retaliation he'd ripped an arm off Lucy's doll. The mothers began to soothe their respective offspring while the children continued to poke tongues and call each other rude names. Tears fell.

Janetta took her leave first. "Goodbye, Tillie. I hope you do well with your baby. Gwenna, it's been nice to see you again after so long. I hear you live in Onehunga these days. You must tell me about it some day. I hear it's frightful. Lovely to see you too, Mam. I wish you would call on me. We could go somewhere and have high tea if you'd like. I can promise it would be peaceful."

Louisa couldn't contain herself. "Good riddance to you, Janie Lewis. I'll not be taking tea with you again until you climb down off your high horse."

Gwenna came close to spluttering out loud. Louisa was the one who most often sat on her high horse, boasting about all the fancy new things she could purchase, thanks to how well the butchery was doing and the increase in wages Albert had received. Neither of them cared two hoots about Mam; they were too busy trying to outdo each other. But Janetta wasn't to be outdone.

"I'm surprised you don't suffer from giddiness with your head so far in the clouds. You'll come crashing back to earth one day, you'll see."

Huffing and puffing, Louisa gathered her two daughters and left in Janetta's wake. "You'll regret that comment, Janie Lewis. That you will."

"Ta-ta then, girls," Bethan called from the doorstep, in a strong Welsh accent. "Glad I was to be seeing you. You be good now."

Tillie and Gwenna burst out laughing. The scowl Louisa had thrown over her shoulder at her mother had been withering, but the girls regretted their mirth when they saw their mam's face.

"They don't set out to be mean," Tillie consoled her.

"They are just so wrapped up in themselves and their world, they don't consider anyone else," echoed Gwenna. Any thoughts about her birthday: gone.

"Thank you, girls. I know you mean well, but it still hurts to see how they have turned out. Now, let's get this mess cleaned up."

Bethan bustled about gathering the used cups and saucers, while Tillie saw to Olwen and Gwenna packed the leftover food into tins.

A few minutes later, Tillie returned to the kitchen. "Are you staying another night then, Gwennie? You've not heard from Johnno, I take it."

Gwenna stopped, hand hovering in mid-air, and stared in dismay at her sister. For the first time in ages, Johnno had slipped from her mind. She was having so much fun staying with Tom and Tillie, and seeing her mam every day, she'd blocked out her new life, her future life. That same dread feeling she'd experienced before sank into her stomach.

"No. I haven't. Oh, my goodness, Tillie. I've not heard a word. What can it mean?"

Bethan and Tillie were quick to assure her it meant nothing. Maybe Mavis hadn't noticed the telegram delivery or hadn't got around to sending one of her own. Maybe Jack had asked Johnno to stay another day.

"There could be dozens of reasons," said her mam. "Stay the night. You can go home in the daylight, and by the time you get organised, you'll find Johnno on your doorstep before you know it."

13

WHEN CIRCUMSTANCES COULDN'T GET ANY WORSE

14 April 1900

Gwenna arrived home on Saturday towards the middle of the day and set about preparing the house, opening windows, lighting the fire and making bread. She set the meat she'd bought from the butcher in Karangahape Road to simmer on the range with onion, potato and carrots. The succulent smells made her stomach rumble.

By mid-afternoon, when everything could be left unattended for a while, she walked over to Mavis's place, hoping to get some milk.

"Gwenna, dear. I was just thinking about you. The hens were busy this morning so I put aside a few eggs. Come in. Sit yourself down."

Mavis handed a bag of eggs to her young neighbour. "Thank you," said Gwenna. "You are so good to me. Is there any chance you might have a little milk to spare too? I couldn't carry anything else back from town."

"Of course, dear, of course. Hang on a minute while I find a jar to put it in."

Mavis bustled around her kitchen until she'd found one and poured in the fresh milk from their house cow.

"Now tell me the news from Auckland while I put the kettle on."

Any news from town was good for gossip, and Mavis laughed over some of baby Olwen's antics. They sighed together about not being able to attend the Easter Fair, the chrysanthemum show or Pollard's Opera Company comic opera production, *The Geisha*. They tutted over the alarming, ongoing news about rats coming ashore off ships arriving from Sydney. Fears they might carry the plague dominated the headlines, but people were assured stringent controls were in place.

"At least no one's got sick or died here. I feel for those poor folk over in Australia, with so many dead. Must be a worry, it must."

"The papers say they are offering a penny reward for every rat caught," said Gwenna.

The two women chatted for another ten minutes, relaxed in each other's company.

"Thanks for the cuppa," said Gwenna, finishing her tea, "but I can't stop any longer; I've got meat cooking and I'm expecting Johnno home any time now."

"Have you heard from him, then?"

Gwenna shook her head. "But it doesn't mean anything. He said he'd be home tonight at the latest."

Dusk fell, day turned to night in the blink of an eye, and still no sign of Johnno. Gwenna paced the floor, straightened the cutlery on the table set ready for supper, and lifted the lid on the stew pot for the third time in as many minutes. Ignoring her stomach rumbling at the aroma, she refused to eat until she could share the meal with Johnno. She just hoped his father wouldn't be with him.

Another hour passed. As the minutes ticked by, she accepted he wouldn't be coming home that night. She banked up the fire with the last of the coal, lowered the flue damper and went to bed.

Neither she nor the baby rested easy. While the baby kicked and turned, so did Gwenna.

One minute she needed the blankets, the next she'd kicked them off. She fell into a fitful sleep in the hour approaching dawn and was beset with dreams: the sound of crying in an empty space with a single beam of light breaking the darkness; children laughing and playing Ring a Ring o' Roses, to be swallowed by the earth when they fell down; a flower seller's barrow re-forming into a fast-growing wilderness, spreading its tentacles to cover everything in its path – gates, fences, wagons, people.

She woke with a start. A fine layer of sweat covered her face, and her nightdress clung to her. The room felt cold even though the sun was well up. She shivered. After a moment, her brain grasped where she was, and what had disturbed her.

She could hear someone shouting.

"Where is he?"

Was that Jack's voice?

"Where're you hiding him?"

Her skin crawled.

The back door of the kitchen burst open. She scrambled out of bed, grabbed her wrap dress and hurried down the hall doing up buttons as she went.

Jack stood in the middle of the room. He was more dishevelled than usual and she could smell the sweat and dirt from the doorway. Underneath the awful greyish-green greatcoat he always wore, his clothes were filthy and he hadn't shaved in days, but it was his eyes that set off alarm bells. They were troubled – and red, as though they had grit in them or he hadn't slept, or both.

"Where is he?" Jack rasped, his throat dry and rough, but he sounded more annoyed than worried.

"Johnno? You mean Johnno?" Panic put an edge on her words.

"Who else, you stupid girl?" Jack pulled out a chair and sank into it, lowering his head; he stared at the section of floor between his feet. His hat hung in his hand.

"He's not here, if that's what you think," she snapped, anger and fear competing for dominance. "He's supposed to be with you."

She stoked up the fire, more for something to do than any other reason. Her hands shook as she filled the kettle and set it on the range, and with every beat of her heart, her uneasiness grew. The disquiet of her dreams added to her anxiety. She couldn't bring herself to ask the question because she didn't want to hear the answer.

The kettle boiled and broke the silence that had grown between them. She threw a handful of tea leaves into the pot and poured in the hot water. Turning the teapot around a few times, she tipped the strong, black tea into a mug and banged it on the table in front of Jack, spilling some on the clean tablecloth still set from the night before.

She poured a cup for herself and, holding it in both hands, leaned against the bench as far away from him as possible. Her jaw ached; her throat burned. A convulsive gasp escaped her lips as she took a deep breath; her whole frame shook with the effort not to lose control.

She could stand it no longer. Through gritted teeth, she breathed, "When did you see him last?"

Jack's head shot up at the sound of her voice, as if he'd forgotten she was there, or even where he was. He stared at her, his eyes distant and empty. "Monday. Afore last."

Two weeks tomorrow. Gwenna gulped in extra air.

"He was here on the Wednesday night before the rain set in. He left first thing the next morning. He said he had to collect a consignment from the wharf."

Jack nodded. "Aye. It was urgent. I told him to be back by Friday. It was important."

"So where is he?" She couldn't hold back any longer.

Jack turned his head away as if she no longer mattered. "He's ruined everything, he has. Wait till I get hold of him."

Gwenna let her fear and fury out. "You should be worried about your son, not your stupid business. What's happened to him?" she screamed.

"What are you talking about, woman? Nothing's happened to him. He's playing games, that's all. Trying to cheat me."

Gwenna couldn't believe her ears. His son, her Johnno, was missing, and the only thing his father could think about was the money he'd lose. "Johnno would never cheat anyone, you selfish old man," she seethed. "We need to find him. And if you won't, then I will."

She sped down the hall to her bedroom to get dressed. Her hands were shaking so much she struggled to tie the laces on her corset. A minute or two later, she dropped her blouse over her head and fastened her skirt. She was buttoning her shoes when she heard hoof beats.

Her heart lifted – was that Johnno?

Tottering towards the window with one shoe in her hand, her spirits plummeted as she caught sight of Black Jack whipping his horse into a gallop and disappearing down the road in a cloud of dust.

She was alone again – with no idea how or where to start looking for her husband.

14

COMING TO TERMS WITH REALITY

Mid-April 1900

Elias mounted his horse and clip-clopped along the back streets past St Benedict's Church towards the cabinetmakers just off Mt Eden Road, wondering where his life had gone so wrong.

After his father died, Elias felt he owed it to him to carry on the business – in his name: the Hughes name – but he'd failed. Everyone had been against him – his Mam, Charlie, even Hugh, but most of all, that bitch Gwenna. It wasn't his fault. He'd tried. He really had tried. Between them, they had taken away any control he once had, although he didn't mention any of that to the stranger at the bar.

He'd met Thomas Woodman by chance in The Edinburgh Castle roughly six months earlier. He'd gone there to get drunk after another clash with Gwenna. Never mind that her very presence annoyed him, or her talent for making sweets far exceeded his, or that his own mother had turned on him. He hated his life. He hated himself. He felt useless and unworthy and loathed the whole confectionery business. Trade was going downhill, and he had no idea how he was going to stop the slide or improve his life.

For some time, the sickly sweetness of the sugar boiling had set Elias's teeth on edge, and his hands and forearms had developed an itchy rash. He'd kept his shirtsleeves rolled down so neither Gwenna nor his mother noticed, but Hugh had, and he offered to take over Elias's work as well. Damn the man. At least he'd gone, but it had left the business short-handed. Elias had made Gwenna work harder, hoping she'd fail and he could blame losing the business on her.

She hadn't failed, but the stupid bitch had got herself pregnant.

He hadn't known why Gwenna was so uncharacteristically slow to get started in the mornings and snappy when spoken to, until he'd quizzed Charlie.

The boy was keen to share the news. "Shh. It's a secret. Don't tell anyone I told you."

The dawning realisation there was nothing he could do to save the business tipped Elias over the edge. He took solace in whatever way he could. He started drinking more heavily. He even resorted to seeking out one or two of those voluptuous women who called out to him as he staggered home late at night, but nothing had provided the answers he sought.

The more he drank, the angrier he got, and the more he lost his temper. The unfairness of the situation consumed him to the point where he'd even threatened Charlie. Poor kid. He'd done nothing wrong. Except now, after what he, Elias, had done, everyone thought him the worst kind of scoundrel, but it wasn't his fault. The situation had been against him from the start. No one understood him.

Until that night in the pub.

Thomas Woodman had understood. "Call me Woody," the man said.

"Eli," he'd responded using a name no one else called him.

"You've got to love what you do, lad, to be successful. You should think about selling up."

"And do what? I've a mother who relies on me. And there's a stepsister and a half-brother." Elias had shrugged his shoulders, the ones that carried the weight of his conscience, and ordered more ale. As the night wore on, Thomas talked about his love – wood.

"I've even got the right name for it – Woodman. Get it?" he laughed. "But a piece of wood talks to you. It tells you what it's best suited for as soon as you start to work it." He paused to take a mouthful of his ale and wipe his lips. "But like all business, it's not always the way *you* want it. Sometimes you have to make a table or a cabinet the way the customer wants it, but even then, there's joy in the feel and smell of working a good piece. There's nothing like a perfectly crafted bit of furniture with a good coat of varnish to bring out the colour."

Their conversation had haunted Elias, and in the weeks following he sought out the man who would become his liberator.

"Why don't you come along to the workshop with me?" said Woody. "I'll show you what I mean."

As soon as the door opened on that early December afternoon and Elias smelt the aroma of fresh wood shavings, something changed within him. Hours passed while he watched and listened as Woody handled a piece of kauri.

"This is real soft wood, so it's easy to work with." Thomas rounded the edge to make a circular top for a side table. "But just as easy to make mistakes, too. Look at the colour, see the way the grain flows."

He clamped a block of macrocarpa on the workbench and gave the smoothing plane to Elias. "Here, have a go. You've got to go with the grain. Just ease it along, lad."

With the plane resting in his hands the way Thomas showed him, Elias pushed it forward. A thin curl came away and fell, then another, and with each sweep of the plane, the wood seemed to come alive under his fingers. He stopped and ran his hand over the surface, surprised at how sleek it felt. He'd never come across anything like this before, nor felt as emotional. No wonder Woody was so fervent.

"You have the knack, Eli," said Woody, watching Elias turn the legs of a writing desk. "You're a natural. I wish you'd come work for me full time."

As the wood took shape in his hands, Elias allowed himself to envisage how he could do what Thomas – and he – wanted. "I will one day, Woody. I just need a bit more time to work things through."

During his last conversation with Bethan, he'd almost – almost – told her what he was doing and about his newfound love for wood. She often asked him where he went or what had put him in such a good mood, but so far he'd resisted telling her.

Life with Mam since Gwenna and Charlie had gone was as near perfect as a man could expect. He still filled the regular monthly orders from stock left over after Gwenna's efforts, which kept the business running for the time being. If he couldn't match the request, he sometimes got Bethan to make a few varieties, but it couldn't last much longer. Time was running out. He'd stopped making anything months ago. Not since Hugh had gone, in fact.

But he was finding he couldn't do either role justice. He felt like a different person when he was working with the wood – and he was becoming more skilled with every stroke and turn – but he couldn't get away from the sweet business often enough to practise. He was torn between what he should do and what he wanted to do.

Thomas understood, and let Elias come and go to suit. He paid him when he'd completed something worth selling, and Elias gave the extra money to Bethan for housekeeping.

He smiled, content, for now. It was a new feeling. One he had still to come to terms with.

The older man slapped Elias on the back. "Don't think too hard, or too long. The answers'll come to you, lad. They always do."

But Elias couldn't stop thinking.

Shaking his head to clear his mind of memories, Elias stood up to stretch, ran his fingers through his hair and shook his head to get rid of the sawdust. Bethan was always on at him about his clothes: 'They're so dusty. Where do you go to get so mucky?' but he didn't care.

Mam would know soon enough. They all would.

"Here you go, Dad," said Alice Woodman as she placed the basket on the workbench. "There's fresh scones this morning. And I brought butter and jam." She walked over to the wood-burning stove where Thomas burnt the offcuts and moved the kettle into place to boil.

She came every morning with food for her father, who preferred not to clean up to eat in the house during the day, even though it was but a few steps away. Some days, Woody worked like a demon until his aching body could no longer stand, then he would clean up in the wash house at the back of the workshop, eat his supper early and go to bed. Other days, satisfied with his efforts, he would finish earlier and visit the pub before supper. The Edinburgh Castle, where he'd met Elias, was his favourite.

"Eli, would you care to wash your hands while I make the tea?" With a small, shy smile, Alice handed him a towel. Ever since Elias had first seen her when she'd come to collect the basket that first afternoon, he'd been smitten. Petite and dark-haired, she stirred a memory of happy times he couldn't identify, a time in his childhood.

He was still nervous in Alice's presence and often stumbled over his words, but then she'd look at him a certain way, and he began to believe she felt as he did.

"Thank you, Alice. I will. Your scones are nice. You're a good cook."

Elias didn't know what had happened to Alice's mother, but the girl ran the household, doing all the cooking and cleaning. "I'm glad you like them. I made them specially this morning."

But what Elias liked most was that she liked to spend time in the workshop. Her main task involved sweeping up the ever-accumulating sawdust, but she was a dab hand at the fine finish sanding and loved doing the staining and lacquering. She understood the business inside out.

"You look pretty today, Miss Alice," said Elias, admiring the trim figure emphasised by the well-cut gored skirt and pleated blouse.

Pulling an apron from the basket and tying it on, she blushed under his gaze. When he still hadn't moved, she broke a small piece off the side of the freshly baked fruit cake and held it up. He opened his mouth and she popped in it. "That should keep you going for a minute. Now away and wash your hands."

Her father watched the scene from the other side of the workshop. "Don't get too keen on him, young Alice." His eyes stared fixedly beyond the door where Elias had gone. "The boy has problems he needs to work through before he'll make marriage material."

She stood on tiptoe and kissed her father on the cheek. "You worry too much, but I love you for it. Now, go wash your hands."

15

FORTUNE OR FATE

16 April 1900

"Elias!" yelled his mother, breathless and anxious. "Elias, where have you been? I need you."

By fortune or fate, he'd arrived back in the yard and was still unsaddling his horse when Bethan rushed outside.

"You've got to help," she gabbled without preamble. "There's a telegram from Gwenna and it's got me fair worried." The pleading expression on Bethan's face halted the terse response on the tip of Elias's tongue. "Will you hitch up the cart and take me to her? Please, Elias, *bach*. I don't ask much of you, but I do ask this."

Not so long ago, he'd not have lifted a finger to help Gwenna in any way, but working with Thomas and meeting Alice had tempered his anger – towards his mother, if no one else.

"What's *she* got herself mixed up in?" He continued to groom the horse, moving around the stable area to avoid making eye contact with his mother, while he tried to decide how to answer.

"I don't know what's happened. The telegram says: 'Johnno missing. Desperate to find him. Pains started.' I've got to go to her ... Elias? ... Please?"

The action of grooming reminded him of the effect the plane and sanding had on him. He couldn't explain why it should be so, but the continual, slow, back and forth movement calmed him and allowed him to think more clearly. If he did this favour for his mother, then she - and Gwenna - would owe him something in return. It might be worth it.

He stopped to stare at Bethan, the brush still in his hand. Moments passed before he grunted ungraciously, "Help me take the cover off."

Bethan complained the preparations were taking far too long as she rushed about helping him ready the cart, and packing her things and everything she thought she would need for Gwenna. They began their journey with little daylight remaining.

"What does she mean, Johnno's missing? And how can she find him if she doesn't know where he is? And, oh dear, she shouldn't be having pains yet. She's not even seven months."

Bethan chatted away incessantly beside him, but Elias didn't want to be drawn into any conversation about Gwenna. Not yet. His time would come.

"You won't travel back tonight in the dark, will you, Elias? I don't want to worry about you too. You'll stay, won't you? At least for a while, until I can find out what's going on. And what I should do. We might have to bring Gwenna back with us. Oh dear, but then, she might be too far gone. Maybe her neighbour, Mrs Mavis Milligan's her name, will be a help."

Elias was amazed his mother could talk so much and

barely take a breath. He'd forgotten she could get like this when she was worried. He'd not spent so much time in her company of late. Not for many years. A flicker of regret passed through him for all he'd lost, only to be replaced by exasperation. He hoped he wouldn't rue his decision.

With a twitch of impatience at his wild, random thoughts, he shook the reins over the back of the mare, urging her to a faster pace. They arrived at the house a little less than an hour and a half later.

Partway up the driveway, Bethan clambered down while the cart was still moving. She ran up the front steps and through the door while he drove around the back. With no plans of staying, he didn't unhitch the horse but led it to the water trough. Leaving the animal to its own devices, he entered the house.

He found Bethan, Gwenna and another woman in the kitchen. He'd not seen Gwenna for months, not since that horror night when he'd lost all sense of anything decent. He'd been appalled when his mother slapped him and he realised what he'd done. Not that he'd let on to them how he felt, but seeing Gwenna now, he was struck by how thin she was, despite being heavily pregnant.

"Um, I should get going," he said, feeling awkward and out of place, and unsure about the propriety of his being there in the first place.

"Don't be silly, Elias," snapped his mother. "You can't leave yet. Give me a chance to decide what's best. Stoke up the fire for me. I might need it. And see if you can find some more coal. Or wood."

Grateful for something to do, he went back outside. With daylight almost gone, the pitch-black interior of the old shed beside the tank stand revealed little through the half-broken door. He'd need a lamp if he were to find anything useful inside. He could smell coal but had no idea how much was there. Much of the pile of wood stacked along the outside wall was still too green and would smoke, but he picked out the driest logs by weight and smell.

Going inside again he dumped the logs in the basket, picked up the poker and stirred the embers, adding more fuel as the flames took hold. After a few moments, the fire settled and burned steadily.

Behind him the women were helping Gwenna walk up and down the kitchen, encouraging her to breathe slowly. He didn't want to be in the room with women doing whatever women did in this situation, so he lit a lamp and took it outside.

He stroked the horse's neck and whispered into its ear. "Aye, girl. How ya doing? Better'n me, I bet. I wish it were you that was birthing. I'd know what to do then. I remember helping my da when I was a little fella." Now his thoughts had taken him back, he opened the box of memories from his youth. Life was great back then, when it was just Mam and Da, and his two giggly sisters. He'd not been quite so happy when Samuel had been born – another boy to steal Da's attention – but he'd turned out all right in the end. "It's a silly thing to say after all these years, but I miss my da …" Elias patted the mare and began to undo the buckles. He'd be here for hours yet and should release the animal from the shafts. "It was my fault. You know that, don't you. It was my fault Da died …" Heavy-hearted, he led the horse into the field at the back and let her loose. "It's never been the same since."

"Elias? Are you there, Elias?" His mother's voice reached him from the back door. As he emerged from the darkness, she breathed a sigh of relief. "Oh, thank goodness. For a moment, I thought you'd gone. Come inside. We need to talk."

"I'll stay out here."

The relationship between the two of them had improved in the last few months, but she was still wary of his reactions. So was he.

"Please, Elias. We need your help."

Misunderstanding her meaning, he stepped back in alarm. "I want nothing to do with any woman's work or babies. There's nothing I can do."

His mother smiled. "It's not woman's work I want you to do, *bach*. It's man's work. Mrs Milligan and I can manage here. What you have to do is far more important."

Mollified, he followed her up the steps.

Elias listened to Gwenna's version of events when Black Jack had returned without Johnno, and Mavis's story about how she'd found Gwenna after seeing Jack leave in such a hurry.

"It was just as well I came round, it was," Mavis preened, glad to be involved in something quite shocking. "Young Gwenna here was in such a state. Dishevelled and half-dressed, and determined to go after that man. It took me all my time to stop her. What was she going to do, after all? He was long gone and she on foot. That's when the first pains started. Well, she obviously couldn't go anywhere then, could she? So that's when I sent the telegram to you like she asked." Despite asking several rhetorical questions, Mavis had not paused long enough for anyone to agree or disagree. Until this trip, Elias had no idea women could talk so much, so quickly. Alice didn't.

During it all, Gwenna suffered more, but still infrequent pains.

Bethan reassured her they were still too far apart to be concerned about. "There's plenty of time yet. Just keep breathing like I said; it'll help."

"I'm that scared for him." Gwenna eyed Elias warily, as uncertain about his presence as he was. "We have to find him. We have to find Johnno."

"Do you know where Jack was, or who he was meeting?" asked Elias.

Gwenna shook her head.

"Or the route Johnno might have taken?" he pressed.

"No. Nothing. South, he said, but he wouldn't tell me more. Jack had made him promise." She gazed at Elias, imploring. "But I had a terrible dream last night. I saw Johnno swallowed up by the earth, lying covered in vines and creepers or such like, completely hidden from view. Please, Elias. Find him for me?"

"I can't promise anything, but I'll ask around."

Elias got up to leave, but Bethan put her hand on his arm. "Wait until morning, son. There's nothing you can do tonight." She stood and led him to one side of the room. "And I'd like to take Gwenna home with me in the morning. The baby's not coming any time soon. Will you let her come and stay, Elias? I can do more for her there than here. Will you?"

Turning his head towards Gwenna – thin, frightened, desolate – she looked a different person to the girl he'd known. And she was visibly wretched.

"Very well. If it makes you happy."

120

How Elias managed to control his temper while Bethan and Mavis fussed over how the quilts should be folded on the floor of the cart and where the pillows should be placed so Gwenna wasn't shaken around too much, he did not know. Eventually, with him driving, Bethan sitting beside him and Gwenna lying in the back, they left for Auckland not long after eight o'clock the next morning.

Mavis stood at the gate waving them goodbye, disappointed the diverting commotion was leaving her behind.

After a long half hour or so, Elias urged the horse beyond the dawdling pace they had so far maintained.

"Don't go so fast," protested Bethan. "Think of Gwenna."

How could he not think of her! Bethan never ceased to remind him every few moments about poor Gwenna. For a while last evening, Elias had almost believed his animosity towards her was fading, but his mother was doing a good job of stirring it up again.

"We'll never get there at this rate," he snapped. "And since you expect me to go haring off all over the place in search of someone I barely remember and care even less about, then leave me alone."

By the time they reached North Street, the morning was well advanced. Bethan continued to fuss over Gwenna until even she showed signs of crossness.

"I'm all right, Mam. Honestly, I can walk by myself," Elias overheard her say as they entered the house, but he wasn't off the hook yet either.

"Elias, bring the quilts and cushions inside for me," Bethan shouted over her shoulder. "And don't forget our bags," she added as an afterthought.

Elias unhitched the wagon, fed, groomed and watered his horse, and did as his mother asked. "I'm 'way round to the King's Arms," he told her after dumping everything in the middle of the floor.

"What're you going there for?" Bethan sounded piqued. "Don't you want to get on the road? There's no telling how far Johnno has got."

Elias took a deep breath. He didn't want to argue with his mother, but his patience was wearing thin. And he wanted to see Alice before he went anywhere. "Don't you think I know that?" he snapped in a much sharper and louder voice than necessary. "But there's no point in riding off willy-nilly. I need some clues about Jack Jones and his business dealings, or who his associates are, before I head off."

Elias saw the alarm in Bethan's eyes. "I'm sorry, Elias. Of course, you know what's best," she soothed, still wary of the bad-tempered brute of a few months ago.

"Yes. I. Do." He turned on his heel and left in case he said anything that might upset their fragile relationship.

Alice did not offer him the solace he'd hoped for. Quite the opposite. Feeling as confused and out of sorts as when he'd left home, he needed to drown a few sorrows before heading off on a journey he didn't want to undertake.

Tuesday lunchtime was not the greatest time to catch men idling at the pub. Elias started with the King's Head at the bottom end of France Street but drew a blank, so he headed towards the Newton Hotel, his nearest local, on the corner of East Street. While having a half-pint of ale and picking up another comment to add to his list, he briefly considered going into the Naval and Family

Hotel on the corner of Pitt Street but decided Black Jack was unlikely to have frequented it. The pub was too new and too well known, so he headed further east along Karangahape Road to the Star Hotel, near the corner of Newton Road. This end of the road had a reputation for being a bit rough and the perfect setting for some of the money-lending dealings Black Jack got into.

And he was right.

It cost him a few bob to get the rest of the information he needed, but Elias walked out of there with knowledge, if not comfort.

16

ON THE ROAD TO DISCOVERY

17 April 1900

Elias did not linger when he returned to North Street to gather his belongings and the food Bethan had prepared.

"Gwenna's resting," said Bethan, helping him pack the saddlebags. "Her pains have stopped for now, but hurry, Elias. Do your best. She is fair grieving and it's not helping matters."

With only a few hours of daylight left, Elias made his way south, following the Great South Road. Along the way, he counted on meeting people who could add to the information he'd already gathered. He didn't fancy going to some of the remoter places without good reason.

The busy road resounded with the scrunching of wood and metal rolling along the dusty road. Voices called out in greeting, bullocks and horses snorted and snickered, and cyclists rang their bells in warning. The noise of the traffic and rattling farm machinery passing the milestones, heading whichever way their destination took them, sounded louder than normal and stretched his nerves as he rode along.

He was eager to get further south, beyond the towns and into the rolling hills and farmland, where he could hear the wind rustling the trees and the birds singing above the clip-clop of his horse's hooves. In the meantime, Elias cast his eyes across everyone travelling towards Auckland, looking for other traders who might help him.

"Have you seen Jack Jones's wagon?" he called out a few times.

"Not lately." Or "Can't remember when," came most of the replies.

"What you want with that no-gooder?" asked one, and another told him, "You'll want nowt to do with 'im."

With the reins loose in his hands, Elias let his horse amble its way along the road. If he got a move on, he could make Papatoetoe or even Manurewa before it was too dark, but the more he thought about it, the more he decided against it. He might well have another hour or so of twilight beyond Otahuhu, but he would not have anywhere decent to stay or get a drink. And he needed a drink.

The two-storey Star Hotel in Otahuhu was as unlike its namesake in Newton Road as possible, and much grander. The place was busy and well lit up when he arrived, but Henry Syms, the obliging landlord, soon found him a room and led him up the staircase. Its ornately carved banister attracted Elias's newly trained eye for quality workmanship, and he stopped to admire it before being shown into a fresh and commodious bedroom.

After arranging with Henry to have his horse stabled, he dropped his saddlebags on the floor. Pulling his shirt off over his head, Elias threw it across the bed and eased the creaks from his body. It had been a long day. Tipping water from the ewer into the matching bowl, he washed the dirt off his face, neck and hands, and pulled on a clean shirt. He would enjoy himself tonight – he might not have the opportunity to sleep in such salubrious surroundings on the road ahead.

Back in the bar, buzzing with chatter and the clink of glasses, he ordered a cold ale to quench his thirst and a whisky to boost his spirits. What he'd heard about Black Jack so far didn't bode well. The man had a dirty reputation for being mean-spirited and hard-nosed when it came to charging interest on his loans and getting his money back.

Jack exploited the weaknesses of running a small business in isolated rural areas. Local storekeepers in need of new or specific goods to attract customers often ordered goods before they had the money to pay for them. Jack's game was to lend them the money for the supplies he delivered, add on his delivery costs, then he charged huge amounts of interest, increasing daily if they couldn't pay on time. Sometimes, Jack bought the goods in advance, paying the supplier with his own money, so the store owner was entirely beholden. Many later discovered, to their despair, they were paying interest only and none of the principal.

His dealings with men trying to make business ends meet were bad enough, but lately, Elias had heard of cases where Jack had picked on struggling widows.

He lent the women a few pennies for food or heating supplies in exchange for a bill of sale over an item of furniture and charged hefty interest on the money, increasing monthly. Word and anger spread, and Jack was openly scorned. In retaliation, Jack cancelled the loans and called them in, charging interest by the day until either someone paid him off or he seized the furniture, leaving the widows further bereft.

While waiting for his second ale to be poured Elias gazed around the room. He spotted Robert Kernow, a carrier he'd sometimes used, sitting with a couple of men Elias didn't know.

"Hello, Bob," Elias said, after making his way through the crowd. "Do you mind if I join you?"

The last time the two of them had spoken Elias had been less than friendly. He assumed the man would not hold it against him. A faint frown crossed Robert's face as Elias extended his hand. "No hard feelings, I hope."

Whatever thoughts Bob had, they faded from his face as he shook Elias's outstretched hand. "Sit down, lad," he smiled, and made the introductions. "This is Fred and Dave. Which way are you headed?"

"Towards Pokeno."

Fred extended a hand in greeting. "Got a wagon with you?"

"Not this time. Just my horse."

"Business or pleasure?" Bob indicated Elias should pull up a chair.

"A bit of both. Got some messages to deliver and looking out for fresh business while I'm at it," said Elias.

"Well, watch yourself. Weather's been bad down that way."

"'Tis true," said Fred. "I heard there were a terrible storm in Thames a week or so back. Streets flooded at the Shortland end, and some houses in Richmond Street, and all thanks to that revolting Noke Noke Creek overflowing. It fair stinks, I can tell you. A man'd take his life in his hands trying to get through it. It's right treacherous. And this road's not much better. All ruts and mud."

The men shared their views on the general quality of the roads and streets found in most small towns: lack of drainage, the appalling conditions of the creeks and streams filled up with debris and effluent, and the health risks it caused.

"The council should do something about it," said Dave, thumping the table. "It's just not good enough."

"Yeah, but where's the money coming from?" argued Fred.

The talk of councils and government, and how useless they all were, drifted to plans for the Plague Hospital in Auckland.

"They want to build it in the Auckland Domain. Of all places!" said Bob. "The locals won't have it, I tell you. They'll win the day, you mark my words."

"But what if it strikes here like it has across the Tasman?" asked Fred. "I've been reading how widespread it's become in Australia. Hundreds of deaths."

"It won't get here. Don't think about it," dismissed Bob, changing the subject. "This here war against the Boers in South Africa is something to think about, though."

The only thought Elias had given the war, even though it was constantly in the papers, was that Hugh's absence was proving a greater loss than Elias had first thought. For all the difficulties they'd had, Hugh was a master, well versed in the sugar business, as well as a good worker. Maybe he'd come back after his year was up and Elias could get out of the whole sticky business.

"Of course we should have gone," said Bob, determined not to be swayed by any doubts about the wisdom of New Zealanders being killed in a war that had nothing to do with them. "Aren't we bound to Britain, like Seddon says, for our own security? We're like a Britain of the South. If England goes, we go. It'll be over by the end of the year."

"I'll believe that when I see it. We've already sent five contingents over there," argued Fred. "The last one left a few weeks ago. And there's plans to send more."

"Won't be needed, I reckon," said Dave. "After all, how many troops does it take to defeat a bunch of Dutch farmers anyway?"

Not having much interest in the war discussion raging on around him, Elias let his thoughts drift towards Alice, and he almost missed what Fred was saying.

"It's about time they introduced that Money-Lenders Bill they've been talking about to curb those greedy shent-per-shent men," said Dave. "It sickens me what they get away with."

Keen to keep them on the subject, Elias ordered another round of ale. It would be worth the expense if he could pick up some useful information. "Do you know of anyone getting caught?"

"Yeah, as a matter of fact, I do. It were my brother's wife's sister. She got cheated by that black-hearted swindler, Jack Jones."

It didn't take much persuasion for Dave to elaborate on the story, and it differed little from the stories Elias had already been told about how Jack preyed on his victims. And, it seemed, he was adding more women to his list on a regular basis.

"I'll take to him with my bare hands if I ever get hold of him. As if it's not bad enough, she'd lost her husband, but then to lose everything she owns to the likes of him is beyond bearing."

"He's not worth the risk," said Fred. "You'd swing if you did him any harm, even if he is a scoundrel."

"I know. I know." Dave pointed his finger. "But do you know how much interest he charged her? Thirty-three per cent! Payable monthly, and she still hadn't paid any principal off. He waited three months before he took the lot. Miserable bastard. I'd kill him, I would. Risk or no risk. If it would make any difference, but it's too late … too late." Dave fell silent and swallowed the rest of his beer in one go.

"Does anyone know where I could find Jack Jones?"

Elias's question surprised Bob. "Why on earth would you want to do that?"

"Business reasons," shrugged Elias. He didn't want to mention Johnno if he could avoid it, in case he implicated the boy. Not that he cared much either way, but Bethan was adamant Johnno was nothing like his father and needed saving – both from himself and from his father – but mostly for Gwenna.

Gwenna … what was it about that girl that irritated him so much? She was good-looking in her own way, pretty even. Her mastery of the trade was without doubt, and she had been more than a kind stepdaughter to Mam. She worked hard and was willing, but she brought the worst out in him …

Nobody had seen Jack. The men continued to harangue each other for a while longer, but soon the conversation turned to the prices at the auctions and the saleyards, none of which interested Elias.

"You'll have to excuse me, gentlemen. I've an early start in the morning."

"Would you care to stay for a game or two of cards?" Bob invited.

"No, thanks." Elias pushed his chair back and got to his feet.

"Well, take care as you go, lad," said Fred. "Something went over the edge along the Razorback a while ago."

Elias promptly sat down again, a bad feeling sending a shiver down his spine. "Where exactly?" Maybe he still had a chance to pick up a clue.

"It was on the steep part; you'll know it - on the bend," said Fred. "I wouldn't have noticed except it was muddy after the deluge and I moved closer to the verge for a while to get away from the ruts. I saw gouge marks where the grass had been flattened, and bits of the edge had broken away.

"When I got onto the straight further along I stopped and walked back. I tried to see into the bush, but I couldn't see nowt beyond a few broken branches, and it were too steep for me to try and scramble down. Whatever it was has gone now."

"And when did you say it happened?" Elias prompted Fred to tell him more, taking care not to sound too eager.

"A week or two maybe, going by the damage." Fred shrugged. "It wouldn't have been easy to spot. Not on the bend like that. Watch out for those ruts. They're bad. Maybe it was nothing. Just take care."

Elias thanked Fred and said another goodnight to the others. As he was leaving he turned. "Do any of you know anything about a Johnno Jones?"

"Ya mean Black Jack's son?" asked Dave.

"Is he?" Elias pretended not to know. "That's a pity. I was told he'd be a good lad to take on for driving. I've been doing it myself, but it takes me away from the business too much. I need someone while my worker is overseas with this war."

"How Johnno turned out a good 'un is beyond my understanding," said Dave. "But the lad's all right. He used to do deliveries for his father. He's worth talking to."

"Thanks for the help. Any idea where I might find him?"

"Haven't seen him in a while, come to think of it. Not for a month or so."

No one else at the table had seen him either.

Elias bid them a final goodnight and left.

17

A DAY OF RECKONING

18 April 1900

Elias swallowed a large bowl of porridge swimming in creamy milk and washed down with two cups of tea. After saying his thank yous to the cook for the additional breads, cold meats and cheese he'd ordered for the road, he headed for the stables.

The early morning sun on his back was a treat at this time of the year, and he kicked his mare into a steady trot. The sooner he reached the spot on the Razorback Fred had described, the better. Elias wanted to see the damage for himself. It might be nothing, but he had his suspicions he might find something more sinister.

The roughly twenty-mile journey would take well over two hours, at best, with the long climb up the Bombay Hills and along the winding Razorback. If he found nothing, his journey ahead would be much longer. He groaned at the thought. He was not used to riding long distances, and he could feel the muscles in his legs aching before he'd begun. Elias started to plan where he would stop for the night long before he'd reached the hills.

To distract himself, he let his thoughts dwell on the conversation he'd had with Alice before he'd left. "What should I do, Alice?" He explained his problem, anticipating she would tell him not to go. "I mean, I don't even know this lad. I've not seen him in years and don't think I would recognise him now if I did meet him. And for all I know, he could be on legitimate business and already back with his father. I'm not at all keen to go interfering."

"That may be so, but your mam and your sister ..." Alice put her hand up to stop him interrupting before he could correct her and say 'stepsister'. In his mind, calling Gwenna 'stepsister' had put her one place removed from him, and not a real part of the family. "Stop it," said Alice. "For goodness' sake, Eli. By law, by time and by all that is right, she is still your sister. You've got to stop thinking any differently."

Elias sighed. "You're too soft-hearted by far."

Alice smiled, and put a gentle hand on his shoulder. "You know I'm right. Now, as I was saying, your mam and Gwenna have asked you to find Johnno. That's all you need to know. Your family has turned to you to help them in a time of need. How could you not do as they ask?"

He didn't know what to think any more. For so many years he'd lived by his own rules and considered behaviour showing any kind of sentiment as a sign of weakness – and a successful business couldn't afford to have a weak man at its helm. He needed to be strong, resolute, even hard-hearted, to be a man. Except in the back of his mind niggled the realisation he wasn't a successful businessman in any way. Whatever the reasons, he had failed.

But how could he admit such a thing, especially to Alice?

These uncomfortable notions did nothing to settle his mind, or help him feel in control. Somehow, he'd let himself be bullied into searching for Johnno. It wasn't something he wanted to do – and there was one reason why he would.

"Would you go if I asked you?" asked Alice.

"Of course, I would," he'd replied. "I'd do anything for you. You know that."

"Then go. Not because of me, but because your mam asked you. Because Gwenna asked. And if all is well, nothing is lost, and if all is not well and you can save the day, then you will be the hero."

And, he admitted, because a creeping suspicion of something not being quite right had settled awkwardly in his gut.

He kicked his horse into a canter. The rolling green hills dotted with sheep and cattle, and the darker hues of the bush backdrop flashed past. Elias found the sight of them much more enjoyable than either the busy city and its crammed-in buildings or the sad little towns, many still with makeshift living quarters.

With the hills approaching, he slowed the mare to a walk, wriggled in the saddle and stood in the stirrups trying to stretch his knees and ease his aching muscles. He pushed on nevertheless. Suspense rising, he urged the animal into a fast walk.

At the top of the Bombays, Elias dismounted and loosened the girth. The view was stunning, stretching all the way back to Auckland, and in the far distance, he could make out the hazy shape of Rangitoto Island in the gulf.

He breathed in the air, smelling of the newly turned soil from the market garden harvests, the fresh fragrance of the karapapa with its clusters of red berries hiding somewhere in the undergrowth, and the flowers of cabbage trees standing tall and alone. Taking the food from his saddlebags, he sat on the ground and a feeling of peace dropped over him.

He and Hugh had travelled this road with the wagon when supplying goods to the Franklin area, but they'd never stopped. He'd always pushed to keep going to the pub at Tuakau for the night. Elias found traipsing around the small towns and villages plying their wares, selling a little bit here and there and drumming up new business, tedious in the extreme. He'd not been down this way since Hugh's last trip, which was one of the reasons the business wasn't doing so well.

Taking a bite from the fresh-made bread and breaking off a piece of cheese, Elias watched the stream of passing traffic – people walking, several riders, a few cyclists and an assortment of wagons, coaches and drays travelling at various speeds. He waved to a few as they passed, but he'd never made friends with any of the carters. In fact, he had no one he could truly call a friend. He had drinking mates, and he had Woody – the only person who knew his secret – but no close friends.

From the beginning, Elias had found settling into a new country more of a challenge than the girls. Aged eighteen when the family had arrived, and still angry with his mother for marrying George less than a year earlier, Elias had resented working for his stepfather. Even though, he now admitted – at least, to himself – George had been a reasonable man who could have taught him a lot more if only Elias had listened. George had been a good confectioner and a genial businessman who nurtured his clients. Something Elias had not mastered, which served to increase his hostility and ensured people kept their distance.

His bad feelings extended beyond Bethan and George to include his younger sisters, who fell in love with the sunshine and lifestyle and soon made friends among the ladies' groups and church community when Elias couldn't. Even Gwenna and Sam had their schoolfriends, but his lot was working in an adult world, trapped halfway between boy and man. His isolation grew when Charlie was born. He took it as an insult, but Alice had made him see it wasn't Charlie's fault.

All his brooding of late was getting on his nerves. The one thing he wanted from life was to be like his father, but when boiled down, there were so many things he couldn't remember about his father. His memories were blurred and damaged. His image of his father was near perfect, but Bethan often said George was the better sweet maker and businessman. Now Elias didn't know what he wanted - except he didn't want to be a confectioner.

"Elias. Is that you?" A voice called from behind.

He scrambled to his feet and turned around to greet Joe Miller. "Hello, Joe. Good to see you again. What's the latest?" Admiring the two beautifully matched dray horses pulling the delivery cart, Elias stood by their heads and stroked them.

"There's been an accident along Razorback and they need extra hands," explained Joe. "I'm on my way back to Auckland with this load so couldn't stop."

Elias felt an invisible finger creep down his spine. "I was just heading that way. What happened?"

"Two delivery vans passing each other on that tricky corner. You know the one. One went over," Joe said. "It's not looking good. I'll send the doc with his cart."

Elias knew it had to be the same corner Fred had talked about last night. "Righto, Joe. I'll get a move on and see what I can do."

The men parted company, promising to catch up at the King's Arms next week. Elias had stuffed his things in the saddlebags, tightened the girth, mounted and headed south before Joe's wagon was out of sight.

In a hurry now, he kicked his horse into a canter and, not long after, arrived at the scene where a delivery wagon, a private carriage and two riderless horses stood.

Elias dismounted and ran towards the men. "I was told you need extra hands. What's happened?"

"Don't know for sure," said the first man. "I arrived after it happened, but I'm told a downhill vehicle collided with an uphill vehicle on the bend."

The second man said, "The driver going down said the man swerved to avoid him on the corner and the wheels went over. They're down there somewhere," he gestured. "The whole lot – horse, wagon and driver."

"What can I do?"

"Ask the fella standing over there." He nodded to a well-dressed man peering into the gully.

In a few strides, Elias covered the distance to stand beside the man, whom he suspected belonged to the private carriage. Elias could see broken branches and crushed greenery swept aside in a swathe, and the rear end of a delivery wagon which, miraculously, was still upright.

"Who needs a hand?" he asked.

The deep ruts in the road Fred had told him about

were clearly visible, and dangerous. Less visible, and with fresh tracks over the top, were the lines of wheels going over the verge – just as Fred had described. Whether the first cart had gone down the bank or just skidded over the edge, Elias couldn't decide. Movement off to one side attracted his eye.

"The man down there said he'd need a hand to get the driver up," replied the smartly dressed man, pointing.

Adrenalin pumping, Elias pulled his jacket off and began to edge his way down the steep bank, careful to test foot- and handholds as he went. Once he was level with the vehicle, the ground evened out and was nowhere near as steep. Elias could stand more or less normally. He could see the shafts of the van had snapped, and the horse, with an obviously broken leg, had been put out of its misery. Somebody had chocked the wheels.

"Hello?" Elias called. "Where's the driver?"

"Over here."

Clambering around the dead horse, Elias found a man seated on the ground, leaning against a tree trunk.

"Where are you hurt?" asked Elias, crouching beside him, casting an eye over the injuries.

The man nursed one arm. His face and hands were covered in scratches, and a blood-soaked shirt bound one leg. "Dislocated shoulder probably," the stranger answered. "The gash will need proper patching but I'll live." He gave the bush above him the once-over. "Don't think I can climb out, though."

Elias's eyes followed the man's gaze up the slope but could see little. A bit of blue sky through the canopy, and the climb appeared a lot steeper going up than coming down.

"We'll figure out a way," said Elias. "Is there anyone else down here to help us?"

"Yeah, one fella further down. Something went over before me. He's gone to investigate."

Elias felt the now-familiar feeling creeping down his spine. "Wait here," he said needlessly.

He found the other man standing near a wagon. It lay on one sideboard, exposing the axle, the shafts pointing uphill. A few boxes lay scattered around, but at first glance nothing else. No horses, no driver, nothing to explain what it was doing there.

"Name's Eli," he said, extending his hand. "I was sent down to help with the injured man."

"Bill," came the reply, as they shook hands. "Thanks. I came straight down as soon as I saw the man go over. Did you see him?"

Elias nodded. "He's not bad, considering. I gather it's your shirt binding his leg."

"Yeah. He's lucky. Injuries could've been much worse."

Elias pointed to the overturned dray in front of him. "What's this?" he asked, hoping for a different answer to the one he expected.

Bill removed his cap and scratched his head. "Beats me. I can't figure out how it got here."

"Can we turn it upright?" Elias scanned the ground and up the bank behind him. "Might be easier to drag it out that way. It doesn't look too badly damaged."

"Odd that, don't you think?" said Bill, putting his cap back on.

Elias twitched his nose. "Do you smell anything?"

"It'll be damp ground and a bit of rotting vegetation somewhere, I expect." Bill headed to the front of the wagon. "Righto, let's see what's what."

Clambering over a few broken branches and low bushes to the other side of the shafts, Bill selected some sturdy branches, one strong enough to use as a lever and another to act as a fulcrum. He jammed one branch into place and raised the front end while Elias jammed a wedge under it.

"Phwaw, *something's* fair rotten around here," said Bill, wrinkling his nose. "Let's do the same at the back."

They moved towards the rear end, but the sight greeting them had both men gagging within moments. Sticking out from under the wagon were the lower legs and one hand of a male body grotesquely bloated, blackened and crawling with insects.

Covering their noses and mouths with the crook of their elbows, they made their way uphill again, as far away from the foul cadaver as they could. Collapsing to the ground next to the injured driver, they gasped for fresh air.

"Oh my God! Who's that?" panted Bill, lying spread-eagled.

Elias sat, knees raised, his arms folded across the top, shaking inside like a blancmange. His mind flooded with memories of the accident that killed his father all those years ago. He ran his fingers through his hair, wiped his face, trying to wipe away the horror, but the image stayed with him.

"I've a good idea who it might be, unfortunately," wheezed Elias, turning shades of pale. "The name on the wagon gives it away." He hoped it would be Black Jack; his gut feeling told him it would be Johnno, since Gwenna had said he was driving it, but Elias kept that piece of information to himself.

"You talking about Black Jack Jones?"

Elias had almost forgotten the injured driver. "I am. Why? Do you know something?"

"Nothing exactly," he began, easing his back against the tree and wincing with the movement.

Bill sat up, interested in the stranger's answer. "There's something not quite right about the whole thing, that's for sure."

"I've heard rumours."

"About what?" Suspicion festered in Elias's mind. He rubbed his hands through his hair again.

The injured man stared at them, pain clouding his eyes. "Do ya think you could get me out of here before we start worryin' about rumours and dead men?"

Apologising, both men scrambled to their feet.

"I'm Eli, by the way, and you are …?"

"Dan. Dan Davies," he grunted. "Pardon me for not shaking ya hand."

Bill and Elias discussed what they would need and how many men they could rally to help.

"Get a move on then, lad," said Bill. "Up you go."

As Elias headed up the bank he turned to the injured driver. "Sorry, Dan. It'll be a bit of a rough ride, nem'mind how we do it."

Dan nodded grimly.

Deep in conversation, the group hadn't noticed Elias as he climbed over the bank and onto the roadway. "What's everyone doing?" he called, seeing a queue of traffic forming and more men milling around.

"We're trying to get enough hands together to bring the cart up." The suited man was enjoying his role as self-imposed leader without having to lift a finger.

Elias didn't rise to the bait. "Good. The wheels are chocked so it won't fall further. And Jack Jones's dray is down there too." He decided not to tell them about the body – he didn't want anyone distracted from the task at hand. He'd much rather the police handled the whole affair, but the scene haunted him, and he struggled to make sense of what had happened. "Let's get the driver of this cart out before we think about anything else. He can't walk."

The second of the two riders was the first to move away from the group. "What do you need?"

Within minutes, Elias was climbing back down the bank with the equipment he'd gathered. Bill grabbed the machete, lopped off two long branches and two cross branches and created a makeshift litter by lacing a blanket to the poles with the bailing twine. Elias attached rope to both stretcher poles and took another trip to the top with the other ends.

Bill removed Dan's belt and tied it around his arm and shoulder. "That should hold it for a bit, I hope. Better than having it flop around, anyway."

While Bill was strapping Dan, Elias came back with two more men. Elias and Bill took the front end of the stretcher and the two strangers the back. Those at the top would pull the rope.

It was tough work. His muscles strained, sweat poured from his brow and his stomach churned. Elias was sure he could smell the stench of rotting flesh. Busy as he was, the further they moved up the bank, away from Jack's wagon, the more Elias's thoughts returned to the body lying a matter of yards away. There was nothing recognisable about the parts he'd seen, even for someone who knew the man. And he hoped he was wrong – that it wasn't Johnno – but there was no way he'd go anywhere near the remains to check.

After several stops and starts, the stretcher crew crept closer to the crest. The ropes were doing their job now and had taken the strain. Dan gritted his teeth in an effort not to call out at every jolt, complaining his body was on fire, but one particularly heavy jarring was more than he could bear and he screamed in agony.

As soon as they were within reach, many hands reached out to help lift Dan onto the roadway. The four carriers followed and slumped to the ground to regain their breath. While everyone was discussing what to do next, a four-wheeled cart appeared over the brow of the hill.

"Great timing. Joe Miller said he'd send someone," said Elias.

"Glad to see you, Doc," said Bill shaking hands with the man.

After a quick examination, the doctor asked for help to transfer Dan into his cart and, with thanks to the rescuers, he trotted off the way he had come.

With the rescue complete and the danger over, people were keen to get away.

The suited man was the first to leave. "Well done, everyone. The rescue went quite satisfactorily, I feel, but I must be on my way. I've a meeting in Auckland and I've wasted enough time. Good day to you all." He tipped his hat, climbed into his carriage and with a click-click of his tongue set his horse moving.

Before anyone else could follow the man's lead, Bill tied a rope across the road, blocking the passage for the queue of vehicles. "Right. I'm not leaving until that van is back on the road, too. Who's gonna help?"

To speed up their departure, several people offered and it was all hands to the rope. Bill and Elias elected to head down into the bush yet another time. They emptied the goods out to be dealt with later, unharnessed the dead horse, dismantled what was left of the shafts and attached the rope to the axle. Bit by bit, as the men on the road took the strain of the rope and Bill and Elias chocked the wheels as they progressed, the vehicle jerked its way to the top. The toughest part was getting it over the edge and safely lodged out of the way of passing traffic.

All the while, Elias kept thinking about Jack Jones's wagon still lying at the bottom of the gully, and who would collect the body – and, more to the point, how he would tell Gwenna.

After hearty congratulations all round, slaps on the backs and calls to get moving, the newcomers made their farewells, happy to have played a minor role.

Bill, Elias and the two riders who'd been first on the scene were the only ones left. They stood watching while the traffic recommenced its journey, kicking up dust as it went.

"We can tell the authorities about this if you like," the first man said, sounding a little too keen to Elias, suspicious even. "We're heading towards Papakura."

There was something about him Elias didn't trust. "That's not necessary," he said, wondering what the man was so keen to tell the police. "I'm sure Joe Miller would have reported it already, since he sent the doctor."

"And if he hasn't, then I will," said Bill. "It was because of me it happened in the first place. I'll go see them anyway."

"Fair enough," replied the second man. Eager to get away, he nudged his companion.

The four men shook hands, thanking each other for their help.

"Before I go," said the first man, "you said there's another wagon still down there? Are you going to haul that out too?"

Bill nodded. "No. Not me. I'll report it to the authorities. They can deal with it."

The man turned to Elias and squinted. "What's the story there? You seemed to know who it belonged to."

"Can't say as I knew him." Only then did Elias remember he'd not spoken to Dan again after they'd brought him up the bank. "The name was written on the side."

"Nothing to tell," said Bill, knowing there was indeed more but choosing not to say anything. "I'd say it's been down there a long time."

Within minutes of the two riders leaving, the dust from their horses' hooves still hovering in the air, Elias was also keen to get away. "I'm off too."

Bill put a hand on Elias' shoulder. "Wait up a bit, lad. You seem to know a lot more about that wagon than you're letting on. There's something not right about it, and I want to know what it is."

Elias shook his head. "I don't know anything more than you. All I know is, Jack Jones's wagon went missing a couple of weeks back."

"So, where are you off to in such a hurry?"

"Chasing rumours."

18

Should he, shouldn't he?

18 April 1900

Elias had no doubt Dan Davies knew something. He kicked himself for not checking where they would take Dan, or asking where the man lived. The signage on the rescued delivery van said Pokeno General Store, which seemed as good a place as any to start asking questions. It was no more than an hour's ride away.

For a few moments, as he trotted down the road, Elias wondered if his journey was over. He'd been sent to find Johnno. Instead, he'd found Jack Jones's wagon and a body.

Gwenna said Johnno had driven off in the cart on the Thursday before Easter. Jack hadn't seen him since the Monday before that. The boy had been missing for at least ten days, and Jack's wagon now lay at the bottom of the gully.

Elias hoped against hope that Jack *had* caught up with Johnno on that Sunday when he'd galloped away from the house - and that Jack had been driving when it went over - but Elias struggled to convince himself such a miracle had happened. His gut feeling told him the grisly remains would be identified as Johnno's, never mind how many times he tried to rewrite the scene in his head.

Maybe he should take the easy way out now – go home, and forget about the whole business. He felt sick at the thought of it all, but who was he kidding? Telling Gwenna and Bethan he'd found a rotting body he thought was Johnno's was hardly the easy way out. In fact, he hoped he wouldn't have to tell them at all. He hoped the authorities would get there first. It wouldn't take the police long to put two and two together. They'd soon be knocking on the door of Jack's house in Onehunga, and learn that Gwenna was married to the son. Mavis Milligan, if no one else, would be sure to tell them.

"Stop being a coward, Elias Hughes," he said out loud as he urged his horse into a canter. All he had was rumour and speculation. He needed to be sure of his facts, to *know* what had happened before he said anything to anyone. The question was: where should he start?

If he went south to Mercer, or west through the small settlements of Franklin, searching for a solution, he could be away for weeks – if he could get anyone to tell a stranger anything. If he returned to Auckland, Dan might be more forthcoming; he owed Elias a debt of gratitude. Or he could leave the whole sorry affair to the police. Except the tingle that crept down his spine at the mention of Jack Jones remained.

Indecision weighed heavily on his shoulders.

In Auckland, he would have to face Gwenna.

The dairy-farming town of Pokeno held little interest for him. While its monthly sales brought people from all around the district, the main sources of employment were the creamery, the railway station, where the post and telegraph offices were, and at William Dean's flax mill. Although it had three churches, a town hall and a school, there was little else of note for travellers - apart from the general store. He didn't expect the storekeeper to recall his name. All the confectionery was sold under the G *Price & Family* brand, and Hugh had done the deliveries.

"Good afternoon," said Elias to the man behind the counter. "My name is Elias Hughes."

"Brown. James Brown." The storekeeper extended his hand. "And how can I help you?"

"Do you know a man by the name of Dan Davies?"

"I do, aye. What's Dan been up to this time?" he chuckled.

"He's had a bit of an accident."

Elias proceeded to explain to James Brown what had happened at the top of the Razorback, and where he'd find his goods and the damaged, but movable delivery vehicle.

"Thank you for telling me. I'd better get it seen to right away," said James, untying his long white apron and calling for his wife to take over the store.

Mr Brown, Elias learnt, was a member of the local road board, a piece of information that might be of use, even if Elias couldn't yet see how.

"That corner is treacherous," said Mr Brown. "It's been giving us cause for concern for a while. I guess we'll have to look into it more thoroughly after this."

Elias wasn't sure anyone should be ferreting around while Jack's wagon was still in the bush - not until the police turned up - but he didn't say anything. It wasn't any of his business.

"Before you go, can you tell me where Dan lives, or where I might find any of his acquaintances?"

James Brown's face darkened. "I can tell you where he lives, but his acquaintances are people I would prefer not to know. Davies is my odd-job driver. Ask at the Mercer pub. They might be able to help you better. Here." James scribbled Dan's address on a scrap of paper and handed it to Elias.

Elias thanked him, and was about to leave when another question popped into his mind. "Do you employ other carriers sometimes then?"

James Brown confirmed he did.

"Any chance you know Jack Jones?"

If Elias thought James Brown's reaction to Dan's friends was uncompromising, his response to the name Jack Jones was downright hostile.

"I have nothing whatsoever to do with that man. He is despicable beyond words and is banned from entering these premises. Now, if you'll excuse me …"

Outside on the verandah, Elias weighed up his options. He was no closer to finding Dan's friends, nor learning what any of them might have heard about Black Jack or the accident. Someone definitely knew something. Bill had been adamant. Given the angle of the wagon, the lack of damage and the way the body lay face down underneath the tail end, Bill swore he'd not been alone at the time.

Elias glanced at his fob watch: three-thirty. He sighed with relief. It was too late to travel far and he could delay his return home for another day without any remorse.

He remounted and turned his horse towards Tuakau, the town he liked best in this area. A smile creased his face. The Tuakau tavern attracted travellers from every direction.

Back in the 1840s, when the place had a vibrant flax-milling industry – long before the wars with the Māori in the 1860s and the construction of the nearby Alexander Redoubt – the main landing area had been situated on the banks of the Waikato River. The centre of town had since moved a mile and a half or so inland where they'd built the railway station, which suited him better.

Within the hour Elias had settled into his room, taken a bath and now stood in the bar room with a glass of whisky in his hand. The day was still not quite done, and he had the bar mostly to himself. Outside, the gathering clouds obscuring the setting sun had turned day into a gloomy twilight, which soon turned to darkness. Inside, while not as up to date as the Star in Otahuhu, the two-storey pub was comfortable, and he intended to make himself very snug. In fact, if the weather turned bad, he might stay another day.

Ordering another whisky and ale, he sat in the armchair by the fireplace, letting his head fall against the wingback, and contemplated his day. His whole body ached, and his heavy limbs and tired mind cried out for rest, but he felt ill at ease. He didn't care about Johnno Jones one way or the other, and less about his father, but finding a body like that had turned his stomach. And Bill's comments worried him. It had looked like an accident, clean and simple, except he, too, sensed there was more to it.

The bar started to fill and Elias recognised some of the men. The night ahead could be more interesting than he'd first anticipated. Soon after, seated in the dining room with half a dozen others, tucking into a hearty roast dinner with lashings of gravy and slabs of freshly made bread, Elias listened to the local gossip and waited for an opportunity to talk about Jack Jones.

"Frost was lucky all the engines and machinery were saved from the fire at the flax mill back in February," said Jim, the man opposite him. "At least he's managed to keep everybody on while he rebuilds the sheds. Wouldn't do to lose employment around here at the moment."

Elias had read about the fire but said nothing. The other men nodded and muttered about what little enough work was available.

"Did you see the advertisement in the paper last week?" asked Frank from the end of the table. "The government is calling for tenders to build a bridge over the Waikato River just a couple of miles from here. Whoever wins the contract will need men to do the hard grunt."

Most of them had seen the notice; it had been the talk of the town. A few wild guesses were tossed around as to who might win it, and everyone hoped it would go to a local.

"Bet it doesn't," muttered Will Cunningham, next to Elias. "I've heard that Orlando Wells bloke from Auckland is putting in for it. If he is, he'll undercut anyone around here. Bet you anything he'll win it."

More nods as the others agreed and contemplated what it would mean. Elias watched their spirits droop at the thought of outside workers coming into town and taking their jobs, until someone mentioned the local rugby match. Elias had little knowledge of the sport or the people involved, but was content to listen. In time, when everyone was relaxed and in a happy frame of mind after a few more drinks, he could start asking questions.

He was beginning to think he'd been wasting his time when the conversation turned to a show the musical theatre group in Pukekohe had put on, the dance at the Pokeno hall, and the Papakura races, but none of it lasted long and his luck turned.

Dinner finished, Will suggested they move to the lounge. Three men declined and said their farewells, which left Jim McFadyen and his brother Arthur, who hailed from Waiuku, Will Cunningham, whom Elias had come across before, and Frank, whom Elias didn't know at all.

With a fresh round of drinks lined up in front of them, the conversation turned to trade. Frank was a cabinetmaker, and Elias itched to talk about how he treated certain woods or the way he turned a shape or made a dovetail drawer, but such a conversation would have to wait. Jim and Arthur ran the local blacksmith and ironmongery, and Will Cunningham was a carrier. If anyone could tell him something, Will was the most likely candidate.

"Don't know's as if I can survive much longer," said Will, who was getting on in years. He had been a carter in the heyday of Mercer, when the boats brought the goods down the river as far as the township and travelled the rest of the way by land. "What with the railway through all the way now – and being extended every time I look – and the roads being improved, there's more competition than ever. I'm getting past it all." He shrugged and took a swallow of beer.

The story was the same everywhere. The railway could ship goods faster, and the more places it went, the quicker and easier it became for people and their wares to get from place to place. In the early days, carriers had been needed to disperse products to farms and villages, and transport goods to and from the steamers calling in to the small harbour ports. These days, with more railway stations available, people could collect their own goods or hire a local man. Old-style, long-distance carters like Will and Jack Jones were in less demand than ever before.

"Yeah, and a few of those cocky young 'uns who know nothing about carting get me mad," said Frank. "The way they stack the goods is enough to make you cringe. It's how things get damaged."

Elias agreed with him. Some woods, like kauri, although beautiful when turned into furniture, were soft and easily dented or scratched. Whatever the owner did with their furniture after delivery was their responsibility, but they wouldn't accept goods which arrived damaged.

"Although, it's not so much damaged goods for us," said Arthur. "It's hard to damage most of the items we send out, but we have lost stock. The worst one for that was Jack Jones. Total scumbag. Don't ever trust him."

Elias's ears pricked at the name. His chance had come. His heart rate increased, but he took care not to show how important the answer was to him.

"Did you have any dealings with Johnno Jones?"

"Some," said Jim. "He's a nice lad. Not cut out to be his father's dogsbody, though. He should get hisself away from his ol' man."

"Yeah. I've met him a few times," added Frank. "Got a right cheeky grin. Unlike his old man, grumpy, bad-tempered bugger that he is."

So far, Elias had learnt nothing he didn't already

know. "Yeah, even in Auckland I've heard rumours about Jack. Didn't know if any of 'em were true or not."

"Believe me, whatever they are, they're true." Arthur sounded distinctly testy.

"How d'ya know if you don't know what they are?" Elias hoped the leading question would draw out the information he needed, but Arthur would not be drawn. His lips tightened and deep frown lines creased his brow.

His brother Jim answered for him. "Trust us. We know – he swindled our poor aunt. I won't go into the details, but we're more than willing to make sure his reputation goes before him and he never works in our area again."

Elias didn't want to sound too inquisitive but, needing to keep the discussion going, he pushed the brothers. "I'd heard he was a hard-nosed moneylender. Why did your aunt need money from the likes of him?" said Elias, interlacing his fingers to steady his nerves.

Arthur sat forward in his chair, pointing his finger, and snarled. "Are you accusing us of neglecting our family? Because if you are, I'll call you out on that."

Hands up in surrender mode, Elias tried to pacify the man. "Not at all, mate. Not me. There's no love lost between 'im and me neither."

Arthur and Jim visibly relaxed. The brothers eyed each other and then glanced at the other men. Arthur nodded.

"We've heard a few stories," said Jim. "'Twas thanks to Johnno he got any carting work at all. But nobody's seen neither one for weeks now. The boy's done himself a disservice there, he has. People aren't gonna hang around waiting for him to turn up to get their goods sent off."

"From what I hear, it's not unusual for Black Jack to disappear," said Frank. "If he's not been seen in a while, you can count the days before you hear about another swindle."

Elias considered this new information. If Jack Jones was as devious as everyone said, was there a chance Jack had sent his own wagon over the top and he and Johnno were in hiding together somewhere? But then who was the body lying underneath? The more Elias thought about it, the more unlikely it became, but he was grasping at any idea to avoid telling Gwenna he thought Johnno was dead.

"Someone's going to get him one day, that's for sure," said Arthur. "I've heard lots of talk about it. Sooner or later the talk'll stop. Someone will get riled up enough to take the law into their own hands."

"As long as it's not you, Art," said his brother.

"That's fighting talk," said Elias. "Do you honestly believe someone would attack him?"

"Wouldn't surprise me if they did," said Will. "He's cheated too many people for too long. He's done for, one way or the other. He won't work around here again. He'll have to move to new pastures."

Jack Jones was more disliked than Elias had thought, but none of this was helping him find out what or who had forced Jack's cart off the road. "Do any of you know Dan Davies?" Elias threw out another hook.

"The guy who drives for Jim Brown in Pokeno sometimes?" queried Frank.

"Yeah, that's the fellow. Me and a few others just fished him out of the bush up the Razorback." Elias explained about the accident, which sent the conversation off track while they discussed the dangers of the road, and that corner in particular, and what the road board should do to improve matters. Everyone had an opinion on the state of the roads and the conversation turned to the chaos cyclists caused.

"Ridiculous things," said Will. "Give me a horse any day."

"I like cycling," said Frank. "It's more convenient." Will grunted, but Frank ignored him. "A bicycle has lots of advantages over a horse: it's easier to store, you don't need stables, or have to go out and catch it when you want it, and it doesn't need feeding."

"Yeah, but they get in the way, and those bells scare the horses," said Will, unconvinced. "Useless things. And you can't carry anything on them, neither. Maybe around the towns they might work, but not on the open roads. I nearly ran one off the side the other day – wobbling around all over the place it was."

"I'll agree with you on that one, I suppose," growled Frank. "Bloody horses. But it's the ruts created by the wheels on your wagons what causes the problem. Not t'other way round. Get stuck in one of those and you know all about it."

Sensing an argument brewing, Elias jumped straight in. "Talking about ruts, I spoke to Dan Davies before he got taken off by the doctor," said Elias, dragging the exchange back to the topic. "He was saying he'd heard rumours about Jack Jones getting his comeuppance, and now you fellas are saying the same thing. You got anything more specific to go on?"

Suspicion appeared on Will's face. "What's with all the questions? Why d'ya want to know?"

Elias shrugged as nonchalantly as he could even though his insides were churning. "Just curious. A man

157

in the pub in Otahuhu warned me there'd been an accident on the same spot a week or two back. When we rescued Dan, we found a wagon down the bottom of the gully as well. Strange to have two go over in the same place, don't you think?"

"Maybe. Maybe not. It's a treacherous piece of road, specially in the wet," said Will. "Whose wagon was it?"

"Jack Jones's," answered Elias.

"What!" exclaimed Will, spluttering over his beer.

Disbelief echoed around the table.

"So where's Jack?" asked Frank.

Elias tossed back his whisky. "Dunno," he said and shuddered, either from the sharp taste of the alcohol or because of what he'd seen, but he hoped the distressing images he carried in his head would fade soon. "But there was a body lying underneath it." His voice was almost a whisper.

While all the talk had been going on around him, Elias had debated whether to tell the men about the body or not, but the story would come out soon enough and he could see no reason to keep it a secret. And he might get more information if he did. The shock on the men's faces achieved what Elias had hoped for.

"Are you saying Jack Jones is dead?" asked Arthur, almost gleefully.

"No, I'm not. I'm saying we saw a body. The police'll have to identify it. At least they know where to start."

Will checked to make sure no one else was listening. Leaning forward, he lowered his voice. "You'll not get anyone admitting to knowing anything - and it might not mean anything - but ..." He tapped the side of his nose. "I overheard someone in the Drury pub say we wouldn't have to worry no more. Him and his mates had made sure a certain scourge wouldn't bother us again. They'd clinked their glasses together and toasted each other, and started talking about something else. No names were mentioned; nothing to give a hint about what they were talking about, but it's got me wondering, that's all. When you put it all together."

"When did that happen?" Elias asked.

The story was not much to go on, but if so many people were talking about Black Jack and what might be done about him, then Bill's suspicions that the accident was no accident were correct. Elias shuddered again. He didn't want to think about the possibility of murder.

"Couple weeks back," Will replied. "Yeah. 'Twere Thursday afore last. I remember, 'cos I don't often stop at Drury, but weather were that bad I didn't push on."

"Those days fit about right, from what I was told," said Elias, mentally calculating what Gwenna had told him. "The weather was bad, you said. I don't remember. Bad how?"

"Wet. We'd had showers on and off for a couple of days, but that day the clouds burst. Those that were on the road – and there wasn't many, it were that slippery – were wrapped up in their wet weather gear, head down trying to get wherever they was going as safely as possible."

"Did you recognise anyone?" Elias tried to keep his voice calm and not let on what he was thinking. Maybe if the road was that wet, it could have been an accident after all.

"You kidding me? No one was looking like anyone that day. I could have passed me own mother and not seen her," said Will.

"So if there'd been a crash, like someone going over a bank, would anyone notice?"

"Not likely. Not then at least. Maybe in a day or two, if someone had cared to look. But most likely the rain would have hidden any evidence to the casual passer-by," answered Will. "What're you getting at?"

"Just thinkin' out loud," said Elias, almost relieved. It sounded more like an accident to him. "I'm not local. I'm from Karangahape Road, but I hear things too. I need a new driver to help out with the sales and deliveries, and someone recommended Johnno Jones, but I can't find him."

It wasn't completely untrue. He did want a driver. He was tired of doing the deliveries himself, even those near to home, since it took him away from his woodworking, but it wouldn't be Johnno.

"I remember now," said Arthur. "I thought I knew you from somewhere. You're the lolly man. You had another guy who used to come down here visiting all the villages and such. You came with him a few times, I seem to recall."

Elias didn't show his surprise at being identified. "Yeah, that's right. I've got my own van, but the driving takes me away from what I should be doing, so I've not been around lately. Hugh, the guy you're talking about, is off with the war. Won't be back until November, if I'm lucky, and if he's lucky enough to survive it all. There's an awful lot who don't. That's why I need someone meanwhile."

Elias detected a slight shift once they became aware of who he was. Frank suggested another round of drinks. Someone banked up the fire, and even though it wasn't cold enough, the fire was relaxing.

Too wound up to let the conversation go off track for long, Elias drank a deep draught of his ale and steered the topic away from the casualties of war back to Johnno Jones. "Will, if I heard you correctly, coming up two weeks ago you heard people in the pub talking about removing a scourge. Right?" Will agreed. "And you believe they meant Black Jack?" pushed Elias.

"I never said that," replied Will, too swiftly.

Elias lifted an eyebrow in query.

"Possibly," Will conceded.

"So, if something, let's say, untoward, has happened to help Black Jack 'disappear', then where's Johnno?" asked Elias, planting a seed of doubt.

"Where are you heading with this?" Jim eyed Elias uncertainly.

"Not sure. All I know is, you've said two men haven't been seen in weeks. I know their wagon is at the bottom of the gully. So what happened? Is one of them dead? If so, where's the other one? And whose body is it?"

The four men gawped at one another, consternation written on their faces.

"Well, if it were that day I was talking about," ventured Will, "anything's possible. But ..." He paused. "Wait up. I remember now. I saw him on Sunday. Yes, I'm sure it was Sunday. I was heading down this way with a shipment, and he came roaring past me at a flat gallop. His horse was frothing at the mouth. And if he came the whole way up the hills at that pace, it's no wonder."

"Never mind about the horse," said Arthur irritated. "Who did you see?"

"Jack Jones. Who else do you think I'm talking about?"

"Are you certain it was him?" His heart pumping, Elias sat on the edge of his seat.

For a moment, Will appeared taken aback. He hesitated. "I ... well. Yes. Yes, I am. He was wearing that funny old greatcoat of his. I remembered it. It's the only one I've seen like it."

Everyone recalled the tatty wool coat Jack wore, with its tarnished brass buttons he never did up. It was unmistakable. The shoulder cape, torn on one side, hung lopsided and flew about in the wind, and would have been the final giveaway.

"And you do mean Sunday gone? Three days ago?" checked Elias, wanting to be absolutely sure.

"I said so, didn't I? How many times do I have ta tell ya? Sunday."

Elias downed the rest of his schooner and ordered more.

"Well, well. That's a turn-up," said Jim. "Where was he going in such a hurry, I wonder?"

"Good riddance, I say. The further he goes, the better. We're well shot of him," muttered Arthur. "For a moment there, I thought he was out of everyone's hair for good." Arthur's face turned grey and grim.

"I'm guessing he wasn't looking for his son, at any rate," said Elias, the beer in his gut turning sour.

"What if Will is right in what he said about overhearing those blokes?" said Frank who'd been listening to the exchange without saying a word. "What if they did do something that day in the rain? Jack Jones's wagon had his name painted on it, but if the fella driving it was wrapped up in oilskins, like Will said, and no one could see him properly, could they have thought it was Jack when in fact it was Johnno? It could be a case of mistaken identity."

Elias felt the shiver down his spine again as the scene fell into place. The wagon going over the top could well have been an accident, forced off the road in the wet.

Except there was no horse, and the body had deliberately been put under the wagon.

"Are you thinking he might have been murdered? By mistake?" asked Will.

No one answered.

Elias tossed back another whisky as he took it all in.

The target was Jack.

But the victim was Johnno.

19

THE AGREEMENT

20 April 1900

"What news?" Bethan ran into the courtyard before Elias had dismounted.

Gwenna stood on the step, her knuckles, clenched over her grossly enlarged stomach in a gaunt body, were turning white. She trapped her bottom lip between her teeth and tensed her shoulders in readiness for his answer.

Anger flared in Elias's gut. He had wanted to avoid this situation, and now he'd landed right in the middle of it. Damn and blast! She seemed so desperate standing there waiting for him to destroy her world, he wanted to get right back on his horse and go anywhere other than here. He'd deliberately stayed away longer to get drunk, in the hope that by Friday evening someone in authority would have been in touch with Gwenna. But he was wrong.

About to snap out a reply designed to hurt her, his thoughts drifted to Alice. How he wished he could go to her right now. Alice, he sighed, as the words she'd said resounded: *"She is your way out."* Maybe he didn't have to destroy Gwenna just yet. Maybe they could both get what they wanted if he played his cards right. "It's a long story. Too long to talk about out here. Go back inside, Mam."

Elias hedged but Bethan pushed him. "Tell us, Elias. Please. What did you find?"

"Don't press me, Mam," he said through gritted teeth. "It's been a hard few days. I need to clean up first," Elias added trying to control his mounting frustration. "I'll see to my horse and come in shortly."

But Gwenna would not budge either. "For once in your life, stop being a coward, Elias Hughes, and be honest."

By God, she riled him. "Coward! You dare to call me a coward. After what I've been through."

He dropped the saddle over the rail with a clatter and turned to face her, an echo of the truth ringing in his brain. With a gap of ten feet between them, tension crackled. "You want the honest truth, do you? Well, let's have it then, shall we?"

Standing square, feet apart and arms spread six inches away from his body, he clenched and unclenched his fists. Every nerve, every fibre stood on edge ready to fight like a beast against the oncoming foe.

"Elias ..." Bethan put a restraining hand on his arm.

He shook it off, his eyes never leaving Gwenna. "Not now, Mam," he growled.

To Gwenna, he said, "Come on then, out with it."

The stepsiblings stared at one another, neither prepared to give the other the advantage. Each could read past resentments in the other's eyes, and in those moments they made a bargain.

"He's dead, isn't he?" Gwenna's voice sounded hollow, coming somewhere from deep inside her, but flat, as if any emotion, any movement would cause her to disintegrate.

He struggled to remain calm and resist his instinct to shout at her. He wanted to rid himself of all his hurts, all the injustices, tell them exactly how he felt deep inside, and throw away the shackles that bound him. But he didn't. He surprised himself with his self-control. "*Ie*. I can't say for sure, but I believe so. The police will have to investigate what happened first. They'll have the final say."

Elias watched her warily. Only her eyes changed. As if a light had gone out. They appeared grey and colourless where usually they sparkled as blue as a sunny sky.

Bethan hurried to her side. "Come along, Gwenna, *bach*; come inside and rest. You don't want to stir things up again."

Gwenna refused to move.

"So what happens now, Elias?"

Even he understood the question was greater than the obvious. She wasn't only referring to Johnno.

"You stay. I'll go."

If Gwenna hadn't heard Elias say those words with her own ears, she would never have believed them.

"You won't change my mind," said Elias, when Bethan refused to accept such an outcome possible, or necessary. "And we'll need more than tea, Mam. Pour us a drink. We're gonna need it." He pulled up a chair.

Bethan fussed about getting the glasses, ale and whisky for Elias, and a brandy for herself and Gwenna. When they were all settled, Elias told them in a curiously indifferent manner what he'd learnt about Black Jack and the accident, keeping his suspicions and the gory details to himself.

His was the lone voice, and it seemed to go on and on as the clock ticked down time. He admitted he'd been learning furniture making and told them about Woody, about his dreams, and lastly about Alice.

Overwhelmed and disconnected, Gwenna said nothing. She sat motionless, her face blank. A small tear escaped, and she wiped it away. Her body, numb. Her mind, a void. A notion she should feel distraught and rail at the world for her loss, or become hysterical, hovered vaguely in her head, but she couldn't find a single spark to light the fire. She doubted she would feel warm ever again. Her blood, if any still ran in her veins, felt icy, her heart a lump of stone.

In contrast, Bethan needed to keep busy when she was upset, to cushion the shock - too many shocks. Jabbering about what she'd heard, Bethan rustled up another drink for Elias, made a pot of tea for Gwenna, sweet and strong, and gathered together bread, cold meats, cheeses and pickles to keep up their strength, even though no one was hungry and nobody touched any of it. She poured herself another brandy and sat in the armchair, quite flustered.

Elias refused to say anything further about Johnno or Jack and turned the conversation to his plans. "So that's it," he said at length. "Plainly and simply, I no longer wish to make sweets. I intend to make furniture. As far as I'm concerned, you're welcome to the business, what's left of it. And I make no apologies on that account. You must meet all the costs, including the lease. I wipe my hands of it. I will remain under this roof until such time as Alice agrees to marry me and we make our home elsewhere. You keep out of my way and I'll keep out of yours. Is that a reasonable deal?"

167

Bethan interrupted several times but gave up after being ignored, talked over or told to hush.

"This is between me and Gwenna, Mam. I know you'd like a different outcome, but this is a far better arrangement than what we had before. Don't you agree, Gwenna?"

How could she not agree? Without saying so, Elias confessed to how bad things had got between them. He provided reasons without excuses, outlined his intentions, leaving no room for argument and offered an arrangement which freed them both.

Elias stood, swallowed the last of his ale, folded a piece of meat into a slice of bread, and waited. Gwenna looked up at him trying to assess what it all meant. Her pains had stopped after he and Bethan had rescued her from that dreadful house. False labour, they said, which could strike again, but she would know the difference when her time came.

"*Ie*, 'tis. There's so much to think about, Elias. My head is fair spinning. And my heart is right aggrieved." Two days earlier had been her birthday. She'd refused any kind of acknowledgement as exhaustion and grief drained her mind and body of all resolve. "Can you give us some time – at least ..."

At least, what? At least until after the police investigation: it could take months? Until after the baby was born, which was still weeks away if she rested well? And what about a funeral?

Even if she managed all those difficulties, taking up the reins of a failing business – if things were as bad as she expected – would take more strength than she had right now. But she couldn't give up this chance. Her future, and that of her child, rested on it.

20

HIDING THE TRUTH

23 April 1900

Neither of them had the grace of time. On Monday morning, a knock sounded.

"Is a Mr Elias Hughes at home?" queried the man who stood at the door checking his notebook.

Bethan stood back, opening the door wider.

Elias rose from the table, still cluttered with breakfast dishes, and took a few steps forward. "I am he."

"Detective Lawrence Scott." The man, dressed in a tweed jacket and bowler hat, showed his badge. "Could we have a word, sir?"

With a wave of his hand, Elias allowed the man entry and made the introductions.

Bethan scurried to clear the table. "Would you care for a cup of tea?"

"Thank you, ma'am. That would be very kind."

Once Elias and the detective were seated, Bethan made a fresh pot of tea, placed it on the table next to a plate of biscuits and moved the sugar and milk within reach. Gwenna watched, aware that fussing over the little details kept Bethan's anxiety at bay.

"Now, sir. I understand you were in the vicinity of an accident on Wednesday on the Razorback." The man added some milk, took a sip of tea and picked up a biscuit.

"I was, yes. We've been expecting you."

"Oh, and why is that, sir?" He didn't pay attention to Elias as he asked the question and proceeded to dunk his biscuit in the tea and suck it.

Elias frowned. "Well, about the wagon I discovered down in the gully. I was helping rescue a man from down the bank when we saw it. I presumed you wanted to talk about that."

"We know all there is to know about the rescue. Mr Davies has kindly advised us of the details. Mr Dean also."

"How is Dan?" enquired Elias.

"I believe Mr Davies is recovering and will be returning home shortly."

"Good, I'm glad. Which one was Dean? I didn't get everyone's name."

"I understand he was the driver of the other vehicle."

"In which case, what brings you to my door?" Elias fidgeted restlessly in his chair.

"I'm here on another matter." The man paused and dunked another biscuit. "We've received a report of some suspicious activities involving you."

"What suspicious activities?" Elias was undeniably taken aback.

"We could go to the station if you would prefer."

"Station?" exclaimed Bethan. "Whatever for? What are you accusing him of?"

"Nothing yet, ma'am. We are simply making enquiries. It seems Mr Hughes failed to mention the body he found in, shall we say, unusual circumstances."

A strange, strangled sound escaped Gwenna's lips as though someone had squeezed what little life remained from her.

"Are you well, ma'am?" For a moment, the officer sounded alarmed.

Gwenna didn't answer.

"Really, detective," snapped Elias. "Have some decency."

Scott remained unruffled. "It seems you may also have omitted to tell the ladies here about your, er, 'find'."

"On the contrary, sir. I *have* informed Mrs Jones …" Elias waved a hand towards Gwenna, "… that I believed her husband was no longer with us, and the police would formally advise her in due course – which I had supposed was the purpose of your visit. However, I chose not to supply the less-than-pleasant details of *how* I reached my conclusion."

The detective had enough propriety to apologise. "Forgive me, ma'am, for the shock, but police business must take precedence."

"Pompous fool," Gwenna muffled under her breath, irritated by his manner. This was her husband, her Johnno, that ghastly man was talking about. Her back straightened. "I understand, Detective Scott, but surely, you could have found a more suitable way."

The officer would not be cowed, however. "I did not comprehend you had not been informed. My apologies, but I am here on more important business."

In his haste and anger, Elias knocked over his chair when he stood up. "Let us go elsewhere, detective. This conversation is completely out of order."

Shocked out of her lethargy, Gwenna held up a staying hand. "No. Stay. I want to hear what happened.

Elias, I know you are trying to protect me – and I thank you – but Johnno is gone and nothing is going to bring him back. I want to know how and why. Maybe you can tell me, detective."

In the few days since he'd rescued her from Onehunga, Gwenna and Elias had rubbed along together, if not comfortably, at least not acrimoniously. They would never be close, and probably never friends either, but she hoped they were no longer enemies. He spent most of his time away from the house – seeing Alice and working at the workshop, he'd said – so the police finding him at home was pure chance.

To Gwenna's mind, there was no doubt Alice's stabilising and calming influence over Elias had changed him. He was a different man to the one Gwenna had lived with, but that in itself scared her; it had been so sudden, and she worried the old Elias would reappear if anyone crossed him. So far, she'd not seen any evidence of the violence returning, but she had noticed the effort it took him to control his tongue on occasions.

He'd appeared that morning in a particularly good mood, so she had asked him to stay and teach her how he managed the accounts, the stock, sales and deliveries and all the other details he had kept from her. She had no doubts about her skill in making the lollies or any style of sweet-tasting treat, for that matter, but while Pa had taught her about weights and measurements, about cost efficiencies and the value of freshness, she had never had anything to do with the running of the business. She would now have to take into account the cost of running the home, the lease, the telephone, owning the neglected delivery van and caring for a horse, as well as managing the orders. The task seemed insurmountable, but the more plans she made, the more hopeful she became. She had so many ideas she was near to bursting with them all. Dragging her down – apart from her despair over Johnno and worry about how she would raise a baby without a husband – was her self-doubt after so many years under Elias's authority.

"Are you sure, Gwenna, love?" Bethan plainly didn't want to know. "Some things are best left as they are. The less you know, the better, in my experience."

Bethan had good reasons. She too had lost a husband to an accident and, in truth, lost her son at the same time. She lost another husband to sickness and had to learn to live with that same son under, at times, harrowing circumstances. Bethan had adapted, learnt to cope with whatever life threw at her, without complaint, and in the process had lost herself. She no longer had any say over anything. Gwenna didn't want that to happen to her.

Two bright spots of anger coloured her cheeks. "I'm sure, Mam. I need to know. I have to learn to take control of my life. Please, Elias. Sit down. If you'd prefer, Detective Scott can tell me what he knows, or you can tell me. It's up to you."

Elias began by explaining how the events on the day of the rescue had unfolded, including seeing a body, which he believed was Johnno's. "I left it to the man named Bill to report the accident with Dan Davies, and what else we'd found, to the police. I didn't consider it necessary for both of us to do so."

As the story developed, the detective appeared to relax. He took notes and occasionally asked a couple of questions, but mainly left Elias to do the talking.

"It was only much later, in a conversation in the Tuakau pub, did I learn about the terrible storm everyone believed had caused the first accident - and when Jack Jones's wagon had more than likely gone over the edge."

Sometimes Elias hesitated, and Gwenna could only surmise what detail he'd left out for her benefit - or could there be a more sinister reason? If so, the officer didn't pick up on it, but he didn't know Elias the way she did. He wouldn't interpret the nuances she had learnt to read to protect herself, but for whatever reason, Elias was lying. Or at least not telling the whole truth.

"In my opinion, the wagon went over in the wet and trapped the driver," concluded Elias.

"I concur with your assessment, young man. The wagon at the bottom of the gully did belong to J Jones Esq., senior. Mr Jones is currently being sought by the police for questioning concerning his dealings, which are contrary to the proposed new laws of moneylending. He is not a registered trader and will have to answer to the courts when the bill is passed. However, he has not been sighted for some time, except it seems by Mr William Cunningham, if what you say is correct. We will follow up this sighting with Mr Cunningham."

He folded his notebook, slipped it into his pocket and extended his hand towards Elias as he stood up. "Combined with our investigations and what you've told me, I believe we can now safely identify the person involved as Mr John Jones. You will be formally notified, Mrs Jones."

The two men shook hands before the officer turned to Gwenna and Bethan. "Thank you, Mrs Jones, and you, Mrs Price, ma'am. Sorry to have intruded upon you, but police business must be attended to," he repeated for the third time.

As soon as he took a step forward, Bethan jumped up to open the door for him.

"Just a moment, detective," said Gwenna, who remained seated at the table. "I was not feeling my best when you arrived, and I'm even more shaky now, given what I have learnt. However, if I'm not mistaken, at the start you indicated Mr Hughes had some suspicious activity to account for, did you not?"

The detective fiddled with his hat. "I did, ma'am."

"And do you still believe it to be the case?" Gwenna noted the man's embarrassment and used it to get what she wanted.

"No. I do not."

"Then you owe Mr Hughes an apology. He did nothing other than to keep some of the more gruesome details to himself."

The man nodded and again extended his hand towards Elias, which, this time, Elias did not accept. Detective Scott dropped his hand to his side. "No hard feelings, I hope, sir. You will understand, I'm sure, I was simply following orders and doing my duty. I thank you for your co-operation and apologise for taking up your time unnecessarily."

It would do.

"Thank you," said Gwenna. "Forgive me if I don't see you to the door. As you can see, I'm heavy with child."

The man glanced between Elias and Gwenna, flabbergasted and shocked at her effrontery.

Elias smiled. "You assume incorrectly, detective. Twice. I am not head of this household. Mrs Jones holds that position. Good day."

When Bethan shut the door behind him, Elias let out an odd-sounding burst of air, which caused Bethan to squawk. Gwenna managed a small twitch of the lips at the noises they made, even though she had no desire to laugh. Death was no laughing matter, but it broke the tension that once again had surfaced.

"I'm sorry you had to go through all that on my behalf, Elias. I never realised how bad it must have been for you." Gwenna had again slumped in her chair, exhausted.

"And I'm sorry you had to suffer that fool," said Elias. "I'd have kept the details from you and Mam if I'd had my way. No woman should face such things. You handled it graciously."

Gwenna stared at him in astonishment. What on earth had Alice said to him? Never in a lifetime would she have expected Elias to compliment her. She was grateful he no longer hit her.

"I didn't thank you for finding him. I should have. I am grateful, and obliged to you." For a few moments, she sat motionless. "I still can't quite believe it - even though I dreamt it." Gwenna had known something was going to happen, some instinct she hadn't known she possessed. An inner sense made her try to stop Johnno from going. "Remember, I told you about my dream: the one where the wilderness spread its tentacles over everything in its path - even wagons and people."

If Johnno hadn't done his father's bidding that day, none of this would have happened, but he had and he'd been killed. All because of his father. She would never forgive the man.

Gwenna's greatest ordeal began later that day when the police arrived.

As Detective Scott had indicated, two officers appeared on her doorstep announcing a body had been recovered, identified and was available for burial.

"We've provided a suitable box, ma'am, but regret you will not be able to view the body. Where should we send it?"

After the morning's fiasco, Bethan nearly fainted with shock. Tillie, who'd hurried around as soon as she'd heard about the detective's visit, supported her stepmother while Gwenna staggered to a chair. They all struggled to gather their wits to answer after the man's bluntness.

Eventually, Tillie came to her senses first. "I will ask my husband, Mr Thomas Griffiths, to contact you as soon as possible."

Tom proved to be his usual tower of strength and organised for the body to be sent to the undertakers, who advised the somewhat malodorous and miserable box should be interred as soon as possible. Following their advice, Tom arranged a speedy and private burial and persuaded the minister to present himself at the house to hold a small service. At the best of times, women were not expected to attend funerals, and there were no men to speak of, other than Tom. They didn't even post a notice in the newspapers. There seemed no point. No one, Gwenna included, wanted Black Jack to see it and turn up unexpectedly. He would not have been welcome.

For Gwenna, it was a day to forget.

In many ways, Johnno's funeral was a painful non-event. She did not have the luxury to indulge in the lengthy and elaborate funeral rituals of the past, nor could she afford to shut herself away from view for a year or more, mourning her loss while she could lose the very business that kept her going.

She rejected the traditional symbols of mourning. She didn't have a lock of hair or a photograph or any memento. All she had were memories – and few enough of those. And since she didn't know when Johnno died, she couldn't stop the clock. Neither would she drape the windows and mirrors after death.

Feeling empty inside, she could not bring herself to show any emotion, and the others followed her lead. Awkwardness was the overriding feature of the day.

21

A NEW LIFE WITHIN REACH

Late May 1900

The tortuous weeks that followed nearly broke Gwenna's spirit.

"Stop fretting, little sister," said Tillie, now a constant visitor to North Street, and Gwenna's crutch. "You are the strongest of all of us. And anyway, you and I have a thing or two to prove to those snobby stepsisters of ours."

Disgusted that Louisa and Janetta had chosen to stay away – 'for the sake of propriety' – Tillie became more determined than ever that the Price sisters would succeed. "Sorry, Mam, I know they're your daughters, and I shouldn't speak badly of them, but they are no friends of ours."

Tillie assured Bethan Charlie could continue living with her and Tom. "Unless you want him home with you." She had been as astounded as all of them with the change in Elias. "And I'm right gladdened to know Elias has found something – and someone, by all accounts – to make him happy in life. Maybe now he can forget his earlier troubles."

In the end, they decided Charlie should remain with Tillie and Tom.

"He's happy and that's what counts," said Bethan. "Between Gwenna, the baby – when it arrives – and the sugar boiling, there's more than enough to do around here. I couldn't give him the time he deserves. And Tom is good to him. Charlie needs a man to show him the proper ways, and so he can start to forget the things he saw Elias do."

"So that's sorted. Now what are we going to do with you, Gwenna, *bach*?" said Tillie.

Gwenna had no suggestions. Her increasingly restless unborn child kept her awake at night, and on edge during the day. "I still can't believe Johnno's gone – before we even started. He's like a ghost in my head. He spent so much time away from me, with his father, I'm beginning to think he only married me because of the baby. Did he ever truly love me?"

"Of course Johnno loved you. I know he did."

Deep in her heart, Gwenna admitted Tillie was right. And she had loved Johnno in return, but sometimes she didn't know what to believe.

It didn't help that Elias refused to talk any further about the whole affair and spent every waking hour away from the house.

"I don't know what to do. I can't afford the time to go into mourning for twelve months. Not now Elias has walked away from the business. I can't lose it now."

"People will understand when they know. And I'll do what I can to help."

Gwenna held her sister's hand. "I know you will, Tillie, dear, but you have a husband and Olwen to care for. You can't neglect them."

"I won't. But you've talked and talked about bringing Pa's dreams to life ever since he died, and we are a team – are we not? That grandchild of his you're carrying will arrive any day now. Surely that's more than enough reason for you to start anew – even if you have to flaunt convention a little."

Refreshed by Tillie's comments, Gwenna rallied and began to make a few trays of toffee and caramels, but she just didn't have the strength to stretch the sugar the way she usually did to make the hard sweets – not the way she liked. Yet between them, she and Bethan began replenishing the dwindling stock, adding a few chocolates and Tillie's fudge to the mix to expand the range.

Bethan fussed over her as only a mother can. "You must rest as much as possible, Gwenna. You don't want those false pains to start up again. And eat – you must eat. You are so thin, my dear, you won't have the strength to do what you must, otherwise. Try some of this soup, at least."

Bethan did her best to help with all the things Elias usually took care of, but she wouldn't answer the telephone. Not that it rang much these days. Except for the few loyal customers who continued to place orders.

"Thank you, Mr Green. I appreciate your custom," said Gwenna, scribbling the order on a piece of paper as she hung up the phone. Word had not yet got around that a woman would be responsible for the business from now on. She counted on the men accepting her in this more enlightened age. Meanwhile, she needed to fulfil the orders coming in.

Tossing and turning in her bed on the first day of winter, she sensed something momentous was about to happen but, unlike her other dream, she couldn't quite grasp its essence and awoke gasping. Sleep eluded her, and when the pains started she instinctively knew they were real this time. Unwilling to waken Bethan, Gwenna rolled to the side of bed and pushed herself into a sitting position. With the next pain, she grasped the bedpost and stood up.

Shortly after, a gush of warm water flowed down her legs onto the rag rug. A random thought she would have to wash it next time the copper was lit flitted through her head. She wouldn't ask Mam; it was too much to expect. Pacing the floor, she stopped on every second turn to peer out the window. She could see little. The cloudy night obliterated the stars, and the moon only shone its light briefly when the wind shifted the clouds.

Ever since arriving in New Zealand, she'd loved the sky. Clear and blue during the day and with a fathomless depth at night, drawing her eyes further and further into the darkness, past so many stars she couldn't name. Even the rain – and it rained a lot during the winter and spring months – fell differently from the soft rains of her childhood. Here the grass grew greener, the trees grew taller and the crops grew in abundance thanks to the sun and the life-giving rain. She loved her new home, despite all she had lost.

Regardless of all that, there were times when she felt the strange pull of her homeland even though she would never return. There was a word for it in the old language – *hiraeth* – a special word, a word she'd never forget. There was no other word to describe the feeling of intense longing; an unbreakable bond for a place you belonged to. There was something about the essence of that land, its mountains and valleys, its rivers and streams, that spoke to her, just like it did here.

She whispered a wish her child would feel as strongly about its birthplace, with its generous light, its life-giving heart and indomitable spirit. One could only but thrive in this country. And thrive she must.

As the pains became stronger and more regular, she recommenced her pacing, the floorboards creaking under her weight, a feeling of heaviness in her limbs. At some stage during her march, Bethan appeared. In the periphery of her mind, Bethan came and went. Hot water appeared, and towels. Someone wiped her brow with a cool cloth and helped her change into a dry nightdress. A teacup against her lips, a glass of cold water. She swallowed gratefully. Slippers warmed her feet. She couldn't rest. Sitting became a torment, lying down impossible. Time passed and daylight crept through the window. And still, the crushing, squeezing pressure persisted.

"Gwenna, dear, you must lie down. You're exhausted. You can't bring a baby into the world like this. Gwenna. Stop."

Through eyes stinging with hundreds of tiny pinpricks, Bethan's face wavered in and out of focus. Hands touched, pushed; voices urged; noises swirled. Stars danced on the ceiling above her head. Her head pounded with the sound of a thousand hammers, and the solid band around her body tightened with each breath. Every sinew strained against the torment. Neck arched, hands clenched, her jaw bit down. A mist appeared and darkness fell.

Through the window, a faint glimmer heralded the dawn. Gwenna could hear a few birds singing their morning chorus in the lone tree at the corner. Slumped in the high-backed wooden armchair slept Bethan, but *her* snores hadn't woken Gwenna.

Turning on her side, she felt an unfamiliar tightening in her breasts at the sight of her newborn. The baby lay sleeping in the dresser drawer on the floor beside the bed, wrapped in the exquisite shawl Bethan had crocheted. A tiny fist escaped its covers and blindly rubbed at a pint-sized mouth and nose from which came the snuffling, mewing sounds that had woken her. "Hello precious," she whispered, a faint smile crossing her lips.

"Ah, so you're awake now, are you? Welcome back." A stranger's voice came from behind her. The woman moved quietly around the bed to where Gwenna could see her. "I'm Mary Williams, the midwife. Mrs Price called me – day before yesterday – and I'm glad she did. You were in a right poor way when I got here. Do you remember any of it?"

Gwenna shook her head. "Everything's pretty much a blur. I was aware of sounds and feelings rather than anything real. And then nothing, until now."

Bethan woke at the sound of Gwenna's voice. "Thanks be to God. I thought we'd lost you."

While the two women fussed about, helping Gwenna to sit up and guiding the baby to her breast, they filled in the gaps in her memory. Tillie had spent almost as much time with Gwenna as in her own house, bringing food to save Bethan from cooking, and fudge to build up the stock. Elias, too, had called, which surprised them all.

"You nearly left us, Gwenna, *bach*. I was that afraid, I thought the fairy folk had come for you. But you're a plucky one, our Gwenna. You are that."

Gwenna smiled weakly. She had no intentions of going anywhere just yet, and she wasn't sure she believed in fairy folk.

"That tightening is your milk coming through," said Mary. "We need to encourage it. We've been feeding your son with a bottle for the last forty-eight hours, hoping you'd pull through on your own. He's a fighter, this one. Like you, by the sounds of things, but he's a long way to go. He's very little and underweight."

A son. She had a son.

Overjoyed, Gwenna did as she was told, knowing something special, magical even, had just happened, but she had no words to explain it. Whatever this feeling meant, it would be something between her and this child. She'd never considered herself a fighter, nor an ancient who could foretell things, but maybe she was wrong – on both counts. Her future lay in her arms, and she would fight anyone who tried to take it away.

"What will you call him?" Bethan bent down over the baby and ran a gentle finger over his cheek.

In her son, Gwenna saw echoes of Johnno. She recalled the fateful morning, the morning Johnno left forever when she'd stared at him, committing every detail to memory as if she sensed he would not return.

Tears flowed down her face, but she left them unchecked. For the first time in many months, these were tears of joy and fulfilment, even if they were still tinged with sadness. Johnno had been a glorious interlude in her life, someone she had hardly known, but this happiness would live on in his son.

"George. After Pa."

〰〰〰〰〰

22

AGAINST THE TIDE

3 June 1900

To Gwenna's frustration, neither Bethan nor Mary would let her out of bed.

"You're to have complete bed rest for at least seven days," ordered Mary. "And your mam has no say in the matter either. So even if you could persuade her around to your way of thinking, it isn't going to happen."

The risk her son might not thrive as well, otherwise, convinced Gwenna to do as she was told. In truth, her body told her the same. After living with anxiety and exhaustion for so long, she had little energy left, and if Georgie needed her, then she would get strong again for him.

In the hours when he lay by her side and she watched him sleep, sometimes dozing herself, a new sense of purpose and resolve bubbled inside her. From now on, when all her doubts and fears rose to the surface, as she was sure they would, she would remember she wasn't working just to fulfil Pa's dreams, nor for her benefit alone. Everything she did, everything she planned and everything she achieved would be for her son, and she would let no one stand in her way.

She had refused to consider naming her son John. That evil man, known as Black Jack Jones, still roamed freely somewhere. She wouldn't let the boy be held back by sharing the same name as the man who, by law, was his grandfather but who would never lay eyes on him if she had her way. Gwenna would also keep her Price name – G *Price & Family*. That had been what George stood for, what Pa wanted to give Gwenna, and it would be her legacy to George junior.

Bethan had been delighted. "Baby George will keep your father's memory alive and give you both something to strive for. Your pa was one of a kind."

Tillie, too, supported her decision when she brought around a layette for the baby.

"Oh, Tillie, this is so beautiful. You shouldn't have." Tears flowed down Gwenna's face again, and she wiped them away. She was doing too much crying these days.

"Of course, I should. Georgie is my nephew and deserves the best. As do you. Don't cry, sweet sister. There are benefits to being a widow, you'll see. You are mistress of your own destiny now."

Taking advantage of her recovery time, she and Tillie spent hours closeted in her room while Georgie and Olwen slept. Between them they wrote down all the ideas they could remember their father giving them, adding several more of their own. They calculated the costs, itemised the risks and considered the threats. Every time, they found the positive column outstripped the negative.

"So why is the business in such a state?" Tillie turned another page and chewed on the end of the pencil. "Gwenna, you're the one for figures. You could calculate the weights in your head quicker than we could on paper. What is the problem here?"

They poured over the accounts, evaluated the errors and missing information, and reached the conclusion Elias had no idea about running a business.

"No wonder he was losing money," said Gwenna. "He either overcharged and lost the client or undercharged and was taken advantage of. Sometimes, he clean forgot to invoice the customer at all."

"Let's hope he's better at his furniture making, then." Tillie laughed, but Gwenna took it seriously.

"He will be," Gwenna assured her. "They are higher priced items and he doesn't have to calculate the costs. Either Mr Woodman will do all that, or I suspect, Miss Woodman."

"Have you met her?"

"No, not yet. Why, have you?"

"I have," said Tillie. "I overheard her name in the fabric department of Smith & Caughey and introduced myself. I found her quite charming."

"So she sews, too? What was she buying?" Gwenna was curious what sort of girl could tame Elias so easily.

"She makes the most beautiful patchwork quilts. Her stitching is finer than mine. I admired the section of quilting she had brought along to match up with some new colours and pattern. She was so easy to talk to, quite open and natural." Tillie went on to describe Alice in detail: petite, dark-haired, dark gentle eyes, with a soft, thoughtful voice. "Her dress was well made, too, and fitted her perfectly. She wore a pretty pastel yellow, I recall. I can see why she would be good for Elias."

"All that, after one meeting? I'll look forward to the experience."

"I will not stay in bed a minute longer." Gwenna threw back the covers and climbed out of bed to the protests of both Bethan and Mary. "I've finished my seven days. I've eaten. I've slept. I've rested. But no more. There is work to be done."

"At least a bit of colour has returned to her cheeks," the two older women agreed, ignoring the younger one. "And she is certainly full of energy again."

"I'll be keeping a close eye on her, though," said Bethan sternly. "And I'll make sure she eats well and conforms to some sense of propriety."

"And she must rest every afternoon after Georgie's feed," insisted Mary.

Satisfied they had Gwenna's next few days under their control, Mary relented. "Just promise me you won't overexert yourself."

Gwenna closed her eyes. *There was little chance of that happening*, she thought, but with Georgie to feed and boxes of sweets to sell, sitting around wouldn't get things done either.

"I'll have to go out, Mam. I have work to do. But no, I won't go to parties and the theatre. I don't want to anyway."

Sometimes the restrictions placed on women by laws and society, despite the fact women now had a real say in those laws, infuriated Gwenna. She would never be able to take control of her life and make progress as a businesswoman if she was constantly held back.

A new determination to make Pa's dreams come alive infused her whole being, although for 'the sake of propriety', as Louisa was so fond of saying, Gwenna agreed to wear black. Tillie had come to her aid yet again by making a suitable day dress and draping a hat, while Bethan dyed two of Gwenna's cotton house dresses.

The first task Gwenna set herself was to contact all the clients listed in the books. Most she wrote to, some she visited in person and others who had telephones she steeled herself to call.

She wrote explaining how, as the daughter of George Price, she would now handle the family business. "Elias Hughes has chosen to seek his own business venture elsewhere."

She didn't elaborate. He could drum up his own business if he wanted to – or let Alice handle that side of things. As long as he didn't get on his high horse about being head of the household again, but it wasn't her problem – not any more.

She signed her name, Gwenna Price.

By tradition, in Wales, and in the north in particular, married women could retain their maiden name if they chose to. The tradition did not apply in New Zealand, but neither was it against the law. Since her marriage had been short, barely four months, and no notices had been placed in any of the newspapers for the wedding or the funeral, and few people knew of her married name, she decided to keep the one she loved the most. As Mrs Price, she could still protect her son and it would endow her with the benefits and freedoms a widow could expect.

Unused to doing so much writing, Gwenna's hand cramped as she held the latest style fountain pen. She would much have preferred to write with a pencil, but doing so would not be considered businesslike. While the pen was easier to use than the old quill, filling it with an eyedropper was far too messy, and the pen left blots on the page and stained her fingers if she wasn't careful.

"Honestly, this is too much to bear." Gwenna laid the pen down to massage her palm, and rolled her head to ease her neck. She viewed her stained hands in disgust. She couldn't risk transferring the ink from her hands into the sugar, and her hands were so sore from writing, she couldn't do much more.

"I'm going out," she announced to Bethan, putting on her newly draped bonnet and coat, and wrapping a scarf around her neck. She avoided the mirror, knowing black stripped all colour from her face, leaving her pallid. In contrast, her eyes seemed larger and brighter with her hair tucked away out of sight.

"Where are you off to this time?"

"I'm sick of writing letters. I'll post a couple of them along the way, but I want to talk to Edward Turner."

"The greengrocer?" Bethan sounded surprised.

"Well, Smeeton wasn't keen on dealing with me, so I'll go to his opposition and see what happens."

"But you wouldn't expect to find lollies at the greengrocer's. That's not like a regular grocery shop." Bethan sounded puzzled.

"No, you wouldn't. But if you did, would you buy some?" Gwenna tingled with the idea. It was a novel concept, but it could work.

Edward Turner had an even better idea.

⬥⬥⬥⬥⬥⬥⬥⬥

23

SURPRISES

Mid-June 1900

"Eli's been arrested!"

Gwenna stared at the distressed girl standing before her breathing hard and fast. Strands of hair clung to her face, still sweaty and red from the exertion of running. "What for?" she demanded, her pulse racing. She knew who this girl was talking about, even if she herself never called him Eli.

"Accessory after the fact," the girl panted. "At least, I think that's what they said. But I got such a fright when they said murder, I didn't listen any more."

Murder? Gwenna shuddered and goose pimples rose on her arms. No one had mentioned murder.

With her breathing under control, the girl tilted her head to one side. "You're Gwenna, aren't you? I'm Alice Woodman."

The two women assessed each other over the doorstep. Going by her appearance, Alice hadn't stopped long enough to change. She wore a simple checked skirt, apron and white blouse, and looked precisely as Tillie had described, and Gwenna instantly took a liking to the girl.

"You'd better come in, Miss Woodman." Gwenna stood back and opened the door wider.

Introductions were made and Bethan made a fresh pot of tea. With a tea cup in their hands to hide behind, the women relaxed a little.

"I've never seen Eli so furious," said Alice. "I thought he would hit one of the policemen until my father stepped in."

Gwenna heard the new name and asked herself whether being Eli was part of his new identity, his new life – like hers.

Bethan was too agitated to listen. "Did Elias send you?"

Alice shook her head. "Oh. No. He didn't want me to come, but I had to. You need to know. I hope you don't mind my intrusion. My father has gone with him. He'll find out what's going on."

"I'm sure I'm grateful to Mr Woodman, but we should go ourselves," said Gwenna, replacing her cup on the saucer.

Shocked, Alice sounded sharper than she intended. "You can't go there. It's a dreadful place."

Bethan appeared confused. "Which place? Haven't they taken him to the new police station in Princes Street? The one they opened earlier this year?"

"I hadn't thought of that. I just assumed they'd take him to the prison in Mount Eden. Horrible stone place that it is." She shuddered. "I can see a glimpse of it from our upstairs window."

"Well, I suppose we'd better find out." About to rise, Gwenna realised Alice had no intention of moving just yet.

"I saw a side of Eli this morning I'd not seen before. Has he been angry like that in the past?"

Bethan and Gwenna glanced at each other. Should they warn her about Elias's temper, or could they consider the change in him permanent? Thanks to the very girl who was asking the question.

Bethan cleared her throat. "Elias had many disappointments in life at an early age. He was too young to understand and often lost his temper when he couldn't cope. I thought he'd grow out of it, in time, and he has for the most part. But he still has his moments."

Gwenna respected how much it hurt Bethan to reveal her son's weaknesses to a stranger, but if what Elias had told them was true, this girl might not be a stranger for long. "He's learnt to control it a lot better in the last six months. Much of it is thanks to you. He speaks of you often."

A soft blush tinged Alice's cheeks, and she briefly lowered her lashes. Her eyes were large, dark globes with hints of sunshine, and perfectly formed. "I believe I have made some changes to his manner. When I first met Eli – he asked me to call him Eli, you know – he was sombre and withdrawn, but he's different now. I know you call him Elias. I've wondered if that's part of it. Does he feel a different person using a different name?" Alice asked, echoing Gwenna's thoughts.

Gwenna would have struggled to consider anyone could change so much or so fast if she hadn't seen and heard it for herself. From her own experience, a name mattered. "I can't answer for him, but yes, quite possibly."

"When he first came," Alice continued, "Eli stumbled over words, but his eyes followed me all the time, without him speaking. He talks a lot more these days. He told me about your husband, Mrs Jones. I am so sorry for your loss."

"Thank you. But please call me Gwenna, and …" She hesitated. Alice's unexpected visit had just strengthened Gwenna's resolve to keep her maiden name. "For business reasons, I will be known as Mrs Price. I'm keeping my name." Gwenna shuddered at the thought of Black Jack Jones and all the trouble he'd caused. "But getting back to why you are here. Are you saying the police believe Elias is responsible for this murder?"

Fear put an edge on Gwenna's words. For all his faults, and he had several, the greatest of which was the chip he carried on his shoulder, she couldn't bring herself to conceive Elias capable of murder, however unintentional. Even in his worst fits of temper, once he'd cowed her, the steam went out of him and he was no longer violent.

"Not responsible as such," said Alice. "But they claim he knew about it and kept it a secret. I'm sure Eli and Dad will sort it out and he'll be back with us before day's end." Alice dismissed Gwenna's concern and smiled, turning the edges of her lips up by the merest amount. Whatever was going on in Alice's mind, Gwenna saw the girl's shoulders relax and sereneness cross her face.

"May I see the baby?" Alice's eyes turned to the basket on the floor where Georgie slept.

"Of course, but please don't wake him."

As nimble as a butterfly, Alice fell to her knees beside the basket and stared at Georgie as though he was a rare and precious doll. Her face softened as she leaned over him to breathe in the fresh smell of soap and rosewater and that characteristic baby smell. Alice was older than Gwenna by three or four years and yearned for a child of her own.

However, they had more pressing business to attend to.

"Shouldn't we at least try to find out why Elias has been arrested?" pressed Gwenna.

"We know why. I told you, the police think he knows something," Alice answered over her shoulder without taking her eyes off Georgie. "Dad and Eli need to convince them otherwise. There is nothing we can do. The police won't talk to us."

"Oh, surely they must talk to his mother," said Bethan, kneading her hands in her apron.

"Is it worth the risk? And you'd have to take Georgie to those awful places. The authorities will deal with it as they see fit. I'm sure we women would get in the way."

The girl was far too infuriatingly pragmatic to suit Gwenna's mood, but Gwenna did admire her logic and calm. Yet another reason to consider Alice would be good for Elias – like water and fire. Fire to keep the water warm, and water to calm the fiery beast.

Despite Alice's rational viewpoint, Bethan and Gwenna still wanted to find Elias.

"I feel it's my duty," said Bethan. "He doesn't have a father to stand up for him."

"Dad's doing that," Alice said breezily. "He likes Eli. He won't let anything untoward happen."

"I could at least take them some food," said Bethan, meandering from task to task, clutching for any reason to go. "They'll be hungry. It's been a long time since breakfast."

"Mam. Calm yourself." Gwenna took her stepmother's hands in hers to steady the uncontrolled fluttering. "It's no good. Much as I hate to admit it, Miss Woodman is right. Whatever happens, Mr Woodman will tell us when the time is right. I can't take Georgie out into the cold weather without knowing where to start."

In the end, they agreed rushing down to the police station or the gaol, or wherever Elias could have been taken, would not be in his best interests.

"Dad says if we repeated anything Eli told us it wouldn't help. We've only heard his version of events. Dad will vouch for Eli."

Gwenna hoped Alice was right.

They waited throughout the endless day. Gwenna made more jars of boiled sweets between feeding Georgie. The rhythm of pulling and twisting the sugar mixture suited her mood and kept the worst of her agitation at bay. Bethan baked and prepared the meat for dinner with enough vegetables to feed an army. Warm, homely aromas filled the air, and the three women knitted together as they worked.

Alice threw them off guard by sweeping and dusting, but for much of the time she watched Georgie and chattered about Eli. "He's been such a godsend to Dad. I can't tell you what a difference he's made."

Alice prattled about how her father loved his furniture making, but he was getting tired, he said.

"But it's not a physical tiredness, it's a subconscious thought. He was worried there'd be no one to take over the business. And he couldn't see the point in carrying on."

"But your father can't be old," said Bethan. "What if you marry and have children one day?"

"Wouldn't matter. Unless it was to another wood-loving man. Dad says a piece of wood has its own energy, and a good wood-man knows how to find the heart. It's not something that can be taught. But once you lose the desire to find it, it's gone for good."

Gwenna heard her father's voice echo in her head at Alice's words, and understood. *You have to love what you do to succeed, Gwenna, bach. If you don't have the heart for it, you'll always find an excuse not to do it.*

Bethan couldn't bear to admit this slip of a girl could know more about her son than she did. "So what's Elias got to do with it? He's never known one piece of wood from the next, except to split it for firewood."

"No disrespect, Mrs Price, but I believe you're wrong. Dad reckons Eli has a natural ability to draw it out in abundance. It's given him a new lease on life to teach Eli how to develop it."

A suspicion crept into Gwenna's mind. "How long has Elias been working for your father?"

"Since last December. I remember because it wasn't long after the election. Dad says ..."

Gwenna was getting a little tired of 'Dad says' and interrupted. "And if you don't mind me asking, who keeps the ledger?"

"I do." A slight frown marred Alice's forehead. "Dad can measure something to within an eensy amount to make a table stand square, or mitre a join, but he can't add up a column of figures and get the right answer."

Mr Woodman and Elias would be two peas in the same pod in that case, chuckled Gwenna to herself. "And you do sell the furniture he makes, don't you?"

Alice frowned, perplexed. "Of course. How else do you run a business?"

But Gwenna hadn't quite finished. "And who works out the costs of time and materials so you know what price to charge?"

"I do. Dad made me go to school and learn my numbers properly."

Gwenna nodded, satisfied. In hindsight, she could now piece together when Elias started to change and become a better person. Bethan had been right in her assessment that something was making him happy. And Gwenna's leaving wasn't the cause.

"Why all the questions?"

"Just curious, Miss Woodman. Just curious." Gwenna smiled. "However, I suggest you don't let Elias anywhere near the ledger either."

From her position seated on the floor next to the sleeping Georgie, Alice tilted her head to one side. The radiant smile that lit her face and reached deep into her eyes startled Gwenna with its brilliance. "Now, why would I let him do that? To each his own, I believe the saying goes."

No wonder Elias was smitten.

At the point of suggesting either Alice return home before dark, or inviting her to stay the night, Gwenna heard the latch click on the door. As soon as the two men entered, Bethan rose from her chair preparing to go to her son, but hesitated, unsure of her welcome. Alice leapt to her feet and stood beaming from ear to ear before Elias, her hands folded behind her back. Gwenna felt sure Alice would have preferred to wrap her arms around Elias's neck but restrained herself at the last moment. A vacant, lost expression dulled his eyes, and his face sagged with exhaustion. He began to tremble as all three women threw questions at him.

"What news?"

"Are you all right?"

"What happened?"

An awkward laugh filled the void.

"All is well," answered the older man.

"Thanks to Woody," confirmed a relieved young man.

Gwenna extended her hand as she approached Alice's father.

He was nothing like she had imagined. His neatly trimmed, auburn beard and moustache suited his lined, craggy face, even while his thick mop of hair stuck out at strange angles, but the warmth in his eyes was what drew Gwenna to him. "Welcome, Mr Woodman. We've heard a lot about you. Thank you for rushing to Elias's aid."

Thomas held his trilby against his chest as he took Gwenna's hand, bowing slightly in a stiff, old-fashioned way. "Mrs Jones. I am delighted to make your acquaintance and be of service to your family."

"Please, call me Gwenna." She would explain about being Mrs Price later. "I feel I know you already, and you've done so much for this family."

For a few moments, nobody moved. Elias and Alice were too intent on staring at one another while Bethan wrung her hands.

"My brother seems to have forgotten his manners. Please take a seat and tell us about the day's events."

Bethan began making a pot of tea and emptying the cake tins onto plates. Gwenna watched her from the corner of her eye, wishing she would sit down but, from experience, knew she wouldn't.

Thomas Woodman repeated what Alice had told them about the police turning up at his workshop, accusing Elias of being an 'accessory after the fact' and wishing to talk to him down at the station. Despite Alice's interpretation, they had not in fact formally arrested Elias, but Thomas had, nevertheless, considered it prudent to attend the police station. During his explanation, tea was poured and cake handed around, both of which helped fill the momentary silences when no one could decide what to say.

"Something funny is definitely going on," said Elias as their tale came to an end. "I've always had my suspicions that Jack's wagon did not go over the edge by itself."

"You have?" Gwenna's voice rose to an unusually high pitch. The tea cup clanked in the saucer as she replaced it.

The expression of horror crossing Elias's face at that moment told her more than any words. He *was* hiding something, but was it just from her or was he trying to protect Alice – and Bethan – from the details?

"I'm sorry. I didn't tell you before, Gwenna, just like I tried to spare you the details of what I found, but they've come out now anyway." Elias rubbed his hands through his hair.

"I apologise to you too, Alice. Mam. There's no point trying to keep any of it from you any more. It's got too involved."

At length, he reached the point in his story where he related the conversation in the Tuakau pub. Bit by bit, Gwenna learnt how others had feared and loathed Black Jack as much as she did. She wouldn't be sorry if she never saw the man again, but to discover people meant him serious harm came as a shock.

"We all agreed someone, or maybe more than one person, would sooner or later teach Jack Jones a lesson," said Elias. "But after Will remembered seeing Black Jack only a matter of days earlier, I realised the accident was more than likely a case of mistaken identity. Johnno had been in the wrong place at the wrong time.

"My problem was I had no way of proving it, so I said nothing," admitted Elias. "And apparently, that was their problem, even though Bill reported the accident and told them about finding Jack's wagon. Someone - one of the men who helped haul the Pokeno Store's delivery van out of the bush, I suspect, but it could have been anyone at the pub - reported me to the police saying I was hiding something."

Thomas Woodman picked up the story, telling them how he had argued finding a wagon in the bush was not a crime. Nor was finding a body, even one the police were now saying could have been suspiciously placed.

"Suspiciously placed?" Gwenna couldn't believe the nightmare was continuing.

The shock of knowing Johnno was dead was bad enough, but to learn someone may have deliberately caused the accident and tried to conceal it was much worse. It was almost beyond belief, but believe it she must. Nothing would change the outcome. And if she was honest, she had always suspected there was more to the tale than anyone was telling her.

She listened as Mr Woodman and Elias finished their story.

"Mrs Jones, er ... Gwenna," interrupted Mr Woodman. "I'm sorry for your loss, and I'm sure this is all a great shock to you - and you, Mrs Price. It's a terrible thing to see your children suffer, whatever causes their suffering. I do understand."

Bethan smiled, and Gwenna could read the relief in

her eyes, knowing someone shared her distress for her son. Her shoulders relaxed.

"But I believe in Eli, if it's any help. He has a future as a woodturner, and I am sure we eventually convinced the police Eli had not committed a crime in any way. He reported what he'd found and told them all he knew. It was not his place to cast suspicion or suggest foul play."

"Are you certain?" asked Gwenna. "This family has had more than its share of upheavals of late. We cannot move on with our lives with anything more hanging over our heads."

Thomas Woodman smiled. He turned his head towards Elias and Alice who had drifted into their own world made for two. Gwenna followed his gaze towards the unusually quiet and now pale Alice and Eli, this new person Gwenna would one day get to know better – and maybe even like.

"Yes. I'm certain," said Mr Woodman.

24

THE MARKET TURNS

Mid-June 1900 – the next day

In the cold, early morning light, Gwenna scurried down Grey Street towards the huge central marketplace filling the interior of an entire block at the bottom of the hill. She was running late. Her watch said it was already six minutes past seven, and the market would be well under way before she got there. While Mr Turner still maintained his greengrocery shop in Karangahape Road, he had recently begun holding auctions three days a week at the central market. He'd invited Gwenna to meet him.

Rushing through the south entrance from Cook Street, past the hay and corn hall, she came to a standstill. The cross-shaped timber building with its lean-to extensions on either side had been badly built many years ago, and was quite unsanitary thanks to the Wai Horotiu swamp, often called the Liger creek. Although the ground had been well drained since those earlier days, the area was still unpleasant and often stank. She shivered in the cold air.

The place was bursting at the seams with stalls of every kind set out in aisles and crammed into every nook and corner. Voices were raised as Chinese market gardeners offering fruit and vegetables vied with European growers for space and customers. Alongside were the flower sellers, the butchers and poulterers, and other food suppliers, but she hadn't expected to find fancy goods, second-hand goods and furniture dealers among them. Gwenna sneezed at the varied and strange aromas confusing her nose, and her ears rang. Adding to the noise, hucksters peddled and entertainers performed before passing the hat around.

How would she ever find him in this crowd? The place was chaotic.

She wandered up the southern aisle and watched groups of people gathered round one auctioneer, bidding for the crate of cauliflower at his feet. The next caller, with a change of pitch and tone, captured her attention and her eyes followed her ears to where he stood, selling boxes of carrots. Behind her, another auctioneer raised his voice offering a fresh sack of kumara, those amazing sweet potatoes, so creamy and tasty, that she loved. As she moved around, she discovered a sense of order among the cacophony.

The bidders knew what they wanted, and the sellers knew how to get them to buy. A nod here, a finger there, and the deal was done. Although how this all related to her, she had no idea.

"Mrs Price … Mrs Price." Someone called her name. "Over here, Mrs Price."

She scanned the space around her, unable to place where the voice had come from until she saw an arm waving. Having reached the central section where the east-west halls crossed with the north–south halls, she saw just how large the market was, and how busy. From her vantage point, she could see the separate but connected buildings on each of the outside four corners.

"Mr Turner. Thank goodness I've found you. What did you want of me?"

"No time to talk now. Just stand here and watch. I'll explain later."

Two hours passed in a flash. Auctioneers kept up the call, and the men behind the tables shifted the sold boxes and heaved fresh stock into place. After a while, she began to recognise certain voices and patterns. Although how they spoke so fast and how the buyers heard anything intelligible was beyond her comprehension. The timing of the end of each sale and the start of the next was finely tuned to the second. Buyers paid for their goods, barrows came and went, creating more disorder, but somehow the system worked. At long last, Mr Turner was free.

"The boys'll take over now. I do the calling, but they can handle the paperwork and delivery. Come, Mrs Price, join me in a cup of tea."

Edward Turner led her to the café area. Gwenna could see many work-weary faces and dirty hands taking a well-earned break, eating a late breakfast of bacon and eggs and fried potatoes.

"We start early – often around four o'clock. The auctions have to be quick so people can get the goods back to their shops and on the shelves while they are fresh. By this time of the day, we're starving. Would you like something to eat?"

They joined the queue; Edward ordered two teas, a full English breakfast for himself and a boiled egg for Gwenna with a slice of fresh bread. Finding a table proved as difficult as finding Mr Turner in the first place, but people were willing to move for Edward Turner, and he soon found somewhere for them to talk. He spooned two large teaspoons of sugar into his milky tea and stirred while he spoke. "This is the way of the future, Mrs Price."

"I don't see how it helps me, though, Mr Turner."

Between mouthfuls of food, with his fork pointing this way and that, he outlined his plans. How she envied his foresight, and the way his four elder sons, although still young – and he had younger ones still at home out west in Huia, he said – were already involved and planning their collective future.

"Mark my words, Mrs Price. The Turner name will become synonymous with auctions for wholesale fruit and vegetable at markets like these." He patted the side of his nose and chuckled. "Although as many deals are done over a cup of tea as on the floor – but that's good for business, too." His eyes sparkled with devilment.

Around her, voices competed with each other above the sounds of tea cups rattling in their saucers, the squeaky clatter of cutlery on plates and chairs scraping the floor. She asked a few questions, hoping they were pertinent, but Edward didn't seem to mind what she said. He kept talking.

"Add-ons are what you need in this world. Haven't you noticed how every shopkeeper has something that doesn't quite fit? I know nothing about flowers, but I always have some in my shop. A little extra for the little lady to take home, or the man walking past who needs to apologise."

Put that way, Gwenna could see his point. Canned foods appeared amongst the fresh food. Ready-made fizzy drinks lined the counter to entice customers to buy, and sweets could be found at the tobacconists and the pharmacy.

"When you came to me the other day, I thought to myself, this girl's got pluck. Nobody else ever asked me if I'd stock sweets. And since Smeeton seems to prefer another source, I thought, why not. But then I thought, I can do better."

Gwenna's heart leapt and her eyes teared up, but she batted them away. She hadn't realised how tense she'd felt until this moment and forced her clenched hands to relax. She had taken a wild chance, but she would be no worse off for asking. Now it seems she would be better off. "Do I take it you are prepared to offer my sweets in your store?"

"In time. I haven't quite decided how it would work for me yet."

Gwenna's spirits fell as rapidly as they had risen. She took a sip of tea to conceal her disappointment and swallowed hard, forcing back the tightening sensation in her throat and the tingle in her jaw. She must not cry.

"But I've a better idea. It's not been done before – and it may not work – but it's worth a shot."

Gwenna's emotions see-sawed so fast she couldn't decide how she felt. Maybe she would just cry later, whichever way it went. Happy. Sad. Tears came regardless, these days. Bethan said it was because of breastfeeding. With that thought in mind, she felt her breasts fill, and she would need to hurry away soon to feed Georgie.

"Mr Turner. Please? What are you talking about?"

"The auctions, Mrs Price. I could auction your sweets for you, then you wouldn't have to worry about the marketing and delivery. It all gets done here."

He raised both hands in the air to encompass the building, the open-air space, the market area and the people. "Deal?" he asked, extending his hand.

"I couldn't shake his hand fast enough or hard enough," Gwenna said as soon as she'd finished her story.

A satiated Georgie lay sleeping in his cot.

Bethan, as usual, fussed around doing chores and making herself indispensable. "I don't understand it all, of course," she said, as Gwenna explained the benefits of what Mr Turner offered, "but it sounds like a great chance."

"Oh, it is, Mam. It is that."

Gwenna would have to recalculate the costs of making and packaging to meet Edward Turner's fees, but it was a small price to pay. In exchange, she wouldn't need to employ someone to deliver the goods or take time away from what she did best, to persuade someone to buy them. Not that she could do much selling while she was in mourning. The buyers would be tolerant up to a point, and she was still to see how a woman in charge, and a young one at that, affected her regular customers.

"We'll have to work hard to build the stock up and make sure there's enough available each week. Mr Turner said he would auction them once a week during the Thursday session. He'll even give them a special name. I don't know what it is yet. He said he'd think on it."

Energised by the possibilities, Gwenna scribbled in the notebook she kept, recording what type and quantities she made, and when. Her estimates were pleasing. "This will open the market right up. I could be selling to anyone, rather than a select few. The expansion options are huge. Mr Turner gets buyers coming in from all points south, he says."

"But isn't it risky? Didn't you say no one had sold sweets this way before?" Bethan nervously wiped her hands on her apron.

"I can't see any risk. I've nothing to lose. If they don't sell, they come back here and I can still sell them the old way. But if they *do* sell, then I'm a step closer to my goal. I will open a shop like Pa wanted. I just don't know when, or where, yet."

Gwenna reached out for her stepmother's hand, inviting her to sit beside her at the table. Against her warm, strong hand, Bethan's hand was cool and dry, and surprisingly thin and lightweight given the work they did.

Some days, the weight of responsibility weighed heavier on Gwenna than others. She, Tillie and Charlie were all that remained of Bethan's family. Sam had disappeared from her life. The odd letter was her only connection with him. Her relationship with Louisa had not improved. And where Louisa went, Janetta followed. Bethan still felt like a stranger – more like a faithful old servant who was tolerated, she'd said – than their mother. Their husbands were no more or less polite than they would be to any person of their acquaintance. "And I'm sure the children have no idea I'm their grandmother," Bethan had complained.

And now Elias had gone.

"Don't fret, Mam. Everything will work out fine, you'll see."

—————

25

THE START OF A NEW DREAM

August 1900

"It's time, Tillie. It's time to open our first shop, but I need your help. And Tom's."

Gwenna reminded her sister she'd always believed their front parlour would make a brilliant shop, situated as it was on a corner with direct street access and an excellent three-bay window along the front.

Tom, as usual, was kindness itself. He listened at length to Gwenna's proposition and asked many questions before going off to check some financial details. She'd asked a lot of Tom and Tillie, but since their house was large enough and they rarely used the front reception room, Gwenna kept her fingers crossed Tom would see the benefits. She didn't have to wait long.

"Your concept is a fine one, Gwenna. Go ahead, do what you like. I've secured you a loan and, as your backer, allocated as much money as you require."

Gwenna didn't know how to thank him, or Tillie, but he wouldn't listen to her gratitude. "I'll do all right out of it, Gwenna."

By supporting their scheme, Tom believed he would recoup all he spent and more. He even approved of the name and gave his blessing to Gwenna retaining G *Price & Family*.

"From what I've heard of your father, I'm sure he would be proud of you, and the least said about the Jones family, the better, in my opinion."

Tillie's excitement was as great as Gwenna's when Tom agreed. It would take months to come to fruition, and the sisters lost no time in putting plans into place.

Bethan took over the role of mother and housekeeper for both households. Cooking, cleaning, washing, and caring for Charlie, Olwen and Georgie gave her a new sense of purpose. Her whole manner changed. She was like her old self again.

She no longer wrung her hands or hesitated to speak, and while sometimes the sisters felt as if they too were children again, being told to wash their hands or tidy up before dinner, both Tillie and Gwenna were relieved to see the positive change.

Despite the chaos caused by the builders doing the necessary alterations, Tom too seemed quite happy to come home at the end of a day's work to find his mother-in-law in charge. His only request was for Tillie to spend the day with him on Sundays going to chapel first, and taking a walk if the weather allowed, or just talking, reading aloud and playing a game or two of cards in inclement weather.

All was going to plan, but even the sisters admitted they couldn't have done any of it without the help of Tom and Bethan – nor Edward Turner, who had made it all possible.

Six weeks earlier, astounded at how simple his scheme had been, Gwenna had turned up on the morning Edward designated, with her heart in her mouth and samples of her confectionery in her basket. But he wouldn't let her voice her worries.

"Chin up, Mrs Price, you cannot lose. You have nothing right now, so you can only go up. And I guarantee you will have something by next week, so don't worry your little head about anything. Leave it to me."

Standing on his box, head and shoulders above the crowd, he extolled the virtues of her lollies, inviting 'one and all' to help themselves and sample Gwenna's handmade confectionery.

"Too many have switched to making their product by machine. I'm all for innovation and modernisation, you understand. And mass production is all very well in certain markets. But," he paused, lowering his voice and leaning forward to make the buyers listen more intently, "my friends, listen to me. I'll let you into a little secret. If you want quality, if you want elegance, if you want individuality, then Gwenna's Superior Sweet Treats are for you." He stood up and his voice returned to its normal auctioneer pitch. "Come along now, only by tasting will you believe me."

Her heart swelled with pride to hear her confectionery named after her. When he'd made the suggestion, she expressed doubts at the informality until he assured her the personal touch would make the difference. She watched as her samples disappeared.

"Taste Gwenna's Superior Sweet Treats for yourself and tell me if I'm wrong. I know I'm not. Tell your friends to come along and try for themselves."

In the first week, she sold a dozen or more boxes,

and more the next week, and the one following. As the weeks passed and the shillings kept rolling in, Gwenna's confidence grew.

One day early in September Tom came home feeling exceptionally pleased with himself. After Tillie had helped divest him of his wet raincoat, brush off his bowler hat and shake out the umbrella, he asked them all to sit down. Bethan sat in the armchair with Charlie on the floor beside her, while Tillie and Gwenna took a seat at the dining room table. Tom stood with his back to the fireplace, warming himself after the soaking he'd received. He reached for his pipe sitting on the mantelpiece, tamped down fresh tobacco and struck a match on the striker. "I've made those enquiries you asked of me, Gwenna," he said between breaths, drawing the pipe. "And it seems you are right. I am able to secure the next-door property for a very reasonable sum." He shook the match out and threw it in the fire. "Gwenna, Bethan, you can now give up your residence on North Street. They accepted my offer."

Gwenna beamed. Everything was falling into place nicely. The neighbouring cottage also had stables for the horse and her pa's beloved van. Neither would be needed as much as they once were, but Gwenna was loathe to dispose of them. Tom, she was sure, would find them useful. The cottage had a garden for the children to play and a back porch where she and Bethan could sit. It all made sense. Costs would be less, distances shortened. She couldn't wait to move in - just her, baby Georgie and Bethan.

"But I have a better suggestion, Gwenna," continued Tom. "I am of the opinion it is I and my family who should move next door," he said, thrilled to have solved so many problems at once, "so you, dear sister-in-law, can live in this house and fulfil your dreams."

Baffled, Gwenna wanted to argue. "But ..."

Tom held up his hand to stop any further questions or interruptions. Tillie placed her hand over Gwenna's, trying to contain her own excitement. Her face creased into a wide smile.

"Tillie and I have spoken about this, and we are agreed. The bungalow would much better suit our purposes. The documents are signed and sealed."

Gwenna glanced between the two.

Tillie nodded enthusiastically. "Yes, my dear. You are hearing correctly."

Unable to contain her own exuberance once realisation hit her, Gwenna hugged her sister and leapt to her feet. Her skirt rustled around her feet as she hurried towards her brother-in-law. "Oh, I can't believe it. Thank you. Dear Tom, thank you so much. There will be no way I can repay you for all your generosity."

He took the legal documents from his inside pocket and handed them to Gwenna.

Being under the age of twenty-one, Gwenna was not legally entitled to own property, but Tom's role as titular head of the whole family meant Gwenna had secured bank funds she might not otherwise have been granted, even as a widow.

Waving away her concerns about how she would service the loan, Tom patted her hand. "Make a success of it, my dear. Show those naysayers a thing or two, and it will be all the thanks I need."

Gradually, over the winter months, the project took shape. After a visit to the solicitors where signatures and papers were exchanged, Tom granted Gwenna full use of the house at 18 Beresford Street. The same day she gave notice on the North Street property.

A month later, Tom, Tillie and Olwen moved into the adjacent cottage, which Tillie declared delightful and more conveniently laid out than the corner place. Bethan, Gwenna and baby Georgie moved into the upstairs rooms and rearranged the back rooms of the house during the renovations. Charlie could be found eating or sleeping at either house as the mood took him.

As soon as the builders and decorators finished their tasks at number 18, including adding the latest up-to-date cooking range and fitting Gwenna's confectioner's table, the girls completed the transformation to the shop.

They lined the shelves against the back wall with jar after jar of Gwenna's handmade sweets. On the recently purchased rimu sideboard, plates sat under glass domes in readiness for Tillie's fudge, alongside an assortment of handmade chocolates and delicate cupcakes. Dainty teacups, saucers and side plates adorned their old Welsh dresser against the other wall. The floorboards had been repolished and a large mirror above the mantelpiece reflected light throughout. Adorning the walls was a pale cream wallpaper with burgundy sprigs set against a frieze of large burgundy flowers with dark green leaves and trailing shoots.

"Didn't I tell you this corner would be the place for Pa's dreams to come true?" said Gwenna.

"You did, sister dear, and my heart knew you were right, even if I doubted it would ever happen. But you've done far more than he dreamed about."

Pa had wanted a small shop where he could display his goods and where retailers could inspect, taste and negotiate prices for larger quantities. Gwenna's ideas were far greater. She wanted a large shop, and a tearoom.

"No, Tillie. *We've* done it. I couldn't have done any of this without you and Tom."

"Tom is the most wonderful man, isn't he?"

Gwenna wholeheartedly agreed. "He most certainly is."

The position was perfect. Close to several churches, en route to the park and several schools, and in easy walking distance of the busyness of Karangahape Road, they had plenty of passing traffic. Gwenna imagined the ladies with their parasols and plumed hats sitting at the small round tables sipping tea.

Outside, they stood back and admired the finished building work. With a fresh coat of cream paint contrasting beautifully with dark green window and door trims, the main entrance now came straight off the street into the extended front parlour. The family could go through to the other end of the house, thanks to a new internal door. The elegant three-bay sash windows facing the street were now draped in the fine lace curtains Tillie had made, drawn back to let in light and allow people on the street to peek inside.

They watched the signwriter hang a painted sign between a pair of hanging baskets above the central window.

Gwenna's
for Superior Sweet Treats
G Price Proprietor

She owed so much to Edward Turner.

Tillie agreed to make her specialty fudge but in greater quantities. Bethan's role was to manage the households, and on occasions bake some of her marvellous Welsh cakes, but most of the work fell to Gwenna.

As well as being the sugar boiler, she would also be the front person. "Except I'm still dressed in black."

"Gwenna, *bach*. In all good establishments, the hostess wears black. It's not only for mourning. Take heart, dear one. You will succeed."

26

THE GRAND OPENING

October 1900

Gwenna chose Labour Day, Wednesday October 10th to open her tearooms. "Shops and offices will be closed that day so people can go to the parade," she explained, knowing tearooms and confectioners were exempt from the Shops Act and she could choose her own hours. Thousands of people were expected to attend the parades and she considered it a perfect opportunity. "If they can't go to their usual place, maybe they'll try something new."

Bethan and Tillie were as excited as she and assured her they would be on hand to help. Even so, the butterflies in Gwenna's stomach were causing chaos. Her hands shook and her mind seemed to flit from one thing to another as she checked every detail.

Tom offered to take Charlie to the park before they went to watch the parades. The two babies would be under Bethan's care at the back of the house, where she would keep an eye on them while making the hot chocolate, teas and coffees, but still Gwenna worried.

"Stop fussing, Gwenna. It will be all right," said Tillie. "You already have a good reputation for your handmade sweets, but instead of tasting them down at the markets, or in the grocers, they are coming here. The difference is you're serving a cup of tea or whatever drink they fancy while they sample your treats. An add-on – isn't that what Mr Turner said?"

"I hope you're right, Tillie."

They worked doubly hard to make sure the display of fudge, chocolates, cakes and sweets was perfect. Gwenna made up small paper cones filled with lollies and twisted at the end for people to take away with them as a free gift if they sat in the tearooms, and a pile of small lollipops, one free for every child. The scales were set in the middle of the counter so both she and Tillie could use them when people asked for a 'quarter' pound.

Tillie fussed with the tablecloths and serviettes she'd embroidered with GY in the corners. They'd learnt the art of hot chocolate and coffee making, purchasing some fancy new pots suitable for pouring the liquid, and practised carrying trays loaded with a full set of dishes.

Believing no one would be interested in buying lollies, or having a cup of coffee so soon after breakfast, Gwenna decided a ten o'clock opening would be best.

Seconds after entering the rear of the shop shortly before opening time, Gwenna yelled down the passageway. "Oh, my goodness. Tillie! Come quickly. There's people waiting."

Through the windows, Gwenna could see a party standing around the doorway and others queuing along the window front. She hurried across the floor to unbolt the door. Wearing a half-mourning dress Tillie had made for her with lilac and grey trimming, she looked remarkably pretty. Independence suited her; she had regained most of the weight she'd lost, and with ringlets framing her face, and eyes bluer than the day, she was a picture of confidence, even if she shook with nerves. "Welcome. Welcome, everyone. Do come in," she invited as soon as the door opened wide enough.

Three women, dressed in their finery just as Gwenna had imagined, complete with feathers in their hats, crossed the threshold first. Chattering amongst themselves, they took a turn checking out the fudge and cupcakes under the glass domes, and the array of lollies in bowls along the counter front as well as in the jars lining the shelves.

"We'll have English breakfast tea for three, please, and some of that fudge," one of the women said to Tillie who now stood behind the counter, "and a quarter of each of those three." Her gloved finger pointed to the specific choices she'd made before she joined her two companions who had taken the table in prime position by the window.

A man and his daughter waited, and Gwenna hurried back to the counter to serve them. The girl, with bouncy curls that shook and danced as she moved, eyed the lollipops and boiled sweets. Wearing a short white dress with black T-strap shoes, she hopped from one foot to the other, sometimes biting her lip and sometimes putting a finger to her mouth. At last, she pointed to the brightly coloured and striped boiled lollies and looked questioningly at her father. He nodded and bought a twist of Gwenna's traditional brown and white striped humbugs with a chewy toffee centre, for himself, and a quarter of Swansea mix of fruit drops, acid drops, rhubarb and custard and strawberry and cream balls, mints and sours for the young girl.

Gwenna flashed a smile at the man as they exchanged

money and goods. "Would you like one of these too?" she asked, coming around the side of the counter and bending down to offer the child a small lollipop.

"No, she wouldn't," the man snapped, putting his hand between Gwenna and the child. "I've spent what I'm going to."

Gwenna had been so wound up and worried it could all go wrong she sucked in air and put her hand against her chest. Goggled-eyed with worry, she stood up straight. Blinking away a sharp tingle in her eyes, Gwenna gushed, "No, sir. Oh, no. That's not what I meant. It's free. I'm giving them away to my first customers. I'm sorry if you thought otherwise …"

The man's attitude changed in an instant. "Well, in that case," he grinned. "Thank you, mistress. Thank you." Still smiling, he turned to his daughter. "You may have the lollipop, Cora." The girl accepted the proffered treat and whispered a thank you.

The man eyed Gwenna for a few seconds. "You'll do well if you carry on as you started. Good luck." He tipped his hat and Gwenna watched as the two of them left.

A voice dragged her attention back to the people in front of her and Gwenna forgot about the little girl. An hour later the shop was still teeming and reverberating with chatter, the ding of teacups and the rustle of people and chairs moving. The tinkle of the bell attached to the door announcing more customers added to the background noise. All five of the small tables were occupied and a steady stream of people visited the counter.

Not for one moment had Gwenna dreamt so many customers would come on her first day, despite the numerous advertisements Tom had put in the newspapers on her behalf. She barely had time to breathe as she turned from one client to the next.

Beside her, Tillie was busy measuring out quarters and taking orders for hot drinks and delivering them to the tables when Bethan rang the connecting bell to tell them an order was ready.

"Next, please," said Gwenna as she faced the closest customer.

Mr Turner removed his hat. His face beamed and he turned to the woman beside him. "May I introduce my wife, Mrs Maude Turner. Maude, dear, this is the young lady I was telling you about. Mrs Gwenna Price."

Gwenna recognised the great compliment she'd been paid. Mrs Turner resided at their property at Huia and, by all accounts, rarely came to the city. Gwenna bobbed a quick curtsy.

The room went quiet when Mrs Turner spoke. "How delightful to meet you, Mrs Price," she said. "I've heard so much about you, and now I've visited your charming establishment, I will be certain to tell my friends and acquaintances of its appeal."

Blushing with a mixture of embarrassment and pleasure, Gwenna hid her elation. "Thank you, Mrs Turner. I am honoured by your presence. May I get you something?"

Mr Turner surveyed the room before answering. "You appear exceedingly busy, Mrs Price, so we won't stay to have tea this time, but could you prepare a pound box of your superior treats for Mrs Turner, please."

For the next few minutes, Maude Turner indicated to Gwenna which of the fudge, chocolates, caramels and sweets she wanted. These Gwenna placed into a white cake box and tied it with ribbons suitable for carrying.

"Goodbye, Mrs Price, and thank you," said Mrs Turner accepting the box. "I am sure we will enjoy your treats very much."

Mr Turner replaced his hat, winked at Gwenna and escorted his wife to the door. In a voice loud enough to be heard from across the room, he said, "Good luck, Mrs Price. Although I'm not at all sure you need it. You have a successful business here already."

The moment the door closed behind him the hubbub of voices began again. Gwenna had secured her position thanks to Mrs Turner,

The remaining hours disappeared in a whirl. The parades had been due to start at two o'clock and Gwenna expected trade to drop off, but it hadn't. Her feet throbbed, her head spun and her back ached, but the plates of fudge lay empty and the pile of dirty dishes and the half-empty canisters told their own story. Not long after four o'clock, came the second surprise of the day. Gwenna stared stupidly at the two women standing there until Tillie nudged her into action.

"Louisa. Janie. What an agreeable surprise. How lovely to see you," effused Gwenna, unsettled by their appearance and hoping nothing bad would come of it.

The women kissed the air next to each other's cheek in greeting, while the two older women removed their gloves and scrutinised the premises. All bar one of the tables were now empty.

Tillie left them to serve the two customers who came in to buy a bag of lollies on their way home, while Gwenna talked about the changes she'd made. A few moments later, the last two ladies at the table by the fireplace rose. Leaving Tillie to chat with the stepsisters, Gwenna excused herself and saw the ladies to the door.

"Thank you for coming, today. I do hope you will call again," Gwenna said, handing them a free bag of lollies as she closed the door behind them.

"Would you care for some tea? Or hot chocolate maybe," Tillie offered her siblings.

"Thank you, no. We can't stay," said Louisa, taking in every detail of the room. "We called in to see what all the fuss was about."

Fuss? Good news, Gwenna guessed. *But what had they heard?*

Janetta was kinder. "What a pretty shop, Gwenna. It's so light and airy and I do like your decor." Wandering to the sideboard, she observed the nearly empty plates but made no comment, and ran her hand along the shiny woodwork.

"Where did you purchase this?" she asked. "It's rather lovely. I wouldn't mind something like this for my home."

"You don't have the space for it," snapped Louisa.

"I will one day, Louisa, and in the meantime, I can dream," replied Janetta.

"You don't appear to have anything to offer us anyway, Gwenna," said Louisa, staring pointedly at the sideboard. "Come along, Janetta. I must be going."

Gwenna and Tillie exchanged glances. Tillie imperceptibly shook her head to warn Gwenna not to say anything, but she couldn't resist.

"Goodbye, Louisa. Thank you for stopping by, even for such a short time." Linking her arm with Janetta, Gwenna walked her to the door. "I do hope you will come again, Janie, and I bought the sideboard from Mr Thomas Woodman, in Burleigh St, off Mt Eden Road." Janetta could find out for herself who the craftsman was.

They didn't close until after five o'clock, as it happened, because another influx of people arrived just as Louisa and Janetta were leaving, to Louisa's dismay.

"Don't glare, sister dear," Gwenna heard Janetta say as they stepped down into the street. "Frown lines will spoil your lovely face."

Astounded by the change in Janetta, Gwenna could not begin to guess what had happened to give Janie the upper hand.

Later, after they'd finished cleaning up and Gwenna had changed her lace-up heeled boots for a pair of comfortable brocade slippers, she chatted with Tillie, Tom and Bethan about their day over a welcome cup of tea in the kitchen.

"Congratulations," said Tillie. "You couldn't have wished for a better day."

All Tillie's fudge sold, and the hot chocolate proved popular. Gwenna had given away numerous lollipops to youngsters coming in with a parent, and most of her free twists of sweets had been distributed to the adults who sat at a table.

"Thank you, Tillie, but my goodness me, I'm glad to sit down." She stretched her feet in front of her and wiggled her toes. "And I'm going to have to be careful which shoes I wear in future; my feet are killing me."

"Mine too," said Tillie, changing her shoes. "I don't remember ever having stood for so long."

Bethan waggled her foot showing a sensible satin pump with a long tongue and decorative buckle on the front. "You'll learn," she chuckled.

"Whatever the state of your feet, ladies, sounds to me like you have a winning combination," said Tom, biting into a piece of ginger slice Bethan had made as an extra.

"Charlie and I had fun too. Didn't we, Charlie?"

Under Tom's care, Charlie had blossomed and become a different child to the thin, sickly boy of not much more than a year ago. Apart from a cough, he'd not been sick over the winter like he used to be. Coming up nine in February, he'd thickened out and grown several inches, but more importantly, the boy was happy. He was succeeding at school, proving to be a great help to Bethan with the babies, whom he adored, and helping Gwenna by running messages.

"Yeah. We did, Tom." Charlie nodded, excited by his day out, but before Tom could continue, Tillie butted in to tell him and Bethan about the other events of the day.

"Mrs Turner played her part so well. Everyone in the room would have heard every word, but I'm positive Mr Turner set it all up. Gwenna is certain to get lots of customers now, once the word gets around. And I'm sure it will."

Gwenna hoped Tillie was right. So much rested on the shop being successful, reminding her she still had work to do this evening to prepare for the morning.

"But you should have been there when Louisa and Janetta arrived. Louisa pouted as if she had a sour plum in her mouth, but she couldn't resist coming in to sneer."

Gwenna rested her hand on Bethan's and gave it a little squeeze. The family had fragmented so much since Pa died, sometimes they forgot Bethan was the mother to seven. From the first day little Georgie was born, Gwenna had understood what they meant by a 'mother's love', likewise for Tillie and Olwen. And it wasn't something that went away, never mind what happened. Gwenna's heart ached for Bethan. How could Louisa be so disagreeable when her mother didn't have an unkind thought in her whole being?

"I feel sorry for that girl," said Bethan. "Something is wrong in her life for her to be so unpleasant, especially to you, Gwenna. She doted on you when you were little."

Gwenna hadn't considered that possibility. Could Louisa's nastiness be a sign of unhappiness?

"So why doesn't Janie say something?" asked Tillie. "They're always together."

"Janie worshipped her older sister and wanted to be just like her," explained Bethan. "When they were little, Louisa was the sparkling one. Always so bright and cheerful, and even more so when she was the centre of attention, but she could get terribly jealous at times. Janie was the shy one in comparison and followed in her sister's wake, hoping the sun would fall on her sometimes. She still does, but Janie underestimated herself. She has a loving heart."

The more Gwenna listened to Bethan's reasoning, the more it made sense. Louisa behaved badly when she needed attention, until someone – most often Janetta – gave her the comfort she craved. Hers was a recipe for control. Gwenna could see it all now, but what did any of it have to do with her or the shop? A small niggle squirmed. Something wasn't right.

While her thoughts meandered, Gwenna paid little heed to Tom describing the colourful parade floats, the flags and bunting flying from the many buildings, the noise from the brass and Highland bands and the street sellers, but she was all ears when Charlie spoke.

"There was a boy my age down there with a tray hung around his neck selling lollies and sherberts and them sore throat lollies in little papers bags. Can I do that, Gwenna?"

Gwenna tried to find out who sent the boy out selling, and which shop the lollies came from, but Charlie shrugged his shoulders. "I dunno, do I? I didn't ask, but I could do better, I reckon."

He had it all worked out. "This boy just stood with his back against a wall and waited for people to pass by before he'd ask if they wanted some. But I'd do what Mr Turner does and call out. And move amongst the crowd too. Bit of a risk someone would swipe a bag or two, but you gotta make sure you're noticed."

Three adults chuckled at his tale, but Gwenna took him seriously.

"Do you know what, young Charlie, maybe next time you could."

"What on earth are you contemplating now?" asked Tillie.

"Precisely what Charlie said. Street selling. Give me time to figure out how it would work best, what the costs would be, and what the tray could look like, but it could be achievable." Gwenna stretched her aching back and put her hand to her mouth to stifle a yawn. "But I can't think about it now, I've work to do."

Gwenna rose when Georgie stirred with the dawn. The early morning time when he first woke warm and soft became their special time. She would feed him, bathe him with orange or violet water, use Vaseline on any rashes, rub him over with Bethan's special skin lotion and dress him in fresh clothes. After lots of cuddles, he soon snuggled back to sleep, and she could attend to her own ablutions.

Thankful for running water in the house, even if it didn't have a separate bathroom, she'd bought herself a new washstand with a particularly pretty ewer and bowl, decorated with mauve roses the exact colour of the dress she was longing to wear again, the one Tillie had made for her wedding, which seemed a lifetime ago but was less than a year.

She dashed into the privy built onto the end of the back verandah next to the laundry, collected hot water from the copper tank beside the firebox, mixed it with cold water from the scullery and returned to her room. Adding a few drops of the scented water Bethan had made to the bowl, Gwenna sponged herself from top to toe. Feeling fresh and revived, she dressed in her usual black silk dress trimmed with purple, which had become her staple for working in the shop, and styled her hair into her favourite shape. Brushing it softly back from her face, she let her naturally curly hair fall in wavy ringlets down the back of her head. Fastening a pair of small, dangly jet earrings in place, she patted the front of her hair into shape with a touch of oil and left the room, taking the bowl with her.

In the kitchen, she donned a large white apron and settled into the sugar boiling routine she and Tillie had worked out. The whole operation was still new and raw, and they made mistakes. Gwenna blistered her hand more than once, when in too much of a hurry to turn and stretch the sugar before it cooled enough, and Tillie's fudge failed one morning because she'd overslept and was in a rush, and they ran out. As the weeks passed, Bethan complained Gwenna wasn't eating enough and offered to bring her a cup of tea, or some bread and cheese, or a bowl of soup, but Gwenna was too busy to stop. To help out, Bethan had, at long last, agreed to answer the telephone if neither Gwenna nor Tillie were around. She wrote the requests in the order book, tore out the top page, clipped the orders together and hung them from the hook above Gwenna's hot plate for her to fill. Thankfully, orders from the markets had increased, and her regular customers remained steady, both of which kept the books healthy, but she found it a struggle to keep up with the orders mounting up on the hook, and she fretted about the shop.

She longed for the words 'let's meet at Gwenna's' to trip off many a tongue before the summer season arrived, but they'd not had a crowd waiting at the door since their first day. While she still believed a ten o'clock opening was early enough, fewer customers came to her door and trade was inconsistent, despite Mrs Turner's visit.

Bit by bit, Gwenna discovered which days needed more provisions than others, and which flavours were the most popular. Despite not knowing how many customers they would have or when they would arrive, and to keep the customers guessing and coming back for more, she introduced Bethan's Welsh cakes sprinkled with caster sugar, and her bara brith fruit loaf, on alternate days. On Saturday half-holiday everything was available, including her own specialty caramels and Tillie's fudge, which Gwenna made exclusive to the shop.

But it seemed, never mind what she did, nothing turned out quite as planned.

⸙⸙⸙⸙⸙⸙⸙

27

SUCCESS COMES TO THOSE WHO TRY

October 1900

Elias could hardly believe what Woody was saying.

"The rimu sideboard you made has been sold. Didn't I tell you it would be the first to go?"

Most of the time, Elias made the smaller items: side tables, wall racks, coat and hatstands, and portable writing boxes. He'd learnt a lot in the last ten months but he still had more to learn. He wanted perfection, but Woody assured him his skills were far superior to many who'd been at the lathe a lot longer.

One day, Woody suggested Elias try his hand at a larger piece. The timber Woody offered him had suited his idea perfectly, but the project had taken longer than Elias had expected, and he'd only finished it a few days earlier. "Sold? Already. My goodness. Who to?"

"Didn't I tell you it was a fine piece and would be snapped up. It went to a new establishment about to open. The owner said it would be ideal for the purpose."

Woody didn't elaborate and Elias didn't ask any further questions. For the first time, he felt as if he was doing something worthwhile, and which would bring greater rewards to the business.

Working on the sideboard had kept him sane and given him purpose. The intricacies of the cupboards and getting the hinges to sit so the doors shut exactly against the shelves, the dovetailing of the drawers and the polishing of the long top, brought him a degree of satisfaction out of the wasteland he'd created.

After the exhausting and traumatic events surrounding the death of Johnno Jones, he'd felt all his anger and hatred returning. He wanted to lash out – at the police, at Gwenna, at anyone he could point the finger at – even, obscurely, Woody, for seeing his shame. Alice had been shocked by what she'd learnt after Woody had dragged him away from the clutches of the police. She'd sat and listened, saying nothing, getting paler by the moment.

The next day she began asking questions, lots of questions, too many questions. "I want to know everything," she said. "It must have been awful for you. You must feel terrible. Talking about it will help, Eli. Truly, it will. Tell me."

She meant well, but he couldn't. He tried, but his anger made him tongue-tied. In the end, he stopped talking altogether. He'd had nothing to do with Johnno's death but he'd ended up involved up to his neck. His newfound happiness and sense of satisfaction dissolved, and a vacant, unfulfilled void entered his being.

He'd moved out of the house in North Street, where Gwenna and Bethan were still living, and found a boarding house. He didn't want to ask Woody if he could move in with him. He couldn't – not until he and Alice reached an understanding – if they ever did. He'd been too scared to speak to her since, to ask her to marry him, even though he felt sure she would accept him. He believed Woody would approve, but something kept holding him back.

Alice, upset by his behaviour, kept asking what was wrong, but he had no answers. He couldn't bring himself to say anything kindly or meet her eye to eye. Now she barely spoke to him. Her eyes beseeched him sometimes when she caught him watching her. He yearned to say something, but couldn't.

Fear kept him mute. If his temper still resided at the edge of his control and he lost it every time something went wrong, Alice would suffer. And he couldn't bear the thought. It would be better she was hurt by his silence than by his fists.

He turned his attention to the large, turned leg of a dining table he was working on and dismissed all the conflicting thoughts from his mind. When he was under the spell of the timber, he felt at rest. The noise from the planer, the leveller and the saw became a panacea, and the turmoil inside his head faded into the background. Swirling dust tickled his nose and sawdust lay around his feet, clinging obstinately to parts of his clothing and sticking in his hair, but he didn't notice. The world outside no longer existed. His timber world was all that mattered.

28

LEARNING TO FORGIVE

November 1900

"Eli. Come through, would you please," called Woody.

Elias put down his sandpaper, wiped his hands on his apron and walked through the adjoining door. Woody had created a space at the front of the work area for people to view finished products without having to come through to the dusty workshop. Elias was not convinced about it at all. The working space was now smaller and more cramped, and the larger pieces of furniture they were working on took up more space. It all seemed back to front to Elias, but they were managing. And the furniture was selling.

"I'd like you to meet Mrs Lewis," Woody said as soon as he entered. "Mrs Lewis, Eli Hughes is the craftsman who made the particular sideboard you are describing."

For a split second Elias didn't recognise the woman, but something in her expression transported him back to childhood days and, like a series of pictures, memories flooded his mind. Benumbed and dimwitted, he continued to stare at his sister for several seconds before Janetta found her senses.

"There's no need for introductions, Mr Woodman. After all, we know each other quite well, don't we, Elias? Although I confess, I did not know my brother was a craftsman. At least, not with wood."

Woody considered it prudent to say nothing, and Elias couldn't quite get his tongue to work either.

"How are you, Elias?" Janetta enquired when it became evident Elias wasn't going to speak. "I haven't heard much about you lately. You've kept very much to yourself, I fear. How surprising to find you here, of all places. But then no one told me you'd become a woodturner."

Eli couldn't decide whether she was offended because she didn't know, or receptive to renewing their association.

Clearing his throat he rasped, "Hello, Janetta," but couldn't find any other words of welcome. He swallowed again. "What are you doing here?"

Seeing Eli's bewilderment, Woody said, "Mrs Lewis was asking if we made furniture to order. She'd seen a particularly fine piece recently and the owner informed her where to come."

Janetta viewed the two men with a puzzled expression Elias couldn't interpret.

"You want me to make something for you?" he asked, still sounding perplexed.

"Well, I didn't know it was you, did I? But yes, that's why I came here." Again, Janetta appealed to Mr Woodman to see if he would say something more helpful. "Mr Lewis and I want a sideboard, smaller than the one Gwenna has, but if …"

"Gwenna! What's Gwenna got to do with this?"

"For goodness' sake, Elias. Will you listen," snapped

Janetta, sounding totally exasperated with him, exactly like she used to get when she still lived at home. "Gwenna has a sideboard I liked in the shop."

"What shop?" interrupted Elias for the second time, feeling his head spin with all the new information.

"The tearooms and sweet shop. Didn't you know? No, I suppose not. It's only been open a few weeks. She told me she'd bought the sideboard from Mr Woodman here, so I came here to order one like it." She turned to address Mr Woodman. "That is, if you are willing to accept an order from me."

Further stupefied at the news Gwenna had opened a shop but not wanting to know any more about it, he turned on his heel and left Janetta and Woody talking. Woody would tell him what he wanted him to make. It didn't matter who bought it. Nothing mattered any more. All Elias cared about was whether the wood responded the way he wanted it to. He couldn't even bear to think about Alice.

He'd pushed her away – for her own good, he'd argued – and had crushed the one person he wanted most in his life. The one person he truly loved. All he had left were the remains of something else that once lived – the wood.

Determined to put Gwenna out of his mind, he picked up his tools and resumed work. Memories of Janetta and growing up before everything went wrong grew into happier and more pleasant images. The five-year age gap between him and Sam didn't allow for friendship, but Elias had enjoyed his sisters' teasing and laughter. Sam was the loner, stuck between two older sisters and two younger stepsisters. Those two sisters had been thick as thieves even then, but good-natured and kindly, including Gwenna, despite her stubbornness. Not until his father's death had things gone bad. Those memories he shut out. But he could not avoid the truth: it was he who had changed, not them.

As usual, the more he stroked and shaped the wood under his hands, the more contented he became. And the more absorbed he got, the more the world retreated.

Some time later, Eli sensed a ghostly shadow behind him, as if a memory had come alive. He spun around to find Alice standing there, hand reaching out ready to touch him, her bottom lip caught between her teeth.

Unsure of her welcome, a small smile shaped her lips, but when the light reached her eyes, he was lost. She hadn't come into the workshop for more than a week. Not since they'd argued about his increasing indifference and, in desperation, he told her to leave him alone - an outburst that had torn him apart ever since, but he'd had no idea how to rectify the situation.

"Eli," Alice murmured, "can you not find it in your heart to forgive me?"

Forgive her? She'd done nothing that needed forgiveness. It was himself he couldn't forgive.

Alice took a step closer. "I'm not sure what I've done or said, but I fear I've offended you somehow. I'm sorry, Eli. Whatever it is, please, can we go back to how we were?"

The unexpected pain in his throat prevented him from speaking, but his eyes piercing hers spoke volumes. He wanted her so much. He loved her. More than anything in his life before - more than he had words for - but doubts overrode his desire. He couldn't believe he deserved someone so perfect. And he didn't trust himself. Seeing Janetta brought back all the memories and reminded him of all he'd lost.

He now recognised the terrible empty feeling of living apart from everything around him as loneliness, and he didn't want to live in this bleak void for the rest of his life.

His arms reached around her waist and he pulled her closer to him until he could bury his face in her hair. She tilted her head back and brought her hand up to touch his mouth, her finger following the outline of his lips. He closed his eyes in rapture and imagined what it would be like to kiss her. To hold her like this in his arms forever more.

Her hand crept along his jawline and fingers slid through his hair, clasping the back of his head. He lowered his head to hers until his lips touched hers, softly, tenderly, touching again. Deeper and more intensely their lips sought each other; she melted into his arms. Whatever doubts he once had faded with her kiss. No one could be so trusting and not have faith in their own judgement. He would trust her, even if he didn't believe in himself.

"It's you who should forgive me, Alice. I never meant to hurt you. I love you, but you need to see me as I am – I'm not a good person …"

"Shush." She stroked his hair as she spoke, like a mother calming her child. "I know who you are. I know you better than you know yourself. I know what you are capable of, and I love you because of it."

Elias felt like a new man. His heart felt lighter, and a sense of urgency stirred within him. He wanted to make up for lost time, for lost moments.

"Thank goodness you sorted yourself at last," said Woody, watching Eli work, "and asked that lovelorn girl of mine to marry you. I was getting desperate I'd have to do it for you, the rate you were going."

Elias laughed, but his reply was serious. "It was all her doing. And yours. I'm grateful for your faith in me. And I will repay you both, I promise. You have my loyalty, and she has my love. I won't let you down."

Woody clapped Elias on the shoulder. "I've known that for a long time, Eli. It's yourself you've let down, lad. Now you've found your will again, greater success and greater rewards will come your way. And it will show in your work. Just you wait and see."

Alice couldn't stay away from the workshop. She swept and tidied, helped hold pieces she didn't need to hold, brought more food than they needed and took every opportunity to be near him, to fleetingly touch him like a feather floating past in the air. They hadn't set a wedding date yet, both wanting to nurture and strengthen the bond between them before they declared it to the world. His happiness soared every time she came near him.

One day at the beginning of December, Woody came through from the front shop. Elias had been busy with a range of small items again: consoles, bedside tables, occasional tables, bookstands and davenports, all which sold well as Christmas presents.

People rarely ordered custom-made furniture any more. Not now machinery had sped up the process and ready-made furniture could be bought from the likes of Tonson Garlick's massive store in Queen Street. Thomas Woodman was a small operator by comparison, but by limiting the use of machinery, his point of difference was the quality of his handmade products. He liked the old ways. It might take longer, but the finished product was more personal.

"Eli. Take a look at this, will you?" He handed Elias a photograph of an elaborate chiffonier. "There's a man out front who wants to know if you can make something like this."

Elias studied the photograph and shook his head. "No, I can't do all that fancy carving, but I wouldn't, even if I could. It'd ruin the line and colour of the wood. And I don't like those overly ornate spindles everywhere propping up the out-of-balance top section."

Elias handed the photo back to Woody searching his face for a reaction. Had he overstepped the line? After all, it wasn't his choice, it was what the customer wanted that mattered.

"Fair enough," said Woody, surprising Elias. "What would you do instead?"

"I'd do something plain with curves rather than curlicues, with a back to it. I'd keep the panels simple with a bit of moulding." He took a pencil from behind his ear and crossed the floor to one of the work tables. Ripping a sheet of paper from a pile tied together on a peg, he drew a rough sketch to show Woody what he was talking about. "Drawers here just under the top, and more inside one of the cupboards and shelving space for platters and terrines."

Woody took it without saying anything. A few minutes later he came back. "Eli, come with me."

Again, Elias laid down his tools and followed Woody out to the front shop.

"This is Mr John Court." Woody introduced Elias. "Mr Court, Eli Hughes is my craftsman. He is a fine carpenter and turner, and I respect his opinion."

Elias didn't like it when Woody sang his praises. He was aware of how many mistakes he made, and that he had a lot more to learn. He and Woody worked well together. Sometimes one of them made the legs, or fashioned drawers or fitted hinges to doors, while the other sanded and shaped and cut the door fronts or table tops. Never mind how many times Woody told him he was a natural, Eli knew Woody fixed up his errors without comment. If anyone was the master, it was Woody.

Elias shook the extended hand. "Mr Court," he said with a nod.

"Nice to meet you, Mr Hughes," acknowledged the man. "My wife speaks highly of your skill. She has bought several articles of yours, which others have admired, and now wishes something larger."

Elias said nothing, hoping it would not be construed as rude, but embarrassment tied his tongue. Woody must have told the man Elias had refused to copy the picture.

"Mr Woodman tells me New Zealand woods do not lend themselves to anything as ornate as this."

Elias glanced at Woody, whose slight smile disappeared almost before it had begun. It wasn't entirely true, of course – any good woodworker could create whatever he wanted from any wood, New Zealand or not, but native wood naturally lent itself to plainer finishes. The ruse was clever, nevertheless, and provided a reason for Elias's point-blank refusal.

"Well, I … that is …" Elias stammered.

Mr Court continued. "I like the style of this drawing. I know it's a rough sketch, but it sits far more comfortably with me than this thing my wife found. I'd like to commission you to make it for me."

Elias glanced at Woody for the second time. An

242

imperceptible nod confirmed he should accept. "Thank you, sir. I'm honoured."

Elias talked with Mr Court for a short while about the specifics of height and length, and left Woody to negotiate the price and delivery time.

"Thank you, Mr Hughes," said the man, "I will ask Mrs Court to provide the details of her requirements for the size, but rest assured she will adore the idea of a one-off piece made just for her."

Later that evening, over a drink in The Edinburgh Castle, Woody congratulated Elias on winning his second commission.

"Second?" queried Elias.

"Oh yes. Didn't I tell you?" Woody swallowed a mouthful of ale and pondered for a moment or two. "No, I don't suppose I did."

Elias could tell Woody had deliberately not told him about it.

"Well? Out with it, what's the other one?"

"A sideboard. But not on the scale of the one Mr Court has ordered, but you should be able to cut the sections at the same time."

"So, who's it for?"

"Never you mind for now, just be happy your work is being noticed and people are asking for you by name. It's not doing me no harm either," added Woody. "It's bringing in the cash, I can tell you."

Eli tried to find out who the commission came from, but Woody wouldn't be drawn.

"It doesn't matter right now. You make it, I sell it. Who buys it makes no difference."

He recalled Janetta coming into the shop six weeks ago. Could it be her? Eli shrugged. He didn't care.

The men chatted convivially over another couple of beers before Woody got around to telling Elias his next plans. "After the success of last year's Auckland industrial exhibition, I've put your name forward for the next one."

The man never ceased to surprise.

29

THE BURDEN OF RESPONSIBILITY

December 1900

Close to two months after the shop had opened, the women had settled into a regular system, but Gwenna was working far more hours than was healthy. And the paperwork was starting to overwhelm her to the point that Tom offered to tackle it.

"Gwenna. Don't be stubborn. You can't do everything yourself. Let me help. I can do invoices over a few evenings, and it's one less task for you to worry about."

Tom had offered before, but Gwenna always refused. Now she gave in. She wasn't so keen on getting someone else to help, though.

"Honestly, Gwenna. You can't keep going like this," said Tillie one evening as they sat around the table after supper.

"I don't know why I bother cooking sometimes," said Bethan, staring at Gwenna's plate. "You eat less than a sparrow these days. It's not good, I tell you. No good will come of it."

"You need someone to help," echoed Tillie. "Either in the shop, so you can make the goods, or in the kitchen, so you can run the shop. You can't do both. You could do with someone to help with the distribution, too. And you shouldn't rely on carriers you have to pay. It's ridiculous when you have a perfectly good delivery van – and horse, might I remind you – sorely neglected in our backyard."

Tom rode the horse to keep it exercised, but in all honesty, he wasn't much of a rider and chose to walk to and from his job at Smith & Caughey's on a daily basis. He occasionally hitched up the van and did a few deliveries on a Saturday afternoon for Gwenna, but he preferred to spend his half-holiday with Charlie, when the women were working. And he refused to use it for personal use when it was emblazoned with G *Price & Family, Confectioners.*

"I know that," Gwenna snapped, "but it can't be helped right now. I can't afford to employ anyone else yet – some days we don't take enough to pay for the ingredients, let alone make a profit. If it wasn't for the wholesale orders coming in, we wouldn't be able to continue."

Gwenna hated admitting she was close to defeat. The wholesale side had picked up considerably, thanks to Edward Turner's auctions, even if the business wasn't quite back to the level her father once enjoyed. On his half-day, with Charlie's help, Tom packed the orders into boxes ready for the carter to deliver them if he couldn't do the deliveries himself. Some evenings, too, one or more of them helped Gwenna parcel up the sweets she'd made, label and store them.

But she couldn't decide whether the shop helped or hindered since the shop itself had not yet turned into the dream she'd held for so long. Some days she was rushed off her feet, others she hardly saw a soul. While she'd never say so, even paying Tillie was a stretch, but since Tillie had given up her piecework sewing job, Gwenna felt honour-bound to contribute to the household. More so, if Tom did her paperwork as well.

"Don't expect miracles, Gwenna," said Tom in his usual calm manner. "Give it time. The spring weather has been awful. I'm sure the sunshine will help bring people in, but …" Tom paused and Gwenna felt her stomach flip. "… may I offer you some advice?"

Gwenna sat up straighter in her chair and nodded. What was wrong?

"I've noticed you are not advertising any more, or at least only on Saturday mornings, which is why I think trade is better. You need to spend money to make money, Gwenna. You need to advertise during the week. It's cheaper then, so try placing an advertisement on Mondays and Thursdays and see if it helps. And…" he continued, "Charlie wants to say something."

Until this moment, Gwenna had forgotten Charlie was in the room. He was patiently entertaining Georgie and Olwen, who gurgled and murmured in the background. At nine months old, Olwen was starting to crawl and needed constant watching.

"Yes, Charlie, what is it?"

Charlie had changed so much in the last twelve months there was little left to recognise of the old version. "I didn't want to say anything, but Tom says I should." Charlie hesitated as if unsure, which was not like him, which in turn made Gwenna more nervous.

"Go on," she encouraged.

"None of the kids from school will come to the shop. They say it's too grand and they aren't allowed. They buy their lollies from the likes of Smeeton's and the other grocers. But yours are better."

Having always been wholesalers, Gwenna had never thought about children buying lollies from her before. She had targeted the tearooms to the ladies, but now Charlie made her think about it – children only came with a parent.

"You could be right, Charlie. Children don't come to the shop by themselves. And you think that matters?"

Charlie sat Olwen on the floor between his legs so he could keep hold of her and gave her toys to play with. The serious expression on his face almost made Gwenna laugh, but she didn't.

"Of course. Who likes lollies the best? Kids, of course. If they *can* buy your lollies, they'll ask their mums and dads for the money. They'll ask why and where from and then everyone will know about Gwenna's," said Charlie, having given his idea a lot of thought. "So the trick is to get the kids to the shop."

"And how do you suggest I do that?" chuckled Gwenna, feeling more relaxed.

Charlie turned to Bethan to gauge her reaction. "Mam, can you look after Georgie and Olwen after school without me?"

"I'm always grateful for your help, Charlie, but you don't have to if you don't want to," said Bethan.

"It's not I don't want to help, it's I think I can help Gwenna better."

Intrigued by his idea, everyone was all ears to how he thought his plan would work. "Set me up with a tray thing or a box on a table and I can stand in the street. I'll sell them all in no time, I reckon, once the kids get to hear about it. I'll tell them all at school when and where

248

they can get the best lollies. Then there's the workers walking home, and the mums and dads coming along to see what's going on. And I reckon some of those broken and funny-shaped sweets and stuff that goes wrong sometimes could be sold off cheap in little bags once a week, right on closing time."

Throughout his explanation, he'd continued to shake a rattle with Olwen and pick up things she'd thrown, paying little attention to what the adults were doing or saying, but he'd made his point.

Tom sat at the table, head propped on an elbow, with one ankle resting on his other knee, drawing on his pipe and smiling as if it had been his idea. Bethan made a moue of uncertainty. Tillie's clap of her hands and enthusiastic face showed she thought it a superb idea, and Gwenna … Gwenna didn't know what to say, silenced by the simplicity of the boy's idea.

"It's an original idea, Charlie, but I'm not so convinced. What happens when the weather's bad? And I can't have you giving up your afternoons to work for me. You're too young."

Charlie shrugged his shoulders. "I don't go anywhere else after school; I come home and help Mam. I'm not too young for that. Why am I too young to help make money?"

Damn. The boy had a point. Other boys his age were expected to work, and much harder than anything she'd ask of Charlie. Some of them didn't always get to go to school because they had to work for their parents. Gwenna wasn't having that, but maybe it was time to stop coddling him.

"And if it's raining I can move under the verandah up the road, but it's summer soon and holiday time coming up, so it shouldn't matter," finished Charlie.

The image of a small handcart painted up with her name on it flashed into her mind. She'd have to be careful not to upset any of the other shopkeepers.

"And, Gwenna?"

"Hmm, yes, Charlie," Gwenna murmured, her thoughts having already drifted towards the possibilities.

"Can I get a cut of everything I sell?"

The adults all burst out laughing.

"Yes, Charlie, my little go-getter. You can."

"Leave it to me," declared Bethan, insisting she would do all the preparation for the Christmas celebrations. "You girls will be in too much of a tizzy to do it properly anyway."

Gwenna breathed a sigh of relief. The closer it got to Christmas, the more frazzled she became. So much had happened in the last twelve months or so, her head spun. She'd gone from underdog, to bride, to widow, to mother, to businesswoman, in such a short time, and fluctuated between jubilation and despair so often, she doubted she had any control over her life.

As usual, when beset by doubts and worry, Gwenna made sweets. Unable to sleep, she headed for the kitchen. The routine soothed her mind as she bent to her task with a naturalness the others didn't possess. While she heated the sugar, prepared the flavourings and calculated the quantities, her heart rate slowed, and a calmness came over her, allowing her to think without getting agitated.

The trauma of the months leading up to her Christmas Eve wedding a year ago filled her mind. Even though Johnno's death had been Gwenna's saddest and most difficult time, and the day Elias was arrested scared her more than she thought possible, in amongst it all were many things she could be grateful for. Her beautiful boy Georgie, a new home and fulfilling a dream she'd held for many years, along with the ever-changing dynamics within the family. Gwenna had nothing to complain about, and yet something was keeping her awake at night.

Charlie was her greatest surprise – next to Elias. Nearly every day, she could see changes in him as he grew more confident, more cheerful and more carefree, as if he'd forgotten all his previous misfortunes. For that, she could only thank Tom. How any man could be so willing, so caring and so agreeable was completely beyond Gwenna's experience of men – even her father. Except Tom was all of those things.

He once said, "Happiness breeds happiness. I'm a happy man. Happy in my work, happy in my home. It's easy to spread such happiness around."

Tom was also the most loving of men towards Tillie and Olwen, and Charlie, whom he treated more like his own son than a younger brother-in-law.

At least she didn't have to worry about them. And Mam was in good spirits. Although, on occasions, Gwenna suspected they were false. As for the others, well … some days, she didn't know where to start.

Gwenna hadn't seen Elias for many months, but Alice popped in from time to time. The girl was so transparent, Gwenna could tell by the way she walked how happy she felt, and she hadn't been happy in some time. Many a time, she was sure Alice was on the tip of saying something but held her tongue. Gwenna suspected Elias and Alice were having troubles, and had been since the day of Elias's arrest. His continued transformation still amazed her, but for now, Gwenna was happy to leave him at a distance. Her life was confused enough, thanks in part to her stepsisters.

Gwenna sensed a change in Janetta, who had called twice since, without Louisa, and who hinted of something afoot. This morning, she called in again.

"Gwenna, I have to say I was surprised, nay, shocked, to find Elias at the workshop you sent me to. Did you know Elias had made your sideboard?"

"Not until after, if I'm honest. When Alice Woodman found out I was looking for furniture for the shop, she told me her father had a unit in his display room I might like. It wasn't until after Mr Woodman delivered it did he tell me Elias had made it."

"So you knew when you sent me there." Janetta bit her bottom lip and frowned, visibly bothered by the whole issue.

"Does it matter who made it? It's a piece of furniture and it serves its purpose. It's well made and often admired. I'm the one getting the credit; I can afford to send a little his way, can't I?"

Janetta still hesitated. "But ... I'm not so sure. After what he was like. Why should I give him my business?" Janetta sounded unusually critical and disparaging.

"Janie, this isn't like you. What's changed?"

"It's just ... Oh dear, I don't know. Percy said it was up to me, he didn't care one way or the other. If I wanted a new cabinet, I should get the one I liked best. But Louisa ..."

Gwenna sighed. "What's Louisa said now?"

"Nothing. That's what worries me. I'd ask her advice, but she's stopped going out, and hardly talks to me. When I call, she is polite but withdrawn. Last

252

time I visited, she looked awfully tired. I wondered if she was with child again, but then she said something very strange – she said, 'the family are unworthy of my attention'. What does she mean?"

Gwenna didn't like the sound of it, whatever it meant.

"I don't know, Janie, but Mam says there's something wrong too. Does her husband treat her right? Or is it money, or his father – or mother? Is she ill? Could be lots of things."

"She's certainly not said anything," answered Janetta, "but then …" Janetta didn't finish what she was saying.

She left soon after. "Goodbye, Gwenna. I'll see you again soon."

She had watched her stepsister leave, aware Janetta had not spoken to any of the others, least of all their Mam. Irritably, Gwenna pounded the sugar into shape – as if she didn't have enough on her plate without having to worry about everyone else in the family.

The next few days passed in a whirl. Shop trade picked up in the middle of December, in particular for her bags of lollies, but in her weary state Gwenna functioned lethargically, without her usual vivacity. She had even forgotten about Charlie's idea about a hawker's tray and barrow. Tillie and Bethan worked around her and, she suspected, did more than their share. Lack of sleep dragged her down.

Every time she lay her head on the pillow confused dreams from the past of the fun-loving Johnno, the embittered Elias, the sickly Charlie and the unhappy Bethan filled her head. Sometimes the stern, uncompromising expression Hugh wore when he'd caught Elias out flashed into view. What woke her, however – sweating and with her heart pounding – were the fleeting images of Black Jack. None of it made sense.

At least, they had a lot of stock on hand, thanks to her nightly efforts.

Two days later, one worry fell from Gwenna's shoulders.

Alice literally bounced into the shop. The heels of her tiny feet encased in her soft leather pumps barely touched the ground as she walked and she seemed to find joy in everything around her. "You'll never guess," she said, doing a little twirl, both hands held against her chest. "Eli and I are engaged." Another couple of bounces on the balls of her feet and a clap of her hands before she announced, "We're getting married. I couldn't tell you before, because … well, because … I wanted to, but …"

"Congratulations, Alice," Gwenna cut the girl short. "And you don't need to explain. I'm just happy for you both; that's if you're sure it's what you want."

"Oh, it is. Well, it is now. The ordeal Eli had to go through after Johnno …" Alice clapped her hand to her mouth and her eyes widened. "Sorry, Gwenna. I didn't mean to bring Johnno up, but the whole affair unsettled Eli terribly. It took him a long time to get over it."

Gwenna forced a smile to her lips. Elias wasn't the only one unsettled. "It's all right, Alice. Johnno's been on my mind a lot lately. But I agree, Elias shouldn't have had to go through it, and I hope he can put it behind him. It's over now. It took months, but the coroner's inquest finally ruled accidental death."

What she didn't admit to Alice was the date the coroner had written on the certificate. 18th April 1900: her birthday. Gwenna had been horrified when the official notice arrived. Why had they chosen that one, of all dates, when he'd been missing since the first week of April?

Alice, relieved by Gwenna's reassurances, scanned her up and down. "Are *you* well, Gwenna?" she asked. "You've lost weight … If I may be so bold as to mention it," she added, embarrassed by her outspokenness.

"Well enough, thank you." Tillie and Bethan had been on at her about the same thing. At that moment more customers came into the shop, giving Gwenna the chance to avoid further questioning. "And congratulations again. Now, you'll have to excuse me."

Gwenna felt sure she would feel better once the new year began. Although why she should be so distressed, she couldn't explain. By the end of the week, Gwenna struggled to move her feet. Charlie had been called in to stay with the babies so Bethan could help Tillie, and Tillie forced Gwenna to retreat to the sitting room.

"Mam and I can finish up, you need to rest. Put your feet up awhile and see if you can grab forty winks."

Too tired to argue, Gwenna lay on the sofa and closed her eyelids to ease her stinging eyes and pounding headache. Some time later she stirred, surprised to see the clock on the mantel said seven thirty. Cross that Tillie had let her sleep so long, Gwenna got to her feet with a vague sense of unease.

Unable to hear any noise, she made her way along the dim corridor. She didn't like being alone after dark when all the memories of the house in Onehunga came back. Entering the shop, goose pimples rose on her arms.

255

The place was deserted and locked up for the night. All appeared as it should have, except for the silence. About to check the kitchen for any sign of life, Gwenna saw a shape in the window behind the lace curtains. Hazy and uncertain in the gathering dusk, like something from her dreams, the shape moved.

Black Jack, her subconscious shrieked. She held her breath and blinked, twice. When she looked again, the shape had gone. She stood, frozen to the spot, afraid to move, worried her mind was playing tricks. The silence echoed around her and she fled to the kitchen. It, too, was deserted. Without pause, she hurried down the steps, leaving the back door swinging open behind her in her haste to reach Tillie's house.

She turned her head, certain someone was chasing her in the gloaming and ran headlong into something solid. Her head spun round as a scream erupted from deep inside her, followed by another, and another.

Sitting bolt upright, thanks to the smelling salts Bethan waved under her nose, Gwenna found herself on the sofa in Tillie's living room surrounded by worried faces: Tom, Charlie, Tillie, Bethan – and Hugh.

"What's going on?" she asked, sounding brittle even to her ears. She blinked rapidly and tried to assemble her thoughts.

"We're hoping you can tell us," said Tillie. "Mr Powell saw you running out the back door like you were being chased. You ran straight into him. Your screams brought us all running, but you'd fainted. Mr Powell carried you in. What on earth scared you so much?"

Gwenna shook her head, gazing at each face until she stopped at Hugh's. Worry etched his features and he looked ghastly: hollow-eyed and worn down, and nothing like the Hugh she'd known. A whole string of questions formed, but they could wait.

"Gwenna. What happened?" urged Tillie when she didn't reply.

"I don't know. I saw something. At least, I thought I did. A shadow in the window. It was getting dark and the house was empty …"

She shuddered at the memory and burst into tears. She couldn't begin to explain her certainty that she'd seen Black Jack. No one would believe her. Bethan sat beside her, put an arm around her stepdaughter and let the girl sob into her shoulder.

"There, there, Gwenna, *bach*. All will be well." She handed the girl a handkerchief. "You've worked yourself to a standstill, you have, my dear. You're exhausted."

Tillie brought her a cup of tea, Charlie sat on the floor beside her and rested his head on her lap, and Hugh stood uncomfortably holding his hat until Gwenna's tears subsided.

"Mr Powell," said Tom, "won't you take a seat? You are welcome in my home."

"Yes. Please," echoed Tillie. "Do sit down and have a cup of tea. You look all in."

But Hugh declined. "I'm sorry to have given you a fright, Miss, Mrs …" He hesitated, unsure how to address Gwenna. "It wasn't me at the window, just so you know. I was in your garden, but it wasn't my intention to scare you."

"What were you doing in the garden?" asked Tom, surprise putting an edge to his voice.

Hugh shifted uneasily from foot to foot. "I've just got back … sir."

Tom nodded, having read in the paper that some of the early contingents sent to South Africa were returning after their twelve-month assignment. It explained a lot about Hugh's appearance.

"The people in the old place told me the family had shifted. I wanted to see where you lived and if …" Hugh stopped.

"If what, Mr Powell?" pushed Tom.

"If Miss Gwenna, um, if the family were well. I should be on my way now, I guess. Thank you for inviting me in, but I should be going."

"Where are you staying, Mr Powell?" asked Bethan.

"In the hostel, Mrs Price, ma'am. Until I find something suitable."

"Well, then, you'd better come and see us again tomorrow. In the daylight. After church would be best. And do come to the door, there's a good chap. There's a lot to talk about."

Throughout the discussion, Gwenna sat in a daze. The last time weird dreams haunted her was leading up to Johnno's accident. She started to shake, scared her visions meant something sinister would happen again. After all, she'd seen Hugh's face in her dreams – his old face, at least; not the one she'd seen this evening – and now he'd appeared without warning.

Her skin crawled as those strange feelings of unease returned.

Black Jack would be next.

30

HAPPIER TIMES

Mid-December 1900

Hugh returned after church the next day, as Bethan had asked. Gwenna had only vaguely taken in his appearance the night before and hoped he hadn't noticed her shock when she saw him in the light of day. His upper body drooped and his jacket hung loosely on the once broad, strong shoulders. With dark bags under his eyes and sallow skin, he looked ... well, 'haunted', was the word, but the vacant expression in his eyes upset her the most.

Hugh had been back in the country for a month, and while the government talked of returned soldiers being offered a plot of land to farm, Hugh was a townie and he didn't want to move to the country. Not that he looked fit enough to do any manual labour, to her. Without hesitation, Gwenna asked him to help her again, just like he used to – if he felt up to it.

Briefly, light entered his eyes and he pulled his shoulders back momentarily before they sagged again. He assured them he was fit and well enough to do whatever they wanted of him.

Over the next few days, in an effort to fatten him up, Bethan made sure he had more food than he could eat, and Gwenna found that, while not as strong as he once was, Hugh was more than willing. Having been forced to package her sweets into smaller boxes so she and Bethan could lift them, they found Hugh lifted the larger boxes effortlessly.

They developed a pattern she'd forgotten they possessed. He could read her needs before she asked, placing the sacks of sugar and other ingredients within easy reach, and improved on the system of labelling and order of storing the sweets waiting for despatch. One day, he rescued a pot of sugar Gwenna had left on the heat when she'd been called through to the shop. When she returned, he was working the sugar almost in the way he always had, except she could see he'd adjusted his pull-and-wrap rhythm, as if one arm was not as supple as it once had been. Whatever the problem, his batch of sweets was still as good as ever.

But he hated noise. If she accidentally banged pots together, or a metal spoon scraped the bottom of a pan, he would recoil. Sometimes, for no apparent reason, he'd step away from what he was doing and, leaning forward in a crouch, would put his hands over his ears. Other times, he'd stand frozen to the spot, staring at something she couldn't see, or shudder violently. He never explained his reaction and returned to what he'd been doing. Never mind how many times she asked, he refused to talk about what happened in South Africa.

Whatever his demons, Gwenna was happy to have him back working with her. The difference he made in less than two weeks was impressive, and she hoped for longer-term effects. The one aspect that had hardly changed at all was that he rarely spoke unless spoken to first. She could cope with that, happy to work in companionable silence, knowing he was there.

In the days since the shadow from her dreams had scared her half to death, and Hugh had appeared out of nowhere, she'd been run off her feet in the shop. She'd not had a spare moment to worry or fret over anything, except ensuring the customers were served. The tables were full with ladies ordering teas, coffees and hot chocolate, even though the summer temperatures reached the high seventies.

Mrs Turner had called again, bringing two acquaintances. Gwenna later found out one was the wife of Mr Ernest Yates, the seed merchant, and prominent in social circles, and the other, Mrs Annabella Geddes, whom Maude Turner referred to as Mary. Gwenna had met Mr John McKail Geddes once or twice in passing after purchasing coffee and tea supplies from the firm still known as Brown Barrett, even though Mr Geddes was the sole owner. The Geddeses were a wealthy, influential couple. Mrs Geddes was known for her patronage of the welfare of women even if her Māori heritage was often a topic of discussion. A simple word from either Mrs Yates or Mrs Geddes would make all the difference to Gwenna's clientele.

Apart from that pleasing but singular episode, Gwenna recognised several women from church. She hadn't noticed their absence until they started to become regulars but had no idea why they hadn't come in the first place.

Gwenna asked Janetta about it as they left church together after the Christmas service.

"Because of Louisa."

"Sorry, Janie, you'll have to explain better than that. What's because of Louisa?"

They paused in their conversation to shake hands with the minister and comment on the sermon before continuing their walk down the path and onto the street, where they waited for Bethan and the others. Percy Lewis stood talking to three gentlemen, Tom and Tillie were passing time with another couple Gwenna didn't know, Bethan held Janetta's two youngsters by the hand, while Charlie, excited by what the rest of the day would offer, bounced alongside.

"Really, Gwenna, sometimes you are so clever, but other times you're too gullible. Louisa is the leader of the Ladies Committee."

"Why should that matter?"

Janetta rolled her eyes. "Honestly, Gwenna. You're too good to be true. Do you remember the day we came to the shop when you first opened and Louisa was all snippy?"

"Yes, but then Louisa can be difficult when she wants to be."

"Exactly. That's what I'm saying. She took it into her head that you didn't deserve to have so much luck. She was jealous. Like she used to get sometimes when we were kids." Janetta moved them further down the street in case they were overheard. "I don't know what she said, but I suspect she threatened the other ladies with their position on the committee. Saying it was in jeopardy if they patronised your shop."

Gwenna couldn't believe her ears. "Surely not?

Louisa isn't spiteful. I know we haven't always got on, not since she married Mr Evans, and I get so cross with the way she treats Mam, but I can't believe she'd deliberately do something quite so mean."

"Well, she did, Gwenna. She did. But, much to my surprise, she also did the reverse."

Now Gwenna was utterly confused. "You mean she's since told them they *can* come to the shop?"

Janetta nodded. "Word gets around and your name – or rather the shop's name – has come up a few times at meetings. You know, someone said they'd overheard someone else say how good it was, and so on. Lately, she's basked in the associated glory of telling everyone she's related to you, and suggesting they were, indeed, missing out if they didn't patronise the place."

"Why would she do that? And didn't anyone take her to task for her about-turn?" Such behaviour was beyond Gwenna.

Janetta shook her head. "Some of the ladies value their social positions, however false they may be, and follow the most vocal opinions in order to be part of the crowd. I'm just not sure what's happened to change Louisa's mind. But something has. And something is definitely wrong. I'm certain of it."

Sitting around the dining table later on Christmas day, Gwenna admired the miniature pine tree Charlie had decorated. Its aroma filled the room. Fresh foliage interspersed with the clusters of red stamens of the pohutukawa flowers festooned the mantelpiece. Other more traditional decorations sat on tabletops and cabinets, and Bethan's precious cards and letters from the home country hung on a string above the fireplace, to be read and reread many times.

"You've excelled yourself, Mam. The place is very festive," Gwenna congratulated Bethan, thankful to be surrounded by her family who helped block out memories of the Christmas she and Johnno had shared last year. Still euphoric and wrapped in new love at the time, she'd pretended it didn't matter, never mind how bleak and cheerless their day had been. She hadn't fooled herself and she doubted she'd fooled Johnno either. "And the food is magnificent," she added, in an attempt to rid her mind of the past.

Tom ceremoniously carried the roast turkey, surrounded by potatoes and carrots from the garden, and set it on the table next to a bowl of peas and a jug of gravy. Expertly carving slices from the bird, he placed two on each plate, until everyone was served.

"Can we pull the crackers now?" asked Charlie, once Tom had sat down.

"Course you can," said his mam.

Bethan had made them herself, and Charlie would find the best gifts inside his – a whistle, a marble or two and a miniature puzzle, at least – on top of the comics she'd given him earlier.

Tillie had given him a new set of clothes since he'd grown again, and he adored Gwenna's box of toy soldiers, but his favourite present was the hand-painted, cast-iron fire wagon Tom had given him.

"Look, Mam. The wheels turn and the ladder can be swivelled around and extended. And look at the little firemen sitting up top. Even their buttons are painted on. Oh, thank you, Tom. What fun."

After they said grace, Tom raised his glass. "To family, to posterity, and to you, Gwenna."

"Me?"

"Yes, Gwenna. You. Despite all the setbacks, all the hardships and all the anguish you've suffered, you have risen above it all and come out on top. I'm honoured to know you and call you sister-in-law. May the coming year bring you both joy and success."

Bethan and Tillie echoed Tom's praises, and the clink of glasses tinkled amid the laughter and babbling from Georgie and Olwen. Gwenna smiled through eyes wet with happiness, relief and optimism.

Maybe the tide had turned.

⸺⸻⸺

31

New love overshadows the past

New Year 1900

At precisely midnight, Elias handed Alice a small, flat packet wrapped in plain brown paper. While the crowd stood in awe of the fireworks, entertained by the blast of sound coming from ships' horns, clanging bells, harsh whistles and chiming clocks, Elias and Alice only had eyes for each other.

"What's this?" she shouted into his ear.

"Open it and see." He held his breath, waiting, eager for her response.

Pulling the string tie open and unfolding the paper, she gasped at the sight of the intricately carved lovespoon lying in her hand. The Welsh tradition of a lovespoon, proof of the carver's skill as well as a gift of love, said more than any words he could have used. Each of the symbols had a meaning: a horseshoe for luck, a cross for faith, bells for marriage, hearts for love, a wheel, supporting a loved one and a lock for security – and he'd used them all.

Alice's hair bobbed up and down as she bounced on her toes, and she flung her arms around Elias's neck, ignoring the stares and sniggers from people around her.

"Oh, Eli. It's beautiful. Thank you so much."

As soon as the fireworks finished, the Garrison Band, under the baton of Mr Hunter, picked up their instruments and started playing again, while the paddle steamer *Eagle* continued its excursion around the harbour.

The open top deck was crammed almost elbow to elbow, but Eli couldn't have been happier. He'd booked two places aboard the boat on the second trip of the night so Alice could see the fireworks. He'd wanted, no, needed, to tell Alice how much he loved her and explain how guilt-ridden he felt about his earlier detachment but, unable to put any of it into words, he had to come up with a different plan.

The newspaper advertisement for the New Year's Eve excursion had sparked one idea, but the lovespoon had been entirely his. Out of the blue, a memory had come to him one day of the simple lovespoon his father had given his mam when they wed – the one he, their son, had snapped into pieces in a rage and thrown in the fire when his mam married George Price.

He'd watched the tears trickle down her face, but she said nothing. She had never reprimanded him or mentioned it since, even though she must have been heartbroken. Only now was he beginning to accept the power of love over the potency of hate. He never wanted to feel hatred like that again. It had nearly destroyed him and everything he once loved.

He had much to regret, and even more to make amends for, but the mythical folklore surrounding the custom became significant. Whether as an act of contrition, a form of retribution or as a pledge, Elias couldn't decide, but the urge to make a lovespoon for Alice was too strong to resist. Like her.

267

Wrapping his arms around her, his heart soared and his mind cleared. For the first time, Elias truly believed he could make something more of his life – with Alice beside him, and a new century ahead of him.

A few days later, taking a break from the oppressive heat inside the workshop, Elias sat in the shade in the courtyard reading the newspaper. Since Woody had built the display room out the front, the workshop had become unbearable in summer. He would have to hint to Alice they should find better premises one day soon.

Elias read about several remarkable and unremarkable events, but the editorial in the *Observer* saying farewell to the old year and 'the death of the Nineteenth Century', and welcoming the twentieth, held his attention and he read from beginning to end.

It is a momentous moment in the history of the world. Looking backward upon the records of history, it is impossible to view the passing away of the Nineteenth Century with other than feelings of regret, for it has been a hundred years unparalleled for marvellous scientific discovery, for the rapid evolution of religious and political freedom, and for a wonderful improvement in the social condition of the peoples of the world.

It is sad to think that the closing hours of the century should be embittered by bloodshed and strife, but so it is for, with all our advancement and enlightenment, we have not yet reached that idealistic era when the sword shall be beaten into the ploughshare and racial hatred and carnage shall give place to universal love and brotherhood. However, let us hope that the new century may see an end to war and its horrors and bring about that happy period when international quarrels shall no longer be submitted to the arbitrament of the sword.

To us in New Zealand, far removed from scenes of bloodshed, the closing year has been gratifying and prosperous, and we must always look back to it as one of the brightest and most progressive periods in our history. Whether the credit is due to the prevailing administration, or to the better conditions of trade and commerce, the fact remains that New Zealand finances were never more buoyant than they are today, and the people were never more prosperous and contented. Let it be hoped that this condition of things will be maintained, that the wellbeing of the people will continue to advance, and that the destinies of this young and self-reliant country will be moulded into a noble and glorious future by the wisdom and sagacity of our legislators.

We in Auckland have every reason to think well of 1900, for it has increased our prosperity, and left us vigorous, happy and hopeful. During the twelve months our city has advanced by leaps and bounds, the development of our natural resources has been profitably proceeded with on an expanding scale, while the last few months has witnessed the gradual recovery of the mining industry, upon which we so largely depend. Employment is plentiful, wages are good, and the working classes in this country never lived in greater comfort or more free from poverty.

> Under these circumstances, there is a peculiar
> sadness associated with the death of the Old Year.
> We owe it much, it has been a kindly friend to us,
> and we cannot part from it without a pang of regret
>
> The Old Year must die, and all that is left
> to us is to speed the parting, while we welcome
> the coming guest.

Elias, of course, couldn't agree with half of what he'd read. He was never more pleased to see the back of a year. Despite whatever scientific and social advances had been made during the last century, his life had been a series of disasters. He hoped a new century would bring about the changes and prosperity and comfort, the writer so ardently championed, but he doubted it. Nor, in his view, would mankind learn any lessons from the ravages of war.

Of more interest were two other announcements taking effect from 1 January 1901 – the Federation of Australia, that New Zealand had stood apart from, which mattered little to Elias, and the release of the Universal Penny Postage, announced by Joseph Ward, which mattered a lot.

According to the newspapers, both inland and overseas postage were now set at one penny throughout the British Empire, and Postmaster-General Ward would be opening new post office buildings in celebration up and down the country throughout the coming year.

Exempt from the new penny postage would be Australia, now it had become a federation of its own, and other foreign territories such as the United States of America, France and Germany, who chose not to take part and who were accused of protecting a falsely perceived fall in their postal revenues. Telephone connection numbers were expected to boom.

If the fact that Woody had recently installed a new telephone connection was anything to go by, the papers were right. Woody didn't like modern inventions, he liked to do things the traditional way. Alice had been responsible for persuading him otherwise. She could cajole both of them into anything she wanted.

Putting aside the newspaper, Elias returned to the workshop to resume where he'd left off shaping the smaller of the two cabinets he'd been commissioned to make. Woody insisted the smaller one should be finished first, to Elias's consternation, since Mr Court's larger order would bring in more reward. But it wasn't his place to question.

Again, under the spell and aroma of the native timbers Elias loved the most, his thoughts could wander. After the most glorious of New Year's Eve celebrations, the next day he and Alice had attended the picnic at Matiatia Bay on Waiheke Island.

Against all his instincts, Elias enjoyed the trip. The passengers experienced an unusual sense of movement and power aboard the SS *Kawau* as it surged through the gentle waves of the Waitematā, creating a white-water wake like a snow-laden road after being ploughed. Elias found the jaunt by steamship far more exhilarating than the paddle steamer the evening before. The *Eagle* had also churned up the water like lather but the slow, unwieldy vessel hadn't excited him like this.

The expanse of water and smell of the ocean brought back memories of the ship that had brought him to New Zealand ten years earlier. In those days, his anger and resentment battled against anything remotely agreeable and he turned his bitterness into animosity: for the water, the ship and the people who had taken him across the world. He had never fathomed Gwenna's love for the harbour, until now.

But it wasn't only the joys of the harbour, the natural bushland of Waiheke Island, its beaches and festivities that had made the day so successful. He and Alice had also set a wedding date. Rather than wait, they agreed on Saturday February 2nd. Alice's reasoning was more emotional than practical.

"Two for Two," she said. It was all they needed, two people together. The rest would simply fall into place.

Elias had no idea what had come over Janetta. Whether the changes in him had triggered a change in her, or whether something else had sparked the shift, he couldn't say, but since her first visit back in November, Janetta now called in to the workshop most weeks. The two of them had almost reached the point of being comfortable, if not friendly.

Alice offered her a cup of tea or some other refreshment.

"Thank you, dear, but I won't be staying. I just want to catch up with Elias for a few minutes."

Woody never objected. As long as Alice was happy.

"I won't keep Elias long, Mr Woodman, I promise, but it's so good to talk to him without the rest of the family interfering. No offence, Alice, dear. I meant my sister mostly, who would interrupt and correct me."

Elias inwardly cringed whenever anyone referred to family as something whole and worthwhile.

Janetta told him innumerable stories about Gwenna and Louisa. Elias learnt something new about their state of flux with every conversation, but he rarely heard anything about Mam. He wondered why, but he couldn't quite bring himself to ask about her, yet.

Those months after Gwenna and Charlie had left … Elias shuddered, remembering the time when the devil had reached so far into his soul that he'd mutated into a beast he'd rather forget. Those months when there'd been the two of them living in the house – him and Mam – had been the turning point in their relationship. Since then, other people had come between them again and he'd maintained a distance.

On the few occasions he'd stood watching the shop and all Gwenna had achieved, hoping to catch Bethan on her own, he'd been disappointed. Every time she left the house she had someone with her: two infants in a double baby carriage, who Janetta had told him were Tillie's Olwen and Gwenna's George; or Charlie, often; or Tillie; sometimes Tom Griffiths; and of late Hugh Powell. Elias couldn't fit Hugh into the picture. Janetta had not mentioned him, but obviously, he'd returned from the war.

Never once had Elias seen Bethan by herself, and he recoiled from exposing his shame in front of anyone else. In the end, he would turn on his heel and return to Alice and Woody, who only knew the recreated Eli.

"Elias?" Janetta began haltingly, dragging him back to the present. "Do you remember how Louisa could get when things didn't go her way?"

"What about it?"

"She's behaving like that now. All snappy and argumentative. Restless. Impatient even. Have you heard anything?"

Elias shook his head. He had less to do with Louisa now than ever. He couldn't even remember her married name. Wed a butcher, he vaguely recalled. "What's it to me?"

"Nothing, I suppose. Except … well …" Janetta explained, "This family's had enough of its share of troubles and upsets, don't you think? I don't want to see a second generation caught up in a similar turmoil. Isn't it time we all made amends?"

Elias questioned why Janetta needed to make amends. His faults he acknowledged. He doubted Gwenna needed to make amends to anyone – if anything, she was the one sinned against, and not only by him. He had refused to accept it for a long time, but he and Gwenna were alike in many ways, both proud and stubborn.

At the cusp of starting a new life with Alice, he wondered what Janie wanted from life. For so long he'd shoved his family away, kept them all at arm's length, not caring for one moment what happened to them. All he'd cared about was his hurts, his problems, but being with Alice had made him see beauty in the people and things around him, things he'd not noticed before.

Tillie loved beautiful things. In her perfect world, people would live in harmony with one another. Gwenna would fulfil her father's dream – she was driven enough to fight off any naysayers. By Janetta's account, Louisa had numerous friends and loved being the centre of attention. It wasn't all he remembered. Independent was the word he'd use to describe her – she'd hated being restricted or bound by rules, even as a youngster.

But Janie? He couldn't decide about her. She wasn't creative like Tillie, Gwenna or him, nor as self-reliant as Louisa, but she was more than capable, with far more common sense.

"What are you getting at, Janie?"

"I just thought, what with you getting married soon … you are, aren't you?"

Elias nodded without giving the date away.

"Maybe we could gather together to welcome Alice into the family. I'm sure Gwenna would allow us to meet in her shop, there's room there, and Mam would love it. She'd put on a feast I'm sure. And … we'd have to talk to Alice, of course," Janie rattled on. Now she had the chance to give her thoughts free rein there would be no stopping the floodgates until she'd finished. "But it's a chance for absolution for all the wrongs we've done each other."

Elias said nothing, but he thought plenty. *There's no way I could put myself through that. And what has Janie done?*

"Oh, Elias. Please," begged Janetta. "So much has changed – none of us are the same people we used to be. Look at you – if you hadn't made the change, none of us would be as we are today. Is there a chance each of us can learn to forgive, if not forget?"

Elias gazed at her for several moments in total bewilderment. "You're asking the wrong person, Janetta. I can accept people might need to forgive me, but who do I need to forgive?"

By openly admitting fault, his contrition and humiliation were complete. He bade her good day and returned to his work, her final word ringing in his ears.

"Yourself, Elias. Forgive yourself."

275

32

CAUGHT IN A WHIRLWIND

January 1901

Whatever plans anyone had for the week or even for the rest of the month, Tuesday January 22nd put a stop to all of them. As news of the death of Queen Victoria filtered through, the entire country went into mourning. The papers wrote endless columns about her reign and her achievements, detailing her life from child to queen, and all she endured. Crowds gathered in open places, black armbands appeared on the sleeves of men from the lowliest workers to the highest in political power. Women draped in black, talked and wept for the poor woman who had lived a long and dignified life as a much-loved and respected monarch, but who suffered in her personal life. Workplaces closed, and the New Zealand ensign flew at half mast alongside the Union Jack on poles tied with black crape.

As the days passed, people sought news of every detail of what would happen next and the all-important question of when her funeral would take place. Albert, her estranged eldest son, whom she blamed for causing her beloved husband's death decades earlier, had become the new monarch as Edward VII. His reputation as a playboy gave cause for much speculation and a healthy degree of cynicism.

Alice paid little heed to anything other than the date of Queen Victoria's funeral: Saturday February 2nd.

"Oh, Eli. What shall we do?" Visibly distressed, Alice took both Elias's hands in hers. "We can't get married on the same day as the funeral. It wouldn't be seemly, not that anyone would marry us anyway."

Elias wrapped his arms around Alice and nestled her against his shoulder. She was much shorter than him and he loved the protective feeling coursing through his veins whenever he held her like this. She fixed her arms around his waist and tilted her head back. With their faces close together and their breath entwined, their lips were drawn to each other like a magnet. They kissed long and deep, their hands and arms in constant motion in an effort to draw closer to each other.

"Well then, my little sweet pea," said Elias, when they separated their lips long enough to breathe, "my suggestion is we get married sooner. Today if we can."

"Oh, Eli. Can we?" sighed Alice, dewy-eyed, taking a step back.

"Why not? Everything is in place, is it not? You have a dress to wear, I have the licence. What more do we need?"

Alice, always a little more practical than him, knew what was and what wasn't possible. Her curls bounced as she shook her head. "We need a minister or registrar to start with, and witnesses and oh, I don't know what else right this minute – but we could do the day after tomorrow." Her eyes shone the more she thought about the possibilities. "Wednesday January 30th – it's a half-holiday – and ..." Her inflection changed. "Eli?"

Still holding her hands in front of him, Elias laughed. "What are you angling for now?"

"I'd like to ask … that is, you … No … I should …" For once Alice didn't quite know how to say what was on her mind.

"Come on, out with it. What're you talking about?"

Alice took a deep breath. "Would you mind if Gwenna came?" she said in a rush.

"Gwenna?" First Janetta, and now Alice. *What plan are these women hatching?* He let her go and rubbed his hands through his hair.

"I want her to be my bridesmaid or matron of honour or whatever you call a married woman, except she isn't married any more. Oh dear. And," Alice rushed on without a break. "I'd like a hot chocolate after the ceremony with some of Tillie's fudge, and your mam's Welsh cakes and try those Glamorgan sausages I've heard about and …"

He put his hands on her shoulders and bent down to face her, eye to eye. "Slow down, Alice. This is the first I've heard of any of this. What are you talking about?"

She blushed a bright pink from her chest all the way up to her hairline. Alice dropped her head, before raising it again to find him at her eye level. "I've been talking with …"

Elias's hands dropped from her shoulders. "Janetta," he interrupted as he straightened up, recalling his sister's suggestion. "That explains it. What's she persuaded you into?"

"She's not persuaded me, Eli. One day, Janie called when you were out with Dad and we got talking. I love Gwenna's sweet shop."

"What? You've been there?" Elias was bewildered. There was so much he didn't know.

"Oh yes, all the time," admitted Alice. "And I want to be part of who they are. I want us to be part of a whole family. Please, Eli. For me. It's truly what I want."

Elias still struggled with his old thoughts and feelings of blame towards the people who personified all he hated about himself. Now Alice wanted to drag him back into their fold. He couldn't do it - he just couldn't.

He turned away from her, paced, took deep breaths. "Alice. Do you have any idea what you're asking?"

"Of course. But it's nothing more than you are capable of, Eli."

Alice sounded so calm, so sure, Elias struggled to comprehend they were talking about the same subject. He was also battling to keep his temper controlled.

"That's not the point. You've said what you want, but what about what *I* want, Alice? What about me?"

She moved towards him and placed a hand on his arm. "This is about you, Eli. You'll be better for …"

"Better! You have no idea what you're talking about. I want nothing to do with the Price family." He brushed her hand from his arm and glared at her.

But Alice wasn't easily put off. "Your mother is a Price, and I know you want to see her. Gwenna technically is a Jones, even if she has kept the Price name - it's the name of a business - not a trap. And what's Tillie done to you? Or Janetta for that matter? And hasn't she asked your advice about Mrs Evans? I've not met her, but she sounds nice. And the little ones - and Charlie. What did they ever do to wrong you?"

His head ached with all her questions. "Alice. You must listen. I want nothing to do with any of them. My life was ruined because of them. I won't go back. I won't.

279

All I want is you as my wife, wood to work and a future together, just you and me."

"Honestly, Eli. You're being silly now. They didn't ruin your life. Nobody did. You simply hadn't found what you wanted to do before. But you have now. And you can't isolate yourself from reality. They are your family. They exist. They live a few streets away. You can't pretend they don't."

The more Alice talked, the more agitated and perplexed he became.

"I can and I will." He grabbed his hat from the peg on the door and left before he could say anything he would later regret.

But once outside and striding up the road, he didn't quite know where to go. It was too early in the day to go to the pub – not that he wanted to any more. He enjoyed a quiet ale at the end of the day with Woody, but he didn't want to get drunk any longer. For one thing, Alice complained at the smell and refused to come close to him for days. But mostly because it reminded him of the person he'd once been.

Passing The Edinburgh Castle reeking of that potent brewery smell Alice objected to, he strode the length of Newton Road. The climb up the hill to the junction of Ponsonby Road had him panting, but today he was glad of the exercise. The fresh air in his lungs stirred his brain into action.

One block along Ponsonby Road he stood and stared across the tops of the trees growing in Western Park and admired the harbour that had captured his affection after so many years of blaming it for his problems. He'd discovered so much about himself of late, thanks to Alice. A sense of peace filled him.

He'd never been known for soul-searching. His attendance at church had been more for appearances than true faith, and he'd never been certain what the words faith and truth meant.

Reflecting on what had brought him so low, he could see how his guilt had obscured much of the truth. Now, embarrassment and shame held him back from admitting fault to anyone.

How could a man, a real man, confess to such failure?

But Janetta believed he could. She had asked him to forgive – and, specifically, to forgive himself – if not forget, and to allow them to welcome Alice into the family circle. Alice had asked him to do the same. Could he trust them not to look at him with contempt as they used to look at the other person he used to be? Could he trust them not to tell Alice what he'd been like? Could he trust Alice to continue to love him when she learnt how contemptible he had once been? And she would, one day she would. Could he forgive himself and let the past go?

"Mr Hughes?" a voice queried behind him.

He turned to be greeted by Hugh Powell.

Elias felt a wave of pity fill his heart. The man was half what he used to be. Elias extended his hand, which Hugh accepted limply. "It's good to see you back, Hugh. How are you?"

Hugh nodded, acknowledging Elias's words, but made no comment.

"I've seen you around, watching the shop," said Hugh without any recrimination. "I hear you are quite successful these days."

"I wouldn't say that," began Elias, surprised by the other man's acclaim.

"I'm glad for your good fortune. And I want to thank you," said Hugh.

"Thank me?" Astonishment complete, Elias blurted, "Whatever for?"

"For giving Gwenna … begging your pardon, sir, Mrs Price, that is … for giving her a chance and the … well, freedom, I suppose is the word, to fulfil her dreams. It was good of you to walk away and hand the business over to her. She won't let you down."

Elias was too dumbfounded to comment.

Hugh raised his hat. "Good day, Mr Hughes. And I believe congratulations are in order, too."

The ability to speak escaped him. Elias touched his hat and watched the other man walk off towards Karangahape Road. Why would anyone – Gwenna most of all – care one way or the other about letting him down?

He couldn't make sense of the encounter any more than he could fathom why Janie and Alice thought him worthy of forgiveness. Hugh had just given Elias credit for something he had done for himself. His motives had been entirely selfish, an act of self-preservation rather than anything noble or honest. Yet his decision had earned their respect.

Just then, a group of young men in a jovial frame of mind walked past him, heading down Ponsonby Road.

One of them slapped Elias on the shoulder. "The Queen is dead, long live the King," he chanted, dancing round in a circle. "Change is coming, I can feel it in the air."

For the second time in as many minutes, Elias seemed unable to form a coherent thought, and his mouth was too dry to wrap his tongue around any words he might have formed.

Another of the young men said, "Cheer up, man. We're sorry the Queen is dead too, but we're on the brink of a new era and the possibilities are endless. We've a new King and a chance our luck will change."

They carried on their way leaving Elias staring after them, with the words 'new' and 'chance' and 'change' swirling in his head. After a few minutes, he headed along Karangahape Road with a new resolve.

33

ACCEPTANCE

January 1901

"Gwenna. Oh, Gwenna. What am I going to do? I fear I've ruined everything."

"Hello, Alice, dear. What brings you here today?" Gwenna came out from behind the counter hoping to prevent the breathless girl from saying anything more in front of customers. With a glance at Tillie, she said, "Come through and tell me what's bothering you." Taking Alice by the arm, Gwenna led her into the house.

Alice burst into tears seconds after the door closed behind them. Guiding her into the sitting room, Gwenna sat beside her on the sofa and patted her hand while the girl mopped up her tears with a handkerchief.

Alice related the conversation between her and Elias over a pot of tea and plate of biscuits. "I'd so hoped I could arrange a reconciliation with everyone. You are such a dear, dear friend, I couldn't bear for you to be estranged from the man I love more than anything in the world."

Gwenna was taken aback to think Alice considered her in such a light, and would speak so openly about her most intimate feelings.

"You would always be welcome here, Alice, even if Elias chose not to call," Gwenna said. "I bear no ill will towards him. I have my life to lead and he has his. We don't need to share our lives to be happy."

"But, I … oh, dear. I've got it all so wrong. I wanted you to be my matron of honour. Oh, please, don't look so shocked," said Alice, seeing the surprise in Gwenna's face. "It's true. I don't have any other friends I could ask. It's always just been Dad and me since my mother died. Until Eli came along. And I want to share my happiness with those who love him too."

Gwenna wasn't so certain any of his sisters would admit to loving Elias, but they didn't wish him harm either. Life was just so much less complicated without his anger and bullying, and they all avoided putting themselves in his way. Alice was right on one count, though: his mother would welcome him and feel her world complete if Elias was a regular part of her life again.

"Is it what Elias wants?" asked Gwenna.

Alice lowered her head and shook it slowly. "No. And now he's so mad at me - I don't mean angry mad - more bothered mad. Vexed, I suppose. I want one thing; he wants another. He wants to please me, but I've pushed him too far. He's left me," she wailed, suddenly lurching into Gwenna's shoulder.

Gwenna put her arms around her and patted her shoulder. "There, there, Alice. I don't believe that for one minute. Now tell me what happened?"

Between hiccups and deep breaths, Gwenna gleaned how Elias had walked out while they were still arguing. In Alice's eyes, the glower he'd given her and the way he slapped his hat on his head and stormed out the door, slamming it loudly behind him, meant he'd gone for good. In Gwenna's eyes, it meant the opposite.

"He'll be back, Alice. He used to do that as a young boy when things got too hard for him. He still did it as a man, after rowing with me or Mam. It's his way of calming down." Gwenna didn't want to alert Alice to the extent of Elias's violence in the past – as far as she was aware, Alice had never been told what Elias had done – but she did want to assure her all was not lost.

Alice immediately lightened. She dabbed at her eyes once more. "Do you think so?" Hope turned her dark eyes into gold. "Truly?"

Gwenna reassured her, "I do. Trust me, he'll be back." Silently, she prayed she was right.

Bethan popped her head around the door. "Gwenna, could you come into the shop? There's someone you need to see."

"Is it necessary?" asked Gwenna, not wanting to leave Alice just yet. "Can you or Tillie deal with whoever it is?"

"No, dear, we can't."

Gwenna stood and smoothed her hands over the skirts of her navy and teal trimmed dress. Since the start of the new year, she no longer wore mourning. Johnno had been gone for eight months, and since she was the only one who mourned him, she believed the time had come to live her own life. Out of respect for the Queen, she would wear a black armband in the shop and don a black cape when she ventured out, but nothing else black.

Leaving Alice to Bethan, but with her mind still on her distress, Gwenna entered the shop. She didn't need to ask Tillie who wanted to see her. She blinked twice to make sure she wasn't imagining anything, but larger than life and equally as nervous, Elias stood facing her. Seconds passed.

"What are you doing here …?" began Gwenna at the same time as Elias said, "I can't find her …"

They both stopped, each waiting for the other to speak again. Frantic with worry, Elias couldn't keep still, twiddling with his hat or running his hands through his hair and stepping one forward, one back.

Gwenna put two and two together, but aware people were listening, she indicated he should follow her. She led him outside and around to the side gate. "If you are searching for Alice, she's here."

Relief flooded his face and his shoulders relaxed. "Can I … may I see her?"

"Maybe," Gwenna hesitated and saw his jaw clench. She couldn't resist making him suffer for a little longer. He had to learn to stop making women weep. "But after what I've heard, will she want to see you?"

The sight of his crestfallen face made her feel rather mean, but she justified her action for Alice's sake, if it meant he came to his senses once and for all.

"No. I suppose not. But will you ask her? Please, Gwenna. Ask her for me."

Pushing her luck a little further, she feigned surprise. "Are you asking me to do you a favour?"

She didn't need to explain. He turned every colour from milk to puce and back again, but Gwenna saw the huge effort he made to control his anger and not walk away. She could see he truly did love the tiny, dark-haired girl in the sitting room and would swallow his pride if it made Alice happy.

"I'm a different man now, Gwenna. If you knew how different, you'd understand why I ask."

She stared at him while she sorted out the war going on in her brain. If she only gave thought to herself, inviting Elias back into her life was a risk and not something she wanted to consider. They were both better people without the other – but when she thought about Alice, who clearly adored him, and Mam, who would never stop loving her firstborn, then the picture blurred.

She had the others to consider as well. Janie believed Elias had changed. Tillie had warmed to the idea. They all wanted to include him in their lives. The surprising viewpoint, and the one to hold the most sway, was Hugh's.

Hugh rarely expressed an opinion, being content to work alongside her and do her bidding. No amount of cajoling had enticed him to speak about his experiences in South Africa, and he would still jump at unexpected noises, so when he did say something, Gwenna listened.

She recalled the day when Hugh, choosing his words with care, had explained how she was honour-bound to their fathers – hers and Elias's – to make the business a success. That part Gwenna grasped. What she had failed to see, and what Hugh emphasised, was how Elias had handed Gwenna her destiny when he gave her the business. She couldn't let him down either.

Even if that decision had been for Elias's benefit to start with, he could have insisted on keeping the business or selling it, instead of letting her have it. Gwenna had married Johnno, was about to become a mother, and even as a widow could never have expected to share in what was his by law. Elias took his chance by leaving and had given Gwenna hers in return.

All these thoughts flashed through her mind in a

matter of seconds while his eyes remained fixed on hers. She sighed. She had no choice. She owed it to the others.

But she wasn't going to let him off the hook easily. "And how am I supposed to get to know this different man you profess to be if you won't have anything to do with anyone you should call family?" she goaded.

Every muscle in his body tensed. She heard the sharp intake of air and held her breath waiting for the explosion. Instead, he dropped his shoulders, hung his head and let the fight drain out of him. Watching him twirl his hat between his fingers, it took all her effort not to smile. Her point had hit home, but the situation was too serious to laugh at.

"Truce?" offered Gwenna, extending her hand.

Elias raised his head and stared at her, assessing her motives. "Truce," he mumbled at length, hesitating before grasping Gwenna's hand for the briefest of moments.

"Let's be honest, Elias," said Gwenna, "we bring out the worst in each other and will never see eye to eye, but for the sake of Alice, Mam and all the others, shall we agree to at least be civil?"

Elias continued to stare at her. She couldn't quite read what was going on in his mind behind those shuttered eyes but trusted he would reach the same conclusions she had, and for the same reasons.

"If it means Alice is happy and Mam will see me, then yes," he concurred. "But let's agree to avoid each other as much as possible, too. I can't guarantee you won't push me too far one day."

"Agreed," she said, in accord with his analysis. "Come with me."

Picking up her skirts, Gwenna led him up the back steps, through the kitchen and into the sitting room where Bethan and Alice sat talking. The joy, relief and adoration on Alice's face when she saw Elias was reward enough for Gwenna. So, too, was Bethan's expression, which mirrored young Alice's, even as tension and doubt edged its way in.

Whatever Elias and Alice said to each other in her sitting room, Gwenna would never know but, to her surprise, Elias asked her to be Alice's attendant. He surprised them even more when he asked Tillie if she would kindly allow them to gather at her home after the ceremony, or at least in the garden.

"Of course, Elias. I'm sure we can accommodate everyone," said Tillie, mentally ticking off what would be needed after checking how many people would be there.

"Alice would like to invite you all – Mam, Louisa, Janie and Mr Lewis, Tillie and Mr Griffiths, Charlie and you, Gwenna. Woody will be there naturally, but we want to keep it small."

Alice had pulled Gwenna aside while the others were talking. She wanted to explain that getting together in Gwenna's shop was one step too far for Elias. He didn't want to be surrounded by jars of sweets and reminders of the past, but he had allowed Alice her choice of guests.

"It's perfectly all right, Alice," said Gwenna. "I understand why he feels like he does. And since you're having a midday ceremony, it makes sense to spend the rest of the day in the garden. Tillie and Mam will make you proud. And I'm honoured to stand at your side."

Within forty-eight hours every detail had been attended to, invitations sent and acknowledged. Gwenna took the brave step of placing a notice in the newspaper on Tuesday to say she would be closed all day Wednesday for a family occasion – hoping it wouldn't affect trade too much. Hugh had offered to keep the shop open, but Gwenna felt it was asking too much of him. Gwenna often did a fair trade on Wednesdays, thanks to half-day closing for most offices and businesses, but while Hugh was a great sweet maker, he would struggle being around so many people, let alone making the teas, coffees and hot chocolates. The lack of staff was something she might have to consider sometime.

After securing the minister and placing notices in the newspaper, Woody and Elias kept to themselves in the workshop until they were needed. Elias started on Mr Court's sideboard and Woody on replacement stock for the shop. The smaller sideboard Elias had made sat finished in the shop with a 'Sold' sign on it.

"I will," said Elias in answer to the minister and, to the sound of church bells, the couple found the happiness they sought. Alice looked radiant as Elias lifted her veil, attached to a circlet of orange blossom and roses, and with all eyes on them they walked together down the aisle as man and wife.

Outside, the family were ready with the rice and rose petals to scatter over the pair. Dressed in a simple ivory silk gown and long kid gloves, Alice turned around on the church step and threw the herb and floral nosegay Bethan had made.

Gwenna hadn't meant to catch it. She coloured as laughter and teasing rang in her ears. "I've no intention of marrying anyone, never mind what the old wives' tale says," she said emphatically.

Before they began the procession from the church back to the house, Bethan and Tillie handed out the traditional boxes of wedding cake they'd made with favours inside. Janie gushed with delight and hugged her mother. "What a wonderful day it is, to have us all here. I'm so happy I could cry."

Louisa looked like she could cry, too, but not with happiness. Gwenna had no idea how Janie had managed to persuade Louisa to attend. There was no sign of Albert Evans, which Louisa explained away by saying he had stayed with the children. Janie had left her two at home with her mother-in-law, and Hugh, bless him, agreed to keep an eye on ten-month-old Olwen and eight-month-old Georgie as they amused themselves in their playpen during the ceremony.

Alice and Elias led the party up Nelson Street, Thomas Woodman extended his arm to Bethan, and they fell into place behind the couple. Charlie, feeling very important as Elias's best man, held his arm out to escort his sister in the correct manner, even though he wasn't quite tall enough. Amid giggles and a tangle of arms, he and Gwenna were forced to swap, so he linked his arm through hers and they could walk side by side in comfort. Janie and Percy Lewis dropped in behind them, leaving Louisa to walk with Tillie and Tom. As usual, Tom, putting others before himself, graciously stood aside and encouraged Tillie and Louisa to walk together while he followed.

By the time they reached the garden, where Hugh had earlier placed an assortment of tables and chairs under the trees, any formality had disappeared and chatter had taken over. Tillie and Gwenna rushed inside to check on their children and put them down for an afternoon nap, Bethan and Janie, aided by Hugh, carried the food out to the tables, while Tom, Percy and Woody poured the drinks set out on another table: ales for the men, home-made lemonade and punch in pottery urns, as well as sherries and port, for the women. The men would partake of their whisky or brandy indoors later, over a pipe and cigar. Charlie, hovering around the men hoping to be given a taste of beer, listened in on their conversation. Alice and Elias only had eyes for each other.

Emerging from the back of the house, Gwenna saw Louisa sitting on her own away from everyone else. She looked as fragile as a glass ornament glittering in the sun, perched on the edge of a precipice. Her hat was placed at such an angle that with the merest tilt of her head she could hide behind its brim.

Gwenna was prevented from going to her at that moment by Bethan who called them all to take their seats. "Come along, everyone. The food is ready. Take your seats for the speeches."

Janie and Percy pulled up a chair each at Louisa's table. Alice and Eli were given a table of their own, Tillie and Tom sat with Thomas Woodman at the next table, leaving Charlie, Bethan and Gwenna to sit together.

Hugh's placement of the tables, whether by luck or forethought, meant everyone sat in an unformed semicircle facing the bride and groom, and no one had their backs to anyone.

Charlie reached his hand out to grab a piece of pie, but Bethan tapped it away, whispering, "Wait till we say grace, and Mr Woodman has to speak first."

Thomas rose to his feet. "Alice, my dear, you look beautiful. You have always given me every reason to be proud of you, and I have no doubt you will continue to do so. I thank Eli's family, Mrs Price in particular, and Mrs Gwenna Price and Charlie for standing up today with the bride and groom. Thanks also to the ladies who prepared all this lovely food. I won't say much more, only that I am happy to welcome Eli into my household and as a wedding gift to the happy couple, I am offering Eli a partnership in the business."

Applause met his words, while Elias's mouth dropped open. He struggled to believe he'd heard correctly. He rose to his feet. "Woody ... Mr Woodman. I don't know what to say. I'm honoured you allowed me to marry you daughter, who I agree is the most beautiful person I've ever known, but to favour me with a partnership is beyond my wildest dreams. I can't thank you enough."

He sat down abruptly, but Alice plucked at his sleeve, whispered something in his ear and Elias stood up again. "Sorry. I'm so overwhelmed, I forgot. Alice," he grinned, "um, that is ... Mrs Hughes and I ..." he hesitated, turning to his bride who nodded encouragingly at him. "... that is, we are grateful to you for sharing this day with us ..." Elias fidgeted with his jacket and tried to loosen his necktie. "I never believed it would happen. I got so many things wrong ..." Elias tapered off, unable to continue, and sat down again.

In the momentary silence, Tom stood up. "Mr Hughes – Eli, if I may. We are not well acquainted. I know little of you beyond what my wife and Mrs Price senior have told me. But a man who admits to the errors of his ways and takes steps to correct those mistakes is worthy of a second chance. You have proven yourself worthy of late, and I speak on behalf of the ladies here today when I say they welcome their son and brother home."

More gentle applause while Tom paused.

He put his fist to his mouth and cleared his throat. "But a word of warning, Mr Hughes. I expect greater things of you in the future. Should you ever falter, I will be watching."

The two men stared at one another, each acknowledging the other's meaning. Elias nodded and Tom retook his seat.

To break the awkwardness, Woody jumped up. "A toast to the bride and groom. May they have a happy life."

Once the toast was over, Bethan led a quick prayer to bless the food. "Help yourself, everyone. There's plenty."

Once everyone had had their fill of all the delicious food and the plates had been cleared, it wasn't long before the group split again. The men resumed their conversation under the trees, while the ladies put away the remainder of the food. Bethan's attention was claimed by the younger children. Tillie, Janie and Alice had their heads bent together talking over something, which left Louisa and Gwenna alone. She'd had no opportunity to ask Tillie what she and Louisa had discussed on the short walk back from the church, but Gwenna couldn't leave the woman standing there forlorn.

"Louisa, you look lovely today. Who made your outfit?" asked Gwenna hoping to get her stepsister talking.

"My usual dressmaker, although it's not new. I couldn't …" Louisa stopped, unable or unwilling to finish her sentence.

"New isn't necessary. It's the fact we are all here that matters. It's been a long time."

Louisa didn't respond, nor did she face Gwenna. The garden took her eye instead.

"Louisa, dear, I don't wish to rake over old coals, there is no reward in discussing what can't be changed," said Gwenna softly, "but I would so like us to speak freely to each other again. Please, Louisa, you appear unhappy. Will you tell me what's wrong?"

Louisa turned her head sharply towards Gwenna, her eyes glistening and her face flaming. "What's Janetta been telling you?"

Taking a step back from her stepsister's sudden hostility, Gwenna replied, "Nothing. I don't know anything other than Janie said she was concerned. I have no idea why she should be, except for her comment you were a little short-tempered lately. Which I've just seen for myself."

Louisa's head tilted and her face disappeared behind the brim of her hat. Her shoulders began to shake.

"Shall I fetch Mam?" asked Gwenna. "Would you talk with her?"

Without lifting her head, Louisa gripped Gwenna's arm. Gwenna waited.

After a few moments, Louisa's hand disappeared into her reticule and she pulled out a fine lace handkerchief and dabbed her eyes. She lifted her head, her eyes sad and red-rimmed. "I'm sorry, Gwenna."

"Whatever for? There's no need to apologise. You're upset. Let me help you."

Louisa shook her head and took a deep breath. "You don't understand. I've not been a very nice person at all. I've spoken badly of you too many times."

Gwenna stopped Louisa from saying anything further. "All that is in the past, and I don't want to hear any more about it. We're in a new year, a new century, and we have two people who are about to embark on a new life. We should take heed. New possibilities and opportunities await." Gwenna smiled warmly, with a sparkle in her eye.

"Why are you being so kind to me?"

"I'm not being kind, Louisa. I'm being realistic. Truly I am. It's better for us all if we get along." Gwenna turned her head to find Alice and Elias and saw how happy they were together. Alice brought out the best in him and, to Gwenna's mind, their future was secure. Now all she had to do was sort out her own. "Look at those two, Louisa. Are they not a picture? Alice has taught me much since I've known her. She's practical, her eyes are wide open and she's loyal. And I've learnt the importance of family from someone who doesn't have one."

Taking Louisa by the arm, Gwenna led her to one of the tables. On her way to fetch a glass of sherry for them, Gwenna caught Tillie's eye; she saw what Gwenna was doing and eased the others further away.

Gwenna explained to Louisa how Janetta had beseeched her to forgive Elias, how Alice had persuaded Elias to bring them all together today, and how she and Elias had reached an agreement. "Alice wanted the family together for reasons of her own, and she made it happen. It mattered to her enough to throw caution to the wind and fight for it. Can't we do the same?"

Louisa remained silent.

Gwenna carried on talking about the difference Charlie made to their lives now he was healthy and happy, and how Bethan had blossomed since she had

297

grandchildren to care for and a purpose in life. "I can't tell you what a difference she's made. I couldn't have done what I have without Tillie, and Tillie couldn't have done it without Mam, and behind us both is Tom." *And Hugh*, but Gwenna didn't add his name to the mix. "We're a team – like Eli, Alice and Mr Woodman are a team. What makes it work is we are happy, as individuals and with each other. We like what we do and who we are."

Gwenna detected a shift in Louisa. Not enough for her to say anything, but some of the tension went out of her. She was listening but, more importantly, Gwenna could see she was hearing the message. "Oh, Louisa, I don't want to dwell on the past. There were too many reasons to be unhappy back then. I want to look forward. To build the business up to be strong enough so Charlie can be part of it, and so young Georgie will be the second George Price to run the business. Do you remember my pa's dreams, Louisa? Do you?"

A faint nod was all Gwenna needed.

"Well, I'm following mine; Elias is following his; Tillie already has hers with Tom and Olwen, her sewing and her fudge. Her dreams may not be as grand, but they are hers and she's happy. Janetta, too, has changed. I don't know why yet, but I'll find out. But what are your dreams, Louisa? Will you tell me? What happened to them?"

After several moments when neither of them spoke, Louisa lifted her head. "I lost them," she whispered, staring beyond Gwenna into a distance only she could see.

Unable to say anything more, Louisa surveyed the garden. She watched Charlie playing catch with Mr

Woodman. Percy and Elias were talking about something of great interest, going by the animated conversation. Bethan could have been mistaken for being years younger, with the little ones playing at her feet while she talked with Janie. Tillie and Alice must have gone inside because she couldn't see them, and Tom was walking towards them with fresh glasses in his hand.

"Come on, you two, enough of this sisterly chatter; it's time you joined the others." Turning to Louisa, he said, "Mrs Evans, I can't tell you how delighted I am to have you here at my home for such a joyous occasion. I hope you will continue to visit us. And I look forward to getting to know Mr Evans."

At the mention of Albert Evans, Louisa's face clouded. She swallowed her sherry in a most unladylike manner, turned to Gwenna and said, "I want to come home." She burst into tears and fled into the safety of the house.

"Did I say something wrong?" asked Tom, watching the woman, one hand on her hat and the other holding her skirt, running up the back steps and disappearing into the shadows.

"Actually, Tom, you've more than likely brought everything to a head. Excuse me, I must go to her."

Gwenna didn't get to Louisa. As she walked across the lawn, Janie stopped her. "I've got something to tell you," she said. "When we can find a quiet moment."

That moment passed, too, as Tillie emerged from the house followed by Alice. Clapping her hands to attract everyone's attention, Tillie said, "Can we all gather on the steps, please? It's time to take the photographs."

This turn of events was a surprise to everyone except Tillie. Alice looked as if she'd won the prize of her life. She hurried down the steps towards Elias, almost bouncing with excitement.

The buzz of conversation rose as one turned to another, eager to know more and ask who'd had their photograph taken. It wasn't a new invention, but the idea was still too novel to take for granted. None of them had been photographed before.

Gwenna soon saw who was responsible. Tom stepped forward and retrieved a canvas bag placed under the table where all the drinks had been set out. Those nearby peered over his shoulders as he removed a black leatherette box from its cover. He explained the circle at the front the size of a ha'penny was the lens, and it had a shutter lever, a winding handle on the side for turning the film and a two small viewing lenses – one on the top for vertical images and one on the side for horizontal – with two small latches keeping the back cover shut.

"It's called a Brownie, and the first ones were released by a company called Kodak in America last year. You have a roll of film, which you thread through like this … and there it is, ready to use," said Tom, clicking the latches into place. "No need for any more trips to those stuffy studios with large cameras on tripods, false backgrounds and large lights. And no more fixed stares waiting for the shutter. We can take our own family snaps," he explained, feeling pleased with himself. "Now, can we have everyone on the steps, please."

After issuing instructions as to who should stand and sit where, with Alice and Elias in the middle and Bethan at the front with the two youngest, everyone stood in place.

Tom took several shots before Gwenna pointed out, "Louisa's not here, and we need a photo with you in it, Tom."

Janie scurried off to find Louisa, while Gwenna ran next door to ask Hugh to join them. He would be able to use the camera as well as anyone, Tom assured her. When Gwenna and Hugh returned, Janie had placed Louisa in front of her on a lower step and firmly rested her hands on her sister's shoulders. Louisa's face was a little puffy, but it wouldn't matter in time to come. The important fact was she was there. Janie whispered something in her ear and Louisa's lips flickered into a small smile.

Tom took a few moments to tell Hugh how to operate the camera. "And don't worry when you see us all standing on our heads through this viewfinder. You will see the image upside down, but it prints the right way up. Clever, isn't it?" Tom placed himself in the group. "Smile, everyone."

⊲⊲⊲⊲⊲⊲⊲⊳

34

Home Truths

February 1901

Gwenna had given little thought to the fact Saturday February 2nd had been designated an official day of mourning for the recently deceased Queen Victoria, or that shops, offices and other businesses were expected to close for the day. After having closed all day Wednesday for Alice and Elias's wedding, she was now champing at the bit.

"Honestly, Gwenna," said Tillie. "You're wearing yourself out. Do you realise how much weight you've lost? Mam says you're not eating properly, again. You can't be up making sweets half the night and working in the shop all day."

"I've got Hugh helping. I'm not doing it all by myself," answered Gwenna, moving from bench to shelf, from shelf to worktop, worktop to stretching hook and back again, checking the copper pan heating on the range as she passed.

Tillie paced around after her, trying to get Gwenna to slow down. "Maybe – but you've got him packaging up the goods and out on the road doing deliveries more than he's here with you making them."

"Hugh's doing a good job. If he didn't do those jobs, then I'd have to, or I'd have to hire someone. And he's not doing out-of-town deliveries any more. Haven't you noticed? We're much cleverer these days. Our stock goes by rail or steamer to the nearest station or port," explained Gwenna, proud of her innovations. "And as for the sweet making, my reputation stands on the quality of what I make. I have to do it."

Since her own fudge was at stake in this conversation, Tillie was having none of it. "That doesn't stop you making fudge, even though you say mine is superior. You can charge more for your specialties, like you do with my fudge – relabel them so everyone knows the difference if you want to – but let Hugh make the basics. He's as capable as you."

"I'll think about it," said Gwenna, carrying on as if Tillie had not been there.

"Well, if you won't think of yourself, think of Mam."

Gwenna paused in her work and gaped at Tillie. "Mam? What's the matter with Mam?"

"Haven't you noticed she's ended up being full-time mother to our two? Tom pointed it out to me. I hadn't noticed either, but apart from when Olwen wakes in the morning and I put her to bed at night, it's Mam who looks after her and Georgie. Tom says it's all right for the moment, but Mam's getting older, Gwenna, and our children shouldn't grow up believing she is their mam."

"Mam's not that old, Tillie. She's not fifty until next year." Gwenna continued with her work, walking around Tillie leaning against the long table. "Maybe when the shop's more established, I'll consider it."

"The shop is established. How much busier could we get?"

"But it's still small change, Tillie. I haven't paid back what I owe yet. I can't lose all I've gained by letting up now."

"That's not what Tom tells me, and you know it. He says the business is going very well. And he should know. He's the one who does all the figures. You've done it, Gwenna. You've brought Pa's dreams to life. Ease up a bit. Before you fall over."

Giving into a moment of glee, Gwenna's mischievous smile brightened her eyes to sapphire. She took a stick of rock, twisted it into a figure of eight, held it against her eyes like a pair of glasses and poked her tongue out at Tillie. "Yes, Mrs Griffiths. Whatever you say, Mrs Griffiths," she teased, before becoming serious again. Tom had told her the books were looking good, but Gwenna couldn't bring herself to believe it possible. "Oh, Tillie, I do hope he's right. But I can't let up just yet."

She threw the twisted stick of rock into the air but missed when she reached out to catch it. It split into pieces on the floor sending them both into peals of laughter.

"You must be done here for the day, Gwenna?" urged Tillie, helping pick up the bits of rock. "Do you want to go to the funeral service for Queen Victoria? It's being held at Albert Park; there's a parade carrying the wreaths to be laid at the foot of her statue."

Gwenna shook her head. "Actually, no, I won't. Do you mind? I know Mam wants to go. Could you and Tom go with her? You could take the babies in the pram. I'd like to slip around to Janie's. She said she had something to tell me at the wedding but we never got the chance to talk again. And I want to try and find out how Louisa is. Poor woman. Something's not right."

304

"You're with child again, aren't you?" Gwenna cried as soon as she saw her stepsister and gave her a hug. Janie's face was a little rounder, her skin a shade pinker and her eyes appeared darker than ever.

Clutching her hands before her, Janetta nodded enthusiastically. "How did you guess? I wanted to tell you at the wedding, but it never seemed the right time."

"You look so happy, Janie. Congratulations."

The two sat in Janie's parlour with John, a year older than Georgie, playing on the floor. Billy, now four, had gone with his father to the funeral service, leaving the household peaceful. Over a cup of tea, the women chatted about the wedding and all the gifts the pair had received, from linens to glassware and a six-piece dinner set, to the glorious bed quilt Tillie admitted to making in secret, in the hope the pair would eventually set a date.

"The partnership Mr Woodman gave Elias will set him up for life now," said Gwenna. "Alice will have her hands full keeping both men on track, but she will. She is so good with figures, and she can still do the books even once they start having a family – and I bet they start soon. Elias might not realise it, but Alice can't wait."

"Mr Woodman told me why he'd decided to give Elias the partnership," said Janie. "He says Elias is destined to become a well-known name in the industry and he wanted to make sure the firm would be recognised as the best in bespoke furniture. But also to give Elias something to 'perpetuate' – is that the word? – after he, Mr Woodman, that is, retired."

Above all these things, though, was the standout surprise gift of the sideboard.

"What sideboard?" asked Gwenna, unaware of the gift, having never visited the workshop and seen the work in progress.

"The one Elias made." Janie explained how she had first gone to his workshop after falling in love with Gwenna's sideboard. "I used it as an excuse to visit Elias," she said. "I go there quite often."

"You two always did get on the best as children," said Gwenna. "But if Elias made it, who bought it?"

"Guess."

Gwenna shook her head. "I've no idea."

"Louisa," said Janie, keeping her voice down.

Gwenna's voice sounded too loud in the quiet. "She did? Why on earth would she do that? She never had anything to do with Elias after she married Mr Evans. And she certainly didn't look like any happy gift-giver at the wedding."

"Shh." Janie put her fingers to her lips. "Louisa's asleep in the back bedroom."

Gwenna's mouth dropped open and she spluttered. "Why is she here? What's going on, Janie?"

Gwenna sat aghast as Janie revealed Louisa's story.

It all began when Louisa heard about the thrashing Elias had given Gwenna back in October 1899. Pity for herself, mingled with pity for Gwenna. She, too, suffered – at the hands of Albert Evans.

According to Janie, Albert's mother, a tyrant at the best of times, had taken control of the household, the children and the money. Louisa was expected to keep up appearances and be the epitome of the society lady and do exactly as she was told. She didn't always measure up.

Butchering made Albert strong, but he made sure never to leave visible marks. Bruises on her upper arms where he squeezed too tightly, and on her back and shoulders, a punch to the stomach. Afterwards, Albert would buy Louisa a gift to say sorry, and life would go back to normal. Except the beatings had become more frequent.

"Louisa hid it all behind a facade of prosperity, too ashamed to admit what her life was like," explained Janie.

Gwenna bit her lip. She felt guilty she'd never noticed. Should she have recognised the signs?

"Remember what she was like at our get-together in Tillie's house, just after Olwen was born? All so uppity and angry, and she couldn't control the children," continued Janie.

Gwenna nodded. She remembered Bethan had said something was wrong that day.

"It was going on back then. She had been on the verge of confessing to Mam many times but couldn't bring herself to say anything. It's only in quite recent times I've learnt about all of it myself."

Janie topped up the teacups and pressed on with her story.

"But it was after you married Johnno, and everything else that followed – and then Elias decided to run off and become his own man – that Louisa became jealous. Every time you turned your hand to anything, you succeeded. Worse still, it seemed Elias was becoming successful too, while her life narrowed. It turned her mean."

Everything started to fall into place in Gwenna's mind: the moods, the nastiness, the absences – they all made sense now. "Has Louisa left him? Is that why she's here?"

Janie nodded. "He hit her the morning of the wedding, and her mother-in-law had forbidden her to

307

attend. She defied his mother but paid for it later that night."

"Oh, that's terrible, but I still don't understand about the sideboard," said Gwenna, frowning in confusion.

"It goes back to the day you opened the shop," said Janie. "Louisa also admired the sideboard. Not that she would have told you – or me, for that matter. She ordered one, a smaller one, for her own home, without knowing Elias was the maker. She found out later when I started telling her about my visits to the workshop and how well Elias was doing. That's when she started to behave out of character."

Gwenna recalled the conversation she and Janetta had had after the Christmas service: She'd said Louisa had started being nice to Janie and telling everyone to visit Gwenna's shop, totally opposite to what she'd done in the previous months.

"I don't know what happened to change things, maybe the violence got worse, but the invitation to Elias and Alice's wedding did it."

Gwenna's exasperation with Janie's convoluted tale erupted. "Did what, Janie? For goodness' sake, get on with it."

"Forced her to leave, of course. Louisa has told me since she's wanted to leave her husband for some time but couldn't see a way out. But when Mr Woodman contacted her to ask about delivery of the sideboard, she had an idea. Since it was already paid for, she told them to keep it as a present. And I don't know what you said to her, but whatever it was, it gave her the strength to leave."

"And I'm never going back," said Louisa, standing by the door. She had arrived so quietly in stockinged feet, Janie and Gwenna jumped at the sound of her voice.

Gwenna rose to her feet and crossed the room to wrap her arms around Louisa and guide her to the sofa. Tears fell. "I'm sorry, Lou. I never knew."

"How could you? I hid it from you all, but after what you said about happiness being the key to fulfilling your dreams, I just couldn't stay there any longer. No one is happy. Not me, not the children, not Albert or his mother. I have no idea about his father, but he's so wrapped up in the business maybe he is."

The afternoon disappeared as the three sisters talked. Percy returned, popped his head into the sitting room and promptly left them alone again. More tea was made and drunk as Louisa filled in the unhappy moments in her life. She was adamant she would not go back. She would miss the children and would ask to see them, but they'd been alienated from her already and she doubted the children would care. They were still too young to have any say.

As they talked, Gwenna schemed. "Louisa. Have you thought about what you want to do, or where you're going to live?"

"I don't know what to think."

"Three days ago, you said you wanted to come home. What did you mean?"

Louisa's crestfallen face crumpled. "They were only words, Gwenna. I don't have a home any more. I'll have to find lodgings and get a job, I suppose. Can I stay for a few days, Janie? Until I get my head together."

Janie assured her she could, but Gwenna went one better.

"Before you get too carried away, I have an idea which would suit us both. My house is big enough; you could come and live with me and Mam, and Georgie.

309

Charlie, too, when he's in the house. He spends most of his time with Tom. But in return, I need your help. I need someone extra to work in the shop and help Hugh put the orders together. It would give me more time to spend making sweets and being a mother to Georgie, so Mam has time to do what she wants. Does it sound like something you'd like?"

"Truly?" asked Louisa, trying to grasp what Gwenna offered. "You'd do that for me?"

Gwenna smiled. "Only if you do me the favour in return and work your hands to the bone."

Louisa didn't smile. "Why would you do me any favours, Gwenna?"

"Because you're family. I've known you all my life, and because someone did me a favour not so long ago, and now I'm doing one in return."

The following Wednesday half-day, they celebrated Charlie's birthday. For the first time in years, six step- and half-siblings sat in the same room without daggers being drawn. Bethan's dreams had finally come true. If her absent son Samuel had been there too she would have felt complete, but having Louisa home again, and Janie expecting another child, was enough.

Gwenna invited them all to share in her latest experiment – lime with a chocolate centre. The shape and balance weren't quite right yet, but taste was her main objective. "Do you like it?" she asked, eagerly awaiting their reaction.

"Mmmm. Lovely," said Charlie. "All sweet and sour. I like it."

Percy wasn't at all keen, and Alice's face puckered when the lime juice hit her taste buds. "Too sharp for me, but the chocolate's nice."

Elias ate his and took a second and then a third one, murmuring something unintelligible, so Gwenna assumed he liked them. Tillie and Tom had been her tasters while she perfected the combination, and approved. Janie, Bethan and Louisa were rather more non-committal. They didn't dislike it but couldn't say it would be a favourite. While not quite the response she'd wished for, Gwenna could not consider it a failure either.

After tea and cakes, the men decided to wander down to the park with Charlie for a game of cricket, leaving a restless Alice, a still downhearted Louisa and a radiant Janie talking about Tillie's latest quilt and complimenting Bethan on the fine lace shawl unfolding from her crochet hook. Gwenna sat at the table sketching an idea for the barrow Charlie insisted upon, with only one ear on the conversation.

"I'm nine now," he'd argued earlier, disappointed he wasn't getting a barrow for his birthday. "And summer is more than half over, and school's in and you promised. You promised, Gwenna. But it never happened. Louisa's here now and helps Mam, and you've got more time to make things. I can tell. Why won't you let me?"

Gwenna sighed. She *had* promised him. She had even thought it a clever idea, but somewhere in the whirlwind of life, she had forgotten. Pushed aside to make space for other more important things. "There's time, Charlie, *bach*. You're still young. It's a great idea and I will come up with an idea or two, but be patient with me."

Never mind which way she explained it – she wanted him to have a childhood of freedom and fun, not a time spent standing on street corners hawking her sweets – he came back with a counterargument.

"But Gwenna, I want to. I need money of my own. I've got ideas. And I want to know how to make sweets, and how to run a business so I can help when I'm older. Gwenna. Please?"

Not until she'd talked to Hugh, who agreed to make something suitable, had she conceded. "Very well. But I'm not teaching you how to boil sugar until you're twelve. Do you understand?"

Charlie's face lit up with delight and he scampered off.

In the meantime, Hugh had created a simple tray from a cardboard box and attached a strap to go around Charlie's neck, and painted it dark green. Gwenna would give it to Charlie this coming weekend, after signwriting 'Gwenna's Confectionery' along the front.

Snatches of conversation drifted into Gwenna's consciousness as she turned her attention away from the barrow and started to scribble down combinations of flavours to go with this and a texture to go with that.

Alice had brought the wedding photographs, which were passed around to be oohed and aahed at. "Dad says he's entering Mr Court's commissioned sideboard into the Industry Awards at the next exhibition. If Elias wins, there's a monetary prize as well …"

Gwenna looked at the snaps and saw for herself what Tillie and Bethan had been telling her for some time. She had lost weight. She also saw one Hugh had taken where she was the central image, rather than the bride and groom. It unnerved her how Hugh had focused on her to the detriment of the bride, but she couldn't decide what it meant.

"Percy and I've agreed to have at least six children. I do so hope this one is a little girl. I love the boys dearly, but …"

Gwenna passed the photos on and turned the page to jot down more ideas. She liked experimenting with new options, even if some of them didn't work.

"Tom said they were rushed off their feet at Smith & Caughey's annual sale yesterday. He came home exhausted."

Louisa had been almost silent since she'd moved in upstairs, so when Gwenna heard her muffled voice, she stopped writing and listened.

"I'm grateful …"

Gwenna had given Louisa the room at the back, the quietest and sunniest, and where she had a view across the tops of houses towards Western Park.

Between them, Bethan and Gwenna had agreed not to question Louisa. She would talk if she wanted to, and if she didn't, then as long as she settled in and was happy, they would be content. Janie had told them enough for now.

What Louisa wanted to do with her life from now on, Gwenna couldn't begin to guess. For now, Louisa was a willing worker and surprisingly cheerful with the customers, but getting her clothes and personal possessions from her mother-in-law had proved an upsetting challenge. Wives who deserted their husbands and families were frowned upon, regardless of the circumstances. Divorce would be out of the question.

"I feel like I'm in a storybook," said Louisa. "I'd accepted my lot, living in a rut I couldn't escape, but here I am, and I don't know what happens next."

Bethan stopped her crocheting and patted her daughter's hand. "You take one day at a time, Louisa. We've all spent time in a rut not of our making, but something always happens to change it. Sometimes it's good and sometimes not; we just have to wait and see what life brings us."

35

OPPORTUNITIES COME AND GO

April 1901

Autumn sunshine extended the warm summer, allowing Charlie to launch his career as a hawker. After a few false starts, he decided on the days he preferred to use the tray and those when he would take the barrow.

Hugh had excelled himself with a lightweight cart with two wheels and shaft-style handles which were easy for Charlie to manage. Painted in the shop colours, with Gwenna's Confectionery written on the sides, and a light canvas roof to keep the sun off the sweets, the effect was stylish and classy.

True to his word, Charlie attracted the children from school and soon had a small but loyal clientele. So far, he'd not run into any trouble - at least, nothing Gwenna heard about - but then he always stood on a different corner, or in a different spot, in the hope of catching a different crowd.

Thanks to Edward Turner, Gwenna's order base through the markets was steady, but for some reason had not increased in several weeks. The battle between imported goods and those locally made continued, and competition was fierce among the big names in confectionery like Rowntree, Cadbury, Halls and Whittaker's. Elias had said the same thing, even though their products were quite distinct from each other. Imported furniture selling in the big stores outsold anything locally made. Both he and Gwenna were determined to establish themselves as worthy rivals to that philosophy. Bespoke 'anything' sold itself by its quality to those who recognised it. The trick was getting people to understand the difference, then persuade them around to the idea of buying New Zealand hand-made products.

Charlie's ploy was to offer free sweets as he marched up and down Queen Street, or walked around the picnickers at the park, or amongst the men playing cricket in the Domain. Often they would buy a small bag or two, and he made sure he handed out Gwenna's trade cards – another of his ideas – to every new customer.

His stack of coins grew every day, and he kept them in a special tin labelled 'Hopes and Dreams'. No one doubted his ability to succeed, but apart from saying he wanted to be a sweet maker like Gwenna, he wouldn't let on what his other hopes and dreams might be.

"And I have to thank you for the increased trade, too, Charlie, my boy," said Gwenna. "I've been surprised by how well you've done."

Life settled into a routine. Louisa fitted into family life as if she'd never left. Her most surprising trait was her ability to handle people. The more fuss she could make of them, the better, and there were times when she undoubtedly enjoyed herself. Gwenna could see how easily she had become a leader of the women's groups she had once belonged to. She'd resigned from them all, removing herself from her past life. When any of the women came into the shop, Louisa was as polite and friendly as ever but refused to engage further. She focused on working in the shop with Tillie, leaving Gwenna to experiment and make a lot more of Gwenna's specialty sweet treats.

As Tillie suggested, Gwenna passed the boiled lolly making over to Hugh who, due to his strength, could manage larger quantities at a time. He no longer looked the forlorn derelict who had turned up on the doorstep all those months ago. Since his return from South Africa, he'd put on weight, and some of the deeper lines on his face had eased. He was still the silent and trustworthy man he'd always been, but he had left something of his true self behind on foreign soil.

Bethan started going out more to women's groups; one day she came home and said she thought she might join the church choir. The girls were thrilled that she was, at last, coming out of the dark space she'd lived in for so long. They all were.

Only one blemish clouded Gwenna's peace of mind: the dreams had returned and once again fear haunted her nights. There seemed no explanation. After the night she'd seen the shadow in the window and Hugh had scared the daylights out of her, her dreams had returned to normal. Worry about the figures adding up kept her awake more often.

But lately, her dreams had been far more restless, disturbed by shadows and vague shapes, and snatches of Johnno. During the day she put it all out of her mind, even though the calendar kept telling her Johnno's anniversary was fast approaching, and with it came the memories she'd wished to put behind her.

After a tiring Saturday, which had at times required all three sisters in the shop, Gwenna collapsed into the armchair in the kitchen. Lamenting the fact she'd been feeling more tired than normal, Gwenna remembered she still wanted to tell Louisa what a difference she was making – in particular, with the customers.

Bethan was cooking her usual weekend meal of mutton and boiled potatoes with cabbage from the garden, and lashings of gravy.

"Have you seen Charlie?" she asked, getting the plates ready to serve dinner.

"He'll be with Hugh or Tom," said Gwenna, without moving from her chair. She'd closed her eyes to ease the itchiness, but she wasn't so much sleepy as bone-weary.

She heard Bethan moving around the kitchen, going to and fro to the dining room and standing at the back door calling Charlie, but couldn't stir herself to help. A few minutes later, Bethan rang her little brass handbell, which could be heard at Tillie's, to tell everyone dinner was ready. They all ate together on Saturday night, including Hugh, who was working in the lean-to they'd converted into a storeroom.

"Has anyone seen Charlie?" Bethan asked as everyone came into the kitchen.

A hand on her shoulder disturbed Gwenna enough for her to open her eyes.

"You must come and eat, Gwenna," said Louisa. "Come on, I've got a story to tell you." Louisa offered her hand and pulled Gwenna to her feet.

"Where's Charlie?" asked Bethan again, getting more

panicky as she checked the dining room after everyone had gathered and he still wasn't there.

No one had seen him.

"He must be here somewhere," said Tom. "Let's call him again."

"The last time I saw him, he was heading down Pitt Street," said Hugh. "He said he was going to try his luck on the waterfront."

"What time was that?" asked Gwenna, suddenly alert.

"Earlier this morning. About nine."

"And no one's seen him since?" queried Tom uneasily.

Heads shook and sisters held hands, worry written on every face.

"Where can he be?" fretted Bethan.

"I'll go find him if you like," offered Hugh. "You stay here and have your dinner."

"I'll go too. I'll never forgive myself if anything has happened to him," said Gwenna, heading towards the hallway.

"We'll all go," said Tom.

Dinner forgotten, the others grabbed their hats and were about to head out the door, when Tillie said, "We can't all go. Someone has to stay with the children."

Through eyes watering in despair, Bethan pleaded. "Will you stay, Tillie, dear? Please? I can't sit still knowing he's out there somewhere."

"If you'd rather, Mam. But are you sure you want to go?"

Bethan was sure. She pinned her hat in place, pulled her jacket over her blouse and followed the others to where they stood in a group on the street.

Tom took charge while Hugh passed around hurricane lamps. "Hugh and ..." Tom hesitated. Deciding who should go with whom and understanding Tillie's concern for Bethan, he paired the two. "... Bethan. Go down Pitt and Hobson to the waterfront and back up Nelson. Keep your eyes open up the side streets."

"Gwenna, you come with me. Louisa, go to the Lewises and ask Percy to go with you. Check Queen Street and don't forget the marketplace. It'll be closed up now, but he could be locked inside. Gwenna and I will check Western Park while there's still some daylight. There was a friendly cricket match there this afternoon." He checked the setting sun against his pocket watch. "It's coming up six o'clock. Meet back here in no more than two hours. It'll be too dark to do anything further afield by then. Stay together, at all costs. I don't want anyone on their own."

Everyone murmured their agreement and set off as instructed. Gwenna and Tom set a fast pace, heading along Karangahape Road and down Ponsonby, looking down every side street and alley, before entering the park from the top end. Within moments the dark shadows cast by the trees and the fading light gave Gwenna the shivers. A sense of doom settled in her stomach. "Tom, what if something bad has happened to him. What will I do?"

"Hold fast, Gwenna. He's a clever lad. He's probably rushing home right now, realising how late he is. Don't upset yourself. We'll find him soon."

The further away from the road they got, the more fearful Gwenna became. Tom lit the lamp he carried and pushed on, confident he knew the path in front of them. Feeling better for having a light close by, Gwenna followed, calling Charlie's name over and over.

The shadows at the bottom end of the park were deeper, and the few lights from houses and gas lamps on the ridge looked a long way away. They could see little. About to make their way back up the hill, Tom spotted something pale on the ground. "Look, Gwenna. He's been here. This is one of your bags."

They called Charlie's name again in unison, paused and waited, hoping to hear a response. "I'm just going over to check behind that clump of trees. Keep talking so I know where you are."

Shaking like a leaf blowing in the wind, she blinked several times to adjust her eyes to the sudden darkness. Still calling out and placing one foot carefully in front of the other, she walked a few more steps and found another bag; a third one lay a few feet further along. "Tom, I've found two more."

Tom came rushing back and, taking her hand in his, they ventured further into the darkest shadows, calling Charlie's name. They heard a faint answering cry.

"Wait here," he said, hurrying towards the sound. But Gwenna didn't listen and followed in his footsteps.

They found Charlie lying on the ground.

Tom put the lamp down and, kneeling beside the boy, turned his head towards the light. Gwenna gasped at the sight of the congealed rivulets of blood down the side of a face streaked with tears.

"Is he …?" She couldn't finish the sentence. Memories of Johnno turned her knees to jelly and her tongue thick with fear.

"He'll be fine," Tom assured her.

"Gwenna?" Charlie groaned.

Gwenna dropped to her knees and started to lift him onto her lap.

"Don't do that, Gwenna," said Tom. "Let's see if anything's broken first."

Being careful not to hurt the boy, Tom ran his hands across Charlie's shoulders and down his arms and legs until he discovered what had prevented the boy from returning home. His ankle lay at a sickening angle. Tom raised the lamp higher and Charlie flipped his arm up to hide the light from his eyes.

"Gwenna," he croaked.

"Yes, Charlie, I'm here." Tears flowed down her cheek, and she clutched his hand and kissed the grazed knuckles. "I'm sorry, Charlie. I'm so sorry. I never meant for any harm to come to you."

"The barrow's broken, Gwenna," he sobbed.

In the faint light, Tom spotted what was left of the barrow. The canvas roof lay in a heap, tossed to one side, one shaft had come to rest a foot or two beyond Charlie's head; the side of the barrow had been smashed in.

"No matter, Charlie, *bach*. You're all that matters."

"There was too many of them, Gwenna."

Tom interrupted. "Let's leave the explanations until later, young man. Let's get you home."

Gwenna picked up the lantern while Tom gathered Charlie into his arms. They'd not gone far before Tom realised he wasn't going to make it back up the hill with Charlie positioned as he was.

"Sorry, lad. I'm going to have to toss you over my shoulder. It won't be comfortable and I'll try not to bump your ankle, but I've no choice."

Charlie nodded stoically, biting his lip to suppress a cry as Tom changed positions and leant into the hill. Tom forged ahead up Howe Street with Charlie's head and arms bouncing against his back. Gwenna scurried

322

along behind, holding one of Charlie's hands and reassuring him.

Ten minutes later, Tillie welcomed an out-of-breath Tom into the house, relieved Charlie was safe and equally as concerned at the state of him.

"Put him on the sofa for now," said Tillie, opening the door to the sitting room.

Tom lowered him down while Tillie eased a cushion under Charlie's ankle. After a more thorough investigation, they decided it wasn't broken, just badly sprained.

"You're not going to be able to walk on it properly for some time," said Gwenna, soaking a towel in cold water and wrapping it around the boy's ankle to help reduce the swelling.

Tears rolled down Charlie's face. "They took the lollies. And the money. I couldn't stop them."

Gwenna wiped his face clean with her handkerchief. "Shush, Charlie, *bach*. None of it matters. Only you, my pet."

"Any sign of the others?" panted Tom, still trying to recover his breath.

"No, not yet." Tillie checked the clock. "You said eight, and it's not yet seven thirty."

Getting to his feet, Tom turned for the door. "I'd better go look for them – Hugh and Bethan at least – and tell them I've found him."

"You'll do no such thing, Tom Griffiths," said his wife. "Sit down. Get your breath back first. You don't know for certain where they are and they'll be here soon enough."

A few minutes later, Louisa and Percy arrived back and were overjoyed to learn Charlie was safe.

"We hurried back to tell you we'd been talking to a couple of blokes near the markets," Percy explained. "They said Charlie's been having some trouble with a few of the older lads. Something to do with Charlie taking their trade. They said to check the park, which we knew you were doing."

Within fifteen minutes, Hugh and Bethan returned. Nearly out of her mind with worry, Bethan rushed through to Charlie the second she heard he was safe. Fussing over him eased her nerves, and before long one of her famous poultices had been applied and he'd been given a small dose of laudanum to ease the pain. He fell asleep before he'd finished his story.

"Well, that's it," stated Gwenna. "He's never going hawking again."

"Don't be hasty, Gwenna," said Tom in all seriousness. "It wasn't the lad's fault."

"Of course it wasn't. Why would you even think it was? It's those hooligans. Thugs. Beating up on a little boy. And left lying there on the ground, injured like that, in the dark. It's just too much. The poor boy would have been frightened out of his mind."

"Sounds to me like he stood up to them quite well," said Louisa, who sat smoothing the sleeping Charlie's brow.

"That's not the point, though, is it? He was out there selling *my* sweets and got attacked because of it."

"I'm sure he's not telling us everything," said Tom. "But this is likely to be a bit of rivalry gone wrong. They smashed up his barrow, yes, and they got into a fight. But he gave as good as he got by the state of his knuckles. You can't blame the boys because Charlie tripped over a tree root and twisted his ankle. Nor for the cut on his face.

He probably did that when he fell. It's just a bit of boys' rough and tumble."

Gwenna wasn't convinced, but the others agreed with Tom – Charlie shouldn't be punished for it. "I'm not punishing him," she humphed, indignant at the suggestion.

"Indirectly, you are. And Charlie will certainly think you are. He wants to be out on the streets selling sweets. If you won't let him any more, he'll believe you blame him for it all," said Tom.

"Tom's right, Gwenna, *bach*."

Surprised Mam would agree with Tom, Gwenna stared open-mouthed at Bethan. "Not you, too?"

Bethan smiled. Now Charlie was safe, she could consider the event more rationally. "You don't know little boys very well yet, do you, Gwenna, dear? Charlie's been too sickly till now to be one of the lads, and I'm right glad he is well enough these days," she shrugged. "Boys will be boys. You'll see, when Georgie gets bigger."

"No son of mine is going to be found brawling in the streets." Gwenna folded her arms across her chest in a perfect imitation of her old schoolteacher. No one bothered to cover their mouths or hide their mirth.

Hovering in the background, perched on the edge of a balloon-back chair listening to it all, sat Hugh. "The lad's capable of looking after hisself, Miss Gwenna." If Hugh spoke when the family were together, he always addressed her formally, which sounded odd to her ears. "I've been teaching him a few moves," smiled Hugh – something he didn't do often. "I'd heard about these other lads pestering him, so I figured he needed the odd trick or two up his sleeve. I'll take a bet the others don't look much better. He'd 'ave landed a few punches."

"And you never thought to tell me?" challenged Gwenna.

Hugh shrugged. "It's boy stuff. You'd have stopped me if you'd known."

"Did you suspect something like this might have happened when we set off?" asked Tom, slightly miffed Charlie hadn't asked him, or more to the point that he, Tom, hadn't thought of it. "You didn't say anything."

"I couldn't be certain, and I didn't want to upset Mrs Price till I was sure. I thought we'd find him down amongst the sailors. Charlie'd not said anything in a while about the other lads."

"You mean this has happened before?" squeaked Tillie.

"No. Not like this," Hugh reassured them. "Just a bit of pushing and shoving. He'd lost a few bags of lollies and they took his money once. It was the last straw as far as he was concerned and he asked me what he could do." Hugh coughed to hide his embarrassment. "He thinks the world of you, Miss Gwenna. He'd protect you with his life if he had to."

The unspoken echo, 'and so would I', filled the room.

Exhausted, Gwenna could take no more and burst into tears.

Days passed and nerves settled as Charlie recovered his spirits and chafed against being kept indoors. Even little Olwen and Georgie held no interest for him any longer. He'd grown out of them in the weeks when he'd been helping Gwenna. But never mind what he said, no one, not even his co-conspirator Hugh, would let him go anywhere.

"But I feel fine now," he said, hobbling badly.

"Will you sit down, Charlie!" barked Bethan. "You must not walk on that ankle."

She tended all the cuts and grazes, rubbing balm into his aching muscles and with the uncanny ability of the young, Charlie bounced back quickly. Even Bethan admitted he'd come to no great harm.

The next day, Hugh appeared with a home-made crutch. Charlie was thrilled and soon learnt how to get around the house, annoying them all with his demands to be useful.

In the end, Gwenna gave in, and with a newly made stand Hugh had put together, she allowed Charlie to sit up at the corner of Pitt Street, peddling sweets and waving a sign with an arrow on it pointing to the shop.

"Do not move until someone comes to get you. Do you hear me?" Gwenna was terrified to let him out of her sight in case something happened to him again. She was determined to make him understand. "You are to sit here and wait. Hugh will carry the stand back."

"All right," Charlie said, bemoaning his lot. In all innocence, he gazed at his big sister. "Gwenna? Your eyes are all black. You don't look good."

"I'll see you later," she said, ignoring his comment, and returned to the shop.

She wasn't at all surprised by what Charlie said. She had reached the point of dreading closing her eyes at night. Within minutes of falling asleep, the dreams began. She often woke in a sweat and gasping for air, as if she'd been running, and could only doze from then on until Georgie and the dawn light allowed her to get up.

The anniversary of Johnno's passing was fast approaching. She hoped and prayed once the 18th – the date on Johnno's death certificate, and her twentieth birthday – had passed, she would sleep again. She'd told no one – not Tillie, not Mam, not even Hugh – the date written on that miserable, defining piece of paper, the day when life had pitched her in another direction. It was bad enough that she associated her birthday with such horror, but she wouldn't inflict it on others. Tom knew of course, but he, too, had kept it to himself. Gwenna assumed the others would mark Johnno's funeral date as his day of passing, if they bothered. Johnno meant little to anyone else. Either way, the week ahead would be a trial.

Last year on her birthday, a day of supposed celebration, she'd been alone in the house in Onehunga. This year, she sensed Mam and Tillie had plans for a celebration. She would have to find something inside her to show appreciation for their efforts, even if she was feeling tormented.

⟨⟨⟨⟨⟨⟨⟨

36

NIGHTMARES BECOME REALITY

18 April 1901

This time when she woke, something other than her dreams had disturbed her. Gwenna rose, tied her wrap around her and tiptoed downstairs. Her heart hammered like a pounding steam engine. Certain she'd heard a noise, she stopped to listen. Footsteps? No one else in the house had stirred but, beginning to think she'd imagined it all, she heard the sound again. Like a sack being dragged.

In the months to follow, she would berate herself for not lighting the lamp when she entered the shop through the connecting door as she had done hundreds of times over the previous six months.

The street lamp was no longer lit, and with no moon the solid darkness became impenetrable, but she had this overwhelming need to check the door was bolted. Like a blind person, Gwenna edged her way to the door by feel, reaching out to the table on her right, the mantelpiece on her left.

She sighed with relief when she checked the bolts and they were still in place. She'd taken a few steps on her return journey when an object flew through the window, sending glass flying. Gwenna lost her balance and fell heavily against the table, toppling it as she crashed to the floor with a yell. How she missed landing on the glass she would never know, but before she could fathom what was happening, another object smashed through the second window, and the third. Glass shards flew everywhere. She whimpered with every bump and bang, but whoever was outside, intent on destroying the windows, hadn't finished. The door glass shattered before another attack was launched on the front windows, using what Gwenna assumed was an iron bar, to smash every remaining pane.

Terrified whoever it was would attack her too if they saw her, she lay absolutely still, praying her white nightdress and robe would not give her away. Hearing sounds from the house, her addled brain realised the noise would have disturbed Bethan and Louisa. Georgie would probably be crying. She had to stop them coming through to the shop. She pulled herself into a kneeling position against a chair, taking care to make the least amount of noise as possible. From there she struggled to her feet amidst the tangle of clothing. Pain shot up her leg and she vaguely worried about what damage she'd done. She stood up at the same time as the door opened and her eyes were assaulted by a bright light, and the shadow of a person looming large came towards her.

"Gwenna, wake up. Come on, Gwenna. You're safe now. Wake up, Gwenna, *bach*."

The soothing voice of her mam echoed in the fog behind her eyes until the astringent smelling salts passing under her nose had her sitting upright. Her head exploded with the movement, and she lay back down again, groaning with the pain.

"What …" She licked her lips. Memory returned and with it panic. She tried to sit up once more, but the room spun, and she was forced to close her eyes and lie down to still the clanging in her head.

"Is … every … one …" She seemed unable to find the words.

"Shush, Gwenna. Rest. We're safe. You're safe. The doctor will be here soon. Hugh's gone to get him," soothed her mam.

Louisa pressed a cold compress, smelling faintly of lavender, to Gwenna's forehead. "You fainted when you saw us. The light was too much of a shock."

"What …" Gwenna began again. "Tell …"

"No talking," ordered Louisa, stroking her arm. "You're to rest. And I'm here to make sure you do."

Louisa's voice faded. Oblivion overtook her.

"You should consider yourself very lucky, Mrs Price," said the doctor. "In my opinion, you were headed for a complete nervous breakdown, young lady."

Gwenna only half listened to the doctor lecture her about her ailments and what should be done about them. Today was her birthday. Two years in a row circumstances had ruined it.

"You are exhausted," continued the doctor, "and grossly undernourished. We need to build your strength up. It will be a slow process requiring long-term bed rest. The bruises will heal, but I am a little concerned with the ligament in your knee. Do not put any pressure on it until I tell you. Initially, I'm confining you to bed for one month."

"A month!" Whatever else he had said, that word was enough to bring Gwenna to her senses. "I won't stay in bed for a month. I can't."

"You can, and you will," said Louisa firmly. "I promised Mam."

Louisa had taken on the role of chief carer. Her skills in the kitchen were limited, and she had never learnt how to make lollies.

Not at all happy with being contradicted by his patient, the doctor began to put his instruments back in his bag. Tersely, he said, "I've given Mrs Evans here some tonic to help strengthen your blood and something to help you sleep. She has a list of recommended foods. I strongly suggest you follow my advice, if you know what's good for you. Good day, madam."

Mam and Louisa were constantly in and out of her room, giving her possets of warm, spiced milk laced with brandy, soups of varying tastes and disgusting aspic jellies. The custards were much better, and the sweet milk toast a treat. They allowed her out of bed long enough to use the commode and propped her up on pillows for an hour at a time, but mostly she slept. The soothing lavender oil Louisa put on her pillow and rubbed on her temple and inside her wrists, helped Gwenna's body take control over her mind.

On the third day, Gwenna felt strong enough to push herself into a sitting position and started asking questions.

To begin with, nobody was keen to discuss what had happened in the shop.

"You have to tell me," moaned Gwenna. "I'm going crazy with worry here."

"Don't upset yourself, Gwenna, *bach*," said Bethan. "Get better first."

By the end of a week, only a few bits of information had filtered through to her.

"If someone doesn't tell me what's going on, I will get up and find out for myself."

Gwenna threw the bedclothes back and attempted to stand up. Her head swam and her legs wobbled dangerously. She was forced to balance on the side of the bed, one hand on the bedpost, the other holding her head until the room stood still.

Bethan fussed and bothered, calling Louisa to help her lift Gwenna back into bed, but Gwenna would not be calmed.

"If you won't tell me, send Tom or Hugh to see me."

Bethan was scandalised that Gwenna would even consider admitting Hugh to her bedroom while attired in her nightgown. "You can't do that. It's not done."

But Gwenna had moved beyond the niceties of society, demanding to see one of the men. "At least Hugh will be honest with me, which is more than you two are."

Neither of her carers would give in.

Later in the day, Louisa returned. Sitting on the side of the bed, she faced Gwenna and laid down the law. "I can't have you getting yourself all worked up like this over things you can do nothing about. What's done is done. I've told you the windows have been battened and the place is secure. That's all you need to know. There's to be a police investigation. We can't do much until then."

"The business will be ruined. We have to do something," wailed Gwenna.

"Stop it, Gwenna. Or I won't tell you anything."

At Louisa's threat, Gwenna calmed down and listened.

"To ease your mind and make it simpler for everyone concerned, I've organised a day bed for you in the sitting room. You will be allowed to come down in the morning before luncheon and again in the afternoon, after a nap, until dinner."

Gwenna started to quarrel, but Louisa put her fingers on Gwenna's lips.

"If you argue with me, you won't be allowed down at all. I will help you dress in the day robe Tillie is making. When you're ready, Hugh will carry you downstairs. Yes, Gwenna," she said when Gwenna again attempted to contradict her. "Carry you. You are not walking and that is final."

The next morning Tillie and Louisa dressed Gwenna in her pale-blue wool day dress. Shaped into the waist and flaring out over soft petticoats, it fastened together from neck to toe with tiny frog fastenings. Brocade trim and heelless brocade slippers turned a plain robe into an elegant dress.

"There's no need to wear corsets, my dear," said Tillie. "It's designed for comfort, but you will be able to receive guests now."

Gwenna was thankful, and said so, giving both sisters a hug and a kiss. Hugh lifted her as if she was a feather and carried her gently down the stairs. Gwenna carelessly draped her arm around his neck and felt a faint shiver through his shoulders. She glanced at him in surprise, but Hugh kept his eyes firmly fixed on where he was going until he sat her on the day bed in the sitting room.

Gwenna had never seen the sofa before but fell in love

with it straight away. She must thank Tom, or whoever bought it. Covered in a warm gold velvet, it looked like an armchair with rolled and padded arms and back, but longer, with extra length for her legs. She splayed the skirt of her robe out to drape prettily over the side.

"You're looking better, if I may say so, Miss Gwenna," said Hugh. "There's a bit of colour in your cheeks." And by the way he danced from foot to foot and turned colour himself, he was clearly embarrassed.

"Thank you, Hugh. Will you stay and talk with me? Tell me what's going on."

"Not right now, Miss Gwenna. Mr Griffiths will explain everything." Hugh glanced at Louisa's stern face. "I'd better be going for now."

Louisa plumped pillows behind Gwenna, pulled a side table closer to her and handed her a milk posset and a book. "Is that better?"

"Perfect. Thank you, Louisa," smiled Gwenna. "But when is someone going to tell me what I need to know?"

As if on cue, Tom knocked on the door and entered the room. He kissed Gwenna on the cheeks and, after all the civilities had been covered, pulled up a chair.

Gwenna sat transfixed, almost unable to utter a word, as Tom explained the events of that night.

"We have not been allowed to touch anything. They are taking photographs of all the damage, including the bricks - to see if they can identify where they came from. And a crowbar left behind. We still don't know who it was, or why. There's been no witnesses come forward, other than you …"

"It was Black Jack."

"What? Don't be silly, Gwenna. It can't have been him," Tom said, dismissing her idea. "You're imagining things, girl. No one's seen or heard of Jack Jones in over a year. He's gone."

Gwenna shook her head and sat forward. "It was him, I'm telling you, Tom. He's haunted my dreams for weeks – just like those dreams I had before Johnno disappeared. It was him. I just know it. Even if no one can prove it. And ... the date, Tom." Tom knew what she meant. "Why that date if it wasn't him?"

"Calm yourself, Gwenna. I won't argue with you if you feel sure. Your instincts have been good before, but it's a long shot. I'll suggest it to the police, but don't expect them to take it seriously." Tom paused. "There's one more thing. The other piece of evidence they're following is the word 'Shrew' painted on the wall."

Gwenna gasped, and tears threatened. She wasn't as strong as she thought. What a horrible word to use, and to deface the building was unforgivable. "Is it still there?" she asked in a strained voice.

"Yes, but it's covered up now," Tom assured her. "The police nailed a piece of canvas over it so passers-by won't gawk at it, and they'll also investigate the paint on the footpath where the pot was spilt. They're hoping whoever it was might have got some on a shoe or their clothing."

"Can I see?"

"No. Absolutely not, Gwenna. You've had enough trauma. You heard what the doctor said. Total rest and no upsets. Anyway, your mother and your sisters would kill me if I let you anywhere beyond this room."

Gwenna attempted a smile, but her mind was working overtime.

"I never saw the room afterwards. It was pitch dark until Louisa came through the door with the light and

I fainted. From what I remember while lying on the floor, he smashed every window. I know I knocked one table flying, it'll be broken, and now you tell me the evil man painted the outside too? I can picture it, Tom. The shop's ruined, isn't it. *He's* ruined it. I'm not going to be able to get it up and running again, am I?"

Gwenna saw the sorrow in Tom's face, but he would never conceal the truth from her. "No, Gwenna, you're not. The damage can be fixed but even if you could reinstate the shop, I'm not sure people would come."

At Tom's words, Gwenna's hopes and dreams shattered. The shop was gone. Everything she had worked for, everything she had sacrificed – all gone in one night of wanton destruction.

Like a dam bursting, her courage deserted her, leaving her as emotionally and mentally exhausted as she was physically drained. She lay on the day bed with no idea how she would recover from such a loss.

Over the next few days, Gwenna had a constant stream of visitors. Elias, the most surprising of them all. He didn't stay long, but she valued his coming.

"Alice told me," he said. "I'm sorry you've met such troubles, Gwenna. Never mind what is between us, you don't deserve them."

From Alice, she learnt more about the story of Louisa's sideboard and how Mr Evans had tried to claim it since he'd paid for it, he said, but her father had refused. His client, Woody insisted, was Mrs Louisa Evans and since *she* had gifted it to his daughter Alice, that was the end of the matter. Mr Court's sideboard was coming along excellently, and Woody was certain it would win first prize. And Elias and her dad were planning on moving to a bigger workshop - "Which means I'll be able to help choose where we live and what the house looks like. I so want a nicer place. It's been fine for Dad and me, but Elias and me, we're a family now." And finally, breathlessly, Alice thought she was pregnant. "You don't mind me telling you, do you, Gwenna? I know it's too soon to know for certain and I shouldn't tell anyone, but I'm so excited."

From Janie, Gwenna learnt about the redecorations in their house to welcome the new baby. New furniture, new curtaining, new colours. They had scrimped and saved after Percy's increase had come through, and the house they'd bought had been pretty run-down, but the potential had been huge since it had so many bedrooms. "Enough for all the children, and a spare one. Percy says I can get a maid in to help." Dreams were coming to fruition for the Lewis family.

"I'm happy you're prospering, Janie. It's good to see," said Gwenna, increasingly concerned about her own situation.

Bethan told her about the new people she'd met through the choir, and how she was helping the ladies with the church bazaar fundraising. In the hope Gwenna would eat more, Bethan prepared her favourite foods in addition to the life-sustaining diet the doctor recommended. Louisa nursed her as if she was a baby in need of constant attention, and strictly adhered to the times she was allowed downstairs. The only times Gwenna saw Hugh was when he carried her up and down. In those brief moments, which she found awkwardly intimate, Gwenna tried to find out what Hugh was doing but misinterpreted his reticence to mean more than his words. The less he said about how the wholesale side was doing, the more Gwenna fretted.

Even Tillie had news. "Tom's been promoted to Assistant Head of Department. A manager even." Gwenna was delighted with the news. Tom deserved recognition, but would it mean she'd lose Tillie? With Tom in such an elevated position, Gwenna assumed Tillie would no longer want to work – not with sufficient money coming into the house for her to become a society lady if she wished. Gwenna couldn't imagine what she would do without Tillie.

All around her, the family was prospering, yet no one spoke of Gwenna rekindling *her* dreams. No one gave her any hope she would be able to rebuild what she had lost. Her heart ached. She had promised Pa she would care for Mam, and Charlie. Even if Tom had taken over the role, there was still Mam to consider – and Louisa. And she had made a pledge to her son. She had failed them all.

Sleep became her escape, thanks to Louisa's magic medicine.

37

SCHEMES AND DREAMS

May 1901

"I want to talk to Hugh," demanded Gwenna as she lay on the day bed.

Tom recognised the look. "What about? What are you scheming now?"

"I don't know exactly, but I've got to do something." Gwenna's frustration levels were fit to burst. "I've done nothing for weeks except eat revolting mushy food, and sleep. Louisa still won't let me walk up and down the stairs, and the doctor confined me indoors for another two weeks." She pumped her hands beside her, thumping the padding in vexation. "It's so unfair. It'll be the end of May by then and six weeks since we last took a single penny."

While her physical health was still not quite up to par, and she tired far too easily for her liking, her mental acuity had returned in full force. The one aspect Gwenna still doubted was her emotional stability. Anger and tears erupted on a regular basis – she hated her lack of control – and Louisa's magic medicine was now making things worse.

"That's not quite true," answered Tom. "And you know it. I've told you the wholesale side is busy. Turner's are doing a great job at the auctions. Hugh is managing well enough, although he admits to missing your deft touch with some of the mixtures. It's early days yet, Gwenna. You can't expect to recover from long-term exhaustion so soon. Relax. We've told everyone your exclusive range is not available again until later in the year, but they should put their Christmas orders in early if they want supplies."

Even to Gwenna, it made sense.

"I still want to talk with Hugh."

"I'm not the one you should be talking to, Miss Gwenna," said Hugh, sticking with his recently acquired and uncharacteristic formality.

Their relationship had changed in the last weeks since he carried her everywhere. Sometimes she found herself resting her head on his shoulder, her arm around his neck, and she could feel his breath when he inhaled the scent of her hair. She realised how much she had come to rely on him.

Tom was her adviser about things financial and often told her to stop being so impetuous, but Hugh was her strength. He'd always been there for her - except for the year when he'd been in South Africa - and understood her better than many. She felt safe with Hugh around.

Although Hugh agreed with her ideas in principle, the sort of people who could bring about what she asked were the ones with money and contacts. Hugh had neither.

"I'm not asking you to sign the documents, just to find me a place. Look. Look what it says here."

For months, the newspapers had been full of the forthcoming royal visit by the Duke and Duchess of Cornwall and York, but there was something new every day as the date of their arrival crept closer.

Gwenna handed the paper to Hugh. "The school holidays are being altered to fit the dates when the duke and duchess are here, and there's to be parades and welcoming parties. There are plans for three ceremonial arches I've read about so far – one at the bottom of Queen Street by the wharf, the government one further up near Victoria Street, and one in Wellesley Street by the library. And visitors will be pouring into Auckland to see the royal couple We can't miss an opportunity like that."

Hugh never refused her anything and agreed he would see what he could find. The pair drew up plans and debated the best locations, but a lot would depend on what was available. The confectionery business was fickle at the best of times. Small operators would appear and disappear – even the bigger ones, like the Chicago company Elias once detested, who were burnt out of one building and vacated their other premises nearly two years earlier. Names changed and nothing remained the same, but Gwenna was convinced. Somewhere along Karangahape Road, there must be suitable premises.

"I don't want to be too close to a similar store, but close to a fruiterer or grocer would work – and towards the mill end if possible. I heard the duchess may go past the Jewish cemetery on the other corner."

A few days later, Hugh returned, grinning. "I've found you the best location I can."

Several shops east of the junction of Upper Queen Street, Hugh had found an empty shop, between a grocer and a draper on the south side – the sunny side – protected by a fixed verandah. By the time he had finished explaining, Gwenna was ready to throw off her fetters and visit the place for herself. She placed her feet firmly on the floor; for once her head didn't spin, and her legs felt stronger. The doctor had been happy with the way the knee ligament was healing, the bruises had faded and she was feeling more like her normal self. The 'doom merchant', as she called the doctor, kept warning her not to do anything to tire herself out. 'You won't recover quickly or easily, Mrs Price,' he had said. 'I want you to take the year off and concentrate on getting strong again.'

Well, *he* could just think again. Six weeks confined indoors was more than Gwenna could handle, and a year off would mean the end of her dreams. No business would survive a year without constant work and attention, and she wasn't ready to give up. Not by a long way. She'd promised Georgie.

Gwenna was on her feet, already thinking about what she should wear and if she could make it up the stairs without assistance when Hugh held his hand up.

"Don't do that, Miss Gwenna, please. Mrs Evans will have my hide if I let that happen. Mrs Griffiths, she could visit instead, and she would be the best person to talk with Mr Griffiths if you want to go ahead with leasing the place."

Gwenna sat down again with a huff. "I'm going batty, just sitting here with nothing to do, Hugh. You've got to help me."

Over the next couple of days, they spent the time conspiring and planning. Gwenna relaxed in his company, and they laughed together in a natural and uninhibited way. Sometimes she caught him watching her before he dropped his gaze.

While Hugh described the shop in detail, Gwenna mapped out the layout. He told her the walls had previously been lined with shelves, and she was delighted to discover much of the furniture from the parlour was unscathed.

"Because your sideboard was against the wall, it didn't get damaged," said Hugh. "The counter is a little scratched, thanks to all the glass shards, but the jars on the shelves behind are all intact. Unfortunately, most of the glass domes, a few of the bowls and the mirror above the fireplace were all broken."

For the first time in weeks, someone had told her the truth about the state of the shop she had put her heart and soul into. But now she had an even better idea.

Gwenna didn't care about the broken glass. It could all be replaced. As long as the stock in the jars was usable. The fact she could salvage the counter and the sideboard were an added bonus. So, too, the tables and chairs. Hugh had repaired the leg on the table Gwenna had tipped over that night. "And I've built two more barrows. One for Charlie to use; it's a bit sturdier - good luck to any lads who try to smash it - and one other."

After a bit of questioning, Gwenna discovered the other one was for her - a daintier one for inside the shop, or she could put it outside for advertising.

"Mrs Griffiths had the signwriter do them professionally this time," said Hugh.

"So Tillie knows what you've been doing?"

Hugh grinned. "I had to explain it to someone. Mrs Evans and Mrs Price kept asking me where I was going all the time. Mrs Griffiths told them she was getting me to do work for her while you were laid up."

Dearest Tillie. She always had Gwenna's best interests at heart.

The question was, could they do it all within the remaining time frame?

"Gwenna, you're getting ahead of yourself," interrupted Tom as she babbled on about what she wanted done with the style and decoration, and how the sweets and Tillie's fudge should be displayed. "Just listen to me for a minute. I have the papers here to secure the lease if you've got your heart set on this place, but are you sure you're up to it?"

"We've got to give it a try, Tom. I promise I won't do anything more than say hello, and when I get tired, I'll go out the back for a rest." Her smile would have knocked another man off his feet, but Tom's raised eyebrow told Gwenna he knew her too well.

He had already seen Tillie and Hugh in action and could see they were in cahoots. Louisa wasn't any better. Charlie would have become a street crier given half a chance, and Bethan had started baking again too. He couldn't fight them all. Gwenna looked over the table at her resolute family and felt the luckiest woman in the world.

"Sign here," said Tom with a sigh. "I hope you all know what you're doing."

Laughter, claps and cheers greeted his words as they watched Gwenna put her name to the piece of paper that opened up her future again.

But for every step forward, there was one backward. The police had completed their investigations and found no evidence to charge anyone with the crime. No arrests had been made, and as far as they were concerned, the case was closed.

Why wouldn't they listen to her? Just because they couldn't prove anything didn't mean Black Jack hadn't smashed the place up. Gwenna railed against the police decision, angry the evil man would not get his just desserts, but more than that, she couldn't bear the thought he might come back one day.

She'd finally and reluctantly accepted that the Beresford Street house would never be used for her shop again, but she didn't like the idea of changing her living arrangements, even if the new shop came with upstairs accommodation. Discussions had gone round and round in circles while they debated what Gwenna should do for the best.

"It's worked so well here," said Gwenna, biting at the side of her fingernail. "You, Tillie and Olwen in your cottage next door, and Charlie between us. Me and Mam, and Louisa upstairs, and Hugh in the room at the back. I've loved every minute of it, but I'm fearful. When the repairs are done and the front parlour is restored to its former use, what happens if Black Jack returns and one of the children are in there and gets hurt."

"He won't," Tom assured her. "He wouldn't dare, not after what the police know."

She couldn't take the risk.

But there was a problem. The accommodation above the shop wasn't large enough to cater for the three women and Hugh. It was either Hugh on his own and the women stayed, or the house was sold and the women moved.

Hugh, naturally, had his own views. "You don't have to worry about me. I'll go back into digs somewhere."

None of the women were listening. They liked having Hugh around and overtalked each other making alternative suggestions. Even Charlie protested about them moving.

"Let's not rush into anything," advised Tom, trying to hush the conversation. "Let's finish the repairs first. If Hugh wants to, he can move into the accommodation above the shop while he's working there. We can sort out what's best when and if you decide to sell this property."

"Meanwhile, there's no time to lose," said Tillie, eager to get started. "We've got less than three weeks to make the place look like 'Gwenna's Superior Sweet Treats' all over again. Let's get started, everyone."

Everyone except Gwenna.

When Bethan joined her with a tray of tea things, Gwenna was reading the newspaper. Louisa had insisted someone stayed with Gwenna at all times to make sure she didn't attempt to leave the house to see what was going on.

"You can't be trusted," said Louisa, fussing over Gwenna's cushions and pillows and placing a rug over her knee. "Someone will bring you a daily update, but you're to stay put."

The scowl on Gwenna's face would have made a weaker person come up with a compromise, but Louisa would not give in. "It's for your own good, Gwenna. You have to be patient."

Patience was not one of Gwenna's strong points, but since everyone agreed with the doctor, she had little choice. She was glad of Bethan's company.

"They tell me the shelves have been checked," said

her mam. "And Hugh got a man to repair those that were a bit loose. It's a wonder they didn't fall down. You wouldn't want that to happen when they're full of sweet jars, now would you? Tillie says she's cleaned them all, and polished them, ready for the jars to be loaded. They look a treat, so I'm told."

Bethan poured the tea while Gwenna turned the page, half-listening. Sometimes Bethan explained too much.

"Hugh has been moving the stock across. He's such a good fellow. Don't you think? And so much fitter and healthier than when he came back from that dreadful war last year. Does he talk about it to you at all? I'm sure he must, the way he feels about you, but I can't get anything out of him. I have to say, the horse and cart do look smart. I think most of it's in the back room now."

Confused, Gwenna said, "Thanks," as Bethan handed her the teacup. She watched her mam with concern.

Bethan cleaned when worried about something she needed to sort out in her head, often becoming silent; she baked or cooked and made things when she felt happy, but everyone knew she was anxious when she talked incessantly.

"What's wrong, Mam? And what's in the back room?"

"The stock, of course, what else would I be talking about? It's been an awful grey day outside. They say the forecast for the next two weeks is not good. Early winter, they say."

"Yes, but what's troubling you, Mam? You're upset about something," urged Gwenna.

"It's nothing, Gwenna, *bach*. Just an old lady's foible. Don't worry about me, chook."

348

When Bethan refused to say anything further, Gwenna turned the page to the centre spread and the words 'Colliery Explosion' in large capital letters jumped out at her. *150 miners entombed.*

"Oh, Mam. There's been a terrible accident at the Caerphilly mine."

Bethan hurried over to sit beside Gwenna. "Oh, no. I've nephews who work in Caerphilly. Read it to me, Gwenna, *bach*. I can't bear it." Those boys she'd known were men now and, like many others, worked underground, taking the daily risk with their lives to feed their families. Bethan shuddered. New Zealand might not have handed them life on a platter, but no one here needed to risk their lives to put food on the table.

"It's dated the 24th," began Gwenna, "and says a gas explosion occurred in one of the large coal mines and completely closed the mouth of the pit." She scanned the article, paraphrasing as she went. "There were a hundred and fifty men below … none of them had any chance of escape. Rescue operations were promptly begun and they are doing their utmost to reach the miners, but it will take some time before they can get to them because of the large amount of ground that has caved in."

"We'll have to wait for further news," said Gwenna, taking hold of Bethan's hand. It was cold. "Maybe tomorrow or the next day before anything else comes through. I'm sorry, Mam."

Bethan collected her handkerchief and blew her nose. Tears were a waste when nothing could be done, she'd always said. Sometimes, being so far away made life hard for those eagerly awaiting news.

"Tell me more about the shop, Mam," asked Gwenna, wanting to distract Bethan from the accident. Upsetting as it was to hear about such a thing, life back home had little to do with them.

Through her sniffles, Bethan began. "The men Tom employed to paint the front will begin tomorrow if the weather is good enough. They say it will take three days at least, because of drying time. The signwriter will do his part when they've finished. I'm sorry, Gwenna, you'll have to excuse me."

Seeing Bethan so unhappy disturbed Gwenna too much for her to remain resting. She rushed after her stepmother, catching up with her in the kitchen where she sat in her usual armchair by the coal range, mopping up tears. Gwenna crouched down and put her arm around Bethan's shoulder. "Mam, what is it? You've been out of sorts worrying about something for ages. Won't you please tell me what it is?"

Mopping up another tear as it trickled down her face, Bethan took a deep breath. "I don't want to burden you, Gwenna dear. It's the thought my sister could lose her sons that's upset me. That's all."

"No, it isn't. You were upset before you knew about the mine accident. So there's more to it than what you are telling me. Please, Mam, tell me."

The profound anguish in Bethan's eyes nearly broke Gwenna's heart. Her own eyes glistened as she watched.

With a shuddering gasp, Bethan sighed. "I've been so afraid, Gwenna. Afraid I was going to lose you. First when Georgie was born and then again when you collapsed."

Gwenna started to say she was well now, but Bethan interrupted.

"I know you're better, but you're still not strong. I'm being a silly old woman, but I don't know what I'd do if I lost you."

"Oh, Mam. Nothing's going to happen to me. And Tillie and Tom, and Louisa, would take care of you if anything did – which it won't."

"I'm not worried about who would look after me, but how I would cope without you. Gwenna, you are so special. A daughter any mother would be proud to have. I love you so much, and my heart has been sorely tested as I've watched you struggle to survive, struggle to succeed, and struggle to overcome your own doubts. You are such a brave, wonderful girl. Don't ever doubt it, Gwenna, dear. But, I beg of you, don't overdo things to get this new shop of yours up and running. Don't make yourself ill again. Please, I beg you." Bethan burst into shoulder-shaking sobs.

If anything would slow Gwenna down, it was the sight of Bethan so heartbroken. Putting both arms around her stepmother, she swore she would take care of herself. "I promised Pa I would look after you, Mam, just like you've looked after me. I won't let you down."

As June 11th approached, the only news of note in the newspapers was the visit of the Duke and Duchess of Cornwall and York, His Royal Highness Prince George and Her Royal Highness Princess Mary. The weather forecast was not promising, and the authorities worried how they would manage the parades if it should rain, which was quite likely. June was never a good month, usually delivering cold, damp conditions, and this June was no exception.

In the few days since Gwenna had been allowed out, it had drizzled incessantly. After visiting the shop, she hurried home. Once inside the door, she removed her coat and bonnet, tutting at the floppy ribbons, and headed for the warmth of the fire in the dining room.

Over supper, Bethan announced, "I've received a telegram from my sister, who says both my nephews perished." She sniffed a little louder than normal, struggling to hold back her tears. "I can't say I knew them as men, but to lose two of your children is a terrible thing. I can't help feel for her loss."

The news was not a total surprise. The newspapers had since reported three men had been rescued, but more than seventy remained buried. The King had 'expressed his sympathy for the families and admiration for the gallant rescuers'.

Gwenna quietly placed her hand over Bethan's and squeezed. They had not spoken again of Bethan's fears, but Gwenna had been a model patient ever since. "I'm sorry, Mam," she whispered.

While the family sympathised, no one else had known the men concerned and had no appreciation of the choices they were forced to make on a daily basis. Once a miner, always a miner, and so on, for the sons and the sons of sons. Mining was a dangerous occupation, but those men had few options.

After a while, the conversation turned to more local matters, in particular the royal visit.

Once they'd settled in the sitting room after their meal, Gwenna picked up the newspaper. She had little interest in what the royal couple did in towns like Rotorua and Wellington but took an avid interest in their Auckland programme.

"They'll be bored to tears by the time they get past all the officials wanting to make endless speeches, but it says the procession will come along Queen Street, turn into Wellesley, up to Symonds Street then cut back through O'Rorke to Princes to take them to Government House," she said. "Pity they aren't coming up to Karangahape Road. Still, there'll be lots of visitors out and about. Let's hope the weather improves."

"That's a sight I'd like to see," said Bethan, intrigued by the idea of more than two-and-a-half-thousand children creating a living Union Jack in Philson Square outside the Municipal Buildings. "All those children dressed in colours and having to stand in just the right place to make themselves like a flag. How wonderful."

"You'd never get close enough to see, Mam," said Louisa. "Not with the archway, and the stand for all those pensioners, and the officials, let alone the actual procession. There'll be hundreds of soldiers with horses and carriages, and guards and bands and who-knows-what-else filling the streets, never mind the crowds. Don't know as I'd want to be in amongst all the nonsense."

"But Louisa, they are royalty. We have to go see them and welcome them," said Bethan, shocked anyone would think otherwise. "And while they're in mourning for Prince George's grandmother. It's so kind of them to visit at such sorrowful times."

"I'd be interested in going down at night to see the illuminations," said Tom, also reading about the programme. "They say the Herald Office will be lit up with electric light. Imagine that. A huge star shape lit with red, white and blue globes, and the South British Insurance Company are showing transparencies of portraits of the King and Queen and the Duke and Duchess. Searchlights will light up other buildings and 'Welcome to Maoriland' will be spelt out in electric light bulbs on the DS building. Along with the regular gas lighting and these extra displays, it should be magnificent, almost like daylight."

"Can I come and see too, Tom?" begged Charlie.

"Of course, you can. We can all go. It's a chance in a lifetime."

"None of this helps us, though, does it?" said Gwenna, biting her quick as she finished reading. The royal programme included a review of the troops, a military demonstration and the firing of cannons at Potter's Parade Ground. The duchess would also be laying the foundation stone at the Queen Victoria School in Parnell.

"What are you expecting?" asked Tom. "That she'll walk past the door and buy your sweets?"

Everyone laughed, except Gwenna, who got a certain glint in her eye when she was scheming. "What a good idea, Tom. I wonder how I could arrange it."

Only Hugh and Charlie took her seriously.

With a matter of days to spare before the SS *Ophir* carrying the royal couple arrived, Gwenna operated like a slave driver. She would have done more herself if she'd been able except Louisa's threats had been more effective, and no one gave her the chance. Gwenna resorted to sitting in a chair in the middle of the shop and giving orders, and on the Monday morning – a day ahead of the royal couple's arrival – they were ready to open for business.

The installation of mirrors along one side gave the shop a light, airy feel, and the glass jars flashed with colour on the shelves opposite. Tillie's fudge, once again, took pride of place under glass domes on the counter.

Initially, they would not serve teas as they had before, so only two tables were provided for those waiting to be served – Gwenna wanted to gauge what demand there was for refreshments in the new position. Instead, they would offer bottles of lemonade and ginger ale as those 'add-ons' Edward Turner had taught her about. Tillie pushed the dainty handcart, with its shelves and canopy, onto the street and parked it beside the entranceway.

Standing outside to admire her handiwork, Gwenna buzzed with excitement. Even she thought the window display was her best effort yet. After she'd studied other displays as she walked from home to the shop, and listened to advice from Tom, who'd collected tips from Smith & Caughey's window trimmer, she put her own ideas into practice.

The window display, with her use of various height boxes and carefully draped satin fabric, would entice the most discerning, and the risk she'd taken in painting the door and window frames in brick red against dark grey had paid off.

"I love it," she'd exclaimed, approving the matching sign along the verandah front.

"It's very smart," agreed Tillie. "Well done."

Up and down the street, bunting and flags flew from every shop, verandah and window, except Partington's windmill, now in a most dilapidated state but still a major landmark nevertheless. Tom told them Smith & Caughey's had turned royal from top to bottom in honour of their visitors.

The sense of relief and satisfaction that they had finished in time almost had Gwenna in tears again, but she fought them back. She would not cry. Not even with happiness. Those days where she had no control were

355

gone. All she needed now was customers.

She didn't have to wait long. Two of their regulars from the previous shop came in to congratulate them. "But I feel it only fair to warn you," said the older lady as they were leaving, "there are some I know who consider you far too young to be responsible enough to have your own business. Not me, of course," she hurried to assure Gwenna, "but the less you say about being the owner, the better, I feel."

Tillie, Louisa and Bethan stood alongside Gwenna and stared at the door where their two customers had just departed, almost too dismayed to say anything.

"Are people still that narrow-minded in this day and age?" asked Gwenna. "I'd never given it any thought."

"Nor me," admitted Bethan. "Even though it's obvious you haven't yet reached the age of majority."

"But widows have greater freedoms," said Louisa more hopefully.

As a wholesaler, her status didn't matter. She was trading under her father's name, and as long as she fulfilled the orders, no one had any complaints. It seemed being seen as 'the person in charge' in a retail environment was more than some people would tolerate, and shouting *Gwenna's* across the signage would not help.

"Is that why Beresford Street didn't work as I'd hoped?" Gwenna wondered. "People thought me too young. I don't feel young. Some days I feel as though I've lived two lifetimes already."

"Don't upset yourself, dear," warned Bethan.

Shaking away her misgivings, Gwenna muttered, "But there's nothing we can do about it."

"Yes there is," said Louisa. "Let Mam be seen as the owner. She is Mrs Price, George's widow. She can say it's called Gwenna's to fulfil your father's wish."

"That's not at all right, Louisa," argued Bethan. "Gwenna deserves all the credit. She's the one with the ideas and the skills. I'd never have done anything like this."

Her sisters ignored the thunderous scowl on Gwenna's face.

"Maybe not, Mam," coaxed Louisa, "but look at it this way: we need to win people back after the disaster at the house …"

"True, Mam. We do," added Tillie. "We can't take the risk of anything putting them off."

"You don't have to say anything that's not true," Louisa encouraged. "Just say you are Mrs Price and your daughter Gwenna is the sweet maker. Over time, it won't matter who the owner is. Meanwhile, I suggest you and I become the face of the shop, and Gwenna and Tillie can go home and do all the work." With a wink and a smile, her teasing was taken in the manner it was intended.

"I'm happy with that," Tillie agreed. "Gwenna isn't strong enough to do both yet, and I'll make enough fudge to match the sales. We're still not going to sell it wholesale, and I can give Mam a rest." Tillie put her arm around Bethan's shoulder. "You won't have to work every day, Mam."

Tillie turned to her sister. "Come on. Cheer up, Gwennie. It's not that bad. We'll have more time to spend with Olwen and Georgie. You'd like that, I know. And Charlie. He'll be happy as Larry running off with his handcart, and I can keep an eye on you and make sure you don't do too much. And you and Hugh are a great team."

The four women reached an agreement, putting Louisa in charge of the roster so the three of them took turns in the shop and Gwenna stayed at home. When she was stronger, and if the business took off as they believed it would, they could re-evaluate the situation. Gwenna still frowned at the suggestions, but at last Bethan saw the value in the arrangement.

At the sound of the bell tinkling above the door, the Price women turned to face the customer coming in. The woman stopped in her tracks in shock at the daunting effect of having four salespeople ready to serve her.

Bethan was the first to recover. "Thank you, girls," she said, waving them away, and walked towards the new customer. "Welcome to Gwenna's. I'm Mrs Price and my daughter Gwenna is the sweet maker. How may I help you?"

Dismissed from the shop, Tillie returned home to relieve Charlie of the job of minding the two little ones. School holidays or not, they couldn't leave him in charge for too long, even with Hugh within calling distance.

Gwenna said she wanted to check out the route of the next day's procession. "They'll be out rehearsing it all today, and I want to see how close we can get. It would be wonderful if Mam could see them."

She didn't mention her other idea to Tillie.

The morning of the royal visit, Gwenna and Hugh had a row – the only time in her life she could remember where they had disagreed so much it was difficult to speak coherently to one another.

"But Hugh, you must," insisted Gwenna.

"I'm not going and that's final."

"But you deserve it. You know you do."

"It's not a matter of whether I deserve it or not, Gwenna. It's the principle. Parading us all in front of the duke at Potter's ground and handing out medals to the contingents who went to South Africa is not the answer."

"Why not? You must tell me, Hugh. Why won't you accept the medal?"

"Gwenna, will you stop. I've told you often enough I don't want to talk about it. I will never talk about it, and neither will I accept their stupid medal."

Hugh grabbed his hat from behind the door and scuttled down the back steps from the kitchen and was out of sight before Gwenna could catch up.

She was about to chase after him when Charlie called her. "Where are we going with these handcarts, Gwenna?"

After walking the one-and-a-half-mile route from the shop to the wharf the afternoon before, Gwenna had come back bubbling with ideas. The streets had been adorned with ceremonial arches and lined with pennants and flags. Schoolchildren had made paper roses to be thrown during the procession, but she'd be disappointed to learn that plans for a display of Māori canoes in the harbour, as part of the welcome, had been suddenly cancelled. The one in the museum was magnificent, and she'd have loved to see the Māori in their canoes on the water.

She'd stood in awe of the display in Kohn's shop showing a pūriri mallet with a white maire handle and silver insert. But what impressed her most was the engraved, solid silver trowel with its polished greenstone handle, which the duchess would use when she laid the foundation stone at the Queen Victoria School for Maori Girls on Wednesday.

So much was happening in the town, with so many activities in so many places. Thousands of visitors would throng the streets; the newspapers wrote of little else. She had to be part of it.

She'd sent Charlie to the shop to collect her handcart with the curved sign fastened over the top and her name painted on both sides. Now, he was back, and she could do nothing about Hugh until later.

Together they filled both handcarts with specially printed bags full of sweets, plus dozens of lollipops of various sizes, and the more economical twists of paper filled with smaller, cheaper lollies. Charlie had a fistful of the trade cards she'd had reprinted with the new location, and so armed, the two of them headed off.

Well ahead of the time when the crowds would gather and long before the procession could be expected, Gwenna and Charlie positioned themselves on the Albert Park corner of Princes Street, opposite the Police Barracks. So far, the rain had not amounted to much, although Gwenna had covered the handcarts with thin, India rubber sheeting to protect them until the crowds arrived.

If all went well, they would see the duke and duchess pass under the grandly decorated archway by the library further down the street and still have time to move along to the corner with O'Rorke Street, where the procession would turn to approach Government House at the far end of Princes Street.

Huge crowds were expected at the start, where the officials were and where all the entertainment would take place. The Municipal Buildings would also attract a much larger crowd than towards the end, but it gave Gwenna space to manoeuvre. She'd not be able to come up with a plan where she could approach the duchess directly, but she'd had another idea.

If all went well, Hugh would capture a photograph of the royal carriage, the handcart and name sign – and Gwenna as she threw handfuls of sweets in the air hoping some would land in the royal carriage. If the newspapers didn't capture the moment, she could give them her photo, and with luck she'd make the headlines.

The proximity to the Police Barracks unnerved Gwenna a little. While she wasn't breaking any laws, if she obstructed the crowds or caused a commotion and attracted their attention, she didn't know what would happen. Neither was she certain she would achieve her aim. It all depended on Hugh. Except now she was worried he wouldn't come, after their row.

She longed to let Charlie stand on the O'Rorke Street corner by himself. That way they could guarantee to be in the right spot, but her concern people would hassle him or take advantage was greater and held her back. Theft was a likely possibility, but losing a few boiled sweets or lollipops didn't worry her as much as Charlie getting hurt again.

He would have to wait until they both moved into position, or Hugh arrived.

Charlie was in his element as a hawker and sold many of the lollies to passers-by and amongst those gathering to wait as the rain fell more heavily. Being small enough, he ducked under umbrellas with ease and squeezed between people to offer his wares. His cheeky, elfin grin won over many of the damp, impatient people.

"Tickle your insides with sweet and tasty treats from Gwenna's," he called. "Ward off the dreaded sniffles with Gwenna's cherry menthol, mint humbugs or aniseed balls."

Charlie could rattle off every sherbert, boiled lolly, hard jube, soft pastille, toffee and brittle that Gwenna made and often gave them unique names, names she then used in the shop.

Gwenna had tried her best to make sure the whole family would have a chance to see the procession, but there were some things beyond her control. She'd told Louisa and Bethan to shut the shop at one o'clock so they could join Tillie and the children to watch. That's if Louisa came – she'd insisted she had no time for royalty and intended to keep the shop open. Gwenna hadn't bothered to argue.

Gwenna could do nothing to help Tom either, who would be lucky to get away from the counter, but the management had promised staff they would see the parade – if only for a few moments.

Standing on the corner, Gwenna could see a large number of children gathering further down Wellesley Street. Seeing the way they were dressed, she realised they would be the living flag children.

"Charlie," she called. "Quick, leave your cart here with mine and run to the shop. Tell Mam to come now. Quick as you can, lad. Never mind the others, they'll manage. Tell her she'll be able to see the children's flag if she does."

Charlie ran off through the lanes and up Liverpool Street, returning half an hour later with a harried and somewhat bedraggled Bethan clutching her hat, an umbrella tucked under her arm.

Gwenna kissed her mother's cheek. "Sorry to hurry you so much, Mam, but look. There." Gwenna pointed lower down and across the street. "You said you wanted to see the children. If you stand your ground here you'll see the duke and duchess pass and, with luck, the procession won't block your view of the children."

An infectious anticipation grew as time passed. Music could be heard in the distance, and people happily chatted with strangers, bunched up as they were under umbrellas. Charlie continued to duck and dive everywhere, returning to the carts when he needed another handful of lollipops or to stuff his pockets with twists.

After the long wait, the mood shifted and tension mounted as people bumped against each other, jostling for the best view. At long last, the parade leaders came into sight. Captain Reid, resplendent in his uniform, came first, followed by two companies of Mounted Rifles, several other mounted officers and outriders, and two carriages carrying people Gwenna did not know. If the heightened noise coming up the street was anything to go by, the royal carriage was approaching. The crowds cheered, hats and handkerchiefs waving.

Gwenna panicked for a moment when she couldn't see Charlie, but then she spotted him through the crowd. When or how he'd got across to the other side of the road she would never know, but he stood comparatively alone next to her cart.

"I can't see the children any more," Bethan protested, rising on tiptoes to get a better view.

About to point towards the royal carriage, where the duke stood facing forward, in uniform, and the duchess, dressed in black holding an umbrella, sat on the other side, Gwenna saw Bethan erupt from the crowd and run across the road in front of the horses.

Gwenna started to follow, intending to pull her back from harm's way, but by then Bethan was standing in the road on the other side of the carriage admiring the living Union Jack in all its glory. Ignoring the rain, and clasping her hands in front of her in glee, Bethan was unaware of the commotion she had caused.

Amid shouts, the rattle of harness, whinnying horses and commands to 'stop', the driver pulled the carriage to a standstill. Gwenna took her chance. To her amazement, Charlie had rushed to Bethan's aid too, pushing her small handcart in front of him.

The three of them stood in the middle of the road – effectively in the middle of the procession, a yard or so from the royal carriage – with Gwenna's name emblazoned at the top of the cart for all to see. Quick-thinking Charlie grabbed several bags of the best and most expensive sweets and ran towards the duchess. An escort rider tried to block his way, but Charlie was too slick.

His young voice could be heard clearly. "Sorry if my mam scared you, duchess. She's so excited to see you. Would you like some of Gwenna's sweets to make up for it?"

The world around them seemed to stop. Gwenna inched towards Charlie, hoping the man on the horse wouldn't push her to one side, but she had to get Charlie away from the carriage before he was arrested or ... or something. She couldn't even begin to imagine what they'd do to a nine-year-old boy.

From nowhere, men with cameras appeared and flashes went off in all directions.

"Who is Gwenna?" asked an English voice, accepting Charlie's proffered bags.

"My sister." Charlie turned his head to see if he could find her. "Here she is. She makes Gwenna's Sweet Treats."

A soggy Gwenna blushed from head to toe as Charlie pointed and all eyes fell on her. She bobbed a curtsy. "I do apologise, Your Royal Highness." She hissed at Charlie. "Come here, Charlie." The duchess nodded in response.

By this time, the guards had dismounted and briskly escorted Gwenna, Bethan and Charlie off the road, while another pushed the handcart out of the way. The procession carried on its way without a backward glance, and Gwenna breathed a sigh of relief they hadn't been taken to the police barracks and thrown in the cells.

The whole event had taken no more than a couple of minutes.

Bethan's eyes bulged like those of a frightened rabbit, Charlie grinned from ear to ear, he was that pleased with himself, and Gwenna couldn't scold either of them. The handcart had tipped over and the remaining sweets scattered on the ground were soon picked up by passing opportunists. Gwenna didn't care.

Nothing had turned out as she planned, but what a story they had to tell. One that would be handed down from generation to generation.

※※※※※※※

38

HOPE REIGNS SUPREME

September 1901

Not long after dawn, Gwenna bounded down the stairs, full of the joys of spring. In the three months since the royal visit, life had turned around, thanks in no small part to their adventure.

The *Auckland Weekly News* was quick to print the photographs of Gwenna curtsying, Charlie handing a package to the duchess, Bethan behind the handcart and Gwenna's name clearly readable. The captions were in awe of a little boy who'd been brave enough to talk to the duchess. Brave wasn't how Gwenna described him – more like reckless and foolhardy.

The affair with the duchess had become the talk of the town, and everyone wanted to see for themselves what all the fuss was about. Stories began circulating about who had seen what; the press interviewed her, and the event grew in people's minds.

The publicity proved advantageous, and the uniformed equerry attracted a lot more attention as he rode along Karangahape Road to deliver a missive from the duchess herself. The handwritten note on royal paper was brief:

Please thank your young brother for presenting me with Gwenna's sweets, which are some of the finest I've tasted. I will remember the occasion with fondness.

HRH Princess Mary, Duchess of Cornwall and York

Gwenna framed the newspaper cuttings and the handwritten note, and displayed them prominently in the window. But the photograph she treasured the most and kept to herself was the one Hugh had taken. He had been there after all.

In the days following, Mam and Louisa performed miracles in the shop while Gwenna, Hugh and Tillie were at a stretch to keep up with the sweet and fudge making. Although they praised Gwenna, in her view, Bethan's and Louisa's engaging way with the customers was responsible for their burgeoning success. By the end of the month, custom had eased to more manageable levels but word had got around and they had orders to fill for weeks ahead. 'Gwenna's' had become a fixture.

The new location was ideal, even with the disruptions caused by men digging up the road in preparation for the expected arrival of the electric trams the following year. Progress is what Johnno would have called it, and while Gwenna would miss the horse trams, she liked the idea of the car she'd seen being driven around town. Maybe, one day, she would own one.

To top off Gwenna's joy, her health was back to normal. The doctor confirmed she was as fit as any young woman should be, which she put down to three things: love, happiness and success.

How could she not respond to the love everyone

showered on her? Which, in turn, gave her the happiness she'd sought but had never opened herself up to. Gone was the anxiety attached to failure and with it returned the enjoyment of life. She was putting on weight and looked as happy as she felt.

Adding to her happiness was Georgie, toddling around and getting into endless mischief with his inquisitive nature, but all he had to say was 'Mam' and he was forgiven.

Bethan was delighted. "It does my heart good to see you recovered, Gwenna. I worried needlessly, it seems, and now your chance has come, my dear. Together, you and Hugh will make something of the business now."

Misinterpreting Bethan's words, Gwenna agreed it was indeed wonderful to have Hugh back. She still had to sort out the living arrangements but that was minor in the scheme of things, and she had been considering that she might need extra staff who could use the accommodation above the shop.

Sharing in her happiness was Alice. "Congratulations, Gwenna," she said, hugging everyone in turn. "I'm so happy for you." She had news too.

She and Elias had found a new workshop and showroom premises in Newmarket, with rooms for Woody above. "And the most delightful cottage for Eli and me, with a picket fence and a garden, a bit out of town. I've painted the nursery pale lemon, but I'm hoping for a little girl," confessed a blushing Alice, glowing with health and pride, anticipating the baby's arrival. "First week of November, I'm told."

But above everything else making Gwenna almost light-headed with glee … the books showed a substantial profit.

As the weeks passed, Louisa's skill with people exceeded Gwenna's expectations, and Bethan's warm nature and ability to chat had won over many who might otherwise have considered Gwenna an upstart. Tillie's fudge was a major drawcard, and Bethan had started to make teas and hot chocolate again, allowing the ladies to sit and enjoy their fudge in a convivial atmosphere. Gwenna would have liked more space for the refreshment area, but it would do for now.

And then there was Hugh.

He'd become so much a part of the fabric of her life she couldn't imagine being without him. He was still as quiet as he'd always been, and when the whole family got together he made excuses, saying he had no place being there. Gwenna didn't agree, of course, but had long since stopped arguing.

Many times she'd tried to analyse her feelings for him, which were entirely different to what she felt for Tom - dear Tom, whom she loved and respected as a brother - and in no way replicated how she had once felt, a long time ago, for Johnno.

Over the years Bethan had tried to tell her that something more than loyalty kept Hugh by her side. While Gwenna ignored that possibility, she had come to rely on him more than she could say. She trusted him to protect what was important to her and cherish her dreams, and she valued his opinion on anything to do with the making of the sweets, even the packaging designs and his ideas about distribution. Theirs was a friendship beyond compare.

Intending to stoke the fire into life and put the large kettle on to boil before Bethan arose, she opened the kitchen door.

She was startled to find Hugh standing across from her, framed in the outside doorway. For a few moments neither of them moved, separated by the kitchen where they spent most of their time together, each trying to guess what the other was thinking.

He held a suitcase.

"Where are you going?" she asked.

"Gwenna ... I'm sorry. I'd planned ..." Hugh struggled to find the right words. "I can't ..." and turned his head away from her.

Gwenna's heart plunged and a sharp, metallic taste burned the back of her throat. "Are you leaving me?" asked Gwenna, her voice rising in panic. "Leaving the business, I mean? Is that what you're saying?"

A soft smile relaxed the lines on his face, that was as familiar to her as her own.

"You'll always be with me, Gwenna, wherever I go."

He was leaving.

The punch of reality struck Gwenna as hard as a physical blow. Bethan's words rang in her ears: 'You'll lose him one day if you don't wake up, girl.'

Gwenna turned the gold band on her finger round and round. She should have taken it off a long time ago. It didn't mean what it once had, and it bound her to the past when she wanted a future. But she hadn't.

Hugh watched her fingers fret over the ring.

The silence lengthened and Gwenna trembled as her agitation rose. "Why ..." she began, her voice so croaky she needed to clear it before she could speak again. She pointed to the suitcase.

Hugh looked down at the leather bag as if he'd forgotten he was still holding it, or as though it would provide the answer to the question. The intensity in his eyes held

Gwenna's, but with his back to the light, she couldn't read the message.

"It's not my place to speak, Gwenna. Not now. It wouldn't be fair."

"Let me be the judge of that," she said, speaking far more sharply than she intended.

The muscles in his face tensed. He gritted his teeth and remained silent.

"Speak, Hugh," she begged. "Please. Where are you going?"

He put the suitcase on the floor and crossed the distance between them. Taking her left hand in his, he placed his thumb over the ring on her finger.

"This is why I can't speak, Gwenna. It gives you freedom, but you are also bound by it. To it. And because of it, I can't live and work beside you, day in day out, any longer. I have to go."

People believed a heart could burst, and, if the noise in her head and the thumping, pounding heaviness in her chest was any indication, then hers was about to explode.

"Why? What have I done?" Her eyes shone with the fervour of every emotion she couldn't begin to put a name to.

"You've done nothing. It's me who is in the wrong." Hugh dropped her hand and wiped his hands down the sides of his trousers. "Let me go, Gwenna, before I say too much."

She reached out and grabbed his arm, wanting to say the words of love that sprang unbidden to the tip of her tongue. "No, Hugh. You can't go ... Please, I ..."

He removed her hand from his arm and held it lightly in his own. "Gwenna, you can do anything you want to in this world, with or without me. Or anyone else, for that matter." His smile broke her heart a little further. "I've watched you develop from a damaged little girl into a determined woman; your class and style sets you as far above me as the stars. And out of my reach."

Gwenna tried to calm the panic inside and make sense of it all. "You're wrong, Hugh. Whatever it is you're trying to say, you're wrong. I would be nothing without you. I'm still that little girl inside, scared I'll fail ..."

Hugh laughed. He actually laughed. When her world was collapsing, he laughed. The sound echoed around the room and in her head – a joyous sound, one that would normally lift her up but today tore her apart.

"My dearest girl. You are so wrong. You are the strength that holds everyone together. Don't you see? You believed it could be done and you did it. You will pass your father's legacy to your son, as you've always dreamed, but until you do that, there is no room in your heart for anything – or anyone – else."

He raised her hand to his lips and kissed it while staring at her, staring in the same way she had once gazed at Johnno, trying to etch his every feature on her memory. "Stay, Hugh. Stay. Please. I can't do it without you. Don't leave me."

Moments passed while their eyes remained locked. Hugh's desolate, hers beseeching.

"I can't, Gwenna, my love. I can't stay. Not without hope. I've loved you from afar for too long. I can't do it any longer."

Her childlike sobs filled the silence.

He picked up his suitcase. "One day you'll understand."

A moment later he was gone.

"I love you," she whispered – too late for him to hear.

She stood frozen, her mind swirling, while her heart splintered. She'd lost the one person who mattered to her the most. Without her realising it, Hugh had become as essential to her as breathing. She couldn't imagine a life without him.

Twisting the ring from her finger, she stared at the empty place where he had stood and vowed to win him back.

⦿⦿⦿⦿⦿⦿⦿

EPILOGUE

FROM THE NEWSPAPERS

BLACK JACK JONES GETS HIS COMEUPPANCE

AT THE COURTS
3 March 1902

Mr John Jones, otherwise known as Black Jack Jones,
carter of Onehunga, was today found guilty, as charged,
with numerous breaches of the Money-lenders Act
1901 and of acquiring moneys by illegal means.

He will be sentenced next month to an expected
term of not less than two years' imprisonment and a
fine of £500.

COMING OF AGE

SOCIETY NEWS
18 April 1902

Mrs Gwenna Price of G Price and Family Confectioners,
was seen at the Savoy Dining Room, in Queen Street,
celebrating her twenty-first birthday.

The supper party guests included her family: Mrs

Bethan Price, Mr Elias Hughes and Mrs Alice Hughes, Mrs Louisa Evans, Mr Percy Lewis and Mrs Janetta Lewis.

Notable business guests included Mr Edward Turner and Mrs Maude Turner, Mr John McKail Geddes and Mrs Annabella Geddes, and Mr & Mrs Ernest Yates.

Surprise guest was Mr Hugh Powell, recently returned to the business after an absence.

GWENNA CELEBRATES

BUSINESS NEWS
1 September 1902

Mrs Gwenna Price of G Price & Family Confectioners is delighted to announce Mr Hugh Powell has returned to the business and will take up his new position as General Manager as of today.

THANK YOU

If you enjoyed this book, discover more unforgettable family heritage stories inspired by immigrants seeking a better life in a foreign land.

THE NEW ZEALAND IMMIGRANT COLLECTION
suspenseful family saga fiction about overcoming the odds.

The Cornish Knot
Portrait of a Man

Brigid The Girl from County Clare
Gwenna The Welsh Confectioner
The Costumier's Gift

The Disenchanted Soldier

* * *

Available at
Amazon.com/vickyadin
www.vickyadin.co.nz

Please consider leaving a customer review.
I'd be delighted if you would sign up for my newsletter
on my website.

* * *

Look out for the upcoming series
THE ART OF SECRETS –
dual-timeline stories about discovering your roots.
First book *The Art of Secrets* available now.

The Costumier's Gift

An absorbing multigenerational dual-timeline family saga

Why does a stranger hold the key to untangling Katie's family secrets?

Continues the lives of *Brigid The Girl from County Clare* and *Gwenna The Welsh Confectioner*

Jane thrives in the one place where she can hide her pain and keep her skeletons to herself. As principal costumier at Auckland's Opera House in its Edwardian heyday, she is content – until the past comes back to haunt her.

Her beloved foster mother Brigid and her best friend Gwenna are anchors in her solitary yet rewarding life. When the burden of carrying secrets becomes too great, Jane surrenders her role as keeper of the untold.

Generations later Katie seeks refuge from her crumbling life with her Granna, who lives in the past with the people in her cherished photographs. Katie discovers she must identify the people behind the gentle smiles and reveal generations of secrets before she can claim her inheritance.

Through Jared, an intriguing new client, Katie revives her stalled career until she learns he holds the key to uncovering her past. Despite an increasing attraction, she shies away from any deeper involvement ... but without him she will never know the truth.

THE NEW ZEALAND IMMIGRANT COLLECTION

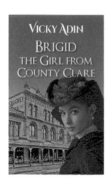

Brigid
The Girl from County Clare

The heart-rending tale of Irish immigration in the 1880s

Like making lace – she pieced together a new life from a single thread of hope

Counterpart to *Gwenna The Welsh Confectioner*
Prequel to *The Costumier's Gift*

Eighteen-year-old Brigid faces an unimaginable choice. If she stays in her beloved Ireland, she is another mouth to feed in a land plagued by starvation and poverty. If she leaves, she will never see her family again. But leave she must.

Heartbroken, she travels by ship with her cousin Jamie to a new life in Australia. On the journey, Brigid meets a rough-and-ready Scots girl who becomes her best friend, a man who beguiles her, and a fellow Irishwoman who causes no end of trouble.

Brigid's skill as a lacemaker soon attracts attention, but it is her selfless nature that draws people to her. When the burden of choice is forced upon her once again, Brigid must find an inner strength if she is to fulfil her dream.

A new start in New Zealand offers hope – until the day she encounters the man who seeks her downfall.

The historical aspects of the story are so accurate and described so perfectly that the reader will frequently need to remind herself/ himself that the story is fiction ... This is a thoroughly satisfying read. It is the kind of story that passes the test as a work of history, and is equally satisfying as a novel that will have your attention from first to last. **** 4 stars – Frank O'Shea, *The Irish Echo*, Sydney

THE NEW ZEALAND IMMIGRANT COLLECTION

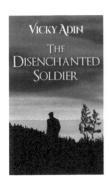

The Disenchanted Soldier

A heart-breaking dual-timeline family saga

From soldier to pacifist

In 1863, young Daniel Adin, a trained British soldier, embarks on an adventure of a lifetime. In pursuit of a new life and land to farm, he travels to New Zealand to fight an unknown enemy – the fearless Māori.

A hundred and thirty years later, Libby is fascinated by the stories of Daniel as he looks down at her from the aged black-and-white photos on the wall. Surrounded by four generations of his large family, she wants to know more, to know what he was really like.

As she researches his past, Daniel's story becomes so much more than she expected.

I loved this book and so will you if you like historical fiction and family sagas set somewhere you likely know little about. This is beautifully and sensitively written. The characters are terrific. The fascinating part to me was how Vicky was able to take us on the family's journey in a thoughtful and non-judgmental way.

***** 5-star Amazon review

THE NEW ZEALAND IMMIGRANT COLLECTION

The Cornish Knot

One woman's emotional quest to discover her family roots

Can one woman's secrets change the life of another a century later?

Prequel to *Portrait of a Man*

A grieving widow, a century old journal, a missing portrait, and an engaging art historian. What will the secrets of the past reveal?

When Megan receives a journal written a century earlier, she sets out on an irresistible path. Following in the footsteps of the diary's author, Megan journeys from her home in New Zealand to Cornwall, France and Italy, uncovering an unsettling past. She meets a fellow countryman in Florence and is soon caught up in the aesthetic world of art where the truth lies hidden beneath the layers of paint.

Charmed by the man her daughter disapproves of, and captivated by a series of unknown paintings, Megan is drawn deeper into the mysteries and conflicts of long ago. As she unravels her family history and reveals its life-changing secrets, can she find love again?

An engaging tale of grief, loss, love and family intrigue ... wonderful story, and a real page-turner, which leads the reader through all the twists and turns of a well-constructed plot. I loved the insightful descriptions of family relationships, the fully realised characters and the various locations in which the action takes place. Seldom have I read such a poignant and faithful account of the effects of bereavement. I can't wait to read more. **** 4-star Amazon review

THE NEW ZEALAND IMMIGRANT COLLECTION

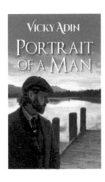

Portrait of a Man

The gripping multigenerational tale of lies, lost chances and misplaced love.

Will the secrets of the past destroy an artist's legacy?

The soul-searching conclusion to *The Cornish Knot*

An Italian artist, a Cornish knot and a Māori koru lead to a shocking exposé. As World War One escalates, can he keep his secrets safe?

In 1863, Matteo Borgoni is a desperate man. If he is to free his beloved wife held captive by her father in Melbourne, his picture framing business must succeed. Haunted by the memory of failure, he has many obstacles to overcome before he can establish himself with the artists of Dunedin, New Zealand and be reunited with his love.

Fifty years on, Luciano, a rakish Italian portrait artist fleeing from a life of lies, turns up at Borgoni Picture Framers seeking refuge. As the ravages of World War One escalate, an unusual friendship and newfound rapport brings unforeseen repercussions. A terrifying pandemic is the last thing they need.

Over a century later, a man recognises a portrait in an Auckland gallery, and demands it back. Amid another global pandemic, a marriage on the brink of failure, and a life-and -death struggle, the portrait exposes generations of family secrets and deceptions with life-changing results.

Portrait of a Man is told over three timelines through the eyes of different generations.

THE NEW ZEALAND IMMIGRANT COLLECTION

The Art of Secrets

An uplifting tale of friendship, grief and lies.

Emma wants to forget; Charlotte never can. Together they remember.

First in the upcoming series THE ART OF SECRETS

A young journalist and an ageing author have little in common, until their secrets tear them apart.

Emma is an enterprising young journalist with a bright future, but her life and career are falling apart. In a last-ditch attempt to save her position, she accepts the assignment to interview the bestselling author, Charlotte Day.

The ageing Charlotte has a reputation for being cantankerous and is highly secretive about her past, one she considers too painful to relive and too shameful to share. Preferring her roses to people, she grudgingly agrees to meet this girl who gets through her defences, forcing her to confront her past.

As Charlotte and Emma's relationship deepens, they become enmeshed in a tangle of secrets that changes their lives.

The art of great writing! ... Adin keeps a tight rein on her leading characters, their actions and reactions credibly grounded in genuine emotions. The change of tone from Emma to Charlotte, from young to old, works, helps the reader see behind the lies and half-truths they tell each other. Their progress from antagonists to friends is seamless, as the layers of the story peel back like petals, exposing the truth at the flower's heart. Bev Robitai, author of *Sunstrike*

Book 1 of THE ART OF SECRETS series

Vicky Adin is a family historian in love with the past. Like the characters in her stories, she too is an immigrant to New Zealand, arriving a century after her first protagonists, and ready to start a new life.

Born in Wales, she grew up in Cornwall until aged 12. Her family emigrated to New Zealand, a country she would call home. Vicky draws on her affinity for these places, in her writing. Fast forward a few years, and she marries a fourth-generation Kiwi bloke with Irish, Scottish and English ancestors and her passion for genealogy flourishes.

The further she digs into the past, the more she wants to record the lives of the people who were the foundations of her new country. Not just her own ancestors, but all those who braved the oceans and became pioneers in a raw new land. Her research into life as it was for those immigrants in the mid-to-late 1800s and early 1900s gave her enough material to write for many years about the land left behind and the birth of a new nation.

Her first book, *The Disenchanted Soldier*, is the most biographical of all her books, inspired by her husband's great-grandfather. For the rest, while the history of the time is accurate, the characters are fictionalised to fit with the events and happenings as they occurred.

Vicky holds an MA(Hons) in English, is a lover of art, antiques, gardens, good food and red wine. She and her husband travel throughout New Zealand in their caravan and travel the world when they can. She hopes younger generations get as much enjoyment learning about the past through her stories, as she did when writing about it.

AUTHOR'S NOTE

The story of *Gwenna* is inspired by the real-life history of my Welsh great-grandmother.

St James's Church in Wellington Street no longer exists. It should not be confused with Hopetoun Alpha in Beresford Street, which was also once known as St James Presbyterian Church. The location of the original St James's Church is where the pōhutukawa sculpture sits at the junction of the Southern Motorway at the top of Hobson Street.

The construction of the Southern Motorway changed many of the streets mentioned in the story, most of which are no longer accessible in the same way. Beresford Street was cut in half and Nelson Street shortened, amongst others. North Street changed its name several times but is now known as Galatos Street. West Street is now a no-exit, narrow lane squeezed next to the motorway overbridge.

Partington's Mill, a major landmark of the time, used by ships as a marker, was demolished in 1950, one hundred years after its construction. The Historic Places Trust was formed in 1957 as a result.

O'Rorke Street has been absorbed into the University of Auckland grounds, as has the original Government House.

The Auckland Domain is the oldest park in Auckland. Western Park was one of the first parks, and opened in November 1879. Myers Park, by comparison, did not come into existence until 1915.

The Auckland Town Hall was built in 1907, and the central markets moved to an area by the railway station in the early 1900s. Edward Turner and his family went on to be known as Turners and Growers Ltd, Fresh Fruit and Vegetable Auctioneers.

The dates of the Auckland Industrial and Mining Exhibition were adjusted to fit the story. The exhibition took place from December 1898 to February 1899. There is no evidence to show a repeat exhibition was held the following year, as suggested. The next Auckland exhibition was not held until 1913-14, but other exhibitions in Wellington, Canterbury and Otago took its place in the interim.

The online 1908 map of Auckland City provided by Auckland Council proved an invaluable reference tool.

bach – *barkh* – little one

cwtch – *cootsh/cutsh* – a special cuddle/a safe place

bara brith – fruit cake

Karangahape Road – *car-rarng-a-har-peh*

www.kroad.com/heritage/the-meaning-of-karangahape/

karapapa – *cah-rarpa-pah* – a native plant belonging to the honeysuckle family

kauri – *kho-ree* – extremely tall New Zealand native tree

maire – *my-ree* – New Zealand native tree

pōhutukawa – *po-hoo-too-car-wah* – New Zealand native tree with red flowers that bloom in summer. It is often referred to as the New Zealand Christmas tree as it flowers in December. Early flowering often means a great summer.

pūriri – *poor-ree-ree* – New Zealand native tree

rimu – *ree-moo* – New Zealand native tree with weeping fronds

shent-per-shent men – loan sharks

REFERENCE TOOLS

Archives

http://archives.govt.nz/events

Auckland Council – 1908 map

http://www.aucklandcity.govt.nz/dbtw-wpd/
CityArchives/1908Map/browse1908map.htm

Auckland Library – Heritage Images

http://www.aucklandcity.govt.nz/dbtw-wpd/HeritageImages/
index.htm

K Road Heritage

http://www.kroad.com/heritage/timeline-of-k-road/

Old Auckland Facebook

https://www.facebook.com/OldAuckCity/?fref=ts

Papers Past – Caerphilly Disaster

COLLIERY EXPLOSION. Auckland Star, Volume XXXII,
    Issue 123, 25 May 1901

https://paperspast.natlib.govt.nz/newspapers/
    AS19010525.2.41?query=caerphilly

Papers Past – New Year 1900 New Century 1901

The FRETFUL PORCUPINE, *Observer*, Volume XXI, Issue
    1149, 5 January 1901

https://paperspast.natlib.govt.nz/newspapers/
    TO19010105.2.16?query=new%20century

Papers Past – The Children's Living Union Jack

https://paperspast.natlib.govt.nz/newspapers/
    AS19010610.2.36.7?query=royal%20visit%20living%20
    Union%20Jack

Papers Past – The Welsh Colliery Disaster

Auckland Star, Volume XXXII, Issue 124, 27 May 1901

https://paperspast.natlib.govt.nz/newspapers/
    AS19010527.2.49.5?query=caerphilly

Te Ara – The Encyclopedia of New Zealand

http://www.teara.govt.nz/en

The New Zealand Herald

www.nzherald.co.nz

Timespanner

http://timespanner.blogspot.co.nz/

https://www.facebook.com/Timespanner/?fref=ts

ACKNOWLEDGEMENTS

My thanks go to my trusted group of supporters: the beta-readers, the editing team and the people who rescue me from my foibles – including my family who remember to feed me when I've forgotten how to cook, and my friends who remind me I need to talk with real people sometimes. You know who you are, and if I name one, I'm bound to miss another. So thank you everyone.

For this book, I owe a special thanks to Lisa Truttman, of Timespanner Blogspot, who pointed me towards information I needed and kept me supplied with old photographs. Hayden Oswin and Bill Gibson-Patmore on Pinterest were also most helpful in providing links to copyright and images they owned.

Thanks, too, to Auckland Library Heritage images who gave me permission to use an early photo of Auckland for the cover design.

Made in United States
Troutdale, OR
08/27/2023

12388488R00219

"The real voyage of discovery consists not in seeking new landscapes, but in having new eyes," said Marcel Proust. During this voyage of discovery to a Secret Naples, Valerio Ceva Grimaldi and Maria Franchini achieve this small miracle: they offer us a new way of looking, leaving us under the spell of the ancient city of the Siren. A revelation for tourists, for all those unfamiliar with Naples, but also for Neapolitans, who'll be able to rediscover themselves and their identity. I've always thought that we Italians are both lucky and a little lazy, the beauty of our artistic cities being rather too familiar. A beauty that we shouldn't take for granted, but rediscover every day. Because beauty lessens our daily concerns and will finally redeem the world.

The co-authors of this invaluable guide (in collaboration with the Geositi project of Napoli Servizi – Comune di Napoli) thus take us by the hand to lead us on a mysterious journey into the belly of Naples, its grottoes, passages, crevices, cisterns, a curious labyrinth in the style of Escher. I must admit that I too have discovered unlikely things. The levels of meaning, the layers that make up Naples, probably have no equivalent: a porous city, it has absorbed a thousand cultures, a thousand suggestions, a thousand styles – Baroque, Gothic, Oriental. Naples must be decrypted. This is an intelligible though esoteric process: like the symbols engraved on the diamond-point projections of the church of Gesù Nuovo or the alchemical mysteries of Raimondo di Sangro, Prince of Sansevero. An atmosphere not only magical but almost pagan, as borne out by the cult of the *capuzzelle* at the church of Santa Maria del Purgatorio ad Arco or at the Fontanelle, but also deeply spiritual and Christian. Naples succeeds in synthesising opposing and pluralistic traditions to compose a unique and fascinating mosaic wherein the pieces are all different. Welcome to the city of which I'm mayor!

Luigi de Magistris
Mayor of Naples

Valerio Ceva Grimaldi Pisanelli di Pietracatella, 38, belongs to an old noble Neapolitan family. A journalist by profession, he worked on the staff of the governor of the Province of Naples, Professor Amato Lamberti, then for the Assessorato all'Ambiente del Comune di Napoli. He also spent two years with Rai TV's *Gap* programme. He was editor-in-chief of the newspaper *Notizie Verdi* and deputy editor of *Terra*, the first environmental daily with a wide distribution. He has published numerous articles and surveys on the City of Naples.
If you would like to visit some of the places in the guide, accompanied by the author, e-mail him at: cevagrimaldi@gmail.com.

Maria Franchini, who has been a guide and lecturer on the monuments of Campania for fifteen years, was born in Naples. A journalist and the author of several books, she is passionate about Neapolitan culture and is also a specialist in Roman civilisation. She works for the Italian Cultural Centre in Paris, where she runs courses in the Neapolitan language, gives lectures and organizes seminars on her favourite subjects.
http://www.sgdl-auteurs.org/maria-franchini/index.php/
maria.franchini@wanadoo.fr

We have taken great pleasure in drawing up
Secret Naples and hope that through its guidance
you will, like us, continue to discover unusual,
hidden or little-known aspects of the city.
Descriptions of certain places are accompanied
by thematic sections highlighting historical details
or anecdotes as an aid to understanding the city in
all its complexity.
Secret Naples also draws attention to the multitude
of details found in places that we may pass every
day without noticing. These are an invitation to look
more closely at the urban landscape and, more
generally, a means of seeing our own city with
the curiosity and attention that we often display
while travelling elsewhere ...

Comments on this guidebook and its contents,
as well as information on places we may not have
mentioned, are more than welcome and will enrich
future editions.
Don't hesitate to contact us:
• Éditions Jonglez, 17, boulevard du Roi,
   78000 Versailles, France
• E-mail: info@jonglezpublishing.com

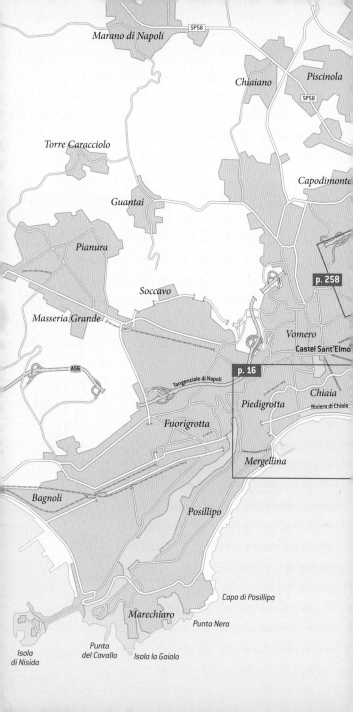

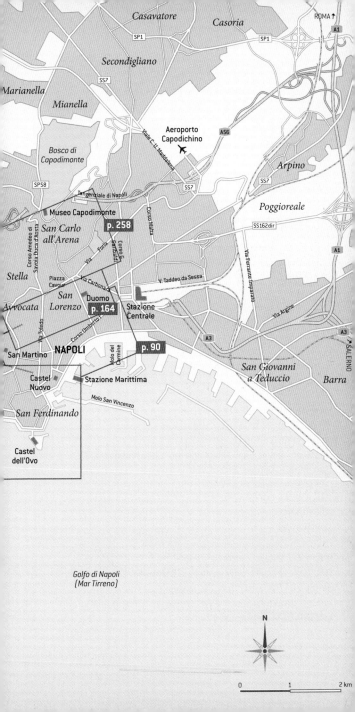

CONTENTS

MERGELLINA, CHIAIA, SAN FERDINANDO

Kayak tours. 18
The cursed villa of Gaiola 19
Is Virgil behind the curse? 19
Ospizio Marino 21
Brother Ludovico da Casoria, an extraordinary character 21
Villa Doria d'Angri 23
Naval Museum of the "Parthenope" University of Naples 23
The devil of Mergellina. 24
Jacopo Sannazaro (1457–1530): the poet of *Arcadia* 25
Epitaph on Virgil's tomb. 27
"Poetry trees" in Virgil's honour 27
Virgil, poet and magician 28
Symbolism of the Crypta Neapolitana 29
When Our Lady lost her shoe: why is Santa Maria di Piedigrotta
so called? 30
Cinderella was born in Naples 31
Private collection of Piaggio Vespas 33
Studio 137A. 35
Every picture tells a story 35
Frescoes at the Stazione Zoologica Anton Dohrn. 36
Palazzo San Teodoro. 39
Female centaurs that caught the attention of the Metropolitan
Museum of Art 39
Palazzo Leonetti staircase and elevator 41
Gay-Odin Museum of Chocolate 41
Museo del Tessile e dell'Abbigliamento *"Elena Aldobrandini"* 43
Traditional Neapolitan chic 43
Palazzo Mannajuolo staircase 45
The early days of Eduardo, "a giant of European theatre" 45
Palestra "Fitness & Beauty" 46
Carafa caves 47
The old city and its ferruginous water 47
Salons of Palazzo Serra di Cassano. 48
Why is the main entrance to Palazzo Serra di Cassano closed?. . . . 48
Sartoria C.T.N. 75 – Canzanella Costumi. 49
Tours of the Galleria Borbonica 51
Remains of an underground tramline 54
Former Aula Magna of the Faculty of Economics and Commerce . . . 56
Museo Orientale "Umberto Scerrato". 57
Museo di Etnopreistoria 57

Byzantine remains in Castel dell'Ovo 57
From Virgil's egg to the Castle of the Egg 58
Archivio Fotografico Parisio. 60
The president's anti-aircraft shelter 63
Vestiges of the former "Suprema" brothel 65
Associazione "Circolo Artistico Politecnico" 66
Giosuè Carducci's revenge. 67
Mascagni, a poor loser 67
Horns against the evil eye 68
Cuckold's horns 68
Corals in the Museo Ascione 69
Lucchesi Palli wing, *Biblioteca Nazionale* Vittorio Emanuele III 71
Aosta collection at the *Biblioteca Nazionale* Vittorio Emanuele III . . 73
Teatro San Carlo clock. 74
Royal access. 75
The new "Giardini room" in the disused carpentry workshop. 75
Naples, world capital of music 76
Circolo Nazionale dell'Unione 79
Bas-relief of a woman 80
Castel Nuovo: a pope imprisoned, Campanella tortured,
Giotto's frescoes, the escapades of Joan of Anjou 82
The crocodile that devoured prisoners 83
Statue of Antonio Toscano 85
Società Napoletana di Storia Patria. 85
Plaque in Vico Pensiero 86
The thinker of Vico Pensiero. 87
Diana and the witches. 87
Naples, a city steeped in spells 88
The *janara*: the legendary witch of nocturnal evildoing 89

TOLEDO, UNIVERSITÀ, BOVIO, GARIBALDI
Museo del Giocattolo di Napoli 93
Giardino dei Cinque Continenti 94
Sister Orsola Benincasa's cell. 95
Antico Laboratorio Scientifico di Scienze Naturali, Fisica e Chimica . 95
Museo della Fondazione Pagliara 95
Museo dell'Opera Universitaria. 95
Reproduction of Lourdes grotto 97
A kitchen garden declared national heritage 97
Chair in the chapel at Santa Lucia al Monte. 99
San Martino vineyard 101

CONTENTS

Largo Baracche gallery 103

Inscription on Palazzo Majorana. 104

Castratos: thousands of children sacrificed in the name of *bel canto* 105

Palazzo Zevallos Stigliano gallery 106

Obscure saga of the last Caravaggio 107

Bust of the goddess known as the "Head of Naples" 108

Secrets of Naples town hall 109

Emeroteca-Biblioteca Tucci 111

Pastrengo barracks 113

Underground altar of the church of Sant'Aspreno 114

Why does Saint Aspren relieve headaches? 115

Saint Aspren: the original aspirin?. 115

Great hall of the Chamber of Commerce. 117

Palazzo Penne. 118

Istituto Magistrale Eleonora Pimentel-Fonseca 120

Antonio Genovesi high school 122

Antonio Genovesi (1712–1769): a philosopher who became the
world's first economics professor 123

Marks on the façade of the church of Gesù Nuovo 125

Bourbon Hall of Fame 126

The Virgin's veil, Guglia dell'Immacolata. 127

When the Virgin belongs to the city and not to the church 127

Archbishop Sisto Riario Sforza's great hall 129

The archbishop who invented microcredit before its time 129

Church of Santi Marcellino e Festo 131

Garments of the miraculous Virgin 133

Cloisters of the former monastery of Saints Marcellino and Festo . 135

Museo di Paleontologia 135

Museo di Antropologia. 137

Museo di Zoologia. 137

Bas-relief of a hairy man 139

Real Museo di Mineralogia 140

Museo di Fisica 141

Accademia Pontaniana library 142

Fontana di Spinacorona. 144

Naples and the myth of the Siren Parthenope. 145

The Giambattista Vico Foundation 146

Giambattista Vico (1668–1744). 147

Land registry of the State Archives. 149

Filangieri room. 150

Souvenir of the terrible explosion of 1943 151

Lo Zingaro, the blacksmith who became an artist for love?. 152

Saint Benedict's plane tree 153
Tasso room 153
Saint George and the Dragon fresco 155
Legends of Porta Nolana 156
Augustissima Compagnia della Disciplina della Santa Croce 157
Greek tower at the Trianon theatre 158
Pay for your pizza eight days later 159
False windows of Corso Umberto 160
Basin of a Roman aqueduct 161
Former Sava wool mill 161
Saint Januarius' missing fingers 161
The miraculous Carmelite crucifix 163
Bungled looting of the remains of Conrad of Hohenstaufen 163

MONTESANTO, DANTE, CAVOUR, DECUMANI

Quartiere Intelligente 166
The "holy land" of the Archconfraternity of Pilgrims 167
Legend of the desiccated pine 167
Italian clock of Spirito Santo conservatory 168
The other two Italian clocks in the city 168
What is the origin of "Italian" clocks? 169
"Holy land" of the Arciconfraternita dei Bianchi 170
Church "holy lands" 171
Former oil tanks 172
Clock in Piazza Dante 173
What is the equation of time? 173
Cloister of the former convent of San Sebastiano 174
Arciconfraternita dei Verdi nel Palazzo Ruffo di Bagnara 175
La Conigliera 175
Hotel Correra aqueduct 176
Pasquale Catalano, a specialist in nativity scenes 177
Where can you see some extraordinary figurines? 177
Church of San Giuseppe delle Scalze 178
Museo Hermann Nitsch 181
Installation seen through a peephole 181
Casts of Parthenon sculptures 182
Gypsotheque of the Academy of Fine Arts 183
Holy Steps of Santa Maria della Sapienza 184
Origin and meaning of the Holy Steps 184
Holy Steps in Naples 185
Underground galleries of Pietrasanta 187

CONTENTS

Cloister of Sant'Andrea delle Dame 188

Seventh Heaven Lane 189

Private tour of Monastero delle Trentatré 190

Why is the number 33 generally associated with nuns
in the Neapolitan lottery? 191

Neapolitan lotto: a history of divination 192

Smorfia: the real meaning of the numbers 194

Incurabili pharmacy 198

Electricity as therapy in the 18th century 198

Naples, the last bastion of *Teriaca* 199

Museo delle Arti Sanitarie degli Incurabili 201

When unhealthy air was believed to cause syphilis 201

Museo di Anatomia Umana 203

Casa Zevola 207

Commemorative plaques at Palazzo Filangieri 208

Gaetano Filangieri 208

Remains of a Dioscuri temple 209

Congregation del Crocefisso della Sciabica 210

Origin of the word "*sciabica*" 211

Artworks by Nathalie de Saint-Phalle 212

Courtyard of Palazzo Spinelli di Laurino 212

The ghost of Bianca 213

Hidden symbolism of Cappella Sansevero 214

Why are two medallions faceless? 216

Sansevero's *Veiled Christ*: from legend to the reality of sudation
and mystical internal fire 217

Triptych of *Christ Unveiled or Hidden Light* 219

Plaque of the church of San Domenico Maggiore 220

Tomb of the first bishop of New York 221

Biblioteca Maurizio Taddei 222

A hotly disputed amputation 222

The duke's study 223

Maradona's hair 225

The Holy Steps of San Gregorio Armeno convent 226

Other curiosities of San Gregorio Armeno 227

Forgotten figurines of the Ferrigno workshop 228

The figure with no gift 229

Symbolism of objects and characters from the Neapolitan
nativity scene 230

Emblems of Naples *sedili* 233

Banksy's *Saint with a Pistol* graffiti 235

Reliquary cabinet at the church of the Gerolamini 235
Palazzo Carafa. 236
The Neapolitan horse: an exceptional animal 238
Shield of the city of Naples. 241
Is that Domenichino's tomb at the chapel entrance? 241
Bars of the Treasury chapel's monumental portal 242
Statue of the Virgin that terrified worshippers 243
"Il Re di Poggioreale", a trafficker who brought the treasure
of Saint Januarius back to Naples 243
Self-portraits on the Treasury chapel altar 244
The dome: each face had its pricce 245
The "Tesoro Vecchio" chapel of San Gennaro. 247
Marble calendar of the 9th century 247
The "*passo da terra*" of the Duomo 248
How is a metre defined? 249
Sala del Lazzaretto of the former della Pace hospital. 251
"May the Lord deliver me from sad neighbours and violinists" . . . 251
Archivo Storico, Banco di Napoli 253
A Neapolitan banking institution older than Monte dei Paschi
di Siena? 253
A Roman villa in the basement of the Banco di Napoli archive 253
Biblioteca Alfredo De Marsico. 255
Lizard in the church of the Santissimi Apostoli 257
Ionic column at Pelletteria Collaro. 257

MATERDEI, SANITÀ, CAPODIMONTE

Crucifix of San Carlo all'Arena church. 261
Why "all'Arena"? 261
Fate Presto: reproduction in the metro of a "Neapolitan" work
by Andy Warhol 261
Piazza Cavour tunnels 262
Bomb shelter in Babuk's garden 265
Events organised by the "Friends of Marcel Proust" 265
Palazzo de' Liguoro di Presicce 267
Studio of painter Massimo d'Orta 268
Little secrets of Palazzo dello Spagnolo. 271
Sirens of Palazzo Sanfelice 271
Greek hypogea in Naples. 272
"Cristallini" hypogea 275
Touching farewell scenes in the Museo Archeologico Nazionale . . 275

CONTENTS

Church of Santa Maria Antesaecula. 276
The fertility chair 279
Other fertility chairs in Naples 279
San Gaudioso catacombs 281
Palazzo de' Liguoro-Santoro staircase 283
Michele Iodice's workshop. 285
Wine tax marker. 285
Torre del Palasciano 287
Ferdinando Palasciano, army doctor of the Two Sicilies 287
Ospedale Leonardo Bianchi 288
Roberto De Simone, bard of Naples 289
Cloister of the Facoltà di Veterinaria (Università Federico II) 291
Museo di Anatomia Veterinaria. 291
Saint Anthony the Hermit's pig. 293
Saint Anthony's monks and the Templars 294
A strange procession and a bungled theft 294
Blessing of the animals. 295
Curiosities of San Gennaro catacombs 297
The noble Cerula and a hitherto unknown Saint Paul 297
La Sanità bridge 298
Model of Battaglino chariot 299
The captain's skull 300
The forgotten history of the Fontanelle 301
The woman killed by gnocchi and other Fontanelle tales 301
The cult of souls in Purgatory: when the dead and the living help
each other to reach Paradise 302
What is "refrisco"? 303
Sweating skulls 303

OUTSIDE THE CENTRE WEST

Neapolitan riding academy 304
Golden cube in the exhibition park 306
Tunnels below Fontana dell'Esedra. 309
A Roman road below the exhibition park 309
Rai production centre 310
Roman baths on Via Terracina 312
Naval basin of the Hydrodynamic Laboratory. 314
Guido Donatone private museum 316
Bas-relief of the Triumph of Death. 318
Sergio Ragni's private collection. 321

Gothic tunnels below San Martino. 323
Della Vicaria tribunal column 325
Meridian of the Carthusians. 327
How does a meridian work? 329
Why was 4 October followed immediately by 15 October
in the year 1582?
Measurement of time and origin of the meridians 330
The highest meridians in the world 331
Why were meridians installed in cathedrals? 331
Parco Viviani 332
Centrale ABC (Acqua Bene Comune Napoli) dello Scudillo 334

OUTSIDE THE CENTRE NORTH & EAST

Casa Museo di Pulcinella 338
The symbolism of *Pulcinella*, exorcist of Neapolitans' existential
angst 338
Maradona "museum" 341
Cimitero delle 366 fosse 342
Keller Architettura studio 345
Origin of the name "Foria" 345
Calabrese enclosed garden 346
Underground passage at San Giovanni a Carbonara 349
Parco di Re Ladislao 351
Archivio Storico del Comune di Napoli 351
Statue of San Gennaro. 353
Hidden symbolism of the cult of San Gennaro. 354
Church of San Carlo Borromeo alle Brecce 356
Symbolism of the fly: from Virgil's golden fly to the Madonna
of the Flies 357
Archivio Nazionale e Storico Enel 359
Art workshops of the Teatro San Carlo 360
Museo Ferroviario Nazionale di Pietrarsa. 362
Naples and the south before 1860: a wealthy and progressive
kingdom 364
Museo Privato delle Carrozze di Villa Bianchi 366

Alphabetical index 368

MERGELLINA, CHIAIA, SAN FERDINANDO

1 KAYAK TOURS. 18
2 OSPIZIO MARINO 21
3 VILLA DORIA D'ANGRI 23
4 NAVAL MUSEUM OF THE "PARTHENOPE" UNIVERSITY OF NAPLES 23
5 THE DEVIL OF MERGELLINA 24
6 EPITAPH ON VIRGIL'S TOMB 27
7 PRIVATE COLLECTION OF PIAGGIO VESPAS 33
8 STUDIO 137A 35
9 EVERY PICTURE TELLS A STORY 35
10 FRESCOES AT THE STAZIONE ZOOLOGICA ANTON DOHRN 36
11 PALAZZO SAN TEODORO 39
12 PALAZZO LEONETTI STAIRCASE AND ELEVATOR 41
13 GAY-ODIN MUSEUM OF CHOCOLATE. 41
14 MUSEO DEL TESSILE E DELL'ABBIGLIAMENTO "*ELENA ALDOBRANDINI*" . . 43
15 PALAZZO MANNAJUOLO STAIRCASE 45
16 PALESTRA "FITNESS & BEAUTY" 46
17 CARAFA CAVES 47

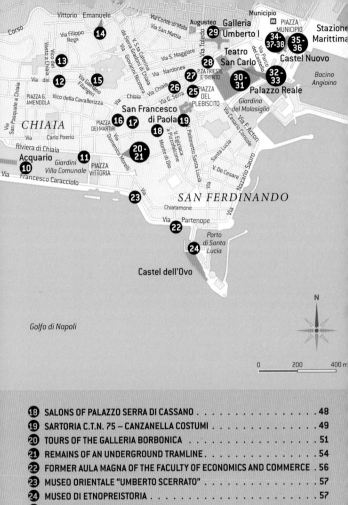

18 SALONS OF PALAZZO SERRA DI CASSANO 48

19 SARTORIA C.T.N. 75 – CANZANELLA COSTUMI 49

20 TOURS OF THE GALLERIA BORBONICA 51

21 REMAINS OF AN UNDERGROUND TRAMLINE 54

22 FORMER AULA MAGNA OF THE FACULTY OF ECONOMICS AND COMMERCE . 56

23 MUSEO ORIENTALE "UMBERTO SCERRATO" 57

24 MUSEO DI ETNOPREISTORIA 57

25 ARCHIVIO FOTOGRAFICO PARISIO 60

26 THE PRESIDENT'S ANTI-AIRCRAFT SHELTER 63

27 VESTIGES OF THE FORMER "SUPREMA" BROTHEL 65

28 *ASSOCIAZIONE* "CIRCOLO ARTISTICO POLITECNICO" 66

29 CORALS IN THE MUSEO ASCIONE 69

30 LUCCHESI PALLI WING, *BIBLIOTECA NAZIONALE* VITTORIO EMANUELE III . 71

31 AOSTA COLLECTION AT THE *BIBLIOTECA NAZIONALE* VITTORIO EMANUELE III 73

32 TEATRO SAN CARLO CLOCK 74

33 CIRCOLO NAZIONALE DELL'UNIONE 79

34 BAS-RELIEF OF A WOMAN 80

35 STATUE OF ANTONIO TOSCANO 85

36 SOCIETÀ NAPOLETANA DI STORIA PATRIA 85

37 PLAQUE IN VICO PENSIERO 86

38 THE THINKER OF VICO PENSIERO 87

KAYAK TOURS ❶

- Bus: 140
- Booking essential: 331 9874271, 338 2109978
- www.kayaknapoli.com
- info@kayaknapoli.com
- Non-swimmers welcome

Discovering
the city
from the sea

A kayak tour along the bay of Capo Posillipo (the city's most scenic district) can't be too highly recommended. Since Roman times these wooded hills overlooking the sea have been dotted with patrician villas concealed among the lush greenery. The tour takes in a stretch of rugged coastline where, nestling in the many creeks, are secluded beaches and grand villas, such as the one commissioned for the Spanish viceroy's wife Donn'Anna di Carafa in the 17th century but never completed. After a few kilometres you reach the beautiful Villa Rosebery, built in 1801, which has become one of three official summer residences of Italian presidents. A little further along is the fishing village of Marechiaro and the famous "*finestrella*" (little window), which inspired the song of that name by the great poet Salvatore Di Giacomo. Next you glide past Palazzo degli Spiriti (Palace of the Spirits), the remains of the nymphaeum of a fabulous Roman villa dating from the 1st century BC. The villa's owner, Publius Vedius Pollio, called it Pausilypon (from the Greek for "the place that brings an end to pain"): the 9-hectare grounds (which Emperor Augustus inherited on Pollio's death) included the two islets of Gaiola, on which stands a 19th-century villa (see p. 19), and extended to the small bay of Cala di Trentaremi where the tour ends. Sometimes these tours are available in the evening. By kayak you can also reach a traditional fishing boat, which serves lunch and dinner.

At certain times of the year you can visit the underwater park of Gaiola in a glass-bottomed boat. As well as offering a great view of the seabed, some of the submerged remains of Villa Pausilypon can also be seen.
Info: 081 2403235; info@areamarinaprotettagaiola.it.

Another company has recently started to organise boat trips along the coast, from a little further out.
Info: 081 4972249; www.alilauro.it.
Villa Pausilypon (36 Discesa Coroglio) can also be reached on foot.
Info: 081 2301030.
Guided tours: 081 2403235; info@areamarinaprotettagaiola.it.

THE CURSED VILLA OF GAIOLA

The villa built in 1874 on the twin islets of Gaiola has never enjoyed a good reputation due to the series of misfortunes that have befallen all who lived there. A business established in the villa by its first owner, Luigi Negri, foundered. In 1911, Marquis Gaspare Albenga grounded his armoured cruiser, the *San Giorgio*, on a nearby sandbank while attempting to give one of his guests a closer view of the coast.

During a storm in 1926 the cable on the funicular linking the mainland with the villa gave way, causing the death of the passenger, a German lady named Elena Von Parish. She had been the guest of the villa's occupants Otto Grumbach and Hans Praun, who both committed suicide, one immediately and the other on returning to Germany. In the 1950s Maurice Sandoz, owner of the well-known pharmaceutical company, lived there for a few years before being admitted to a psychiatric clinic where he too committed suicide, convinced that he'd gone bankrupt. The next owner, Paul Karl Langheim, ended up ruined.

The villa was then bought by Giovanni Agnelli, who, during the few years he owned it, had a number of bereavements in his family. In 1968, Agnelli sold the property to the oil magnate Paul Getty, whose son was kidnapped and had an ear cut off by the kidnappers in 1973.

The last "lucky winner" was Gian Pasquale Grappone, who bought the estate in 1978 but was jailed after complaints from his many creditors. So the villa was auctioned and, on the same day, Signor Grappone's wife died in a car accident.

The villa of Gaiola is now owned by the Campania Region.

IS VIRGIL BEHIND THE CURSE?

Until the 19th century, before it was submerged, you could still see part of a building belonging to Villa Pausilypon that from the Middle Ages was known as "Virgil's school". Virgil, considered a benevolent god in antiquity (see p. 28), was "downgraded" and classed as a necromancer as Christianity asserted itself. To scare the people, who persisted in their belief in the great poet's beneficial powers, a rumour was put about that these ruins were part of the school where Virgil taught black magic, so the place was bewitched.

OSPIZIO MARINO

24 Via Posillipo
• Bus: R2 from Napoli Centrale station; 140 from Piazza Municipio
(Donn'Anna stop)
• Visits on reservation: napolisegreta@gmail.com (authorization
required)

*A hospice
with a view*

I n the most beautiful district of Naples, on the peninsula of Posillipo, an enterprising monk founded the beautiful and little-known Marine Hospice in 1883. Antonio Curri, who was responsible for the construction work, chose an Arabist neo-Gothic style inspired by the famous Cloister of Paradise (Amalfi cathedral) for his beautiful portico of Moorish arches.

To reach the church, which stands just above the beach, you have to descend several long and unusual flights of "Holy Steps" (not a single flight as tradition dictates – see p. 184), with the Stations of the Cross depicted on the walls. The splendid ceramic decoration of the church, site of the founder's tomb, is the work of Brother Angelico Calabrese. On the floor above you can visit the cell where Brother Ludovico (see below) lived, with all his personal effects and a private chapel in polychrome wood.

The complex, which housed sick children and destitute old fishermen, was built on the ruins of a building that had been used as a lazaretto, bought by the founder in 1873. Today the hospice is run by Franciscan nuns who care for the elderly poor.

BROTHER LUDOVICO DA CASORIA, AN EXTRAORDINARY CHARACTER

Arcangelo Palmentieri (later Brother Ludovico) was born in Casoria, on the outskirts of Naples, on 11 March 1811. After a mystical experience in the church of San Giuseppe dei Ruffi in Naples, he devoted himself to saving African children from slavery. He spent the rest of his life fighting for the recognition of the rights and dignity of the poor, inventing such concepts as "professional training" before it was fashionable, placing disadvantaged children with practising artisans.

To finance his Marine Hospice, Palmentieri opened a resort for the clergy on the nearby beach that was even patronised by the Archbishop of Naples. "For my poor people," he would exclaim, "I've even gone into trade!" He was indeed an astute manager and founded over 200 similar institutions without having a penny to his name. He was a friend of King Ferdinand II, who financed a mission in Africa on his behalf, yet when the Bourbon dynasty fell he said: "On behalf of the poor, I kiss the forehead of the Grand Turk and of Victor Emmanuel." Palmentieri also founded the Order of the Grey Friars of Charity, who lived in absolute poverty but took no vows, not even that of celibacy.

Brother Ludovico died in Naples on 30 March 1885 and was beatified in 1993 by Pope John Paul II.

VILLA DORIA D'ANGRI

❸

80 Via Petrarca
- Metro: Line 2 or 6 Mergellina, then Bus: C21 from Piazza Sannazzaro
- Tel: 081 5475418
- antonio.alviani@uniparthenope.it
- Visits by appointment

L ocated in the old village on the heights of Posillipo, in a park of around 2 hectares with sweeping views of the bay, the splendid villa of the Doria d'Angri princes was built in 1833 in a neoclassical style inspired by Palladio and decorated with

The villa where Wagner finished Parsifal

extravagant Pompeian and oriental frescoes. The villa was put up for sale in 1857 and purchased by the Santa Dorotea boarding school for girls. Since 2000, it has housed the "Parthenope" University of Naples.

The original decoration, preserved in only a few rooms, was carried out by renowned artisans such as Gennaro Maldarelli and Gennaro Aveta, who drew their themes from the classical repertoire, closely emulating the style chosen for Palazzo San Teodoro (see p. 39).

There is a plaque in a first-floor corridor in honour of Wagner, who composed the final notes of *Parsifal* during his stay at the villa. The summer house on the terrace overlooking the bay is shaped like a Chinese pagoda, a fashionable style at the time. Its decoration has been lost with the exception of the small bells on the roof.

The church of Santa Dorotea, opposite the main entrance to the villa, can be visited on request. Tel: 081 5475418.

NEARBY

NAVAL MUSEUM OF THE "PARTHENOPE" UNIVERSITY OF NAPLES ❹
- Visits: contact museum director, Prof. Antonio Scamardella: antonio. scamardella@uniparthenope.it

Villa Doria d'Angri also has a very interesting naval museum with 160 model boats, parts of ships and nautical instruments. The museum was established at the time of the founding of the university, which inherited the collections of the arsenals and naval cadet school; it has since been enriched by various other pieces donated by Neapolitan workshops and the C and TT Pattison shipyard.

THE DEVIL OF MERGELLINA ❺

Church of Santa Maria del Parto - 9/b Via Mergellina
• Metro: Line 2 or 6 Mergellina; Buses: R3, 140 (Mergellina stop)
• Open 8.30am–1pm and 4pm–7pm (ring bell at 9/b next to the elevator
or to the left of the church)

**The
cardinal's
demons**

Santa Maria del Parto (Holy Mary of Childbirth), sited far from the beating heart of old Naples, is not much visited although it is of great interest. Its name probably comes from *De partu Virginis* (Childbirth of the Virgin), a poem by Jacopo Sannazaro who had the church built on his land (see opposite).

In the sacristy, the five life-size figurines of saints form part of a magnificent Christmas crib of 1520, when characters other than Mary and Joseph first appeared. The sculptor was Giovanni da Nola, a leading artist of the Neapolitan Renaissance. Behind the altar stands Sannazaro's imposing tomb, clearly inspired by Michelangelo, with a bas-relief depicting a scene from the poet's major work, *Arcadia*. The monument is entirely covered with pagan motifs, leading one of the Spanish viceroys to order its destruction. The monks of the adjoining monastery saved it *in extremis* by engraving the names of David and Judith under the figures of Apollo and Minerva.

The most intriguing detail of this church is the painting of Saint Michael killing the dragon/devil, shown with a woman's head with lovely features. This is in fact the face of Victoria d'Avalos with whom Cardinal Diomede Carafa had fallen hopelessly in love. Initially tantalised and then rejected by the beautiful Victoria, the prelate lost his reason. So he decided to commission this painting from Leonardo da Pistoia in which his female tormentor is killed by the archangel. According to legend, the cardinal's anguish was eased as soon as he could act out his fantasy. He then had this legend inscribed below the canvas: "*et fecit victoriam alleluja*" (I finally won, Hallelujah) – words with a double meaning that may well relate to the victory of faith over the devil.

This is the legend from which the Neapolitan saying "beautiful as the Devil of Mergellina", referring to man-eaters, is derived.

After the suppression of religious orders in the Napoleonic era, part of the monastery was bought by an impresario for the use of Gioachino Rossini – here he could give free rein to his passion for beautiful women and the pleasures of life.

JACOPO SANNAZARO (1457–1530): THE POET OF *ARCADIA*

The poet Sannazaro, famous in his day, was widely imitated by Ronsard and Leopardi as well as other great poets. He was like a brother to King Frederick I of Aragon, who offered him a property at Mergellina, a magical place not far from Virgil's tomb. Sannazaro had a villa built there as well as founding the church of Santa Maria del Parto. Having gone into exile with the king, he returned to Naples in 1505 after the kingdom had been conquered by Charles V. In spite of his resounding success, he stayed loyal to the Aragonese and always kept his distance from the court of the viceroys. A great humanist, he discovered and transcribed the texts of Latin poets. He was extremely versatile and wrote poems as well as plays (known as *farces*) to entertain the Aragonese court. His poem *Arcadia*, where he sings of the beauty of Naples, is considered the archetype of the modern pastoral. In the last years of his life, he wrote only in Latin. *De partu Virginis* enjoyed great popularity with the papacy, as well as in France.

Sepolcro di Virgilio sul Monte Posilipo poco lungi dalla Grotta di Napoli

EPITAPH ON VIRGIL'S TOMB

Roman columbarium
Via Puteolana – behind Mergellina train station
• Metro: Line 2 Mergellina
• Open daily 9am to 1 hour after sunset
• Closed 1 January, Easter Monday, 1 May, 25 December

Virgil's
magical laurel

The Roman columbarium on Via Puteolana, close to the Crypta Neapolitana (see p. 29), is reputed to be the site of Virgil's tomb. The greatest poets of all time gathered there. The epic poet Statius, who was Neapolitan, recounts that the tomb was a sacred place and he made a pilgrimage there himself.

Close to the tomb there once stood a laurel that was said – in both the written and the oral traditions – to have grown spontaneously. According to a belief that endured until the 20th century, women picked the leaves and chewed them for their miraculous powers, as borne out by an epitaph of 1668. This belief was so strong that even Neapolitan emigrants to America were asking for branches from the tree. The demand was so great that the laurel had no chance to regenerate.

Laurel has always been part of the Virgil myth: according to his biographer Donatus, before the poet's birth his mother had dreamed of a laurel branch that grew to full size as soon as it was planted in the ground. However, laurel embodies a profusion of magico-religious symbols. For example, the tree is sacred to Apollo, whose priestesses, the Sibyls, chewed the leaves before prophesying.

As the tree bears no fruit, it incarnates virginity. It is also "eternal" because it doesn't shed its leaves in winter. Finally, it symbolises the underworld kingdom of Persephone, daughter of Demeter, the Great Earth Mother: to escape from her suitor Apollo, Daphne invoked the Great Mother, who turned her into a laurel. Through this tree Virgil brings together all these values: virginity, eternity, fertility and the underworld.

Doubts still linger about Virgil's actual burial site. According to some ancient chroniclers, the poet's remains were placed for safekeeping in the foundations of Castel dell'Ovo (Castle of the Egg), where Virgil had hidden a magic egg (laid by the bird-woman, the Siren, see p. 145). Be that as it may, as expressed in these lines engraved on a marble slab: "*If the tomb was opened, if the urn was broken, what does it matter? This place will always be celebrated for the name of the poet.*"

"POETRY TREES" IN VIRGIL'S HONOUR
In 2012 the municipality bestowed this title on an initiative designed to honour the great Latin poet on his 2,082nd anniversary. Along the path leading to the tomb and crypt were planted some of the trees and shrubs Virgil mentions in his works, among them the male dogwood (*Cornus mas*), which according to the *Aeneid* was used to build the Trojan horse.

VIRGIL, POET AND MAGICIAN

Born in Mantua, Virgil (70–19 BC) spent much of his life in Naples, where he set several episodes of the *Aeneid*. He also asked to be buried there. Carved on his tomb (p. 27) are verses he is thought to have composed: "*Mantua gave me birth; Calabria took me away; and now Naples holds me; I sang of pastures, farms, leaders.*" It was undoubtedly this detail that built up the immense popularity of the Virgil cult in this region, traces of which are still visible today.

His boundless knowledge, the perfection of his poetry and his interest in magico-religious language earned Virgil such admiration from his peers that, according to Pliny the Elder and Ausonius, the Ides* of October were dedicated to him shortly after his death (he was born on 15 October).

In Campania, people even began to associate him with the major cults of the time: the Great Mother (fertility), Apollo (the Sun), the Siren Parthenope (virginity) and the Sibyls (prophecy), so countless supernatural powers were eventually attributed to him.

The poet's saintly aura intensified over time, due largely to the Donatus biography derived from the work of Suetonius. The early Christians themselves saw in his writings – especially in Eclogue IV of the pastoral poems, the *Bucolics* – the orphic and solar elements found in Christianity. Thus, while of the pagan world, Virgil was not rejected by the emerging religion, especially as the Emperor Constantine himself had formalised the acceptance of Christianity: Virgil (and the Sibyls) were henceforth represented among the prophets (notably in the Sistine Chapel in Rome).

Even Virgil's homosexuality, real or imagined, was considered a virtue. He was so chaste, insists Donatus, that he was called Parthenias, the "little virgin". And it is therefore no coincidence that the oral traditions of Campania often mention a "*verginella*" (little virgin) – always a man. The transvestite or hermaphrodite does indeed encapsulate the masculine and the feminine, and therefore the universe. Even today, Neapolitan transvestites play a fundamental role in some popular rites.

The Virgil cult remained in vigour until the year 1000. Then the myths linked to the poet were gradually replaced by legends of saints or madonnas, and the church demoted even Virgil to the role of necromancer. But belief in his benevolent powers was too deep-rooted in the Neapolitan spirit: his memory would often be evoked where churches were established, built in their turn on the ruins of pagan temples.

*Ides: from the Latin word *iduare* (divide), referring to the mid-month position of the Ides. In the Roman calendar, the Ides are reference days falling on the 13th (January, February, April, June, August, September, November, December) or the 15th (March, May, July, October) of each month.

SYMBOLISM OF THE CRYPTA NEAPOLITANA

Following Virgil's death in 19 BC, the construction of the tunnel known as the Neapolitan Crypt was attributed to him. The poet-magician is said to have pierced the hill with a sunbeam in a single night, to give the poor the chance to go through it to have their ailments treated at the Phlegraean Fields (Campi Flegrei, "burning fields"), the site of the defeat of the Titans, where many therapeutic hot springs still bubble.

Many other myths give meaning to this place. Caves, in the popular imagination, have always been associated with the origins of life. This tunnel carved out by Virgil, "the virgin" (see opposite), who is both man and woman at the same time, he who lies at rest close to the crypt, can only be a thousand times more sacred. With its east–west orientation, it is also an initiatory path, because he who takes that route from Naples is heading west and ritually dies with the Sun. But when he returns to the east, "resurrected" by the miraculous waters of Virgil, he is reborn like the sacred star. The crypt thus became one of the main places of worship of the ancient city, where initiatory rites were held for Mithras, Demeter and Dionysus, the deities associated with the Sun and fertility. Even less surprising is the later syncretism with the Madonna of Piedigrotta and the basilica dedicated to her "at the feet of the grotto" (see p. 30).

In the 8th century, when Christianity spread more widely, a chapel dedicated to the Madonna of Idria was erected in the crypt. Idria is derived from *Ogiditria,* meaning "indicates the way". The allusion to the path of the Sun couldn't be clearer. In addition, new mothers and brides gathered at the feet of the Virgin, just as they used to pray to the Sun and the Great Mother. A fresco representing the Madonna of Idria can still be seen to the left of the tunnel entrance, while on the right a saint, probably Luke, is depicted. In the course of various excavations (15th and 17th centuries), a relief from the 3rd century AD was found showing the god Mithras sacrificing the bull (on view at the National Archaeological Museum).

In reality, the 705 m long tunnel, illuminated by two light wells, was built by the military architect Lucius Cocceius on the orders of Emperor Augustus (1st century BC) to connect Neapolis to Puteoliso, which at the time was the most important commercial port of the empire. The crypt has seen tremendous changes over the centuries and was closed in the early 20th century to be replaced by a modern tunnel, which connects Mergellina to the Phlegraean Fields.

WHEN OUR LADY LOST HER SHOE: WHY IS SANTA MARIA DI PIEDIGROTTA SO CALLED?

Maria Santissima
di Piedigrotta.

It was after an apparition of the Virgin to three nuns in 1353 that the basilica of Santa Maria di Piedigrotta was built. Although the word *piedi* (feet) originally referred only to a geographical position (the Madonna "at the feet of the grotto", the legendary cave created by Virgil – see p. 29), it soon took on another sense: the foot and the shoe (a woman's) are an allegory of the path in all its meanings, but also of fertility (as they trample the earth) and the cave (symbol of death and birth).

We also find this attribute in a local legend that the Virgin would appear to fishermen at night, leaving a shoe to mark her passage. Now Persephone, in Greek mythology, before she returned to the underworld at the end of summer, also left a shoe in token of her promise to fertilise the land the following year. And until recently a little shoe (called "*o scarpunciello d''a Maronna*") was offered to pregnant women

to ease the pains of childbirth, and to brides to ward off sterility. Prayers were also written inside a footprint.

From its earliest days, in order to be accepted more widely, Christianity tried to assimilate and transform pagan cults rather than eradicating them: besides Persephone, here the Virgin replaced a certain Virgil, who was also a "virgin" (see p. 28), and whose crypt (Crypta Neapolitana) is nearby.

So it is no surprise that the greatest festival of the year was dedicated to the Madonna di Piedigrotta: the date of 8 September was chosen because it corresponded to other pagan feasts in honour of solar and underworld deities, always in the name of fertility and all united under the sign of Virgil. Even the representation of the Madonna of Piedigrotta brings together key magico-religious elements: the babe in arms like the Great Mother, the Sun to the right and the Moon to the left, allegories of Heaven and the underworld, and with the bare foot showing.

This ritual chant recorded by Roberto De Simone (see p. 289) in 1970 makes clear allusions to the shoe as symbol of the path travelled by the Sun:

The sun has risen behind the mountains
There are shoemakers
Who know how to make shoes
With golden tips like the Sun ...

The great festivities in honour of the Madonna of Piedigrotta took place on the night of 7–8 September, and were not far removed from Dionysian rites: torchlight processions to the sound of loud instruments, erotic dances and songs. Cheering crowds wended their way to the church on decorated floats, men and women separately. Everyone then gathered before Virgil's tomb, where chanting took place. Then came dancing in the cave where, for one night, all taboos were swept away.

Outside the tunnel/cave, the festivities adopted the same symbols but in a more refined manner. All Neapolitans participated, including the bourgeoisie.

Carts decorated in carnival style rolled through the streets, banter was allowed but must never exceed the bounds of propriety. The traditional torches were replaced by sumptuous lighting; music and songs took pride of place. From the 19th century onwards, the best-known Neapolitan songs had been composed for this occasion. Today this Madonna is still celebrated, but the festive events have become much more low-key since the 1970s.

CINDERELLA WAS BORN IN NAPLES

The tale of Cinderella with her famous glass slipper comes from Naples (the storytellers called her "Cinderella Cat"). The first written version (in the Neapolitan dialect) is attributed to Giambattista Basile, author of the *Pentameron* (17th century), a collection of folk tales from the oral tradition.

PRIVATE COLLECTION OF PIAGGIO VESPAS

• Booking essential: napolisegreta@gmail.com

*A rare
wartime Vespa*

A very secret private garage in the depths of a building occupied by the town hall of the Chiaia–San Ferdinando–Posillipo district houses one of Italy's most extraordinary – and virtually unknown – collections of motorcycles. It contains around seventy Piaggio Vespas dating from the 1940s to the 1990s. The collection specialises in models produced by Piaggio plants abroad, particularly in France, Spain, Germany and the UK. But there is also an extremely rare Ape, made in the USSR in the 1950s.

All the Vespas on show are in working order and have a certificate of origin. The oldest, the "Vespa 98" (number corresponding to engine size), dates back to 1946 and is one of 15,000 units produced by the Sestri Ponente factory (near Genoa) between 1946 and 1948, before a 125 cc engine was developed.

The most interesting example is undeniably the "Vespa TAP" (Airborne Troops), produced for the French troops who fought in Vietnam. These very light two-wheelers with reinforced parts were parachuted in behind enemy lines, and allowed soldiers to ride over terrain that was very steep and difficult to access. These incredible "war Vespas" were manufactured from 1956 by ACMA (Ateliers de Construction de Motocycles et Automobiles), already a Piaggio franchise.

The bikes were armed with a cannon similar to the "Super Bazooka" that could pierce armour-plating up to a centimetre thick. The gun was mounted under the seat at a slight angle, extending more than a metre beyond the windshield that supported it.

The TAP could carry two riders and the luggage rack held six large missiles. The removable support could be converted into a tripod for aiming the weapon. Six hundred of these Vespas were produced, all painted in the camouflage colours of green and beige.

STUDIO 137A

(former City Hall Café)
137A Corso Vittorio Emanuele
• Metro: Line 2 Amedeo
• Funicular Chiaia: Parco Margherita
• Visits on reservation
• info@137a.it

8

> *Arts workshop in a historic meeting place*

Following the "coworking" principle, several artists, designers, architects, photographers and stylists share the large open-plan space at 137A, where a wide range of events is organised: arts workshops, cinema sets, exhibitions ...

137A occupies the premises that belonged a few years ago to the famous City Hall Café, a historic location where Andy Warhol met Joseph Beuys and where Chet Baker, Paolo Conte, Dizzy Gillespie, Stan Getz, Dave Holland, Sam Rivers and many other big names performed.

The current occupants have kept the original architecture, but added vintage artefacts, photographs and contemporary artworks. You can ask to have a coffee or an aperitif in the lovely small garden/terrace.

NEARBY

EVERY PICTURE TELLS A STORY

9

A few steps away, at No. 141C, is a small workshop for restoring vintage objects. On request, the owner Giovanni Rinaldi will give you a slide show with a French stereoscopic device from the early 20th century. The extremely rare images show significant events in the city's history during the last century, such as the eruption of Vesuvius in 1944 and numerous views of Naples of yesteryear. For reservations, phone Signor Rinaldi: 347 3839827.

FRESCOES AT THE STAZIONE ZOOLOGICA ANTON DOHRN ⑩

Villa Comunale
• Metro: Line 2 Amedeo • Funicular Chiaia: Parco Margherita
• Open 9.30am–6pm; closed Mondays
• Visits to frescoes on reservation
• Tel: 081 5833111 / 081 5833218
• www.szn.it • stazione.zoologica@szn.it

> *A beautiful reading room in the aquarium*

The Stazione Zoologica Anton Dohrn, which houses Europe's only 19th-century aquarium still open to the public, also has spectacular frescoes on the walls of the library's reading room: the themes coincide perfectly with the ideology of its founder, German zoologist Anton Dohrn. As a supporter of Darwin's evolutionary theories, he aspired to combine science with art, so in 1873 he asked the painter Hans von Marées and the architect Adolf von Hildebrand to decorate the room accordingly.

In a decor featuring loggias surrounded by a frieze of marine plants and animals, a number of different scenes are painted: to the right of the entrance, muscular fishermen roll up their nets and push a boat out onto the water; they are next seen with a mysterious woman at the end of their working day.

Fishermen push the boat out

The other wall features *Pergola*: a group of friends seated in a tavern near Palazzo Donn'Anna in Posillipo (Anton Dohrn with his colleagues, Kleinenberg and Grant, as well as the two artists, von Marées and von Hildebrand, are recognisable). Finally, on the wall opposite the entrance is an orange grove where two women chat while three male figures, an allegory of the three ages of man, are working.

This frescoed room is directly above the aquarium, which – almost uniquely – has kept its original 1874 structure. Here you can admire all the marine species from the Mediterranean, including some that are extremely rare.

The orange grove: the three ages of man

PALAZZO SAN TEODORO

281 Riviera di Chiaia
- Metro: Line 2 Amedeo • Funicular Chiaia: Parco Margherita
- Visits on reservation
- Tel: 081 3604134 / 081 3604135
- info@palazzosanteodoro.it

*A palazzo
in Pompeian style*

Built in 1826 in a style reminiscent of Roman patrician houses by the Florentine architect Guglielmo Bechi, a great admirer of antiquity, the beautiful residence which belonged to Duke Caracciolo of San Teodoro is unknown to most Neapolitans.

Much of the palazzo is now private apartments, with the exception of the first-floor rooms which can be hired for receptions and are therefore open to the public. At the top of an elegant marble staircase, you enter the large lavishly decorated dining room with terracotta tiles in imitation of Pompeian houses. In the middle of the ceiling hangs an imposing chandelier, a gift from King Ferdinand II. Walk through into the music room, which gives the impression of being in a Roman villa: columns, frescoed mythological themes dominated by Pompeian red, a ceiling decoration emulating Nero's Domus Aurea (Golden House) ...

FEMALE CENTAURS THAT CAUGHT THE ATTENTION OF THE METROPOLITAN MUSEUM OF ART

Guglielmo Bechi, known for his anti-conformism, had female centaurs painted on the ceiling of one of the rooms leading from the dining room to the music room. The fresco so impressed the directors of New York's Metropolitan Museum that they published a long article on the subject.

PALAZZO LEONETTI STAIRCASE AND ELEVATOR

⓬

40 Via dei Mille
• Metro: Line 2 Amedeo
• Funicular Chiaia: Parco Margherita
• Visits during caretaker's working hours

> *A staircase and an elevator "suspended in space"*

The self-supporting staircase of Palazzo Leonetti, built in 1910 by architect Giulio Ulisse Arata, is a work of great ingenuity. The steps of the Liberty-style staircase, whose elegant railing is decorated with floral motifs, seem to emerge from the wall, giving the impression of being suspended in space along with the elevator structure which is supported by the steps.

This system is used in both wings of the building, which is U-shaped, an unusual architectural form for Naples.

Palazzo Leonetti, one of the city's most elegant palazzi, is home to two consulates – British and Spanish. While initially designed as a luxury hotel, it was then used to accommodate the residents of the Pendino neighbourhood when it was demolished during the Risanamento (see p. 222). For financial reasons it was sold to the family of the Leonetti counts in 1916.

NEARBY

GAY-ODIN MUSEUM OF CHOCOLATE

⓭

12 Via Vetriera
• Metro: Line 2 Amedeo • Funicular Chiaia: Parco Margherita
• Tel: 081 417843
• info@gayodin.it
• Visits during shop opening hours

Fabbrica Cioccolato Gay-Odin, one of the oldest chocolate manufacturers in the city, was founded in 1894 by a Piedmontese couple, Isidoro Odin and Onorina Gay. It has occupied the current premises since 1922. Besides the house specialities, visitors are offered the chance to visit a small museum with a collection of old wooden and bronze machines that show the different stages of manufacturing chocolate: a large bean grinder from 1837, a measuring device for liqueurs, etc. Visitors are shown how the machines work: the cocoa powder was separated from the fat (cocoa butter) in the beans, then, with the bronze wheel heated in the fire, the hot ingredients were mixed to make the chocolates.

Among the specialities is the "*foresta*" (forest), a small log composed of superfine layers of chocolate fashioned with a granite roller. Gay-Odin is also known for its 3 m tall Easter egg, displayed every year in the shop window and decorated with a different greeting every time.

Gay-Odin was sold in the 1950s to the Maglietta family, who still produce their chocolates in the traditional way. It was declared a national monument in 1993.

MUSEO DEL TESSILE E DELL'ABBIGLIAMENTO🄬
"ELENA ALDOBRANDINI"

18 Piazzetta Mondragone
- Metro: Line 2 Amedeo • Funicular Chiaia: Parco Margherita
- Tel: 081 4976104 • www.fondazionemondragone.it
- Visits Monday to Friday 9.30am–1pm and 3pm–5pm;
Saturday 9am–1pm (but telephone in advance to check opening hours)
- Admission: €5

> *A trip through the history of Neapolitan haute couture*

Since 2003, the rooms on the first and second floors of the building occupied by the Fondazione Mondragone – set up in 1655 by Elena Aldobrandini, wife of the Duke of Mondragone and Prince of Stigliano – have housed the Museum of Textiles and Clothing. There are major collections by famous Neapolitan fashion designers, together with photographs and various documents that trace the evolution of local fashion from the end of the 19th century up to the mid-20th century. You can also admire beautiful upholstery fabrics, all manufactured in Neapolitan factories between the late 19th and mid-20th centuries, as well as robes and sacred objects from the church of Santa Maria delle Grazie a Mondragone, which is part of the foundation.

Be sure not to miss the fabulous garden whose beauty was praised by a number of chroniclers in antiquity – access is by a flight of steps in the courtyard. Outdoor concerts are organised here in summer.

TRADITIONAL NEAPOLITAN CHIC
The international fame of Neapolitan couture is due in part to the existence of London House, frequented by celebrities such as the princes of Savoy, Eduardo De Filippo, Vittorio De Sica and many others. The establishment was founded in the early 1930s by Gennaro Rubinacci, whose grandfather imported silk fabrics from the East in the first half of the 19th century.

PALAZZO MANNAJUOLO STAIRCASE

36 Via Filangieri
• Metro: Line 2 Amedeo • Funicular Chiaia: Parco Margherita
• Visits during caretaker's working hours

> *An*
> *Art Nouveau*
> *gem*

Palazzo Mannajuolo, built between 1909 and 1911, takes its name from one of the three engineers who designed it.

This beautiful piece of architecture, located on the city's most exclusive street, is not on the tourist trail or even on the itineraries that cultural associations organise for locals.

However, the corbelled, elliptical marble staircase, with its wrought-iron railings in Art Nouveau style, is a real gem. The whole design is one of great boldness and elegance: seen from below, the curved flights blend with horizontal planes against a fake blue sky.

THE EARLY DAYS OF EDUARDO, "A GIANT OF EUROPEAN THEATRE"

In 1925, part of Palazzo Mannajuolo was converted into a cinema/theatre (the Kursaal), now the Filangieri cinema. It was here in 1931 that one of the giants of Italian theatre, Eduardo De Filippo (1900–1984), known to Neapolitans simply as "Eduardo", made his debut as a worthy successor to Pirandello. His plays, nearly all in the Neapolitan dialect, have always met with resounding success worldwide, as far away as India and Japan. In the UK it was Laurence Olivier who, through Eduardo, triumphed with *Saturday, Sunday, Monday*; in the US, critics heralded him as "a giant of European theatre".

Such was the playwright's fame (and that of his company, which included his brother Peppino and sister Titina) that under the fascist regime, when the law banned "dialects" and Eduardo blithely ignored this censorship, Mussolini himself was obliged to declare: "We don't touch the De Filippo family!"

PALESTRA "FITNESS & BEAUTY" ⑯

26 Vico Santa Maria a Cappella Vecchia
• Metro: Line 2 Amedeo • Funicular Chiaia: Parco Margherita
• Visits on request during opening hours
• Tel: 081 7646580

A sports venue in a deconsecrated church

In what is now the chic neighbourhood of Piazza dei Martiri, the early Christians built a chapel near a cave which, according to some writers (such as Jacopo Sannazzaro, see p. 25), was dedicated to the Egyptian god Serapis. Later, Basilian monks enlarged the chapel, which became a church and then a monastery. The complex then passed to the Benedictines and the Olivetans. In the 19th century, the monastery was sold to the Marquis di Sessa (owner of the neighbouring palazzo).

The church itself was handed over to a religious congregation. Now deconsecrated, it has become a gym and sports centre, although the 18th-century stucco and the Gothic portico can still be seen.

CARAFA CAVES

30/M Vico Santa Maria a Cappella Vecchia, c/o Gran Garage
- Metro: Line 2 Amedeo • Funicular Chiaia: Parco Margherita
- Monday to Saturday open 24/7; best to visit during daylight hours
- Admission free

A magical site

A narrow tunnel and a winding lane lead to the Carafa caves – spectacular former underground quarries that were converted into a parking lot some decades ago. To see their full extent, go up to the second level (artificially created to make better use of the space), from where you can

appreciate the impressive height of the vaults supported by huge stone arches.

Since antiquity, the people of Naples have excavated the local yellow and grey tuff, a soft but durable volcanic stone that is ideal for all kinds of construction work. The Romans used it to build water tanks for their fleet.

According to some sources, during the Angevin domination in the 13th century this quarry supplied the materials to enlarge the port and build Castel Nuovo (New Castle, the royal palace of the time). The Military Academy of Nunziatella, the Military Archives, the Madeleine bridge (which spanned the Sebeto river at the entrance to the city) and Palazzo Carafa (hence the name of the caves) were all built with tuff from these quarries.

THE OLD CITY AND ITS FERRUGINOUS WATER

The Carafa caves were cut into the hill of Pizzofalcone (formerly known as Monte Echia), part of the territory where, in the 7th century BC, the Greeks founded a place they named after the Siren Parthenope (see p. 145). In Roman times the hill became the setting for the sumptuous residence of General Lucullus, famous for his proverbial banquets. The remains of his villa are still visible from the most panoramic viewpoint of Pizzofalcone. The natural caves at the foot of the hill, inhabited in the Neolithic period, were closed in the 17th century. Monte Echia was the source of the ferruginous water much enjoyed by Neapolitans, which was collected and stored in earthenware pot-bellied jugs – part of the memories of old Naples – to be sold from small kiosks dotted around the city. The source, which was suspected of being polluted, was sealed off in the 1970s.

SALONS OF PALAZZO SERRA DI CASSANO

Istituto Italiano per gli Studi Filosofici
14 Via Monte di Dio (side entrance)
• Metro: Line 1 Toledo • Funicular Centrale: Augusteo
• Tel: 081 7642652 / 7642654 • info@iisf.it
• To visit, contact Istituto Italiano per gli Studi Filosofici: www.iisf.it

Palace
of the revolutionary
nobles

Palazzo Serra di Cassano, meeting place of the Neapolitan Republicans in the late 18th century, is now the home of the Italian Institute of Philosophical Studies, founded and directed by Maître Gerardo Marotta who donated his personal library of 300,000 volumes to the institute.

Although the sumptuous ballroom is familiar to participants of the congresses held there, two other magnificent great rooms are almost unknown: the Rococo "Sala dei Capitoli", decorated with stucco-work framing paintings by Giacinto Diano showing episodes from the life of Scipio Africanus (1700); and the "Salone Direttorio", with its furniture of rare elegance and monochrome pictorial decoration of the 18th century. The palazzo is the work of the famous architect Ferdinando Sanfelice, who also designed the splendid monumental "double staircase".

WHY IS THE MAIN ENTRANCE TO PALAZZO SERRA DI CASSANO CLOSED?

The main entrance to Palazzo Serra di Cassano, at 67 Via Egiziaca a Pizzofalcone (the side nearest to Palazzo Reale), was closed in perpetuity in 1799: this was done as an expression of grief after this aristocratic family's son and heir, Gennaro Serra, was executed, on the orders of the king, for taking part in the proclamation of the Parthenopean Republic. Since then, the doors have only been opened on two occasions: the evening of 3 September 1960 to celebrate the Sailing Olympics, attended by a number of personalities including Maria Callas accompanied by Aristide Onassis; and in 1999 during a formal commemoration of the bicentenary of the Parthenopean Revolution.

SARTORIA C.T.N. 75 – CANZANELLA COSTUMI ⑲

39 Via Solitaria; moving to 7 Piazza Sant'Eligio
• Metro: Lines 1 and 2 Garibaldi
• Visits by appointment • Tel: 081 7645173 • info@ctn75.com

Vincenzo Canzanella's haute couture workshop – Naples' oldest workshop specialising in costumes for cinema, theatre, opera and TV – opens its doors (booking essential) onto a magical world of silks, velvets, brocades, hats from another age and pearl-studded fans … all displayed among 19th-century console tables and gilded mirrors. Fifteen thousand costumes worn by A-list stars of cinema and theatre take the visitor on a journey through time.

Dream dresses for divas

Signor Canzanella is always proud to show people round, and loves to point out the famous dazzling white dress worn by Claudia Cardinale for the ball scene of Visconti's film *The Leopard*. Years later, Kim Basinger asked if she could borrow the dress (suitably altered to fit her) when she went to accept an award at Taormina (Sicily) – needless to say, the request was granted.

The list is long: you'll be bowled over by the countless other costumes, such as those of Sophia Loren in Vittorio De Sica's film *Il Viaggio* (The Journey, 1974), Ingrid Bergman in Roberto Rossellini's *Giovanna d'Arco al rogo* (Joan of Arc at the Stake, 1954) and Audrey Hepburn in William Wyler's *Roman Holiday* (1953).

The highlight is undoubtedly the ballgown ordered for a concert by Maria Callas, who in 1963 weighed 106 kg and wanted at all costs to appear slim. The obliging Signor Canzanella worked for over a month to satisfy the diva, who was thrilled with her dress embroidered with metallic thread, glass beads and sequins, despite its weighing 6 kg.

Besides these unique pieces there are costumes for numerous lyric operas and the plays of the great Eduardo De Filippo, in addition to those made for the Shah of Iran in 1968 and many others …

TOURS OF THE GALLERIA BORBONICA ❷⓪

"Standard" tour organised by the Associazione Culturale Borbonica
Sotterranea
40 Via Domenico Morelli (entrance in Morelli parking garage)
• Metro: Line 2 Amedeo • Funicular Chiaia: Parco Margherita
• Tel: 366 2484151, 081 7645808 • mail@galleriaborbonica.it
• www.galleriaborbonica.com
• Guided tours: Friday, Saturday, Sunday and public holidays 10am,
12 noon, 3.30pm, 5.30pm (duration 1 h 20 min)
• 60% of the route is wheelchair accessible

*The
king's secret
passage*

The Bourbon Tunnel is part of a strategic design by the Bourbon King Ferdinand II: in 1853 he commissioned architect Errico Alvino to excavate an underground passage beneath Monte Echia, between Palazzo Reale and Piazza Vittoria, which as well as opening onto the sea was also close to the barracks. The passage was designed to allow the troops stationed in the barracks on Via Pace (today Via Domenico Morelli) quick access to the royal residence; it was also a means of escape for the royal family if they were in danger from a foreign invasion. The work, carried out entirely by hand, was often delayed by technical problems, such as the huge cisterns over which bridges had to be built and which can still be seen today. The 431 m long tunnel ran down to Piazza Carolina, behind the columned portico of Piazza del Plebiscito, but it was never completed due to the excessive cost and the unstable political situation.

The tunnel had no exit until the Second World War, when it was used as an air-raid shelter and fitted with electricity and toilets, still there today. After the war and until 1970, the tunnel was used by the city council to store objects found in the rubble of buildings destroyed by the 200 bombardments the city had suffered. These abandoned objects are still there – cars and motorbikes by the dozen, many statues from different eras, and the funerary monument of Captain Aurelio Padovani, founder of the Neapolitan branch of the Fascist Party.

The association runs three different tours exploring this section of the "underground city": Standard (see above), Adventure (*Avventura*) (see p. 54) and Caving (*Speleo*) (see p. 63). The Adventure option includes a raft ride through part of the tunnel, whereas the Standard tour lets you walk the full length of it.

REMAINS OF AN UNDERGROUND TRAMLINE

"Adventure" tour organised by the Associazione Culturale Borbonica Sotterranea
40 Via Domenico Morelli (entrance in Morelli parking garage)
• Metro: Line 2 Amedeo • Funicular Chiaia: Parco Margherita
• Tel: 366 2484151, 081 7645808
• mail@galleria borbonica.it • www.galleriaborbonica.com
• Guided tours: Saturday and Sunday 10am, 12noon, 3.30pm and 5.30pm (duration 1 h 20 min)

On a raft 20 m below Piazza del Plebiscito

In the late 1980s, a metro line was planned below Piazza del Plebiscito, or rather an underground tram line that was supposed – on the occasion of the 1990 World Cup – to connect the western districts to the city centre and run on to the east side. The work was never completed. As the tunnel is partly flooded from the groundwater table, a raft ride is part of this tour in the "underbelly" of Naples.

A short walk through the tunnel leads to a jetty where you board a raft for the crossing (which only takes a few minutes), before continuing on foot as far as a gallery where you can still see traces of the construction site.

The "Adventure" tour helps you understand the extent of this underground city. Naples in fact sits on an unimaginable maze of tunnels, aqueducts

and cisterns carved out of the tuff over the centuries since the founding of the Greek city, and even earlier, as the first traces of human presence date back to the third millennium BC. At all periods the excavated volcanic stone was reused for building at street level. The cisterns, which were in use until the 19th century, were closed in 1885 during a severe cholera epidemic and replaced by a modern aqueduct. During the Second World War, some of the tunnels were used as air-raid shelters.

The association runs three different tours exploring this section of the "underground city": Standard (see p. 51), Adventure (*Avventura*) (see above) and Caving (*Speleo*) (see p. 63). The Adventure option includes a raft ride through part of the tunnel, whereas the Standard tour lets you walk the full length of it.

FORMER AULA MAGNA OF THE FACULTY OF ECONOMICS AND COMMERCE

㉒

Centro Congressi Federico II - 36 Via Partenope
• Bus: C25 or 140
• Metro: Line 1 Toledo • Funicular Chiaia: Parco Margherita
• Visits by appointment: 081 2535706
• Monday to Friday 9am to 7pm

A ceiling worthy of a royal palace

The Conference Centre of the University of Naples Federico II, built by Roberto Pane in 1937, boasts ambitious architecture typical of the Mussolini era: a vast columned hall with a grand staircase and a room with a stunning coffered wooden ceiling 22.5 m long.

The current occupants are recent, as the building formerly housed the Faculty of Economics and Commerce – the first in Europe (see opposite).

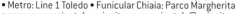

NEARBY

MUSEO ORIENTALE "UMBERTO SCERRATO"
61/62 Via Chiatamone (entrance on Via Partenope)
• Metro: Line 1 Toledo • Funicular Chiaia: Parco Margherita
• www.museorientale.unior.it • museorientale@unior.it
• Admission free • Open Thursday and Friday 11am–2pm; other days by appointment

The Umberto Scerrato Museum, which belongs to the University of Naples "L'Orientale", opened in November 2012. It brings together over 300 pieces in addition to various collections previously acquired by the university but scattered around different sites and not open to the public.

Among the most interesting is a collection of Mesopotamian seals (2002 BC–5th century AD) that is unique in Italy. Some gemstone seals served as good-luck talismans, as borne out by the inscription on one of them: "Long life to the owner of this seal." In the 19th century it was very fashionable to set such objects in jewellery. The collection of Egyptian and Islamic

stelae is also interesting: the smallest of the Islamic steles, displayed at the museum entrance and dating from AD 819, is among the oldest found to date.

The University of Naples "L'Orientale", founded in 1732, is Europe's first seat of learning dedicated to the study of non-European cultures and remains one of the most important in Italy.

MUSEO DI ETNOPREISTORIA
• Tel: 081 7645343 • museo@cainapoli.it
• Open Saturday and Sunday 10am to 1pm; other days by appointment

Since 1972 the wonderful Castel dell'Ovo has housed the "Alfonso Piciocchi" Ethno-Prehistory Museum run by the Neapolitan Speleological Association (Naples branch of the Club Alpino Italiano, CAI).

The displays include artefacts from the Lower Palaeolithic to the Iron Age. Of particular note are the fossil animals and many Villanovan ceramics from the Catena site. The museum also offers visitors an innovative approach to archaeology that reveals how our ancestors lived.

BYZANTINE REMAINS IN CASTEL DELL'OVO

Traces of the Byzantine church of San Salvatore (a stone arch, two pillars and three small Roman columns) can be found in the Castle of the Egg. Access to this part of the fortress is only authorised on certain occasions such as Maggio dei Monumenti (Monuments in May). Info: www.comune.napoli.it.

For the connection between Castel dell'Ovo and Virgil's egg, see following double-page spread.

FROM VIRGIL'S EGG TO THE CASTLE OF THE EGG

The name Castel dell'Ovo (Castle of the Egg) derives from a legend known only in outline. Virgil, the great benefactor of Naples, is supposed to have placed an egg in a glass carafe, then locked the carafe in a cage hung from the roof of a tunnel over which this castle was later built, right in the city centre near the waterfront.

The egg is a recurring symbol in many religious rites in Naples and elsewhere. It is the ultimate symbol of life and, with its perfect shape, a representation of the universe: part of it is yellow like the Sun and part is white like the Moon, the two celestial bodies that personify male and female respectively.

In Naples the egg is linked to various cults, notably that of the Siren Parthenope (see p. 145), the founder of Naples, a deity half-woman and half-bird who, before dying, had laid a sacred egg at the spot where they later built her tomb. So it would be a very inauspicious omen if the egg was stolen or broken.

This belief persisted until the 14th century, a time when attempts were being made to eradicate the pagan cults. It is said that when Queen Joan I of Anjou rebuilt the castle after it was destroyed by a tidal wave, she hung a cage containing an egg in the tunnels under the fortress in order to save the city. In any case, the islet was renamed "Il Salvatore" (The Saviour) after the church, which was incorporated into the fortress. A chapel dedicated to the Madonna dell'Uovo (Our Lady of the Egg) was also built to keep both clergy and people happy. Today, no trace of the chapel remains, though the legend continues to haunt the castle vaults.

The Castle of the Egg was built by the Normans (12th century) on the ruins of a Basilian monastery, built in turn on the remains of an estate that belonged to the Roman general Lucullus. The huge estate stretched from the existing islet to the hill of Pizzofalcone and probably as far as Castel Nuovo (Piazza Municipio). Lucullus bred moray eels in saltwater lakes dotted around his grounds. In his splendid gardens he had planted the very first peach trees to be imported from Persia, as well as the first cherry trees from Pontus, a region bordering the Black Sea. This love of gastronomy earned Lucullus such a reputation that the word "Lucullan" now means "lavish" or "gourmet".

ARCHIVIO FOTOGRAFICO PARISIO

10 Piazza Carolina – Porticato di San Francesco di Paola
- Metro: Line 1 Toledo • Funicular Centrale: Augusteo
- Tel: 081 0324427, 329 4776984 • info@archiviofotograficoparisio.it
- www.archiviofotograficoparisio.it
- Open Monday to Friday 9.30am–1.30pm and 2.30pm–5pm
- Admission free

A hundred years of Neapolitan history in a million negatives

The headquarters of the Archivio Fotografico Parisio association, located behind the portico of the church of San Francesco di Paola, is not only a must for anyone wanting to know Naples better – it is also a small architectural jewel, with many fine early-19th-century elements. More than a million negatives and hundreds of photographs, together with vintage equipment, are preserved within its walls. A permanent photographic exhibition traces the past hundred years of the city's history.

The archive was created out of two complementary collections: that of Giulio Parisio (1919–1965), an internationally renowned contemporary photographer who set up his studio on the premises, and that of the brothers Vincenzo and Guglielmo Troncone, who (from 1926 to 1996) had a photographic studio nearby and recorded scenes of human interest. This archive allows the visitor to rediscover the traditions and transformations, festivals, crafts and old neighbourhoods of Naples from the early 1920s to the end of the 1980s.

Most of the images are digitised and you can buy reproductions.

THE PRESIDENT'S ANTI-AIRCRAFT SHELTER

"Caving" (Speleo) tour organised by the Associazione Culturale
Borbonica Sotterranea
4 Vico Grottone
• Funicular Centrale: Augusteo
• Tel: 366 2484151, 081 7645808
• mail@galleria borbonica.it • www.galleriaborbonica.com
• Guided tours: Saturday and Sunday at 11am and 4pm (duration
2½ hours)

> **Hoisted
> by cable 35 m
> underground**

The Caving tour organised by the Associazione Culturale Borbonica Sotterranea requires equipment that is provided by the association itself (helmet with lamp, overalls and harness). You start down a narrow 17th-century staircase that leads to the cisterns 35 m below. You then go through a maze of pipes and cisterns once used to supply the city with water, before reaching a bomb shelter used during the Second World War by the famous writer Curzio Malaparte and the current President of the Italian Republic, Giorgio Napolitano.

Next is a small gallery with thousands of shells piled high, thrown out from a 19th-century goldsmith's that specialised in buttons and cameos: the workshop was located just above the tunnel and was linked to it by means of a well. Then you have to crawl along increasingly narrow tunnels belonging to the ancient Bolla aqueduct, where in some places there are mysterious (religious?) signs on the walls, probably made by the *pozzari*, the men who looked after the underground aqueducts. Finally, you cross a huge cave via a wooden bridge suspended 6 m above the ground and return by cable lift.

The association runs three different tours exploring this section of the "underground city": Standard (see p. 51), Adventure (*Avventura*) (see p. 54) and Caving (*Speleo*) (see above). The Adventure option includes a raft ride through part of the tunnel, whereas the Standard tour lets you walk the full length of it.

VESTIGES OF THE FORMER "SUPREMA" BROTHEL

㉗

Chiaja Hotel de Charme - Antica Casa Lecaldano Sasso La Terza
216 Via Chiaia – 80121 Napoli
• Metro: Line 1 Toledo • Funicular Centrale: Augusteo • Bus: R2 from
Napoli Centrale station
• Tel: 081 415555 / 081 422344 • info@hotelchiaia.it

T he up-market "Suprema" brothel in the Spanish quarter was one of the most elegant and luxurious in the city. Although at the time you entered by the door which now leads to the kitchen of the famous Pizzeria Brandi, access today is via the Chiaja Hotel de Charme (address above), whose staff are happy to show visitors around.

De Crescenzo said: 'The evening before, Saint Januarius failed to work his miracle'

In 1958, the Suprema was closed, like all the brothels in Italy, to the chagrin of many fans, including Luciano De Crescenzo. This illustrious Neapolitan author wrote that on 19 September 1958, Saint Januarius (the city's patron saint, see p. 354) had failed to work his biannual miracle, presumably in protest at the unjust closures that would take place next day.

But fate had decided that the Suprema would live again. One day, a contractor who was converting a large apartment block into a hotel heard that the adjacent premises were being offered for sale at auction. He managed to buy the place only to discover that it was the former brothel.

Given its historical value, the hotel's interiors have been restored in spirit, with their garish colours and even a price list. You can see some original objects such as mirrors, a small piece of furniture and the bidet where prostitutes washed their clients (in the first half of the 20th century, venereal disease was widespread and greatly feared). Don't miss the original sign, which has been carefully restored.

The rooms with their flashy decor – around ten in all – have plaques with the "stage name" of each girl. They read: Mimì of Vesuvius (alias the anti-fascist, Gelsomina), Anastasia the Friulian, Dorina of Sorrento …

At the beginning of the corridor, to the left, a little bridge connects two small terraces that used to overlook the courtyard: from here the girls would display their charms while the clients, down below in the lobby, made their choice.

Further along the corridor you can admire a beautiful Art Nouveau glass door, which has also been restored. A staircase, which now leads to the hotel's emergency exit, at the time led to a door reserved for personalities or celebrities who didn't want to be seen in such a place.

ASSOCIAZIONE "CIRCOLO ARTISTICO POLITECNICO"

48 Piazza Trieste e Trento
- Metro: Line 1 Toledo
- Funicular Centrale: Augusteo • Bus: R2 from Napoli Centrale station
- Visits on reservation by e-mail or phone
- associazionecircoloartistico@gmail.com • Tel: 081 426543
- www.associazionecircoloartistico.it

A meeting place under the sign of art and culture

Established on 22 December 1888 under the name Società Napoletana degli Artisti by a group of famous artists including Antonio Mancini and Domenico Morelli, the Circolo Artistico Politecnico association, housed on the second floor of the palazzo of Cardinal Zapata (viceroy of Naples in the 17th century), has a museum, historical archives, a library and a photographic collection. It also awards scholarships and organises cultural events, art exhibitions, concerts and plays.

The elegant Liberty-style salon dates from 1912 and was designed by the architect Giovan Battista Comencini. The museum displays over 500 works by Neapolitan painters and sculptors of the early 19th to early 20th centuries. The photographic collection includes signed portraits of famous people such as Enrico De Nicola, Giorgio Napolitano, Enrico Caruso, Eduardo De Filippo and Giacomo Puccini.

The library is dedicated to the poet, journalist and writer Ferdinando Russo, a founder member of the circle. It holds 3,000 volumes, including rare editions from 1687.

GIOSUÈ CARDUCCI'S REVENGE

The guest of honour at a poetry conference held in 1887 was the great Tuscan poet Giosuè Carducci, who was visiting Naples with his girlfriend Annie Vivanti. Ferdinando Russo was struck by her beauty and straightaway wrote a song especially for her, *Scetate* (Wake Up), set to music by Mario Costa. One night, Russo sang his composition below the balcony of the hotel where Carducci and his girlfriend were staying. When he attended the conference next day, the furious Carducci declared that poetry "was the prerogative of people living in cold and meditative regions".

MASCAGNI, A POOR LOSER

The Italian operatic composer Pietro Mascagni was a tireless card player, and could spend all night at "*Lo Scopone scientifico*" (see the 1972 film of that name directed by Luigi Comencini), which is played by two couples with Neapolitan cards. Mascagni always claimed he was unbeatable at this game, but whenever he happened to lose he attacked his partner, calling him "a nullity who deserves an end like Turiddu", alluding to his opera *Cavalleria rusticana*.

HORNS AGAINST THE EVIL EYE

The number of Neapolitans who have never owned a red horn can be counted on the fingers of one hand. Even fewer have never mimicked horns, pointing the index and little fingers towards the ground, an automatic gesture for them as soon as they feel threatened by a curse, real or imaginary. And the phrase "I'm making the *corna*" (sign of the horns) is used instead of "Touch wood". The people of Naples certainly didn't invent this symbol, which was once almost universal, but have simply developed it in their own way and perpetuated its use over time, to make it the ultimate "talisman".

Animal horns were displayed over house entrances as far back as the Neolithic period. They were believed to be a powerful natural weapon in driving out enemies and the forces of evil. By warding off misfortune, they brought happiness and therefore fertility, which was indispensable for survival.

Warriors in most parts of the world wore horned helmets and the animals that supplied the horns themselves became objects of worship.

In ancient Egypt, horns also became an attribute of female fertility: Isis, the Great Mother, a very popular deity in Rome and Naples, wore horns on her head with the Moon set between them. In addition, many goddesses are represented with a crescent Moon, an allusion to the horn.

The little Neapolitan version, in order to be effective, must be red, hollow, twisted, pointed and received as a gift. It derives from the Roman phallus, attribute of the god Priapus, a ubiquitous amulet in Roman culture. At Pompeii, phalluses were carved on doors, walls and even the cobbled streets. In people's homes, many objects were decorated with huge priapic symbols in marble or bronze. Women wore the symbol around their necks as red coral pendants.

With the coming of Christianity, propriety required the phallus to be replaced by a horn. In the Middle Ages, Neapolitan jewellers were renowned for their necklaces made from miniature red horns, which were exported throughout Europe.

CUCKOLD'S HORNS

Whereas to ward off the *iettatura* (curse of the evil eye, from Neapolitan *jettare*, to throw, or hurl), the two-fingered gesture points to the ground, pointing the fingers up at someone is to treat them as a cuckold. Originally this gesture branded a man as an ox and therefore impotent.

In Italy, Saint Martin, Bishop of Tours, became the patron of deceived husbands. Each city has its own legend to justify this practice. In Naples it is said that the husbands of unfaithful women would lock themselves in the Certosa di San Martino (Saint Martin's Charterhouse, see p. 319).

CORALS IN THE MUSEO ASCIONE

Ascione 1855 SrL - 19 Piazzetta Matilde Serao (inside Galleria Umberto I)
• Metro: Line 1 Toledo, Line 2 Montesanto • Funicular Centrale: Augusteo
• Bus: R2 from Napoli Centrale station
• Visits on reservation • Tel: 081 421111
• napoli@ascione.com • www.ascione.com

A coral display in the city centre

I n premises located on the second floor inside Galleria Umberto I, in the museum run by the house of Ascione, you can admire over 300 designs in coral, lava stone (very popular with Queen Victoria) and cameos – so many choice pieces from a production that spread over a century and a half from the early 19th century to the 1940s. The Ascione workshop is the oldest in the town of Torre del Greco (between Pompeii and Naples), world capital of coral and cameos.

Here you'll find a superb chain created in 1938 for Princess Maria José on the occasion of her visit to Naples; a precious coral necklace presented to Queen Farida of Egypt (two copies of this were made in case the original was lost); and a 1920 cameo considered to be one of the prettiest in the world, *Immortal Love*, by Antonio Mennella. Note also a splendid medusa in coral, emblem of the house, which alludes to the Medusa of Greek mythology whose blood turned into coral when she was killed by Perseus.

A browse through the information section will reveal corals of different types and provenances, ancient techniques for collecting the coral (which used to be found in abundance along the coast) and tools for working the precious material ... an entire room is devoted to cameos and the art of engraving them.

LUCCHESI PALLI WING, *BIBLIOTECA NAZIONALE* VITTORIO EMANUELE III

1 Piazza del Plebiscito
- Metro: Line 1 Toledo, Line 2 Montesanto • Funicular Centrale: Augusteo
- Bus: R2 from Napoli Centrale station
- Tel: 081 7819266 (administration), 081 7819240 / 7819267
- bn-na.lucchesipalli@beniculturali.it
- Open Monday to Friday 8.30am–6.45pm (last distribution 5.30pm)

> *A splendid but virtually unknown collection*

This wing of the Victor Emmanuel III National Library holds the valuable and little-known Lucchesi Palli collection, established in 1888 when Count Febo Edoardo Lucchesi Palli of the Campofranco (Sicily) noble family donated his extensive library to the state. The count gave not only his books and manuscripts, but also furniture and shelving from his library, having them transported and adapted at his own expense. The rooms were then embellished by the city's most sought-after artisans.

The original collection consisted of over 30,000 volumes (librettos, theatrical works and Japanese literature in the original language). It has since developed considerably as a result of acquisitions and other donations, to become a reference for music, theatre and cinema.

The collection includes many letters in Giuseppe Verdi's own hand; all the manuscripts and publications of the celebrated poet Salvatore Di Giacomo (see p. 76), who was also the librarian of this section; some 2,500 scripts of plays from the early 19th century; the Raffaele Viviani archive (see p. 333), tracing the entire career of the great Neapolitan actor and writer; as well as a collection of over 25,000 *Piedigrotte* – Neapolitan songs mainly written for the Piedigrotta festival (see p. 30).

AOSTA COLLECTION AT THE *BIBLIOTECA NAZIONALE* VITTORIO EMANUELE III

1 Piazza del Plebiscito
• Metro: Line 1 Toledo, Line 2 Montesanto • Funicular Centrale: Augusteo
• Bus: R2 from Napoli Centrale station
• Guided tours on reservation at Ufficio per le Relazioni con il Pubblico
(URP). The visit is not for the faint-hearted!
• Tel: 081 7819231

> *The enchanted Africa of Hélène, Duchess of Aosta*

A tiger skin and head, the heads of an elephant and a rare three-horned rhinoceros, antelopes, giraffes and other stuffed animals of the savannah together with weapons (daggers, machetes, spears, guns, a sword with a horn hilt and an emerald set in the blade), African musical instruments, Inca artefacts, a rock inscription in the Berber language from the 11th century BC (one of the oldest in the world, found in the Algerian Sahara) ... All these objects were donated to the National Library by the Duchess of Aosta, Princess Hélène of Orléans, a world traveller (known as "the Bedouin princess"), photographer, hunter and benefactor (she was an inspector for the Red Cross). She died at Naples in 1951, aged nearly 80, and is buried in the church of Santa Maria Incoronata at Capodimonte.

The extraordinary Aosta collection was originally assembled in the Reggia (royal palace) at Capodimonte, where the duchess lived with her husband, Prince Emanuele Filiberto of Savoy-Aosta. In 1947, everything was entrusted

to one of her friends, Guerriera Guerrieri, the museum's director. It is now displayed in the five frescoed rooms that formerly comprised the private cabinet of King Ferdinand I of Bourbon.

The collection also includes 11,000 books and 10,000 photographs: private documents that reveal a unique image of the cadet branch of the Savoy dynasty. Hélène of Orléans was a precursor of the Danish Baroness Karen Blixen, who was also a writer and inspired the film *Out of Africa*. In Hélène's memoirs, she describes her journeys and continues to dream of Africa, where "my wandering soul could stop, live, enjoy the passing of time".

TEATRO SAN CARLO CLOCK

98/F Via San Carlo
• Metro: Line 1 Toledo • Funicular Centrale: Augusteo • Bus: R2 from
Napoli Centrale station
• biglietteria@teatrosancarlo.it
• promozionepubblico@teatrosancarlo.it
• Booking office opening hours: Monday to Saturday 10am–7pm;
Sunday 10am–3.30pm • Tel: 081 7972331

The clock face turns, not the hands

In the San Carlo theatre, the clock under the proscenium arch has a feature that few Neapolitans know about: instead of the clock hands moving, as tradition dictates, here the dial rotates around a fixed pointer in the form of the right arm of a winged female figure.

The most plausible explanation for this is that the Siren (lower left) is inviting Time to stop and enjoy the pleasure of the arts, while pointing out to him the Muses of poetry, music and dance. Time, in the centre and surrounded by six female figures, indicates the passing of the hours, which are represented as signs of the zodiac.

Originally, the predominant colours of the San Carlo theatre were blue and silver: these colours are still displayed on the royal coat of arms above the proscenium arch.

The current red and gold decoration dates from 1849, a year of great political upheaval.

ROYAL ACCESS

The San Carlo theatre is linked to Palazzo Reale by an underground passage excavated on the orders of the Bourbon King Charles III. The passage, intended to connect the royal family's apartments to the box reserved for the king and his entourage, was commissioned from the architect Antonio Medrano by the king himself, who paid 32,000 ducats from his own pocket for the privilege.

THE NEW "GIARDINI ROOM" IN THE DISUSED CARPENTRY WORKSHOP

In 2011, the premises formerly occupied by the San Carlo theatre's carpentry workshop were converted into rehearsal and recording rooms. Below the "romantic garden" of Palazzo Reale, they can be glimpsed through a window near the sculpture *Prova d'orchestra* by Mimmo Paladino.

For more on music in Naples, see following double-page spread.

NAPLES, WORLD CAPITAL OF MUSIC

Of course, not all Neapolitans are musicians or singers, but music and singing are deeply rooted in their culture. In this region people pray, protest and even sell their wares in song.

In the 19th and 20th centuries, song production was in full swing and some melodies travelled from one end of the planet to the other in the baggage of the world's most famous tenors. The lyricists of this period were often poets of great stature such as Salvatore Di Giacomo to whom we owe, among other works, the delightful *Marechiaro*. It is said that E. A. Mario wrote about two thousand songs, among which is the hugely popular *Santa Lucia Iuntana*.

Many of the lyrics revolve around love, but there are others that celebrate Naples as its people are attached to their city in a way that borders on the absurd. Songs such as *Santa Lucia Iuntana*, dedicated to emigrants torn apart by homesickness, are a poignant testimony to this.

The echo of Neapolitan music spread around Europe from the early 16th century, when the first *villanelles* – pastoral songs – were transcribed and recovered by professional composers.

From the late 16th century onwards, Naples never ceased to produce great composers. Carlo Gesualdo, Prince of Venosa, was an innovative and unparalleled madrigalist, despite having been involved in a horrific crime: in his palazzo at 9 Piazza San Domenico, the prince surprised his wife Maria d'Avalos with her lover, Duke Fabrizio Carafa, and brutally murdered them both.

In the following centuries, the four Neapolitan conservatories (the first of which, Santa Maria di Loreto, was founded in 1537) echoed to the music of Pergolesi, Vinci, Scarlatti, Jommelli, Porpora, Cimarosa, Paisiello, Bellini, Leoncavallo, Cilea ... almost 300 of them in all.

Jean-Jacques Rousseau exclaimed in his 1768 *Dictionnaire de musique*: "Run, fly to Naples and listen to the masterpieces of Leo, Durante, Jommelli, Pergolesi ..." The 18th-century French writer Charles de Brosses called Naples the "world capital of music". For Stendhal, writing in the first half of the 19th century, the San Carlo was simply incomparable. This theatre, built in 1737, was also the world's first opera house (Milan's La Scala dates from 1778 and Venice's La Fenice from 1792).

By the 15th century, music had already charmed the Aragonese (Spanish) court, and in the 13th and 14th centuries musical plays, predecessors of the lyric opera, were heard in the royal castle of the Angevin (French) dynasty. From the time of the founding of the city by the Greeks, the people had never stopped singing. Only a few pieces of this very early musical heritage have been recovered by the maestro Roberto De Simone (see p. 289) because it belonged to a strictly oral tradition.

Even today, during religious festivals, the words of ritual songs are improvised by the performers who, although following a traditional model, can't repeat what they have just sung. During these celebrations, the tarantella or "*tammurriata*" dance is performed in a frenzy, in bygone days with the aim of inducing a trance and communicating with the gods. These dances, considered "diabolical" by the Church, were even banned at one time, before ending up in the traditional music repertoire. Nowadays, in certain small towns of Campania, devotional dances are still performed as in Graeco-Roman times. The instruments are the same too – large and small tambourines, castanets, the double flute and vertical flute, and others with untranslatable Neapolitan names (*putipù, scetavajasse, triccabballacche*). When street vendors still walked the city, you could hear rhythmic poetry chanted to advertise their wares, with lines such as: "*Maiateche 'e cerase! Che belli voce! Sientele, segno c'abbrile trase*" (I'm selling these cherries in pairs! Listen to their beautiful voices! They say that April has arrived). The religious songs and the street vendors' voices are very similar to ancient Greek monody, even directly emulating it.

In their day, both Livy and Virgil recorded that they were moved by the wonderful songs they heard at Naples. Seneca complained of Neapolitans deserting places of high culture to squeeze into theatres where singers were performing. Nero came to Naples in a public relations exercise and recruited hordes of Alexandrians to his cause, because they applauded by making a terrific din with their instruments (hence the derivation of those untranslatable names above) – so it was Nero who invented "rent-a-crowd" applause on his visit to Naples.

This passion for music is rooted in the founding myth associated with the Siren Parthenope (see p. 145), one of the first deities of the ancient city. Just as the Sirens sang to sweeten the passing of the dying, the priestesses who worshipped at their shrine chanted prophecies. No wonder that singing is considered sacred in Naples.

Modern technology has not dried up the musical vein of ancient Parthenope. Excellent musicians and singers carry on the tradition. Riccardo Muti is a product of the Neapolitan music schools, as is maestro Roberto De Simone, one of the most eclectic geniuses of our time (see p. 289).

CIRCOLO NAZIONALE DELL'UNIONE

99 Via San Carlo
• Metro: Line 1 Toledo • Funicular Centrale: Augusteo
• Access only on request during Maggio dei Monumenti: phone or email to get authorization
• Tel: 081 415693 / 081 413329 • circolonazionaleunione@yahoo.it

> *A historic club faithful to ancient traditions*

The Circolo Nazionale dell'Unione, considered the most beautiful private club in the city, has hosted numerous heads of state in its extremely lavish rooms.

An ancient wooden elevator with velvet-covered seats leads to the first floor with its reading room, meeting room, library, and the large salon of breathtaking riches – crystal chandeliers, vast mirrors in golden frames and stucco decoration. From the terrace of this salon you can enjoy an incomparable view of Palazzo Reale, Castel Nuovo and Piazza del Plebiscito.

This place was built to host the court on the orders of King Ferdinand IV (who became Ferdinand I after the Congress of Vienna) by the architect Antonio Niccolini, who was also responsible for the reconstruction of the San Carlo theatre after it burned down in 1816. Later, King Francis I of Bourbon gave the building to the Accademia delle Dame e dei Cavalieri (Academy of Dames and Knights), an aristocratic association that organised receptions, especially in honour of foreign dignitaries visiting Naples.

After the unification of Italy, Victor Emmanuel II hired out the building to a new association, the Casino dell'Unione, founded by union supporter Carlo Poerio. In 1947, the Casino and the Circolo Nazionale merged to create the Circolo Nazionale dell'Unione, whose vocation is still hospitality in the form of receptions in honour of high-ranking visitors. The club is members only but visits can be arranged on request or during the Maggio dei Monumenti open day in May. Certain rules are mandatory, such as the dress code (black tie for gentlemen, formal dress for ladies).

BAS-RELIEF OF A WOMAN

Triumphal arch at the entrance of Castel Nuovo – Piazza Municipio
• Metro: Line 1 Toledo, Line 2 Montesanto
• Funicular Centrale (Augusteo) or Funicular Montesanto (Montesanto)

> *Lucrezia d'Alagno, lover of King Alfonso I?*

The monumental gateway of the Arco di Trionfo (Triumphal Arch) at Castel Nuovo (the royal palace in the Angevin and Aragonese periods), a masterpiece of the Neapolitan Renaissance, commemorates Alfonso of Aragon's victorious entry to the city in 1443.

He is followed by pages, eminent citizens, soldiers, horsemen ... and one woman – the only one. She is shown in the foreground just in front of the horses pulling the triumphal chariot. Given the height of the arch, you won't be able to see her with the naked eye. Historians are in agreement that the suggestion of her being an allegory of the Siren Parthenope is highly unlikely as she has never been shown fully clothed like this mysterious female figure: most experts think she represents Lucrezia d'Alagno, King Alfonso I's great love.

She was 18 and he was 53 when they met for the first time on 23 June 1448. On this Saint John's Eve, it is said, the beautiful and noble Lucrezia was begging in the street with the other girls, as tradition required. The king, who was passing by, accepted the small plant that the lovely beggar handed him and in exchange offered her a purseful of Alfonsos, the gold coins of his reign. Lucrezia opened the purse, pulled out a single coin and gave the rest back to the king, saying that one Alfonso was enough for her. Even if the story of this meeting is shrouded in legend, the king was indeed deeply in love with Lucrezia. Their love story lasted for ten years, until the death of the monarch.

All those who knew her, even Pope Paul II, were ready to swear to Lucrezia's virtue as she never allowed Alfonso to share her bed. Be that as it may, the beautiful lady not only became immensely rich and powerful, but she was introduced to the king's court and he had her sit at his right hand during official ceremonies. But he could never marry his beloved, because, although he was separated from his wife of thirty years, the pope obstinately refused to grant him an annulment. Lucrezia, emboldened by her many influential connections, even tried her luck by going to Rome herself. Alfonso provided her with an escort of the noblest ladies of the kingdom, an army of servants and 500 horsemen, such were the depths of his passion. But Calixtus III was unimpressed and unyielding. On the king's death, Lucrezia's power diminished and she ended her days in a convent.

CASTEL NUOVO: A POPE IMPRISONED, CAMPANELLA TORTURED, GIOTTO'S FRESCOES, THE ESCAPADES OF JOAN OF ANJOU …

It is said that the future Boniface VIII ordered his spies to intimidate the rather gullible Pope Celestine V while he was being held at the court of King Charles II of Anjou in Castel Nuovo. So under cover of night these minions introduced a long speaking tube into the room of the pope, who believed he was hearing the voice of God commanding him to renounce the papacy. Celestine made his decision to abdicate in December 1294 and died two years later while interned on the orders of Boniface VIII.

Giotto, who in 1328 was the official court painter, completed no less than three cycles of paintings in Castel Nuovo: a series of portraits of famous people in the Great Hall, scenes from the Old and New Testaments in the Palatine Chapel and a number of frescoes in the king's apartments. Everything was lost in a fire before the castle was rebuilt in the 15th century.

Joan I (1327?–1382) of Anjou (Queen of Naples and titular Queen of Jerusalem, Countess of Provence), the granddaughter of Robert the Wise, had four husbands and, it is said, several lovers. Her reputation as a lustful woman was such that people attributed her death to a horse she had tried to mate with in the castle stables (when in fact she was dethroned, imprisoned and assassinated). For centuries, playwrights, writers and historians, Spanish, English, French and German, perpetuated these defamatory rumours. Joan, however, was simply the victim of her youth (propelled onto the throne at only 16), the libertinism at court and a very disadvantageous historical context.

Joan II of Anjou-Duras (1371–1435) acceded to the throne at the age of 41 on the death of her brother Ladislas. She, too, had a renowned libido and it was she who, according to legend, got rid of her discarded lovers by having them fall into a trap that led to the "crocodile pit" (see opposite). Dethroned in her turn, she was buried in the church of the Annunziata at Naples, unlike Joan I whose body simply disappeared.

It was also in a Castel Nuovo cell that the philosopher Tommaso Campanella was imprisoned and brutally tortured, accused of inciting his countrymen to revolt against Spanish rule. He survived by feigning madness, which demanded incredible courage given the constant supervision to which he was subjected. In 1602, having recovered from the injuries inflicted by his torturers, he was incarcerated for twenty-seven years in a cell where he wrote the utopian treatise *La Città del sole* (The City of the Sun).

THE CROCODILE THAT DEVOURED PRISONERS

Prints of Castel Nuovo up to the mid-19th century show a stuffed crocodile hanging above the main doorway. No historian has ever been able to provide a rational explanation of what this exotic animal was doing or when it was put there.

A symbolic act, some say. But to symbolise what? It is true that in the castle's underground passages a trapdoor leads to a well of some kind which is connected with the sea, and this place, from an unspecified period, was known as the "crocodile pit".

Chroniclers of different eras (including Alexandre Dumas *père* in his history of the Bourbons of Naples) reported that Queen Joan II of Anjou cast the lovers she tired of into the pit. The unfortunate suitors were then devoured by a huge crocodile which, after being imported by traders in exotic animals, had escaped and hidden in a cave on the shore next to the castle.

This very reptile would probably have dealt with any number of prisoners who needed to be "disappeared" with no fuss. Later – exactly when is not known – it was decided to kill the animal using a horse's thigh as bait. Might the mummified remains of the beast then have been placed at this strategic spot to feed the legend and discourage enemies of the kingdom?

The mystery remains, and still haunts Neapolitans to such an extent that, on 21 March 2004, they immediately jumped to the conclusion that evidence had been found of the famous crocodile's existence when the skeleton of a large animal was discovered during excavations for the construction of a metro station in Piazza Municipio. The daily *Il Corriere della Sera*, which heralded the sensational discovery, published a retraction the next day, as soon as it was clear that this was simply a mammal whose bones happened to be there.

STATUE OF ANTONIO TOSCANO

Museo Civico di Castel Nuovo
Piazza Municipio
• Metro: Line 1 Toledo, Line 2 Montesanto
• Funicular Centrale (Augusteo) or Funicular Montesanto (Montesanto)
• Visits Monday to Saturday 9am–7pm
• Tel: 081 7955877

> *Portrait of an intransigent republican*

Among its numerous works of art, the Museo Civico di Castel Nuovo's second-floor display of portrait busts includes a little-known statue by Francesco Jerace (1857–1937), depicting a man with his left arm raised to protect his head.

Antonio Toscano was a Calabrian priest and committed republican who sacrificed his own life and that of his companions to avoid falling into the hands of the enemy. In 1799, with the proclamation of the Parthenopean Republic, Toscano was entrenched with his garrison at Fort Vigliena, south of the city. On 13 June of the same year, Cardinal Fabrizio Ruffo, at the head of his troops supporting the king (known as Sanfedisti, i.e. members of the "Holy Faith"), gave the order to attack the fort and broke down the walls. Seeing that all was lost, Toscano managed to reach the powder magazine and blew it up.

In the same room, the glass floor allows you to see the Roman remains (1st century BC and 5th century AD) found beneath the castle.

NEARBY

SOCIETÀ NAPOLETANA DI STORIA PATRIA ⬤36

Castel Nuovo
Piazza Municipio
• Metro: Line 1 Toledo, Line 2 Montesanto
• Funicular Centrale (Augusteo) or Funicular Montesanto (Montesanto)
• Tel: 081 5510353
• info@storiapatrianapoli.it
• Open Tuesday and Wednesday 10am–6pm

Housed in the "San Giorgio" and "di Mezzo" towers of Castel Nuovo (also known as Maschio Angioino), the Neapolitan Society of National History, founded in 1875, holds the first book to be printed in Italy: Saint Augustine's *De Civitate Dei* (The City of God), published in 1467 by C. Sweynheym and A. Pannartz at Subiaco (near Rome).

This private library, which also organises conferences and cultural events, has the richest literary heritage in southern Italy, consisting of about 350,000 works ranging from monographs to manuscripts, scrolls, prints and drawings. One of the most important collections is that of the library of French seismologist Alexis Perrey (1807–1882), which includes a letter written to him by Charles Darwin.

PLAQUE IN VICO PENSIERO

Società Napoletana di Storia Patria - Castel Nuovo - Piazza Municipio
• Metro: Line 1 Toledo, Line 2 Montesanto
• Funicular Centrale (Augusteo) or Funicular Montesanto (Montesanto)
• Open to the public Tuesday and Wednesday 10am–6pm

A lover's despair engraved in stone

In the ancient heart of Naples, where almost 3,000 years of stratified history is frozen in time, part of Via dei Tribunali (the main east–west axis crossing the Graeco-Roman city) is closely associated with stories of witchcraft (see below). Here (before it was swept away by the wave of modernisation that engulfed the city in 1890) was Vico Pensiero (Thought Lane), a dark alley so called because of a plaque bearing the enigmatic Neapolitan lines "*Povero pensiero me fu arrubato pe no le fare le spese me l'à tornato*" (Poor thought stolen from me and then returned to avoid paying the price). No one yet knows either the origin or the author, or even the date of this plaque, now kept in the premises of the Società Napoletana di Storia Patria (SNSP, Neapolitan Society of National History).

The active Neapolitan imagination couldn't ignore such a mystery, so people took it upon themselves to find an explanation: one evening in the year 1500, a young poet strolling through the neighbourhood came upon the alley in question. Suddenly he heard a meow and saw a kitten crouched in a corner. He picked it up and sheltered it under his coat. Before he had even turned away, a door opened and a girl came out. She had jet-black hair down to her hips and jade-green sparkling eyes. In the voice of an angel, she thanked the young man for taking care of her cat. Literally thunderstruck, he stayed for a long while chatting with the beautiful stranger, who arranged to meet him the next day at the same time.

For months on end the poet lived for these nocturnal meetings, obsessed with one idea: to marry the sublime creature who had captivated him. One day, however, she vanished without warning. Enquiries around the neighbourhood came to nothing: no one had ever seen this girl. He had surely been the victim, he was told, of a witch who wanted to capture the spirit of a handsome young man for her own amusement. But the poet would have none of it and almost went insane: emaciated, in scruffy clothes, he spent all his time sitting at the place where he'd met the girl. One night, in the depths of despair, he took up a stone and engraved the words that can still be read today, then disappeared without a trace.

NEARBY

THE THINKER OF VICO PENSIERO

Above the plaque in Vico Pensiero, a bas-relief called *Thought* depicts a seated man with a pensive air.

Could the mysterious plaque-inscriber have written these words after the theft and subsequent return of the sculpture? This is the hypothesis put forward by Ludovico de la Ville-sur-Yllon (one of the founders, with Benedetto Croce, of the prestigious journal *Napoli Nobilissima*), when he wrote an article about it in 1893. The "*poor thought*" would actually have been the statuette that was thought to have been "stolen and then returned to avoid paying the price", i.e. to avoid punishment by the law.

DIANA AND THE WITCHES

The ruins of the temple of Diana below the church of Santa Maria Maggiore (see p. 89), a short distance from the site of Vico Pensiero, are not unrelated to the web of legends woven by the popular imagination over the centuries. The cult of Diana, followed by women who celebrated nocturnal rites, was demonised by the early Christians, who associated these moonlit ceremonies with the witches' sabbath. In the Neapolitan dialect, in fact, the word *janara* (wicked witch) derives from *dianaria* (follower of Diana).

NAPLES, A CITY STEEPED IN SPELLS

The celebrated writer Matilde Serao (1856–1927), who understood the Neapolitan soul so well, wrote in her book *Il Ventre di Napoli* (The Belly of Naples, 1884): "The Neapolitans, women in particular, believe in witchcraft. The *fattura* [spell] has its fervent adherents: *fattucchiere* [witches] abound.

"A woman wants her husband to remain faithful while away from home? The *fattucchiera* gives her a piece of cord knotted in several places to stitch into the lining of her husband's jacket. Another wants a man to fall in love with her? The *fattucchiera* burns a strand of her hair, pulverises it and mixes it with other ingredients to dissolve in a glass of wine and give it to the uninterested man to drink. You want to win a lawsuit? You have to psychologically tongue-tie the adversary's counsel: make fifteen knots in a length of string and invoke the devil, a terrible incantation.

"Do you wish for the death of a faithless lover? You must fill a small pot with poisonous herbs and boil them up in front of his door at midnight precisely. Do you wish for the death of a woman who's your rival? Pierce a fresh lemon with a few pins to form the silhouette of your enemy, then attach a scrap of her clothing to the fruit, and finally throw the whole lot into her well. The *fattura* ... is found in all districts of the city, she has a solution for every need, emotional or violent, and can satisfy all desires, well-meaning or cruel.

"That's all. Or rather, that's not all. If all that has just been said was multiplied twentyfold, you might not be near the mark."

THE *JANARA*: THE LEGENDARY WITCH OF NOCTURNAL EVILDOING

In the towns and villages of Campania, where people worshipped the goddess Diana — known also as Hecate by the Romans — the legend arose of the *janare* (probably a corruption of *dianare*), diabolical and supernatural creatures, so different from the very real *fattucchiere* (see opposite).

Hecate, a lunar deity like Diana, embodied both fertility and the Black Moon, which was associated with darkness, ghosts and nightmares.

The *janare* originated in Benevento, 80 km east of Naples. There, under a walnut tree in a deep gorge of the Sebeto river (probably the source of the word sabbath as associated with witches), these fearsome she-devils assembled on Saint John's Eve. In Naples, on the very spot where the church of Santa Maria Maggiore stands today, was a temple dedicated to Diana/Hecate. With the advent of Christianity, the women who performed nocturnal rites in honour of the deity began to be demonised and called *janare*.

In both town and country they were greatly feared: it was said that after 11pm every Tuesday and Friday (unlucky days for the superstitious), when their husbands and children were sleeping, they stripped off completely, smeared their bodies with magical olive oil and rode out on their broomsticks to spread evil. As they could liquefy their bodies, they'd find their way into homes through the keyhole of the door, leaving behind sickly babies with stunted growth. If someone felt oppressed during the night, it was the *janara* leaning with all her weight on the unfortunate victim's chest. When a horse looked half-dead and its mane was tousled, that was because a *janara* had exhausted it by galloping all night. These terrifying creatures could also metamorphose into women of great beauty to drive men wild with desire (see Vico Pensiero, p. 86).

At dawn their powers would disappear and they again became ordinary women. But there were tricks to confuse them. If you managed to catch one in the act, you just needed to say: "Come and fetch some salt tomorrow." The next day the witch, in her normal guise, had to come and ask for a handful of salt. If you dared grab her by the hair, you had to be shrewder than her and not reply "Your hair" to her question "What are you holding me by?" Otherwise she'd vanish.

To ward off evil spells, metal objects and a pious image were hung around children's necks. A broom made from rice straw was also placed in front of the door: the *janare* were compelled by their infernal rules to count the stalks one by one. As this task took them until dawn, you could easily stop them without fearing their powers, which would be neutralised by daylight.

It seems that the Russian composer Modest Mussorgsky, after staying at Montecalvo Irpino (near Benevento), in the palazzo of the Duchess Isabella Pignatelli, daughter of Tsar Nicolas II's adviser, was so impressed by these legends that he was inspired to compose the symphonic poem *Night on Bald Mountain* (Montecalvo means "Bald Mountain").

TOLEDO, UNIVERSITÀ, BOVIO, GARIBALDI

1 MUSEO DEL GIOCATTOLO DI NAPOLI 93
2 GIARDINO DEI CINQUE CONTINENTI. 94
3 SISTER ORSOLA BENINCASA'S CELL 95
4 ANTICO LABORATORIO SCIENTIFICO DI SCIENZE NATURALI, FISICA E CHIMICA. 95
5 MUSEO DELLA FONDAZIONE PAGLIARA 95
6 MUSEO DELL'OPERA UNIVERSITARIA 95
7 REPRODUCTION OF LOURDES GROTTO 97
8 A KITCHEN GARDEN DECLARED NATIONAL HERITAGE 97
9 CHAIR IN THE CHAPEL AT SANTA LUCIA AL MONTE 99
10 SAN MARTINO VINEYARD. 101
11 LARGO BARACCHE GALLERY. 103
12 INSCRIPTION ON PALAZZO MAJORANA 104
13 PALAZZO ZEVALLOS STIGLIANO GALLERY 106
14 BUST OF THE GODDESS KNOWN AS THE "HEAD OF NAPLES" 108
15 SECRETS OF NAPLES TOWN HALL. 109
16 EMEROTECA-BIBLIOTECA TUCCI 111
17 PASTRENGO BARRACKS 113
18 UNDERGROUND ALTAR OF THE CHURCH OF SANT'ASPRENO 114
19 GREAT HALL OF THE CHAMBER OF COMMERCE 117
20 PALAZZO PENNE 118
21 ISTITUTO MAGISTRALE ELEONORA PIMENTEL-FONSECA 120
22 ANTONIO GENOVESI HIGH SCHOOL 122
23 MARKS ON THE FAÇADE OF THE CHURCH OF GESÙ NUOVO 125

24 BOURBON HALL OF FAME 126
25 THE VIRGIN'S VEIL, GUGLIA DELL'IMMACOLATA 127
26 ARCHBISHOP SISTO RIARIO SFORZA'S GREAT HALL 129
27 CHURCH OF SANTI MARCELLINO E FESTO 131
28 GARMENTS OF THE MIRACULOUS VIRGIN 133
29 CLOISTERS OF THE FORMER MONASTERY OF SAINTS MARCELLINO AND FESTO 135
30 MUSEO DI PALEONTOLOGIA 135
31 MUSEO DI ANTROPOLOGIA 137
32 MUSEO DI ZOOLOGIA 137
33 BAS-RELIEF OF A HAIRY MAN 139
34 REAL MUSEO DI MINERALOGIA 140
35 MUSEO DI FISICA 141
36 ACCADEMIA PONTANIANA LIBRARY 142
37 FONTANA DI SPINACORONA 144
38 THE GIAMBATTISTA VICO FOUNDATION 146
39 LAND REGISTRY OF THE STATE ARCHIVES 149
40 FILANGIERI ROOM 150
41 SOUVENIR OF THE TERRIBLE EXPLOSION OF 1943 151
42 SAINT BENEDICT'S PLANE TREE 153
43 TASSO ROOM 153
44 *SAINT GEORGE AND THE DRAGON* FRESCO 155
45 AUGUSTISSIMA COMPAGNIA DELLA DISCIPLINA DELLA SANTA CROCE . 157
46 GREEK TOWER AT THE TRIANON THEATRE 158
47 FALSE WINDOWS OF CORSO UMBERTO 160
48 BASIN OF A ROMAN AQUEDUCT 161
49 SAINT JANUARIUS' MISSING FINGERS 161
50 THE MIRACULOUS CARMELITE CRUCIFIX 163

MUSEO DEL GIOCATTOLO DI NAPOLI

Università degli Studi Suor Orsola Benincasa
10 Via Suor Orsola
• Funicular: Centrale or Montesanto (Corso Vittorio Emanuele)
• Visits on reservation: 081 2522308

Yesterday's toys in an unexpected place

The Suor Orsola Benincasa Institute has four museums (see following double-page spread), of which the most unusual and unexpected is the Museo del Giocattolo (Toy Museum). The collection brings together 1,238 historic items from Italy and abroad: dolls and dolls' houses with a vast range of accessories, wooden and tin toys, board games and lead soldiers.

The museum also has a doll manufactured by the house of Kämmer & Reinhardt in the 1930s, bought in Germany by the great Neapolitan philosopher Benedetto Croce for his daughter Silvia. She later donated her doll to the museum where it can be seen today, perfectly restored.

GIARDINO DEI CINQUE CONTINENTI ❷

Istituto Suor Orsola Benincasa
10 Via Suor Orsola
• Funicular: Centrale or Montesanto (Corso Vittorio Emanuele)
• Open Monday, Wednesday and Friday by appointment: 081 2522288

A hanging botanical garden

In 2001, a "Garden of the Five Continents" was planted on the top-floor terrace of the former convent of Suor Orsola Benincasa, featuring rare species of trees and flowers from around the world. It is accessed through a rose garden with thirty different varieties, in a place that was once devoted to the meditation of nuns. The convent, which was founded in 1582, was converted in the early 20th century to an academic institute specialising in education and the natural and human sciences.

NEARBY

SISTER ORSOLA BENINCASA'S CELL ❸
• Visits on reservation: 081 2522288

A small staircase in the Immacolata Concezione leads from Saint Michael's chapel, which Sister Orsola (1547–1618) had built, to the cell where she lived. In a room near the sacristy is a clothed wooden statue of Sister Orsola sitting in a wheelchair. The sculpture was made soon after the death of the renowned founder of the Order of the Oblates of Santissima Concezione. As the nuns of the order were bound by the most rigorous rule of seclusion, Sister Orsola's motto was: "To live in bliss, you must live in silence and solitude."

ANTICO LABORATORIO SCIENTIFICO DI SCIENZE NATURALI, FISICA E ❹
CHIMICA
Istituto Suor Orsola Benincasa
• Visits on reservation: 081 2522288 / 335 5855499

The Laboratory of Natural Sciences, Physics and Chemistry holds a collection of scientific instruments that were still in use at the end of the 19th century.

MUSEO DELLA FONDAZIONE PAGLIARA ❺
• Visits on reservation: 081 2522288

The Rocco Pagliara collection of prestigious art includes Old Masters such as El Greco, Claude Lorrain, Camille Corot, Giacinto Gigante and Antonio Mancini.

MUSEO DELL'OPERA UNIVERSITARIA ❻
• Visits on reservation: 081 2522288

In the Historical Museum of Suor Orsola Benincasa, many objects trace the history of the former convent and the school that succeeded it. One of the most remarkable pieces is probably *Descent from the Cross*, a wooden sculpture by Giacomo Colombo dating from 1698. There is also a notable painting of Orsola Benincasa interceding with the Virgin on behalf of the Neapolitans, who vowed to worship this woman to such a point that they placed her among the patron saints of their city. The museum is housed in the former parlour where you can see a perfectly preserved rotating pass-through hatch, the nuns' sole point of contact with the outside world.

REPRODUCTION OF LOURDES GROTTO

Monastic complex of San Nicola da Tolentino
9 Via Suor Orsola
• Funicular: Centrale (Corso Vittorio Emanuele)
• Open on certain occasions only: see www.fondoambiente.it

A stone from the original grotto

Built in 1618 by Neapolitan architect Gian Giacomo da Conforto, the monastic complex of San Nicola da Tolentino has a small shrine dedicated to the Virgin of Lourdes, as well as a reproduction of the cave in which she appeared to Bernadette Soubirous in 1858. In 1873, the monks displayed an image of the Virgin for the first time in their church. A group of the faithful, returning from a pilgrimage to Lourdes, brought back a statue of Mary which was installed on its present site and a stone from the grotto into which a marble plaque was set.

The monastery is also home to about 3,000 marble ex-votos. For lack of space, the monks are now obliged to refuse all new ex-votos that the worshippers continue to offer.

From the monastery belvedere you can enjoy a stunning view of the Bay of Naples.

NEARBY

A KITCHEN GARDEN DECLARED NATIONAL HERITAGE ❽

The impeccably maintained kitchen garden of San Nicola da Tolentino monastery, laid out on two terraces, is always shown in old maps and sketches of Naples such as the famous "Tavola Strozzi" (on view at the San Martino Museum). The garden was declared national heritage in 2010.

CHAIR IN THE CHAPEL AT SANTA LUCIA AL MONTE

Hotel San Francesco al Monte
328 Corso Vittorio Emanuele
• Funicular Centrale and Montesanto (Corso Vittorio Emanuele)
• Tel: 081 4239111
• info@hotelsanfrancesco.it • www.sanfrancescoalmonte.it/

A miraculous chair for pregnant women

The charming Hotel San Francesco al Monte, set on the hillside just below the San Martino vineyard (see p. 101), was built over the remains of Santa Lucia al Monte monastery, built in the 16th century by the Friars Minor Conventual. Among the well-preserved structures that have been incorporated into the modern building, you can visit the chapel of San Giovanni Giuseppe della Croce, built in the 18th century in the cell where the saint lived. Here, miraculously unmarked by the passage of time, is the chair where he prayed and which is linked to the legend of the "apricot prodigy" – one winter's day, in the presence of the holy man, a pregnant woman was seized by an irrepressible desire for apricots, which were out of season. Saint Giovanni Giuseppe then gave her a little tree on which apricots immediately began to grow.

When this monk was beatified in 1789, the chair became a cult object which, it was believed, had the power to protect pregnant women who came to sit there from time to time.

The convent developed from a small cell dug into the tuff hillside by Friar Agostino Maglianico that became the church of Santa Lucia al Monte, which can still be visited. Later, with the help of Father Francesco of Perugia, a monastery was built around the church. In this still tranquil place, Saint Giovanni Giuseppe della Croce lived for twelve years until his death in 1734, when he became the patron saint of the island of Ischia.

In a corridor dug into the tuff is another chapel, the site of the original cell that gave rise to the church and monastery.

In the former refectory there is still a huge fresco depicting Jesus offering food to Saint Peter of Alcantara and Saint Pascal, with Saint Teresa of Ávila. Behind this room was the entrance, now sealed up, to a secret passage leading to the Certosa di San Martino (Saint Martin's Charterhouse, see p. 319).

From the hotel terrace the view takes in the entire city, to such an extent that during the popular insurrection of 1647 led by Masaniello, Spanish soldiers used this monastery as a base from which to bombard the dissenters entrenched in the city centre.

SAN MARTINO VINEYARD

Communità Rurale Urbana Vigna di San Martino
340 Corso Vittorio Emanuele
• Funicular Centrale and Montesanto (Corso Vittorio Emanuele)
• Tel: 338 5621757
• www.piediperlaterra.org • piediperlaterra@gmail.com
• Open all year round (but obtain authorization first)

> **A verdant oasis of peace**

Although the San Martino vineyard was once part of the Charterhouse of the same name (see p. 319), these 7 hectares (privately owned) lie on the slopes of Vomero, a densely populated residential neighbourhood. It's hard to imagine that behind a gate on a busy avenue is an agricultural business with terraces bounded by ancient supporting arches of tuff.

Orchards, vegetable gardens, olive groves, vineyards, herb gardens and even donkeys and farmyard animals make this place a verdant oasis of peace that has miraculously escaped real-estate speculation thanks to its owner. It has been declared a national monument by the Ministry of Culture.

Within the farm, the association Piedi per la Terra (Feet on the Earth) has for several years organised walks and courses on environmental culture for children, as well as other events. The association and the farm have partnered to create the Urban Rural Community of San Martino, a centre for disseminating an ecological culture and alternative economy, building a relationship between the land and the city. The Community offers a range of initiatives organised around environmental protection, not to mention artistic events.

The vineyard also boasts an exceptional and unusual view of the city: between the high walls that flank Suor Orsola Benincasa University is a sweeping vista of the bay in which the island of Capri seems to be suspended.

LARGO BARACCHE GALLERY

Largo Baracche
largobaracche@gmail.com
• Metro: Line 1 Toledo • Funicular Centrale (Augusteo)
• For opening hours and visits, enquire at 393 3641664

> *A bomb shelter converted into an art gallery*

The Largo Baracche workshop and gallery is located in a small square at the heart of the Spanish Quarter. Originally a bomb shelter, it was occasionally used after the Second World War to store goods. It was restored in 2001.

Since 2006, young artists have joined together to rehabilitate the square and the underground space of 200 m², staging exhibitions, shows and even film festivals there. A staircase incorporated into a modern multicoloured structure leads to the first gallery from which you can access other whitewashed areas, giving an impression of great clarity thanks to the very well-planned play of light.

INSCRIPTION ON PALAZZO MAJORANA

15 Via Carlo Cesare
• Metro: Line 1 Toledo • Funicular Centrale (Augusteo) or Montesanto (Montesanto)

Caffarelli's monstrous ego

Caffarelli, whose real name was Gaetano Majorana (1710–1783), had one of the purest voices in the history of Italian opera. Apulian by birth (from the old Puglia), he studied in Naples where he was castrated, the price for keeping his magnificent voice. He is remembered in the city by the palace he built in 1754.

The extremely narcissistic singer had these words to his own glory inscribed on the gateway: *Amphyon Thebas Ego Domum* – literally "Amphion Thebes Myself this House" – by which he meant: "If Amphion built the walls of Thebes with the mere sound of his lyre, I have built this palace with the sound of my voice."

A number of contemporary writers, including Lalande in his *Voyage en Italie*, mention that a mischievous spirit had written this comment on the double doors: *ille cum, tu sine* ("him with, you without"), alluding to Amphion's intact male attributes, unlike those of Caffarelli. But no trace remains of this witticism.

Caffarelli, a cad and an insolent brawler, was the subject of much gossip that delighted all the scandalmongers of the time. A story doing the rounds in Europe claimed that he refused the gift of a valuable snuffbox from Louis XV on the pretext that it had no portrait of the king. When it was pointed out to him that His Majesty only granted such an honour to ambassadors, Caffarelli retorted: "Well, let His Majesty make the ambassadors sing!"

In 1739, during a concert at the prestigious church of Donna Regina, Caffarelli came to blows with his rival, Reginelli. In 1741, he had to be handcuffed and locked up because during an opera performance at the San Carlo theatre, he shouted at the audience, jeered the other singers and exhibited openly lecherous behaviour towards one of the women. Two years later, again on stage in front of the spectators, he changed the music to confuse his partner, just for the hell of it.

CASTRATOS: THOUSANDS OF CHILDREN SACRIFICED IN THE NAME OF *BEL CANTO*

The practice of castration, introduced to Italy by the Arabs, was adopted by the Church as it was anxious to cover the full range demanded by polyphonic music without using female voices, which had traditionally been banned since the Middle Ages.

The rise of melodrama, which demanded a vocal range inaccessible to women (the castrato voice was capable of an octave higher), was the origin of the exponential spread of this practice in the 17th and 18th centuries. If the career of these "angelic monsters" was decided in Naples, the Papal States held the record for castration (42%).

As the church prohibited the operation in monasteries (at the time, the four Neapolitan conservatories were religious institutions – see p. 168), children between 8 and 10 years of age were operated on in rural clinics or sometimes in large city hospitals. The operation took place in unspeakable sanitary conditions without anaesthetic.

At best, opium was given to the young patients but in the main they just had the carotid artery compressed until they lost consciousness. Most of these children came from poor families who were willing to sacrifice them for money or in the belief that it was the only possible future for their sons. Of the thousands of children operated on, only a few kept an exceptional tone and some even lost their voice. Many of them were psychologically devastated and committed suicide, went crazy, shut themselves up in a monastery or ended up in the streets to swell the ranks of prostitutes.

Those who did become famous at the cost of exhausting work (four to six hours per day) would reap veritable fortunes. They were adored by powerful men and even by women, who had no hesitation in marrying them. Some are true legends in the style of Caffarelli, Porporino or Farinelli who, as President de Brosses wrote, "had seven notes more than a normal voice". And as for Gaspare Pacchiarotti, on some evenings he made

members of the orchestra weep with his angelic voice.

In 1798, castration was abolished although the last of the great castrati, Giovanni Battista Velluti, sang at the San Carlo from time to time until 1808. The reason for the demise of the castrati was not really a moral issue, but rather the advent of romanticism, which no longer required artifice, illusions or vocal ambiguity.

PALAZZO ZEVALLOS STIGLIANO GALLERY

"Gallerie d'Italia"
185 Via Toledo
• Metro: Line 1 Dante or Toledo, Line 2 Montesanto • Funicular Centrale
(Augusteo)
• Tel: 800 454229 / 081 7917233 • info@palazzozevallos.com
• Open Tuesday to Sunday 10am–6pm, Saturday until 8pm
• Admission €4, concessions €3

Ups
and downs
of Palazzo Zevallos

The only remaining original feature of Palazzo Zevallos Stigliano (1637) is Cosimo Fanzago's gargoyled doorway. The palazzo is located in Via Toledo – of which Stendhal said in *Rome, Naples, and Florence*: "I shall not forget Via Toledo, nor any other of the parts of Naples; to my eyes this city has no equal and is the most beautiful city in the universe." The numerous changes in ownership have significantly altered the interior design, including the loss of frescoes by Luca Giordano (17th century). In the early 19th century, the palazzo was even divided into apartments. Finally, in 1898, it was bought by the Banca Commerciale, which undertook major work to convert the hall (formerly open to the sky), the monumental staircase and the first floor into what we see today. Only the *Apotheosis of Sappho*, the large fresco by Giuseppe Cammarano that decorates the ceiling, is from an earlier date (1832). Having been completely renovated in neoclassical style by the Cariplo e Intesa Bank, the building now houses a prestigious museum/gallery where you can see the last work of Michelangelo Merisi, better known as Caravaggio (see opposite), several landscapes by Gaspar van Wittel and Anton Smink Pitloo, two great masters who had a decisive influence on the Neapolitan school of the 19th century, and a fresco by Ezechiele Guardascione (1875–1948), which shows the palazzo as it was before being bought by the Banca Commerciale.

OBSCURE SAGA OF THE LAST CARAVAGGIO

Now displayed in the gallery of the Intesa Bank on the first floor of Palazzo Zevallos, *The Martyrdom of Saint Ursula*, the last work by Caravaggio painted just before his tragic death at Porto Ercole (Tuscany), has a troubled history. The picture, commissioned in 1610 by the son of the Doge of Genoa, Marcantonio Doria, who left it to his son Nicolò, Prince of Angri and Duke of Eboli, seemed to disappear during the 18th century. It abruptly reappeared in 1814, wrongly attributed to Mattia Preti, in the legacy of Giovanni Maria Doria. In 1854, it turned up at Naples in the Palazzo Doria d'Angri before being moved to this family's country estate at Eboli (90 km south of Naples). After the Second World War, the villa and the painting were sold to Baron Romano Avezzano. The badly damaged painting, its provenance still uncertain, was sold to the Banca Commerciale in 1972 for the modest sum of 8 million lire (equivalent to about 4,000 Euros).

Meanwhile, irrefutable evidence (letters, wills, etc.) were used to validate the thesis of Professor Bologna, who since 1954 had been fighting for the recognition of Caravaggio as the author of *The Martyrdom of Saint Ursula*. Caravaggio had, moreover, included his self-portrait, without any scars, in the guise of a soldier standing just behind the saint.

In 2004, the painting was painstakingly restored and finally recaptured its original radiance. It had suffered a number of accidents in its lifetime: Caravaggio, in a hurry to leave the city – because he'd been badly beaten up by thugs from the family of the man he killed in a duel at Rome – delivered the canvas without waiting for the varnish to dry completely. In order to expedite its transfer to Genoa, Prince Doria's agents in Naples left it out in the sun to dry, thinking they were doing the right thing. But the varnish softened further and the painter was asked to repair the damage. As the condition of the remaining paint was still unsatisfactory, however, it was subjected to much "tinkering" that partly led to those false attributions.

The Martyrdom of Saint Ursula is one of three Caravaggio paintings to be found in Naples (the others are *The Flagellation of Christ* in Capodimonte Museum and *The Seven Acts of Mercy* in the church of Pio Monte della Misericordia), although the artist completed dozens of works during the two periods he spent in the city (1606–1607 and 1609–1610). Two of them have fallen into oblivion (an altarpiece said to be commissioned by Croatian merchant Nicholas Radulovic and *Judith Beheading Holofernes*); another

three in a chapel of the church of Sant'Anna dei Lombardi were destroyed during the earthquake of 1805; *The Denial of Saint Peter* was smuggled out and sold to New York's Metropolitan Museum of Art; and others are scattered throughout Europe.

BUST OF THE GODDESS KNOWN AS THE "HEAD OF NAPLES"

⓮

Palazzo San Giacomo – Piazza Municipio
• Metro: Line 1 Toledo • Funicular Centrale (Augusteo)
• Calendar of guided tours: www.comune.napoli.it

"

Mystery of the Neapolitan Marianne

The Palazzo San Giacomo (Naples town hall) was chosen in 1961 as a safe home for the marble bust of a woman's head previously found in the church of San Giovanni a Mare (where a copy can be seen today). Although the writers of antiquity attributed this head to a colossal statue of the Siren Parthenope, the mythical founder of Naples (see p. 145), it is actually Aphrodite/Venus whose temple was on the acropolis in Roman times. It is not known how the head came to be in a neighbourhood that was originally outside the city walls.

Although this first sculpture was initially known as *Marianna a capa 'e Napule* (Marianne, the Head of Naples), it took the name "Marianne" at an unknown later date.

Intriguingly, the area where the bust is now found is called "Caponapoli", literally "Head of Naples", in the sense that Naples begins here for those arriving from the south. Symbolically, this is also where the head would be of the Siren lying along the city that she personifies (see p. 145).

We also know that when the head was probably near the church of Santa Maria dell'Avvocata, this Madonna was celebrated on the feast day of Saint Anne, 26 July. The women performed a propitiatory rite, dancing around the sculpture, which they decked out with flowers and ribbons. The confusion between Mary and Anne (mother of the Virgin Mary) may have resulted in the name "Marianne".

This bust was meant to embody a very important symbol for the people, who sometimes honoured it and sometimes directed their anger against it, as in the popular revolution of 1799. In that year, a group of

intellectuals wanted to follow the French example by proclaiming a republic against the will of the people, who remained faithful to the king. The counter-revolutionaries then conflated the Neapolitan Marianne and the French Jacobin one. In each revolution, Marianne lost bits of her nose, which was fairly well repaired until she was quite disfigured and became associated with ugliness. The Neapolitans, who are always ready to mock, say that an unattractive woman with a large head looks like "Marianne, the Head of Naples".

SECRETS OF NAPLES TOWN HALL

⑮

Palazzo San Giacomo – Piazza Municipio
• Metro: Line 1 Toledo, Line 2 Montesanto • Funicular Centrale
(Augusteo) or Montesanto (Montesanto)
• Bus: R2 from Napoli Centrale station
• Calendar of guided tours: www.comune.napoli.it

Within Naples town hall, known as Palazzo San Giacomo after the church of that name which forms part of the complex, there are many historical artefacts. The medal collection displayed on the second floor, for example, includes forty-five medals associated with notable events in the former capital as well as the symbolic keys to the city, which used to be handed over to successive conquerors as a sign of surrender. The bow (handgrip) of each key is decorated with a wreath of laurel and oak leaves, together with a crown. An "unbridled" horse, the ancient symbol of Naples, is set inside the bow. The join with the shank is formed by a shield engraved with the monogram CDN for *Città di Napoli* (City of Naples).

A remarkable plaque in a room between the first and second floors shows the location of each of the numerous original offices. It was Ferdinand II's decision to have this building constructed to bring together all the state's ministries and secretariats, previously scattered around the city.

Palazzo San Giacomo, formerly known as the "Royal Building of Ministers of State", had seven entrances, six interior courtyards with two fountains, forty corridors and 846 rooms. It was built between 1819 and 1825 by the architects Stefano and Luigi Gasse, Vincenzo Buonocore and Antonio De Simone.

> The guided tour also includes access to the mayor's office, who welcomes visitors himself when available (otherwise his deputy fills in).

EMEROTECA-BIBLIOTECA TUCCI

Palazzo delle Poste – Piazza Matteotti – 2nd floor
• Metro: Line 1 Toledo, Line 2 Montesanto • Funicular Centrale (Augusteo)
• Tel: 081 5513845 / 081 5511226 • info@emerotecatucci.it
• www.emerotecatucci.it
• Open Monday to Friday 8.30am–6.30pm
• Saturday 8.30am–2.30pm (except July and August)
• Admission free
• Some photographic reproduction is allowed

Newspaper library

The Tucci newspaper library, largely unknown to the general public, keeps 9,500 collections of newspapers, magazines and almanacs, mainly Italian but also French, English, German, Austrian, Russian, etc., published over the last five centuries.

Some 200 of these titles are thought to be the only copies in the world. A real treasure trove is held by this extraordinary library founded in 1909, for professional reasons, by a group of journalists (among them Vincenzo Tucci, correspondent of the *Giornale di Sicilia*, to whom the building was dedicated in 1953). The library moved to its present location in 1936 (previously it was in Palazzo Gravina, which used to be the central Post Office). It has been continually enriched with valuable donations from all over the world, becoming an international study centre of the first order. Periodically it organises literary meetings and round tables.

Furthermore, it publishes documents not for sale (the institution is non-profit), but for sending to researchers, universities and libraries around the world. The archives also contain secret military maps and documents, and signed letters from generals, politicians, writers and poets. Finally, you can visit a small postal museum displaying posters, prints and manuscripts of the 18th century. The very welcoming director, Salvatore Maffei, will be pleased to show visitors the otherwise unobtainable collection of the Neapolitan daily *Il Lampo* (1848–1849), a volume of rare news from various places (1692) and the first Italian edition of Vitruvius' *De Architectura* (1521). The spacious premises, whose showcases are packed with history, also has an art gallery where you can admire, among other works, a canvas by landscape artist Giuseppe Casciaro, *Grapevines*.

In 1999 the archives were declared to be "of remarkable historical interest" by the Ministry of Culture.

PASTRENGO BARRACKS

4 Via Mario Morgantini
• Metro: Line 1 Toledo, Line 2 Montesanto • Funicular Centrale
(Augusteo) or Montesanto (Montesanto)
• provnacdo@carabinieri.it
• Visits by appointment (authorization required): 081 5481111

> *Four
> ancient cloisters
> in the carabinieri
> barracks*

The four beautiful cloisters that used to be part of a monumental religious complex that included the adjacent church of Sant'Anna dei Lombardi (1411) are little known: since 1860, they have been incorporated into the carabinieri headquarters. As this is a military zone, only accompanied visits are allowed.

As soon as you cross the threshold you'd think you were in 16th-century Naples – the so-called Cloister of the Well, in perfect condition thanks to restoration work, is spectacular. Built in the late Renaissance, it is surrounded by arcades of grey volcanic stone (*piperno*) and completed with a beautiful garden in the centre of which stands a white marble well dating from the late 16th century. Even the original wooden bucket is attached to the well chain.

The great 17th-century cloister – known as the Cloister of the Post as one side belongs to the central Post Office – is equally beautiful. Designed by the architect Giacomo Conforto, it stands on a different level to the other three cloisters. The Cloister of the Carabinieri or of the Columns, and the Cloister of the Supreme Court (so called as it was formerly occupied by the judiciary) are also worth a visit.

The vast monastery belonged to the Oliveto monks until 1799, the

year in which this Benedictine Order was suppressed by the king for adhering to revolutionary ideas. It was subsequently occupied by several institutions: the Special Court for passing judgment on the revolutionaries (1799–1800), the Parliament in 1848 and the Education Board (Provveditorato agli studi). The size of the monastery, which originally consisted of seven cloisters, was significantly reduced during the redevelopment of the city in the late 19th century.

Italian epic poet Torquato Tasso wrote part of his *Gerusalemme liberata* (Jerusalem Delivered) a few years before his sojourn there.

UNDERGROUND ALTAR OF THE CHURCH OF SANT'ASPRENO

⑱

Via Sant'Aspreno
• Metro: Line 1 Università, Line 2 Montesanto • Funicular Centrale (Augusteo) or Montesanto (Montesanto)
• Visits Monday to Friday 9am–1pm

The "hole" that cures headaches

Built in the 8th century on the site of a legendary cave inhabited by Saint Aspren, the church of Sant'Aspreno al Porto was incorporated into the current *Borsa* (Stock Exchange) in 1895.

In the crypt, which was probably part of some thermal baths in the Roman period, the altar against the wall is said to have therapeutic properties: people suffering from a headache should kneel down and stick their head into the square "hole" of the altar while invoking the saint's name and the pain will disappear.

You do notice right away the wear and tear caused by many heads rubbing on the stone. The phenomenon is unexplained, but many people believe in the effectiveness of this "therapy".

WHY DOES SAINT ASPREN RELIEVE HEADACHES?

Aspren, the first Bishop of Naples, was also the protector of the city before he was deposed by Saint Januarius in 1673. He is thought to have lived during the reigns of Trajan and Hadrian (1st–2nd centuries AD).

According to legend, Saint Peter, having founded the church of Antioch and before going to Rome with a group of disciples, stopped at Naples. He healed an old lady with an incurable disease who immediately converted to the Christian faith. Later, as Saint Candida the Elder, she begged Saint Peter to heal her friend Aspren, who was also sick. As soon as he was cured of his illness, Aspren embraced the new religion. Before leaving Naples, the apostle named the neophyte as first bishop of this city where the Christianised community was flourishing.

Some say that the gift of curing headaches comes from the fact that Aspren was beheaded because of his conversion to Christianity. Others say he placed a heavy stone on his head as a penance.

His body lies in the vast catacombs of Capodimonte hill, while his solid silver bust is in the Duomo (Naples cathedral) among fifty other busts of saints, also silver (including Saint Januarius).

The Duomo also possesses the staff with which Saint Peter healed Saint Aspren, and there is another site where this saint relieves headaches (see opposite).

SAINT ASPREN: THE ORIGINAL ASPIRIN?

Apparently inspired by Saint Aspren, Bayer laboratories gave the name "aspirin" to the analgesic and anti-inflammatory drug they had just launched on the market in 1899.

GREAT HALL OF THE CHAMBER OF COMMERCE ⑲

2 Via Sant'Aspreno
• Metro: Line 1 Università, Line 2 Montesanto
• Funicular Centrale (Augusteo) or Montesanto (Montesanto)
• segreteria.presidenza@na.camcom.it
• Visits on request

"Hall of cries"

The Chamber of Commerce, Industry, Crafts and Agriculture, built in 1895 over the ruins of the church of the early Christian Saint Aspren (see p. 114) by the architect A. Guerra and engineer L. Ferrara, was opened in 1899. The building also housed the Stock Exchange until 1992, when all trading activities were centralised in Milan.

Few Neapolitans know that it's possible to visit the great "hall of transactions", which were known as "cries". The immense neo-Renaissance hall is surrounded by columns interspersed with caryatids bearing lanterns or anchors, symbolising maritime trade. The boards that listed the stock quotations for major Italian companies are also kept there.

The upper section has windows painted by Neapolitan artists representing allegories of trades and commerce. An imposing staircase leads to the first floor where there are offices, an entirely wood-panelled library with thousands of volumes concerning the activities of the Naples Chamber of Commerce and a beautiful meeting room now used for conferences. The Chamber of Commerce, founded in 1808 by Joseph Bonaparte, had its headquarters in Via Toledo in the Monte dei Poveri Vergognosi ("Shamefaced Poor") building, which was acquired in the 20th century by the Rinascente department store.

The Naples Stock Exchange was launched in 1778, at a time when transactions took place in the religious complex of Saint Thomas Aquinas (between Via Toledo and Via Medina), demolished in 1932. In 1826, the exchange was transferred to its present home in Palazzo San Giacomo (see pp. 108–109). Because the city had a major port and enjoyed stable international relations, its trading activities were very intense, although they declined after Naples was annexed to the Kingdom of Italy.

PALAZZO PENNE

⑳

24 Piazzetta Teodoro Monticelli
- Metro: Line 1 Università
- Admission free (courtyard)

Beelzebub's palace?

Palazzo Penne, built in 1406 for Antonio Penne, the private secretary of King Ladislas of Anjou, is a rare example of the architecture of this period with its blend of Catalan (doorway) and Tuscan (façade bosses) elements. The renowned Antonio Baboccio was probably the designer. Penne's influence at court was such that he was allowed to be buried along with his family in the church of Santa Chiara, a site reserved for the royal dynasty. To get an idea of the size of this building, just think of its stables (in the courtyard) that could accommodate forty horses and six cars. The lily (symbol of the royal dynasty) and the feather (the family emblem – *penne* means "feathers") are engraved all over the façade and entrance. Other carved symbols, revealing both the religiosity and the superstition of this eminent dignitary, probably excited the imagination of ordinary people, who spread a scurrilous tale about him.

Above the doorway, right in the centre, clouds are pierced by rays of light

(divine). On either side of this relief, a hand holds a ribbon on which is engraved a phrase from the Latin poet Martial which warded off the evil eye by these words: "*Avi Ducis Vultu Sinec Auspicis Isca Libenter Omnibus Invideas Nemo Tibi*" (You who do not look favourably on this place, O envious one, then envy everyone, [because] no one will envy you).

The palace is traditionally said to have been built by the devil himself, to whom Antonio Penne appealed by signing a written agreement in his own blood. The noble fell deeply in love with a girl who, not knowing which of her many suitors to choose, imposed unrealistic conditions on all of them. She promised to marry Antonio Penne if he could build a grand palace in a single night. No sooner said than done: Penne charged Beelzebub with the task, although he took the precaution of asking for a small clause to be added. The poor devil, overjoyed to possess such a soul and sure that he was the smartest, accepted and carried out the job. When the next day he asked for his due, the noble Penne first demanded that his clause should be respected. This stipulated that before the debt was paid, the service provider must count grain by grain all the corn spilled in the courtyard of the palace, the number of grains having already been noted in a sealed letter. Beelzebub burst out laughing and in two ticks picked it all up.

But once the letter was opened, he realised that he was five grains short: Penne had very cunningly coated them with pitch so they'd stick under the devil's nails. Satan tried to protest but his overlord made the sign of the Cross and he was forced to disappear.

ISTITUTO MAGISTRALE ELEONORA PIMENTEL-FONSECA

Former Casa Professa
2 Via Benedetto Croce
• Tel: 081 2520054
• Metro: Line 1 Dante, Line 2 Montesanto • Funicular Montesanto
(Montesanto)
• Visits Monday to Saturday 9am–1pm

A rare edition

The former Casa Professa was a Jesuit monastery, another witness to their power in Naples. This beautiful building, now converted into a high school, adjacent to the celebrated church of Gesù Nuovo, still retains the original library with its collection of 50,000 rare volumes, mainly journals and essays concerning the Jesuit Order.

The library, which is on the second floor, is accessed by a monumental staircase leading to a splendid carved wooden door surrounded by a marble portico. This majestic salon impressed all visitors at the time, who considered this library to be the most beautiful in the city (and there were many of them).

The ceiling has frescoes by Antonio Sarnelli (1712–1800), who was also responsible for the very fine patterns on the tiled flooring. The books are arranged over two storeys on shelves set into the walls and decorated with wooden mouldings (1730). The upper storey is surrounded by a balustrade of pierced wood, decorated with medallions and carved birds.

The ensemble was not completed until 1750: between 1685 (when the building was constructed) and the time that serious work began on the fixtures and fittings, chickens were even kept there.

ANTONIO GENOVESI HIGH SCHOOL

House of Congregations
Piazza del Gesù Nuovo (left of Gesù Nuovo church)
• Metro: Line 1 Dante, Line 2 Montesanto • Funicular Montesanto
(Montesanto) • Tel: 081 5514756 • Visits (contact caretaker) Monday to
Saturday 9am–1pm (except public holidays)

Forgotten vestiges of the former House of Congregations

The House of Congregations, occupied since 1888 by the Antonio Genovesi high school, was part of a complex composed of several buildings including the church of Gesù Nuovo. This grand ensemble dating from the 16th century fitted perfectly into the Counter-Reform movement, which promoted the exaltation of the greatness of God by decorative richness beyond measure. Although the church is still in one piece, adjacent buildings have retained only vestiges of their former splendour. Only the Oratory of the Ladies, the sacristy and the Oratory of the Nobles (or Knights) remain of the former House of Congregations.

These lay congregations for charitable work, initially five in number, were placed under the exclusive spiritual direction of the Jesuits, the most powerful order in Naples at the time. They had succeeded in ousting the Dominicans by being more tolerant as confessors to noble families, and taking the side of the Neapolitans (of all classes) who were fiercely opposed to the Inquisition. It was moreover thanks to these astute tactics of the Jesuits that the Inquisition never crossed the borders of the kingdom. The sacristy of the Congregation of Nobles is now the entrance lobby to the Genovesi high school. Its decoration was commissioned from Gian Domenico Vinaccia, a versatile artist among whose designs was the incredible solid silver carved altar of the Cappella di San Gennaro (Chapel of Saint Januarius, also known as the Chapel of the Treasury, in the Duomo). To the left is a bust of the philosopher Antonio Genovesi (see opposite).

Next is the Oratory of the Nobles (now the assembly hall). The ceiling frescoes (1630) are remarkable, with a nativity scene by Battistello Caracciolo (1578–1635) in the centre. This artist, originally a faithful follower of Caravaggio, was seduced by the decidedly Baroque taste of the Carracci brothers while devising his own very personal style. Here Caracciolo created one of his masterpieces, despite the divergent opinion of some critics who accused him of having "stuck an easel painting on the ceiling". In 1640, the Jesuits had the decoration completed by Giovanni Lanfranco (1582–1647), a painter from Parma renowned for his light and delicate touch and to whom we owe the extraordinary fresco of the dome of the Chapel of the Treasury.

Finally you can visit the school library, located in the former Ladies Oratory, where the frescoes were executed by Belisario Corenzio, a painter omnipresent in Naples between the 16th and 17th centuries. Contemporary chroniclers accused him of using unorthodox methods to discourage rivals and win commissions.

ANTONIO GENOVESI (1712–1769): A PHILOSOPHER WHO BECAME THE WORLD'S FIRST ECONOMICS PROFESSOR

Genovesi, born near Salerno to a very modest family, was obliged to enter a religious order to be able to study. A figurehead of the Italian and European Enlightenment and passionate about philosophy, he shone particularly in economics. After teaching metaphysics and ethics at the University of Naples, in 1754 he became the world's first professor of political economics, when King Charles of Bourbon founded this faculty as part of his progressive reforms. Here, for the first time, education was no longer reserved for the clergy and Italian was made obligatory rather than Latin. His major work, *Lezioni di commercio*, was translated into German, Spanish and Portuguese. Catherine II of Russia even sent students to Leipzig, where the innovative theories of this great thinker were taught – he is still studied today.

According to Genovesi, education should be extended to all social classes so that a country could prosper. He was utterly opposed to the privileges of aristocrats, advocating the productivity of the individual for his own good and for that of society. He also took the side of those who sought separation between Church and State: for him the Church was only competent in matters of religion. These ideas earned him accusations of atheism and heresy, although he was never prosecuted. However, at his death he was buried in the church of Sant'Eframo Nuovo (Saint Ephraem) with no epitaph on his tomb.

MARKS ON THE FAÇADE ㉓
OF THE CHURCH OF GESÙ NUOVO

Piazza del Gesù Nuovo
• Metro: Line 1 Dante, Line 2 Montesanto • Funicular Montesanto
(Montesanto)
• Tel: 081 5578111

An
Armenian
musical score?

The façade of the church of Gesù Nuovo (all that remains of Palazzo Sanseverino, built in the 15th century) holds the key to a mystery that was a complete enigma until 2010: some of the diamond-point projections that decorate this façade are marked by incisions about 10 cm long which have been variously interpreted. According to one theory, these marks were thought to have the power to attract positive energy and were part of a secret language known only to the medieval master builders and their descendants. But in justification of the number of natural disasters suffered by this building over the centuries, it is said that the diamond points were installed facing in the wrong direction, which would have distorted the benevolent influence of the incisions.

In 2010, after five years of research, the art historian Vincenzo de Pasquale, supported by two Hungarian researchers, Jesuit Csar Dors and musicologist Loràrt Renz, suggested that these marks are actually letters of the Aramaic alphabet, the language spoken by Jesus of Nazareth, which correspond to musical notes. If read from right to left and bottom to top, they would form the extraordinary exploded score of a 45-minute concerto that its discoverers named *Enigma*.

However, this theory is not accepted by other art historians.

Diamond-point rustication, hitherto little known in the Kingdom of Naples, was depicted on the 10,000 lira notes issued from 1976 to 1984.

BOURBON HALL OF FAME ㉔

Church of Santa Chiara
49/c Via Santa Chiara
• Metro: Line 1 Dante, Line 2 Montesanto
• Open 7.30am–1pm and 4.30pm–8pm

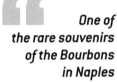

One of the rare souvenirs of the Bourbons in Naples

It has not been established how the bodies of the last of the Bourbons of Naples – the exiled Francis II and his wife Maria Sophia of Bavaria – were repatriated in 1984 and interred alongside their family in the Chapel of Saint Thomas in Santa Chiara, the church that had been chosen by the Angevin kings as their final resting place. This is one of the few reminders of the Bourbons in Naples.

For some time now, the reputation of the Bourbon dynasty (which ruled Naples from 1734 to 1860) is starting to be reassessed: it is known, for example, that the King of the Two Sicilies, Ferdinand II (died 1859), was so renowned for his liberal ideas that when the early unificationists offered him the throne of Italy he refused, faithful to his non-expansionist policy.

Religious ceremonies in honour of the kings of Naples are regularly held at Santa Chiara.

THE VIRGIN'S VEIL, GUGLIA DELL'IMMACOLATA

㉕

Piazza del Gesù Nuovo
• Metro: Line 1 Dante, Line 2 Montesanto

A menacing shadow over the square

The 30 m monument to the Immaculate Virgin, right in the middle of Piazza del Gesù Nuovo, is regarded as one of the most outstanding examples of Neapolitan Baroque.

Legend has it that if you look at the back of the Virgin's statue on top of the spire, you get a menacing feeling of being watched that can only be shaken off some distance away. The veil that covers her head does indeed seem to bear the outline of a face, staring at passers-by, which could be a carbon copy of death.

According to the most superstitious local residents, this sinister joke was orchestrated by the family of the Princes of Sanseverino, who had been forced to give up their palace to make way for the church of Gesù Nuovo on that site. The Jesuits kept only the façade as a reminder of the greatness of the Sanseverinos, who were disgraced for joining a conspiracy against Don Ferrante of Aragon (King Ferdinand I of Naples) in the late 15th century.

WHEN THE VIRGIN BELONGS TO THE CITY AND NOT TO THE CHURCH

Every 8 December the city of Naples, represented by the mayor, pays tribute to the Virgin Mary by offering her a bouquet of roses placed in the arms of the copper statue by firemen on an extending ladder. The monument is owned by the city and not by the Jesuits who commissioned it, as indicated on the shield carved on the surrounding railings. This decision sprang from an agreement signed by Pope Pius VII and the Bourbon King Ferdinand I in 1818.

ARCHBISHOP SISTO RIARIO SFORZA'S GREAT ㉖ HALL

Decumani Boutique Hotel
15 Via San Giovanni Maggiore Pignatelli
• Metro: Line 1 Dante or Università • Funicular Montesanto (Montesanto)
• Tel: 081 5518188 • info@decumani.com

> **One of the most sumptuous salons in Italy**

I n the palace that was once the residence of Sisto Riario Sforza (1810–1877), the last Archbishop of Naples before the unification of Italy, you can see one of the vastest salons in Italy, with its 9 m high ceiling. The prelate's magnificent reception room was first used for the official presentation of certificates to graduates of the University of Naples "L'Orientale" before it became part of a high school, during which time the palace deteriorated somewhat. Today, the superb salon – decorated with frescoes and enriched with stucco and fine gold-framed mirrors – has a new lease of life, thanks to the restoration work (undertaken in collaboration with the authorities) by a private company that has converted part of the palace into a hotel.

In the vaulted ceiling of the hall, note the fresco with the arms of the Riario family and those of the powerful Sforza family (sky-blue viper).

THE ARCHBISHOP WHO INVENTED MICROCREDIT BEFORE ITS TIME

Sisto Riario Sforza was very popular: during his long sojourn as archbishop (1846–1879), he greatly helped the poor, whose number continued to grow after three eruptions of Vesuvius and four cholera epidemics. After giving away all his personal property, the archbishop borrowed 12,000 ducats from Baron Rothschild, who lived in Naples. With these funds he created a "bank for the poor", which lent small sums to people without means who wanted to start a small business. On learning what his money was being used for, Baron Rothschild refused any repayments.

The current Cardinal of Naples has also set up a privately funded "bank for the poor" and named it after the archbishop.

CHURCH OF SANTI MARCELLINO E FESTO

University of Naples Federico II
10 Largo San Marcellino
• Metro: Line 1 Università • Bus: R2 from Napoli Centrale station
• Visits on reservation (authorization required, by phone or email):
081 2537395 / 081 2535706 (Ufficio eventi Rettorato); eventi@unina.it

> **Sacred art
> in the heart
> of the university**

The church of Saints Marcellino and Festo, now incorporated in the Faculty of Sciences at the University of Naples Federico II (founded in 1224), was part of a large religious complex for women which was given its current name in 1565, when two adjacent monasteries, both built in the 8th century, were joined together: that of Saints Festo and Desiderio, which belonged to the Benedictines, and Saints Marcellino and Pietro, occupied by the Basilians (monks who follow the rule of Saint Basil of Caesarea or any Byzantine rite).

The church, which is open only on special occasions or on reservation, is richly decorated with gilded stucco, carved woodwork and grandiose frescoes. The vault and dome feature paintings by Belisario Corenzio representing different saints and episodes from the life of Saint Benedict. The walls were painted by Massimo Stanzione. The wooden ceiling is breathtaking, as is the main altar bursting with precious marble and bronze. The remarkable tabernacle, with its statues of Saint Marcellino and Saint Festo, was carved in 1666 by Dionisio Lazzaro.

Don't miss the extraordinary majolica floor of the choir, dating from the second half of the 18th century. The church was completed by Pietro D'Apuzzo, probably following a design by Giacomo di Conforto, and restored by renowned architect Luigi Vanvitelli in 1767.

GARMENTS OF THE MIRACULOUS VIRGIN

Church of Gesù Vecchio
38 Via Giovanni Paladino
• Metro: Line 1 Università
• Tel: 081 5526639
• Open 10am–12 noon, 4pm–6pm
• Closed on Sunday afternoons except the 11th of each month

> *Placido Baccher, "apostle of the Immaculate Virgin"*

On the altar of the church of Gesù Vecchio, the miraculous statue of the Virgin was commissioned by Don Placido Baccher, who disseminated the cult of Mary around Naples.

Placido Baccher (1781–1851) was a very pious man, his devotion to the Virgin so great that he was known as the "apostle of the Immaculate Virgin". During the 1799 revolution, when he was 18, he was unjustly arrested, sentenced to death and imprisoned in Capuano castle. The night before his execution, he dreamed of the Virgin, who promised to save him. The next day his judges, recognising their error, did indeed free him. But the presiding judge, seeing that there were only sixteen condemned men instead of seventeen, ordered Placido's re-arrest. He tried to escape the guards by climbing down a rope from a balcony but fell, seriously injuring his head. Again, the Virgin appeared in his dreams and healed him.

Placido was ordained as a priest in 1806 and came to the church of Gesù Vecchio five years later. At that time he instituted the cult of the Immaculate Conception and commissioned a statue of the Virgin wearing ornate gilded garments, just like those he had seen in his dream, from sculptor Nicola Ingaldi.

Today, that Madonna still watches over the tomb of Placido Baccher, who devoted his entire life to the cause of the poor and the sick, notably during cholera epidemics. Thanks to him, the cult of this Madonna is still very much alive in the church – the Saturday following 30 December is commemorated as the day when the Virgin, during the solemn crowning of her statue authorised by Pope Leo XII, spoke these words in the presence of the officials, the court and the devout: "Blessed be the priests who officiate at my altar and the faithful who take communion on the Saturday after my coronation." On that day, known as "Special Saturday", you can witness a veritable pilgrimage in which all the worshippers receive communion. Another very popular ceremony is that of 8 December, the Feast of the Immaculate Conception.

CLOISTERS OF THE FORMER MONASTERY OF SAINTS MARCELLINO AND FESTO

University of Naples Federico II
10 Largo San Marcellino
• Metro: Line 1 Università • Bus: R2 from Napoli Centrale station
• Tel: 081 2537231
• Open Monday to Friday 9am–5pm

Within the Faculty of Sciences of the University of Naples Federico II are two cloisters that belonged to the former monastery of Saints Marcellino and Festo. The largest of the two, built in 1567 by the architect Vincenzo della Monica, is square and surrounded by arches of grey volcanic stone (*piperno*); it is now part of the Faculty of Political Science.

A sublime yet forgotten cloister

The second cloister has an elegant double staircase. The Museum of Palaeontology (see below) is in the former chapter house.

NEARBY

MUSEO DI PALEONTOLOGIA

8 Via Mezzocannone
• Metro: Line 1 Università • Bus: R2 from Napoli Centrale station
• Tel: 081 2535245
• Open Monday to Friday 9am–1.30pm
• Monday and Thursday 2.30pm–4.50pm also
• Guided tours on request

Few people know that within the remarkable Centro Musei delle Scienze Naturali – the University of Naples Science Museums – the Palaeontology Museum holds the only dinosaur skeleton in central and southern Italy. It has been suspended from the ceiling of the chapter house of the former monastery of Saints Marcellino and Festo to preserve the magnificent 18th-century majolica floor covered with floral motifs and landscapes, a work of the Massa brothers. The giant skeleton (8.5 m long and 3.4 m tall) is that of an *Allosaurus fragilis* found in 1993 in the United States, on the border between Wyoming and Utah, and which lived about 140 million years ago.

In an adjoining room you can see the cast of Wolly, a small mammoth found in Siberia in 1977. Note also the Middle Triassic fossils of fish dating back over 210 million years from the Salerno region (at Giffoni Valle Piana).

NEARBY

MUSEO DI ANTROPOLOGIA

8 Via Mezzocannone
• Metro: Line 1 Università • Bus: R2 from Napoli Centrale station
• Tel: 081 2535205 • Open Monday to Friday 9am–1.30pm
• Monday and Thursday 2.30pm–4.50pm also

The Anthropology Museum opened in 1994 in one wing of the Jesuit college. Among the most interesting pieces are two human skeletons dating back 11,000 to 12,000 years, found in the Romanelli caves (Puglia/Apulia), an 8th-century mummy found at Tiwanaku in the Bolivian Andes, and stone artefacts of the 3rd millennium BC from an Anatolian-Aegean site: these were bequeathed to the museum by Heinrich Schliemann, the German archaeologist who discovered Troy and Mycenae, and died at Naples in 1890.

MUSEO DI ZOOLOGIA

8 Via Mezzocannone
• Tel: 081 2535164 • Open Monday to Friday 9am–1.30pm
• Monday and Thursday 2.30pm–4.50pm also

The Zoology Museum, founded in 1813, has an extraordinary, huge "mammals room" (47 m long and 10 m wide), surrounded by two levels of elegant walnut cabinets in neoclassical style. Notable in the large collection of vertebrates (consisting of rare animals) is the skeleton of a rorqual grounded on the beach of Maratea (Calabria) in 1846, and another whale, *Eubalaena glacialis*, the only museum specimen in the world and the sole member of its species to be killed in the Mediterranean. Hundreds of rifle and pistol rounds were needed to finish off the immense cetacean that had the misfortune to swim into the Gulf of Taranto in 1877.

The carcass yielded 3,521 kg of oil before its bones and internal organs were sold to the University of Naples. Other curiosities not to be missed: two mummified heads of Nile crocodiles (dating from 1758), and the skeleton of an Indian elephant offered in 1742 to Charles of Bourbon by Sultan Muhammad V in exchange for a few pieces of precious marble. The elephant, which was kept in the gardens of the Royal Palace of Portici (near Naples), died prematurely in 1756. Its presence and its death greatly affected the Neapolitans who, when a hand-out ends abruptly, exclaim *"Capurà, è muorto ll'alifante"* (Corporal, the elephant is dead), in memory of the poor soldier who guarded the beast and who, on its sudden death, no longer collected tips from the many onlookers jostling at the gates of the gardens to admire it.

CURIA NOBILIUM DE PORTU
HEIC UBI OLIM NAVIUM STATIO FUERAT
FUNDATA
INVENTOQUE IN EFFOSSIONIBUS ORIONIS SIGNO
DISTINCTA
NUNC SEDE IN ELEGANTIOREM URBIS REGIONEM
TRANSLATA
NE CONVERSO IN PRIVATOS USUS LOCO
LONGAEVA VETUSTATE FACTI FAMA ABOLERETUR
ÆTERNUM APUD SEROS NEPOTES TESTEM
HUNC LAPIDEM ESSE
UOLUIT
ANNO ÆRÆ CHRIST. CIƆƆCCXLII.

BAS-RELIEF OF A HAIRY MAN

③③

9 Via Mezzocannone
• Metro: Line 1 Università

> *Legend
> of the merman
> Cola Pesce*

An inscription at 9 Via Mezzocannone records that the bas-relief above, depicting a hairy man with a long knife in his hand, was found in the vicinity and became the emblem of the "Sedile di Porto", one of the city's administrative districts (see p. 233). The carving, the original of which is kept in the San Martino Museum (see p. 319), may represent the giant hunter Orion who, to escape the wrath of Apollo, took refuge in the sea. Here he was killed by an arrow from Diana who, repentant, transformed him into a constellation. Be that as it may, this character was commonly known as Cola (or Niccolò) Pesce, featuring in a popular legend.

Based on extensive research by Benedetto Croce, the great Neapolitan philosopher and historian, the first traces of this myth (with some variations) are to be found in 12th-century Spain (Cadiz). The legend then spread to France (Côte d'Azur), Sicily and Naples. In this city where it was still very much alive until the 17th century, it was said that a boy, as a consequence of spending all day in the sea, angered his mother who told him not to set foot on land again.

Cola (or Niccolò) Pesce travelled over long distances by being swallowed by a big fish – when it reached its destination he disembowelled it with his long knife. From time to time he left the water to talk to the fishermen, telling them that the caves under the island of Castel dell'Ovo (see p. 58) were bursting with treasure. One day the king, to whom Cola Pesce often presented gems he'd found underwater, wanted to test the boy's skills and asked him to fetch a cannonball fired from the top of the hill. The boy agreed, but just as he was about to reach his target, the water closed over him like a tombstone and he remained a prisoner of the sea forever.

The author of *Esoterica Napoli* (Esoteric Naples), Mario Buonoconto, gives his own version of this legend. He thinks that Cola Pesce belongs to a mysterious brotherhood formed in the early Middle Ages, whose members were followers of the cult of the Siren Parthenope and known as *e figli 'e Nettuno* (Neptune's children). According to Buonoconto, these men were the only ones to know the properties of a kind of seaweed with which they could stop their vital functions while remaining conscious. This allowed them to stay underwater for a long time, enrich themselves with the treasures lying at the bottom of the sea and practise their secret rites. Mating with the sirenians (sea-cows) who once inhabited the Bay of Naples was one of these ceremonies.

REAL MUSEO DI MINERALOGIA

8 Via Mezzocannone
- Metro: Line 1 Università • Bus: R2 from Napoli Centrale station
- Tel: 081 2535245 • Open Monday to Friday 9am–1.30pm
- Monday and Thursday 2.30pm–4.50pm also
- Guided tours by appointment: 081 2537587

> *Rare minerals in the Jesuit College*

The Royal Museum of Mineralogy, founded by the Bourbon King Ferdinand I, is a spectacular place. A library has been installed in the magnificent 17th-century hall where the Jesuit College met and the first meetings of the Chamber of Deputies were held when Ferdinand II granted the constitution of 1848.

Among the museum's 25,000 exhibits, note two hyaline (glassy) quartz crystals from Madagascar, each weighing 482 kg (a gift to Charles III of

Bourbon in 1740); several lava "bombs" from eruptions of Vesuvius; the fragment of a 7.5 kg meteorite found at Toluca, Mexico, in 1784; and cameos, a Neapolitan artisan speciality. Some of the cameos are carved out of lava stone, such as those depicting the faces of the Bourbon King Ferdinand IV and his wife Maria Carolina (sister of Marie Antoinette), and a satyr's head in white Carrara marble and quartz, the work of Antonio Canova.

NEARBY

MUSEO DI FISICA
(35)
8 Via Mezzocannone
• Tel: 081 2536256
• Open Monday and Thursday 9am–1pm and 2pm–5pm • Tuesday, Wednesday and Friday 9am–1pm

The Physics Museum has around 700 instruments dating from the 17th to 19th centuries: microscopes, electromagnetic, acoustic and mechanical devices, current testers ... Note the two astronomical telescopes, one of which was developed by the physicist and mathematician Evangelista Torricelli, inventor of the barometer (1608–1647).

ACCADEMIA PONTANIANA LIBRARY

8 Via Mezzocannone
- Metro: Line 1 Università • Bus: R2 from Napoli Centrale station
- Tel: 081 5525015 • info@accademiapontaniana.it
- accademia@pontaniana.unina.it • sbordone@unina.it
- www.pontaniana.unina.it
- Visits on reservation by e-mail or phone

The oldest academy in Italy

The aim of the Accademia Pontaniana, housed at the University of Naples Federico II in architecturally austere rooms, is to promote cultural development in the Mezzogiorno (southern Italy).

Since it was founded in the 15th century, the academy has produced many major works of literature. Among its early members were the eminent man of letters Giovanni Pontano (after whom the institution is named), Pietro Summonte, Jacopo Sannazaro (see p. 25), Scipione Capece, Vincenzo Cuoco, Benedetto Croce, Renato Caccioppoli and Maria Bakunin.

The academy, originally known as the "Alfonsine", was set up around 1443 when King Alfonso of Aragon brought the leading researchers of the time to participate in round tables at Castel Nuovo. The first president was the poet, historian and writer Antonio Beccadelli, known as Il Panormita (a poetic form, meaning "The Palermitan").

FONTANA DI SPINACORONA

37

Via Guacci Nobile
Fountain on the wall of the church of Santa Caterina della Spinacorona
• Metro: Line 1 Università • Bus: C55 (Università stop)

> **The lactating fountain: Parthenope extinguishing the fires of Vesuvius**

The Spinacorona fountain, installed on the orders of Viceroy Don Pedro de Toledo in 1498, is the least known of the three Naples fountains representing the Siren Parthenope (see opposite). It is also the only one that has remained in its "original version", i.e. with wings and bird legs. Some historians of antiquity claim that there was already a fountain on this site dating back to a more distant time, but this hypothesis is disputed.

Jets of water spring from the breasts of the Siren Parthenope and flow down over Vesuvius carved in high relief. At the foot of the statue, a viola symbolises music, an inseparable element of the myth. A Latin inscription that used to be there, *dum vesevi syrena incendia mulcet*, encouraged the divinity to

extinguish the destructive fires of the volcano.

It may seem that Don Pedro de Toledo was expressing his desire to calm the ardour of the very volcanic Neapolitans by gentleness. But they apparently didn't take the hint, because it has always been popularly known as the "fountain of the tits".

Don Pedro perhaps didn't know which way to turn at a time when Saint Januarius hadn't yet proved himself (see p. 354), the Virgil cult had waned and the Madonna had never before pulled off a miracle where eruptions of Vesuvius were concerned.

The statue here is a copy; the original is on display at the remarkable San Martino Museum, the museum of the history of Naples.

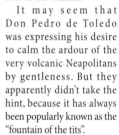

NAPLES AND THE MYTH OF THE SIREN PARTHENOPE

Homer tells how, after failing to shipwreck Ulysses, the three Sirens drowned and the lifeless body of one of them, Parthenope, was washed ashore near the island of Megaris (site of Castel dell'Ovo, now Megaride peninsula). The Greek colonists then erected a tomb to house the remains of the virgin Siren (*parthenos* = virgin in Greek) and gave her name to the city they founded near the monument.

Parthenope worship ran so high in Naples that festivities and gymnastic games were introduced in her honour — an unusual and unexplained phenomenon in Hellenic civilisation, as even in Greece there wasn't the slightest trace of such a cult. This reverence for the Siren partly explains the salient points of Neapolitan culture, which developed under the sign of a virgin who, in spite of her virginity, left the legacy of the egg/Palladium (Palladium being a symbol representing the city: see p. 58), thus becoming the mother of a city and a people.

Centuries later, the Virgin Mary gave birth to a child who was expected to save the world, a parallel that may throw light on the Neapolitan predilection for the Madonna.

The Siren dies, but the city is founded on her tomb. In Naples, death is therefore not a taboo but is respected as part of life. Worship of the dead is common and not a terrifying thing: people pray to the dead as they do to the saints.

The Siren accompanies souls to the underworld after bewitching the dying with her singing. She is a bird-woman (before transmutation into a mermaid in the Middle Ages) and, like all birds, encodes omens in her singing. As ships pass by, she sings with her companions: "... no one has yet passed by here with their black boat without hearing our song that flows from our lips like honey ... and we know all that is happening in every corner of this Earth ...".

Why then be surprised at the Neapolitans' great love of music and their predilection for premonitions? And doesn't the saying "See Naples and die" allude to Parthenope who, with her divine voice, enchanted those who had to make the final journey?

Even today, we find traces of the city being identified with the Siren. In the popular imagination, the parts of the prone body of Parthenope/Naples were in three districts of the city. Their symbolic names are still in use: the feet rest in the western outskirts, at "Piedigrotta" (see p. 30), while the head is at "Caponapoli" (Head of Naples) and the rest of the body lies in the centre of the old city, in the Nile district, known as the "Corpo di Napoli" (Body of Naples).

Moreover, Neapolitans are known as "Parthenopeans" and when at the beginning of the 20th century the city was extended down to the sea, the name "Partenope" was given to the new street running alongside Castel dell'Ovo. Three fountains are dedicated to the Siren: the first, which is very old, was restored in the 15th century (see opposite); the second, which dates from the 19th century, majestically dominates the centre of Piazza Sannazzaro near Mergellina marina (its original site was near the central station at the south entrance to Naples); and the third, which is ultramodern, graces the shopping mall at Napoli Centrale station that was refurbished a few years ago.

THE GIAMBATTISTA VICO FOUNDATION

35 Via San Gregorio Armeno
• Metro: Line 1 Dante, Line 2 Montesanto • Funicular Montesanto
(Montesanto)
• Tel: 081 19804664 • fondazionegbviconapoli@gmail.com
• Visits by appointment: Monday to Saturday 9am–1pm and 3pm–7pm

Foundation aid to reopen a church

The 7th-century church of San Gennaro dell'Olmo, originally known as San Gennaro ad Diaconiam, was the first early Christian basilica dedicated to Saint Januarius in the city centre. In the 8th century, Basilian nuns persecuted by Eastern iconoclasts settled within its walls. Until the 14th century, Mass was celebrated there in Latin and Greek. Around that time the church was given its present name, Saint Januarius of the Elm, apparently because just in front of the building there stood an elm where tournament winners used to hang their prizes. In the 17th century, the church was completely rebuilt in the style of the time, although the neoclassical façade dates from the early 20th century. The church was closed and neglected for forty years, but reopened and restored thanks to the Giambattista Vico Foundation. Under the building are the remains of the temple of Augustus, not yet cleared of rubble.

The chapel that is now dedicated to San Biagio (Saint Blaise) originally belonged to San Gennaro dell'Olmo. The Basilian nuns had kept the skull of Saint Blaise there, brought back from the East with the remains of Saint Gregory.

In 1543, the pope ceded the chapel to the confraternity of booksellers, of whom there were many in the area, hence the name of the street at a right angle to the church, San Biagio dei Librai (Saint Blaise of the Booksellers). The confreres were collecting funds for the upkeep of the chapel and for the dowries of poor young girls. As Saint Blaise was growing in popularity, the

present church was built (1631–1632). His success was due to a belief that attributed him with the power to heal sore throats. According to his hagiography, he is thought to have saved a child who was about to choke on a fishbone. Worshippers were falling over themselves to get into the chapel (and later the church) so that the priest would protect them from throat infections, in the name of the saint, by placing two crossed candles under their chin. Giambattista Vico was baptised in this church.

NEARBY

Giambattista Vico spent the early years of his life in this neighbourhood. Along with his eight brothers and sisters, he lived in a room above his father's small bookshop, as indicated by the plaque at 31 Via San Biagio dei Librai.

GIAMBATTISTA VICO FOUNDATION

Thanks to the perseverance of a group of enthusiasts, the two adjacent churches of San Gennaro dell'Olmo and San Biagio were saved from oblivion (see opposite). Now deconsecrated and restored, they host cultural events organised by the Giambattista Vico Foundation, which also has its headquarters there. This non-profit association, in addition to running exhibitions and conferences, aims to restore monuments and set up museums.

GIAMBATTISTA VICO (1668–1744): A GREAT BUT NEGLECTED PHILOSOPHER

Nothing seemed to predestine the young Giambattista to be the great philosopher he became. At the age of 7, after a severe fall that fractured his skull, he was bedridden for three years. This accident was probably the reason for his chronic melancholy. After studying with the Jesuits, he worked all his life to support his large family but never had a job that fulfilled his potential – he was appointed to the Chair of Rhetoric, the least well-paid post at the University of Naples. He died, consumed by throat cancer, before seeing the revised edition of his 1725 masterpiece, *Scienza nuova* (New Science), on the common cultural history of nations.

Montesquieu, unaware that Vico was dead, came to Naples to meet him. He bought a copy of *New Science*, which greatly inspired his *L'Esprit des lois* (The Spirit of Laws, 1750).

Vico is regarded as a prophet of modern thought. As an innovator, he completely ignored the philosophical currents of his time and denounced in particular the limits of Cartesian theories. He anticipated Marxist ideas in announcing the end of caste and the rise of social struggles which,

according to his reasoning, would lead to social equality.

Vico rejected inequality between peoples, stating that all men have a common way of thinking and acting. In his far-sighted and progressive way, he wrote that a civilisation, even the most advanced, should never be considered as the best or even as unsurpassable.

Although his work was neglected for over a century, he was extensively studied in the 19th and 20th centuries, notably by Hegel.

LAND REGISTRY OF THE STATE ARCHIVES

5 Piazzetta Grande Archivio
• Metro: Line 1 Museo, Dante or Università
• Tel: 081 5638256 or 081 5638301 • as-na@beniculturali.it
• Guided tours Monday and Thursday at 9am and 11.30am
• During Heritage Days and on 1 May, you can visit rooms normally closed to the public

Temple of art and history

The State Archives, opened in 1845, are housed in the premises of the Benedictine monastery of Saints Severino and Sossio, built in 902 and rebuilt in the 16th century.

The splendid old chapter house, which dates back to the 16th and 17th centuries (now the land registry), is decorated with frescoes depicting the precepts of Benedictine rule. The paintings were executed in 1608 by Belisario Corenzio who, the legend goes, fell to his death from the scaffolding while painting the transept of the church adjoining the monastery.

Some 9,000 volumes belonging to the *onciario* register are of great historical interest. This collection of documents, written between 1740 and 1752 as part of a reform initiated by King Charles III of Bourbon, identify all property, movable and immovable, belonging to the inhabitants of the kingdom, in order to impose fair taxation. This name *onciario* is derived from *oncia*, one of the currencies of the time used for the valuation of goods.

The monastery church, which has recently been restored, is occasionally open to the public.

FILANGIERI ROOM

5 Piazzetta Grande Archivio
• Metro: Line 1 Museo, Dante or Università
• Tel: 081 5638256 / 081 5638301 • as-na@beniculturali.it
• Guided tours Monday and Thursday at 9am and 11.30am
• During Heritage Days and on 1 May, you can visit rooms normally closed to the public

> **Former refectory of the monastery of Saints Severino and Sossio**

In the stately Filangieri room, once the refectory of the Benedictine monastery of Saints Severino and Sossio (see previous page), the impressive fresco decorating the vault was painted in the 17th century by Belisario Corenzio: it depicts the multiplication of loaves and fishes, and Saint Benedict distributing bread to the religious

orders, the nobles and the people. One hundred and seventeen figures can be distinguished in all. Around the walls, filed on carved wooden shelves, are the *atti governativi* (royal decrees and dispatches) dating from the beginning of the 16th century until the unification of Italy (1861).

Other official documents, precious scrolls, watercolours and a very interesting collection of noble families' coats of arms are also kept in this room.

NEARBY

SOUVENIR OF THE TERRIBLE EXPLOSION OF 1943   41

In a corner of the first cloister of the archives (in the direction of the tour), known as the "Marble Cloister", you can still see the remains of huge chains belonging to a warship, the *Caterina Costa*. The ship was bombed while anchored in the harbour on 28 March 1943. Following the terrible explosion that ensued, the port was totally devastated and debris was hurled around the city, killing 600 civilians. On the outer left wall of Castel Nuovo (see p. 82), the scars left by the explosion can still be seen.

LO ZINGARO, THE BLACKSMITH WHO BECAME AN ARTIST FOR LOVE?

The remarkable frescoes that decorate the Chiostro del Platano (Cloister of the Plane Tree, built in 1460) in the former monastery of Saints Severino and Sossio – now the State Archives (see p. 149) – are attributed to Antonio Solario, nicknamed *Lo Zingaro* (The Gypsy). But this attribution cannot be verified as the artist is shrouded in a mystery that no expert has ever penetrated due to lack of documentation. Even his first name (Andrea or Antonio?) and his place and date of birth are uncertain: Abruzzo for some, Venice for others, whereas in Lombardy several artists can be found named Solari, Solaro or Solario. He is thought to have stayed in Naples, where several major works have been attributed to him without any supporting evidence.

The art historian Bernardo De Dominici (18th century), a notorious raconteur whose biographies are filled with anachronisms and fanciful details, reported a romantic story about this artist: at the time of Ladislas of Anjou, King of Naples from 1386 to 1414, Antonio Solario was a blacksmith at the court (a trade usually followed by the gypsies, hence his nickname) and rather admired by the king's sister, Joan, who on the death of her brother became queen as Joan II.

Colantonio del Fiore, a renowned painter (another great artist whose biography is unclear) who was regularly seen at court, was enthused by the work of the young blacksmith and invited him home. Solario then fell deeply in love with his host's daughter, but Del Fiore stated that he would only give the hand of his daughter to a well-established and respected artist. Solario, determined to marry the young woman, accepted the challenge and obtained Colantonio's firm promise that he wouldn't marry off his daughter before the artist came back for her.

For ten long years *Lo Zingaro* paced Italy from north to south in search of the best teachers to learn the art of painting. Finally he made it back to the Naples court, where he showed a little picture he had painted to his patron, now queen. Joan II, won over by the beauty of the painting and familiar with

Solario's story, summoned Colantonio and showed him the picture without revealing the name of the artist. Del Fiore, who greatly admired the work, was commanded by the sovereign to consent to the marriage of the two lovers. Thus the blacksmith became a celebrated artist from whom works on a grand scale were commissioned.

This story is scarcely credible because, on the one hand, the historical dates do not match the reality, and on the other, the obvious similarity to the story of Flemish painter Quentin Massys suggests that De Dominici took advantage of the lack of information on Solario and conflated the two artists.

NEARBY

SAINT BENEDICT'S PLANE TREE

The Oriental plane tree that dominates the courtyard of the main cloister replaced the thousand-year-old tree said to have been planted by Saint Benedict himself. The original, ravaged by pests and cut down in 1959, although it was indeed ancient, couldn't really have been planted there by Saint Benedict as he never came to Naples. The cloister is known as "del Platano" because a grove of plane trees was probably growing on the site and the monks kept one of them.

Around the cloister are beautiful frescoes depicting episodes from the life of Saint Benedict, executed at the end of the 15th or early 17th century by Antonio (or Andrea) Solario, nicknamed *Lo Zingaro* (see opposite).

TASSO ROOM

Near the Chiostro di Marmo (Marble Cloister) of the State Archives, you can visit a pretty room in which the poet Torquato Tasso (author of *Jerusalem Delivered*) lived from June to October 1594. On display is the Code of Saint Martha, a set of seventy-two illuminated sheets on which are reproduced the coats of arms of kings, queens and aristocratic members of the confraternity of that name between the 15th and 17th centuries. On the third floor, another unique object stands at the entrance to the director's office: the *Carta lapidaria* is an 8th-century marble table engraved on both sides with a contract for the sale of a building at Cumae (20 km from Naples).

SAINT GEORGE AND THE DRAGON FRESCO 🕮

Church of San Giorgio Maggiore
• Entrance to Piazza Crocelle ai Mannesi
• Metro: Line 1 Museo, Line 2 Cavour
• Tel: 081 287932
• Open Monday and Thursday, 9am—2pm
• To see the hidden fresco, contact the caretaker

> **One stunning image hides another**

The choir of the church of San Giorgio Maggiore conceals an extraordinary secret: behind the main altar, the huge *Saint George Slaying the Dragon*, a 40 m² canvas, can be opened like the page of a book, thanks to a hinged mechanism (activated by the sacristan on request), to reveal a fresco by Aniello Falcone (see below) on the same subject. This was painted during the reconstruction of the church to a design by Cosimo Fanzago after the fire of 1640. The unfinished building work resumed a century later, when Alessio D'Elia executed his *Saint Severus* and *Saint George* under which, during further restoration work in 1993, Falcone's fresco was discovered.

San Giorgio Maggiore, founded by Emperor Constantine and enlarged by Bishop Severus in the 5th century, was one of the city's four main churches of the early Christian period. In the 1640 restoration the church's orientation was reversed: this explains the position of the entrance, which now leads directly to the apse, the only original section and of great architectural interest.

The paintings of Aniello Falcone, an artist famous for his depictions of battles and scenes of everyday life, are rare in Neapolitan religious buildings and they are clearly distinguishable from those of his contemporaries. The story goes (as revealed by the highly controversial De Dominici: see p. 152) that Falcone and his contemporaries belonged to a revolutionary group, the "Death Company", whose aim was to kill the Spanish occupiers of Naples.

LEGENDS OF PORTA NOLANA: FROM THE Y OF THE PYTHAGOREAN SCHOOL TO VIRGIL'S SERPENT

Porta Nolana is now opposite Circumvesuviana station (the first railway line in Italy, 1826). You can still see reliefs from the 15th century, when it was moved to this site. Previously it was in the Forcella ("small fork") district, whose emblem was a forked stick (still visible on the exterior of the church of San Lorenzo Maggiore, Via dei Tribunali, see p. 233). The letter Y echoed the topography of the site, i.e. a very long street (known as Spaccanapoli, cutting through the old city from east to west) that forked just at the site of the gate in question.

Today Forcella is a working-class district, teeming with life. According to some historians, it was once home to the Pythagorean school represented by Y. This letter embodies a plethora of symbols: in addition to the tree of life, it was associated with the Christian Cross as well as the golden bough that Aeneas had to seek before returning to the underworld (Virgil's *Aeneid*). Until the late 18th century, local residents carved a Y on their doors or their shields to exorcise evil. Y also has the same shape as a sorcerer's wand – which locates water and therefore life, as well as the type of stick used to catch snakes.

Several medieval chroniclers, from the 11th century onwards, recounted a legend whereby Virgil had chained a snake under Porta Nolana to rid the city of all creeping vermin.

In the 14th century this enduring belief was replaced by the story of a miracle performed by the Madonna, an extraordinary event that served as a pretext to build a church near the gateway. According to this legend, a worshipper, after praying to the Virgin, returned home safely although he had passed through a swamp where a monstrous serpent killer of men was lurking. The church was dedicated to Santa Maria dell'Agnone (Our Lady of the Swamp, a word derived from the Latin *anguis*). Today, the building is no longer there, but the alley that ran alongside it is still called Vico della Serpe (Snake Alley), and locals tell the story of a magician who killed a snake just as it was about to bite the king.

But Virgil had not only charmed the snakes, he had also placed two marble heads in niches flanking the gateway, on the right a grinning male and, on the left, a grimacing female. These two sculptures were useful in divination: if you go through the gate on the left, there'll be nothing but trouble, whereas if you go through the one on the right, everything you undertake will turn out well. The man's head clearly represented the Sun and therefore the light, while the woman embodied the Moon, and thus the night and darkness. The position of the two stars is the same in the painting of Christ and the Madonna (see Santa Maria di Piedigrotta, p. 30).

Note that in Roman times people were strongly discouraged from entering a city on the left foot (incidentally, even if the meaning is slightly corrupted, the English idiom is still "get out of bed on the wrong side"). Both sculptures were moved to the royal residence of Poggioreale, but all trace of them has been lost over the centuries.

AUGUSTISSIMA COMPAGNIA DELLA DISCIPLINA DELLA SANTA CROCE

45

9 Via Cesare Sersale
• Metro: Line 1 Garibaldi or Università
• Visits on reservation with Signora Stefania Como
• Tel: 339 8690373 • stefania.como@yahoo.it

The city's oldest congregation

Founded in 1290, the August Company of the Discipline of the Holy Cross is the oldest congregation in the city. But it remains virtually unnoticed, access being through an anonymous building.

To reach the church, you pass through a lovely garden surrounded by walls decorated with 17th-century frescoes, in the centre of which stands a beautiful 16th-century well. The main entrance was blocked up after the 1980 earthquake. The church, built in 1420 over part of an older oratory, was subjected to a number of alterations carried out by Dionisio Lazzari and Arcangelo Guglielmelli in the 17th and 18th centuries. Set into the majolica floor is a tombstone dating from 1367. Through a door (now walled up) and spiral staircase leading to the dome, the church communicated with that of Sant'Agostino alla Zecca, one of the oldest and largest in the city (closed for repairs). The real treasure of the congregation, which is awaiting restoration, is a canvas in the San Martino Museum: *The Deposition of Christ*.

Painted in 1465 by Pietro Bifulco, it was a gift of Don Ferrante of Aragon (Ferdinand I), who is depicted along with his court dignitaries.

Although the Compagnia della Disciplina, which preaches penance and charity, has secular origins, its members include many illustrious Neapolitans and three popes: Clement XIV, Pius IX and Leo XIII. According to some historians, one of the meetings of participants in the so-called "Barons' Conspiracy" against the Aragonese king took place within this institution in 1485. Following this foiled plot, the congregation's activities were prohibited until the fall of the Aragonese dynasty at the beginning of the 16th century.

GREEK TOWER AT THE TRIANON THEATRE ⑯

9 Piazza Vincenzo Calenda
- Metro: Line 1 Garibaldi or Università
- Tel: 081 2258285 • trianon@teatrotrianon.org
- Open daily, except public holidays, 10am–1.30pm and 4pm–7.30pm
- Call or e-mail for current opening hours

The only Greek watchtower in the region

The Trianon theatre, in the centre of a large building complex, is surrounded by houses whose balconies and windows can be seen from the auditorium and which overlook the dome surmounting the property. Apart from this curious feature, the theatre also possesses the remains of a watchtower, known as the "Siren's Tower", which was part of the Greek walls (5th–4th centuries BC). These ruins were incorporated into the theatre during its construction in 1911. The tower, enclosed by a glass screen and visible from the auditorium, is the only one in the Neapolitan area that survives from the Greek era.

The remains of the ancient Greek fortifications (which flanked Porta Herculanensis or Furcellensis) that can be seen in Piazza Vincenzo Calenda are known as "'*o cippo a Furcella*" (Forcella district cippus, or boundary stone) by the people, who see them as the ultimate symbols of antiquity – when Neapolitans want to accuse something of being obsolete (whether an object or an event), they say "*s'arricorda 'o cippo 'e Furcella*" (this dates back to the Forcella cippus). The term "cippus" probably derives from the pillars on either side of the door.

Other remains of a corner tower from antiquity can be seen at 14 Via Costantinopoli, in the courtyard of the Second University of Naples' Faculty of Medicine.

PAY FOR YOUR PIZZA EIGHT DAYS LATER
Pizzeria d"e Figliole
39 Via Giudecca Vecchia
Closed Sunday
Fried pizza + one drink, €6
Tel: 081 286721
Pizzeria d"e Figliole, founded in 1860, serves only fried stuffed pizzas for which, by tacit agreement, you can pay eight days later.
This old custom dates from the time when this kind of pizzeria was only open one day a week and the most loyal customers were allowed to pay their bill "'*a agge a otto*" (in a week starting from today), i.e. on the next opening day.

FALSE WINDOWS OF CORSO UMBERTO

272 Corso Umberto
• Metro: Line 1 Garibaldi

Aesthetic astuteness

Looking through the top-floor windows of the building at 272 Corso Umberto, it becomes obvious that you can't see the ceiling of an apartment but simply the sky. These are actually the windows of a fake storey that was added in 1884 to harmonise with its neighbours. At that time, the authorities of the newly unified Italy launched a city regeneration programme (the Risanamento: see p. 41) and built this new thoroughfare from scratch.

NEARBY

BASIN OF A ROMAN AQUEDUCT ❹❽
46 Piazza Enrico de Nicola – Lanificio 25
• Tel: 081 6582915 • Visits on reservation: info@lanificio25.it
• www.lanificio25.it

The church of Santa Caterina a Formiello is flanked by buildings belonging to the now disused convent of the same name. Recent excavations near the old cloister that now serves as the headquarters of the Lanificio 25 association (which seeks to upgrade these completely unknown historic places) have uncovered, at a depth of about 10 m, a large basin dating from the Roman era. It was probably part of the Bolla aqueduct built at the time of Augustus, the remains of which can still be seen above the arcades.

The name "a Formiello" derives from the Latin *ad formis*, literally "near the canals", i.e. near the ancient conduits of the Bolla aqueduct that supplied the city's water.

FORMER SAVA WOOL MILL
Santa Caterina a Formiello monastery, occupied by the Dominicans until 1809 and renowned throughout Europe for the quality of medicinal remedies produced there, has over the centuries undergone major transformations that have altered its beautiful architecture. Although the main cloister has become a parking lot, you can still see the monumental arches surrounding it. In the centre, two tall chimneys bear witness to the former presence of a wool mill leased to Baron Sava at the time of the Bourbons. The quality of the work, produced exclusively by women, was famed throughout Europe. The plant closed after the unification of Italy was proclaimed in 1861.

NEARBY

SAINT JANUARIUS' MISSING FINGERS ❹❾
Church of Santa Caterina a Formiello - 49 Piazza Enrico De Nicola
• Metro: Line 1 Museo, Line 2 Cavour
• Tel: 081 444297
Legend has it that during the 1795 eruption of Vesuvius, the lava would have enveloped the city if the patron saint of Naples, Saint Januarius, had not intervened to halt the impending catastrophe. Once the miracle had occurred, as a sign of thanks a bust of the saint was placed in front of the church, facing in the direction of Vesuvius. This statue has a peculiar feature – it lacks the fingers on both hands. According to another legend, the saint is said to have hurled them at a miscreant who dared to curse his image.

THE MIRACULOUS CARMELITE CRUCIFIX

Basilica Santuario del Carmine Maggiore
2 Piazza del Carmine
• Metro: Line 1 Garibaldi
• Tel: 081 201196 / 081 201942 • info@santuariocarminemaggiore.it
• Visible from 26 December to 2 January, and Ash Wednesday

> **When the crucified Christ ducked to avoid a cannonball**

I n the basilica of Our Lady of Mount Carmel, a 14th-century wooden crucifix displayed for only a few days a year bears an unusual figure of Christ with his head bent over to the right. The legend goes that on 17 October 1439, Christ leaned over to dodge a cannonball fired from a Spanish warship when the Aragonese were trying to dislodge René of Anjou and his men, holed up in the church. The legend also says that the missile (still kept in the crypt) headed straight for the crucifix after smashing through the apse. At that moment Christ must have ducked, leaving his head as we see it today.

The order to fire on the church was given by Pedro of Castile, brother of Alfonso of Aragon, pretender to the crown of Naples. It seems that the next day, before again ordering the bombardment of the church, Peter's head was blown off by an enemy cannonball. Three years later, Alfonso triumphantly entered the city. Learning of his brother's blasphemous act, he decided to protect the crucifix by building a tabernacle. This was not completed until 26 December 1459, after the king's death. Since then, the crucifix has been on show to the public every year from 26 December to 2 January.

It is also displayed on the first day of Lent to celebrate the day in 1679 when this very crucifix is thought to have saved the city as it was about to be destroyed by a violent storm.

BUNGLED LOOTING OF THE REMAINS OF CONRAD OF HOHENSTAUFEN

In the Carmelite church lies the tomb of Conradin (King Conrad the Younger), the last Swabian heir to the throne of the Kingdom of Naples and Sicily. Dethroned by the Angevins, he was executed in 1268 by order of Charles of Anjou. In September 1943, a group of German soldiers burst into the church to claim the remains of the king they considered one of their own. The sole guardian of the church, Father Elia Alleva, was forced to lead them to the tomb surmounted by Conrad's statue. On reading the epitaph, the soldiers thought they understood that the king was buried *dietro* (behind) the monument, so they moved the pedestal and statue and damaged other tombstones (the reason why one of them, still to be seen, is broken). When they failed to find what they were looking for, they left empty-handed. What the looters didn't realise was that Conrad's remains were *dentro* (inside) the pedestal, rather than *dietro*.

MONTESANTO, DANTE, CAVOUR, DECUMANI

1 QUARTIERE INTELLIGENTE. 166
2 THE "HOLY LAND" OF THE ARCHCONFRATERNITY OF PILGRIMS 167
3 ITALIAN CLOCK OF SPIRITO SANTO CONSERVATORY 168
4 "HOLY LAND" OF THE ARCICONFRATERNITA DEI BIANCHI. 170
5 FORMER OIL TANKS 172
6 CLOCK IN PIAZZA DANTE. 173
7 CLOISTER OF THE FORMER CONVENT OF SAN SEBASTIANO 174
8 ARCICONFRATERNITA DEI VERDI NEL PALAZZO RUFFO DI BAGNARA. . 175
9 LA CONIGLIERA 175
10 HOTEL CORRERA AQUEDUCT. 176
11 PASQUALE CATALANO, A SPECIALIST IN NATIVITY SCENES . . . 177
12 CHURCH OF SAN GIUSEPPE DELLE SCALZE 178
13 MUSEO HERMANN NITSCH 181
14 CASTS OF PARTHENON SCULPTURES 182
15 GYPSOTHEQUE OF THE ACADEMY OF FINE ARTS 183
16 HOLY STEPS OF SANTA MARIA DELLA SAPIENZA 184
17 UNDERGROUND GALLERIES OF PIETRASANTA. 187
18 CLOISTER OF SANT'ANDREA DELLE DAME. 188
19 PRIVATE TOUR OF MONASTERO DELLE TRENTATRÉ. 190
20 INCURABILI PHARMACY 198
21 MUSEO DELLE ARTI SANITARIE DEGLI INCURABILI 201
22 MUSEO DI ANATOMIA UMANA 203
23 CASA ZEVOLA. 207
24 COMMEMORATIVE PLAQUES AT PALAZZO FILANGIERI 208

TELLA

25 REMAINS OF A DIOSCURI TEMPLE 209
26 CONGREGATION DEL CROCEFISSO DELLA SCIABICA 210
27 ARTWORKS BY NATHALIE DE SAINT-PHALLE. 212
28 HIDDEN SYMBOLISM OF CAPPELLA SANSEVERO. 214
29 TRIPTYCH OF CHRIST UNVEILED OR HIDDEN LIGHT 219
30 PLAQUE OF THE CHURCH OF SAN DOMENICO MAGGIORE . . . 220
31 TOMB OF THE FIRST BISHOP OF NEW YORK 221
32 BIBLIOTECA MAURIZIO TADDEI 222
33 THE DUKE'S STUDY 223
34 MARADONA'S HAIR 225
35 THE HOLY STEPS OF SAN GREGORIO ARMENO CONVENT . . . 226
36 FORGOTTEN FIGURINES OF THE FERRIGNO WORKSHOP 228
37 EMBLEMS OF NAPLES SEDILI 233
38 BANKSY'S SAINT WITH A PISTOL GRAFFITI 235
39 RELIQUARY CABINET AT THE CHURCH OF THE GEROLAMINI . 235
40 PALAZZO CARAFA 236
41 SHIELD OF THE CITY OF NAPLES 241
42 BARS OF THE TREASURY CHAPEL'S MONUMENTAL PORTAL . . 242
43 SELF-PORTRAITS ON THE TREASURY CHAPEL ALTAR 244
44 THE "TESORO VECCHIO" CHAPEL OF SAN GENNARO 247
45 MARBLE CALENDAR OF THE 9TH CENTURY 247
46 THE "PASSO DA TERRA" OF THE DUOMO. 248
47 SALA DEL LAZZARETTO OF THE FORMER DELLA PACE HOSPITAL 251
48 ARCHIVO STORICO, BANCO DI NAPOLI. 253
49 A ROMAN VILLA IN THE BASEMENT OF THE BANCO DI NAPOLI ARCHIVE . 253
50 BIBLIOTECA ALFREDO DE MARSICO. 255
51 LIZARD IN THE CHURCH OF THE SANTISSIMI APOSTOLI. . . 257
52 IONIC COLUMN AT PELLETTERIA COLLARO 257

QUARTIERE INTELLIGENTE ❶

3 Scala Montesanto
• Metro: Line 1 Dante, Line 2 Montesanto
• Funicular Montesanto (Montesanto)
• Tel: 327 0407003 • quartiereintelligente@gmail.com

"Green intelligence" in a built-up area

Looking down from Scala Montesanto, the monumental flight of steps (built in 1869 by Gaetano Filangieri, Prince of Satriano) that connects the Montesanto neighbourhood with Corso Vittorio Emanuele, you may be surprised to see an amazing place known as the Quartiere Intelligente ("Smart Neighbourhood"), set up on a derelict site that had until the 1980s been home to a bus garage and a glove factory.

Since June 2013, following major rehabilitation work on one person's initiative, you can stroll through a lovely park, part garden and part vegetable plot, and relax sitting in the "Nest", a work by the artist Michele Iodice (see p. 285) entitled *Migrazioni*.

As yet little known, largely because it's tucked away in overcrowded Montesanto, the Q.I. association, which campaigns for environmental compatibility, uses the large white wall of an adjoining building as a screen to project videos by contemporary artists on ecological solidarity and the relationship between man and nature.

The association also organises various activities: cultural events, shows, markets for organic and recycled products, gardening courses for schools, and creative workshops.

THE "HOLY LAND" ❷
OF THE ARCHCONFRATERNITY OF PILGRIMS

41 Via Portamedina alla Pignasecca
• Metro: Line 1 Dante, Line 2 Montesanto • Funicular Montesanto
(Montesanto) • Visits 9am–2pm on reservation: 081 5518957
• museo@arciconfraternitapellegrini.org

A "holy land" in the heart of the historic centre

I n the crypt of the church of the Santissima Trinità (rebuilt in the 18th century) in the courtyard of Pellegrini hospital (another entrance at 44 Via Ninni), the plots of land enclosed by fencing are known as the "holy land" (see p. 281) where deceased members of the Archconfraternity Augustissima Trinità dei Pellegrini (pilgrims) were buried. Until the 17th century, the bodies of the most prominent were dried, dressed in their red serge garments and stood upright in niches coloured red to symbolise the blood Christ shed for humanity, and thus for the charity. The modern confreres still wear these garments during their ceremonies.

After the restoration work, to avoid the bodies decaying further, the niches all around the crypt were closed with panels of wood – except one, which is

fitted with a window so that people can see inside.

Today, Pellegrini hospital, in the Pignasecca district (see box), is a modern building standing on the remains of a religious and hospitaller complex, founded in the 16th century by the archconfraternity. The primary purpose of this association was, among other charitable works, to aid pilgrims to the Holy Land. Every year, from 1600 onwards, this hospital took in 80,000 pilgrims. Of the original complex two churches remain: the 16th-century Materdomini (entrance on Piazzetta Fabrizio Pignatelli) and the Santissima Trinità mentioned above.

LEGEND OF THE DESICCATED PINE

According to legend, a pine tree grew in this district outside the city wall. A great many magpies hid in its branches, constantly stealing things from the local residents.

The ecclesiastical authorities, however, believed that the thieves were human and excommunicated the alleged perpetrators. Notice of the sentence was displayed on a pine branch, which soon withered. The district has been known ever since as "Pignasecca", the desiccated pine.

ITALIAN CLOCK
OF SPIRITO SANTO CONSERVATORY

❸

Faculty of Architecture, University of Naples Federico II
402 Via Toledo
• Metro: Line 1 Dante, Line 2 Montesanto • Funicular Montesanto
(Montesanto) or Centrale (Augusteo)

*A clock
displaying
only six hours*

A very fine clock with a so-called "Italian" face, divided into six sections, can be seen set high up on the façade of the new Faculty of Architecture of the University of Naples Federico II, housed in the Spirito Santo conservatory. (See opposite for the origin of these clocks.)

The conservatory was one of the city's numerous charitable institutions, dedicated to the care and education of destitute young girls. It was built in 1563 on the initiative of the Illuminati dello Spirito Santo, who received the go-ahead from Pope Pius IV. Pietro di Giovanni was responsible for the project and Mario Goffredo was commissioned to enlarge the adjacent church whose dome is a fine piece of architecture.

In 1590 the Congregation of the Illuminati also opened a Monte di Pietà (charitable institution). Later, King Ferdinand IV of Bourbon abolished the religious orders and the Monti di Pietà. The building was then ceded to the Bank of Naples, which until 1856 continued to shelter young girls.

THE OTHER TWO ITALIAN CLOCKS IN THE CITY
There are two more clocks with six-hour faces in Naples: one in the large cloister of the Charterhouse of San Martino and the other on the left tower of the church of Gerolamini.

WHAT IS THE ORIGIN OF "ITALIAN" CLOCKS?

The subdivision of the day into hours goes back to antiquity and was probably introduced by the Chaldeans. Whereas the Babylonians and Chinese measured time in double hours, twelve *kaspars* a day for the former and twelve *tokis* for the latter, the Greeks and Romans divided the day into two equal parts of twelve hours each. As the time from sunrise to sunset varied with the season, daylight hours in summer were longer than the hours of darkness, while the reverse held true in winter.

The rigorous discipline of monastic orders, especially the Benedictines, led to a radical upheaval in ways of measuring time. The hour began to be calculated by sundials that did not show the hour, but the religious duty to be fulfilled at various moments of day and night (matins, vespers, etc.). At the end of the 13th century, mechanical clocks made their appearance in Europe. This was a true revolution, as from then on the hour had a fixed duration, to such an extent that by the end of the 14th century most towns had abandoned the solar hour indicated by a gnomon to organise themselves by the striking of the church tower clock.

The day began at sunset and was divided into twenty-four hours: consequently the clock faces were graduated from I to XXIV. However people soon got tired of counting twenty-four chimes, not to mention the innumerable errors that occurred.

So from the 15th century the system was modified so that the clock would strike only six times a day instead of twenty-four. Little time was wasted in applying this simplification and so clock faces began to be numbered I to VI. During the Napoleonic campaigns, "Italian" time was replaced by "French-style" time, where clocks were numbered I to XII and the day started at midnight.

"HOLY LAND"
OF THE ARCICONFRATERNITA DEI BIANCHI

4

Vico dei Bianchi allo Spirito Santo
• Metro: Line 1 Dante, Line 2 Montesanto
• Funicular Montesanto (Montesanto)
• Visits on reservation (authorization required): 081 5524570

One of the most secret "holy lands"

A sturdy double flight of steps, similar to Neapolitan palazzo staircases of the 16th century, leads to underground rooms of the Reale Compagnia e Arciconfraternita dei Bianchi ("the Whites"), where the funeral rites of confreres were celebrated. On each side of the altar more steps lead to the "holy land" (see opposite), where the bodies were interred. The very fine 18th-century floor

tiles and the three paintings attributed to Francesco Solimena make the place less austere.

The church can only be reached through the archconfraternity offices. On the ground floor, you can admire altars of precious marble and paintings by 17th-century masters. In the adjoining assembly hall is a striking demi-lune painting, *The Washing of Feet*, attributed to Belisario Corenzio (around 1630).

The archconfraternity is the successor to an earlier charity, the Compagnia dello Spirito Santo, which dates back to 1555.

CHURCH "HOLY LANDS"

The "holy land" is an enclosed plot in the crypt of certain churches, where the dead used to be buried before their remains were exhumed and placed in ossuaries (see also p. 281).

FORMER OIL TANKS

5

Boutique De Luca – 5a/5b Via Cisterna dell'Olio
• Metro: Line 1 Dante, Line 2 Montesanto
• Funicular Montesanto (Montesanto)
• Tel: 081 5520196 / 081 5520642 / 081 5520382
• pasqualedelucasrl@virgilio.it • www.delucaparati.it • www.dldesign.it
• Visits during shop opening hours (authorization required)

> **Stocks
> of oil below
> the city streets**

In the basement of the De Luca fabric shop, you can visit two of the five refractory-brick tanks where, in the 18th century, the oil produced in the Kingdom of Naples and the Two Sicilies was stored. Contrary to general belief, the oil was for consumption rather than for lighting – streetlights weren't introduced until fifty years later. An elevator takes visitors, accompanied by an employee, down to 15 m below ground level. In these premises, now used as a warehouse, you can clearly see the large openings for pouring the oil into the tanks, the mouth of the hole blackened by contact with the oil. Other smaller openings

were used to draw off buckets of oil for sale.

Also in the shop, two contemporary plaques indicate the capacity of each tank in *stara* (1 *stara* was equivalent to about 10.5 litres): the largest could hold 125,000 litres of oil. On the shop floor you can see two openings covered by a glass plate for checking the condition of the oil. This storage system allowed the precious commodity to be taken off the market or rapidly "fed back" when the commodity price fluctuated as it tended to do in the Kingdom of Naples.

The disused tanks ended up as storage space, as here, or even entertainment venues like the Modernissimo cinema nearby.

CLOCK IN PIAZZA DANTE   ❻

14 Piazza Dante
• Metro: Line 1 Dante, Line 2 Montesanto
• Funicular Montesanto (Montesanto)
• Tel: 081 5491740

> *A rare mechanism that follows the equation of time*

On the façade of the Convitto Nazionale Vittorio Emanuele II tower (formerly a monument commemorating the Bourbon King Charles III), there are two clocks, one large and the other small, bearing the inscription *EQUAZIONE DEL TEMPO*. The face, with its single hand, displays on each side the same series of three numbers: 5, 10, 15. The clock's extremely sophisticated mechanism always shows the discrepancy between apparent solar time (as measured by observation of the Sun or a sundial) and local mean solar time (as kept by conventional timepieces), expressed as a correction never exceeding 16 minutes. When the

hand indicates a negative value, the Sun is in the west, so a sundial will appear "fast"; whereas positive values indicate that the Sun is in the east and therefore "slow". This clock, which is the only one in Europe, came into operation in 1853. It was out of action for years until an astronomical geography teacher from Convitto, Daniela Salvatore, wrote a short treatise on the subject. Thanks to this publication, a senior official at the Banco di Napoli (Bank of Naples), Egidio Mitidieri, decided to fund the clock repairs and it has been in working order since 2008.

WHAT IS THE EQUATION OF TIME?

The equation of time is the difference between apparent solar time and conventional local time. This difference arises from the inclination of the Earth's axis and variations in the speed of its orbit around the Sun.
Since antiquity, astronomers have studied this phenomenon by measuring sidereal time and solar time, but it was only from the 17th century that a mathematical method was invented to calculate these variations. Dutch mathematician Christiaan Huygens was responsible for drawing up the first tables of equation of time values for each day of the year, published in his 1658 work *Horologium Oscillatorium*.

CLOISTER OF THE FORMER CONVENT OF SAN SEBASTIANO

14 Piazza Dante
• Metro: Line 1 Dante, Line 2 Montesanto
• Funicular Montesanto (Montesanto)
• Visits by appointment (booking essential) • Tel: 081 5491740

A
well-hidden
gem

Inside Convitto Nazionale Vittorio Emanuele II there is still a charming medieval cloister which formed part of San Sebastian convent. The church, dating from the time of Constantine, was destroyed in 1941. The small cloister, spanning two centuries (13th and 14th) during the Angevin domination, is surrounded by twenty-five columns built from recovered materials dating from the time of the "Low Empire" (the Dominate) to the Roman era. In the vaults, there are still some frescoes with naturalistic motifs of flowers and birds.

Today the cloister has two storeys, but the second is more recent. A half-moon relief decorates the upper section of one of the entrances. This work, carried out in the 15th century and attributed to Tommaso Malvito, probably belonged to a funerary monument that no longer exists.

ARCICONFRATERNITA DEI VERDI NEL PALAZZO RUFFO DI BAGNARA
Piazza Dante

Between the two churches of San Domenico Soriano and Santa Maria di Caravaggio, in Palazzo Ruffo di Bagnara, is the 17th-century chapel of Saint Ruffo. Today it belongs to the archconfraternity of the "Verdi" (Greens), formerly housed in the Complesso dello Spirito Santo, in Via Toledo. The archconfraternity takes its name from the green homespun cloth worn by members, who used to raise money for the dowries of young girls in need. The altarpiece representing Saint Ruffo is the work of Francesco Solimena, a major figure in Neapolitan Baroque.

LA CONIGLIERA
7 Vico Luperano
• Visits on request (knock at main entrance)

On request, in Palazzo Leporano (or Luperano) you can visit the remains of the 15th-century Palazzo della Conigliera, the extramural residence of King Alfonso II of Aragon. On his death in 1495, the building was inhabited by the Luperano family who renovated it, keeping some elements of the original building, to the design of the renowned architect Giuliano da Maiano.

HOTEL CORRERA AQUEDUCT

241 Via Francesco Saverio Correra
• Metro: Line 1 Dante, Line 2 Montesanto • Funicular Montesanto
(Montesanto)
• Tel: 081 19562842 • info@correra.it
• Admission free • Ask at reception for a guide

A Roman aqueduct integrated into a hotel

Hotel Correra, a short distance from Piazza Dante, backs up against a wall of tuff. Inside, remains of the Graeco-Roman city walls have been incorporated in the décor and stones have even been left exposed in some of the rooms.

From the lobby, there is access to a 10 m long underground gallery where, during construction of the hotel in 2003, other remains were found – from a Roman aqueduct, according to some archaeologists. Although this little tunnel has even been used as a carpenter's storeroom, exhibitions are currently organised there. The gallery is assumed to be longer than 10 m, but for the moment no further excavations have been carried out.

Also in the lobby, a "cocktail corner" has been set up in a cave left just as it was found.

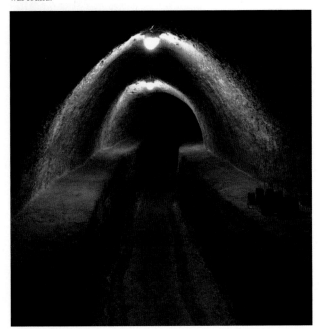

PASQUALE CATALANO, A SPECIALIST IN NATIVITY SCENES

5 Via Francesco Saverio Correra
• Metro: Line 1 Dante, Line 2 Montesanto • Funicular Montesanto (Montesanto)
• Visits December to June on reservation by phone or e-mail
• pasqualecat@libero.it
• Tel: 081 5495593, mobile 338 1156884

> *Just like an authentic 18th-century crib*

Pasquale Catalano is a master of the art of nativity scenes (known as *presepiale* art from *presepe*, Italian for crib). Every year at his home, he spends forty days building a new nativity 4.5 m long, respecting a tradition born at the court of Naples in the 18th century. While the décor varies from year to year, the essentials remain the same: the scene is always set in a hovel or the ruins of a temple; the cave immediately below the ground, the home of disturbing presences to be repelled (originally the devil was placed there to symbolise the subterranean Evil defeated by Good); the inn and the innkeeper, those too an incarnation of Evil (see p. 231); the three washerwomen, an allegory of Purification.

Signor Catalano explains that a crib in this style must pinpoint the moment of the birth of Christ; therefore anything that moves, like water flowing from a fountain or animated figurines, is banned. These variations, he adds, belong to a commercial trend departing from the tradition whose origins date

back to King Charles of Bourbon. Charles did in fact like to collect the figurines that were not only made by renowned sculptors, but were dressed in costumes of pure silk and adorned with real jewellery. The taste for figurines and cribs spread first among the aristocracy then through all social strata, handed down to us today in various interpretations.

WHERE CAN YOU SEE SOME EXTRAORDINARY FIGURINES?
"Le voci di dentro" by Alessandro Flaminio
111 Via San Biagio dei Librai • Metro: Line 1 Dante, Line 2 Montesanto
La scarabattola
50 Via dei Tribunali • Metro: Line 1 Dante
"Presepiando e non solo" by Aldo Caliro
85/c Via San Biagio dei Librai • Metro: Line 1 Dante, Line 2 Montesanto
(Aldo Caliro is in the Guinness Book of Records for his cribs that fit on a pinhead or an optical fibre.)

CHURCH OF SAN GIUSEPPE DELLE SCALZE ⑫

65 Salita Pontecorvo
• Metro: Line 1 Dante, Line 2 Montesanto
• Visits by appointment only
• Contact any of the following associations: Archintorno, Forum
Tarsia (posta@forumtarsia.it), Mammamà, Medici senza Frontiere,
Duomimatto, Ramblas, Altra Definizione

A forgotten gem

At first sight the church of San Giuseppe delle Scalze, surrounded as it is by imposing scaffolding, gives the impression of being under repair. But the scaffolding is just a simple precaution because the monument is so dilapidated. You can, however, visit it by appointment.

The entire church was built for the monastic Order of Discalced Carmelites by the Bergamo architect and sculptor Cosimo Fanzago, who worked mainly in Naples.

This gem of a building, with its very unusual stucco interior embellished with grand arches presided over by statues of Saint Joseph, Saint Peter of Alcantara and Saint Theresa, is considered one of the best examples of Neapolitan Baroque. The impressive central nave is as remarkable as the three sculptures.

The church (which was closed after suffering serious damage in the 1980 earthquake) was built in 1660 on the site of a palazzo that the nuns had bought from Marquis Spinelli for 16,000 ducats. As Fanzago the architect had failed to find a suitable plot to build the convent as the Carmelites wished, he was obliged to make use of the structure of the existing palazzo. The order was suppressed from 1808, and in 1820 the building was taken over by the Barnabite Fathers. It was later converted into a boarding school and finally a day school. Although the church is closed for worship, it has never been formally deconsecrated.

The ceiling, destroyed in 1980, was decorated with frescoes by Luca Giordano and Francesco De Maria. They are now on display in the gallery of the Museo Nazionale (National Museum) at Capodimonte.

MUSEO HERMANN NITSCH

29/d Vico Lungo Pontecorvo
• Metro: Line 1 Dante
• Tel: 081 5641655
• Open Monday to Friday 10am–7pm, Saturday 10am–2pm
• Closed 3 August to 1 September
• Admission €10, concessions €5

> **A stunning contemporary art venue**

The museum founded by Giuseppe Morra (also owner of the San Martino vineyard, see p. 101) opened in 2008 in a power station that had been shut down since the beginning of the 20th century. There are large-format photos of the idiosyncratic performances of contemporary Austrian artist Hermann Nitsch with whom Morra worked from 1974. Also displayed in the various rooms, covering an area of 2,000 m², are objects used by Nitsch for his street theatre performances in several cities around the world, including Naples. Be warned that these images, aimed precisely at shocking spectators, might upset sensitive souls!

The plant was built in 1885 (the date can still be seen on some of the original pillars that have been preserved) by the engineer Paolo Boubée, who also designed the beautiful dome of Galleria Umberto I in Naples.

Hermann Nitsch (Vienna 1938) is the co-founder of the Viennese Actionism movement and the inventor of the Theatre of Orgies and Mysteries, which included all artforms. Among these, the most contentious performances involved public participation, witnessing the actual slaughter of animals whose blood was spread on huge canvases. The horror and disgust raised by this bloody spectacle, according to Nitsch, would initiate a counter-reaction of catharsis and purification.

INSTALLATION SEEN THROUGH A PEEPHOLE

Several spaces on the first floor of the Nitsch Museum were loaned to artists in order to create a work. The most original of these is a secret library called *Scriptorium dell'adepto*, an installation that you can only see as a whole by looking through a peephole. The conceptual artist responsible for it, Luca Maria Patella, who was already active in the 1960s, wanted to pay tribute to Marcel Duchamp's last work, *Étant donné eau et gaz*. The door of the room is in four colours, corresponding to Jung's four psychological functions. In the library you can consult Patella's writings on aesthetics, psychology and artistic avant-garde movements.

CASTS OF PARTHENON SCULPTURES

Accademia delle Belle Arti – 36 Via Bellini
• Metro: Line 1 Dante, Line 2 Montesanto • Funicular Montesanto
(Montesanto)
• Visits on reservation: 081 441900 / 081 441887

Casts of Phidias' masterpiece in Naples since 1820

On the walls of the lecture hall of the Academy of Fine Arts (founded in 1752 by Charles of Bourbon) are displayed beautiful casts of the sculptural decoration of the Parthenon in Athens. All but three sections of the frieze, and the metopes and tympanum sculptures, belong to the series of casts executed on the spot by British diplomat Lord Elgin (1766–1841) before they were taken to London. The Neapolitan casts were offered to the Bourbon King Ferdinand I by the British King George IV in 1820.

NEARBY

GYPSOTHEQUE OF THE ACADEMY OF FINE ARTS

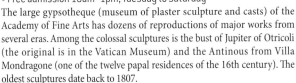

• Free admission 10am–1pm, Tuesday to Saturday

The large gypsotheque (museum of plaster sculpture and casts) of the Academy of Fine Arts has dozens of reproductions of major works from several eras. Among the colossal sculptures is the bust of Jupiter of Otricoli (the original is in the Vatican Museum) and the Antinous from Villa Mondragone (one of the twelve papal residences of the 16th century). The oldest sculptures date back to 1807.

The Academy's gallery of modern art holds a number of masters. An entire room is given over to Filippo Palizzi of the Neapolitan landscape school. These paintings were bequeathed to the museum by the artist himself. Canvases by his brothers, Giuseppe, Nicola and Paolo, all accomplished artists, also form part of the collection. The gallery also has twenty-eight older works from the 15th to 18th centuries.

HOLY STEPS
OF SANTA MARIA DELLA SAPIENZA

Convento delle Ancelle del Sacro Cuore di Santa Caterina Volpicelli
47 Via Sapienza
• Metro: Line 1 Dante or Museo
• Visits by appointment (authorization required)
• Tel: 081 459362

*Little-known
Holy Steps*

You can book a visit to the monastery of Santa Maria della Sapienza, founded in the 16th century by Maria Carafa. This building contains virtually unknown wonders: the Holy Steps and a splendid church, considered one of the temples to Neapolitan Baroque. The church was remodelled and decorated in the 17th century by two great artists, Francesco Grimaldi and Cosimo Fanzago. Although badly damaged, it is now being restored.

The Holy Steps, twenty-eight of them, are in a vaulted corridor frescoed by a pupil of Francesco Solimena, Andrea D'Aste. The pictorial decoration, commissioned by Mother Marie-Thérèse Carafa, consists of a fresco in the vault depicting the Resurrection, a Crucifixion altarpiece at the top of the steps, and six oval paintings (now missing) representing the Passion of Christ.

To the right of the main altar, the original access to the Holy Steps is now closed off.

ORIGIN AND MEANING OF THE HOLY STEPS

In Christian tradition the Holy Steps led to the tribunal where Christ was taken for interrogation by Pontius Pilate before being crucified. In AD 326 Saint Helena, mother of Emperor Constantine, is thought to have brought the stone steps to Rome, where they were placed in the Santuario della Scala Santa near the basilica of Saint John Lateran. After the Council of Trent (1545–1563), called by Pope Paul III in response to Protestant reforms and to suppress the worldly excesses of the clergy, the Church tightened up ecclesiastical discipline by encouraging penitential practices. These included the dissemination of Holy Steps, reproductions of Rome's Scala Santa, of which there are still a couple of dozen around the world. Besides those in Naples (see opposite), there are stairs in Jerusalem (part of the original flight), Bastia and Lourdes in France, and in Italy at Prato, Turin, Mantua, Varallo ... Traditionally, in order to gain indulgences or forgiveness, worshippers had to climb the steps on their knees while reciting prayers in order to reach an altar or a simple crucifix at the top.

HOLY STEPS IN NAPLES

- Santa Maria della Sapienza (see opposite).
- San Gregorio Armeno (p. 226).
- Arciconfraternita dell'Ecce Homo al Cerriglio. The Holy Steps connect the small chapel in the monastery of Santa Maria la Nova (12 Via del Cerriglio – Metro: Line 1 Università).
- Arciconfraternita dei Bianchi dei Santi Francesco e Matteo della Scala Santa. Founded in 1606, by concession of Pope Paul V (20 Vico Giardinetto – Metro: Line 1 Toledo).
- Former monastery of Santi Marcellino e Festo, where part of a 17th-century Holy Stair is preserved, restored by Luigi Vanvitelli in 1772, near the demolished oratory (10 Largo San Marcellino – Metro: Line 1 Università).

UNDERGROUND GALLERIES OF PIETRASANTA ⑰

Piazzetta Pietrasanta
• Metro: Line 1 Dante, Line 2 Montesanto
• Funicular Montesanto (Montesanto)
• Tel: 347 6455332 • info@lamacchinadeltempo.info
• Visits on reservation

A
10,000 m²
network
of underground
galleries

To the right of the entrance to the Pietrasanta (Holy Stone) church, a hatch gives access to the early Christian chapel built in AD 533. In the 1960s a landslide caused the collapse of the right aisle, revealing the earlier building and the underground galleries.

In the course of restoration, the chapel has been converted into an exhibition space for objects found during the excavations: a Roman house and remains of the Greek city walls. From this first level about 5 m deep, you can descend another 30 m to take a trip through the bowels of the ancient city, on tracks dug into the rock wall by the *pozzari* (the men who maintained the wells and tanks). The total surface area of this intricate network of tunnels, part of which was used as a bomb shelter during the Second World War, is over 10,000 m². Of particular note is the jaw-dropping, strangely convoluted section where the wall forms "waves", which is why it's called ONDE M. A. (WAVE M. A.) by the cavers, who think this route could be 2,000 years old.

At a fork in the tunnels, on the wall at the entrance to the right-hand gallery, an engraved cross is followed by twelve groups of linked or intersecting crosses spread over several hundred metres. The twisting path runs along the axis of the palace of Raimondo di Sangro, Prince of Sansevero (see p. 214) and then straightens out to end under the altar of the church. The twelve groups of crosses seem to correspond to another sign carved on a white marble plaque set in the wall of the church bell tower on Piazza Miraglia side: a Greek cross with arms terminating in fleurs-de-lis, the emblem of the Military Order of Calatrava (the Castilian city where the order was founded). Experts calculate that the underground route marked out by the crosses is a link to the bell tower.

CLOISTER OF SANT'ANDREA DELLE DAME

Sant'Andrea delle Dame university campus - 7 Via Luigi De Crecchio
• Metro: Line 1 Dante, Line 2 Montesanto
• Funicular Montesanto (Montesanto)
• Open weekdays 9am–4pm

A spectacular double row of palm trees

The cloister of Sant'Andrea delle Dame ("of the Ladies"), home of the Second University of Naples medical school, is all that remains of a monastic complex for young girls from upper-class families founded in 1583 by Giulia, Lucrezia, Laura and Claudia Parascandolo, the four daughters of a wealthy lawyer.

Initially known as Sant'Andrea delle Monache ("of the Nuns"), the convent was renamed for the "Ladies" in honour of its founders. Its religious vocation

was suppressed during the Napoleonic period and the building was later converted into a medical school.

The bright and spacious cloister, bordered by tall pillars of grey stone and embellished by a magnificent double row of palms, was decorated by the Flemish painter Pietro Mennes. This place, although open to all, is pretty well unknown except by university students.

SEVENTH HEAVEN LANE

Via De Crecchio, named in honour of an eminent 19th-century rector of the University of Naples Federico II, was formerly called Vico Settimo Cielo (Seventh Heaven Lane), probably derived from *Settimio Celio* Gaudioso, an African bishop of the 5th century who founded the monastery of Saint Gaudioso in this district. There is, however, a legend that the seven heavens refer to those of the Iris that appeared as a blinding light on 13 December 596, while they celebrated the funeral rites of the future Saint Agnello in the church of Santa Maria Intercede.

PRIVATE TOUR
OF MONASTERO DELLE TRENTATRÉ

19

8 Via Pisanelli
• Metro: Line 1 Museo, Line 2 Cavour
• Tel: 081 299963 • francesco33i@alice.it
• Visits on reservation for groups, one Saturday per month for individuals

A true rarity

The long history of the Trentatré (Thirty-three), founded in 1535, has made this convent quite a rarity. Although the site has always been closed to the public due to the strict Rule observed by the nuns, guided tours have been allowed for a decade or so, but only on certain dates. Many Neapolitans are even unaware of its existence.

Thirteen nuns still live there at present, supported by charity, and the founder Maria Lorenza Longo is on the way to beatification.

The building stands on the ancient Greek acropolis of the city, close to the remains of the Roman theatre. Besides the church, the tour takes in the refectory (where you can admire the fine *Supper at Emmaus* painted by Giuseppe Bonito in the 16th century), the cellars, the very pretty cloister and the parlour with its grille still in place where a few believers still come to ask the nuns to pray for them. Another curiosity is a small exhibition of baby Jesus waxworks, quantities of which have been made by the nuns since the 18th century. The figurines, which are offered to benefactors as Christmas gifts, differ from the Neapolitan artisan use of mainly plaster, terracotta and papier-mâché.

The adjacent church of Santa Maria di Gerusalemme, rebuilt in the 17th century, also complies with the Rule that imposes austerity and poverty: the decorative elements are basically stucco and wood, humble materials.

In 1518, the noblewoman Maria Lorenza Longo, after experiencing a miracle, founded the Ospedale degli Incurabili (Hospital for Incurables) for patients with syphilis. She designated some rooms in this building for the use of a small number of Capuchin Poor Clares, who observed strict cloistering.

In 1538, Paul III limited the number of nuns to thirty-three, as many as the years of Christ's life, hence the popular name of the convent. Another notable feature was that these nuns were all poor girls, including rehabilitated prostitutes. The reputation of holiness of the Thirty-three spread throughout Europe and led to the founding of numerous convents on the same model. There were 200 of them in the 18th century.

WHY IS THE NUMBER 33 GENERALLY ASSOCIATED WITH NUNS IN THE NEAPOLITAN LOTTERY?

Over the centuries, the popularity of this convent has become so rooted in the city's culture that number 33 in the Neapolitan Book of Dreams, the Smorfia (where each number has one or more meanings – see pp. 194–197), is associated, among other things, with nuns in general. Furthermore, the expression "like one of the thirty-three nuns" is used of people who are constantly asking the time: it seems that the nuns of the convent passed their time counting the quarter hours. The invention of the delicious sfogliatelle, a local pastry speciality, is also attributed to these nuns.

NEAPOLITAN LOTTO: A HISTORY OF DIVINATION

In Naples, the lottery has always been a kind of esoteric practice where Christian faith and paganism intermingle. The choice of numbers calls on cabalistic laws or numerology derived from Pythagorean theories.

So the numbers you play must always be inferred from a dream, an exceptional event or a news story. To achieve this you have to consult the *Smorfia* (Book of Dreams), which lists all the things that correspond to the numbers 1 to 90, in words and images, so that even non-readers can use it. This numerological interpretation is sometimes very complex, especially as winning combinations range from one to five numbers. Neapolitans, particularly residents of the *centro storico* (historic centre), then sometimes turn to an *assistito* (helped by [God]): those whom it is believed communicate with the dead, who in turn are supposed to intercede with the Almighty to change their family's fortune by making them rich. If there have been no dreams or significant events, the "assisted", a veritable soothsayer, always guided by the souls of the dead, generates words or actions – necessarily ambiguous – to which the punter will attach a meaning by consulting the *Smorfia* at home. The delusional nature of these predictions has given rise to a common way of describing someone who rambles on: in the Neapolitan dialect, they're "dishing out numbers".

Generally, the "assisted", who don't have the right to play on their own account, are only paid with a percentage of the sum collected for a successful prediction.

Having procured the "good numbers", to increase your chances you must invoke the Madonna, a patron saint, souls in Purgatory (see pp. 302–303) or an imp called the *munaciello* (little monk). God is never directly responsible. Prayers may be spontaneous or follow a model such as this: "Today it's the Moon / tomorrow it'll be Mars / and my chance will come / it'll come by sea / it'll come by land / come into my dream without scaring me / three beautiful numbers make me dream."

Stories abound relating to the Neapolitans' unbridled love of the lottery, for example:

Charles Dickens describes how in 1845 he witnessed a rider fall from his horse. As the hapless victim lay in a pool of blood, a passer-by asked his age before even offering to help, as he needed a third number to play – the other two being 56 (a fall) and 18 (blood).

On 29 April 1994, when John Paul II slipped in the bathroom and broke his hip, the *ricevitorie* (lottery offices) were taken by storm. Everyone played 56 (a fall), 32 (the pope), 90 (broken hip) and 29 (date of the accident). According to the *Corriere della Sera* reporter who wrote up this incident, if all the numbers had come up, the state would have gone bankrupt.

The celebrated Neapolitan author Matilde Serao has written: "The Neapolitans are sober, they aren't corrupted by spirits, they don't die of delirium tremens, they're corrupted and die of lotto."

When a law was passed in 1734 to ban gambling over Christmas, Neapolitans invented the family game of *tombola*. This custom, which still thrives around Christmastime, involves all levels of society. To play, the numbers 1 to 90 (engraved on small wooden cylinders) are extracted from a conical basket with a hole at the top. The players buy one or more cards with fifteen numbers printed on each. The money collected makes up the pot, which is then divided into five prizes. As each number is drawn, if it appears on their card(s), the players cover it with a bean from the pile in front of them. The winner is the first to cover two, three, four or five numbers in the same row. The jackpot is won by completing a whole card. Each number is traditionally called along with its meaning. In the old neighbourhoods, where the traditional culture hasn't yet broken down, a transsexual, or an elderly woman, is always responsible for the draw.

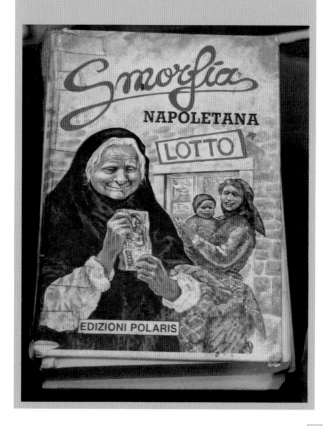

SMORFIA: THE REAL MEANING OF THE NUMBERS

The complete version of the *Smorfia* (a word derived from Morpheus, the god of sleep and therefore of dreams) is a veritable key to dreams in which each number has several meanings, and each meaning can be applied to many situations. There nevertheless is a classic popular version – the one used in the "family" lotto mentioned on the previous page – where each number refers to traditional beliefs, local culture, and life itself. Sexual allegories are common because many ancient rites were dedicated to the gods of fertility. Some topics need an explanation, while others are self-explanatory. The origin of these meanings is not always known. Note that women feature far more than men, traditional society in Campania being matriarchal.

1: Italy Before the unification of Italy (1861), 1 corresponded to the Sun, which was the subject of a primitive cult in antiquity.

2: little girl

3: cat In Neapolitan dialect, *gatta* (cat) is feminine and has a clear sexual connotation.

4: pig This was the sacred animal of Demeter, one of the main deities once worshipped in Naples. With the arrival of Christianity, Saint Anthony the Hermit took over from Demeter, so the pig was dedicated to him (see p. 293).

5: hand The number 5 refers to the five fingers. A magical symbol for thousands of years (hands are depicted in several prehistoric caves).

6: her that always looks down (female genitals).

7: vase An essential object that featured, like weapons, among the first "creations" of *Homo sapiens*.

8: Madonna The Virgin has replaced almost all pagan deities. Her feast days are 8 May, 8 October and 8 December.

9: offspring

10: dried beans They symbolise immortality because they "come back to life" in water after drying. Roman women wore bean-shaped pendants for luck. Beans are used to cover the drawn numbers when playing lotto with the family.

11: mice By running back and forth at high speed from the light to the shadows, they symbolically ensure the uninterrupted link between these two worlds, and therefore between spirit and matter, Good and Evil.

12: soldiers

13: Saint Anthony (of Padua). A particularly well-loved saint in Naples, whose feast day falls on 13 June.

14: drunkard In the Dionysian rites of old, very common in Graeco-Roman Naples, drunkenness, synonymous with loss of consciousness, was a way of communicating with God.

15: little boy

16: buttocks "To have buttocks" means to be lucky.

17: misfortune Although in Naples as elsewhere there shouldn't be 13 seated at table, it is Friday the 17th the Neapolitans dread. The number 17 is however associated with happiness in the Kabbalah, and some say that its bad reputation comes from the Roman numeral XVII, of which the anagram VIXI (I lived) means "I'm [now] dead."

18: blood - 19: laughter - 20: festival - 21: naked woman

22: madman - 23: idiot - 24: Carabinieri

25: Christmas The date marking the rebirth of the Sun (winter solstice) was already celebrated in Graeco-Roman Naples.

26: *Nanninella* Diminutive of Anna, the mother of Mary and patron of all female occupations, whose feast day is 26 July.

27: *càntaro* (chamber pot). This is a very common insult, equivalent to "asshole". The term is used in many colourful phrases, e.g. "*scassà 'o càntaro*", meaning "to shit in somebody's boots".

28: women's breasts

29: father of all children (male genitals). In Naples the phallus is still a widespread talisman, as it was in Roman times. Faced with a bad omen, men touch their crotch to ward off their fate, whereas women touch a red horn (see p. 68), the Christian version of the Roman phallus.

30: lieutenant's bullets Metaphor for "testicles". The only purpose of the lieutenant, *tenente*, is to rhyme with *trenta*, given that in Neapolitan the final vowel is not pronounced.

31: owner (real estate). Because the 31st is the day you pay the rent.

32: *capitone* (big eel). The indispensable Christmas Eve meal. This fish is very similar to the serpent, the embodiment of Evil. So to ward off Evil, it is cut up alive.

33: age of Christ This number is also associated with the nun, because in Old Naples there is a convent called the "Thirty-three" (see p. 190).

34: *capa* (head). But also the *glans penis*. In Neapolitan, *capa 'e cazzo* (literally dickhead) is a insult commonly aimed at airheads.

35: bird In many civilisations, birds represent the means of communicating with celestial bodies.

36: castanets Ancient instrument played in ritual dances during religious festivals in antiquity as today.

37: monk In the Campanian popular imagination, monks always have one foot in the world of magic. Some of them, it is believed, had the power to know the winning numbers in advance. *'O munaciello*, the little monk, is the notorious imp who, according to legend, appears in Neapolitan homes to bring happiness or misery, depending on how it is treated.

38: blows (beating up) - **39: hangman's rope**

40: *paposcia* (scrotal hernia). Several Neapolitan words and phrases associated with this condition are a source of ribald jokes. For example, if a man takes a chance by predicting rain, he is laughingly asked if he's got a hernia because, seemingly, it's painful when the weather changes.

41: knife (weapon). This is the weapon used by "men of honour" because it requires more courage than the gun.

42: coffee Neapolitans so love their coffee that, in the bars of the historic centre, regulars pay for two coffees, their own and one for the next customer who mightn't have any money on them.

43: "slut" on the balcony. Equivalent of "easy woman" because in bygone days if a woman lingered on the balcony it was to attract attention or wait for her lover.

44: bars (prison windows).

45: good wine Sacred drink in both the pagan and Christian eras, when it becomes the blood of Christ.

46: money - 47: death - 48: talking dead (in dreams)

49: piece of meat - 50: bread

51: garden Implying the female pubis.

52: mother Key character in Neapolitan culture in which the Great Mother was one of the main deities.

53: old man He personifies wisdom.

54: hat Historically, headgear has always been a distinctive mark of social class.

55: music A fundamental element of Campanian culture (see pp. 76–77). Here, the two 5s represent the ten fingers needed to play an instrument.

56: a fall

57: hunchback Among Neapolitans, who are very superstitious, a hunchback (men only!) brings good luck and, to increase your chances, you even have to caress his hump.

58: parcel Synonymous with the gift that is used to cement social ties, seal pacts, finalise a marriage contract.

59: hairs 60: complaint (lamentation).

61: hunter The hunter always features in the Neapolitan nativity scene (see p. 229), where all the major magico-religious symbols of Campanian culture are found. As the oldest method of getting food, hunting is also often represented in the funerary paintings of antiquity.

62: murder victim   63: bride

64: *sciammeria* (formal dress – frock coat). This word is used to ironise about someone dressed in their Sunday best. A *sciammeria*, being a long jacket "cover-up", is also a synonym for the sex act.

65: tears Especially those of women beating their breast.

66: two single girls The allusion to the two 6s is obvious. The two marriageable girls, one beautiful and the other ugly, is also a recurring theme in Campanian folktales.

67: squid in the guitar A very suggestive phrase to describe the sex act.

68: *zuppa 'e carnacotta*, literally "cooked meat soup". This is traditionally a soup for the poor, made from a few green vegetables, aromatic herbs and thin slices of veal offal. It is served very hot over a layer of traditional *freselle* crackers.

69: upside down A number whose sexual meaning is blindingly obvious.

70: residential building

71: *ommo 'e merda* (manure). A very common insult.

72: wonder Here the meaning is rather that of another state of being as possessed by the divine light. In the nativity scene, in front of the cave of the Baby Jesus, there must be a *pastore d' 'a meraviglia*, an open-mouthed and open-armed shepherd struck by the divine event. In common parlance, the "amazed shepherd" signifies a blissful innocent.

73: hospital

74: cave Natural caves are imbued with a profound religious meaning in many civilisations, particularly in Campania. A number of rites did in fact take place in caves (see Crypta Neapolitana, p. 29). The cave also alludes to the ultimate "cavity", that of the woman who gives life.

75: Pulcinella (Punch, see p. 339).

76: fountain Fountains embody a magical value: apparitions and lovers' trysts take place near them. The fountain is also an essential element of the nativity scene, as it was near a fountain that the angel Gabriel announced to Mary that she was carrying the Baby Jesus.

77: devils This number is also associated with women's thighs, as the supreme temptation, to be resisted by saints and initiates to pagan religions preaching purity (such as Isis worshippers).

78: *bella figliola* (pretty girl). A euphemism to avoid explicitly saying *zoccola* (literally female rat), whore.

79: thief

80: mouth Of all the parts of the human body, the mouth has been chosen for its many essential functions: breathing, eating, talking, laughing, sensuality.

81: flowers They are associated with two critical phases of human life: marriage, from which life is born, and death.

82: set table For Neapolitans, a hearty meal is synonymous with a religious festival, family unity, pleasure, and needless to say an eternal dream for the poor. Tavern tables overflowing with food are never left out of the crib scene.

83: bad weather In the land of Sun-worshippers, bad weather is a poor omen. The Neapolitans make signs to ward off the fates if they wake to see an overcast sky. The number 83 is probably connected with the year 1783, when a downpour followed by a powerful earthquake devastated Calabria (formerly part of the Kingdom of Naples).

84: church - 85: souls in Purgatory (see pp. 302–303).

86: corner shop Another vital place as it contains everything essential to life, not to mention embodying a basic human activity. An authentic Neapolitan nativity scene is always dotted with little shops.

87: *perucchie* (lice). This is one of sixty slang expressions for money. However to Neapolitans *quatte perucchie* (four lice) means something very cheap – *perucchiuso* signifies "miserly".

88: *casecavallo* Euphemism for someone that's a "pain in the neck", as you might say to them in English: "You get on my tits" or "You piss me off". Not only is *casecavallo* (a typical cheese from the Campania region; in Italian, *caciocavallo*) shaped like a distended testicle, but these cheeses are hung up in pairs in shops.

89: little old lady The very old woman is the one who performs the ancient rites: the relatives of Saint Januarius (see p. 354), the Sibyls, the *Befana* who brings gifts to children on 6 January, are all old women.

90: fear and the people If Neapolitans laugh at anything and everything, it's to relieve their angst: worry over the eruptions, earthquakes and endless wars that have raged through this beautiful country. This explains the double meaning of this last *Smorfia* number.

INCURABILI PHARMACY

50 Largo Maria Longo
• Metro: Line 1 Museo, Line 2 Cavour
• Visits by small groups on reservation
• Tel: 081 440647
• info@ilfarodippocrate.it

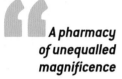

> *A pharmacy of unequalled magnificence*

Built in the 16th century, then enlarged and refurbished (as seen today) between 1740 and 1760, the pharmacy in the Ospedale degli Incurabili (Hospital of the Incurables) is a genuine masterpiece. According to contemporary thinking, the beauty of the many works of art in the pharmacy was aimed at treating patients more effectively.

This marvellous little place is the last of the hundreds of such pharmacies that used to fill the city. The only proof of their existence is the many ceramic vases dispersed in public and private collections around the world. The two-room pharmacy, closed for over thirty years, was reopened to the public in 2011.

A monumental grey stone staircase takes you to the main salon with its tiled floor made by the prestigious Massa brothers' workshop (also responsible for the majolica work in the celebration cloister of Santa Chiara). At the entrance, two golden sculptures face one another: allegories of the "virgin uterus" and the "post-operative uterus" respectively. In the centre stands a rare walnut table, 5 m long, carved from a single massive trunk. All around the walls is a dazzling display of 420 multicoloured ceramic vases, also by Massa, decorated with scenes from the Old Testament and in a perfect state of conservation: the largest contained ointments, the smaller ones syrups – remedies mainly reserved for hospital patients (see p. 201).

The walls of the salon are covered from top to bottom with beautiful carved walnut cabinets with inlaid shelves, the work of cabinetmaker Agostino Fucito. The ceiling fresco by Pietro Bardellino features scenes from the Trojan War, but with a nod to medicine, as the hero Menelaus (or Achilles) is being cared for by Machaon, a warrior well-versed in the physician's art.

ELECTRICITY AS THERAPY IN THE 18TH CENTURY

At the four corners of the ceiling of the large salon are the portraits of four characters, all with connections to medicine except Italian physicist Alessandro Volta (1745–1827), who earned his place there because certain conditions were already being treated in the late 18th century using heat generated by electricity.

NAPLES, THE LAST BASTION OF *TERIACA*

Note also a large marble vase in which was kept a remedy long considered infallible against poisoning: *Teriaca* (Greek *thériaké*, antidote to poisonous animal bites). Naples was the last Italian city to cease production in 1906. (For more information, see *Secret Venice* in this series of guides.)

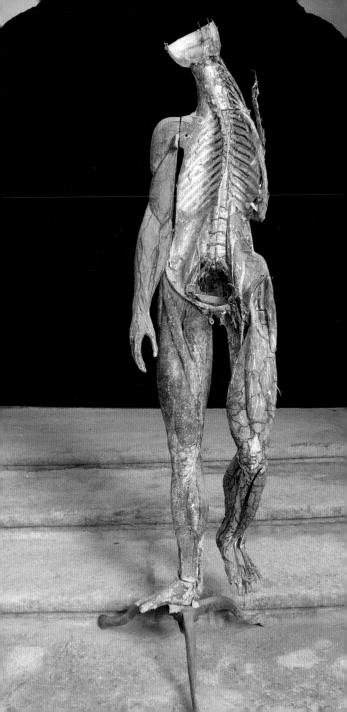

MUSEO DELLE ARTI SANITARIE DEGLI INCURABILI

50 Largo Maria Longo
• Metro: Line 1 Museo, Line 2 Cavour
• Visits on reservation by phone or e-mail
• Tel: 081 440647
• info@ilfarodippocrate.it

A unique anatomical model

In the Hospital for Incurables, besides the pharmacy (see previous double-page spread), a very interesting museum is housed in the premises of the former Convento delle Convertite (convent for reformed prostitutes). It bears testimony to the advanced level of modernity achieved by medicine in 16th-century Naples (the founding of the hospital by Maria Lorenza Longo dates back to 1518 – see p. 190).

The highlight of the Museum of the History of Medicine and Health is an anatomical papier-mâché model built in 1730/1740. This unique educational tool – complete with perfectly represented veins, backbone and muscles, which can be dismantled and articulated – was used in the centre's school of medicine.

Among the many artefacts are rare surgical instruments, a portable pharmacy from the 18th century, one of the first glass feeding bottles in history and an anaesthetic mask, an all-time first.

The hospital, which has been operational since 1518, was one of the largest in Europe, with 1,600 beds when it opened.

In the courtyard, the marble basins can still be seen where, before they were admitted, the sick were washed then dressed in a long white shirt. The doctors washed their hands at the fountains on either side of the courtyard.

WHEN UNHEALTHY AIR WAS BELIEVED TO CAUSE SYPHILIS

The place where the hospital was built, Caponapoli hill, was purposely chosen for its particularly clean air as it was thought to cure syphilis. When the real cause of this terrible condition was discovered, the names of aristocrats and prelates disappeared as if by magic from the hospital records.

NEARBY

In the largest cloister of the Incurabili monastery complex, over a hundred species of medicinal herbs formerly grown here have recently been replanted. In the centre of the garden stands a beautiful camphor tree, planted in 1525, which is the oldest in Italy. The rooms used as a maternity ward give onto the adjacent cloister, referred to as the "cloister of the pregnant women", as indicated by an old plaque.

MUSEO DI ANATOMIA UMANA

Seconda Università degli Studi
5 Via Luciano Armanni
• Metro: Line 1 Museo, Line 2 Cavour
• Tel: 081 5666010
• www.museoanatomico-napoli.it
• Admission free Monday to Friday, 9am–12 noon • Closed August
• Reservation by phone required

> *Human monstrosities*

T he Human Anatomy Museum, founded in 1819 and completely unknown to the general public, figures among the top three in the world for the richness and importance of its collections, put together by eminent anatomists and later bequeathed to the university. They are kept in very elegant 19th-century cabinets in the monastery of Saint Patricia, now closed down.

Among the most impressive pieces is a calcified foetus 10 cm long that remained in the body of the mother for twenty-eight years and was discovered only after her death – an incident recounted in a scientific text of 1658.

There is no lack of eccentricities in these rooms, where you can see "artwork" in macabre taste, to say the least: a low table made from human blood, bile, brains and lungs, on which a female hand is laid, all preserved through a process called "petrifaction".

The many examples of deformities include a number of malformed foetuses preserved in formaldehyde and a skeleton of a woman who died at the age of 90 with severe arthritis.

In the section on anatomical dissection (417 dried samples dating back to the 18th century), two bodies are on display: their vascular system is revealed following injection with coloured dyes. The rarest exhibit is a humerus attributed in the archives to a skeleton prepared by Andreas Vesalius, the father of modern anatomy, in 1544 at Basle. As far as is known, this is unique in the world.

Note also the giant anatomical plates (70 × 100 cm), dated 1823, by the Siena anatomist Paolo Mascagni. There are only two sets in the world, the others (1825) being in Pisa.

Other curiosities include the skulls of four criminals known as the "Vicaria four". They were the protagonists of an incident that made headlines in the early 19th century: with the help of her lover, her father and a young surgeon who had fallen for her, Giuditta Guastamacchia planned her husband's murder. The four culprits were executed on Via dei Tribunali on 19 April 1800. Note the marks drawn on their skulls by criminology physiognomists.

Thanks to the work of the director of the institute, Professor Vincenzo Esposito, the museum was reopened to the public in 1997.

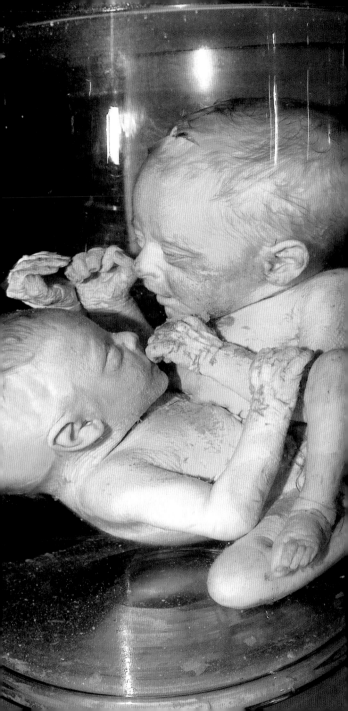

CASA ZEVOLA

31 Via Atri
• Metro: Line 1 Dante or Università, Line 2 Montesanto
• Funicular Montesanto (Montesanto)
• Further information by e-mail: napolisegreta@gmail.com

> **The incredible apartment/ museum of a modern "disciple" of Giordano Bruno**

The large apartment of Giuseppe Zevola, Neapolitan painter, poet and philosopher, is a clever extravaganza: family furniture, Baroque mirrors and other unique objects hang from the ceiling, such as the "Lady Philosophy", made entirely from mirrors and round mosaics on a golden background swaying back and forth. All the doors and windows are painted in bright colours, as are the chairs, tables, tablecloths and plates. There is an abundance of chandeliers and rotating centrepieces on the tables, while on the walls the heroes of Indian mythology rub shoulders with saints and heretics. Zevola considers his amazing residence, which he calls *Muta domus*, to be his personal theatre.

As an unconditional admirer of the great philosopher Giordano Bruno, Zevola commits to memory and publishes extracts from his works. Having worked for ten years in the Historical Archive of the Banco di Napoli (see p. 253), the artist managed to assemble a collection of drawings, poems, puns, even doodles, left in the margins of their ledgers by former employees of the "*Banchi pubblici*" (old-time banks) from 1538 to 1861. The collection was published under the title *Piaceri di noia* (Pleasures of Boredom).

Since 2002, one of Giuseppe Zevola's works has been on display at Rione Alto (Line 1 of the metro), known as the "art" station.

COMMEMORATIVE PLAQUES AT PALAZZO FILANGIERI

23 Via Atri
• Metro: Line 1 Museo, Line 2 Cavour

The palazzo where great minds met

The façade of Palazzo Filangieri, built in the 18th century by the Filangieri family of Arianiello, is studded with commemorative plaques dedicated to personalities who lived here between the 18th and 20th centuries: the one above on the right concerns the jurist and philosopher Gaetano Filangieri, born in 1752 (see below); the one below states that the celebrated philosopher Benedetto Croce (1866–1952) had an apartment there from 1900 to 1912.

The bottom-left plaque records that Goethe was a guest of the Filangieri family. In his *Italian Journey*, Goethe had indeed written that Gaetano Filangieri, whom he met on 5 March 1787, was worthy of the highest consideration and aspired to man's happiness without losing sight of the concept of freedom. Still on the left, the inscription above commemorates physicist and mathematician Nicola Trudi, professor of infinitesimal calculus at the University of Naples, who was well known for his treatises on "determinants" (the Trudi determinants).

GAETANO FILANGIERI: A NEAPOLITAN WHO INSPIRED THE AMERICAN CONSTITUTION

GAETANO FILANGIERI

Gaetano Filangieri is omnipresent in Naples: a beautiful street, a museum, a school and a lavish salon in the State Archives (see p. 253) all bear his name. However, the scope of this great philosopher has not been fully recognised – a leading figure of the Enlightenment in its specifically Neapolitan aspect, Filangieri was one of the most eminent jurists of his time. He was an enthusiastic reformer and advocated education for all, and the equitable redistribution of land and taxation based solely on income, revolutionary concepts at the time. His major work, *La Scienza della legislazione* (The Science of Legislation), was translated into several languages and was a major influence on the fathers of the American Constitution. Benjamin Franklin regularly consulted the Neapolitan thinker and highly esteemed his advice. Filangieri died in 1788 at Vico Equense on the Sorrento coast, where he had retired. He was only 36 years old.

REMAINS OF A DIOSCURI TEMPLE

"Limonè" limoncello factory
Piazza San Gaetano 72
• Metro: Line 1 Museo, Line 2 Cavour
• Tel: 081 299429
• limoncellodinapoli@yahoo.it
• Visits during normal shop opening hours

Below the church of San Paolo Maggiore (Saint Paul the Greater), corresponding to the left nave, the "back shop" of the Limonè *limoncello* (a local lemon liqueur) manufacturers is a narrow corridor 6 m long with some vestiges of a Dioscuri temple: large

> *Reminders of the 1st century in the back shop*

blocks of yellow tuff from the foundations, a water tank and a well about 20 m deep in which you can still see the water mark, and a wall built in *opus reticulatum* (diamond-shaped brickwork). The site of the temple, dating from the 1st century AD, had probably already been used by the Greeks in the 5th century BC and it was near the Graeco-Roman forum of Neapolis – today Piazza San Gaetano. The present church was built in around the 8th century over the ruins of the pagan temple.

In Greek and Roman mythology, the twins Castor and Pollux were known as the Dioscuri, i.e. Sons of Zeus. They were both the sons of Leda and the brothers of Clytemnestra and Helen: Castor was the son of Tyndareus, a Spartan king, whereas Pollux was the son of Zeus, king of the gods.

CONGREGATION DEL CROCIFISSO DELLA SCIABICA

76 Via dei Tribunali
• Metro: Line 1 Museo or Dante, Line 2 Cavour
• Tel: 338 3647883
• Visits Wednesday 3pm–5pm, Sunday 9am–12 noon
• Admission free

Body socks

A green door on the landing of the steps leading to the church of San Paolo Maggiore forecourt gives access to the Congregation del Crocifisso della Sciabica, founded in 1623 for pauper burials.

This charitable institution houses a chapel and small church built in the *cella* (inner chamber) of the Roman temple of the Dioscuri (see p. 209) where the remains of bodies that had been buried nearby in consecrated ground, now disused and inaccessible, are laid to rest.

Inside a glass case you can see a skeleton whose skull (never recovered) was replaced by a plaster mask. This body, dressed in a wedding gown, is that of

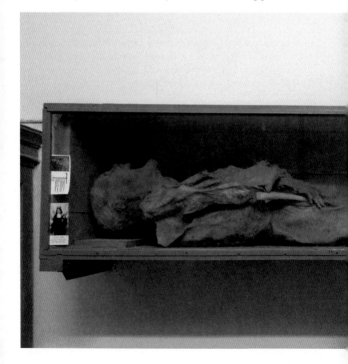

Maria Felice, last descendant of the Ricciardi family, who in 1833 was felled by a heart attack during her wedding in this very church. In another case lies the withered corpse of a priest who officiated for the congregation at an unknown date. The body was found intact except for the feet. Some kind soul has covered the stumps with socks so that he wouldn't look like an amputee.

ORIGIN OF THE WORD *"SCIABICA"*

The *sciabica* is a fishing net with very fine mesh used to catch any small fry. By using that name, the founders of the Crocefisso congregation intended to metaphorically save even those souls who had fallen through the usual "net".

In front of the church of San Paolo Maggiore, apart from the two columns at the entrance from the Dioscuri temple, there are also the remains of three large sections of marble pavement (stylobate). Two of these have been placed at the entrance to the church, while the third seems to have been used as a base for the statue of Saint Cajetan, second patron saint of Naples, to be found in the square named after it, Piazza San Gaetano.

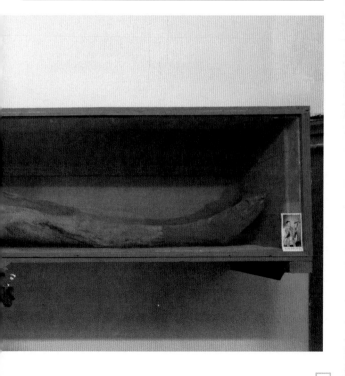

ARTWORKS BY NATHALIE DE SAINT-PHALLE ㉗

Palazzo Spinelli di Laurino
362 Via dei Tribunali
• Metro: Line 1 Museo, Line 2 Cavour or Montesanto
• Visits on reservation by phone or e-mail
• Tel: 081 299579 • nhsp@aol.com

Dedicated
to art

The large top-floor apartment of Palazzo Spinelli di Laurino has been dedicated to art thanks to Nathalie de Saint-Phalle, a writer of French origin who has lived in Naples since 1993. Canvases, books, catalogues, musical instruments and other creations of great originality form a pot-pourri of works of art enhanced by the shimmering colours of the carpets.

Many artists, several of whom are very well known, have displayed their work in this large open space. Some have donated their works, thus contributing to the atmosphere of cosmopolitan "cultural contagion". These artists include Neapolitan painter Giuseppe Zevola (see p. 207), American poet John Giorno and Neapolitan photographer/sculptor Beatrice Caracciolo. Other works in the collection were previously exhibited in another apartment (Il Purgatorio, used as a B&B until 2011) of Palazzo Marigliano, which still belongs to Nathalie de Sant-Phalle.

A lovely room in the Palazzo Spinelli apartment can be booked for the night.

COURTYARD OF PALAZZO SPINELLI DI LAURINO

Although all Neapolitans know where to find Palazzo Spinelli (as they often queue outside one of the city's most famous pizzerias), only insiders are aware that that through the carriage door of the palazzo is a detail that you won't find in any of the city's other old palazzi: a superb elliptical courtyard. The owner of the building, Troiano Spinelli, the last Duke of Laurino, whose commemorative plaque can be found between the two flights of stairs, had his palazzo restored by the celebrated architect Ferdinando Sanfelice (see p. 271). A true original, Sanfelice turned the square courtyard into an ellipse, a tribute to Romanness particularly appreciated by Duke Troiano, true humanist that he was.

THE GHOST OF BIANCA

The legend goes that a ghostly woman wandered around near the staircase at Palazzo Spinelli. This would have been Bianca, the young lady companion of Lorenza Spinelli, Troiano's wife. Bianca was taken in as an orphan by the duke, but as she grew up her beauty aroused Lorenza's jealousy.

To be rid of her rival, the duchess spread the rumour that Bianca was trying to seduce her husband so had to be sent away. One night, with the complicity of a deaf-mute servant, she gagged and bound the girl before walling her up alive in one of the niches of the entrance hall. The unfortunate girl managed to untie her bonds and remove the gag, cursing her torturer thus: *"This wall is not enough to make me disappear. I will return, and when you see me, you will know what to expect. When you see me, you or someone else."*

HIDDEN SYMBOLISM
OF CAPPELLA SANSEVERO

28

Chapel of Sansevero - 19/21 Via Francesco De Sanctis
• Metro: Line 1 Dante, Line 2 Montesanto
• Funicular Montesanto (Montesanto)
• Tel: 081 5518470
• info@museosansevero.it • www.museosansevero.it
• Open Monday to Saturday 10am–17.40pm, Sundays and holidays
10am–1.10pm • Closed Tuesday

> *Veiled*
> *hermetism*
> *of Raimondo*
> *di Sangro*

The Sansevero chapel, built in 1590, was enlarged and embellished by Raimondo di Sangro in 1744 with an extensive collection of statues all dedicated to Mary, mother of Jesus. Beyond the religious orthodoxy of the statuary, there are a series of symbols of the hermetic heterodoxy that characterised the esoteric thinking of di Sangro, one of the founders of Freemasonry in Naples and an avowed practitioner of alchemy.

On the left side of the chapel is the statue of *Decoro* (Decorum), a young man with a lion's skin thrown over his shoulders in an allegory of Hercules, which symbolises Strength, intellectual Power. Opposite, *Amor divino* (Divine Love), holding up a flaming heart, symbolises the Power of the Spirit and the Heart that makes it possible to achieve chemical Marriage and Divinity, here embodied by the Divine Mother, patron of alchemists. A little further along is *Liberalità* (Liberality): the coin (*moneda*) and compass represent the Monad, Spirit of Man and the circle of the action of the Divine Will where its presence is diffused.

On the opposite side is *Educazione* (Education), which transmits

to the child, the neophyte, the elemental assumptions of hermetic Initiation – respect for freedom of thought and feelings of our fellow beings, with decorum and love in the service of Divine Wisdom symbolised by the Virgin. These principles are reinforced by the presence of other statues, those of *Sincerità* (Sincerity), *Soavità del giogo coniugale* (Sweetness of the Marital Yoke), *Zelo della religione* (Religious Zeal) and *Dominio di se stessi* (Self-control). Whoever does not possess these qualities will inevitably fail the Initiation that the symbolism evokes.

Sincerity, a caduceus in his right

hand and a heart in the left, represents spiritual introspection, the request for hermetic Illumination by the Initiate seeking to unite with the God within, in an act of absolute sincerity. *Sweetness of the Marital Yoke*, helmet on head and yoke in hand, indicates that gently but firmly, like a sacred warrior, he must gradually transform the life-energy into life-consciousness in the yoke of real life. *Religious Zeal* carries a torch evoking acquired knowledge and the duty to preserve it, without adulterating it with foreign elements, while respecting the freedom of thought which conforms to free will in general. *Self-control* (of one's baser tendencies) is the greatest and most sublime of battles that a man can fight, which is why this statue features a warrior holding a chained lion at his feet and an inverted torch, expressing the Love that emanates from the tamed beast (exterior and interior). This is the allegory of the triumph of Love and Wisdom over brute force, the ultimate transformation of the profane to the Initiate.

The abandonment of ordinary life for a spiritual existence is symbolised by the *Disinganno* (Disillusionment) statue, which represents a man releasing himself from the mesh of a net with the help of a winged genie, allegory of the divine Spirit. This is represented below by a bas-relief of Christ giving sight to the blind, transmitting the Light of Truth to those who live in the darkness of ignorance, the greatest blindness of all.

Finally, *Pudicizia* (Modesty) brings together all initiatory Wisdom, whose Light is sought by the neophyte wishing to become an Enlightened One.

WHY ARE TWO MEDALLIONS FACELESS?
Some of the statues in the chapel have associated medallions representing characters linked with the allegory. The medallions of Raimondo di Sangro's daughter-in-law and his wife, Carlotta Gaetani, nevertheless bear no images – at the time, it was considered bad luck to physically represent those who were still alive.

The statue of *Disillusionment* has also been interpreted by some as a reference to Masonic initiation in the 18th century: the neophyte did indeed go into the initiation ceremony blindfolded. He rang at the Lodge door, saying he was a blind man who wanted to see the light again. Once inside, the blindfold was removed. The ritual required that he should also have one shoulder bared in the same way as the statue.

The monument to Cecco di Sangro emerging armed from a sarcophagus commemorates the incident when, feigning death during the siege of Amiens in 1597, Cecco was locked in a crate that was then brought into the city. He climbed out during the night and opened the gates for his comrades in arms, who could then seize the city.

The statue of *Modesty* by Antonio Corradini represents Cecilia Gaetani d'Aragona, mother of Raimondo di Sangro, who died at the age of 20 (26 December 1710), when he was just 11 months old: the broken marble slab symbolises life cut short.
The statue also alludes to the goddess Isis (veiled), deity of the initiatory sciences: according to tradition, in Greek Neapolis *Modesty* was usually placed in the same setting as Isis.

SANSEVERO'S *VEILED CHRIST*: FROM LEGEND TO THE REALITY OF SUDA-TION AND MYSTICAL INTERNAL FIRE

The *Veiled Christ* statue in the Sansevero chapel, carved from a single block of marble by the Neapolitan Giuseppe Sanmartino (1720–1793), is considered the great masterpiece of 18th-century European sculpture.

It is said that Raimondo di Sangro (1710–1771), an avowed alchemist who had commissioned the sculpture, knew how to turn materials into stone and he was thought to have taught the sculptor how to calcify cloth into marble crystals. This supposed secret seduced the artists of the day, including Antonio Canova, who tried to get to the bottom of it, saying he was ready to give ten years of his life in exchange for the mysterious procedure so he could create this strikingly unusual masterpiece.

The legend of the petrifaction of cloth is above all linked to the deeper significance, not of the shroud, but of *sudation* (perspiration), which arises from proximity to the heat of the Mystic Fire coiling up within the human organism (the Hindu *kundalini*). The link between sudation and petrifaction is understood as follows: the internal heat is so intense that the body perspires and its crystals calcify or petrify. The ancient alchemists explained this phenomenon by the biblical story of Lot's wife fleeing Sodom, who was turned into a pillar of salt when she looked back. The word "sudation", the consequence of which is that materials or bodies turn to stone, is derived from Sodom or Sod.

The steam bath is one of the basic techniques for increasing this mystical heat, with the result that sweating is occasionally given an ultimately "Creationist" value. In many religious and mythological traditions, the first man was created by God following an intensive sudation. This idea of divine creation was eventually popularised by the use of steam baths, which held the same significance for the peoples of northern Asia and of Europe.

The realm of fire, of insensitivity to heat and hence to mystic heat, which makes extreme cold or glowing embers bearable, constitutes a magico-mystical virtue, which along with other no less miraculous qualities (ascension, levitation, etc.), translates in terms of the senses the fact that the mystic is already part of the spiritual world and its immaterial inhabitants. This is perhaps why the steam bath and sudation had a sacrificial meaning for the classical civilisations of antiquity – the believer offered his sweat to the Supreme Sun God, a gesture of purifying and merciful value that allowed him to enter that invisible world bodily and with no qualms and to evolve there, leaving behind the "dormition" of the physical senses by a definitive spiritual awakening, like a Christ or an Enlightened One throwing off the shackles of the flesh and the rule of death.

SINE ANTIQUA ARTE NON EST NOVA ARS

TRIPTYCH OF *CHRIST UNVEILED* OR HIDDEN LIGHT

Church of Monte Manso di Scala Foundation
34 Via Nilo
• Metro: Line 1 Dante or Museo • Funicular Montesanto (Montesanto)
• Visits by appointment (phone)
• Tel: 348 1149647 (Maria Girardo, Associazione Terramia)
• info@terramia.napoli.it

> *Christ unveiled versus Christ veiled*

The lovely church of the Monte Manso di Scala Foundation, where you can book a visit, is incongruously sited on the third floor of a very elegant palazzo in the historic centre, just above the famous Sansevero chapel whose owner, alchemist Prince Raimondo di Sangro, let the Jesuits use the space. In agreement with Pope Benedict XIV, they wished to counteract the prince's openly Masonic tastes by building a church exalting the Christian faith. The contemporary sculpture by Giuseppe Corcione, a triptych entitled *Christ Unveiled or Hidden Light* set three floors above the famous *Veiled Christ*, was another way of opposing the unorthodox ideas of the sulphurous Prince of Sansevero.

The institution of Monte Manso di Scala, founded in 1608 by Giovanni Battista Manso, was originally dedicated to charitable works, but later became a seminary for young nobles whose religious education was entrusted to the Jesuits. To this day the foundation, true to its spirit of solidarity, awards scholarships to young Neapolitans from impoverished aristocratic families.

The elliptical and light-flooded church, closed since 1959, was seriously damaged by the earthquake of 1980. It reopened in 2009 after lengthy restoration work funded by the foundation.

The Rococo altarpiece of the main altar, *Madonna in gloria con santi gesuiti*, representing the Virgin in glory with Jesuit saints, was painted by Francesco de Mura (1696–1782).

PLAQUE OF THE CHURCH
OF SAN DOMENICO MAGGIORE

30

18 Vico San Domenico
• Metro: Line 1 Dante, Line 2 Montesanto

A mysterious plaque and hermetic verses

On the wall to the left of the main entrance of the church of San Domenico Maggiore (the most used access is in Piazza San Domenico, opposite) is a marble plaque inscribed with Latin verses whose meaning has totally baffled even the most eminent researchers from the 17th century to this day. The plaque itself is also a mystery as nobody knows its provenance, author or exact date. In the 17th century, Giovanni Antonio Summonte wrote in his *Historia di Napoli* (History of Naples) that in 1560, while the Dominican owners of the convent were having restoration work done on the church, this inscription was found below the marble slabs covering the floor. Also featured at the bottom left is a man wearing a sort of homespun robe, kneeling and with his hands clasped in prayer. As the monks thought it had something to do with water, they placed the plaque near the cloister's well. In 1605 it was moved to its present site.

Here is a literal translation:

"*The bringer of storms begrudged me the Sun, dear to God, and with the rain he carried far away the human bodies submerged in the sea. Now we suffer less cruel calamities; and beware the sinister Trojan line scattered under the sky. With my voice I beg the spirits and the guiding lights above, who with sin purged can pave the way to heaven. As the radiant Sun shines again, penetrating the water, the ice melts with the heat.*"

The lettering is in mid-15th century style, but some words suggest that this could be copied from a 13th-century inscription.

Philosophers and historians of different periods have put forward a number of hypotheses. Some went for the simplest explanation: a mischievous soul wanted posterity to rack its brains. Others saw in it the story of a shipwreck by a survivor who, perhaps for superstitious reasons, didn't want to be understood. Philologist A. S. Mazzocchi (18th century) went so far as to assign the four couplets to Petrarch, who reportedly described the terrible storm of 1345 during the reign of Joan I of Anjou.

For his part, historian S. Volpicella (19th century) interpreted it as a denunciation of the supposed poisoning of Saint Thomas Aquinas by Charles I of Anjou (*the bringer of storms*), of the Capetian line (*sinister Trojan line*). The Dominican C. Di Gregorio (17th century), careless of anachronism, claimed it was probably directions written by his confreres to find extremely valuable sacred objects hidden during the siege of Naples by Marshal Lautrec's troops in 1528. The list of alternative versions goes on …

The sumptuously decorated complex of San Domenico Maggiore, whose construction began in 1283, is of major historical interest. This Dominican monastery, where Thomas Aquinas, Giordano Bruno and Tommaso Campanella all spoke from the pulpit, was a peerless centre of philosophical study for centuries.

NEARBY

TOMB OF THE FIRST BISHOP OF NEW YORK

In the Treasure Room (access through the vestry) of San Domenico Maggiore is the striking tomb of Richard Luke Concanen. This Dominican priest (born in Ireland in 1747) was appointed first Bishop of New York in 1808 by Pope Pius VII while he was prior of the Dominican monastery in Rome. But he never managed to leave for the United States because he was held prisoner in Naples by the Napoleonic troops occupying the city, and had to administer his diocese by correspondence. He died two years later and was buried in the Dominican church of San Domenico Maggiore. Don't miss the mural on the Treasure Room ceiling, one of the most impressive works of Francesco Solimena, depicting the triumph of faith over heresy thanks to the Dominicans.

BIBLIOTECA MAURIZIO TADDEI

Palazzo Saluzzo di Corigliano
12 Piazza San Domenico Maggiore
• Metro: Line 1 Dante or Università, Line 2 Montesanto
• Funicular Montesanto (Montesanto)
• www.unior.it
• Visits on reservation

Gilded mythology

I n the 17th-century palazzo that once belonged to the Duke of Corigliano and is now occupied by the University of Naples "L'Orientale", the Maurizio Taddei library has been set up on the fourth

floor, in a 1,000 m² space with a superb gallery known as the *galleria grande*. This example of pure Rococo has beautiful gilded stucco and frescoes depicting a battle between gods and giants (gigantomachy) and scenes from the *Aeneid*. The walls are also decorated with mythological themes, the four seasons, together with allegories of the works and virtues of the duke. The bibliographic heritage includes some 230,000 volumes, as well as newspapers, manuscripts and rare 16th-century editions in Chinese.

A HOTLY DISPUTED AMPUTATION

Built in the second half of the 18th century by Mario Gioffredo, Palazzo Casacalenda (17 Piazza San Domenico Maggiore), which belonged to the Dukes of Sangro Casacalenda e Campolieto, was restored by the renowned architect Luigi Vanvitelli. At the end of the 19th century, during the urban renewal project known as the Risanamento (see p. 41), it was decided to demolish two wings of the palazzo. Neapolitan historians, led by philosopher Benedetto Croce, firmly opposed this amputation that would have destroyed magnificent frescoes and an early Christian chapel, built on the ruins of a circular Greek temple dedicated to Eumelus of Corinth and incorporated in the building. Nevertheless one wing was demolished and part of the temple converted into a shop. So today on Via Mezzocannone you can see a strange barber's shop topped by a small circular tower in early 20th-century style.

THE DUKE'S STUDY

Palazzo Saluzzo di Corigliano
12 Piazza San Domenico Maggiore
• Metro: Line 1 Dante or Università, Line 2 Montesanto
• Funicular Montesanto (Montesanto)
• www.unior.it
• Visits on reservation

*Rococo
marvel*

On the second floor of Palazzo Saluzzo di Corigliano, home of the University of Naples "L'Orientale", the "duke's study" is a pure Rococo marvel: the walls of the 5 × 5 m room are totally covered by gilded mirrors, a veritable set-piece created by architect and designer Filippo Buonocore. The room, which is miraculously still intact with its gilded wood carvings by Bartolomeo Granucci, was the private study of the former owner, the Duke of Corigliano.

The palazzo originally belonged to Duke Giovanni di Sangro Vietri, who commissioned it from the architect Giovanni Donadio, known as Mormando. The building was badly damaged by the 1688 earthquake. It was purchased in 1727 by Agostino Saluzzo, Duke of Corigliano, who completely renovated it. After a period of neglect (1935 to 1977), the palazzo was given a new lease of life when the university moved in.

MARADONA'S HAIR ③④

Altar of the Nilo bar – 129 Via San Biagio dei Librai
• Metro: Line 1 Dante or Line 2 Montesanto
• Funicular Montesanto (Montesanto)
• Tel: 081 5517029

> **A footballer venerated like a saint**

Just in front of the Nile statue in the district known as the "Corpo di Napoli" (Body of Naples), Signor Bruno Alcidi, owner of the Nilo bar, built an altar in 1987 dedicated to Diego Armando Maradona: among other "relics" kept in a glass box is a hair from the football idol of Neapolitan *tifosi* (supporters). It was plucked directly from Maradona's head twenty-five years ago, when Signor Alcidi found himself on the same plane as the Naples team returning from a game in Como.

On the altar at the entrance to the Nilo bar, other than the hair, there are pennants, pictures, a vial containing real Neapolitans' tears of joy as a lucky charm, a prayer to San Gennaro (Saint Januarius) in the local dialect …

According to Signor Alcidi, setting up the little shrine did some good because Napoli won the first cup in its history just afterwards, and three years later the second.

The altar was recently redesigned after the fulfilment of a vow that the entire Alcidi family made when Maradona fell ill in 2000. Once the vow was made, says Signor Alcidi, the health of the *Pibe de Oro* (Golden Boy) improved and he was fully recovered by 2004.

Signor Alcidi has also posted an invitation on the altar, translated into several languages, to come and have a drink in the Nilo bar where other mementoes of the Argentine footballer are on display: posters, pictures, badges … all set off by the warm welcome from the bar's owner, who's always happy to tell the story of his altar.

THE HOLY STEPS
OF SAN GREGORIO ARMENO CONVENT

35

1 Via San Gregorio Armeno
• Metro: Line 1 Museo, Università or Line 2 Cavour
• Tel: 081 5520186 • sspsae-na.santelmo@beniculturali.it
• Church open Monday to Thursday 9am–12 noon, Saturday and Sunday 9am–1pm, closed Friday • Cloister: daily 9.30am–12 noon
• Visits to some parts of the convent on request. Visits to the church ambulatory and adjacent premises on 25 August only

Memories of cloistered nuns

Following the Council of Trent (1545–1563), the convent of San Gregorio Armeno, like many other convents, underwent far-reaching reforms such as the institution of mandatory penances. Among these was the construction of "Holy Steps" that the nuns of San Gregorio Armeno had to climb on their knees every Friday in March (a custom that lasted until the 19th century). The lower section of the staircase, built in 1692, is decorated with paintings of angels and there are symbols of the Passion of Christ in a small room to the left of the altar, reached through the presbytery of the eponymous church (one of the most extraordinary examples of Neapolitan Baroque). The so-called "treasure room", where many sacred relics and objects are on display, is worth a visit.

OTHER CURIOSITIES OF SAN GREGORIO ARMENO

In a long room known as the "nuns' corridor" (access through the presbytery), between the grilles that allowed them to attend Mass without being seen, note the wooden altars with various objects set on them: clothed statues of saints, a Madonna wearing shoes and a silk dress in the fashion of the 18th century, Baby Jesuses with period wigs, opaline vases with flowers made from coloured beads and miniature furniture belonging to the young novices condemned to live cut off from the world.

In the cloister of San Gregorio Armeno convent, a plaque indicates that from the second week of December, Advent, the large and small ovens were for the exclusive use of the abbess, as she was not called to fasting like the other nuns.

The left wall of the staircase leading to the convent is decorated with frescoes featuring views and windows with dogs and cats sitting on the sill, probably an abbess's nod to her lost freedom. At the top of the steps, on both sides of the main entrance, you'll notice two small doors: hidden behind them are the "wheels" (a kind of dumb waiter) to receive deliveries of food, clothes and other objects, the nuns' only means of communication with the outside world.

The convent was founded in the 8th century by Basilian nuns who'd fled Constantinople because of the war between iconoclasts and iconodules (those in favour of religious images). It was dedicated to Saint Gregory, to whom we owe the birth of the world's first Christian state, Armenia, which in AD 301, well before the Edict of Constantine (Edict of Milan, AD 313), adopted Christianity as its official religion.

FORGOTTEN FIGURINES OF THE FERRIGNO WORKSHOP ③⑥

Giuseppe and Marco Ferrigno
8 Via San Gregorio Armeno
• Metro: Line 1 Dante or Line 2 Montesanto
• Tel: 081 5523148 • info@arteferrigno.it

> **Figurines as they used to be**

The Ferrigno artisanal workshop (*bottega*), founded in 1836, is unusual in that it still produces the type of figurine forgotten even by most Neapolitans. Often they have delightful popular legends attached. Some of the most endearing forgotten characters are described here.

THE FIGURE WITH NO GIFT

There is one character in the nativity scene whose only gift is his wonder at the extraordinary event taking place before his eyes: the birth of Christ. The legend goes that the *pastore della meraviglia* (shepherd full of wonder), as the Neapolitans call him, was reprimanded by all the other characters for daring to appear empty-handed before the Virgin. But Mary had only kind words for him: "The world will remain beautiful as long as there are men and women who are capable of wonder."

Stefania

According to the Apocrypha, only married women who'd had children were allowed to visit the Virgin Mary. Stefania, a childless widow, still wanted at all costs to honour Mary, who was also her friend. So she decided to wrap a stone the size of a child in a blanket. Mary noticed this ploy, but took pity on the widow who longed for a child and told her that she'd soon have her wish. When Stefania went back home, the stone sneezed and turned into a baby. This is why Saint Stephen (Santo Stefano in Italian) is celebrated on Boxing Day.

The woman without hands

The poor woman, it is said, would have liked to help Mary give birth, but she couldn't as she had no hands. The Madonna gave her two new hands to thank her.

The wife of the black Magus

In the nativity scenes of yesteryear, notably those of nobles and the affluent classes, the black Magus on horseback was followed by a small group of four pages bearing a chair on which the king's wife was seated with a little dog. Over time, because this set was expensive to make, it was less and less in demand until it disappeared from the traditional crib. But you can see a beautiful example in the Ferrigno shop.

The perfect crib scene

Another character that is never missing from even the simplest crib scene is Benino the shepherd, sleeping on a hillside made of cork. Traditionally, Benino is said to dream forever of a wonderful manger with twelve sheep as white as snow (an allusion to pure souls) grazing around him. The shepherd's dream come true is precisely what you can see at Ferrigno's. Another fine rarity.

For the symbolism of the Neapolitan crib, see following double-page spread.

SYMBOLISM OF OBJECTS AND CHARACTERS FROM THE NEAPOLITAN NATIVITY SCENE

"Christmas is a time outwith History, a time in suspension where good and evil coexist," writes Roberto De Simone, the ultimate specialist in Campanian popular traditions.

In Naples, where the boundary between sacred and profane is blurred and flexible, there are different kinds of nativity scene. There are those of the nobles and wealthy bourgeois, spectacularly rich in detail with figurines carved by recognised artists, which include some traditional themes without transgressing Christian dogma. And then there are the cribs for ordinary people, featuring a crowd of jostling figurines with rather rudimentary features, but so touching with their limbs glued back on over the years. This kind of scene is packed with myths, superstitions and even symbols that are an outlet for collective fears (the devil, for example).

The landscape of the Neapolitan nativity scene says it all: made from cork, it is mountainous and full of winding roads dotted with figurines on their way down to the cave, always at the bottom in the foreground. Because you must first descend into the darkness (the tortuous paths) before reaching the light, or rebirth (represented by the Baby Jesus).

The well represents the link between the surface and the underground waters from which malefic spirits may emerge during Christmas night, because that's the time when Evil wanders abroad before the birth of Good. In the countryside, children are kept away from wells and no water is drawn on that night. The presence of "Madonnas of the Well" in many places around the city of Naples and throughout Campania shows the concern to protect this disturbing place.

The fountain with the woman. According to the Apocrypha, the angel Gabriel announced the birth of Christ to the Virgin near a fountain. In Campanian folktales, lovers' trysts and fantastic apparitions always take place close to fountains.

The bridge is a passage that leads to the "other side", and therefore also into the beyond, into the unknown. On Christmas night, it's said, terrifying encounters happen there: a nun displaying the head of her beheaded lover, werewolves, ghosts of suicides or hanged men … Throughout Europe there are legends about bridges built in one night by the devil or other evil spirits (e.g. at Cahors in France).

The windmill has arms that turn round like time, the time that's reborn on Christmas morning. It produces flour, which is as white as death but also life-giving as it's used to make bread, the universal food.

The river carries water which is life, but it can also be underground like the Styx, the river of Hades.

The inn is overflowing with food eaten at the Christmas feast. This banquet is actually funereal, burying time that dies before its renewal. The inn also symbolises the risks of travel. In folk tales, ogres disguised as innkeepers chop up children to eat them, but Saint Nicholas puts a stop to that by sticking together the pieces of the innocent victims and resurrecting them.

The Magi ride horses of different colours, white like the rising Sun, chestnut like the sunset and black as the night. They symbolise the journey of the star which, like the Magi, starts out from the East. At the end of the night, the three kings are led before the Christ, who is the Sun reborn. In older nativity scenes there was also a queen (see p. 229), personification of the Moon, which follows the path of the Sun.

The washerwomen stand for the midwives who rush to help the Virgin. They spread out white linen, symbol of Mary's virginity.

The gypsy is an allegory of the prophecy embodied in the sacred representations of the past by the Sibyls. According to legend, a Sibyl foretold the birth of Christ. But the gypsy in the crib has iron tools in her hand, foreseeing the Passion of Christ.

The hunter and the fisherman embody, among other features, the two most ancient of human activities.

The food sellers always number twelve, because they stand for the twelve months of the year. For example, the tomato seller represents July, the watermelon seller August, and the roasted chestnut seller November ...

EMBLEMS OF NAPLES *SEDILI*

Piazza San Gaetano
• Metro: Line 1 Dante or Museo, Line 2 Montesanto

> *Historical symbols of the oldest neighbourhoods in Naples*

Above the entrance to the Opera di San Lorenzo Maggiore Museum (not to be missed) are the crests of the seven *sedili* (municipal districts, also called *seggi*) of the city of Naples. Each of these institutions brought together representatives of the noble families who lived in the corresponding neighbourhood. These were derived from the very old *fratries* (brotherhoods) that governed the city in Graeco-Roman times and which, according to historian Filippo Pagano, became *sedili* in the 9th century. The *sedili* were abolished in 1800 by Ferdinand IV of Bourbon. It was in 1808, during the Napoleonic era, that the first town hall was established.

The "Y", a millennial symbol of great complexity, corresponded to the *sedile* of Forcella ("little fork") where there was a Pythagorean school using this letter as its insignia. The letter could also be an allusion to the gallows, because it was at Forcella that condemned men were executed by hanging (see also p. 156).

The "P" represented the one and only *sedile* of the people; the "door" crest symbolised Portanova (created when a new gate was cut in the city walls at the seafront); the "mountain" was the crest of Montagna, so called because of its elevated location; the "hairy man" was linked to the Porto (port) area; the "white horse" to Capuana (called after the powerful Capuano family); and the black rearing horse was the emblem of Nilo (or Nido) *sedile*, where many Alexandrians lived in Roman times. The colour of the two horses is strictly related to the geographical position of these two districts (see p. 237).

The *sedile* was also the building where the elected representatives met. It was squarely built and consisted of two rooms, one small and the other large, for important occasions.

At the beginning of Vico Sedil Capuano stands a column surmounted by an arch (now incorporated into a modern building) that used to be part of Capuano *sedile*. A wall plaque in Piazza Portanova commemorates the *sedile* of that name.

BANKSY'S *SAINT WITH A PISTOL* GRAFFITI

112 Piazza Girolamini
• Metro: Line 1 Dante or Museo, Line 2 Cavour

> *Street art in the historic centre*

A t the base of the wall to the right of the church and convent of the Gerolamini, the celebrated artist Banksy has painted a figure inspired by Saint Agnes (whose church is in Piazza Navona in Rome). The image is surmounted by a pistol with a gear-wheel halo. This artist, who has become very well known and sought after in the art world, has left work on the walls of many cities around the world. In Italy he chose Naples, where apart from Saint Agnes he painted Saint Teresa lying near a pile of fast-food packaging. This image, unfortunately covered by the graffiti of a rival artist (not by vandals), is on the wall opposite the church of Santa Chiara in Via Benedetto Croce.

Banksy, about whom little is known, not even his real name, was born in Bristol in 1974 or 1975. The artist's anti-establishment and provocative graffiti express his rebellion against consumerism and corruption.

NEARBY

RELIQUARY CABINET AT THE CHURCH OF THE GEROLAMINI

142/144 Via Duomo
• Metro: Line 2 Cavour, Line 1 Museo, Università, Dante
• Tel: 3334338049
• mn-gir@beniculturali.it
• Open (church, monumental cloister & art gallery) 8.30am–2pm, closed Wednesday

In the monastery church of the Gerolamini, the reliquary cabinet in the so-called martyrs' chapel (right side of the transept) is an absolute rarity. The cabinet, built into the altar, is fitted with a mechanism of weights and counter-weights by which the altarpiece can be moved to reveal polychrome wooden busts of the martyrs. The sculptures containing their relics are invaluable as the decoration was carried out using a very specialised technique common in Spain in the 17th and 18th centuries, *estofado de oro*, which involved imitating the richness of inlaid garments by means of pure gold leaf and red, emerald green and azure blue lacquers. The mechanism is currently out of use, but funds are being raised to repair it. Two of the busts are on display in a chapel in the left nave and the others are being restored.

Note that the name of the square is spelled differently on two nameplates – Gerolomini and Gerolamini – because so far nobody has been able to decide which is correct.

PALAZZO CARAFA ④⓪

121 Via San Biagio dei Librai
• Bus: 149 or 24 (Sant'Anna dei Lombardi stop)
• Metro: Line 1 Dante, Line 2 Montesanto

The head of Virgil's horse

The fine Renaissance Palazzo Carafa holds a copy of the horse's head originally exhibited in Naples National Archaeological Museum (see p. 275) in the 18th century. Considered as the symbol of the city (see below), the provenance of the head has always been disputed: some have seen it as a Greek original while others (including 16th-century art historian Giorgio Vasari) attributed it to Donatello. Since 2012, archival documents have confirmed the second hypothesis.

Before it was deleted, this inscription could be read on the base on which the sculpture now rests:

This head shows
All the nobility and immensity of his body,
A barbarian forced the bit on me
Superstition and greed put me to death,
The regrets of the good increased my value
Here you see my head,
The cathedral bells keep my body
The symbol of the city perished with me …

There is a rumour that on some days a horse is heard whinnying when the cathedral bells ring out. Be that as it may, this horse is legendary.

Until the 14th century, in a square near the cathedral stood a huge bronze horse that had the power to heal sick animals, give immunity to healthy ones and increase the fertility of males. This bronze was thought to have been carved by Virgil, who later placed it on this site.

For centuries, Neapolitans would bring along their beasts, harnesses hung with little crescent loaves and garlands of flowers, to have them walk three times around the monument. According to Virgil's biographer Donatus, the loaves evoked the symbolic bread that the Emperor Augustus gave Virgil when the poet cured several of his horses of a mysterious ailment.

This ritual lasted until 1322, the year when the body of the statue was destroyed, in line with the Angevin monarchs' determination to eradicate all traces of pagan beliefs.

The legend goes that it was a cardinal, annoyed by this horse that was more popular than Saint Januarius, who had the bronze melted down to make the cathedral bells. Another version blames the blacksmiths, who were envious of the horse's powers that stopped them making a living.

The free and unrestrained horse is one of the most significant and persistent symbols in Neapolitan mythology. The people saw themselves in this untamed bronze horse, as borne out when two of the city's conquerors, Conrad of Swabia

(1253) and Charles of Anjou (1266), had a bit fitted to the horse to ratify their conquest and point out to the Neapolitan rebels that they had to submit to Christianity.

Once the horse was gone, the cult moved to the church of Sant'Eligio Maggiore (Saint Eligius, protector of blacksmiths). On 1 December, unshod horses were brought in and their shoes hung on doors. Gradually, Saint Eloi was replaced by Saint Anthony the Abbot, whose church was built in the district named after him during the Angevin period (see pp. 293–295). This saint has the power to heal all animals and on 17 January, his feast day, a number are brought to the priest to be blessed. Until some forty years ago, the animals were dressed up in the kind of finery worn at the time of the bronze horse and, as before, they turned three times around the church …

The blessing of the horses also exorcises the dangers of travel: once horses were no longer used as a means of transport, all kinds of vehicles continued to be blessed. This ritual is still practised today but in a very low-key fashion.

Until the 18th century, the horse was the emblem of two neighbourhoods: Nilo and Porto Capuana. The first was black, the second white. They symbolised the darkness and the light, black on the left and white on the right (facing the city, back to the sea), exactly as the Moon and the Sun frame the Madonna of Piedigrotta (see p. 30).

For more on the Neapolitan horse, see following double-page spread.

THE NEAPOLITAN HORSE: AN EXCEPTIONAL ANIMAL

If riding reached new heights in Naples, it was thanks to the Neapolitan horse, an exceptional animal of majestic grace, both lightweight and powerful. The finest mounts were raised on the plains of Capua, where the extraordinary fertility of the land led the Romans to call this region "Campania Felix". These ideal geographical conditions were complemented by the expertise of farmers who for thousands of years had carried out felicitous crosses between the robust local horses and the elegant oriental animals imported by the Etruscans (who had settled in the Campanian hinterlands).

The Romans added the finishing touches when they crossed these horses with the Barb breed, famous for its stamina and power, which they bought in North Africa. Incidentally it was among these horses of Capua that Roman senators chose their mounts for triumphal parades.

In the 14th century, the reputation of Neapolitan breeders was confirmed by Boccaccio in *The Decameron* (Andreuccio da Perugia, day II, story V). In this story, the horse dealer comes to Naples seeking a bargain among these valuable animals, as his purse contains the tidy sum of 500 gold florins (by way of comparison, the queen of Naples, Joan of Anjou, sold Provence to the papacy for 80,000 florins a few decades later). Chroniclers down the ages have subsequently celebrated these magnificent animals coveted by all the kings of Naples to the extent that they severely punished anyone who took them out of the kingdom. And the prices people were willing to pay for a "Neapolitan" were often exorbitant.

Even today, this horse is legendary for all lovers of dressage, particularly in other countries, and even more so because the breed was thought to have died out in the early 20th century.

Then, in the 1990s, a miracle occurred. A coffee importer from Piano di Sorrento, Giuseppe Maresca, launched a wild challenge to revive the glorious Neapolitan horse. Against all odds, despite the many sceptics, overcoming huge numbers of difficulties and with no public or private funding, he managed to replace this missing piece in the mosaic of Neapolitan history.

Deep in Serbia, just as the country was about to be plunged into the horrors of war, Maresca located a direct descendant of a Neapolitan stallion. His name was Neapolitano and he was 20 years old. After surmounting the bureaucratic red tape, in 1990 Neapolitano "Il Vecchio" returned to the country of his ancestors, which had left for Austria 200 years earlier. Waiting for the old stallion were a few mares, amazingly saved from extinction by Capuan peasants. Before he died, the stallion sired Neapolitano I di Vicalvano and a lovely mare, Cianciosa di Vicalvano. The miracle had come to pass.

Today the Neapolitan has its studbook like any other officially recognised breed. The precious horses of the Maresca breeders, who seem to have stepped by magic out of an old engraving, live in classy stables on Vicalvano hill, a paradisiacal site between Sorrento and Amalfi.

The only thing left to do now is to set up a Neapolitan academy that can compete with those of Vienna, Versailles and Jerez, as Maresca has dreamed of for years. At present the "Federico Grisone" academy exists only on paper, but to put this remarkable project into practice what place would be better suited than the former Bianchini barracks at 178 Via Amerigo Vespucci? The 16th-century building, today partly occupied by Treasury offices (after being converted into barracks), was intended as a site for training the thousands of horses from the kingdom's many breeders. Not many people know that the first covered riding school in Europe (and probably in the world) was built at this "*Cavallerizza*" so that horses could be trained even in bad weather.

It was also in 16th-century Naples that the equestrian Federico Grisone wrote the first riding treatise in history since Xenophon (4th century BC).

Signor Maresca is pleased to show visitors around his horses (at Piano di Sorrento, 45 km from Naples): maresca.giuseppema@tiscali.it

SHIELD OF THE CITY OF NAPLES

Cappella del Tesoro di San Gennaro
147 Via Duomo
• Metro: Line 1 Museo or Università, Line 2 Cavour
• Tel: 081 449065
• Open 9am–12 noon and 4.30pm–7pm

> *A place
> of worship
> that doesn't belong
> to the church*

At the entrance to the Treasury chapel, the shield of the city engraved on the floor marks the boundary between the secular and the ecclesiastical. The chapel has in fact always belonged to the city, represented by a "Deputation", which originally consisted of twelve members, two for each area of Naples (formerly called *sedili* – see p. 233). Since 1601, this city institution has watched over the relics of Saint Januarius, including a vial containing his blood, and manages everything relating to the worship and treasure of the patron saint of Naples.

1526 was a terrible year: the French were besieging Naples and the plague was resurgent. So the Neapolitans pledged to erect a magnificent chapel dedicated to San Gennaro if he liberated them from these scourges. As calmer times returned, on 13 January 1527 funds were collected and the promise was formalised in a notarised document. But construction work on the chapel didn't start until 1608 under the direction of the Deputation. The treasure, formerly preserved in one of the bell towers, wasn't installed in the chapel until 13 December 1646.

IS THAT DOMENICHINO'S TOMB AT THE CHAPEL ENTRANCE?

When the elected members of the Deputation decided to entrust the paintings that decorate the chapel to non-Neapolitans, local artists felt gravely insulted. It seems that they exerted strong pressure on their "foreign" competitors. The less experienced of these soon abandoned the idea of accepting the commission, as in the case of Il Giuseppino (Cavaliere d'Arpino), and Guido Reni, who left Naples in haste after one of his collaborators was attacked with a knife. Although Domenico Zampieri, known as Il Domenichino, complained that he had received a threatening letter, he was persuaded by the Deputation, who promised him close protection. Yet Domenichino, the Baroque master of the Bolognese School, died suddenly on 6 April 1641, poisoned, it is said. He is thought to have been buried somewhere in the chapel, but exactly where isn't known. But just before the entrance door you can see a tombstone without a name, apparently untouched, fitted with four metal rings to open it ...

BARS OF THE TREASURY CHAPEL'S MONUMENTAL PORTAL

42

Cappella del Tesoro di San Gennaro
147 Via Duomo
• Metro: Line 1 Museo or Università, Line 2 Cavour
• Tel: 081 449065
• Open 9am–12 noon and 4.30pm–7pm

> *A door that resonates like a xylophone*

The Treasury chapel of San Gennaro was also one of the Neapolitan temples of music where the teachers were none other than Scarlatti, Cimarosa, Paisiello (author of the concert for the coronation of Napoleon Bonaparte), Provenzale …

The entrance to the chapel is a masterpiece by the famous architect Cosimo Fanzago, who wanted to blow away his contemporaries with a feature as unusual as it was surprising: when struck with a metal object, the bars emit a sound like a xylophone, and each bar corresponds to a different note. Although this extraordinary instrument was probably never used, it still achieved its designer's aim of astounding visitors.

STATUE OF THE VIRGIN THAT TERRIFIED WORSHIPPERS

Of the fifty-four solid silver busts stored in the Treasury chapel, two represent the Virgin Mary. On one of these busts only the head was originally in silver, the body being pasteboard covered with a layer of silver. But this "economical" ploy didn't work, as during processions the heavier head would fall off the body and sow panic among the worshippers. So the Deputation commissioned a headless torso, which was completed by Tommaso Treglia in 1717.

"IL RE DI POGGIOREALE", A TRAFFICKER WHO BROUGHT THE TREASURE OF SAINT JANUARIUS BACK TO NAPLES

According to the latest valuation, dating back to 2010, the treasure of Saint Januarius is thought to be the most valuable in the world, even exceeding that of the British Crown Jewels or the Russian tsars.

Over the centuries, donations from eminent personalities and ordinary people have enriched the treasure chest, now consisting of 21,160 pieces. This vast heritage has remained intact since 1305, never stolen or used to pay for wars.

There are endless anecdotes about Neapolitans' faith in their patron saint and the determining role of the Deputation. The least well known of these concerns a trafficker who was dubbed the "King of Poggioreale" (Royal Hill). During the Second World War, a German captain took the treasure to the Vatican for protection. Once the conflict had ended, despite the insistent demands of the Deputation and Cardinal Ascalesi to repatriate the Neapolitan heritage, the Vatican turned a deaf ear. One day, a certain Giuseppe Navarra, known to have grown rich on the black market (hence his nickname – the 1961 film on the subject was internationally released

DINO DE LAURENTIIS PRESENTA

IL RE DI POGGIOREALE

ERNEST BORGNINE

as *Black City*) – offered to bring the treasure back to Naples. The Deputation and the cardinal agreed.

A few days later it was discovered that the man, seemingly disguised as a bishop, had managed to get hold of the treasure. But there was no further news of him, which worried the citizens greatly. Then, completely unexpectedly, he suddenly resurfaced with great ceremony, his car at the head of a procession of truckloads of treasure. The "King of Poggioreale" explained that he'd had to travel by small mountain roads to avoid criminals and the Allied troops who could have confiscated the precious load. Giuseppe Navarra died in poverty, forgotten by all.

SELF-PORTRAITS
ON THE TREASURY CHAPEL ALTAR

43

Cappella del Tesoro di San Gennaro
147 Via Duomo
• Metro: Line 1 Museo or Università, Line 2 Cavour
• Tel: 081 449065 • Open 9am–12 noon and 4.30pm–7pm

*Hidden
self-portraits
by the artist*

Gian Domenico Vinaccia, having worked for three years on the front of the solid silver altar, died in 1695 a few days before seeing his work in the Treasury chapel, and before he could enjoy the much anticipated celebrity. However, the talented sculptor and engraver managed to escape oblivion by theatrically appearing in his own masterpiece: the man in glasses with his head emerging in front of that of the horse ridden by Cardinal Alessandro Carafa (the main figure in the procession bringing the relics of Saint Januarius back to Naples) is a self-portrait. And that's also the artist with hat in hand, bowing to observers.

THE DOME: EACH FACE HAD ITS PRICE

After the death of Domenichino, the Deputation commissioned Giovanni Lanfranco to fresco the dome to represent Paradise. This work is populated by countless faces because, it seems, the celebrated painter had signed a lucrative contract stipulating that his fee would vary depending on the number of characters he painted.

THE "TESORO VECCHIO" CHAPEL OF SAN GENNARO

Duomo
147 Via Duomo
• Metro: Line 1 Museo or Università, Line 2 Cavour
• Tel: 081 449097
• Cathedral open daily 9am–1.30pm and 4pm–7.30pm
• Visits to the Tesoro Vecchio on request

> *The very first treasury chapel of San Gennaro*

U p on the wall of the cathedral's left nave you can see the shutters of a blocked-up window that formed part of an upper floor of the chapel known as the "Tesoro Vecchio". From here, before the construction of the present Treasury chapel, the cardinal showed the faithful the miraculous liquefaction of the blood of Saint Januarius (see pp. 354–355).

Access to this floor is near the left tower, where a spiral staircase leads to the oratory of the Archconfraternity of Santa Restituta dei Neri (the "Blacks") whose members always wore black habits. The confreres' main occupation was to arrange the burial of those with no means of their own who had met with a sudden death. The interior of the oratory is decorated with Mannerist and Baroque paintings (including a canvas by Francesco Solimena), all beautifully framed in stucco; the altarpiece is a *Nativity* by Fabrizio Santafede. In the sacristy of the Archconfraternity is a fine portrait of the viceroy, the Duke of Alba, and his wife Maria.

NEARBY

MARBLE CALENDAR OF THE 9TH CENTURY

The door in the left aisle leads to the courtyard of the Archbishop's Palace, where a section of paved Roman road can be seen among other archaeological remains, as well as various pieces of architecture from antiquity. On one wall hangs a rare marble calendar of the 9th century, from the church of San Giorgio Maggiore. Fantastical animals are carved on one side of the calendar, while on the other the liturgical celebrations of the Neapolitan Church are given, notably those relating to the Greek rite. This artefact is a major historical document in that it gives information on the saints venerated at that time, as well as the death dates of twenty-three Bishops of Naples. In the inner rooms is a permanent exhibition of carriages that once belonged to cardinals.

THE *"PASSO DA TERRA"* OF THE DUOMO

147 Via Duomo
• Metro: Line 1 Museo, Line 2 Cavour
• Tel: 081 449097
• Open daily from 9am–1.30pm and 4pm–7.30pm

> **Unit of measurement in Naples before the metric system**

In the last pillar of the cathedral's left nave, the metal bar that can be seen embedded along its length is an instrument of land measurement (see below), known as *passus ferreus* or *passo da terra*: since Roman times units of measurement had been installed in sacred places to deter fraud.

The use of the *passo* dates back to the Byzantine duchy (established in the 6th century, it gradually became autonomous and lasted five centuries), during which Naples adopted the provisions regarding weights and measures listed in the *Pragmatica Sanctio* (edict) of the Roman Emperor Justinian. According to some archival documents, the *passus ferreus* was set in a column of the basilica of Santa Restituta that was later incorporated into the cathedral. The column was then moved into the Caracciolo Pisquizy chapel and finally to its present site in the 14th century, when construction work on the new cathedral was completed by Robert of Anjou.

In 1480, the King of Naples Don Ferrante of Aragon (Ferdinand I) restored some order to the different measurement systems and determined that from now on there would only be two measures: the *passo di terra* equivalent to

7.33 palms (1.85448 m) for dividing neighbouring land, and the *passo itinerario* corresponding to 7 palms (1.84569 m), used to define the limits of large properties. The palm, in the Kingdom of Naples, was equivalent to 12 onces (26.36 cm), the average hand size of a man about 1.80 m tall.

The current metric system was devised in 1791 in France. For his part, the Bourbon King Ferdinand IV – exiled to Sicily during the Napoleonic period – launched the "Sicilian metric system" that was applied throughout the Kingdom of the Two Sicilies only to be abolished on the unification of Italy (see p. 364).

HOW IS A METRE DEFINED?

It is all too often forgotten that the metre is a French invention, being defined by the Paris Académie des Sciences in 1791 as one ten millionth of a quarter of a meridian of the earth. By this definition, the circumference (that is, meridian) of the Earth was 40,000km. After the establishment of the first standard metre, it was 1875 before seventeen other nations signed the "Convention du Mètre". In 1899, the Bureau of Weights and Measures had a standard metre cast in platinum-iridium alloy, which was held to be subject to only infinitesimal variations; that original bar can still be seen at the Pavillon de Breteuil in Sèvres (Hauts-de-Seine). With the advent of laser technology, the Conférence Générale des Poids et Mesures (CGPM) in 1960 gave a definition of the metre that is rather less comprehensible to the layman: 1,650,763.73 wavelengths of orange-coloured radiation emitted by the krypton 86 atom.

In 1983 came an even more esoteric definition: the metre is the length of the path travelled by light in vacuum during a time interval of 1/299,792,458 of a second. According to the theory of relativity, the speed of light in vacuum is the same at all points, so this definition is considered to be more accurate.

SALA DEL LAZZARETTO
OF THE FORMER DELLA PACE HOSPITAL

226 Via dei Tribunali
• Metro: Line 1 Museo, Line 2 Cavour
• Tel: 081 7951321 / 081 7951996 • municipalita4@comune.napoli.it
• www.comune.napoli.it
• Visits during certain cultural events or on request

*Lepers
cared for
in a luxurious
city centre hall*

Behind the 15th-century palace that belonged to Sergianni Caracciolo, favourite of Queen Joan II of Anjou, the buildings currently occupied by the local municipal offices once belonged to the hospital of the Brothers Hospitallers (built in 1587), an impressive complex comprising two cloisters and a Baroque church, of which only a small section is open to the public. On request, you can visit the huge lazaretto, the only place in the city that accepted lepers and patients struck down by the plague and other infectious diseases. The impressive dimensions of the Sala del Lazzaretto, richly decorated with paintings depicting the Virgin and the saints of the Order of Saint John of God by Giacinto Diano and Andrea Viola, are 12 m high, 60 m long and 10 m wide. At the far end, a beautiful 18th-century marble altar used to conceal the surgery. The raised gallery that runs around the walls was used by the staff to distribute meals to avoid contagion.

"MAY THE LORD DELIVER ME FROM SAD NEIGHBOURS AND VIOLINISTS"

At the end of the courtyard of the former della Pace hospital, these words in the regional dialect of the 16th century can be read on a wall plaque: *"God deliver me from canine jealousy, bad neighbours, and the lies of a respectable man."* In the 17th century, the historian Carlo Celano wrote that these words were traditionally said to have been engraved by an honest man unjustly sentenced to death after false accusations. He is thought to have left all his property to the nearby hospital on condition that the brothers display the inscription on the wall outside their hospital (the present inscription is a copy of the original, which was moved inside the hospital in 1893) and ensure that it stayed there forever. He had even specified that if the plaque had to be destroyed, all his assets would pass to the Ospedale degli Incurabili. It is said that until the 19th century the administration of this institution regularly sent a courier to check if the inscription was still in place.

The historian Bartolomeo Capasso, however, thought that the condemned innocent had played the violin all day long, oblivious to the exasperation of his neighbours. One of them, a tailor who could no longer concentrate on his work, is thought to have taken advantage of a murder on the street to denounce the violinist and be rid of him for good. A story that seems to bear out perfectly the Neapolitan saying: "May the Lord deliver me from sad neighbours and violinists."

ARCHIVO STORICO, BANCO DI NAPOLI

213 Via dei Tribunali
• Metro: Line 1 Museo, Line 2 Cavour
• Visits on reservation only
• info@ibnaf.it • Tel: 081 449400

> **The best-endowed bank archive in the world**

The Historical Archive of the Banco di Napoli, the largest archive in the world, occupies 336 huge rooms (of which only a few can be visited), on seven floors of two adjacent monumental palaces: Palazzo Ricca and Palazzo Como (or Cuomo). The documents stored here range over 500 years, from the 17th century to the present day.

In the vast central hall, the table and shelves where the old files are stacked are the originals, offering a virtual voyage back in time. Some ledgers of clients' accounts are a metre tall, each corresponding to a single semester (the initials "PP" indicate the first half, "P2" the second). You'll also be intrigued by a huge paper "sausage" displayed in a glass case: these are receipts which were threaded on hemp ropes and hung from the ceiling out of the reach of rodents.

A NEAPOLITAN BANKING INSTITUTION OLDER THAN MONTE DEI PASCHI DI SIENA?

Two financial experts, D. De Marco and E. Nappi, have found documents in the State Archives pertaining to deposits and withdrawals that concern the charitable institution Casa Santa dell'Annunziata, including a receipt for the refund of a deposit dated 19 March 1493. This discovery makes it possible to claim that the origin of the Neapolitan Monti di Pietà, which merged to form the Banco di Napoli in the 16th century, were the "savings banks" of charitable institutions (Casa Santa dell'Annunziata, Conservatorio di Sant'Eligio, Ospedale degli Incurabili). Neapolitan banking is therefore thought to be nine years ahead of the Monte dei Paschi di Siena, considered to be the first bank in Italy.

NEARBY

A ROMAN VILLA IN THE BASEMENT OF THE BANCO DI NAPOLI ARCHIVE
• To visit, contact Gruppo Archeologico Napoletano
• Tel: 081 5529002 or 338 4031994 (mobile)

On some occasions, you can visit the excavations beneath Palazzo Ricca, which belongs to the Banco di Napoli archive. These vestiges of the Roman era (2nd century BC), the frescoed walls and remnants of thermal baths, used to be part of a patrician villa.

BIBLIOTECA ALFREDO DE MARSICO

Castel Capuano
Piazza Enrico de Nicola, access by Castel Capuano
• Metro: Lines 1 and 2 Garibaldi
• Visits by appointment (by phone or e-mail)
• Tel: 081 269416
• bibliotecademarsico@tin.it

> **The essence of Neapolitan advocacy**

Housed in Castel Capuano, the Norman royal palace (2nd century), which was converted into the Palace of Justice in the 16th century (itself transferred in 2000 to the business centre on the outskirts of the city), the exceptional Alfredo De Marsico library owes its name to the eminent jurist of that name (1888–1985).

The library, opened on 19 July 1986 in the beautiful hall of the Criminal Court where the Council of Queen Joan of Anjou sat in the 14th century, houses over 80,000 volumes dating from the 16th to the 20th centuries. Some rare editions are even cited by the British National Library as the only copies in the world. They are also invaluable for their precious bindings and refined typography.

This bibliographic heritage has been enriched over the centuries through donations from illustrious lawyers. Among them are the last memoirs of Giovanni Napolitano, father of Giorgio, current President of the Italian Republic.

Not only does the library contain legal works, it also has collections of authoritative philosophical and literary treatises, ancient codes of law, monographs, encyclopedias and four rare editions (1612, 1622, 1683, 1759) of John Calvin's writings.

The frescoed vaults of the two rooms at the entrance to the library, painted by Belisario Corenzio, represent the Judgment of Solomon, the Judgment of David, allegories of the virtues and coats of arms. In the 16th century, the so-called "small throne" room was designed for individuals attending the trial of those indicted for serious threats to social order. This "small throne" in red velvet with gold armrests, which had probably belonged to Francis II of Bourbon, was confiscated from a mob boss. The artefact was exhibited in June 2013 in the basement of Castel Capuano as part of a stunning display on various notorious news items. Among the most original were a life-sized wooden jaguar in whose belly had been hidden a large quantity of cocaine, counterfeit cigarettes, and a rubber mask with the face of actor Lino Banfi, used for a hold-up.

LIZARD IN THE CHURCH OF THE SANTISSIMI APOSTOLI (51)

8 Largo Santi Apostoli
• Metro: Line 1 Museo, Line 2 Cavour
• Tel: 081 299375
• Open weekdays 9am–12 noon and 5pm–8pm, weekends and public holidays 9am–1pm

A calcified lizard in church

In the church of Santissimi Apostoli (Holy Apostles) is a strange phenomenon: on the handrail of the carved balustrade of the wooden choir (1640) a lizard has been caught in the thick layer of dust that accumulated during the long years the church was closed. The little reptile, in a perfect state of preservation, is now an integral part of the furnishings and was left in place during the restoration of the choir, completed in 2013.

The church was built in the 5th century over Roman ruins, probably a temple dedicated to Mercury. Although the façade is fairly anonymous, the interior is notable for the frescoes of Giovanni Lanfranco and paintings by Francesco Solimena and Luca Giordano, three major representatives of Neapolitan Baroque.

In the left transept of the sacristy, the remarkable Filomarino altar (1646), the only work signed by Borromini in Naples, is worth a visit.

NEARBY

IONIC COLUMN AT PELLETTERIA COLLARO (52)

224 Via Duomo
• Metro: Line 1 Museo, Line 2 Cavour
• Tel: 081 266276

During refurbishment of the Collaro premises in the early 1950s, a beautiful old column was discovered in an excellent state of conservation. Today you can still see the refined Ionic capital sitting majestically among bags, briefcases and suitcases, now restored by the owners who almost look upon it as a family heirloom.

The date of the column is uncertain, as is its provenance. Some suggest the Graeco-Roman period, others Roman thermal baths or perhaps a 19th-century private mansion.

MATERDEI, SANITÀ, CAPODIMONTE

1 CRUCIFIX OF SAN CARLO ALL'ARENA CHURCH 261
2 *FATE PRESTO*: REPRODUCTION IN THE METRO OF A "NEAPOLITAN" WORK
   BY ANDY WARHOL. 261
3 PIAZZA CAVOUR TUNNELS 262
4 BOMB SHELTER IN BABUK'S GARDEN 265
5 PALAZZO DE' LIGUORO DI PRESICCE 267
6 STUDIO OF PAINTER MASSIMO D'ORTA 268
7 LITTLE SECRETS OF PALAZZO DELLO SPAGNOLO. 271
8 SIRENS OF PALAZZO SANFELICE 271
9 GREEK HYPOGEA IN NAPLES. 272
10 "CRISTALLINI" HYPOGEA. 275
11 CHURCH OF SANTA MARIA ANTESAECULA 276
12 THE FERTILITY CHAIR 279

13 SAN GAUDIOSO CATACOMBS 281

14 PALAZZO DE' LIGUORO-SANTORO STAIRCASE 283

15 MICHELE IODICE'S WORKSHOP 285

16 WINE TAX MARKER 285

17 TORRE DEL PALASCIANO 287

18 OSPEDALE LEONARDO BIANCHI 288

19 CLOISTER OF THE FACOLTÀ DI VETERINARIA (UNIVERSITÀ FEDERICO II) . 291

20 MUSEO DI ANATOMIA VETERINARIA 291

21 SAINT ANTHONY THE HERMIT'S PIG 293

22 CURIOSITIES OF SAN GENNARO CATACOMBS 297

23 LA SANITÀ BRIDGE 298

24 MODEL OF BATTAGLINO CHARIOT 299

25 THE CAPTAIN'S SKULL 300

CRUCIFIX OF SAN CARLO ALL'ARENA CHURCH ❶

70 Via Foria
• Metro: Line 1 Museo, Line 2 Cavour
• Visits 7.30am—11am and 5pm—7pm

The wounded Christ

On 11 November 1923, the church of San Carlo all'Arena was badly affected by fire, which among other damage brought down a precious crucifix that shattered on the floor. The figure of Christ carved by Michelangelo Naccherino in 1599 from a single block of marble, which originally stood in Spirito Santo basilica, is so realistic that it has even been compared with the famous *Veiled Christ* statue in the Sansevero chapel (see p. 217). After extremely skilful restoration work, the statue was returned to its many devoted followers. The new and inevitable injuries "inflicted" on the statue have only accentuated its dramatic effect. The sculpture is in the fifth chapel, dedicated to Saint Charles Borromeo (16th-century Archbishop of Milan), whose shroud is said to have been kept in one of the other chapels.

The church was laid waste when it was occupied by the French troops, who used it as a barracks. It was was almost entirely rebuilt by Francesco De Cesare in 1837.

WHY "ALL'ARENA"?

The church of San Carlo all'Arena, so called to distinguish it from the church of San Carlo a Mortelle, was commissioned from Fra' Giuseppe Nuvolo in 1631 by the Carthusian monks. The name "all'Arena" (of the arena) alludes to the sandy clay on which the church was built – an alluvial sediment that slid down from the surrounding hills and was generally known as the "Lava of Vergini".

NEARBY

FATE PRESTO: REPRODUCTION IN THE METRO OF A "NEAPOLITAN" WORK BY ANDY WARHOL ❷

The hundreds of passengers who hurry every day along the corridor connecting Line 1 to Line 2 of the metro (between Museo and Cavour stations) don't take much notice of a large poster reproducing the front page of the local daily *Il Mattino*, which came out in the aftermath of the 1980 earthquake. Although most Neapolitans think it's a simple tribute to the many victims of the disaster, the poster is actually a reproduction of a work by Andy Warhol (the original is in the Royal Palace of Caserta).

The pop art celebrity was so touched by the simple yet meaningful title *Fate Presto* (Hurry Up) that he decided to immortalise this tragic event in the history of southern Italy. Warhol later made a series of eighteen paintings representing the Vesuvius eruption at different hours of the day, one of which is displayed at the Capodimonte gallery.

PIAZZA CAVOUR TUNNELS

③

La Macchina Del Tempo
Il Museo del Sottosuolo
140 Piazza Cavour
• Metro: Line 1 Museo, Line 2 Cavour
• info@ilmuseodelsottosuolo.com
• Info for timetables and opening: 320 5741842
or at www.ilmuseodelsottosuolo.com

The
underground
museum

Nobody would think that the little door behind the two metro stations in Piazza Cavour leads to a extensive underground world, much less well-known than the other passages under the city streets. A long stairway leads down 20 m to an intricate network of tunnels, galleries and caverns hewn in the tuff, the largest of which covers 3,600 m².

Some of this space was used as an air-raid shelter during the Second World War, when over a thousand people took refuge there. The site has now become a museum, founded by Clemente Esposito, president of the Southern Speleological Society.

Glass cases display artefacts found during the excavations: an old gun, vials belonging to an ancient pharmacy that stored its goods in one of the underground quarries, as well as tools, oil lamps and crockery.

Further down, you end up in a quarry with walls 8 m high, around which benches have been dug out of the tuff walls to serve as makeshift beds during the war.

This is the only network of tunnels under the city where the modern aqueduct (Carmignano) runs over the remains of the aqueducts of antiquity. Another distinctive feature is that it's the only quarry outside the city walls, excavated in the 17th century when exploitation of the caverns under the city was banned for fear of subsidence.

BOMB SHELTER IN BABUK'S GARDEN ❹

55 Via Giuseppe Piazzi
• Metro: Line 1 Museo, Line 2 Cavour
• Visits by reservation only: 347 5597231

*A shelter
for the elite*

Behind a 16th-century palace that belonged to the Caracciolo del Sole family there is a little garden, measuring about 1,000 m², full of lemon trees, flowers and beautiful fountains: a charming hideaway among the many modern buildings.

The restoration work was carried out by Professor Gennaro Oliviero, President of the "Friends of Marcel Proust" association, which since 2009 has organised visits and events. Professor Oliviero wished to name this garden after his cat, Babuk, to which he was very attached.

Among the greenery is the entrance to a 17th-century underground quarry, which was later converted to a 700,000 litre cistern. This was abandoned after the 1884 cholera epidemic, when the Serino aqueduct was built. In those days the steps were extended to reach the bottom of the tank at a depth of 14 m.

During the Second World War, the space was used as an air-raid shelter, as borne out by objects found during repair work. It was called the "elite" shelter because it was reserved for the wealthy of the neighbourhood. After the war, the old quarry was completely forgotten.

On the walls, still coated with waterproofing material, you can still see the marks left by the stonemasons and the outline of steps cut out by the cistern maintenance workers. There are also strange carvings in the tuff, such as crosses or salamanders. The main chamber led to galleries, some of which are still piled with old gravel. Only one of them has been cleared and leads to a small quarry that you can arrange to visit.

EVENTS ORGANISED BY THE "FRIENDS OF MARCEL PROUST"
The association occasionally organises very agreeable literary events or performances: www.amicidimarcelproust.it

PALAZZO DE' LIGUORO DI PRESICCE

12 Via Arena della Sanità
- Metro: Line 1 Museo, Line 2 Cavour
- Visits on request
- pdeliguorodipresicce@gmail.com

Home of "the saintliest of Neapolitans and most Neapolitan of saints"

At the heart of the Vergini district with its streets teeming with life and chaotic traffic, the Palazzo de' Liguoro di Presicce is not only a discovery, but a genuine experience, because you touch on the very essence of "*napoletanità*" (being, feeling a real Neapolitan). This is entirely due to the owner, Princess Paola di' Liguoro di Presicce, who has restored this superb 16th-century residence and welcomes visitors with exquisite courtesy.

The princess is a direct descendant of Saint Alphonsus Maria de' Liguori, known as "the saintliest of Neapolitans and most Neapolitan of saints", who lived in this building. His statue still stands in a niche in the staircase wall.

Although only a few traces remain of the palace chapel, the first-floor rooms still have the elegant 17th-century decoration attributed to Domenico De Mare. The princess's own large apartment, part of which can be visited on request, is a treasure trove of huge mirrors, 17th-century inlaid furniture, imposing bookcases and sparkling chandeliers. As for the ballroom with its frescoed vault, you'd think it had come straight out of Visconti's *The Leopard*.

Madame de' Liguoro, having lived in Rome for a number of years, chose to settle here, because, she says, "In Vergini we breathe the air of truth." She is devoted body and soul to the rehabilitation of the neighbourhood, weighed down as it was with far too many unfounded prejudices rooted in the minds

of Neapolitans themselves. To this end, she funds a number of cultural events such as putting on plays.

The princess also rents the other apartments in the palace to artists or writers, thus creating a fantastic reserve of culture and creativity without equal in the city.

STUDIO OF PAINTER MASSIMO D'ORTA ⑥

43a Vico Santa Maria del Pozzo
• Metro: Line 1 Museo, Line 2 Cavour
• Visits on request
• dorta.massimo@libero.it

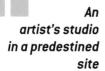

*An
artist's studio
in a predestined
site*

The painter Massimo D'Orta – brother of Marcello D'Orta, author of the 1990 bestseller *Io speriamo che me la cavo* [I'm hoping I get out of this], who died in 2013 – willingly welcomes visitors to his workshop, which he also calls home, in Palazzo de' Liguoro di Presicce (see previous double-page spread).

The artist works in the salon of the large apartment with a ceiling that retains traces of earlier frescoes. When Massimo D'Orta first visited the

apartment in 2000, he refused to live there because of the terrible state it was in. Then, after a few days, he returned to have a better look round. As he entered the salon, all of a sudden he distinctly heard a voice whispering: "I was expecting you." When he got over his bewilderment, he decided to buy and restore the apartment. Less than a week later, the representatives of a wealthy Texas businessman, having seen Massimo D'Orta paintings in an exhibition, commissioned a life-size copy (2×3 m) of Caravaggio's *Descent from the Cross*, a work that the artist had always dreamed of reproducing. What's more, the fee for this commission easily covered the significant cost of the restoration work. D'Orta later discovered that in this apartment had lived a disciple of Saint Alphonsus de' Liguoro, Saint Gerard Majella (1726–1755), much loved in the neighbourhood for his work helping the poor. His benevolent presence, they say, still protects this former palace.

From the painter's workshop, you can admire a beautiful magnolia around 500 years old and over 20 m high.

LITTLE SECRETS
OF PALAZZO DELLO SPAGNOLO

❼

19 Via Vergini
• Metro: Line 1 Museo, Line 2 Cavour
• Admission free

To reach Capodimonte hill, where he had a palace built to display the works of art inherited from his mother, Elisabeth Farnese, Charles I of Bourbon had to travel along Via Vergini. This street with its silted-up surface was so steep that even the horses couldn't make it: only oxen could.

When the king changed horses for oxen to climb the Vergini slopes

At the superb Palazzo dello Spagnolo (Palace of the Spaniard – don't miss the famous and strikingly original external staircase), at the beginning of the slope, the king stopped to exchange his beautiful horses for these humble bovines. For the residents of this house and the whole neighbourhood, it was the perfect opportunity to get a close look at the king.

But every good thing comes to an end: when Joachim Murat ascended the throne of the kingdom of Naples, he had a much more accessible new road built linking the city centre to Capodimonte. The palace where the oxen awaited the king, designed in 1738 by Ferdinando Sanfelice, is so named because it was occupied in the 19th century by a Spanish nobleman, Tommaso Atienza, known for his eccentricity.

NEARBY

SIRENS OF PALAZZO SANFELICE

❽

2/6 Via Sanità

Ferdinando Sanfelice (1675–1748), born into a family of the old Neapolitan nobility and an enlightened Freemason with innovative and bold ideas, was known for the audacity of his projects, notably his staircases that were so outrageous that, fearing they would collapse at any moment, people nicknamed them: "*Sanfelì lievet' 'a sotto*" (Sanfelice, don't stay under there). He built the eponymous palazzo for his own family, or rather two palazzi with identical portals – one built from scratch and another restored next door. Some obscure details: the pediment of the two portals is flanked by two Sirens who are represented with wings and a fishtail, which is very rare because in iconography Sirens are usually either bird-women or mermaids (see p. 145). Also note in the vault of the entrance hall the eight-branched star, a symbol with multiple meanings familiar to both Templars and Freemasons.

GREEK HYPOGEA IN NAPLES

❾

126/129 Via Santa Maria Antesaecula
- Metro: Line 1 Museo, Line 2 Cavour
- Tel: 347 5597231
- Guided tours by appointment with the Celanapoli association
- celanapoli@libero.it

Greek tombs under buildings in the historic centre

In the Vergini district, a steep flight of steps leads to the two hypogea in the care of the Celanapoli association. The underground tombs, discovered when checks were carried out after the 1980 earthquake, are part of a great Hellenistic necropolis (4th century BC) that was once in the open. It was in use until the 2nd century AD, then gradually covered by 10 m of sediment. In the 16th century, when building began in this area, the tuff layer was excavated and much of the necropolis was destroyed.

A number of these tombs, many of which were converted into cisterns by the inhabitants of the stately palazzi of the 18th century, had been known since at least 1649, when the historian Carlo Celano was already mentioning grave robbers being arrested by the authorities. So there are not many intact tombs left. Furthermore, although the water stored in these chambers preserved their decoration for a few centuries, the worst damage occurred after the cholera epidemic of 1884, when water storage was banned for reasons of hygiene.

From then on, these precious relics would become a dumping ground for rubble, which also makes the current excavations extremely complex.

The tombs, all monumental and certainly belonging to notables, were dug into the tuff wall that stretched along the extramural perimeter from north to east of the ancient city of Neapolis (now Via dei Cristallini, Vico Traetta, Via Santa Maria Antesaecula). To imagine what this necropolis was like, think of the excavations at Petra in Jordan, whereas their decoration is reminiscent of Macedonian art. In fact, these structures have no equal to this day.

The first hypogeum is called "dei Togati" because of the extraordinary high relief depicting a lifesize man and woman, both draped in togas. The upper section is regrettably hidden by a supporting arch from the building above. On one side, you can make out a very poorly preserved panther, an allusion to the Dionysian cult. The burial chamber, measuring 15 m², is still filled with rubble.

The tomb known as the "Melograno" (pomegranate) is better preserved. In the burial chamber, once entirely covered with frescoes, you can still see a frieze of pomegranates, pine cones, lotus flowers and eggs, as well as an unidentified fruit, all evoking fertility.

In another inaccessible section are traces of the sarcophagi. Descending to a depth of about 20 m, you reach the place that until the early 20th century was used as a cold store for meat and charcuterie. Cattle bones can still be seen there.

Four tombs from the same Hellenistic necropolis are accessible at 133 Via dei Cristallini (see following double-page spread).

"CRISTALLINI" HYPOGEA

133 Via dei Cristallini
• Metro: Line 1 Museo, Line 2 Cavour
• Visits can be booked during the first and third Saturdays of May only
• napolisegreta@gmail.com

A unique tomb

Four exceptional tombs from the Hellenistic necropolis of Vergini district (see previous double-page spread) were discovered in perfect condition in 1888 when cleaning out the well underneath Baron Giovanni di Donato's palace. The site, 11 m below street level, is down a flight of steps in the courtyard of the building.

Like all the other tombs, these are constructed on two levels. The atrium chambers that once stood on the ground floor, intended for funeral rites, are connected to the burial chamber by a passageway (*dromos*). The first atrium was decorated with eight bas-reliefs, only one of which remains. The associated tomb has been almost completely destroyed by stone-masons. The second is stunning in its incredible state of conservation (funerary urns, frescoes and altars). In the third, covered by a pitched roof rather than a barrel vault, are superb bas-reliefs including one of a farewell scene (see below). Its unique tomb of incomparable beauty features bas-reliefs, sarcophagi with ornamental marble pillows, and paintings, including a magnificent Medusa, that seem freshly restored. The last vault is completely different, surrounded by the niches (columbaria) typical of Roman cemeteries, proof that they reused the site. Among the many objects found there are painted vases, statuettes, terracotta fruits and eggs, jars of ointment and inscriptions in honour of the deceased.

TOUCHING FAREWELL SCENES IN THE MUSEO ARCHEOLOGICO NAZIONALE

Metro: Line 1 Museo, Line 2 Cavour

The "Napoli antica" section of the Archaeological Museum of Naples (the world's most important repository of Graeco-Roman art), inaugurated in 1999, is still little known although of major interest. The most notable exhibits include the so-called "*de commiato*" (farewell) bas-reliefs from the tombs of Vergini and La Sanità. Most of these show two people shaking hands. The most touching scene is that of two men, with a woman caressing the cheek of one of them, most likely the deceased. Not to be missed.

CHURCH OF SANTA MARIA ANTESAECULA

Dispensaire Asl
48 Via Santa Maria Antesaecula
• Metro: Line 1 Museo, Line 2 Cavour
• Viviquartiere association
• Visits on reservation by phone or e-mail
• Tel: 339 6304072 • viviquartiere@libero.it

> *A*
> ***former church***
> ***in a health centre***

Within a modern public building you'll be amazed to find the vestiges of a large 17th-century convent – the construction date of 1622 can still be read on the original gate. In that year, to escape the epidemics that were constantly breaking out in the city, the girls' boarding school in the Vicaria Vecchia district, founded in 1275 by Charles I of Anjou's chancellor Pierleone Sicola, was moved to the present location because of its reputation for hygiene.

The original name of this institution, Santa Maria a Sicola (after the founder), was changed to Santa Maria Antesaecula in memory of the Virgin Mary's words: *"ab inizio et ante saecula creata sum"* (At the beginning of time, before the world was, I was created). The property later became a Dominican monastery. There's not much of the old structure left.

The church (entrance in one of the offices), rebuilt on several occasions and closed for a long period, is used today for cultural events. Urbanisation has also spared part of the original garden. At the end of the Second World War, reconstruction work exposed the crypt that served as a burial ground, with its pierced seats used for drying out corpses (see also San Gaudioso catacombs, p. 281), which were left in place.

At 109 Via Santa Maria Antesaecula, a plaque marks the building where the famous comedian Totò lived.

THE FERTILITY CHAIR

Church of Santa Maria della Sanità
14 Piazza della Sanità
• Metro: Line 1 Museo, Line 2 Cavour
• Tel: 081 7443714 • info@catacombedinapoli.it
• Open daily, 10am—5pm

I n the chapel dedicated to Saint Thomas Aquinas at Santa Maria della Sanità church is a chair made from volcanic stone dating from the early Christian period, originally an episcopal chair in the catacombs beneath. The Dominicans moved it to its current location in the 17th century.

Sit in this chair if you want to bear a child

According to legend, the chair has the power to cure sterility in women who sit in it. This belief, which endured until the last decade or so, is no longer so widespread. Nowadays the chair is even behind a barrier.

OTHER FERTILITY CHAIRS IN NAPLES

In Vico Tre Re a Toledo in the Spanish quarter, women are commonly seen queuing in front of the church of Santa Maria Francesca delle Cinque Piaghe di Gesù to sit on a wooden chair that had belonged to Sister Maria Francesca, the saint addressed by women wishing to bear a child. In this church, the relics of a lock of hair and one of the saint's vertebrae form part of the same ritual. For the miracle to happen, the vertebra should brush against the belly of the would-be mother. The home of Maria Francesca (also known as "Santarella" – little saint), next to the church, is open to all those who wish to visit or pay homage to the saint born on 25 March 1715. She is said to have received the stigmata. There is no longer any trace of a third chair that used to be in Santa Maria della Catena church.

SAN GAUDIOSO CATACOMBS

14 Piazza della Sanità
Entrance in Santa Maria della Sanità church
- Metro: Line 1 Museo, Line 2 Cavour
- Tel: 081 7443714 • info@catacombedinapoli.it
- Open 10am–1.30pm: last guided tour of catacombs 12.30pm
- Admission: €10 valid for one year, includes San Gennaro catacombs

> **Skeletons in fancy dress**

Access to San Gaudioso catacombs is by a flight of steps below the presbytery of Santa Maria della Sanità (17th century). In the early 16th century, these vast underground galleries were used to preserve the dead, using a Spanish method that had been adopted by the Dominican and Capuchin monks.

While the bodies of the poor were crammed into ossuaries, the aristocrats were carried into these underground tunnels to undergo a very special treatment: after sitting the corpse in a niche made for this purpose (which can still be seen today), it was pierced. Apparently the bodies were burst open to empty them of all fluids, hence the Neapolitan term *schiattamuorto* for undertaker (corpse-piercer) and a fairly common and unsavoury insult: *puozze schiattà* or *puozze sculà*, "go and bust a gut" or "go and drip".

As the Dominicans considered the soil as a gift from God that shouldn't be contaminated by sinful man, these bodily fluids were drained into a pot placed under the seated corpse. Once the body had dried out, the head (seat of the soul) was detached and inserted in the wall of a tunnel next to the main chamber. Then a life-size mural was painted of the deceased's fully clothed body under its own head and a few explanatory details were inscribed on the wall.

The first mural depicts Donna Sveva Gesualdo, Princess of Montesarchio, who paid 600 ducats to benefit from this treatment. Note also the spouses holding hands. There's a legend that these two saw a terrifying and unwelcome guest arrive at their wedding, the ghost of the captain whose head is preserved in the nearby Fontanelle cemetery (see p. 300). On the left is a magistrate, Diego Longobardo, with his robes and judge's gavel, dead in 1632; next come Marco Antonio d'Aponte, Scipione Brancaccio with his sword, Alessandro d'Afflitto and the painter Giovanni Balducci with his ruler and palette.

In 1637, this practice was abolished because of the Dominicans constantly knocking holes in the walls to insert the aristocrats' heads (which, incidentally, brought the monks a significant extra income) and threatening the stability of the whole district. Besides, the damp tunnels became a breeding ground for germs because of this method of treating corpses.

In 2002, the pastor of Santa Maria della Sanità church founded a cooperative, the Paranza, with the aim of training young people and raising funds with which to restore and reopen monuments. The cooperative also manages a B&B, Casa del Monacone – an exemplary start-up of a very useful business, regrettably little known.

PALAZZO DE' LIGUORO-SANTORO STAIRCASE ⑭

8/10 Salita Capodimonte
• Metro: Line 1 Museo, Line 2 Cavour
• Tel: 347 5597231 • celanapoli@libero.it
• Guided tour on reservation with the Celanapoli association

Extraordinary architecture carved out of the tuff

Built into the tuff hillside of Capodimonte, Palazzo de' Liguoro-Santoro (named after its successive owners) dates back to at least 1746, as indicated by the marble inscription at the entrance. You'll immediately realise that the building is totally different to its neighbours. In the entrance hall, entirely hollowed out of the tuff, a closed door on the left leads to the old cemeteries also dug into the hillside. A small altar stands in the centre, and to the right a few steps will take you to one of the most original and most spectacular stairwells in the city: a spiral staircase carved out of the tuff and covered with lava stone of unparalleled grace and perfection.

Another peculiarity is that on climbing to the top floor, instead of being plunged into darkness as in most buildings, you're bathed in the light streaming through the circular openings. The staircase leads to a private roof garden with a beautiful view over the city centre. During guided tours you can sometimes visit this garden.

MICHELE IODICE'S WORKSHOP

132 Salita Capodimonte
- Bus: C63, 2M, 178, R4
- Visits on reservation
- mic.iodice@gmail.com

*Sculptures
in a stable*

A former quarry, first used as a stable and then a slaughterhouse and accessed through the entrance hall of a building, has been converted into a studio by a Neapolitan artist who displays hundreds of sculptures along the tuff walls. Michele Iodice, the sculptor, has also brightened up his studio with towering plants that add to its originality. Local people say that this was where the replacement oxen were stabled while they waited to be harnessed to the king's carriage whenever he and his family took the only road up to the Royal Palace of Capodimonte, which was too steep for the horses (see p. 271).

NEARBY

WINE TAX MARKER

Further along Salita Capodimonte you come to Via Sant'Antonio a Capodimonte where, between 1 Salita Capodimonte and 111 Via Sant'Antonio, a plaque marks the boundary of the "wine tax". Among the earliest collectors of this tax, which was payable on the sale of carafes and casks of wine in the City of Naples, was Gregorio Carafa di Stadera, an aristocrat who lived in the 12th century.

TORRE DEL PALASCIANO

B&B La Torre di Rò
53 Salita Moiariello
• Metro: Line 1 Museo, then Bus C63
• Tel: 081 457711, 335 6957720
• www.latorrediro.com
• Reservation by e-mail: info@latorrediro.com

> *A strange tower inspired by Palazzo della Signoria*

Built to the plans of architect Antonio Cipolla for Ferdinando Palasciano (see below), the extraordinary Palumbo tower that flanks a palazzo dating from 1868 is clearly inspired by the medieval Palazzo della Signoria in Florence. The enchanting verdant garden all around the tower, with its beautiful trees – oaks, oranges and laurels – is just a short distance from the Royal Palace of Capodimonte. Although the tower stands out against the Neapolitan landscape and can be seen from afar, not many locals know that it is open to the public: it has recently been restored and converted into a B&B.

Through the entrance hall to the left, near the wall, stands a grey stone obelisk (1868) engraved with the names of famous people. The beautiful staircase leads to the three guest rooms (each located on a different floor and all with private bathrooms). At the top is a panoramic terrace with a parapet pierced with niches known as Ghibellines. From here, Palasciano's wife Olga de Wavilow could even see the monumental tomb of her beloved husband, located in the so-called "corner of illustrious men" in the city's main cemetery at Poggioreale. Indeed the statue of the deceased, on a pedestal 5 m high, is hard to miss.

FERDINANDO PALASCIANO, ARMY DOCTOR OF THE TWO SICILIES

Dr Ferdinando Palasciano (1815–1891), appointed army doctor of the Kingdom of the Two Sicilies, was in Sicily during the riots of 1848. He cared for the enemy wounded against the orders of General Carlo Filangieri and so found himself accused of insubordination. Condemned to be shot, he was rescued by King Ferdinand II, who commuted his sentence to a year in prison. This incident laid the foundations of the Geneva Convention of 1864, which in turn gave rise to the Red Cross.

The care that Dr Palasciano lavished on Garibaldi, after he was seriously injured fighting at Aspromonte, led to a growing friendship between the two men and they corresponded over a long period. Their letters are preserved in the San Martino Museum (see pp. 319).

OSPEDALE LEONARDO BIANCHI ⑱

230 Calata Capodichino
• Bus 125 from Napoli Centrale station (Calata Capodichino stop)
• Visits: contact offices of Divisione Sanitaria – Dottoressa Sicolo,
9am–2pm • Tel: 081 2546118 / 081 2546147

A hospital theatre

For the past fifteen years, Roberto De Simone has rehearsed his performances in the abandoned Leonardo Bianchi psychiatric hospital. The new life of this vast hospital complex (fifty-four buildings over 20 hectares) began in the 1990s with the abolition of asylums. Before the hospital was permanently decommissioned, its administrative rooms were opened up for artists to rehearse in front of the patients. This experiment was designed to help them make a smooth transition to the "outside world". De Simone was one of the first to accept the challenge. What was supposed to be a temporary experiment then became a ongoing palliative.

The asylum, built in 1902 and commissioned in 1909, was one of the most important in southern Italy. Its archives contain thousands of documents considered to be a valuable asset, essential to studying the history of psychiatry. After the patients had gone, some buildings were used by the social security services. The current director of this branch of public health, Dr Anna Sicolo, is striving to set up a museum to save these symbols of human incarceration from oblivion.

Two books have now been published on this site, which clearly fascinates artists: *Folia/Follia: Il patrimonio culturale dell'ex ospedale psichiatrico "Leonardo Bianchi" di Napoli,* by G. Villone and M. Sessa, published by Gaia; and *Libera Viva*, which documents a photographic/archival project by Italian artist Elisabeth Hölzl, published by Verlag für Moderne Kunst (in English).

ROBERTO DE SIMONE, BARD OF NAPLES

Composer and concert pianist, conductor and founder of vocal groups, musicologist, essayist and mythologist, playwright and director, Roberto De Simone turns everything he touches to gold. All his works cover the full range of performance arts: dramatic style and colourful language, song and dance, intellectual and popular culture, obscenity and refinement are all in harmony in the hands of such a prodigy. Roberto De Simone dares to try anything and succeeds in everything, which has prompted Giulio Baffi, Italy's most respected theatre critic, to say that "the theatre will be eternally indebted to Roberto De Simone".

De Simone has also safeguarded an invaluable cultural heritage that would otherwise have been lost for ever: in the 1960s, he tirelessly roamed around the region to record and transcribe tales and songs from the oral tradition. In addition to his discoveries in the countryside are the nuggets he unearthed in libraries and archives, real assets to leave to posterity. To make these forgotten treasures better known, he launched the Nuova Compagnia di Canto Popolare, an extraordinary group of singers. Success was global. In 1976, it was the turn of *La Gatta Cenerentola* (Cinderella), a musical in which De Simone wove a web of the most significant magico-religious symbols from the ancient culture of his homeland. In Naples, *La Gatta* became a rare phenomenon in that it appealed to intellectuals as much as to ordinary people. (It came to London's Sadler's Wells theatre in 1999.) Riccardo Muti hit the nail on the head in saying that De Simone is "the soul of his city".

De Simone, an artist of inexhaustible talent, constantly renews himself and success follows success. So far he has to his credit twenty musicals (composed and directed), a dozen concertos and an opera, not to mention the plethora of operatic productions for the most prestigious national and international theatres. The value placed on his many essays, among which *Il segno di Virgilio* (The Sign of Virgil) is a veritable bible of Neapolitan mythology, is such that they sell out as soon as they appear. His books are never reissued, like his shows, which are rarely repeated. He's keen to preserve the authenticity that might succumb to rampant commercialisation.

De Simone's love of folk traditions has inspired him to collect a mass of objects that he wants to make accessible to the public in a museum devoted to folk art. The Naples city hall had promised him a space in the historic centre, where he'd be able to fulfil another dream: setting up a music school. The promise is now dead in the water, as he's accepted an offer from the nearby municipality of Portici, site of the summer residence of the kings of Naples. The mayor of Portici has offered to make available a beautiful 18th-century villa because, he says, "Roberto De Simone forms part of the heritage of humanity." So Naples has missed a unique opportunity to embrace one of its exceptional sons, who has devoted his soul and his genius to the city.

CLOISTER OF THE FACOLTÀ DI VETERINARIA ⑲ (UNIVERSITÀ FEDERICO II)

1 Via Delpino
- Metro: Line 1 Museo or Garibaldi, Line 2 Cavour or Garibaldi
- Tel: 081 2531111
- Open Monday to Friday 8.30am–6.30pm

> **One of the city's best-preserved and least-known cloisters**

At the former monastic complex of Santa Maria degli Angeli alle Croci, now home to the Faculty of Veterinary Science, you can visit one of the best-preserved cloisters in the city. Built in 1581, it was extended and embellished a century later by Cosimo Fanzago. The arches of the cloister, surrounded by a covered gallery with grey volcanic stone columns, are decorated with 17th-century frescoes attributed to Belisario Corenzio and depicting episodes from the Bible. Each keystone (thirty-six in all) is in the form of a shield

with the corresponding family name, in gratitude for donations received from the aristocrats who contributed to the restoration of the monastery.

Following the suppression of the monastic orders under Napoleon, this complex was chosen to host the veterinary school for military and civilian use, a decision that was confirmed by Ferdinand IV of Bourbon when he recovered his throne. In 1935, the school became a faculty of the University of Naples Federico II.

NEARBY

MUSEO DI ANATOMIA VETERINARIA ⑳

1 Via Delpino
- Tel: 081 5644238 • Visits on request
- Open Tuesday to Friday 9am–2pm; also Tuesday and Thursday 3pm–5pm
- Admission free

The Museum of Veterinary Anatomy, on the third floor of the building that houses the Faculty of Veterinary Science, preserves the bodies of various animal species that have been injected with plasticised liquids so that the arterial and vascular systems are revealed. The museum also has a collection of Mediterranean fauna, mainly marine, either dry or preserved in formalin.

SAINT ANTHONY THE HERMIT'S PIG

㉑

Church of Sant'Antonio Abate – 302 Via Foria
• Metro: Line 1 Museo, Line 2 Cavour

*Fire
and pork fat*

The church of Sant'Antonio Abate (Saint Anthony the Hermit), built at the time of King Robert of Anjou (14th century) and refurbished in the Baroque style after a fire, became extremely popular after Virgil's bronze horse was banned (see p. 237). In order to heal their sick horses, people began to celebrate a ritual around this church identical to the one previously held around the statue attributed to Virgil. Although the animals' harnesses were originally decorated with little crescent loaves, these have morphed into biscuits coated with white icing that are sold on the steps of the church on 17 January, the saint's feast day. This is the same date when animals are taken there to be blessed. Despite this background, it's a pig, not a horse, that stands at the saint's feet –representing all the other animals. The healing power attributed to Saint Anthony is indeed strictly linked to the pig: the monks of Saint Anthony, to whom the Angevin king had assigned the religious complex with its hospital, were known for their ointment prepared from pork fat, with which they treated burns and wounds.

Interestingly, shingles is called "Saint Anthony's fire" in the Neapolitan dialect, because the other attribute of this saint is just that – fire. The legend goes that Saint Anthony the Hermit, in his desert retreat, struggled with the Devil tempting him in the guise of a pig. So Anthony descended to Hell to retrieve the souls taken by Lucifer and stole fire by lighting his *tau*-shaped staff (see box p. 294), which explains his reputation as the Devil's worst enemy and healer of conditions associated with fire.

With their taste for esotericism, the Neapolitans couldn't help but be captivated by this charming myth. They raised pigs in the street and particularly appreciated those with distinctive marks on their coats, more so if they formed the letter *tau*.

On 17 January, the pigs were decked out with ribbons and offered to the monks. The same day, huge bonfires were lit to burn the evil, after the statue of the saint was paraded on a white horse (nowadays a great fire is still lit but under the strict control of firefighters, and a white horse is no longer used to carry the statue). Sacred pigs proliferated in the city and were only banned in 1663–1664 because of an accident: during the solemn procession in honour of Saint Januarius, a piglet slipped between the legs of a bishop who fell over with a great crash.

Gradually, the monks who took over from the early followers of Saint Anthony lost their predecessors' pharmaceutical knowledge. However, belief in the benefits of pork fat was so tenacious that until the end of the 19th century, every 17 January, a monk offered worshippers a small piece of bacon wrapped in a image of the saint folded into a cone.

SAINT ANTHONY'S MONKS AND THE TEMPLARS

The Knights of Saint Anthony belonged to an ecclesiastical and hospitaller order founded in 1095 at Vienne in the south of France. They were called to Naples by the Angevin kings but driven out by the Aragonese in the 15th century. Wearing a white cloak bearing a distinctive blue *tau* (known as Saint Anthony's Cross), the last letter of the Hebrew alphabet (modern *tav*), the main vocation of these noble laymen was to care for the sick – they founded some 370 hospitals throughout Europe.

It is possible that some Templars, after the suppression of their order, converted to monks of the Order of Hospitallers of Saint Anthony.

At Naples, the wounded brought back from the Holy Land were treated in the hospital opposite the church of Sant'Antonio Abate (Saint Anthony the Hermit). There seem to have been some Templars among them who, according to the local elders, are thought to have left traces of their passage in the underground tunnels criss-crossing Borgo Sant'Antonio Abate. So it could have been the Templars who revealed the secret of the miraculous ointment to the monks.

A STRANGE PROCESSION AND A BUNGLED THEFT

Neapolitans' devotion to this saint in whose honour they held the first winter festival was such that the procession lasted ten days! It began on 6 January and ended on the 16th, the eve of the feast itself.

On the first day, the gilded silver statue of Saint Anthony was brought from the cathedral and set on the right of Saint Janarius, then paraded in a carriage drawn by a white horse preceded by a band of trumpeters. The procession passed through all the city neighbourhoods where the merchants competed for the "visit of the saint", who was supposed to protect them from misfortune. The luckiest ones welcomed the statue by showering it with gifts and money. In the evening, Saint Anthony was housed in the first convenient church along the route.

The crowd meanwhile jubilantly cheered the procession along by lighting fires. On the evening of the 16th, the statue was displayed in its home church; during this final part of the route, people were invited to throw out all their old wooden goods for burning in the grand closing bonfire, so as to destroy all the negative vibes from the previous year. On the 17th, the blessing of the animals took place.

In 1808, as the statue stood in the church of Sant'Antonio Abate, thieves stole the silver bust of Saint Blaise and then tried to make off with Saint Anthony, hauling the statue up with ropes they had slipped through one of the church windows. But the ropes gave way and the thugs took to their heels. This incident gave rise to the proverb *"Saglia Antuono ca Biase è sagliuto"* (Let Anthony up because Blaise is up), which is repeated when an event or person is expected to follow another event or person.

BLESSING OF THE ANIMALS

Saint Anthony, who was supposed to have healed a dying piglet that a sow left at his feet, was soon attributed with the power to protect pigs and other animals. So in modern Italy and elsewhere, a number of priests conduct a blessing of the animals on 17 January, the saint's feast day (supposed date of his death around AD 340). Where once only farm animals were concerned as they represented a valuable source of income, nowadays all animals are welcome without exception: dogs, cats, rabbits, horses, even snakes, camels and other exotic animals that eccentric owners like to keep.

Throughout pre-war southern Italy, Naples included, the ritual was to have the animals turn three times in a circle around the church, the figure 3 and the circle being notorious magical symbols. In Naples, this only concerned horses: every Sunday from 17 January until the first day of Lent, the people celebrated the same ritual around this church as previously held around the statue of Virgil's horse. Other relics of that time are in the form of biscuits coated with white icing sold in the streets around the church during the festival (see p. 293). These are copies of the crescent loaves with which the horses used to be decorated.

Today, the festivities have been markedly toned down. As the benediction service has replaced the ancient ritual in Naples (as elsewhere), the ceremony takes place at early Mass and the animals are blessed in the church itself.

CURIOSITIES OF SAN GENNARO CATACOMBS

13 Via Tondo di Capodimonte
Basilica of Madre del Buon Consiglio
• Bus: R4, C63, 178 (Capodimonte stop)
• Metro: Line 1 Museo, Line 2 Cavour
• Tel: 081 7443714 • prenotazioni@catacombedinapoli.it
• Guided tours every hour Monday to Saturday, 10am–5pm, Sunday 10am–1pm
• Admission: €8, concessions €5

> **The strange stone phallus and the deaconess's fresco**

I n the catacombs of San Gennaro (which are as vast and rich as Rome's), in the middle of a square room there sits a phallic stele that has intrigued experts ever since its discovery in the 18th century. From the name of the god Priapus cut into the stone to the seemingly meaningless inscription in a language resembling Hebrew, an air of mystery still hangs over the significance of this stele.

Since the Greek god of fertility, Priapus, is associated with orgiastic rites, researchers exclude any connection with the Christian religion and even less with Judaism – not known for its predilection for sexual rites. Professor Lacerenza, an academic expert in Hebrew language and culture, hypothesises that the stele doesn't date from antiquity but from the 18th century, when it was thought to have been taken into the catacombs by clever but naughty eccentrics to have some fun at the expense of posterity. If this is a hoax it has certainly been successful, given the amount of publicity surrounding it.

THE NOBLE CERULA AND A HITHERTO UNKNOWN SAINT PAUL

During restoration work in 2011, in an upper gallery to the left of the extraordinary fresco that adorns a deaconess's tomb, a magnificent fresco of Saint Paul has emerged from under a thick layer of plaster. The exceptionally well-preserved painting is distinctive as much for the brilliance of its colours as for its expressive features.

Cerula, the deaconess, holds two open Gospels – a very unusual occurrence according to the director of the catacombs, Father Antonio Loffredo, in the sense that open Gospels are a prerogative of images of bishops. The veil covering the woman's head and chest is decorated with a purple border with dancing cupids printed (or embroidered) around it. Although this detail is a sign of wealth, it also reflects the Coptic or Eastern origins of Cerula, which at the same time testifies to the presence of Christians fleeing persecution by the Arian Vandals, following their leader Quodvultdeus, the Bishop of Carthage exiled to Naples whose tomb is in the bishops' crypt of these catacombs.

LA SANITÀ BRIDGE

124 Via Sanità
• Metro: Line 1 Museo, Line 2 Cavour

***Bridge
in a cloister***

The so-called "La Sanità" bridge was built in 1807 on the orders of Joseph Bonaparte to connect the city centre with the Royal Palace of Capodimonte, which was very difficult to reach. To achieve this new route that would span the valley of the densely populated La Sanità neighbourhood, architect Nicola Leandro, who was site manager, did not hesitate to "desecrate" the beautiful monastic complex of Santa Maria della Sanità: the grand cloister of the monastery was completely demolished while the smallest and most original cloister, which was oval-shaped, was partially vandalised and disfigured with a huge pillar as seen today.

The La Sanità bridge changed its name in 2011 and is now known as the "Maddalena Cerasuolo" bridge in homage to a member of the resistance who managed to stop the German troops who were preparing to blow it up to cut the city off from the Allies' northern advance.

MODEL OF BATTAGLINO CHARIOT

Church of Sant'Agostino degli Scalzi
Salita San Raffaele, 6 Via Sant'Agostino degli Scalzi
• Metro: Line 1 Dante, Line 2 Montesanto
• Visits: Saturday and Sunday, 10am–12 noon

In the sacristy of Sant'Agostino degli Scalzi is a wooden model of a chariot containing a variety of sacred representations dominated by the statue of the Immaculate Virgin. The sculpture dates from the mid-18th century and the artist is unknown. The model recalls the lavish floats used in the 17th century for Easter Saturday processions,

An unexpected testimony of former ecclesiastical splendour

which were named after the gentleman who introduced them: Pompeo Battaglino, who was also the sponsor of the great pomp of these celebrations.

The Easter procession took on such importance that the most eminent dignitaries from the viceroyalty, the militia of the three Knightly Orders of Spain, the royal guards, the yeomen of the guard, the most eminent prelates of the city and the archconfraternities all took part. Although the procession was abolished in 1749 because of its prohibitive cost, it had become so famous that Italian and European personalities made a special effort to be there.

Until the early 20th century, when a Neapolitan wanted to indicate something grandiose, he would say that "it looked like a Battaglino chariot".

THE CAPTAIN'S SKULL ㉕

Cimitero delle Fontanelle
80 Via Fontanelle
• Metro: Line 1 Museo or Materdei, Line 2 Cavour; Bus: C51
• Tel: 081 5573913
• Open 10am–5pm • Admission free

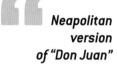

Neapolitan version of "Don Juan"

Among the mass of skulls piled up in the central aisle of Fontanelle cemetery – known as the aisle of the *anime pezzentelle* (see opposite) – the skull of the captain, distinguished by the number of candles placed in front of its *scarabattola* (mini-chapel), is the subject of an amazing legend.

A feisty local youth, who was an incorrigible womaniser, used to meet his conquests in the cemetery. One evening, after that day's lover had left, he wanted to smoke a cigarette. All of a suddenly the eye-sockets of the skulls

around him lit up like eyes of fire and stared at him as a sign of reprobation. The young man laughed and challenged death, inviting it to his coming wedding. On the wedding day, during the feast, a carabineer dressed in black arrived and sat at a table without speaking or eating. Asked who he was, he replied that he'd only reveal that in private to the married couple. So they went with the carabineer to a room away from the crowd and he asked the youth if he remembered the invitation he had issued in the cemetery. Once again the miscreant laughed at the stranger and even offered to shake his hand. The captain took off his uniform, revealing his skeleton, and struck the couple down on the spot (adapted from Roberto De Simone, *Novelle K666*, Einaudi, 2007).

THE FORGOTTEN HISTORY OF THE FONTANELLE

The 16th and 17th centuries were particularly disastrous for Naples: earthquakes, eruptions, famines and epidemics followed one another (the 1656 plague alone killed 250,000 out of 400,000 residents), with everything made worse by the negligence of the Spanish viceroys. As the church cemeteries were full to capacity, gravediggers exhumed bodies by night, without the knowledge of the families, and threw them into the mass grave in the old Fontanelle quarry (outside the city walls at the time). They were so numerous and so crudely buried that whenever there was a heavy storm, the torrents of silty water flowing down from Capodimonte hill washed out the corpses that the terrified residents then saw floating down the streets.

When in 1837 church burial grounds were demolished, according to Amedeo Colella (*Manuale di napoletanità*, 2010), Fontanelle cemetery is thought to have held 8 million skeletons.

In 1872, the ossuary was redesigned by Father Gaetano Barbati with the support of local women and divided into three sections. To the left, the "priests' aisle" houses all the bones from the churches and their congregations, with at the bottom a very evocative cave known as the "Tribunal". It is here that, for over a century, the Camorra (Neapolitan criminal organisation) godfathers would meet for their initiatory rites and oaths of allegiance in blood, as well as to issue death warrants. In the centre, the "plague aisle" takes in all the victims of epidemics. To the right, in the *"anime pezzentelle"* (poor little souls) aisle, a chapel is festooned with thousands of femurs, stacked like books, surmounted by skulls which are said to be arranged in male/female pairs. "This is the library of the dead who are engaged [to be married], not of dead fiancés", declared a young boy who showed Roberto De Simone round in the 1970s (see p. 289).

After its closure following the ban imposed by the Church in 1968 (see p. 303), the ossuary was restored and it was reopened to the public in 2011.

THE WOMAN KILLED BY GNOCCHI AND OTHER FONTANELLE TALES

During the Second World War, an American soldier came to pray for the souls of the "library fiancés" (see above) to heal his daughter, who had an incurable disease. His prayers were answered and the daughter recovered. So the soldier hastened back to the cemetery to thank the "fiancés", but he suffered a heart attack and dropped dead in front of them. "He died of joy," exclaimed Michelino, Roberto De Simone's young guide, "and now you can see his picture here." There were indeed stacks of photos in the Fontanelle at the time (according to Roberto De Simone, *Novelle K666*, Einaudi, 2007). Although the corpses in Fontanelle cemetery are usually unnamed, those laid to rest in a glass coffin in the "priests' aisle" on the left are the Count of Cerreto, Filippo Carafa and his wife Margherita Petrucci, who died at the end of the 18th century. The mummified body of the woman with a gaping mouth, as if she was vomiting, fired people's imagination. They explained this oddity in their own way: the countess must have choked on her gnocchi ...

For the cult of souls in Purgatory, see following double-page spread.

THE CULT OF SOULS IN PURGATORY: WHEN THE DEAD AND THE LIVING HELP EACH OTHER TO REACH PARADISE

Although the cult of the dead is practised in different ways in other regions of Italy and around the world, that of the souls in Purgatory exists only in Naples, the city where death cohabits particularly lightly with life. And Purgatory – middle Earth between Hell and Paradise – is the ideal point where the living and the dead are not too far removed.

In Neapolitan culture the dead have always been honoured as they were in life and "friendly" relations maintained with the deceased, but from the 17th century the souls in Purgatory came to the forefront in popular beliefs. At that time, survivors of the many plagues that befell Naples began to develop a symbiotic relationship with the dead: the living, thanks to their prayers and devotion, would help the dead to ascend to Heaven; once up there, the dead would intercede on behalf of their benefactor with the saints and the Virgin. The souls in Purgatory would thus heal the sick, find good husbands for young women, bring back an unfaithful lover and even give out winning lotto numbers (see p. 192), the only way for the impoverished to aspire to a better life.

This cult is physically expressed in two ways: by mini-chapels still scattered around the streets of the historic centre, and specific signs of devotion that can be seen in the hypogea of some churches and in Fontanelle cemetery (see p. 301). In the mini-chapels, the statuettes or paintings of souls in Purgatory are all in a similar style: surrounded by flames with arms raised to the sky, where there is a holy image, each representing a trade or social situation (public writer, fisherman, priest, mother and daughter, married couple ...). In the ossuaries you can see skulls placed in mini-chapels with rosaries, embroidered handkerchiefs, flowers, candles and ex-votos set before them.

This ritual was practised by women, known as *'e maste* (the bosses): every Monday (the day formerly devoted to lunar deities of darkness, such as Hecate or Diana) they would go into the ossuaries and after carefully cleaning their "chosen one", recite prayers to him or her until they reached a peak of histrionics, sometimes culminating in a trance. The pact between the *masta* and the deceased was only sealed under certain conditions: she began by choosing a skull from among the thousands piled up in the tomb, cleaned it with alcohol and covered it with a white cloth – preference being given to children, who, since antiquity, have been considered as intermediaries between the two worlds. If at night the *masta* dreamed of a stranger who revealed his or her identity and life-story, the link with

the "chosen one" was established: the following Monday, the white cloth was replaced with an embroidered handkerchief and the "contract" was signed.

Some of the "chosen" became famous after having accomplished many miracles (see below).

Following the Second Vatican Council (1962–1965), the ecclesiastical court banned the cult of the unknown dead in 1969, calling it "superstitious, arbitrary and therefore inadmissible", because "the holiness of the living person could not be demonstrated". So some ossuaries were closed. But the Neapolitans, used to the art of braving prohibitions that stifle their freedom and culture, have persevered, even if nowadays to a lesser extent.

WHAT IS "REFRISCO"?

The prayers and attention lavished on the dead are referred to as *refrisco* (freshness or coolness) in the Neapolitan dialect because they soothe the suffering caused by the flames of Purgatory. "Refrisco" is derived from the Latin *refrigerium*, a word used by the Romans to describe the funeral rituals designed to assist the deceased in their journey to the next world. The early Christians understood *refrigerium* as "comfort", either spiritual or material (a banquet or alms), to sooth the soul of the deceased.

Incidentally, the typical phrase used by a true Neapolitan who wishes to warmly thank someone is: *"Frisco all'aneme 'e tutte 'e muorte tuoje"* (Comfort and peace to the souls of all your dear departed).

On the other hand, to curse someone, a Neapolitan will utter imprecations against the souls of the dead relatives of the "enemy".

SWEATING SKULLS

Some skulls that don't collect dust but droplets that look like sweat are thought to be miraculous (see, for example, the skull of Donna Concetta in Fontanelle cemetery). This phenomenon is due to the fact that in some places, particularly where there is high humidity, dust simply doesn't lie. As for the "sweat", it's only condensation.

There's a very unusual museum of souls in Purgatory in Rome – see *Secret Rome* in this series of guides.

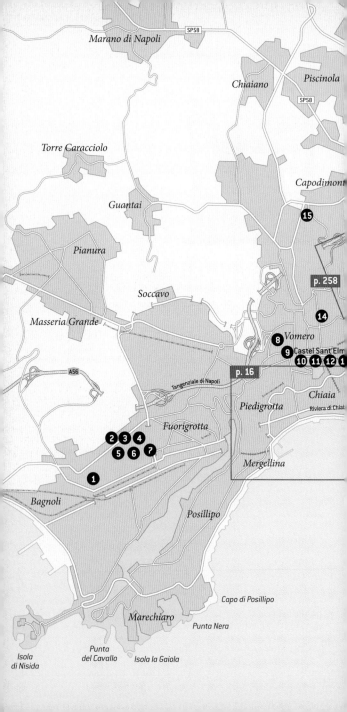

p. 258

p. 16

OUTSIDE THE CENTRE WEST

1 NEAPOLITAN RIDING ACADEMY 304
2 GOLDEN CUBE IN THE EXHIBITION PARK 306
3 TUNNELS BELOW FONTANA DELL'ESEDRA 309
4 A ROMAN ROAD BELOW THE EXHIBITION PARK 309
5 RAI PRODUCTION CENTRE 310
6 ROMAN BATHS ON VIA TERRACINA 312
7 NAVAL BASIN OF THE HYDRODYNAMIC LABORATORY 314
8 GUIDO DONATONE PRIVATE MUSEUM 316
9 BAS-RELIEF OF THE *TRIUMPH OF DEATH* 318
10 SERGIO RAGNI'S PRIVATE COLLECTION 321
11 GOTHIC TUNNELS BELOW SAN MARTINO 323
12 DELLA VICARIA TRIBUNAL COLUMN 325
13 MERIDIAN OF THE CARTHUSIANS 327
14 PARCO VIVIANI 332
15 CENTRALE ABC (ACQUA BENE COMUNE NAPOLI) DELLO SCUDILLO . . . 334

NEAPOLITAN RIDING ACADEMY ①

Circolo "La Staffa"
37 Via Beccadelli (access by Viale della Liberazione)
• Metro: Line 2 Campi Flegrei; Rail: Ferrovia Cumana, from Montesanto (Mostra stop)
• Visits: contact Carla Travierso, Consigliere alla Casa
• Tel: 081 5703619

*A park
with splendid
ancient pines,
home to an elite club*

The "U. De Carolis" Neapolitan riding academy, founded in 1937, is located in a 3 hectare park scattered with ancient pines and cypress-flanked avenues – totally unexpected in a heavily urbanised neighbourhood.

You can book a visit to the attractive premises of the prestigious La Staffa

club. Its large rooms, decorated in typical 19th-century Neapolitan style, are richly furnished with 18th-century pieces bequeathed by the city's most eminent aristocratic families, notably by the academy's founder, the Marquis Riccardo De Luca di Roseto.

You'll also appreciate the pieces made by the Giustiniani, the famous Neapolitan ceramicists. In the main salon, a wide bay window overlooks the large indoor arena where riding lessons and competitions are held.

The Neapolitan Riding Academy, near the Mostra d'Oltremare complex (see p. 307), was opened in 1940 by King Victor Emmanuel III. In the following years it was patronised by the most illustrious Neapolitan and Italian riders, including Prince Umberto of Savoy.

After the Second World War, thanks to its founder the Marquis De Luca (who was the academy's director for over thirty years), the indoor arena, the La Staffa club and the two swimming pools were rebuilt.

GOLDEN CUBE IN THE EXHIBITION PARK

Mostra d'Oltremare
54 Via John Fitzgerald Kennedy
• Metro: Line 2 Campi Flegrei; Rail: Ferrovia Cumana (Mostra stop)
• Tel: 081 7258000
• presidenza@mostradoltremare.it • www.mostradoltremare.it
• Visits from Tuesday to Saturday 6pm–midnight, Sunday and public
holidays 10am–midnight • Admission €1
(NB: access also by Piazzale Vincenzo Tecchio)

**A corner
of Africa**

Some of the attractions in the huge exhibition and recreational park of the Mostra d'Oltremare (Exhibition of Overseas Territories) are still little known to Neapolitans.

The "golden cube", for example, is one of the pavilions devoted to Italian East Africa built during the 1940 Triennial Art Exhibition. Inside, the walls were frescoed by Giovanni Brancaccio with depictions of Julius Caesar and Mussolini on horseback. The exterior of the pavilion is covered with an ochre-

coloured mosaic whose golden reflections in sunny weather earned the building its name. The work is inspired by the architecture of the Ethiopian city of Aksum.

A little further on, the "Fasilides baths" in the centre of a little lake recall the castle of the Emperor Fasilides at Gondar, also in Ethiopia. This monument commemorates the colonisation of the Mussolini era: the city of Gondar, whose castle was restored by Governor Mazzetti in 1938, became the symbol of Italy's occupation of Ethiopia.

Leaving behind the avenue of palm trees, you'll come across the Rhodes pavilion, which is Arabist in style; Giovanni Battista Ceas took the Order of Hospitallers' medieval inns as his model.

The Mostra d'Oltremare, originally known as the Mostra Triennale delle Terre Italiane d'Oltremare (Triennial Exhibition of the Italian Lands Overseas), inaugurated in 1940, is the very image of fascist propaganda. After suffering severe damage during the war, the park was rebuilt and renamed the Mostra Triennale del Lavoro Italiano all'Estero (Triennial Exhibition of Italian Work around the World), becoming an example of Mediterranean post-war rationalism.

TUNNELS BELOW FONTANA DELL'ESEDRA ❸

Mostra d'Oltremare
54 Via John Fitzgerald Kennedy
• Metro: Line 2 Campi Flegrei; Rail: Ferrovia Cumana (Mostra stop)
• Tel: 081 7258000
• info@mostradoltremare.it • www.mostradoltremare.it
• Visits from Tuesday to Saturday 6pm–midnight, Sunday and public holidays 10am–midnight
• Booking required by email: presidenza@mostradoltremare.it
(NB: access also by Piazzale Vincenzo Tecchio)

You can book a visit to the tunnels under the Esedra fountain at the Mostra d'Oltremare. The fountain, 230 m long and 20 m wide and covering 900 m², is one of the largest in the world. The highest water jet reaches 40 m. At certain evening events, when water jets and lights play to the rhythm of music, 140 projectors illuminate the scene.

Below one of the largest fountains in the world

NEARBY

A ROMAN ROAD BELOW THE EXHIBITION PARK ❹

During construction work on the complex, some Roman remains were discovered – a road, a mausoleum and an aqueduct. The stretch of road, which is 200 m long and paved with lava stones, formed part of a highway from Naples to the large commercial port of Pozzuoli, which intersected a secondary route. The surface of the heavily used road is worn in places by chariot wheels. You can also see the remains of a pavement. After the damage caused by the Second World War, the small archaeological park was restored thanks to the renowned archaeologist, Professor Amedeo Maiuri. The mausoleum and chapel opposite were reconstructed following the original model.

RAI PRODUCTION CENTRE

5

9 Viale Guglielmo Marconi
• Metro: Line 2 Campi Flegrei; Rail: Ferrovia Cumana (Mostra stop)
• Visits can be arranged in May during the annual "Maggio dei Monumenti" event
• www.comune.napoli.it
• cpnarainapoli@rai.it

A "television factory"

Construction of the Naples headquarters of Rai (Radiotelevisione italiana, Italy's national broadcasting company), over an area of 18,000 m², began in 1958 and was completed in 1961, when the first recording took place. If it's not in use, you can visit the TV1 studio (area 800 m², 12 m

high), one of the largest in Europe, where such series are made as *Un Posto al sole* (A Place in the Sun), a huge hit since 1996. In the corridor leading to the studio, wall paintings show the main actors and "guest stars" of this TV soap. Among the other areas accessible to visitors is the studio hosting regional news programmes. Original pieces of equipment have been preserved here and there by way of souvenir.

Rai's sound archives of Neapolitan songs, with over 40,000 digitised pieces, also feature in the tour, as does the auditorium where you can admire the organ with 10,000 pipes, the largest in Europe.

ROMAN BATHS ON VIA TERRACINA ⑥

Via Terracina junction with Viale Marconi
• Metro: Line 2 Campi Flegrei; Rail: Ferrovia Cumana (Mostra stop)
• Tel: 081 5529002
• rootsdiscoverycf@gmail.com
• Gruppo Archeologico Napoletano • info@ganapoletano.it
• Open on certain occasions or on reservation with Associazione
Culturale "Roots Discovery"

2,000-year old mod cons

A "rest area" of the Roman era on Via Terracina (2nd century AD) was discovered in 1939 about 2 m below street level during the construction of the Mostra d'Oltremare (see p. 307). These excavations, which had been forgotten for

decades, were recently reopened to the public – although only on certain occasions.

This installation on a busy road linking Naples to the commercial port of Pozzuoli was equipped with baths, latrines and other facilities for the comfort of passing travellers. Black and white mosaics on marine themes can still be seen: in their bathhouses, the Romans generally avoided colourful mosaics that could be damaged by steam and moisture. The building was equipped with an ingenious system to recycle water: after being used for bathing, it poured into small channels used to clean the latrines.

NAVAL BASIN OF THE HYDRODYNAMIC LABORATORY

Faculty of Naval Engineering, University of Naples Federico II
21 Via Claudio
• Metro: Line 2 Campi Flegrei; Rail: Ferrovia Cumana (Mostra stop)
• Tel: 081 7683308 • miranda@unina.it • www.dii.unina.it
• Visits on reservation

Europe's largest university naval engineering facilities

The Faculty of Naval Engineering's facilities are the largest in Europe. The huge pool, opened in 1980 and modernised a few years later, is 147 m long by 9 m wide and 4.20 m deep.

It is equipped with a device known as the "swell absorber", which is capable of reducing the impact of incidental swell by 95% on waves between 5 m and 7 m long.

On the sides of the pool, two rails are used to activate a gantry that can take a load of 28 tonnes: a small-scale boat is attached to it and lowered into the water to be tested under various atmospheric conditions. These tests are for yachts as well as cruisers or merchant ships.

Two beeps warn technicians and visitors when a test is about to be launched: the gantry operates with sudden accelerations that in an instant can reach 7 m per second.

GUIDO DONATONE PRIVATE MUSEUM ⑧

Villa Costanza, 12 Vico Acitillo
• Metro: Line 1 Quattro Giornate
• Tel: 081 5792010 • guido.donatone@alice.it
• Visits only in summer (except August) for cultural associations, on reservation by e-mail or phone
• Collection under anti-theft surveillance 24/7

A rare collection of antique ceramics

Y ou can book a visit to the Guido Donatone private museum, an authentic collection of Neapolitan and Campanian ceramics whose most representative pieces have been declared national heritage by the Italian Ministry of Culture.

The museum's halls still retain the precious 19th-century Colonnese floor tiles from the renowned manufacturers. Among the many wonderful pieces are two huge and eye-catching plates made in Naples in the 18th century, decorated with vignettes taken from French engravings. These plates are known as "imperial" due to their exceptional size – 60 cm in diameter – whereas the largest pieces manufactured in other Italian workshops measure only 45 cm.

Also not to be missed are the stoups of Borrominian inspiration from Cerreto (near Reggio Emilia), the rare 15th-century tiles and, displayed in the centre of one room, a beautiful litter for aristocrat transport – a minor masterpiece of Neapolitan Rococo decorated with paintings of Hercules and Diana the Huntress.

Professor Guido Donatone, who has written a couple of dozen specialised works and is one of the greatest ceramics historians, founded the Centro Studi per la Storia della Ceramica Meridionale (Centre for the Study of Ceramics from Southern Italy), based in Naples. The lengthy research of this dedicated historian led to the rediscovery of Neapolitan and Campanian production from the 15th and 16th centuries. These ceramics, found in museums in Italy and abroad, had always been attributed to artisans from Tuscany or Faenza.

It is thanks to Prof. Donatone that we now know that the production of highly sophisticated earthenware was launched in Naples under the Aragonese kings. Around 1447–1448, Alfonso the Magnanimous, the dynasty's first king, brought a great Arab ceramicist from Manises (near Valencia) who specialised in decorative tiled floors. This craftsman worked in the Aragonese Royal Palace of Castel Nuovo where there are records of a ceramics kiln, which so far hasn't been recovered, under a staircase in the courtyard.

The late neoclassical Villa Costanza, now Prof. Donatone's residence and museum, was built in the early 19th century by Filippo Angelillo, attorney general and advisor to the Bourbon King Ferdinand II. The villa miraculously escaped the rampant urbanisation of the 1950s.

BAS-RELIEF OF THE *TRIUMPH OF DEATH* ⑨

Certosa e Museo Nazionale di San Martino
Largo San Martino
• Funicular: Centrale (Piazza Fuga), Chiaia (Cimarosa), Montesanto (Morghen), then bus V1
• Daily except Wednesday 8.30am–7.30pm

> *Death, which does not yield to the temptation of money*

In the epigraphic section of the remarkable (though little visited) San Martino Museum, the exceptional bas-relief *Triumph of Death* was saved from destruction at the last minute by archaeologist Giuseppe Fiorelli in 1862. In that year, the authorities of recently unified Italy, driven by iconoclastic fury, decided to destroy all sacred pictures "lying about" in the streets of Naples.

The bas-relief was outside the church of San Pietro Martire and dates from 1361. This work, the only bas-relief ever made in Naples, unlike all other similar works in Italy and Europe, is a rare example of folk art: the two characters are addressing one another (instead of the observer) as in a cartoon and the text is written in the vernacular despite its Gothic lettering. The depiction of a mortal who tries to subvert Death is also a first, because all other similar examples date from the 15th century and lack any inscriptions.

Here, Death wears two crowns as a sign of power. The hawk perched on the left arm and the lure in the right hand mean that Death continues its relentless pursuit despite the many victims symbolised by the thirteen corpses lying at its feet. Among these, the crowned head and the prelate indicate that the hunt is indiscriminate and cares little for social status.

To the right is shown the sponsor of the work, Franceschino da Brignale, a Genoese citizen (probably a merchant) who twice survived a shipwreck. He is emptying a bag full of gold coins and saying: "I want to give you all this if you let me go." Death replies: "Even if you gave as much of it as we could ask for, you could not escape death when your hour tolls."

The central inscription, on the other hand, addresses the reader by clearly describing the scene carved on the bas-relief. It ends with a warning and an incentive to behave as a good Christian.

In the border around the carving is the dedication from its sponsor: "I thank God the Father a thousand times […] for twice saving my life while everyone else drowned. I, Franceschino da Brignale, commissioned this work in memory of this received grace, 3 August 1361."

Above, there are two coats of arms of the Dominican Order, to which the church of San Pietro Martire belonged.

In its original setting, the bas-relief was well known. To refuse a request for a loan of money, Neapolitans used to say: "Why don't you ask Death at San Pietro Martire, who has plenty of it?"

The San Martino Museum, established in 1866 when the Certosa di San Martino (now closed down) was declared a national monument, is rarely visited despite being truly remarkable. Saint Martin's charterhouse itself, dating from 1325, is literally bursting with works of art. The building encompasses various architectural styles, each of the highest order (changes were made until the 17th century), forming a harmonious whole. The church, which is wealthy beyond imagination, is considered the essence of Neapolitan Baroque, with collections that encapsulate the glorious history of the city. To top it all, the building stands on the hill of the same name overlooking the Bay of Naples. From the the monastery's terraces, you can enjoy a 180° panorama. A visit is highly recommended.

SERGIO RAGNI'S PRIVATE COLLECTION

56 Via Aniello Falcone
• Funicular: Centrale (Piazza Fuga) or Chiaia (Cimarosa)
• Visits on reservation by phone or e-mail
• Tel: 081 5584442
• elleboro25@libero.it

A remarkable collection of Rossini artefacts

T he stunning collection that Sergio Ragni has put together in his immense apartment, which occupies part of the splendid Villa Belvedere, is a yardstick for many musicologists. It consists of artefacts relating to music, particularly the work of Gioachino Rossini, who lived in Naples from 1815 to 1822.

Among the rarest pieces are autographed scores, such as the alternative ending to *William Tell* written for the Bologna opera house in 1840, and the *Cantata in Honour of Pius IX*, a very rare composition by the maestro after his decision to give up music and the theatre.

The letters written by Rossini (over 150, many addressed to his father) represent one of the largest collections of Rossini correspondence in existence.

There are also hundreds of documents (contracts, orders, correspondence with impresarios) on Rossini's theatrical activities in Italy from 1809 to 1824; the autographs of musicians he frequented, as well as singers trained in his repertoire; rare portraits of his first wife, the famed Spanish soprano Isabella Colbran; letters and the contract signed by Isabella with impresario Barbaja to perform at the San Carlo and the Fondo (now the Mercadante theatre); a quantity of scores, often first editions printed in Italy, France and Germany, revealing the wide range of the composer's work; an impressive set of biographical and critical works from the first edition of Stendhal's *Life of Rossini* to comprehensive studies by the Rossini Foundation of Pesaro, without equal in any Italian library; an almost complete collection of contemporary press cuttings illustrating the maestro's work; an audio archive including all recordings of his music … In one corner, there is even a pair of stiletto heels that belonged to Maria Callas.

Villa Belvedere, built in 1671 by Flemish banker Ferdinando Vandeneynden, then bought by the Carafa family, opens onto one of the most beautiful views of Naples. The Cenacolo Belvedere reception rooms are on the first floor.

GOTHIC TUNNELS BELOW SAN MARTINO

5 Largo San Martino
• Metro: Line 1 Vanvitelli, then bus V1
• Funicular: Centrale (Piazza Fuga), Chiaia (Cimarosa), Montesanto (Morghen) then bus V1
• Tel: 081 2294541
• sspsae-na.sanmartino@beniculturali.it
• Visits on request

The monks' tunnels

A fter thirty years of work, the underground tunnels of the superb Charterhouse and Museum of San Martino were reopened to the public under the name "Gothic Underground" because they date back to the founding of the monastery (1325), which was designed by the renowned architect Tino da Camaino. There is a profusion of statues, architectural fragments and commemorative plaques from buildings lost during the Risanamento in the late 19th century (see p. 41). Between the powerful arcades of this timeless place, these relics tell of 400 years of the history of Naples, from the 14th to 18th centuries. Among the most significant pieces are a Madonna by Tino da Camaino and the *Triumph of Death* bas-relief (see p. 318).

D. ON PETRVS DETHOLETO
MARCHIO VILLE FRANCHIE
GENERE CAESAR IN PRESENTI
REGNO VICE REX LOCVM
TENENS GENERALIS CAN
TANIVS PRINCEPS IVSTISSI
MVS EXCELLENTE MILITE
VID FERDINANDO FIGVE
ROA PALATIO HISPANO
REGENTE MAGNIAM CVRIAM
VICARIE CVRANTE ADILLO
RVM NOBSCH ABOLENDVM
QVICLAM NEMINE SPETTAN
TE BONIS DE BANT HVM
LOCVM · · ERVM IVAN
D'20 · · RDPOSTE PA
benefit · · VT VIOLENT
SCELVS · · IC ITERATO
SPECTA · · ID COMMODVM
MAGN · · VM CVPIDERIO

DELLA VICARIA TRIBUNAL COLUMN

Museo Nazionale di San Martino
5 Largo San Martino
• Metro: Line 1 Vanvitelli
• Funicular: Centrale (Piazza Fuga), Chiaia (Cimarosa), Montesanto (Morghen)
• Open every day except Wednesday, 8.30am–7.30pm (ticket office closes 6.30pm)
• Admission: €6, concessions €3

Debtor's "pillory"

I n the National Museum of San Martino, on the left side of the passageway where two old coaches are displayed, is a column known as the "colonna della Vicaria", which formerly stood in front of Castel Capuano (see pp. 255 and 357). Anyone in debt was subject to an infamous punishment – to avoid being condemned to the galleys, he had to lower his trousers and embrace the column while reciting a formula inviting his creditors to confiscate all his property to recover their dues. This "ceremony" was all the more humiliating in that it attracted a crowd of passers-by whose gibes the hapless debtor had

to endure. The practice was abolished in 1546 and replaced by a public "confession" service, followed by the obligation to always wear a hat with distinctive signs sewn on it, recognisable to all.

The column was also a kind of "morgue": all unidentified bodies were placed there in the hope that someone might recognise them. The corpses were left in place until the smell became unbearable. This macabre function wasn't banned until 1856.

A stone for meting out a similar punishment can also be seen in Florence (see *Secret Florence* in this series of guides).

The humiliating exposure suffered by debtors has marked the souls of the Neapolitans: even today, to indicate somebody going away empty-handed, they say *"se ne ji cu na mana annanze e n'ata arreto"* (to leave with one hand in front and the other behind), implying hide one's private parts.

MERIDIAN OF THE CARTHUSIANS

Museo Nazionale di San Martino
5 Largo San Martino
• Metro: Line 1 Vanvitelli, then bus VI • Funicular: Centrale (Piazza Fuga), Chiaia (Cimarosa), Montesanto (Morghen), then bus V1
• Tel: 848 800288 or 06 39967050
• Open every day except Wednesday 8.30am–7.30pm (ticket office closes 6.30pm) • Admission: €6, concessions €3
• Group reservations from Monday to Saturday 9am–1.30pm and 2.30pm–5pm

Astronomy as an art form

The meridian that features in the former prior's apartment at Saint Martin's Charterhouse (room 33) is a superb work of art as well as an astronomical masterpiece.

Despite being lower than the best-known meridians (see p. 331), it is still one of the most comprehensive and beautiful examples in Italy. It was designed in 1771 by Rocco Bovi, who left his signature in a metal plate set into the magnificent floor with its majolica tiles representing the constellations and signs of the zodiac, made in 1771 by the great ceramicist Leonardo Chiaiese.

On the bronze columnar strips are engraved graduations intrinsic to the diurnal half-day, expressed in hours and minutes in order to determine the daily sunrise and sunset and the height and declination of the Sun.

Note also the indications of the solar cycle, the "Dominical Letter" (assigning the dates on which Sundays fall in a given year following a perpetual calendar), the degrees of the ecliptic that mark the path of the Sun against the background of the celestial sphere, a geometric scale from the Tychonic system (developed in the 16th century by Danish astronomer Tycho Brae to calculate the orbits of the planets as they were known at the time) with respect to the Earth and the Sun, and other related measurements. There are also indications of the winter and summer solstices.

Note also two pretty wind roses in grey marble and copper: on the one with thirty-two winds, four continents (Europe, Africa, Asia and America) are indicated with the north rotated by 90°.

The superb representation of the constellations, defined by little stars along the meridian line, corresponds with the time of year when they transit the local meridian at midnight.

Notable among the various symbols and engraved images are a human face (self-portrait of the artist?), a seascape with boat and seagulls, the Sun with the sign of Cancer and some small houses, as well as a bay (Naples?) and a mountainous landscape: small details that add a poetic note to this superb composition.

For more on meridians and their origin, see following double-page spreads.

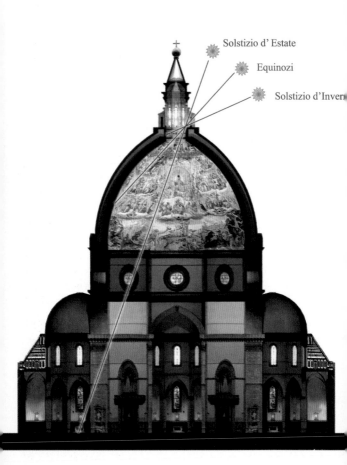

Solstizio d' Estate

Equinozi

Solstizio d'Inver

HOW DOES A MERIDIAN WORK?

Instead of using the shadow of a gnomon, these use a small hole placed at a certain height, through which the Sun's rays fall onto a meridian line (i.e. one aligned exactly north–south. The fact that the Sun's rays perform the function of the shadow in a traditional sundial means that the opening is sometimes referred to as a "gnomonic opening". The higher the opening, the more efficient the meridian, hence the interest in using cathedrals (see "Why were meridians installed in cathedrals?", p. 331); the circumference of the hole had to be no more than one thousandth of the height above the ground. Obviously, the opening had to be installed on the south side of the building in order to let in the rays of the Sun, which lies to the south in the northern hemisphere.

The meridian line should run from the point that stands perpendicularly below the axis of the opening, not always easy to determine using the instruments available to scientists in the past. The length of the line depends on the height of the opening; in some cases, where the building was not long enough to trace the entire meridian line across the floor (as was the case at Saint-Sulpice in Paris), an obelisk was added at the far end, so that the movement of the Sun's rays could then be measured up the vertical. In summer, when the Sun is highest in the sky, the rays fall onto the meridian line closer to the south wall (where that line begins) than in winter, when the Sun is lower over the horizon and the rays tend to strike towards the far end of the meridian line.

The main principle behind the working of the meridian is that at noon, solar time, the Sun is at its apex and, by definition, its rays fall straight along a line running exactly north–south. So the exact moment when those rays strike the meridian line, which does run north–south, indicates solar noon. Furthermore, the exact place on the meridian line where that ray falls makes it possible to determine the day of the year: the point right at the beginning of the line is reached solely on the day of the summer solstice, whereas the exact end of the line is reached on the day of the winter solstice. Experience and observation meant that the meridian line could be calibrated to identify different days of the year.

Once this was done, the line could be used to establish the date of various movable feasts, such as Easter – one of the great scientific and religious uses of meridians. Similarly, the different periods corresponding to the signs of the zodiac could be established, which explains why such signs are indicated along the length of a number of meridian lines.

WHY WAS 4 OCTOBER FOLLOWED IMMEDIATELY BY 15 OCTOBER IN THE YEAR 1582?
MEASUREMENT OF TIME AND ORIGIN OF THE MERIDIANS

The entire problem of the measurement of time and the establishment of calendars arises from the fact that the Earth does not take an exact number of days to orbit the Sun: one orbit in fact takes neither 365 nor 366 days but rather 365 days, 5 hours, 48 minutes and 45 seconds.

At the time of Julius Caesar, Sosigenes of Alexandria calculated this orbit as 365 days and 6 hours. In order to make up for this difference of an extra 6 hours, he proposed an extra day every fourth year: thus the Julian calendar – and the leap year – came into being.

In AD 325, the Council of Nicaea (called by Constantine, the first Roman emperor to embrace Christianity) established the temporal power of the Church. The Church's liturgical year contained fixed feasts such as Christmas, but also movable feasts such as Easter, which was of crucial importance as it commemorated the death and resurrection of Christ, and so the Church decided that it should fall on the first Sunday following the full moon after the spring equinox. That year, the equinox fell on 21 March, which was thus established as its permanent date.

However, over the years, observation of the heavens showed that the equinox (which corresponds with a certain known position of the stars) no longer fell on 21 March ... The 11 minutes and 15 seconds difference between the real and assumed time of the Earth's orbit around the Sun led to an increasing gap between the actual equinox and 21 March. By the 16th century, that gap had increased to ten full days and so Pope Gregory XIII decided to intervene. Quite simply, ten days would be removed from the calendar in 1582, and it would pass directly from 4 to 15 October. It was also decided, on the basis of complex calculations (carried out notably by the Calabrian astronomer Luigi Giglio), that the first year of each century (ending in 00) would not actually be a leap year, even though divisible by four. The exceptions would fall every 400 years, which would mean that in 400 years there would be a total of just 97 (rather than 100) leap years. This came closest to making up the shortfall resulting from the difference between the real and assumed time of orbit. Thus 1700, 1800 and 1900 would not be leap years, but 2000 would.

In order to establish the full credibility of this new calendar – and convince the various Protestant nations that continued to use the Julian calendar – Rome initiated the installation of great meridians within its churches. A wonderful scientific epic had begun ...

The technical name for a leap year is a bissextile year. The term comes from the fact that the additional day was once placed between 24 and 25 February. In Latin, 24 February was the sixth (*sextus*) day before the calends of March, hence the name *bis sextus*, to indicate a supplementary sixth day. The calends were the first day of each month in the Roman calendar.

THE HIGHEST MERIDIANS IN THE WORLD

From the 15th to the 18th centuries, some seventy meridians were installed in churches in France and Italy. Only ten, however, have a gnomonic opening that is more than 10 m above floor level – that height being crucial to the accuracy of the instrument:

Santa Maria del Fiore (Florence)	90.11 m
San Petronio (Bologna)	22.07 m
Saint-Sulpice (Paris)	26.00 m
Monastery of San Nicolo l'Arena (Catania, Sicily)	23.92 m
Cathedral (Milan)	23.82 m
Santa Maria degli Angeli (Rome)	20.34 m
Collège de l'Oratoire (Marseille)	17.00 m
San Giorgio (Modica, Sicily)	14.18 m
Museo Nazionale (Naples)	14.00 m
Cathedral (Palermo)	11.78 m

WHY WERE MERIDIANS INSTALLED IN CATHEDRALS?

To make their measurements more precise, astronomers required enclosed spaces where the point admitting light was as high as possible above the ground: the longer the beam of light, the more accurately they could establish that it was meeting the floor along an exactly perpendicular plane. Cathedrals were soon recognised as the ideal location for such scientific instruments as meridians. The Church had a vested interest as well, because meridians could be used to establish the exact date of Easter.

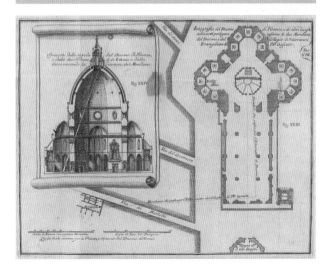

PARCO VIVIANI

14

Via Girolamo Santacroce (main entrance)
Salita di San Antonio ai Monti (side entrance), Via Cupa Vecchia
• Metro: Line 1 Salvator Rosa
• Open 7am–6pm from 1 to 31 March, 7am–7.30pm from 1 April to
30 June, 7am–8.30pm from 1 July to 31 August, 7am–7pm from 1 to
30 September, 7am–6pm from 1 to 31 October, 7am–4.30pm from
1 November to 28 February

A green
oasis
in a sea
of concrete

Viviani is a small park of just 2 hectares on the hillside where some species of Mediterranean shrub, such as agave, olive, pine and rosemary, have been preserved. The site offers panoramic views with very fine glimpses of sea and city.

A flight of steps also leads to a tunnel dug into the tuff by which you descend to the secondary exit below. Other passages, now blocked up, led to the historic centre of the city, thus linking the "upper" residential neighbourhoods with the popular ones "down below". The family that owned this domain spread ghost stories by calling themselves "Spiritillo" (Little Ghost) to scare away children who came to steal the fruit from their trees.

Raffaele Viviani (1888–1950), to whom the park is dedicated, is one of the greatest playwrights and poets in the Neapolitan dialect. He particularly liked this place, which he called "a little garden of happiness". Viviani was very close to the people and denounced their situation of extreme poverty in language of great dramatic energy. This author of immense stature is unknown abroad. The markedly Neapolitan spirit of his work is probably why he's been sidelined at the international level.

CENTRALE ABC (ACQUA BENE COMUNE NAPOLI) DELLO SCUDILLO ⓯

Via Serbatoio dello Scudillo
• By car: Tangenziale, Zona Ospedaliera exit
• Public transport: several buses go to the Ospedale Cardarelli terminus
• Visits only on certain occasions, such as the Fondo Ambiente Italiano (FAI) open days or for school groups (if insured) on request
• Information: www.fondoambiente.it • Tel: 800 884021
• www.abc.napoli.it • info@abc.napoli.it

Underground pools three times the size of a football stadium

You can book a visit to the "dello Scudillo" hydro plant, managed by the municipal company ABC, which supplies water to Naples and the surrounding municipalities, 1.6 million consumers in all.

The tours are rather limited as the site is subject to very strict rules because of the sensitive nature of public health facilities, so much so that up to the early 20th century the guards had orders to shoot intruders.

The part open to the sky is littered with relics of the former aqueduct, including a huge section of cast iron dating from 1885. In the covered parts you'll see bronze meters from the same period (the first in Italy) and old tools, as well as invoices from the 1950s with curious advertisements on the back.

After donning protective headgear, the tour continues down to the huge underground pools (the biggest are 330 m long, three times larger than a football stadium). At the end of a long corridor, you'll see a 310 m basin dug out of the rock face and filled with water. The mechanics of routing water to the higher-level districts are very impressive.

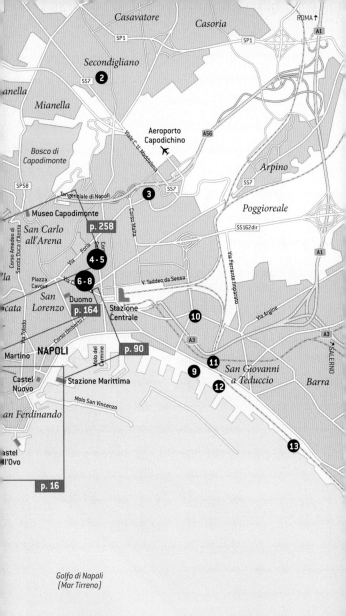

OUTSIDE THE CENTRE NORTH & EAST

1 CASA MUSEO DI PULCINELLA 338
2 MARADONA "MUSEUM" 341
3 CIMITERO DELLE 366 FOSSE 342
4 KELLER ARCHITETTURA STUDIO 345
5 CALABRESE ENCLOSED GARDEN 346
6 UNDERGROUND PASSAGE AT SAN GIOVANNI A CARBONARA 349
7 PARCO DI RE LADISLAO 351
8 ARCHIVIO STORICO DEL COMUNE DI NAPOLI 351
9 STATUE OF SAN GENNARO 353
10 CHURCH OF SAN CARLO BORROMEO ALLE BRECCE 356
11 ARCHIVIO NAZIONALE E STORICO ENEL 359
12 ART WORKSHOPS OF THE TEATRO SAN CARLO 360
13 MUSEO FERROVIARIO NAZIONALE DI PIETRARSA 362
14 MUSEO PRIVATO DELLE CARROZZE DI VILLA BIANCHI 366

CASA MUSEO DI PULCINELLA ❶

Piazza Castello
80011 Acerra (suburbs)
- Bus: 171, A37, A31 from Piazza Garibaldi (Napoli Centrale station)
- Tel: 081 8857249
- Open Monday to Friday 9am–1pm; also Monday, Wednesday, Thursday from 3pm–6pm; weekends by appointment
- Admission free

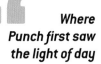

> ### Where Punch first saw the light of day

It was at Acerra, one of the Naples suburbs, where *Pulcinella* (Punch) is thought to have first seen the light of day. So it was at Acerra, in a castle dating back to the 9th century that belonged to the feudal lords of the city, that it was decided to pay tribute to this iconic character in a special section of the Pulcinella, Folklore and Peasant Culture Museum. Legends about his origins, old prints, photos of the most famous *Pulcinella* theatres and puppets from around the world take visitors on a trip through the imagination of a people.

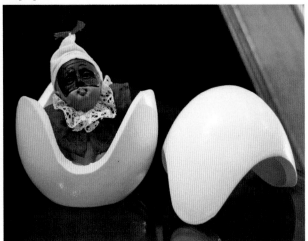

THE SYMBOLISM OF *PULCINELLA*, EXORCIST OF NEAPOLITANS' EXISTENTIAL ANGST

The origins of *Pulcinella* are uncertain. Although the character probably developed from a type of ancient theatre called *atellane* (from Atella, a city near Naples) in the 4th century BC, it was not until the 17th century that he was taken up by the commedia dell'arte. From the 18th century he became the most famous, the most studied and the most represented character (and puppet) in the world.

Far from Naples, he changes his name and sometimes loses some of his typical features. In Paris he's known as *Polichinelle*, in London *Punch*, in Istanbul *Karagoz*, in Spain *Don Cristobal*, in Germany *Kaspar* and in Moscow *Petruska*.

Roberto De Simone (see p. 289), an authority on the subject, claims that *Pulcinella* represents all aspects of Neapolitan popular culture, which, for thousands of years, has exorcised all its existential anxieties by inventing symbols, dances and, in this case, a character.

Pulcinella has in fact a rather funereal aspect: his black face with hooked nose, his spectral complexion, his deformities and his smock as white as a shroud are certainly scary enough; his nasal, croaking voice is not of this world.

His name probably derives from *pulcino* (chick) because, like a chick, he was hatched from a hen's egg – the hen is the creature sacred to Persephone, queen of the underworld (see pp. 58–59). *Pulcinella* thus embodies death and the misfortunes of humanity, but at the same time he wards them off with his cornucopia-shaped cap and his burlesque behaviour. The roles he plays are as numerous as the defects and qualities of a people, for *Pulcinella* is both comic and tragic, simple and smart, affable and arrogant, rich and poor, cowardly and brave, hopelessly stupid and amazingly resourceful, but always able to rise from the ashes, like any genuine Neapolitan.

His inherent and total ambivalence fits perfectly into the Neapolitan culture, where contradictions reign. He has a lover and is frequently lewd, but his Italian name sounds feminine and he is sometimes graphically depicted giving birth to small "clones" from his hump – this is the myth of the hermaphrodite that runs through Neapolitan culture. The androgynous *Pulcinella* also rhymes with *Verginella*, the name the people gave to their great benefactor Virgil, also both man and woman (see p. 28). Moreover, for the alchemists the hermaphrodite is the perfect being insofar as it synthesises man and woman, and therefore the universe.

Pulcinella has a big belly, another allegory of motherhood, but also of hunger because *Pulcinella* is forever hungry. He dreams only of macaroni, an affirmation of his strictly Neapolitan origins. Then, suddenly, his stomach becomes a sign of opulence and he's seen gorging himself on the long steaming ribbons of pasta that he grabs in handfuls to stuff in his mouth. This is what the poor did in the old days when boiled macaroni sprinkled with grated cheese was sold in the streets. Despite this memorable trademark identity, for the great Roman director Maurizio Scaparro *Pulcinella* is "the world's mask". As for Roberto Rossellini, he has his *Pulcinella* say: "I'm a comedian, not a clown" – for the renowned filmmaker, the character always knows how to keep his dignity.

A Naples theatre, the San Carlino, demolished in 1884, was devoted almost exclusively to so-called *Pulcinellate* plays. Many little street theatres for children, known as *guarattelle*, used hand puppets to tell *Pulcinella* stories. The tradition isn't lost as you can still catch these street performances during festivals and sometimes in the summer.

MARADONA "MUSEUM"

Via Lombardia Isolato 1
• Visits by reservation with Signor Massimo Vignati
• Tel: mobile 3381918907
• Admission free

> *A "temple" dedicated to Maradona*

On display in a cellar is the largest collection relating to the history of Neapolitan football, and especially to Diego Armando Maradona, who played for Napoli from 1984 to 1991. This initiative is due to Signor Saverio Vignati, who was caretaker of the city stadium from 1979 to 2006. On his death, his son Massimo brought all the objects collected by his father together in this room.

So on the entrance walls you can see dozens of pennants offered to the Vignati family by the *Pibe de Oro* in person. The most original exhibit is the bench where the famous footballer sat in the stadium locker room – a bench that's become a veritable altar since Signor Vignati placed the portrait of his idol on it when he finally left Naples. Since that day, nobody has ever dared to sit there.

Also kept in the cellar-museum are the boots worn by Maradona at the 1986 World Cup; his team captain's armband; the gloves he wore to keep out the cold during a game in Moscow; his first professional jersey; the mascot of the 1990 World Cup, a present from Pelé; Ciro Ferrara's parting ball; and Napoli jerseys signed by Maradona and well-known players from other teams who, before leaving Naples, donated some souvenirs to the Vignati family "museum".

CIMITERO DELLE 366 FOSSE ❸

50 Via Fontanelle al Trivio
• Tel: 081 7806933 / 333 1606015
• www.cimiterodelle366fosse.com
• Open Saturday and Sunday 8.30am–1pm

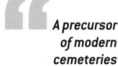

*A precursor
of modern
cemeteries*

Constructed in 1762, half a century before Napoleonic edicts banned burials in urban areas, the cemetery of the "366 graves" consists of an area of 80 m² in which 360 communal graves were dug, all numbered and about 7 m deep. The graves, arranged in nineteen rows (the six remaining are below the cemetery church), were used in turn for a single day and then closed up, to be reopened the

following year. Taking into account the population density of Naples (which, at that time, was the third-largest city in Europe after London and Paris), this rotation lessened the risk of spreading germs.

The capacity of these graves was considerable: 900,000 bodies could be buried there. They were however thrown into the pit any old how, which is why an English lady (name unknown), whom, they say, had lost her daughter or niece in a cholera epidemic in 1875, donated a machine that would lower the bodies into place in a more decorous manner. You can still see the remains of this machine in a corner of the cemetery.

This site, designed by Ferdinando Fuga at the request of Charles III of Bourbon, was the first cemetery exclusively for those with no resources. It was part of the social policy of the king, who had commissioned the same architect to build the huge Albergo dei Poveri (poorhouse: see p. 351) in the city centre. The cemetery was closed down in 1890.

KELLER ARCHITETTURA STUDIO

106 Via Foria
- Metro: Line 1 Museo, Line 2 Cavour
- Visits on reservation by e-mail or phone
- info@kellerarchitettura.it
- Tel: 081 450707

*Art, history
and design
in an 18th-century
palazzo*

O n the second floor of Palazzo Ruffo di Castelcicala, in an apartment of over 400 m², stunning 19th-century majolica floors and French woodwork rub shoulders with prototypes of modern architecture and vintage furniture.

The apartment/office/gallery of architect Antonio Giuseppe Martiniello (Keller Architettura) is typically Neapolitan:

huge rooms, long and very wide corridors and painted ceilings, all decorated with paintings, pop artefacts and a really spectacular suspended bookcase that the owner has had built using the original structure of untreated wood. At the other end of the apartment, the "Nativity" meeting room takes its name from the ceiling decoration. Next come the "Butterfly" and "Four-leafed Clover" rooms. You can book a visit and even have a drink in this exclusive location, unexpected and charming as it is.

The film *Thus Spake Bellavista* by Luciano De Crescenzo, which was a great success in 1980, was shot in the courtyard of the palazzo.

ORIGIN OF THE NAME "FORIA"

The street name "Foria" probably derives from *fuori via* (beyond the streets) – this district used to be outside the city walls. It was only in the 18th century that the Bourbons built this avenue to connect the capital city with the factories that had sprung up to the north.

CALABRESE ENCLOSED GARDEN ⑤

234 Via Foria
- Metro: Line 1 Museo, Line 2 Cavour
- Open 9.30am–4.30pm • Visits to Kaffeehaus and Cabinet Stern:
Tuesday and Friday 10am–3pm • Book with Associazione Culturale LADU
- Tel: 329 3106616 / 349 4296015
- http://ladunapoli.wordpress.com • ladu.associazione@gmail.com

19th-century coffeehouse refinement

Founded in 1864 by Francesco Saverio Calabrese, a keen botanist, the Calabrese vivarium was the first in the city and is the only one still operational. The location is a 16th-century garden just opposite the Orto Botanico (entrance 223 Via Foria, bookings 081 2533937, admission free). Despite being in a densely populated area, the vivarium covers about 4,000 m²

and has seven glasshouses which used to be heated by a coal boiler, now preserved in a small building.

The place is redolent with the memory of Calabrese's daughter-in-law Rita Stern, a highly refined aristocrat of German origins whose receptions were attended by the cream of the Neapolitan aristocracy and the intelligentsia. In her offices within the large garden, recently restored and opened to the public, a number of charming objects, paintings, photos and documents are on display. They trace the history of the family and its relations, who included, among others, Eduardo De Filippo and the great Neapolitan actress Pupella Maggio, who seems to have spent a lot of time in the Kaffeehaus. This exceptional site is now run by the LADU (Laboratorio di Degustazione Urbana) cultural association. The beautiful 18th-century architecture is the work of architect Pompeo Schiantarelli.

UNDERGROUND PASSAGE AT SAN GIOVANNI A CARBONARA

6

Entrance in Bovio-Colletta school
31 Via Carbonara
• Metro: Line 1 Museo, Line 2 Cavour
• Visits can be arranged in May during the annual "Maggio dei Monumenti" event
• Info: 331 8338858 / 347 6455332

> **Belisarius, cunning conqueror of Naples**

A small door in the courtyard of the Bovio-Colletta school leads to a passage that since antiquity has been witness to significant events in the city's history. A long flight of steps leads down into a gallery with the remains of a Roman aqueduct.

In 537, according to the historian Procopius, it was through this tunnel that General Belisarius at the head of his army managed to enter Naples, which subsequently became part of the Byzantine empire.

After twenty days of unsuccessful siege, Belisarius learned from one of his Isaurian soldiers (from an Anatolian tribe) that an underground passage of the Bolla aqueduct led to a well which in turn emerged close to the city walls. So Belisarius' soldiers could surprise and kill the sentries, then climb the walls and enter the city easily.

Some 900 years later, Alfonso of Aragon used the same ruse to win the war against the Angevins. Familiar with the Belisarius story, Alfonso ordered General Diomede Carafa to look for this tunnel. He delegated the job to two *pozzari* (the men responsible for maintaining the aqueduct), who finally came up in a tailor's house near the city walls, right opposite Palazzo Caracciolo d'Oppido, now home to the Bovio-Colletta school. Once the tunnel was discovered, conquest of the city was child's play. That was on 2 June 1442.

NEARBY

A short distance from the Bovio-Colletta school, next to the church of Santi Apostoli, is another entrance to subterranean galleries via a beautiful spiral staircase in the *liceo artistico* (high school). You can also visit this site during "Maggio dei Monumenti".

NEARBY

PARCO DI RE LADISLAO

❼

Junction of Via Cardinale Seripando and Via Pontenuovo I
• Tel: 081 281795
• Open 7am–6pm from 1 to 31 March, 7am–7.30pm from 1 April to
30 June, 7am–8.30pm from 1 July to 31 August, 7am–7pm from 1 to
30 September, 7 am–6pm from 1 to 31 October, 7am–4.30pm from
1 November to 28 February
• Admission free

From the windows of the municipal archives you can see into King Ladislas
park, a rare example of a *hortus conclusus* (literally, a walled kitchen garden)
where the monks of the adjoining monastery cultivated medicinal and
aromatic herbs as well as vegetables. This garden, covering an area of
4,500 m², is now community-owned but quite unknown to Neapolitans and
even many local residents. It is however a restful haven in a chaotic and noisy
neighbourhood.

ARCHIVIO STORICO DEL COMUNE DI NAPOLI

❽

31 Salita Pontenuovo
• Metro: Line 1 Museo, Line 2 Cavour or Garibaldi
• Info: 081 7956502 • archivi.storici.biblioteche@comune.napoli.it
• Admission free with guided tours

The municipal archives, although little known locally, conserve a rich and
varied range of documents on the historic, social and urban development
of the city: administrative records from 1387 to 1860, maps and sketches
from the 18th and 19th centuries, acts concerning charitable institutions set
up over the last four centuries and a fascinating collection of photographs
taken between 1858 and 1987.

In a small room, elegant wooden display cases contain old coins, scrolls
and antique maps – among them, Duke Giovanni Carafa di Noja's precious
topographical map, printed with copper plates in 1775 and considered
fundamental to the study of local town planning. The map, divided into
thirty-five plates, is not only a "snapshot" of Naples as it was at the time, but
shows some public buildings according to their original plan rather than
how they were eventually built. The Albergo dei Poveri (poorhouse), for
example, measuring 100,000 m² and one of Europe's largest buildings in the
17th century, was intended to be even bigger, as shown by the Duke of Noja
– its longest side was supposed to measure 600 m instead of the eventual

384 m (width 150 m). The work was
halted in 1819 and never resumed.
During the Second World War, as a
precaution, the archives were stored
underground in the Beverello tower
adjoining Castel Nuovo. Although
the documents were spared by the
bombing, they were still seriously
damaged by a fire that broke out on
4 March 1946. Some of the exhibits
still bear scorch marks.

STATUE OF SAN GENNARO

Via Ponte della Maddalena
• Bus: 194 or 196 from Napoli Centrale station (Parcheggio Brin stop)

> **The statue that halted the lava flow in 1631**

According to a legend recorded by Conrad of Querfurt (Chancellor to Holy Roman Emperor Henry VI, 1194), Virgil had placed a marble knight at the city gates with his bow arched to shoot a arrow in the direction of Vesuvius, in order to protect Naples from the volcano's anger. But one day a reckless peasant, annoyed by this menacing statue, pulled the string of the bow: the arrow flew off and struck Vesuvius, which immediately began to belch fiery lava.

During the eruption of 1631, when burning lava was at the gates of Naples, San Gennaro (Saint Januarius) wrought a miracle: his statue, which had replaced that of Virgil's archer, raised a hand to stop the flood of destruction.

Today, in memory of this miracle, at the southern entrance of the city in Via Ponte dei Francesi the statue of the saint can still be seen, his hand raised in the direction of the volcano. In gratitude, the Neapolitans clubbed together to offer Saint Januarius one of the most sumptuous chapels ever built in honour of a saint, in the cathedral dedicated to him.

In the small square behind the cathedral, Piazza Sisto Riario Sforza, an obelisk was erected for another statue of Saint Januarius. This is the very site where a bronze horse once stood (see p. 236), a miraculous horse that not only cured all animals, but in the guise of Ennosigaïos (the ground-shaker) had the power to repel earthquakes. Another fine example of the assimilation of pre-existing pagan symbols by nascent Christianity, which in order to establish itself preferred to shrewdly absorb local cults rather than struggle against them.

For more on the symbolism of Saint Januarius (San Gennaro), see following double-page spread.

HIDDEN SYMBOLISM OF THE CULT OF SAN GENNARO

On 19 September (anniversary of the saint's death) and the first Saturday of May, in the sumptuous setting of the Treasury chapel, before a crowd of the faithful at prayer, the blood of the patron saint of Naples liquefies. The oldest reference to this event dates back to 1389. The adoption of this saint by the Neapolitans – frustrated by the abolition of their ancestral cults and always looking for extraordinary events – was instantaneous.

Until the 1950s, the miracle was immediately greeted with histrionics that were a mixture of penance and jubilation: crying women tearing out their hair, men shuffling along on their knees, screams of joy and loud applause. On the other hand, if there was a long delay, some old women known as the *zie di San Gennaro* (kinswomen of Saint Januarius) began to hurl insults at the saint using the epithet "Yellow Face" (the colour of the silver statue yellowed by time). This reflected the people's deep-rooted fear that the city might be in danger if the blood did not liquefy. The fear was so great that people could lash out violently at whoever was supposedly responsible for the non-appearance of the miracle. Sometimes it was believed that the saint was protesting against policies hostile to the pope, so people turned against the authorities, who were often forced to reconsider their decisions.

The liquefaction of blood incorporates a mystical aspect dear to Neapolitans: the oracle (concerning the fate of the city) with her priestesses (the kinswomen) and the blood, a key element in some initiation rites (such as those of Mithra and Cybele). During these ceremonies, novices were baptised by having the blood of a specially sacrificed bull poured over them. Note the strong female presence, a fixture in this city's religious practices. Moreover, when waiting for the miracle, the "kinswomen" invoke the Madonna in these terms: "Beloved Mother, take your cloak and the cape of Saint Januarius, and help us, defend us, shelter us, and rid us of all evils, and save us from a bad death. Beloved mother, let us have a good life and a holy death on behalf of the love Saint Januarius vowed to you." According to archival documents, following the beheading of Januarius in 305, the blood was collected and stored in a vial by Eusebia, an old and pious virgin, as ancient and virginal as the Sibyls and the "kinswomen". The vial in question dates from the 4th century.

The blood-centred ceremony also forms part of a collective propitiatory rite celebrated by the Duke and Bishop of Naples (from the 5th to 11th centuries). This involved swinging an ovoid receptacle containing an egg in the presence of four human skulls representing the "four corners of the world", which were supposed to reunite into a single "universal central body" in the form of the egg.

Nowadays, the vial containing the blood is also ovoid, the cardinal too swings the vial, and liquefaction occurs in the presence of the saint's skull. The Vatican has not spoken out clearly on the subject of this "miracle" and prudently defines it as a "marvel". In 1965, Saint Januarius was even demoted and his cult declared "local and voluntary". This loss of status greatly annoyed the Neapolitans and produced one of the best-known examples of graffiti lining the walls of the city: "*San Gennà futtatenne*" (Saint Januarius, don't worry about it).

In 1991, a group of researchers in Pavia, northern Italy, claimed to have reproduced the phenomenon in the laboratory. The liquid in the vial, they declared, was an ordinary type of gel that flows when shaken and coagulates when the vibrations stop. This process of "thixotropy" was already known to the ancient alchemists. In the 18th century the Prince of Sansevero, renowned Neapolitan alchemist and inventor (see pp. 214–215), reproduced this phenomenon before the astonished gaze of his guests.

But the blood of Saint Januarius doesn't necessarily liquefy every time the cardinal shakes the vial – and sometimes it is already found in the liquid state even before the ceremony. Moreover, spectroscopy carried out in 1988 revealed that the substance was indeed haemoglobin, even though the provenance (animal or human) could not be determined. The explanations are many and varied, from alchemical interpretations to quantum theory, not to mention biochemistry and psychophysics. So the case is far from closed.

The ceremony used to take place four times a year. Besides the two dates mentioned above, the miracle was witnessed on 16 December, anniversary of the day the saint's statue raised a hand to halt the lava flow (see p. 353), and 14 January, anniversary of the transfer of his relics from the sanctuary at Montevergine to Naples.

CHURCH OF SAN CARLO BORROMEO ALLE BRECCE ⑩

102 Via Galileo Ferraris
• Bus: 192 from Napoli Centrale station (Via Ferraris stop)
• Tel: mobile 349 5939227 (Father Serge Baudelaire)
• Open Sunday at 11am (summer), 10am and 12noon (winter)

> *Painting of the Madonna of the Flies*

In the church of San Carlo Borromeo, high up behind the main altar, is a painting of the Madonna of the Flies. This copy (the original canvas was burned in 1850) depicts, alongside the Virgin, Saint Francis of Assisi and Saint Anthony of Padua, as well as the walls of Constantinople and the glow of the blazing city during the Persian invasion that the Virgin is thought to have halted.

In 1650 flies were painted around the image of Mary, who was originally venerated under the name of Our Lady of Constantinople. The legend goes that that was the year of an infestation of flies in the marshes around Naples. The market gardeners, first to be affected by this scourge and fearful of the disease

carried by these insects, promised to build a chapel for the Virgin in return for her help. The miracle came to pass and the chapel was erected in a swampy area where buffaloes were raised. It was demolished during the construction of the Central Station and moved to the site of the present church. In fact, this legend had its roots in a very old myth concerning one of Virgil's miracles (see opposite).

The cult of Saint Mary of Constantinople spread throughout the kingdom from 1452, when a Byzantine icon with her image was found on a Calabrian beach. In Naples, it was believed that this Madonna kept epidemics at bay and a church in the city centre was dedicated to her.

SYMBOLISM OF THE FLY: FROM VIRGIL'S GOLDEN FLY TO THE MADONNA OF THE FLIES

Belzebuth Signore delle mosche

There is a legend that in the Porta Capuana district, near a swamp, Virgil had a fly made of precious metal: he hung it in a window at the castle (Castel Capuano) to drive away these pests that infested the city.

Flies embody uncleanliness, epidemics, putrefaction and therefore death by disease. Symbolic of evil powers (see Apuleius in his book *The Golden Ass*), these insects are linked to Beelzebub, the Lord of the Flies. This was borne out in the Campanian practice of swatting flies from the body of the deceased during a funeral vigil, in order to ward off evil. This gesture was ritualised to the extent that among the mischief allowed during the feast of Our Lady of Piedigrotta (see p. 30), a fly swatter made from strips of coloured paper could be waved in the faces of passers-by.

During the Angevin period the metal fly – a talisman that had actually existed – was removed. A Christian legend tells of a terrible plague of flies on the outskirts of Naples in 1650, so the market gardeners prayed to the Madonna of Constantinople to save their crops and their families. Once she had got rid of the pests, they commissioned a painting depicting the Virgin surrounded by flies. This painting (a copy of the original which was destroyed during the Second World War) was moved to the church of Saint Charles Borromeo (see opposite).

Questioned by Roberto De Simone (see p. 289), the local priest stated that until the 19th century worshippers prayed to this Madonna for protection against infectious diseases. At the end of each summer epidemic, he added, she was offered golden flies by way of thanks. The last such offerings were made after the terrible cholera epidemic of 1884.

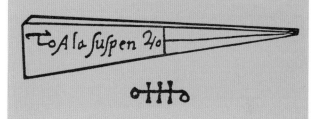

ARCHIVIO NAZIONALE E STORICO ENEL

24 Via Ponte dei Granili
• Metro: Line 2 Gianturco; Bus: 2 or 4
• Tel: 081 3674213
• archiviostoricoenel@enel.com
• paolo.deluce@enel.com
• Visits on reservation

The entire history of the Italian electricity industry

The historical archives of Enel (Ente Nazionale per l'Energia Elettrica – the result of the nationalisation and merger of Italy's 1,270 electricity suppliers in 1962) – contain the complete documentation relating to the history of the Italian electricity industry from the 19th century to the present day. In 2006, the archives of various Enel headquarters throughout Italy were combined with those of Naples to become the national archives. They extend for 13,000 m and contain, among other documents, the first original contract of 1894 for the city lighting, signed by the mayor at the time, about 100,000 photos, thousands of sketches, hundreds of instruments, incandescent lamps for street lighting …

Among the curiosities is a rare example of a 1940s meter with a capacity of 1,382 kilowatts, equipped with a system that let you pay for your electricity consumption with one-lira coins. This device was removed after eighteen months – some very astute Neapolitan consumers had made fake coins the same weight and size that worked perfectly. In the 1980s, a more efficient blue-coloured meter was introduced: technicians called it the "Maradona meter" in honour of the famous footballer of the local team.

ART WORKSHOPS OF THE TEATRO SAN CARLO ⑫

23 Stradone Vigliena – San Giovanni a Teduccio
- Trolleybus: 4 from Piazza Garibaldi
- Tel: 081 7972205
- Visits on request
- Admission: €4

*A former
factory
in the service
of art*

This building, which consists of two rectangles of different heights dating from 1928, belonged to Cirio, a canned food manufacturer which in the 1960s and 1970s was the largest in Europe.

Since the 1990s, Naples' inner industrial suburbs had been largely depopulated and so became run-down. Thanks to a

scheme designed by the prestigious San Carlo theatre, art came to the rescue of this declining district that until the beginning of the 20th century had been renowned for its beautiful beaches. The absurd policy of "industrialisation at any price" had literally made a clean sweep of the most beautiful coastal sites of Naples, both east and west along the bay.

The former Cirio establishment, now rehabilitated, has seen its machines replaced by scenery and its workers by artisans. In this way, Naples has followed the example of other major European cities which have transformed their abandoned factories into creative spaces. Plans are also afoot for these huge premises to host educational exhibitions that are open to the public.

This spectacular site can be visited on request.

MUSEO FERROVIARIO NAZIONALE
DI PIETRARSA

⑬

6 Via Pietrarsa
• From Napoli Centrale station, Salerno–Torre Annunziata line (Pietrarsa stop) • museoferroviariopietrarsa@ferservizi.it • Visits: Friday, Saturday and Sunday 9am–4.30pm; closed public holidays and 29 June
• www.ferroviedellostato.it; http://www.museodipietrarsa.it/
• Guided tours Thursday, on reservation: 081 472003 • Admission: €5, concessions €3.50 (children 6–10 years, senior citizens 65 and over)

Trains from the glory days of Naples

Housed in a disused factory at Pietrarsa, the National Railway Museum is the first in Italy and among the largest in Europe. Among the exhibits are railcars, the first electric trains with a driver's cab, wagons for transporting coal, royal carriages and those of the first "fast" trains, steam locomotives including the "Bayard", twin of the "Vesuvio", which inaugurated the first Italian railway linking Naples to Portici (7.5 km), and a giant model 18 m long that a railway worker spent his entire life building.

Founded in 1840 on the decision of Ferdinand II of Bourbon, the factory, known as the "Real Opificio Borbonico di Pietrarsa", was the most modern steel plant in Italy as well as the largest. It not only produced locomotives, but also steam engines as well as artworks such as the huge cast iron-statue (4.5 m high) of Ferdinand II. The factory was in the vanguard even in the social sphere: the employees – almost 1,000 of them (982 workers, including 224 soldiers and 40 prisoners being reintegrated into society, plus administrative staff) – worked only eight hours a day and were entitled to a pension.

After the unification of Italy in 1861 (see p. 364), the Real Opificio Borbonico was gradually downgraded to the rank of locomotive repair shop: production was relocated to the north of Italy and the staff were reduced to 100. In 1863, the ensuing workers' revolt was bloodily suppressed by the army – seven protesters were killed and twenty seriously wounded (see memorial plaques on the outside wall of the museum). Pietrarsa closed on 15 November 1975.

The site where the factory was built was originally called "Pietra Bianca" (white stone), a name that was changed to "Pietrarsa" (burnt stone) after the terrible 1631 eruption of Vesuvius when the entire area was covered with lava.

NAPLES AND THE SOUTH BEFORE 1860: A WEALTHY AND PROGRESSIVE KINGDOM

Until it was annexed to the Kingdom of Italy on 21 October 1861, the Kingdom of the Two Sicilies had aroused the admiration of many foreign travellers. A prosperous and highly industrialised country with its 9 million inhabitants (among a total of 22 million in what would become Italy), its 5,000 industries employing 51% of the peninsula's population and its 9,174 merchant ships, the kingdom had gold reserves that were twice the size of all the other Italian states combined. The most modern taxation system in Italy, controlled prices of essential goods, the lowest infant mortality in Europe thanks to vaccination (from 1818) and the high number of doctors guaranteed people a very agreeable life. Prestigious universities, a plethora of publishing houses and newspapers (1,289 publishers/printers against Milan's 1,255),[1] and fifteen theatres open nightly, all made Naples a city of culture with an international reputation.

Under these conditions, it isn't surprising that the south put up fierce resistance to the Piedmontese occupier. The price of Italian unification was extremely heavy for the south: indiscriminate acts of barbarism against tens of thousands of resistance fighters and civilians (the former accused of banditry, the latter of complicity), hundreds of villages razed to the ground ... In protest, Austria, France, Prussia and Russia even broke off diplomatic relations with the new government.

But the spoliation of the south didn't stop: its thriving economy was literally destroyed and relocated to the north. All the laws governing the former kingdom were abolished and nothing put in their place, the upkeep of order was entrusted to pardoned criminals and the country, plunged into chaos, has never recovered. Emigration became the only means of survival for millions of southerners, who left their homeland for the first time in thousands of years.

The veils that hid the historical truth have only recently been lifted. These excerpts from testimonies (selected from the hundreds rediscovered to date) are very enlightening:

A. Bianco di Saint-Jorioz (Commander of the Piedmontese army): "The year 1860 found these people dressed, shod, industrious, with economic reserves ... Now it's just the opposite ... Nobles and commoners, rich and poor, all here aspire, with a few rare exceptions, to an imminent return of the Bourbons."[2]

Senator Brignole Sale (during the vote in the Piedmontese Senate for the annexation of the Kingdom of the Two Sicilies): "That kingdom belongs to an independent prince who is still in place, who with a group of loyal soldiers resists the revolutionary hordes. Were we not at peace with him? ... What reason will we invoke to justify such a crime?"[3]

Colonel Massimo d'Azeglio (former Minister of the House of Savoy): "I can understand that Italians have the right to fight against those who would keep the Austrians in Italy, but we do not have the right to shoot Italians who, while remaining Italian, do not wish to join with us."[4]

Napoleon III to General Fleury: "I informed Turin of my reproaches. [...] Not only are misery and anarchy at their height, but the most culpable and unworthy acts are a matter of course ..."[5]

Lord Henry Lennox (speech in the British House of Commons, 8 May 1863): "The so-called Italian unity primarily owes its existence to the moral support and protection of England ... and it is in the name of England that I denounce such barbaric atrocities ... The description of the attitude and condition of the tortured in Dante's Inferno would give the best idea of the scene that presented itself in that prison yard ..."[6]

The socialist Gaetano Salvemini (letter of 1923): "If the Mezzogiorno [the south of Italy] was ruined by unity, Naples was frankly assassinated ..."[7]

G. La Farina (Sicilian unitarist deputy): "... Four or five jobs all done by the same person ... important posts given to minors ... pensions for the wives, sisters and sisters-in-law of so-called patriots although they are not entitled to them [...] Thieves, escaped prisoners, looters and murderers, pardoned by Garibaldi and paid off by Crispi and Mordini, have been implanted in the carabinieri, in the security services, in the revenue guard corps and even in the ministries ..."[8]

Letter (28 October 1861) from Minister Ricasoli to the Prefect of Naples: "... The transfer of these documents to the General Archives could be extremely dangerous ... His Majesty's Government [Victor Emmanuel], which wishes to put an end to the era of Italian discord, cannot allow retrospective recriminations to be constantly fuelled by a publicity of which he alone can determine the shape and opportunity."[9]

Over a thousand books have been published on the subject in Italian, some of which are included in the bibliography on p. 380.

1. Information from CLIO, *Catalogo dei libri italiani dell'ottocento* [Catalogue of Italian books from the nineteenth century] (1801–1900).
2. A report from 1864. See G. Turco, "Brigantaggio, legittima difesa del Sud" [Brigandry, the South's Legitimate Defence], *Il Giglio* magazine, Naples, 2000, p. xxxi (& others).
3. Declaration at the Senate's sitting of 16 October 1860 during the vote to annex the Kingdom of Naples (before the plebiscite of 21 October).
4. Letter of 2 August 1861 to the Hon. Matteucci, published in the *La Patrie* and *Monarchia Nazionale* newspapers.
5. Letter of 21 July 1863 sent from Vichy. See O'Clery, *La Rivoluzione italiana* [The Italian Revolution], Ares, Milan, 2000.
6. O'Clery, *La Rivoluzione italiana*.
7. Letter no. 58, dated 14 June 1923.
8. Account given to Carlo Pisano, 12 January 1861. See A. Pellicciari, *L'Altro Risorgimento* [The Other Risorgimento], Ares, Milan, 2011.
9. *Istituto Storico Italiano per l'Età moderna e contemporanea*, [Italian Historical Institute for the Modern and Contemporary Era], Vol. XVIII, 28 October 1861, no. 401; cited by U. Pontone, "Due Sicilie" [Two Sicilies], *L'Alfiere*, no. 46, Naples, 2003.

MUSEO PRIVATO DELLE CARROZZE DI VILLA BIANCHI ⑭

c/o Clinica Bianchi
342 Via Libertà – Portici (Naples)
• Rail: Circumvesuviana station, direction Torre Annunziata–Sorrento
• Visits (free) on reservation • napolisegreta@gmail.com

Incredible treasures on wheels

Professor Leonardo Bianchi's private collection of carriages, completely overlooked by Neapolitans, definitely merits a visit both for its location (the former stables of the castle where the kings of Naples often stayed on hunting trips) and for its superb vehicles, all in perfect working order. In the 1940s Professor Bianchi, a renowned neurologist and

accomplished horseman, collected unique examples of carriages produced in Italy and abroad between 1820 and 1920. These vehicles have all belonged to eminent personalities of the time, such as the hunting car of the Duke of Aosta, Emmanuel Philibert, who often took part in hunting expeditions organised by the Bianchi family.

Note in particular the splendid black and yellow model that belonged to the Thurn und Taxis (a rich, aristocratic German family who were key players in the postal services of Europe in the 16th century) which the ladies would hire to join their husbands for a picnic lunch after the hunt; and the lovely "Clarence" coupé designed by the English Duke of Clarence, later William IV … not to mention the German "Landau" sedan with its refined upholstery and, among the oldest vehicles in the collection, the small and fast "American" made in New York in the early 19th century.

ALPHABETICAL INDEX

Accademia Pontaniana library 142
Antico Laboratorio Scientifico di Scienze Naturali, Fisica e Chimica . . 95
Antonio Genovesi (1712–1769): a philosopher who became the world's
first economics professor 123
Antonio Genovesi high school. 122
Aosta collection at the *Biblioteca Nazionale* Vittorio Emanuele III. . . . 73
Archbishop Sisto Riario Sforza's great hall 129
Archbishop who invented microcredit before its time. 129
Archivio Fotografico Parisio 60
Archivio Nazionale e Storico Enel 359
Archivio Storico del Comune di Napoli. *351*
Archivo Storico, Banco di Napoli 253
Arciconfraternita dei Verdi nel Palazzo Ruffo di Bagnara. 175
Art workshops of the Teatro San Carlo 360
Artworks by Nathalie de Saint-Phalle 212
Associazione "Circolo Artistico Politecnico" 66
Augustissima Compagnia della Disciplina della Santa Croce 157
Banksy's *Saint with a Pistol* graffiti 235
Bars of the Treasury chapel's monumental portal 242
Basin of a Roman aqueduct 161
Bas-relief of a hairy man 139
Bas-relief of a woman 80
Bas-relief of the *Triumph of Death* 318
Biblioteca Alfredo De Marsico 255
Biblioteca Maurizio Taddei 222
Blessing of the animals 295
Bomb shelter in Babuk's garden 265
Bourbon Hall of Fame 126
Brother Ludovico da Casoria, an extraordinary character 21
Bungled looting of the remains of Conrad of Hohenstaufen 163
Bust of the goddess known as the "Head of Naples". 108
Byzantine remains in Castel dell'Ovo. 57
Calabrese enclosed garden 346
Captain's skull 300
Carafa caves 47
Casa Museo di Pulcinella. 338
Casa Zevola 207
Castel Nuovo: a pope imprisoned, Campanella tortured,
Giotto's frescoes, the escapades of Joan of Anjou 82
Castratos: thousands of children sacrificed in the name of *bel canto* . . 105
Casts of Parthenon sculptures 182
Centrale ABC (Acqua Bene Comune Napoli) dello Scudillo. 334
Chair in the chapel at Santa Lucia al Monte 99
Church "holy lands" 171
Church of San Carlo Borromeo alle Brecce 356
Church of San Giuseppe delle Scalze. 178
Church of Santa Maria Antesaecula 276
Church of Santi Marcellino e Festo 131
Cimitero delle 366 fosse. 342
Cinderella was born in Naples 31
Circolo Nazionale dell'Unione. 79
Clock in Piazza Dante 173

Cloister of Sant'Andrea delle Dame 188
Cloister of the Facoltà di Veterinaria (Università Federico II) 291
Cloister of the former convent of San Sebastiano 174
Cloisters of the former monastery of Saints Marcellino and Festo . . .135
Commemorative plaques at Palazzo Filangieri. 208
Congregation del Crocefisso della Sciabica 210
Conigliera 175
Corals in the Museo Ascione 69
Courtyard of Palazzo Spinelli di Laurino 212
"Cristallini" hypogea. 275
Crocodile that devoured prisoners 83
Crucifix of San Carlo all'Arena church 261
Cuckold's horns 68
Cult of souls in Purgatory: when the dead and the living help each other
to reach Paradise 302
Curiosities of San Gennaro catacombs. 297
Cursed villa of Gaiola. 19
Della Vicaria tribunal column 325
Devil of Mergellina 24
Diana and the witches. 87
Dome: each face had its price. 245
Duke's study 223
Early days of Eduardo, "a giant of European theatre" 45
Electricity as therapy in the 18th century 198
Emblems of Naples sedili. 233
Emeroteca-Biblioteca Tucci 111
Epitaph on Virgil's tomb. 27
Events organised by the "Friends of Marcel Proust". 265
Every picture tells a story 35
False windows of Corso Umberto 160
Fate Presto: reproduction in the metro of a "Neapolitan" work
by Andy Warhol 261
Female centaurs that caught the attention of the Metropolitan Museum
of Art 39
Ferdinando Palasciano, army doctor of the Two Sicilies 287
Fertility chair. 279
Figure with no gift. 229
Filangieri room. 150
Fontana di Spinacorona. 144
Forgotten figurines of the Ferrigno workshop. 228
Forgotten history of the Fontanelle. 301
Former Aula Magna of the Faculty of Economics and Commerce 56
Former oil tanks. 172
Former Sava wool mill 161
Frescoes at the Stazione Zoologica Anton Dohrn 36
From Virgil's egg to the Castle of the Egg 58
Gaetano Filangieri 208
Garments of the miraculous Virgin 133
Gay-Odin Museum of Chocolate 41
Ghost of Bianca 213
Giambattista Vico (1668–1744) 147
Giambattista Vico Foundation 146

ALPHABETICAL INDEX

Giambattista Vico Foundation 147
Giardino dei Cinque Continenti 94
Giosuè Carducci's revenge. 67
Golden cube in the exhibition park. 306
Gothic tunnels below San Martino 323
Great hall of the Chamber of Commerce 117
Greek hypogea in Naples 272
Greek tower at the Trianon theatre 158
Guido Donatone private museum 316
Gypsotheque of the Academy of Fine Arts 183
Hidden symbolism of Cappella Sansevero 214
Hidden symbolism of the cult of San Gennaro 354
Highest meridians in the world 331
"Holy land" of the Archconfraternity of Pilgrims. 167
"Holy land" of the Arciconfraternita dei Bianchi 170
Holy Steps in Naples 185
Holy Steps of San Gregorio Armeno convent 226
Holy Steps of Santa Maria della Sapienza 184
Horns against the evil eye 68
Hotel Correra aqueduct 176
Hotly disputed amputation 222
How does a meridian work? 329
How is a metre defined? 249
"Il Re di Poggioreale", a trafficker who brought the treasure
of Saint Januarius back to Naples 243
Incurabili pharmacy 198
Inscription on Palazzo Majorana. 104
Installation seen through a peephole. 181
Ionic column at Pelletteria Collaro. 257
Is that Domenichino's tomb at the chapel entrance? 241
Is Virgil behind the curse? 19
Istituto Magistrale Eleonora Pimentel-Fonseca. 120
Italian clock of Spirito Santo conservatory 168
Jacopo Sannazaro (1457–1530): the poet of *Arcadia* 25
Janara: the legendary witch of nocturnal evildoing 89
Kayak tours 18
Keller Architettura studio 345
Kitchen garden declared national heritage. 97
Land registry of the State Archives 149
Largo Baracche gallery 103
Legend of the desiccated pine 167
Legends of Porta Nolana 156
Little secrets of Palazzo dello Spagnolo. 271
Lizard in the church of the Santissimi Apostoli 257
Lucchesi Palli wing, *Biblioteca Nazionale* Vittorio Emanuele III. 71
Maradona "museum". 341
Maradona's hair 225
Marble calendar of the 9th century 247
Marks on the façade of the church of Gesù Nuovo 125
Mascagni, a poor loser. 67
"May the Lord deliver me from sad neighbours and violinists" 251
Meridian of the Carthusians 327

Michele Iodice's workshop 285
Miraculous Carmelite crucifix 163
Model of Battaglino chariot 299
Museo del Giocattolo di Napoli 93
Museo del Tessile e dell'Abbigliamento *"Elena Aldobrandini"* 43
Museo dell'Opera Universitaria 95
Museo della Fondazione Pagliara 95
Museo delle Arti Sanitarie degli Incurabili 201
Museo di Anatomia Umana 203
Museo di Anatomia Veterinaria 291
Museo di Antropologia 137
Museo di Etnopreistoria 57
Museo di Fisica 141
Museo di Paleontologia 135
Museo di Zoologia 137
Museo Ferroviario Nazionale di Pietrarsa 362
Museo Hermann Nitsch 181
Museo Orientale "Umberto Scerrato" .57
Museo Privato delle Carrozze di Villa Bianchi 366
Naples and the myth of the Siren Parthenope 145
Naples, a city steeped in spells 88
Naples and the south before 1860: a wealthy and progressive kingdom 364
Naples, the last bastion of *Teriaca* 199
Naples, world capital of music 76
Naval basin of the Hydrodynamic Laboratory 314
Naval Museum of the "Parthenope" University of Naples 23
Neapolitan banking institution older than Monte dei Paschi di Siena? 253
Neapolitan horse: an exceptional animal 238
Neapolitan lotto: a history of divination 192
Neapolitan riding academy 304
New "Giardini room" in the disused carpentry workshop 75
Noble Cerula and a hitherto unknown Saint Paul 297
Obscure saga of the last Caravaggio 107
Old city and its ferruginous water 47
Origin and meaning of the Holy Steps 184
Origin of the name "Foria" 345
Origin of the word *"sciabica"* 211
Ospedale Leonardo Bianchi 288
Ospizio Marino 21
Other curiosities of San Gregorio Armeno 227
Other fertility chairs in Naples 279
Other two Italian clocks in the city 168
Palazzo Carafa 236
Palazzo de' Liguoro di Presicce 267
Palazzo de' Liguoro-Santoro staircase 283
Palazzo Leonetti staircase and elevator 41
Palazzo Mannajuolo staircase 45
Palazzo Penne 118
Palazzo San Teodoro 39
Palazzo Zevallos Stigliano gallery 106
Palestra "Fitness & Beauty" 46
Parco di Re Ladislao 351

ALPHABETICAL INDEX

Parco Viviani 332
Pasquale Catalano, a specialist in nativity scenes. 177
"*Passo da terra*" of the Duomo 248
Pastrengo barracks 113
Pay for your pizza eight days later 159
Piazza Cavour tunnels. 262
Plaque in Vico Pensiero 86
Plaque of the church of San Domenico Maggiore 220
"Poetry trees" in Virgil's honour 27
President's anti-aircraft shelter 63
Private collection of Piaggio Vespas 33
Private tour of Monastero delle Trentatré 190
Quartiere Intelligente 166
Rai production centre 310
Real Museo di Mineralogia 140
Reliquary cabinet at the church of the Gerolamini 235
Remains of a Dioscuri temple 209
Remains of an underground tramline. 54
Reproduction of Lourdes grotto 97
Roberto De Simone, bard of Naples 289
Roman baths on Via Terracina. 312
Roman road below the exhibition park 309
Roman villa in the basement of the Banco di Napoli archive. 253
Royal access 75
Saint Anthony the Hermit's pig 293
Saint Anthony's monks and the Templars 294
Saint Aspren: the original aspirin? 115
Saint Benedict's plane tree 153
Saint George and the Dragon fresco. 155
Saint Januarius' missing fingers 161
Sala del Lazzaretto of the former della Pace hospital 251
Salons of Palazzo Serra di Cassano 48
San Gaudioso catacombs. 281
San Martino vineyard 101
Sanità bridge 298
Sansevero's *Veiled Christ*: from legend to the reality of sudation
and mystical internal fire. 217
Sartoria C.T.N. 75 – Canzanella Costumi 49
Secrets of Naples town hall 109
Self-portraits on the Treasury chapel altar 244
Sergio Ragni's private collection 321
Seventh Heaven Lane 189
Shield of the city of Naples 241
Sirens of Palazzo Sanfelice 271
Sister Orsola Benincasa's cell. 95
Smorfia: the real meaning of the numbers 194
Società Napoletana di Storia Patria 85
Souvenir of the terrible explosion of 1943 151
Statue of Antonio Toscano 85
Statue of San Gennaro 353
Statue of the Virgin that terrified worshippers. 243
Strange procession and a bungled theft. 294

Studio 137A 35
Studio of painter Massimo d'Orta 268
Sweating skulls 303
Symbolism of objects and characters from the Neapolitan
nativity scene 230
Symbolism of *Pulcinella*, exorcist of Neapolitans' existential angst . 338
Symbolism of the Crypta Neapolitana 29
Symbolism of the fly: from Virgil's golden fly to the Madonna
of the Flies 357
Tasso room 153
Teatro San Carlo clock 74
"Tesoro Vecchio" chapel of San Gennaro 247
Thinker of Vico Pensiero 87
Tomb of the first bishop of New York 221
Torre del Palasciano 287
Touching farewell scenes in the Museo Archeologico Nazionale 275
Tours of the Galleria Borbonica 51
Traditional Neapolitan chic 43
Triptych of *Christ Unveiled or Hidden Light* 219
Tunnels below Fontana dell'Esedra 309
Underground altar of the church of Sant'Aspreno 114
Underground galleries of Pietrasanta 187
Underground passage at San Giovanni a Carbonara 349
Vestiges of the former "Suprema" brothel 65
Villa Doria d'Angri 23
Virgil, poet and magician 28
Virgin's veil, Guglia dell'Immacolata 127
What is *"refrisco"*? 303
What is the equation of time? 173
What is the origin of "Italian" clocks? 169
When Our Lady lost her shoe: why is Santa Maria di Piedigrotta
so called? 30
When the Virgin belongs to the city and not to the church 127
When unhealthy air was believed to cause syphilis 201
Where can you see some extraordinary figurines? 177
Why "all'Arena"? 261
Why are two medallions faceless? 216
Why does Saint Aspren relieve headaches? 115
Why is the main entrance to Palazzo Serra di Cassano closed? 48
Why is the number 33 generally associated with nuns in
the Neapolitan lottery? 191
Why was 4 October followed immediately by 15 October in the year 1582?
Measurement of time and origin of the meridians 330
Why were meridians installed in cathedrals? 331
Wine tax marker 285
Woman killed by gnocchi and other Fontanelle tales 301
Zingaro, the blacksmith who became an artist for love? 152

NOTES

NOTES

ACKNOWLEDGEMENTS

Valerio Ceva Grimaldi Pisanelli di Pietracatella

To my grandfather, Ugo Stellato, a remarkable man of culture and a great lover of Naples
To Amato Lamberti, a treasured teacher

Special thanks to:
Fernando Pisacane, Antonio Speranza, Laura Giusti, Augusto Cocozza, Serenella Greco, Roberta Stellato
For their contributions to the texts: Augusto Cocozza, Serenella Greco, Antonio Speranza, Elena Regina Brandstetter, Serena Riviezzo
This guide has been produced in collaboration with the Geositi project of Napoli Servizi – Comune di Napoli, directed by Salvatore Iodice

Also:
Massimo Marrelli, Luigi de Magistris, Fabrizio Vona, Annachiara Alabiso, Rossana Muzii, Fabio Speranza, Simona Golia, Soprintendenza Speciale per il Patrimonio Storico, Artistico ed Etnoantropologico e per il Polo Museale della Città di Napoli e la Reggia di Caserta, Fondo Edifici di Culto del Ministero dell'Interno, Ufficio per i Beni Culturali Ecclesiastici della Diocesi di Napoli for kindly granting reproduction rights, Comando Provinciale dei Carabinieri di Napoli, Francesco Pinto, Antonello Perillo, Carlo Sbordone, Sergio Sciarelli, Lida Viganoni and Università Orientale, Luciano Gaudio, Gennaro Rispoli, Paolo Jorio, Riccardo Carafa d'Andria, Flavio Zanchini, Michele Iodice, Italo Ferraro, Agostino Caracciolo and the entire board of Circolo dell'Unione, Imma Ascione, Paola de' Liguoro di Presicce, Massimo d'Orta, Ignazio Frezza di Sanfelice and secretariat of Arciconfraternita dei Bianchi, Francesco Rossi and Seconda Università degli Studi di Napoli, Nino Daniele, Niccolò Rinaldi, Guido Donatone, Marco de Gemmis, Sergio Ragni, Serena Lucianelli, Rita Pagliari, Mario Pagliari, Manuela Sorice, Natalie de Saint Phalle, Jole Lianza, Andrea Rea, Fondazione Monte Manso di Scala, Carla Travierso, Franco Abbondanza, Arciconfraternita della Santa Croce, Antonio Martiniello, Giuseppe Zevola, Rosaria Russo, Silvano Focardi, Enzo De Nicola, Mimmo Galluzzo, Maria Francesca Stamuli, Università Parthenope, Circolo Artistico Politecnico, Giuseppe Messina, Bernardo Leonardi, Salvatore Miranda, Leonardo Bianchi, Giuseppe Morra, Giampiero Martuscelli, Fabio Chiosi, Mariano Cinque, Gabriele Flaminio, Marina Andria, Susy Cacace, Imma Cuomo, staff of NapoliServizi, Antonio Loffredo, Adelina Pezzillo and staff of San Gennaro and San Gaudioso catacombs, Luca Cuttitta, Gianluca Minin and staff of Galleria Borbonica, Gianpaolo Leonetti, Insolitaguida Napoli, Associazione Nartea, Lello Scuotto, Antonio Caliendo, Maurizio Di Cresce, Francesco Licastro, Giovanni Lucianelli, Gennaro Giorgio, Associazione La Paranza, Pierluigi Sanfelice di Bagnoli, Livio Barone, Carlo Ferrari, Maria D'Ambrosio, Alessio Postiglione, Grazia Formisano, Imma Sansone Perrella, Adriana Pascale, Fulvio Mamone Capria, Palmiro Camerlengo, Enzo Colimoro, Antonella Rizzo, Pietro Fusella, Francesco Russo, Michele Iacobellis, Arturo Castellano, Carlo Leggieri, Daniela Del Monaco, Giuliana Sandulli, Piero Bizzarro, Alessandra Basile, Fabrizio Masucci, Davide Tartaglia, Stefano Cortese, Donatella Monti, Clemente Esposito, Vincenzo Esposito, Giobby Greco, Antonio Gargano, Maria Girardo, Roberto Vernetti, Salvatore Maffei, Carmen Credendino, Luca Marconi, Marco Giglio, Vincenzo Pisano, Rosario Serafino, Trianon – il Teatro della Musica a Napoli, Vincenzo Dina, Angelo Mazzagatti, Francesco (Monastero delle 33), Massimo Vignati, Carmelo Raiti, Giuseppe Serroni, Luciano Iovinella, Gaia Mautone, Nicoletta Diamanti, Lanificio25, Antonio Iaccarino (Locus Iste), Paolo de Luce, Francesco Esposito, Press Office of Teatro San Carlo, Rosaria Torre, Vincenzo and Davide Canzanella, Gianfranco Wurzburger, Pasquale Catalano, Giuseppe Talotti, Pasquale Ferraioli, Silvana Casale, Giuseppe Brancaccio, Antonio Daldanise, Massimo Rippa, Antonio De Gregorio and Paolo Giordano for their collaboration on the text and illustrations for Cimitero delle 366 Fosse, Sisters of Ospizio Marino, Giuliana Ricciardi, Francesco Quaratino, Giulia Milanese, Antonio Moccia, Tiziana Grassi, Pasquale de Luca, Reale Arciconfraternita di Santa Maria del Popolo, Stefania Salvetti, Alice Bartoli, Cristina Di Stasio, Giovanni Brun, Antonio Denunzio, Carla Celestino, Andrea of San Giorgio Maggiore church, Isabella Tarsi, Serena Amabile, Fabiana Mendia, Antonio Pariante and Comitato di Portosalvo, Gruppo Archeologico Napolitano, Associazione Roots Discovery, Carmine G., Saverio Dionizio, Roberto Conte, Università degli Studi Suor Orsola Benincasa, P. Edoardo Parlato, Renato Previtera, Rossana Spadaccini, Agnese Iardino, Davide Lazzaro, Clelia Santoro, Chicca Pagliari, Maria Esposito, Mauro Giancaspro, Gennaro Oliviero, Stefano e Mario de Felice.

Maria Franchini

Special thanks to Maestro Roberto De Simone for his immense contribution to my knowledge of Neapolitan culture.
With great appreciation for their invaluable help: Raffaele Bracale, tireless researcher; Prof. Giuseppina Buonaiuto of Liceo Genovesi; Dr Lucio Fiorile, head of Biblioteca Majoli; Dr Paola Milone of Istituto di Storia Patria; Prof. Mirella Scala of Istituto Pimentel Fonseca; Dr Anna Sicolo of former Ospedale Bianchi; Fondazione Giambattista Vico.

All texts are by Valerio Ceva Grimaldi Pisanelli di Pietracatella except:
pages 19–21, 117, 167, 181, 208, 227, 251, 261, 275, 297 (nearby and thematic boxes), pages 25, 26–27, 28–29, 30–31, 58–59, 68, 76–77, 81, 82–83, 86–87, 88–89, 104–105, 107, 108, 118–119, 120–121, 122–123, 126, 139, 144–145, 146–147, 152, 156, 190–191, 192–193, 194–195, 196–197, 220–221, 230–231, 236–237, 238–239, 271, 272, 288–289, 293, 294–295, 300–301, 302–303, 318–319, 338–339, 352–353, 354–355, 356–357, 364–365 (Maria Franchini), pages 214, 215 and 217 (VMA).

Select bibliography

Aprile, P., *Terroni*, Piemme, Alessandria, 2011

Bianchini Braglia, E., *La verità sugli uomini e sulle cose del Regno d'Italia*, Ass. Solfanelli, Modena, 2010

Capasso, B., *Napoli greco-romana*, Berisio, Naples, 1987

Croce, B., *Storie e leggende napoletane*, Adelphi, Milan, 1990

De Simone, R., *Il segno di Virgilio*, Sezione Editoriale Puteoli, Naples, 1982

Del Boca, L., *Indietro Savoia, controcorrente del Risorgimento italiano*, Piemme, Alessandria, 2004

Di Fiore, G., *Controstia del Risorgimento*, Rizzoli, Milan, 2011

Fatica, M., *Sedi e palazzi dell'Università degli Studi di Napoli l'Orientale*, U. N. O., Naples, 2005

Ferrara, O., *Addio Sud, o briganti o emigranti*, Capone, Turin, 2012

Ferraro, I., *Atlante della città storica*, Oikos, Naples, 2002

Fratta, A., *Il Patrimonio architettonico dell'Ateneo Fridericiano*, Ed. Arte Tipografica, Naples, 2004

Gleijeses, V., *Chiese e palazzi della città di Napoli*, Giglio, Naples, 1978

Gulì, V., *Il Saccheggio del Sud*, Editoriale Campania Bella, Naples, 1998

Liguori, D., *Memento Domine. Le verità negate sulla tragedia del Sud fra Borbone, Savoia e briganti*, Sibylla, Rome, 2007

Molfese, F., *Storia del brigantaggio dopo l'unità*, West Indian, Molinara, 2012

"Napoli Nobilissima" collection, A. Berisio, Naples, 1969

Ressa, G., *Il Sud e l'unità d'Italia*, 2003. See: http://www.olevano.it/biblioteca/Sud-Unita.italia-Ressa.pdf

Viesti, G., *Abolire il Mezzogiorno*, Laterza, Rome, 2003

Zitara, N. *L'unità d'Italia. Nascita di una colonia*, Jaca Book, Milan, 2011